An

A to Z

GRAMMAR for
CHINESE LANGUAGE
LEARNERS

當代中文

語法點全集

 國立臺灣師範大學國語教學中心
Mandarin Training Center National Taiwan Normal University

鄧守信／編著

An A to Z Grammar for Chinese Language Learners

This dictionary lists close to 400 entries of modern Chinese grammar, arranged alphabetically on the basis of Hanyu Pinyin, a phonetic system standard in the field of teaching Chinese as a second language world-wide. This volume has been designed specifically for Chinese language learners, from the very beginning stage of their learning career up to the so-called advanced level, commonly defined in a university curriculum in the West. To fully make use of this dictionary, it is imperative that the users understand and can freely work with the tools employed in this volume, especially when some of the tools used have not been tried in the L2 Chinese field, e.g., Chinese parts of speech.

The Chinese Language[1]

China is a multi-ethnic society, and when people in general study Chinese, 'Chinese' usually refers to the Beijing variety of the language as spoken by the Han 漢 people in China, also known as Mandarin Chinese or simply Mandarin. It is the official language of China, known mostly domestically as the Putonghua 普通話, the lingua franca, or Hanyu 漢語, the Han language. In Taiwan, Guoyu 國語 refers to the national/official language, and Huayu 華語 to either Mandarin Chinese as spoken by Chinese descendants residing overseas, or to Mandarin when taught to non-Chinese learners. The following pages present an outline of the features and properties of Chinese. For further details, readers are advised to consult various and abundant on-line resources.

Language Kinship

Languages in the world are grouped together on the basis of language affiliation, called language-family. Chinese, or rather Hanyu, is a member of the Sino-Tibetan family, which covers most of China today, plus parts of Southeast Asia. Therefore, Tibetan, Burmese, and Thai are genetically related to Hanyu.

---

[1] Many sections below are taken from Teng, Shou-hsin. 2005. An Introduction to the Chinese Language, commissioned for ICLP, Taipei.

Hanyu is spoken in about 75% of the present Chinese territory, by about 75% of the total Chinese population, and it covers 7 major dialects, including the better known Cantonese, Hokkienese, Hakka and Shanghainese.

Historically, Chinese has interacted highly actively with neighboring but unaffiliated languages, such as Japanese, Korean and Vietnamese. The interactions took place in such areas as vocabulary items, phonological structures, a few grammatical features and most importantly the writing script.

Typological Features of Chinese

Languages in the world are also grouped together on the basis of language characteristics, called language typology. Chinese has the following typological traits, which highlight the dissimilarities between Chinese and English.

A. Chinese is a non-tense language.

Tense is a grammatical device such that the verb changes according to the time of the event in relation to the time of utterance. Thus 'He talks nonsense' refers to his habit, while 'He talked nonsense' refers to a time in the past when he behaved that way, but he does not necessarily do that all the time. 'Talked' then is a verb in the past tense. Chinese does not operate with this device but marks the time of events with time expressions such as 'today' or 'tomorrow' in the sentence. The verb remains the same regardless of time of happening. This type of language is labeled as an atensal language, while English and most European languages are tensal languages. Knowing this particular trait can help European learners of Chinese avoid mistakes to do with verbs in Chinese. Thus, in responding to 'What did you do in China last year?' Chinese is 'I teach English (last year)'; and to 'What are you doing now in Japan?' Chinese is again 'I teach English (now)'.

B. Nouns in Chinese are not directly countable.

Nouns in English are either countable, e.g., 2 candies, or non-countable, e.g., *2 salts, while all nouns in Chinese are non-countable. When they are to be counted, a measure, or called classifier, must be used between a noun and a number, e.g., 2-piece-candy. Thus, Chinese is a classifier language. Only non-countable nouns in English are used with measures, e.g., a drop of water.

Therefore it is imperative to learn nouns in Chinese together with their associated measures/classifiers. There are only about 30 high-frequency measures/classifiers in Chinese to be mastered at the initial stage of learning.

C. Chinese is a Topic-Prominent language.

Sentences in Chinese quite often begin with somebody or something that is being talked about, rather than the subject of the verb in the sentence. This item is called a topic in linguistics. Most Asian languages employ topic, while most European languages employ subject. The following bad English sentences, sequenced below per frequency of usage, illustrate the topic structures in Chinese.

*Senator Kennedy, people in Europe also respected.

*Seafood, Taiwanese people love lobsters best.

*President Obama a, he attended Harvard University.

Because of this feature, Chinese people tend to speak 'broken' English, whereas English speakers tend to sound 'complete', if bland and alien, when they talk in Chinese. Through practice and through keen observations of what motivates the use of a topic in Chinese, this feature of Chinese can be acquired eventually.

D. Chinese tends to drop things in the sentence.

The 'broken' tendencies mentioned above also include not using nouns in a sentence where English counterparts are 'complete'. This tendency is called dropping, as illustrated below through bad English sentences.

Are you coming tomorrow? -----   *Come!

What did you buy? -----   *Buy some jeans.

*This bicycle, who rides? -----   *My old professor rides.

The 1st example drops everything except the verb, the 2nd drops the subject, and the 3rd drops the object. Dropping happens when what is dropped is easily recoverable or identifiable from the contexts or circumstances. Not doing this, Europeans are often commented upon that their sentences in Chinese are too often inundated with unwanted pronouns!!

Phonological Characteristics of Chinese

Phonology refers to the system of sound, the pronunciation, of a language. To untrained ears, Chinese language sounds unfamiliar, sort of alien in a way. This is due to the fact that Chinese sound system contains some elements that are not part of the sound systems of European languages, though commonly found on the Asian continent. These features will be explained below.

On the whole, the Chinese sound system is not really very complicated. It has 7 vowels, 5 of which are found in English (i, e, a, o, u), plus 2 which are not (-e, ü); and it has 21 consonants, 15 of which are quite common, plus 6 which are less common (zh, ch, sh, r, z, c). And Chinese has a fairly simple syllable shape, i.e., consonant + vowel plus possible nasals (n or ng). What is most striking to English speakers is that every syllable in Chinese has a 'tone', as will be detailed directly below. But, a word on the sound representation, the pinyin system, first.

A. Hanyu Pinyin 漢語拼音.

Hanyu Pinyin is a variety of Romanization systems that attempt to represent the sound of Chinese through the use of Roman letters (abc...). Since the end of the 19th century, there have been about half a dozen Chinese Romanization systems, including the Wade-Giles, Guoyu Luomazi 國語羅馬字, Yale, Hanyu Pinyin, Lin Yutang, and Zhuyin Fuhao Di'ershi 注音符號第二式, not to mention the German system, the French system etc. Thanks to the consensus of media worldwide, and through the support of the UN, Hanyu Pinyin has become the standard worldwide. Taiwan is probably the only place in the world that does not support nor employ Hanyu Pinyin. Instead, it uses non-Roman symbols to represent the sound, called Zhuyin Fuhao, alias BoPoMoFo. Officially, that is. Hanyu Pinyin represents the Chinese sound as follows.

b, p, m, f   d, t, n, l   g, k, h   j, q, x   zh, ch, sh, r   z, c, s

a, o, -e, e   ai, ei, ao, ou   an, en, ang, eng   -r, i, u, ü

B. Chinese is a tonal language.

A tone refers to the voice pitch contour. Pitch contours are used in many languages, including English, but for different functions in different languages. English uses them to indicate the speaker's viewpoints, e.g., 'well' in different contours may indicate impatience, surprise, doubt etc. Chinese, on the other hand, uses contours to refer to different meanings, words. Pitch contours with different linguistic functions are not transferable from one language to another. Therefore, it would be futile trying to learn Chinese tones by looking for or identifying their contour counterparts in English.

Mandarin Chinese has 4 distinct tones, the fewest among all Han dialects, i.e., level, rising, dipping and falling, marked — ╱ ∨ ╲ , and it has only one tone-change rule, i.e., ∨ ∨ => ╱ ∨ , though the conditions for this change are fairly complicated. In addition to the four tones, Mandarin also has one neutral(ized) tone, i.e., ˙ , pronounced short/unstressed, which is derived, historically if not synchronically, from the 4 tones; hence the term neutralized. Again, the conditions and environments for the neutralization are highly complex and cannot be explored in this space.

C. Syllable final –r effect (vowel retroflexivisation).

The northern variety of Hanyu, esp. in Beijing, is known for its richness in the –r effect 兒化 at the end of a syllable. For example, 'flower' is 'huā' in southern China but 'huār' in Beijing. Given the prominence of the city Beijing, this sound feature tends to be defined as standard nationwide; but that –r effect is rarely attempted in the south. There do not seem to be rigorous rules governing what can and what cannot take the –r effect. It is thus advised that learners of Chinese resort to rote learning in this case, as probably even native speakers of northern Chinese do.

D. Syllables in Chinese do not 'connect'.

'Connect' here refers to the merging of the tail of a syllable with the head of a subsequent syllable, e.g., English pronounces 'at' + 'all' as 'at+tall', 'did' +'you' as 'did+dyou' and 'that'+'is' as 'that+th'is'. On the other hand, syllables in Chinese are isolated from each other and do not connect in this way. Fortunately, this is not a serious problem for English language learners, as the syllable structures in Chinese are rather limited, and there are not many candidates for this merging. We noted above that Chinese syllables take the form of CV plus possible 'n' and 'ng'. CV does not give rise to connecting, not even in English; so be extra cautious when a syllable ends with 'n' or 'g' and a subsequent syllable begins with a V, e.g., MǐnÀo 'Fujian Province and Macao'. Nobody would understand 'min+nao'!!

E. Retroflexive 捲舌 consonants.

'Retroflexive' refers to consonants that are pronounced with the tip of the tongue curled up (-flexive) backwards (retro-). There are altogether 4 such consonants, i.e., zh, ch, sh, and r. The pronunciation of these consonants reveals the geographical origin of native Chinese speakers. Southerners do not have them, merging them with z, c, and s, as is commonly observed in Taiwan. Curling up of the tongue comes in various degrees. Local Beijing dialect is well known for its prominent curling. Imagine curling up the tongue at the beginning of a syllable and curling it up again for the –r effect!! Try 'zhèr-over here', 'zhuōr-table' and 'shuǐr-water'.

On Chinese Grammar

'Grammar' refers to the ways and rules of how words are organized into a string that is a sentence in a language. Given the fact that all languages have sentences, and at the same time non-sentences, all languages including Chinese have grammar. In this section, the most salient and important features and issues of Chinese grammar will be presented, but a summary of basic structures, as referenced against English, is given first.

A. Similarities in Chinese and English.

	English	Chinese
SVO	They sell coffee.	Tāmen mài kāfēi.
AuxV+Verb	You may sit down!	Nǐ kěyǐ zuòxià ō!
Adj+Noun	sour grapes	suān pútáo
Prep+its Noun	at home	zài jiā
Num+Meas+Noun	a piece of cake	yí kuài dàngāo
Demons+Noun	those students	nàxiē xuéshēng

B. Dissimilar structures.

	English	Chinese
RelClause: Noun	the book that you bought	nǐ mǎi de shū
VPhrase: PrepPhrsae	to eat at home	zài jiā chīfàn
Verb: Adverbial	Eat slowly!	Mànmanr chī!
Set: Subset	6th Sept, 1967	1967 nián 9 yuè 6 hào
	Taipei, Taiwan	Táiwān Táiběi
	3 of my friends…	wǒ de péngyǒu, yǒu sān ge…

C. Modifier precedes modified (MPM).

This is one of the most important grammatical principles in Chinese. We see it operating actively in the charts given above, so that adjectives come before nouns they modify, relative clauses also come before the nouns they modify, possessives come before nouns (tā de diànnǎo 'his computer'), auxiliary verbs come before verbs, adverbial phrases before verbs, prepositional phrases come before verbs etc. This principle operates almost without exceptions in Chinese, while in English modifiers sometimes precede and some other times follow the modified.

D. Principle of Temporal Sequence (PTS).

Components of a sentence in Chinese are lined up in accordance with the sequence of time. This principle operates especially when there is a series of verbs contained within a sentence, or when there is a sentential conjunction. First compare the sequence of 'units' of an event in English and that in its Chinese counterpart.

Event: David /went to New York/ by train /from Boston/ to see his sister.

English: 1   2   3   4   5

Chinese: 1   4   2   3   5

Now in real life, David got on a train, the train departed from Boston, it arrived in New York, and finally he visited his sister. This sequence of units is 'natural' time, and the Chinese sentence 'Dàwèi zuò huǒchē cóng Bōshìdùn dào Niǔyuē qù kàn tā de jiějie' follows it, but not English. In other words, Chinese complies strictly with PTS.

When sentences are conjoined, English has various possibilities in organizing the conjunction. First, the scenario. H1N1 hits China badly (event-1), and as a result, many schools were closed (event-2). Now, English has the following possible ways of conjoining to express this, e.g.,

Many schools were closed, because/since H1N1 hit China badly. (E2+E1)

H1N1 hit China badly, so many schools were closed. (E1+E2)

As H1N1 hit China badly, many schools were closed. (E1+E2)

Whereas the only way of expressing the same in Chinese is E1+E2 when both conjunctions are used (yīnwèi…suǒyǐ...), i.e.,

Zhōngguó yīnwèi H1N1 gǎnrǎn yánzhòng (E1), suǒyǐ xǔduō xuéxiào zhànshí guānbì (E2).

PTS then helps explain why 'cause' is always placed before 'consequence' in Chinese.

PTS is also seen operating in the so-called verb-complement constructions in Chinese, e. g. shā-sǐ 'kill+dead', chī-bǎo 'eat+full', dǎ-kū 'hit+cry' etc. The verb represents an action that must have happened first before its consequence.

There is an interesting group of adjectives in Chinese, namely 'zǎo-early', 'wǎn-late', 'kuài-fast', 'màn-slow', 'duō-plenty', and 'shǎo-few', which can be placed either before (as adverbials) or after (as complements) of their associated verbs, e.g.,

Nǐ míngtiān zǎo diǎr lái! (Come earlier tomorrow!)

Wǒ lái zǎo le. Jìnbúqù. (I arrived too early. I could not get in.)

When 'zǎo' is placed before the verb 'lái', the time of arrival is intended, planned, but when it is placed after, the time of arrival is not pre-planned, maybe accidental. The difference complies with PTS. The same difference holds in the case of the other adjectives in the group, e.g.,

Qǐng nǐ duō mǎi liǎng ge! (Please get two extra!)

Wǒ mǎiduō le. Zāotà le! (I bought two too many. Going to be wasted!)

'Duō!' in the first sentence is going to be pre-planned, a pre-event state, while in the second, it's a post-event report. Pre-event and post-event states then are naturally taken care of by PTS. Our last set in the group is more complicated. 'Kuài' and 'màn' can refer to amount of time in addition to manner of action, as illustrated below.

Nǐ kuài diǎr zǒu; yào chídào le! (Hurry up and go! You'll be late (e.g., for work)!

Qǐng nǐ zǒu kuài yìdiǎr! (Please walk faster!)

'Kuài' in the first can be glossed as 'quick, hurry up' (in as little time as possible after the utterance), while that in the second refers to manner of walking. Similarly, 'màn yìdiǎr zǒu-don't leave yet' and 'zǒu màn yìdiǎr-walk more slowly'.

We have seen in this section the very important role in Chinese grammar played by variations in word-order. European languages exhibit rich resources in changing the forms of verbs, adjectives and nouns, and Chinese, like other Asian languages, takes great advantage of word-order.

E. Where to find subjects in existential sentences.

Existential sentences refer to sentences in which the verbs express appearing (e.g., coming), disappearing (e.g., going) and presence (e.g., written (on the wall)). The existential verbs are all intransitive, and thus they are all associated with a subject, without any objects naturally. This type of sentences deserves a mention in this introduction, as they exhibit a unique structure in Chinese. When their subjects are in definite reference (something that can be referred to, e.g., pronouns and nouns with definite article in English) the subject appears at the front of the sentence, i.e., before the existential verb, but when their subjects are in indefinite reference (nothing in particular), the subject appears after the verb. Compare the following pair of sentences in Chinese against their counterparts in English.

Kèrén dōu lái le. Chīfàn ba! (All the guests we invited have arrived. Let's serve the dinner.)

Duìbùqǐ! Láiwǎn le. Jiālǐ láile yí ge kèrén. (Sorry for being late! I had an (unexpected) guest.)

More examples of post-verbal subjects are given below.

Zhè cì táifēng sǐle bù shǎo rén. (Quite a few people died during the typhoon this time.)

Zuótiān wǎnshàng xiàle duōjiǔ de yǔ? (How long did it rain last night?)

Zuótiān wǎnshàng pǎole jǐ ge fànrén? (How many inmates got away last night?)

Chēzi lǐ zuòle duōshǎo rén a? (How many people were in the car?)

Exactly when to place the existential subject after the verb will remain a challenge for learners of Chinese for quite a significant period of time. Again, observe and deduce!! Memorising sentence by sentence would not help!!

The existential subjects presented above are simple enough, e.g., people, a guest, rain and inmates. But when the subject is complex, further complications emerge!! A portion of the complex subject stays in front of the verb, and the remaining goes to the back of the verb, e.g.,

Míngtiān nǐmen qù jǐge rén? (How many of you will be going tomorrow?)

Wǒ zuìjìn diàole bù shǎo tóufǎ. (I lost=fell quite a lot of hair recently.)

Qùnián dìzhèn, tā sǐle sān ge gēge. (He lost=died 3 brothers during the earthquake last year.)

In linguistics, we say that existential sentences in Chinese have a lot of semantic and information structures involved.

F. A tripartite system of verb classifications in Chinese.

English has a clear division between verbs and adjectives, but the boundary in Chinese is quite blurred, which quite seriously misleads English-speaking learners of Chinese. The error in *Wǒ jīntiān shì máng. 'I am busy today.' is a daily observation in Chinese 101! Why is it a common mistake for beginning learners?

What do our téxtbooks and/or teachers do about it, so that the error is discouraged, if not suppressed? Nothing, much! What has not been realized in our profession is that Chinese verb classification is more strongly semantic, rather than more strongly syntactic as in English.

Verbs in Chinese have 3 sub-classes, namely Action Verbs, State Verbs and Process Verbs. Action Verbs are time-sensitive activities (beginning and ending, frozen with a snap-shot, prolonged), are will-controlled (consent or refuse), and usually take human subjects, e.g., 'chī-eat', 'mǎi-buy' and 'xué-learn'. State Verbs are non-time-sensitive physical or mental states, inclusive of the all-famous adjectives as a further sub-class, e.g., 'ài-love', 'xīwàng-hope' and 'liàng-bright'. Process Verbs refer to instantaneous change from one state to another, 'sǐ-die', 'pò-break, burst' and 'wán-finish'.

The new system of parts of speech in Chinese as adopted in this series is built on this very foundation of this tripartite verb classification. Knowing this new system will be immensely helpful in learning quite a few syntactic structures in Chinese that are nicely related to the 3 classes of verbs, as will be illustrated with negation in Chinese in the section below.

The table below presents some of the most important properties of these 3 classes of verbs, as reflected through syntactic behaviour.

Table 1.

	Action Verbs	State Verbs	Process Verbs
Hěn- modification	x	✓	x
Le- completive	✓	x	✓
Zài- progressive	✓	x	x
Reduplication	✓ (tentative)	✓ (intensification)	x
Bù- negation	✓	✓	x
Méi- negation	✓	x	✓

Here are more examples of the 3 classes of verbs.

Action Verbs: mǎi 'buy', zuò 'sit', xué 'learn; imitate', kàn 'look'

State Verbs: xǐhuān 'like', zhīdào 'know', néng 'can', guì 'expensive'

Process Verbs: wàngle 'forget', chén 'sink', bìyè 'graduate', xǐng 'wake up'

G. Negation.

Negation in Chinese is by means of placing a negative adverb immediately in front of a verb. (Remember that adjectives in Chinese are a type of State verbs!) When an action verb is negated with 'bù', the meaning can be either 'intend not to, refuse to' or 'not in a habit of', e.g.,

Nǐ bù mǎi piào, wǒ jiù bú ràng nǐ jìnqù! (If you don't buy a ticket, I won't let you in!)

Tā zuótiān zhěng tiān bù jiē diànhuà. (He did not want to answer the phone all day yesterday.)

Dèng lǎoshī bù hē jiǔ. (Mr. Teng does not drink.)

'Bù' has the meaning above but is independent of temporal reference. The first sentence above refers to the present moment or a minute later after the utterance, and the second to the past. A habit again is panchronic. But when an action verb is negated with 'méi', its time reference must be in the past, meaning 'something did not come to pass', e.g.,

Tā méi lái shàngbān. (He did not come to work.)
Tā méi dài qián lái. (He did not bring any money.)

A state verb can only be negated with 'bù', referring to the non-existence of that state, whether in the past, at present, or in the future, e.g.,
Tā bù zhīdào zhè jiàn shì. (He did not/does not know this.)
Tā bù xiǎng gēn nǐ qù. (He does not want/did not want to go with you.)
Niǔyuē zuìjìn bú rè. (New York was/is/will not be hot.)

A process verb can only be negated with 'méi', referring to the non-happening of a change from one state to another, usually in the past, e.g.,
Yīfú méi pò, nǐ jiù rēng le? (You threw away perfectly good clothes?)
Niǎo hái méi sǐ; nǐ jiù fàng le ba! (The bird is still alive. Why don't you let it free?)
Tā méi bìyè yǐqián, hái děi dǎgōng. (He has to work odd jobs before graduating.)

As can be gathered from the above, negation of verbs in Chinese follows neat patterns, but this is so only after we work with the new system of verb classifications as presented in this series. Here's one more interesting fact about negation in Chinese before closing this section. When some action verbs refer to some activities that result in something stable, e.g., when you put on clothes, you want the clothes to stay on you, the negation of those verbs can be usually translated in the present tense in English, e.g.,

Tā zěnme méi chuān yīfú? (How come he is naked?)
Wǒ jīntiān méi dài qián. (I have no money with me today.)

H. A new system of Parts of Speech in Chinese.

In the system of parts of speech adopted in this series, there are at the highest level a total of 8 parts of speech, as given below. This system includes the following major properties. First and foremost, it is errors-driven and can address some of the most prevailing errors exhibited by learners of Chinese. This characteristic dictates the depth of sub-categories in a system of grammatical categories. Secondly, it employs the concept of 'default'. This property greatly simplifies the over-all framework of the new system, so that it reduces the number of categories used, simplifies the labeling of categories, and takes advantage of the learners' contribution in terms of positive transfer. And lastly, it incorporates both semantic as well as syntactic concepts, so that it bypasses the traditionally problematic category of adjectives by establishing three major semantic types of verbs, viz. action, state and process.

Adv	Adverb (dōu 'all', dàgài 'probably')
Conj	Conjunction (gēn 'and', kěshì 'but')
Det	Determiner (zhè 'this', nà 'that')
M	Measure (ge, tiáo; xià, cì)
N	Noun (wǒ 'I', yǒngqì 'courage')
Ptc	Particle (ma 'question particle', le 'completive verbal particle')
Prep	Preposition (cóng 'from', duìyú 'regarding')
V	Action Verb, transitive (mǎi 'buy', chī 'eat')
Vi	Action Verb, intransitive (kū 'cry', zuò 'sit')
Vaux	Auxiliary Verb (néng 'can', xiǎng 'would like to')
V-sep	Separable Verb (jiéhūn 'get married', shēngqì 'get angry')
Vs	State Verb, intransitive (hǎo 'good', guì 'expensive')
Vst	State Verb, transitive (xǐhuān 'like', zhīdào 'know')
Vs-attr	State Verb, attributive (zhǔyào 'primary', xiùzhēn 'mini-')
Vs-pred	State Verb, predicative (gòu 'enough', duō 'plenty')
Vp	Process Verb, intransitive (sǐ 'die', wán 'finish')

Vpt   Process Verb, transitive (pò (dòng) 'lit. break (hole), liè (fèng) 'lit. crack (a crack))

Table 2. Eight Parts of Speech in Chinese

Parts of Speech	Symbols	Example
Noun	N	水-shuǐ (water), 五-wǔ (five), 昨天-zuótiān (yesterday), 學校-xuéxiào (school), 他-tā (he/him), 幾-jǐ ((a)few)
Verb	V	吃-chī (to eat), 告訴-gàosù (to tell), 容易-róngyì (easy), 快樂 kuàilè (happy), 知道-zhīdào (to know), 破-pò (to be broken)
Adverb	Adv	很-hěn (very), 不-bù (no), 常- cháng (often), 到處-dàochù (everywhere), 也-yě (also), 就-jiù (only/then), 難道-nándào (could it really be that…)
Conjunction	Conj	和-hàn (and), 跟-gēn (and), 而且-érqiě (also), 雖然-suīrán (although), 因為-yīnwèi (because)
Preposition	Prep	從-cóng (from), 對-duì (to), 向-xiàng (to), 跟-gēn (to/with), 在-zài (at), 給-gěi (to)
Measure	M	個-ge (for general), 張-zhāng (for flat objects), 杯-bēi (for cup), 次-cì (for times, occurrences), 頓-dùn (for the duration of a meal/a duration of action), 公尺-gōngchǐ (for length)
Particle	Ptc	的-de (for modification), 得-de (for complement), 啊-a (for sentence final, realization), 嗎-ma (for question), 完-wán (for completion of action), 掉-diào (for separation), 把-bǎ (for disposal), 喂-wèi (for addressing, people especially over the phone)
Determiner	Det	這-zhè (this), 那-nà (that), 某-mǒu (somebody or something), 每-měi (every/each), 哪-nǎ (which)

1. Noun（名詞）

The category noun includes common nouns (一般名詞), numerals (數詞), words indicating time (時間詞), words indicating location (地方詞), and pronouns (代名詞). Nouns can be used as the subject (主語), object (賓語), or an attributive (定語) in a sentence. It is noteworthy to mention that words indicating time or location can be used as an adverbial (狀語) in a sentence. For example, 他明天出國 Tā míngtiān chūguó (He is leaving the country tomorrow). Thus, parts of speech and sentence functions are distinct notions.

2. Measure （量詞）(or linguistically classifiers)

There are measures that modify nouns, such as 一件衣服 yí jiàn yīfú (a shirt) and 一碗飯 yì wǎn fàn (a bowl of rice). There are also classifiers that modify actions, such as 來了一趟 lái le yí tàng (came once). Classifiers appear after determiners and/or numerals.

3. Determiner (限定詞)

Determiners in the Chinese language include 這 zhè (this), 那 nà (that), 哪 nǎ (which), 每 měi (every/each), and 某 mǒu (somebody or something). Determiners have unique syntactic status. They always appear in the far-left position of a noun phrase, e.g., 那三本書是他的。 Nà sān běn shū shì tā de. (Those three books are his).

4. Preposition (介詞)

Prepositions connect a noun to the main verb or verb phrase, by way of specifying its time, place, manner, instrument etc. Common prepositions in Chinese are given in Table 2 above. They in general are placed in front of verb phrases, e.g., 他在家裡看電視。 Tā zài jiā lǐ kàn diànshì. (He is watching TV at home.)

5. Conjunction (連詞)

By definition, conjunctions join elements. There are two types of conjunctions, intra-phrase conjunctions and sentential conjunctions. The former connect two or more similar elements, e.g., 中國跟美國 Zhōngguó gēn Měiguó (China and the United States), 美麗與哀愁 měilì yǔ āichóu (beauty and sadness), and 我或你 wǒ huò nǐ (me or you). The latter bind single sentences into compound sentences; 雖然 suīrán... (although) and 可是 kěshì... (but) are two such conjunctions. Chinese sentential conjunctions usually appear in pairs, with the first (such as 雖然 suīrán (although)) preceding the second (such as 可是 kěshì (but)). First sentence conjunctions such as 不但 búdàn (not only), 因為 yīnwèi (because), 雖然 suīrán (although), 儘管 jǐnguǎn (in spite of), 既然 jìrán (since), 縱使 zòngshǐ (even though), and 如果 rúguǒ (if) may appear before or after the subject of a sentence. Second sentence conjunctions such as 但是 dànshì (however), 所以 suǒyǐ (therefore), 然而 ránér (however), 不過 búguò (but), and 否則 fǒuzé (otherwise) may only appear before the subject. Following are two examples:

➊ 她不但寫字寫得漂亮，而且畫畫也畫得好。
Tā búdàn xiězì xiě de piàoliàng, érqiě huàhuà yě huà de hǎo.
Her penmanship is pretty, and she paints well too.

② 我因為生病，所以沒辦法來上課。

Wǒ yīnwèi shēngbìng, suǒyǐ méi bànfǎ lái shàngkè.

I cannot come to class because I am sick.

When the two sentences do not share the same subject, the conjunctions may only appear before, not after, the subjects. See the following two examples:

③ 我們家的人都喜歡看棒球比賽，不但爸爸喜歡看，而且媽媽也喜歡看。

Wǒ men jiā de rén dōu xǐhuān kàn bàngqiú bǐsài, búdàn bàba xǐhuān kàn, érqiě māma yě xǐhuān kàn.

Our family loves watching baseball. It's not just my dad, my mom likes to watch too.

④ 因為房子倒了，所以他無家可歸。

Yīnwèi fángzi dǎo le, suǒyǐ tā wújiā kěguī.

The house collapsed, so he has no home to return to.

6. Adverb（副詞）

Adverbs modify verb phrases, and modifiers in Chinese always precede the modified. In most cases, adverbs appear between the subject and the verb. Adverbs in Chinese have traditionally been classified into several sub-categories based on meanings. What is noteworthy here is the fact that monosyllabic adverbs such as 才 cái (just, only), 就 jiù (only, merely, then), 再 zài (again, and then), and 還 hái (still, additionally) have multiple meanings, making them very difficult to learn at the initial stage.

Our traditional definition of adverbs is less than perfect, and there are many exceptions to our rules of adverbs. One notable exception relates to a group of adverbs (?) that can be placed at the beginning of a sentence, in violation of our typical rule, e.g., 難道你不想去？Nándào nǐ bù xiǎng qù? (You mean you don't want to go?), in which the adverb 'nándào' not only violates the syntactic rule but also does not follow the functional rule of adverbs that they modify verb phrases. In fact, this adverb expresses the speaker's attitude and expectation. Maybe it's not an adverb after all.

7. Particle（助詞）

Particles are members of closed word classes, and despite their limited number, their importance in syntax warrants a place among the main parts of speech. Particles can be put into the following six categories based on their different functions:

Interjections (感嘆助詞): 喂wèi, 咦yí, 哦ó, 唉āi, 哎āi

Phase particles (時相助詞): 完wán, 好hǎo, 過₂guò, 下去xiàqù

Verb particles (動助詞): 上shàng, 下xià, 起qǐ, 開kāi, 掉diào, 走zǒu, 住zhù, 到dào, 出chū

Aspectual particles (時態助詞): 了₁le, 著zhe, 過₁guò

Structural particles (結構助詞): 的de, 地de, 得de, 把bǎ, 將jiāng, 被bèi, 遭zāo

Sentential particles (句尾助詞): 啊a, 嗎ma, 吧ba, 呢ne, 啦la, 了₂le

Of these six categories, the widely recognizable aspectual particles always appear after the verb of a sentence, indicating the internal temporal structure of an event. For example, 了 le marks completion, 過 guò marks experience, and 著 zhe marks continuation. Phase particles comprise the complement in traditional verb-compliment structure. We categorize these words because their semantic meaning has either disappeared or weakened. Words in this class present the temporal structure of an action and appear after verbs and/or before aspectual particles.

Verb particles (動助詞) are a type of complement (補語). Different verb particles bear different intrinsic meanings, not related to the original, literal meanings. For example, 上shàng and 到 dào are used to express contact (接觸義); 開kāi, 掉diào, 下xià, and 走 zǒu are used to express separation (分離義); 起qǐ and 出chū are used to express emergence (顯現義); and 住zhù is used to express immobility (靜止義). Verb particles express the relationship between a theme or patient (客體) and its source (源點) and goal (終點) (Bolinger, 1971[2] ; Teng, 1977[3]). Here we use Teng's (2012:240)[4] examples to further elaborate:

⑤ a 他把魚尾巴切走了。
      Tā bǎ yú wěibā qiēzǒu le.
      (He cut away the fish tail.)

    b 他把魚尾巴切掉了。
      Tā bǎ yú wěibā qiēdiào le.
      (He cut off the fish tail.)

---

[2] Bolinger, D. (1971). *The Phrasal Verb in English*. Cambridge: Harvard University Press.

[3] Teng, Shou-hsin. (1977). A grammar of verb-particles in Chinese. *Journal of Chinese Linguistics*, Vol.5, 1-25.

[4] 鄧守信（2012），漢語語法論文集（中譯本）。北京市：北京語言大學出版社。

The characteristics of verb particles 走zǒu and 掉diào are explained as follows:

走zǒu: meaning that the theme is separated from the source, but accompanies the action taker.

掉diào: meaning that the theme is separated from the source, and disappears from the speaker or the sphere in which the action takes place.

Here the fish tail can be taken as the object of the sentence, and the fish itself as the source (源點). With this understanding, it is easy to understand the difference between 走zǒu and 掉diào.

Understanding the characteristics of verb particles allows learners to infer sentence meaning through verb-particle collocation, and also helps them discern which particles go with which verbs. When used with aspectual particles, verb particles precede, however, verb particles do not appear with phase particles.

Structural particles include attribute particle (定語助詞) 的de; adverbial particle (狀語助詞) 地de; complement particle (補語助詞) 得de; particles that mark the following noun as a direct object (處置助詞) such as 把bǎ and 將jiāng; and passive particles (被動助詞) 被bèi, 給gěi, and 遭zāo.

8. Verb (動詞)

The syntactic function of verbs is to serve as the main predicate of a sentence. In order for learners to understand the syntactic behaviors marked by verbs, we classify verbs into three sub-classes: action verbs (動作動詞), state verbs (狀態動詞), and process verbs (變化動詞) (Teng, 1974)[5] . Action verbs imply time and will, state verbs imply neither time nor will, and process verbs imply only time.

Action verbs refer to what one performs willfully and intentionally, either physically or mentally. They are transient in the sense that they terminate naturally, e.g., 吃 (chī, to eat) must be done intentionally and the activity ends usually in 30 minutes or so. An action can be prolonged and it can also be terminated abruptly. An action can also be refused by the person involved. These properties are not just whimsical and philosophical. They are directly associated with syntactic/grammatical rules, as will be detailed immediately below.

---

[5] Teng, Shou-hsin. (1974). Verb classification and its pedagogical extensions. *Journal of Chinese Language Teachers Association*, 9 (2), 84-92.

State verbs refer to quality, condition and 'state'. State verbs can be further classified as follows.

Cognitive verbs (認知動詞): 知道zhīdào (to know), 愛ài (to love), 喜歡 xǐhuān (to like), 恨hèn (to hate), 覺得juéde (to feel, to think), 希望xīwàng (to hope)

Modal verbs (能願動詞): 能néng (can), 會huì (can/will), 可以kěyǐ (could/may), 應該yīnggāi (should)

Optative verbs (意願動詞): 想xiǎng (would like to), 要yào (to want to), 願意 yuànyì (willing to), 打算dǎsuàn (to plan to)

Relational verbs (關係動詞): 是shì (to be), 叫jiào (to be called), 姓xìng (to be surnamed), 有yǒu (to have)

Adjectives (形容詞): 小xiǎo (small), 高gāo (tall), 紅hóng (popular), 漂亮 piàoliàng (beautiful), 快樂kuàilè (happy)

Adjectives can be used as predicates (謂詞) or modifiers (修飾語). Most cognitive verbs are transitive state verbs. Modal verbs, which are used to express ability or possibility, and optative verbs, which are used to express a wish, bear syntactic differences to other state verbs. Modal verbs and optative verbs are followed by a main verb, rather than a noun phrase or an aspectual particle. We group these two classes of state verbs as Vaux (助動詞) to show their unique syntactic functions. Vaux, like verbs, can fit in the 'V-not-V' structure (see Table 3), whereas adverbs cannot. Relational verbs do not follow adverbs of degree, i.e.,, they are incompatible with modifiers such as 很hěn (very), bearing different syntactic rules than general state verbs.

The differences between action verbs, state verbs, and process verbs can be seen in their syntactic structures, as shown in Table 3. For example, action verbs can be collocated with 不bù (no), 沒méi (not), 了$_1$ le (verbal particle indicating a completed action), 在zài (progressive aspect verb), 著zhe (a particle indicating progressing or continuation of action), and 把bǎ (disposal particle); state verbs cannot be collocated with 沒méi, 了$_1$ le, 在zài, and 把bǎ; process verbs can be collocated with 沒méi and 了$_1$ le, but cannot be collocated with 不bù. Upon learning that 破pò (to be broken) is a Vp (process verb), a student would never then come up with the sentence: *花瓶不破huāpíng bú pò (*The vase didn't break), and would know that 破pò needs to be collocated with negative modifier 沒méi instead of 不bù .

Table 3. The Three Sub-classes of Verbs and Their Syntactic Rules

	不	沒	很	了₁	在	著	把	請(祈使)	V(一)V	V不V	ABAB	AABB
Action Verbs	v	v	x	v	v	v	v	v	v	v	v	x
State Verbs	v	x	v	x	x	x	x	x	x	v	x	v
Process Verbs	x	v	x	v	x	x	x	x	x	x	x	x

(Table compiled from Teng (1974) and Prof. Teng's class handouts)

It is noteworthy that these rules are not without counter-examples. When there are rules, there are also exceptions. The few exceptions, however, do not take away from the advantage that this table provides.

In addition to the 8 major parts of speech in Chinese, the following lower-level subcategories are employed. The marking –t refers to transitive verbs, whereas –i to intransitive. –pred refers to adjectives (sub-class of State Verbs) that can serve only as predicates, and –attr to adjectives that can serve only as attributes (modifiers). –sep refers to separable intransitive verbs (see below for discussion).

(1) –attr (attributive only, 唯定)

-attr marks state verbs that can only be used as attributives. In general, adjectives (state verbs) are either used as the predicate of a sentence (那女孩很美麗 Nà nǚhái hěn měilì – That girl is very pretty), or the attributive that modifies a noun (她是一個美麗的女孩 Tā shì yí ge měilì de nǚhái – She is a pretty girl). However, some state verbs such as 公共 gōnggòng (public) and 野生 yěshēng (wild) can only be used as attributives. For example, 公共場所 gōnggòng chǎngsuǒ (a public place), 野生品種 yěshēng pǐnzhǒng (a wild breed), and 那是野生的 Nà shì yěshēng de (that is wild). These verbs do not stand on their own as predicates. For example, *那種象很野生 Nà zhǒng xiàng hěn yěshēng (*That breed of elephant is wild) is an incorrect sentence.

(2) –pred (predicative only, 唯謂)

-pred marks state verbs that can only be used as predicates. In contrast to the previous class, adjectives in this class only function as predicates and cannot be used as attributives. A good example for this class of verb is 夠 gòu (enough). When students understand that 夠 gòu (enough) is a Vs-pred, they would not make sentences such as *我有（不）夠的錢。Wǒ yǒu (bú) gòu de qián. (*I do not have enough money) and would instead render the correct sentence: 我的錢（不）夠。Wǒ de qián (bú) gòu. (I do not have enough money).

(3) –sep (separable, 可離)

-sep marks a unique verb class in Chinese. These verbs are traditionally called separable words (離合詞). Words in general, probably universally, do not become separated, e.g., *under-not-stand. But –sep verbs in Chinese can be separated, making it look like the verb-object syntax. Separable words can be interposed by aspectual particles (example ⑥), time duration (example ⑦), recipient of an action (example ⑧), or modifiers indicating amount (example ⑨).

⑥ 我昨天<u>下</u>了<u>課</u>，就和朋友去看電影。
Wǒ zuótiān xià le kè, jiù hàn péngyǒu qù kàn diànyǐng.
Yesterday I went to a movie with friends after class

⑦ 他<u>唱</u>了三小時的<u>歌</u>。很累。
Tā chàng le sān xiǎoshí de gē, hěn lèi.
He sang for three hours. it was exhausting

⑧ 我想<u>見</u>你一<u>面</u>。
Wǒ xiǎng jiàn nǐ yí miàn.
I want to meet up with you

⑨ 這次旅行，他<u>照</u>了一百多張<u>相</u>。
Zhè cì lǚxíng, tā zhào le yìbǎi duō zhāng xiàng.
He took over 100 pictures on this trip

Separable words are intransitive verbs, including action verbs (V-sep), state verbs (Vs-sep), and process verbs (Vp-sep). Understanding separable verbs and their markings helps students avoid making erroneous sentences such as *他唱歌三小時。Tā chànggē sān xiǎo shí. (*He sang for three hours). In Taiwan, however, some separable words have started taking on transitive usage, such as 幫忙 bāngmáng (to help). This new usage is relatively recent and localized, and thus they are classified as intransitive in this volume.

Default Markings

So that we do not give a long string of markings when we specify parts of speech, a system of default markings has been utilized in this volume, as detailed below. To illustrate, when V is presented, it refers to an Action verb that is at the same time transitive.

V: Action verb, transitive, e.g., 買-mǎi (to buy), 做-zuò (to do), 說-shuō (to say)

Vi: Action verb, intransitive, 跑-pǎo (to run), 坐-zuò (to sit), 笑-xiào (to laugh), 睡-shuì (to sleep)

V-sep: Action verb, separable, intransitive, 唱歌-chànggē (to sing), 上網-shàngwǎng (to access the internet), 打架-dǎjià (to engage in a fight)

Vs: State verb, intransitive, 冷-lěng (cold), 高-gāo (tall), 漂亮-piàoliàng (beautiful)

Vst: State verb, transitive, 關心-guānxīn (to be concerned about), 喜歡-xǐhuān (to like), 同意-tóngyì (to agree with)

Vs-attr: State verb, intransitive, attributive only, 野生-yěshēng (wild), 公共-gōnggòng (public), 新興-xīnxīng (emerging)

Vs-pred: State verb, intransitive, predicative only, 夠-gòu (enough), 多-duō (plenty), 少-shǎo (few in number)

Vs-sep: State verb, intransitive, separable, 放心-fàngxīn (not to worry), 幽默-yōumò (humorous), 生氣-shēngqì (angry)

Vaux: State verb, auxiliary, intransitive, 會-huì (can/will), 可以-kěyǐ (could/may), 應該yīnggāi (should)

Vp: Process verb, intransitive, 破-pò (to be broken), 壞-huài (to go bad), 死-sǐ (to die), 感冒-gǎnmào (to catch a cold)

Vpt: Process verb, transitive, 忘記-wàngjì (to forget), 變成-biànchéng (to become), 丟-diū (to have lost something)

Vp-sep: Process verb, intransitive, separable, 結婚-jiéhūn (to get married to), 生病-shēngbìng (to fall ill), 畢業-bìyè (to graduate)

Notes

Default values:

When no marking appears under a category, a default reading takes place, which has been built into the system by observing the commonest patterns of the highest frequency. A default value can be loosely understood as the most likely candidate. A default system results in using fewer symbols, which makes it easy on the eyes, reducing the amount of processing. Our default readings are as follows.

Default transitivity.

When a verb is not marked, i.e., V, it's an action verb. An unmarked action verb, furthermore, is transitive. A state verb is marked as Vs, but if it's not further marked, it's intransitive. The same holds for process verbs, i.e., Vp is by default intransitive.

Default position of adjectives.

Typical adjectives occur as predicates, e.g., 'This is great!' Therefore, unmarked Vs are predicative, and adjectives that cannot be predicates will be marked for this feature, e.g., zhǔyào 'primary' is an adjective but it cannot be a predicate, i.e., *Zhè tiáo lù hěn zhǔyào. '*This road is very primary.' Therefore it is marked Vs-attr, meaning it can only be used attributively, i.e., Zhǔyào dàolù 'primary road'. On the other hand, 'gòu' 'enough' in Chinese can only be used predicatively, not attributively, e.g., 'shíjiān gòu' '*?Time is enough.', but not *gòu shíjiā 'enough time'. Therefore gòu is marked Vs-pred. Employing this new system of parts of speech guarantees good grammar!

Default wordhood.

In English, words cannot be torn apart and be used separately, e.g., *mis- not –understand. Likewise in Chinese, e.g., *xǐbùhuān 'do not like'. However, there is a large group of words in Chinese that are exceptions to this probably universal rule and can be separated. They are called 'separable words', marked -sep in our new system of parts of speech. For example, shēngqì 'angry' is a word, but it is fine to say shēng tā qì 'angry at him'. Jiéhūn 'get married' is a word but it's fine to say jiéguòhūn 'been married before' or jiéguò sān cì hūn 'been married 3 times before'. There are at least a couple of hundred separable words in modern Chinese. Even native speakers have to learn that certain words can be separated. Thus, memorizing them is the only way to deal with them by learners, and our new system of parts of speech helps them along nicely. Go over the vocabulary lists in this series and look for the marking –sep.

Now, what motivates this severing of words? Ask Chinese gods, not your teachers! We only know a little about the syntactic circumstances under which they get separated. First and foremost, separable words are in most cases intransitive verbs, whether action, state or process. When these verbs are further associated with targets (nouns, conceptual objects), frequency (number of times), duration (for how long), occurrence (done, done away with) etc., separation takes pace and these associated elements are inserted in between. More examples are given below.

Wǒ jīnnián yǐjīng kǎoguò 20 cì shì le!! (I've taken 20 exams to date this year!)

Wǒ dàoguò qiàn le; tā hái shēngqì! (I apologized, but he's still mad!)

Fàng sān tiān jià; dàjiā dōu zǒu le. (There will be a break of 3 days, and everyone has left.)

Grammatical Description

In this A to Z dictionary, each grammatical entry contains 3 sub-sections: Function, Structure and Usage.

Function

Instead of merely giving a list of sentence structures, we explain grammatical functions, affording students a clear understanding of a grammar point. Primarily, we aim to answer the question 'What does this grammar item do? What do native speakers use it for?' For example, the complement after 得 de has a complementary function, while adverbials and attributives has a modifying function. Here we can take the reduplicated form of monosyllabic verbs as an example, VV. This is a rather straightforward form, saying a verb twice, but we need to understand the function of the form: *verb reduplication suggests "reduced strength"*. It also suggests that the action is easy to accomplish. When what is expressed is a request/command, verb reduplication softens the tone of the statement and the hearer finds the request/command more moderate. To take another famous example of Chinese grammar, BA-construction. Instead of concentrating on the syntactic structures of this particularly puzzling construction, we first dwell on the question 'What do BA sentences do? What do native speakers use it in their utterances for?'

Structure

Only after functionality do we introduce structures. In this section we first lay out the basic structure of a grammar point, and, in some cases, present them in a linear fashion, such as 'subject + 把bǎ + object + V + 了'. We again list functions, e.g., subject and object, and not merely nouns and verbs. What follow are descriptions of the 'negative structure' and 'interrogative structure' of the given grammar point so that students will know how to voice negativity and to ask questions based on the basic form. For example, we point out that the negative modifier for state verbs is 不bù instead of 沒méi. When introducing phrases or clauses with the word 把, we point out that the negative modifier should appear before 把bǎ instead of before the verb. In terms of interrogative structure, we reserve 嗎ma primarily for the first few lessons, as it is a straightforward, commonly used interrogative expression. Thereafter we tend to use V-not-V, 沒有méi yǒu (used at the end of a sentence), and 是不是shìbúshì as interrogative forms.

Usage

Not to be confused with linguistic pragmatics (語用學), this section points out when to use and when not to use a specific grammar point, and what to be careful of when using it. For example, reduplicated state verbs cannot be used with adverbs of degree, i.e.,, *很輕輕鬆鬆 *hěn qīngqīng sōngsōng (*highly very xxx) is not a grammatically correct expression. Perfective 了le is used to indicate the completion of an action, not an action that has occurred in the past. Some grammar points might be confused with other structures or phrases. When necessary, we also give detailed explanations accordingly. For example, upon learning both 一點yìdiǎn (a bit) and 有一點yǒu yìdiǎn (a little), we explain their respective differences in usage. Extra attention is given to the usage section, and to supplement teacher's experience we have employed interlanguage corpora to provide information that will help students master Chinese. Lastly, we include, if necessary and helpful, comparative and contrastive notes between Chinese and English. It is regrettable that we are not able, at this stage, to provide contrastive notes relating to other languages.

Final Words

This is a very brief introduction to the organization and major contents of our A to Z Chinese Grammar for Learners. This introduction can only highlight the most salient properties of Chinese grammar. It is not our intention to present a coherent, systematic book on the entirety of Chinese grammar. There exist excellent such books, e.g., Li, Charles and Sandra Thompson. 1982. *Mandarin Chinese: a Reference Grammar*. UC Los Angeles Press. (Authorized reprinting by Crane publishing Company, Taipei, Taiwan.) We welcome suggestions for improvements, steng@ntnu.edu.tw.

Shou-hsin Teng, Ph.D., Editor in Chief
National Taiwan Normal University
Chungyuan Christian University, Taiwan
March 2018

Chinese Parts of Speech 2017
漢語詞類

Major 8 Parts of Speech
八大詞類

Symbols	Parts of Speech	八大詞類	Examples
N	noun	名詞	水、五、昨天、學校、他、幾
V	verb	動詞	吃、告訴、容易、快樂，知道、破
Adv	adverb	副詞	很、不、常、到處、也、就、難道
Conj	conjunction	連詞	和、跟，而且、雖然、因為
Prep	preposition	介詞	從、對、向、跟、在、給
M	measure	量詞	個、條、張、次、頓、公尺、碗
Ptc	particle	助詞	的、得、啊、嗎、完、掉、把、喂
Det	determiner	限定詞	這、那、某、每、哪

Verb Classification
動詞分類

Symbols	Classification	動詞分類	Examples
V	transitive action verbs	及物動作詞	買、做、說
Vi	intransitive action verbs	不及物動作詞	跑、坐、睡、笑
V-sep	intransitive action verbs, separable	不及物動作離合詞	唱歌、上網、打架
Vs	intransitive state verbs	不及物狀態詞	冷、高、漂亮
Vst	transitive state verbs	及物狀態動詞	關心、喜歡、同意
Vs-attr	intransitive state verbs, attributive only	唯定不及物狀態動詞	野生、公共、新興
Vs-pred	intransitive state verbs, predicative only	唯謂不及物狀態動詞	夠、多、少
Vs-sep	intransitive state verbs, separable	不及物狀態離合詞	放心、幽默、生氣
Vaux	auxiliary verbs	助動詞	會、能、可以
Vp	intransitive process verbs	不及物變化動詞	破、感冒、壞、死
Vpt	transitive process verbs	及物變化動詞	忘記、變成、丟
Vp-sep	intransitive process verbs, separable	不及物變化離合詞	結婚、生病、畢業

Default Markings
內定值說明

Symbols	Default Values
V	Action Verb, Transitive
Vs	State Verb , Intransitive
Vp	Process Verb, Intransitive
V-sep	Separable Verb, Intransitive

目 次
Contents

A

B

D

O

P

Q

T

W

X

Y

Z

A-not-A Questions

Function

The A-not-A form of making a question is the most neutral way to ask a question in Chinese and closest to yes/no questions in English.

❶ 王先生要不要喝咖啡？
Wáng xiānshēng yào bú yào hē kāfēi?
Does Mr. Wang want to have some coffee?

❷ 這是不是烏龍茶？
Zhè shì bú shì Wūlóng chá?
Is this Oolong tea?

❸ 臺灣人喜歡不喜歡喝茶？
Táiwān rén xǐhuān bù xǐhuān hē chá?
Do Taiwanese people like to drink tea?

Structures

The 'A' in the structure refers to the first verbal element.

❶ 他喝咖啡。　　　　　他喝不喝咖啡？
Tā hē kāfēi.　　　　　Tā hē bù hē kāfēi?
He'll have coffee.　　Does he want to drink coffee?

❷ 你是日本人。　　　　你是不是日本人？
Nǐ shì Rìběn rén.　　Nǐ shì bú shì Rìběn rén?
You are Japanese.　　Are you Japanese?

❸ 他來臺灣。　　　　　他來不來臺灣？
Tā lái Táiwān.　　　　Tā lái bù lái Táiwān?
He came to Taiwan.　Is he coming to Taiwan?

Usage

When the verbal element (A) in an A-not-A question is disyllabic (XY), the second syllable (Y) can be dropped in the first 'A' of the pattern, so 'XY-not-XY' is the same as 'X-not-XY'. For example, 你喜歡不喜歡我？Nǐ xǐhuān bù xǐhuān wǒ? is the same as 你喜不喜歡我？Nǐ xǐ bù xǐhuān wǒ? (Do you like me?)

Answering Questions in Chinese

Affirmative answers can be formed by repeating the main verb in the question, followed by a sentence in the affirmative, e.g.,

❶ A：他是不是臺灣人？/他是臺灣人嗎？
Tā shì bú shì Táiwān rén? Tā shì Táiwān rén ma?
Is he Taiwanese?

B：是，他是臺灣人。
Shì, tā shì Táiwān rén.
Yes, he is Taiwanese.

❷ A：你喜不喜歡臺灣？/你喜歡臺灣嗎？
Nǐ xǐ bù xǐhuān Táiwān? Nǐ xǐhuān Táiwān ma?
Do you like Taiwan?

1

B：喜歡，我喜歡臺灣。
Xǐhuān, wǒ xǐhuān Táiwān.
Yes, I like Taiwan.

❸ A：王先生是不是日本人？／王先生是日本人嗎？
Wáng xiānshēng shì bú shì Rìběn rén?
Wáng xiānshēng shì Rìběn rén ma?
Is Mr. Wang Japanese?

B：是，王先生是日本人。
Shì, Wáng xiānshēng shì Rìběn rén.
Yes, Mr. Wang is Japanese.

❹ A：他喝不喝烏龍茶？／他喝烏龍茶嗎？
Tā hē bù hē Wūlóng chá? Tā hē Wūlóng chá ma?
Does he drink Oolong tea?

B：喝，他喝烏龍茶。
Hē, tā hē Wūlóng chá.
Yes, he drinks Oolong tea.

In Chinese, short answers in the affirmative can be made by simply repeating the verb from the question.

❶ 你是王先生嗎？　　　　　　　是。
Nǐ shì Wáng xiānshēng ma?　　　Shì.
Are you Mr. Wang?　　　　　　 Yes.

❷ 他來不來臺灣？　　　　　　　來。
Tā lái bù lái Táiwān?　　　　　Lái.
Will he come to Taiwan?　　　　Yes.

❸ 他喜歡不喜歡喝茶？　　　　　喜歡。
Tā xǐhuān bù xǐhuān hē chá?　　Xǐhuān.
Does he like tea?　　　　　　　Yes.

Negative replies can be formed by repeating the main verb in its negative form, i.e., 不＋verb, followed by a sentence in the negative. 不 bù is an adverb which is placed before a verb or another adverb, e.g.,

❶ 他是不是李先生？　　　　　　不是，他不是李先生。
Tā shì bú shì Lǐ xiānshēng?　　 Bú shì, tā bú shì Lǐ xiānshēng.
Is he Mr. Li?　　　　　　　　　No, he is not Mr. Li.

❷ 王先生喝茶嗎？　　　　　　　不，他不喝。
Wáng xiānshēng hē chá ma?　　 Bù, tā bù hē.
Does Mr. Wang drink tea?　　　 No, he doesn't drink tea.

❸ 李小姐是不是臺灣人？　　　　不是，李小姐不是臺灣人。
Lǐ xiǎojiě shì bú shì　　　　　　Bú shì. Lǐ xiǎojiě bú shì
Táiwān rén.　　　　　　　　　 Táiwān rén?
Is Miss Li Taiwanese?　　　　　No, Miss Li is not
　　　　　　　　　　　　　　　Taiwanese.

In Chinese, a brief answer to a question can be formed by repeating the verb in the negative or in the positive.

❶ 他要不要喝咖啡？　　　　　　　　不要。
　Tā yào bú yào hē kāfēi?　　　　　　Bú yào.
　Does he want to drink coffee?　　　No.

❷ 你喜歡不喜歡喝烏龍茶？　　　　　不喜歡。
　Nǐ xǐhuān bù xǐhuān hē Wūlóng chá?　Bù xǐhuān
　Do you like to drink Oolong tea?　　No.

❸ 陳小姐是不是美國人？　　　　　　是。
　Chén xiǎojiě shì bú shì Měiguó rén?　Shì.
　Is Miss Chen American?　　　　　　Yes.

Usage　There are some exceptions to the rules above. For example, when the verb is 姓 'to be surnamed' or 叫 'to be called'. When the question is 他姓李嗎？Tā xìng Lǐ ma? 'Is he surnamed Li?', the negative reply should be 不姓李 Bú xìng Lǐ. '(He is) not surnamed Li.', rather than *不姓bú xìng. When the question is 李先生叫開文嗎？Lǐ xiānshēng jiào Kāiwén ma? 'Is Mr. Li called Kaiwen?', the negative reply should be 不叫開文 Bú jiào Kāiwén. '(He is) not called Kaiwen.', rather than *不叫bú jiào.

按照, ànzhào, (Prep), in accordance with

Function　The preposition 按照 refers to 'on the basis of, in accordance with, following'.

❶ 按照醫生說的，你睡覺以前要吃一包藥。
　Ànzhào yīshēng shuō de, nǐ shuìjiào yǐqián yào chī yì bāo yào.
　According to what the doctor said, you need to take a packet of medicine before going to bed.

❷ 我打算按照網路的介紹，自己去花蓮玩玩。
　Wǒ dǎsuàn ànzhào wǎnglù de jièshào, zìjǐ qù Huālián wánwán.
　I plan to visit Hualien on my own and follow the recommendations on the internet.

❸ 按照臺灣的法律，剛來臺灣的外國學生不可以工作。
　Ànzhào Táiwān de fǎlǜ, gāng lái Táiwān de wàiguó xuéshēng bù kěyǐ gōngzuò.
　According to Taiwan law, foreign students who have just arrived in Taiwan cannot work.

Structures　The 按照 prepositional phrase can be placed either at the very beginning of a sentence, or before a verb.

❶ 按照他的旅行計畫，他現在應該在法國。
　Ànzhào tā de lǚxíng jìhuà, tā xiànzài yīnggāi zài Fǎguó.
　According to his travel plan, he should be in France now.

3

❷ 你應該按照老師的建議，練習寫中國字。
Nǐ yīnggāi ànzhào lǎoshī de jiànyì, liànxí xiě Zhōngguó zì.
You should follow the teacher's suggestion and practice writing Chinese characters.

Negation :

❶ 他沒按照老師的建議準備考試。
Tā méi ànzhào lǎoshī de jiànyì zhǔnbèi kǎoshì.
He did not follow the teacher's advice in preparing for the exam.

❷ 我常常不按照老闆說的做事。
Wǒ chángcháng bú ànzhào lǎobǎn shuō de zuòshì.
I often do not follow my supervisor's instructions when working.

❸ 小高沒按照計畫回來工作，他的老闆很不高興。
Xiǎo Gāo méi ànzhào jìhuà huílái gōngzuò, tā de lǎobǎn hěn bù gāoxìng.
Xiao Gao did not return to work as planned and his boss is very unhappy.

Questions : In addition to 嗎, 是不是 is the only other pattern possible when the preposition 按照 is used.

❶ 你是不是按照老師給你的建議練習說話？
Nǐ shìbúshì ànzhào lǎoshī gěi nǐ de jiànyì liànxí shuōhuà?
Are you practicing speaking as per the teacher's suggestion?

❷ 你是不是按照網路上的說明做小籠包？
Nǐ shìbúshì ànzhào wǎnglù shàng de shuōmíng zuò xiǎolóngbāo?
Are you following the instructions from the internet in making the steamed dumplings?

❸ 請你按照我們約的時間在捷運站跟我見面，好嗎？
Qǐng nǐ ànzhào wǒmen yuē de shíjiān zài jiéyùn zhàn gēn wǒ jiànmiàn, hǎo ma?
Please meet me at the MRT Station according to the arranged time, OK?

吧, ba, (Ptc), Making Suggestions

Function ▶ 吧 indicates a suggestion from the speaker.

❶ A：我們去喝咖啡還是喝茶？
Wǒmen qù hē kāfēi háishì hē chá?
Shall we go drink coffee or tea?

B：我們去喝咖啡吧。
Wǒmen qù hē kāfēi ba.
Let's go drink coffee.

❷ A：今天晚上我們看什麼電影？
Jīntiān wǎnshàng wǒmen kàn shénme diànyǐng?
What movie are we watching tonight?

B：我們去看臺灣電影吧！
Wǒmen qù kàn Táiwān diànyǐng ba!
Let's watch a Taiwanese movie.

❸ A：週末我們去打籃球，好不好？
Zhōumò wǒmen qù dǎ lánqiú, hǎo bù hǎo?
Let's go play basketball on the weekend, OK?

B：我不喜歡打籃球，我們打網球吧！
Wǒ bù xǐhuān dǎ lánqiú, wǒmen dǎ wǎngqiú ba!
I don't like to play basketball. Let's play tennis.

Structures ▶ 吧 is placed at the sentence-final position.

Usage ▶ 吧 is used in imperatives to soften the command. For example, 喝吧！Hē ba! 'Go ahead and drink!' An imperative without 吧 sounds harsh and direct and can be impolite, for example, 喝！Hē! 'Drink!'

把, bǎ, (Ptc), To Dispose of Something (1)

Function ▶ This pattern is generally referred to as 把bǎ or disposal construction. It consists of a variety of internal elements and is quite similar to the phrase 'take this (noun) and...' in English, but much more widely used. The most basic structure refers to how a noun, object of the action verb, is disposed of by the subject.

❶ 我把牛肉麵吃了。
Wǒ bǎ niúròu miàn chī le.
I ate the beef noodles. (I took the beef noodles and ate them.)

❷ 他把我的湯喝了。
Tā bǎ wǒ de tāng hē le.
He drank my soup.

❸ 房東把房子賣了。
Fángdōng bǎ fángzi mài le.
The landlord sold the house.

Structures ▶ 把bǎ＋object＋verb＋了le, in which the object is in most cases definite in reference (bare nouns, or nouns with modifiers such as 這個zhè ge 'this', 那個nà ge 'that', 他的tā de 'his', etc.), the verb (bare, i.e., just one character) must be an outward transitive action verb (action away from the actor like selling, buying, and consuming, not inward towards the actor like buying, learning, and listening), and sentence must end with the particle 了.

***Negation* :** The negation uses 沒 or 別 occurs in front of the particle 把bǎ.

❶ 我沒把豬腳麵線吃了。
Wǒ méi bǎ zhūjiǎo miànxiàn chī le.
I didn't eat the pork knuckles with fine noodles.

❷ 別把我的藥吃了。
Bié bǎ wǒ de yào chī le.
Don't take my medicine.

❸ 他沒把書賣了。
Tā méi bǎ shū mài le.
He didn't sell his book.

Questions :　　Question with 把 can be formed by A-not-A or 是不是.

❶ 你把功課寫了沒有？
Nǐ bǎ gōngkè xiěle méi yǒu?
Have you finished your homework?

❷ 你是不是把機車賣了？
Nǐ shìbúshì bǎ jīchē mài le?
You sold the motorcycle, right?

❸ 你是不是把他的早飯吃了？
Nǐ shìbúshì bǎ tā de zǎofàn chī le?
You ate his breakfast, right?

Usage

(1) As mentioned above, the object of 把 must be definite.

❶ 我想把手機賣了。
Wǒ xiǎng bǎ shǒujī mài le.
I want to sell my mobile phone.

❷ 我想把那支手機賣了。
Wǒ xiǎng bǎ nà zhī shǒujī mài le.
I want to sell that mobile phone.

❸ *我想把一支手機賣了。
*Wǒ xiǎng bǎ yì zhī shǒujī mài le.
I want to sell a mobile phone.

(2) The bare verb in 把 sentences must be transitive and outward. They include 賣 mài 'to sell', 吃 chī 'to eat', 喝 hē 'to drink', 寫 xiě 'to write', but not such inward verbs as 買 mǎi 'to buy', 學 xué 'to learn', e.g., *我把中文學了 *Wǒ bǎ Zhōngwén xué le.

(3) The notion 'dispose of' is often indicated using 'do-with', 'do-to', and 'take (noun) and (verb)' in English, e.g., 'What he did with his car was to sell it' or 'He took his car and sold it.'

把, bǎ, (Ptc), Moving an Object to a Location　(2)

Function　　It has been presented that 把 disposes of things. Most typically, disposal results in relocating things.

❶ 我把球踢到學校外面了。
Wǒ bǎ qiú tī dào xuéxiào wàimiàn le.
I kicked the ball out of the school yard.

❷ 他想把公司搬到台南。
　Tā xiǎng bǎ gōngsī bān dào Táinán.
　He wants to move the company to Tainan.

❸ 我打算把這個蛋糕拿到學校請同學吃。
　Wǒ dǎsuàn bǎ zhè ge dàngāo ná dào xuéxiào qǐng tóngxué chī.
　I plan to take this cake to school and treat my classmates to it.

❹ 我要把這包茶送給老師。
　Wǒ yào bǎ zhè bāo chá sòng gěi lǎoshī.
　I want to give this package of tea to my teacher.

❺ 請妳把那件衣服拿給小高。
　Qǐng nǐ bǎ nà jiàn yīfú ná gěi Xiǎo Gāo.
　Please give that dress to Xiao Gao.

❻ 我打算把舊車賣給高先生。
　Wǒ dǎsuàn bǎ jiù chē mài gěi Gāo xiānshēng.
　I plan to sell the old car to Mr. Gao.

❼ 請你把那張椅子放在樓下。
　Qǐng nǐ bǎ nà zhāng yǐzi fàng zài lóuxià.
　Please put that chair downstairs.

❽ 我要把媽媽給我的錢存在銀行裡。
　Wǒ yào bǎ māma gěi wǒ de qián cún zài yínháng lǐ.
　I want to deposit the money Mom gave me in the bank.

Structures The pattern is A＋把＋B＋Verb＋Prep (到, 在, 給)＋Location. 到 and 在 are used with places and 給 with people. Futhermore, 到 is used with 'moving' verbs, and 在 with 'placing' verbs.

Negation :

❶ 他沒把資料帶到學校來，可是還好我帶了。
　Tā méi bǎ zīliào dài dào xuéxiào lái, kěshì háihǎo wǒ dài le.
　He didn't take the documents to the school. It's a good thing I did though.

❷ 別把那本書賣給別人，賣給我吧。
　Bié bǎ nà běn shū mài gěi biérén, mài gěi wǒ ba.
　Don't sell anyone else that book, sell it to me.

❸ 我還沒把這個月的房租拿給房東。
　Wǒ hái méi bǎ zhè ge yuè de fángzū ná gěi fángdōng.
　I haven't given the landlord this month's rent yet.

❹ 他還沒把買電視的錢付給老闆。
　Tā hái méi bǎ mǎi diànshì de qián fù gěi lǎobǎn.
　He hasn't given his boss the money to be spent on a TV.

❺ 別把隨身碟放在桌子上。
　Bié bǎ suíshēndié fàng zài zhuōzi shàng.
　Don't put the flash drive on the desk.

❻ 他沒把錢放在我這裡，他帶回家了。
Tā méi bǎ qián fàng zài wǒ zhèlǐ, tā dàihuí jiā le.
He didn't leave the money here with me, he took it home.

Questions :   Either the pattern A-not-A or 是不是 is used.

❶ 妳是不是把我的書帶到學校來了？
Nǐ shìbúshì bǎ wǒ de shū dài dào xuéxiào lái le?
Did you bring my book to school?

❷ 你把機車騎到公司來了沒有？我等一下要用。
Nǐ bǎ jīchē qí dào gōngsī lái le méi yǒu? Wǒ děng yíxià yào yòng.
Did you ride the motorcycle to work? I need it soon.

❸ 你把那本本子拿給老師了沒有？
Nǐ bǎ nà běn běnzi ná gěi lǎoshī le méi yǒu?
Did you take that notebook to the teacher?

❹ 你是不是把照相機送給她了？
Nǐ shìbúshì bǎ zhàoxiàngjī sòng gěi tā le?
Did you give the camera to her?

❺ 房東是不是把熱水器裝在浴室外面了？
Fángdōng shìbúshì bǎ rèshuǐqì zhuāng zài yùshì wàimiàn le?
Did the landlord install the gas hot water heater outside?

❻ 你把學費用在什麼地方了？
Nǐ bǎ xuéfèi yòng zài shénme dìfāng le?
What did you spend your tuition on?

把, bǎ, (Ptc), with $V_1V_2V_3$ (3)

Function

This is a sub-type of the 把-construction, in which a noun has been moved to a new location, specified by a sequence of V_1 (action), V_2 (direction), and V_3 (in relation to the speaker).

❶ 我把垃圾拿出去了。
Wǒ bǎ lèsè ná chūqù le.
I took the garbage out.

❷ 他把書帶回去了。
Tā bǎ shū dài huíqù le.
He took the book back home.

❸ 高小姐從皮包裡把錢拿出來。
Gāo xiǎojiě cóng píbāo lǐ bǎ qián ná chūlái.
Miss Gao took money out of her purse.

❹ 主任請助教把李小姐的履歷表拿進來。
Zhǔrèn qǐng zhùjiào bǎ Lǐ xiǎojiě de lǚlì biǎo ná jìnlái.
The director had the TA bring in Miss Li's resume.

Structures   The basic pattern is Subj＋把＋Obj＋$V_1V_2V_3$.

*N*egation :

❶ 我沒把書帶回來。
Wǒ méi bǎ shū dài huílái.
I did not bring the book back.

❷ 你別把蛋糕放進背包裡去。
Nǐ bié bǎ dàngāo fàngjìn bēibāo lǐ qù.
Don't put the cake into your backpack.

❸ 她沒把買回來的衣服拿出來給朋友看。
Tā méi bǎ mǎi huílái de yīfú ná chūlái gěi péngyǒu kàn.
She didn't show her friends the new clothes she bought.

*Q*uestions :

❶ 張先生是不是把公司的車開回去了？
Zhāng xiānshēng shìbúshì bǎ gōngsī de chē kāi huíqù le?
Did Mr. Zhang drive the company car back to his place?

❷ 我剛剛請你幫我買一杯咖啡。你把咖啡買回來了嗎？
Wǒ gānggāng qǐng nǐ bāng wǒ mǎi yì bēi kāfēi. Nǐ bǎ kāfēi mǎi huílái le ma?
Did you buy the coffee which I asked for back?

❸ 搬家的時候，你要把這些桌子、椅子都搬過去嗎？
Bānjiā de shíhòu, nǐ yào bǎ zhèxiē zhuōzi, yǐzi dōu bān guòqù ma?
While moving out, would you bring these tables, chairs with you?

> Usage

The object in the 把-construction is always definite, even though a definite noun is sometimes disguised as indefinite.

❶ 我把那本英文書帶回來了。
Wǒ bǎ nà běn Yīngwén shū dài huílái le.
I brought back that English book.

❷ *我把一本英文書帶回來了。
*Wǒ bǎ yì běn Yīngwén shū dài huílái le.
I brought back an English book.

❸ 對不起，我把一件事忘了！
Duìbùqǐ, wǒ bǎ yí jiàn shì wàng le!
Sorry, I forgot something!

把, bǎ, (Ptc), V(一)V, Disposal with Verb Reduplication (4)

> Function

The VV pattern softens the action and also makes it brief. This pattern is often combined with the 把-construction in making requests or orders, indicating 'doing something briefly to a noun'.

❶ 你把那本書看一看，再告訴我好不好看。
Nǐ bǎ nà běn shū kàn yí kàn, zài gàosù wǒ hǎo bù hǎokàn.
Take a look at that book then tell me if it's any good.

❷ 小美把提出來的錢算一算，再去付學費。
Xiǎoměi bǎ tí chūlái de qián suàn yí suàn, zài qù fù xuéfèi.
Xiaomei counted the money she withdrew before going to pay her tuition.

❸ 請你把學校上課的情形跟新同學說一說。
Qǐng nǐ bǎ xuéxiào shàngkè de qíngxíng gēn xīn tóngxué shuō yì shuō.
Please tell the new students about how classes are conducted.

Structures　The verb in 'V一V' has to be monosyllabic. Disyllable verbs are reduplicated as ABAB, e.g., 把東西收拾收拾！Bǎ dōngxi shōushí shōushí! 'Clean up the stuff!'.

Negation :　Not available.

Questions :　Questions are formed with the 嗎 and 是不是 patterns.

❶ 你有空的時候，能不能請你把垃圾倒一倒？
Nǐ yǒu kòng de shíhòu, néng bù néng qǐng nǐ bǎ lèsè dào yí dào?
Could you take out (lit. dump, pour out) the garbage when you're free?

❷ 媽，我是不是先把大白菜拌一拌再加鹽？
Mā, wǒ shìbúshì xiān bǎ dàbáicài bàn yí bàn zài jiā yán?
Mom, should I mix Chinese cabbage first, add salt later?

❸ 媽媽問小孩：「吃東西以前，你把手洗一洗了嗎？」
Māma wèn xiǎohái: 'Chī dōngxi yǐqián, nǐ bǎ shǒu xǐ yì xǐ le ma?'
The mother asks the child, did you wash your hands before eating?

把, bǎ, (Ptc), with Resultative Complements　(5)

Function　In the 把-construction, the complement after the verb may indicate a result of the action. The complements come in 2 forms, V＋C or V＋得＋C.

❶ 媽媽不小心把餃子煮破了。
Māma bù xiǎoxīn bǎ jiǎozi zhǔpò le.
Mom accidentally split the dumplings while cooking them.
(i.e., The dumplings accidently split when Mom was cooking them.)

❷ 請你把白菜洗乾淨，等一下就要用了。
Qǐng nǐ bǎ báicài xǐgānjìng, děng yíxià jiù yào yòng le.
Please wash the cabbage clean, it's going to be used soon.

❸ 他把水餃都包得好難看。
Tā bǎ shuǐjiǎo dōu bāo de hǎo nánkàn.
He did a very bad job wrapping up dumplings.

Structures　The complement indicating the result of action in this construction can be a state verb, a process verb or a phrase/clause following 得de.

❶ 你這麼洗，會把鍋子洗壞。
Nǐ zhème xǐ, huì bǎ guōzi xǐhuài.
You'll ruin your pot washing it like that.

❷ 他第一次做泡菜，把泡菜做得很難吃。
Tā dìyī cì zuò pàocài, bǎ pàocài zuò de hěn nánchī.
The first time he made kimchi it tasted awful.

❸ 你趕快把窗户關好，我們要出去了。
Nǐ gǎnkuài bǎ chuānghù guānhǎo, wǒmen yào chūqù le.
Hurry up and close the window, it's time we get going.

Negation :

❶ 別把菜吃光了，要留一點給別人。
Bié bǎ cài chīguāng le, yào liú yìdiǎn gěi biérén.
Don't eat up all the food. Leave some for others.

❷ 如果我沒把碗洗乾淨，老闆會叫我再洗一次。
Rúguǒ wǒ méi bǎ wǎn xǐ gānjìng, lǎobǎn huì jiào wǒ zài xǐ yí cì.
If I don't wash the bowls really clean, the boss will ask me to rewash them.

❸ 你不把話說完，他不知道你想做什麼。
Nǐ bù bǎ huà shuōwán, tā bù zhīdào nǐ xiǎng zuò shénme.
If you don't finish what you are saying, he won't know what it is you want to do.

Questions :

❶ 你把湯喝完了沒有？
Nǐ bǎ tāng hēwán le méi yǒu?
Have you finished (drinking) the soup?

❷ 他是不是把餃子煮破了？
Tā shìbúshì bǎ jiǎozi zhǔpò le?
The dumplings burst when he cooked them, right?

❸ 你是不是把小籠包都吃光了？
Nǐ shìbúshì bǎ xiǎolóngbāo dōu chīguāng le?
Did you eat all of the steamed dumplings?

> Usage

As can be seen in the examples above, 了 le is often added at the end of a 把 bǎ sentence to express change of state, which is highly compatible with the meaning of resultative complements.

把, bǎ, (Ptc), Unintentional Event (6)

> Function

While most 把 sentences refer to intentional, purposeful, acts on the part of the subject, there are a few occurrences of 把 sentences, but their frequency is rather high.

❶ 我太忙，把先生要我買的東西忘得乾乾淨淨。
Wǒ tài máng, bǎ xiānshēng yào wǒ mǎi de dōngxi wàng de gāngān jìngjìng.
I was so busy that I clean forgot to buy what my husband asked me to.

11

❷ 他把重要的隨身碟掉了，急著到處找。

Tā bǎ zhòngyào de suíshēndié diào le, jízhe dàochù zhǎo.

He lost his flash drive, so he is anxiously looking everywhere for it.

❸ 老師跟學生說：「你回國以後別把學過的中文忘了。」

Lǎoshī gēn xuéshēng shuō: 'Nǐ huíguó yǐhòu bié bǎ xuéguò de Zhōngwén wàng le.'

The teacher told his student, 'Don't forget all the Chinese you learned after you return to your country.'

把 A 當做 B, (bǎ A dàngzuò B), to treat or take A as B (7)

> Function

This pattern takes A to be B, making A in the role of B.

❶ 有不少人把買彩券當做一夜致富的機會。

Yǒu bù shǎo rén bǎ mǎi cǎiquàn dàngzuò yí yè zhìfù de jīhuì.

Lots of people treat the lottery as an opportunity to get rich over night.

❷ 有時候我們把體育館當做辦演唱會的地方。

Yǒu shíhòu wǒmen bǎ tǐyùguǎn dàngzuò bàn yǎnchànghuì de dìfāng.

Sometimes we use the gym as a venue to hold concerts.

❸ 風水學是把利用環境、改造環境當做一門學問。

Fēngshuǐxué shì bǎ lìyòng huánjìng, gǎizào huánjìng dàngzuò yì mén xuéwèn.

Feng Shui takes using and remoulding the environment as an academic discipline.

❹ 沒想到他居然可以把垃圾當做材料，做成藝術品。

Méi xiǎngdào tā jūrán kěyǐ bǎ lèsè dàngzuò cáiliào, zuòchéng yìshùpǐn.

Who would expect that he could use garbage as material for making art objects.

白, bái, (Adv), in vain, all for nothing

> Function

(1) The adverb 白 modifies action verbs and carries the meaning 'to do the action in vain', 'to have no effect at all.'

❶ 我說了那麼多次，你還是聽不懂。我真是白說了。

Wǒ shuōle nàme duōcì, nǐ háishì tīngbùdǒng. Wǒ zhēnshi bái shuō le.

I've told you so many times and you still don't understand. I'm really wasting my breath.

❷ 媽媽做了好多菜，可是家人都沒回來吃。媽媽白做了。

Māma zuòle hǎo duō cài, kěshì jiārén dōu méi huílái chī. Māma bái zuò le.

Mom made a huge meal, but nobody came home to eat, so she basically made it for nothing.

❸ 我們寫的報告老師說不用交了。我們白寫了。

Wǒmen xiě de bàogào lǎoshī shuō bú yòng jiāo le. Wǒmen bái xiě le.

Turns out we don't need to turn in the report the teacher told us to write. We did it for nothing.

❹ 他不知道學校放颱風假，沒開門。他白去了。

Tā bù zhīdào xuéxiào fàng táifēng jià, méi kāi mén. Tā bái qù le.

He didn't know that school closed on account of a typhoon, and he went in for nothing.

❺ 打折的時候買的一些東西都沒用。我都白買了。

Dǎzhé de shíhòu mǎi de yìxiē dōngxi dōu méi yòng. Wǒ dōu bái mǎi le.

I didn't end up using those things that I bought on sale. I bought them in vain.

(2) When used with action verbs such as 吃, 喝, and 住, in contexts where the subject normally pays to do the action, 白＋action verb means to do the action without paying for it, coupled with bad attitude and behavior.

❶ 有些餐廳常碰到白吃的客人，老闆覺得很頭痛。

Yǒuxiē cāntīng cháng pèngdào bái chī de kèrén, lǎobǎn juéde hěn tóutòng.

Some restaurants get a lot of dine-and-dashers. It's such a pain for the managers.

❷ 他已經六個月沒付房租了。房東說不能再讓他白住了。

Tā yǐjīng liù ge yuè méi fù fángzū le. Fángdōng shuō bù néng zài ràng tā bái zhù le.

He hasn't paid rent for six months. The landlord said he's not going to let him mooch any longer.

幫, bāng, (Prep), on behalf of

Function   幫 introduces the beneficiary of an action.

❶ 請幫我微波包子。

Qǐng bāng wǒ wéibō bāozi.

Please microwave the baozi for me.

❷ 請幫我買一杯咖啡。

Qǐng bāng wǒ mǎi yì bēi kāfēi.

Please buy a cup of coffee for me.

❸ 請幫我照相。

Qǐng bāng wǒ zhàoxiàng.

Please take a picture for me.

Negation :

The negation marker 不 is placed before the preposition 幫, not before the verb.

❶ 他不幫我微波包子。　　（*他幫我不微波包子。）
　 Tā bù bāng wǒ wéibō bāozi .
　 He won't microwave the baozi for me.

❷ 姐姐不幫弟弟買咖啡。　　（*姐姐幫弟弟不買咖啡。）
　 Jiějie bù bāng dìdi mǎi kāfēi.
　 Sister won't buy coffee for her brother.

❸ 王先生不幫我照相。　　（*王先生幫我不照相。）
　 Wáng xiānshēng bù bāng wǒ zhàoxiàng.
　 Mr. Wang would not take a picture for me.

Questions :

❶ 你說！你幫不幫他買手機？
　 Nǐ shuō! Nǐ bāng bù bāng tā mǎi shǒujī?
　 Say it! Are you going to buy a cell phone on his behalf?

❷ 他幫你照相嗎？
　 Tā bāng nǐ zhàoxiàng ma?
　 Did he take a photo for you?

❸ 誰能幫我微波包子？
　 Shéi néng bāng wǒ wéibō bāozi?
　 Who can microwave a baozi for me?

被, bèi, (Ptc), A Passive Marker (See 受 shòu entry also)

被 passive sentences express not only the 'affected' meaning but also the 'unfortunate' meaning, especially in ordinary daily speech. The particle 被 is commonly used in translating English passive sentences.

❶ 我的自行車昨天被偷了。
　 Wǒ de zìxíngchē zuótiān bèi tōu le.
　 My bike got stolen yesterday.

❷ 我的腿被他踢得很痛。
　 Wǒ de tuǐ bèi tā tī de hěn tòng.
　 My leg got kicked by him and hurts.

❸ 這些餃子包得不錯，但是被我煮破了。
　 Zhèxiē jiǎozi bāo de búcuò, dànshì bèi wǒ zhǔpò le.
　 These dumplings were wrapped well, but they were split open by me when cooking.

Obj＋被＋(Subj)＋V. The subject is omitted when its identity cannot be established.

Negation :

The negator is 沒, which occurs before 被.

❶ 沒關係，我的錢沒被偷。

Méi guānxi, wǒ de qián méi bèi tōu.

It's OK. My money wasn't stolen.

❷ 那些碗沒被弟弟打破。

Nàxiē wǎn méi bèi dìdi dǎpò.

Those bowls were not broken by my little brother.

❸ 那些學生在打棒球。小心別被球打到。

Nàxiē xuéshēng zài dǎ bàngqiú. Xiǎoxīn bié bèi qiú dǎdào.

Those students are playing baseball, be careful, don't get hit by the ball.

Questions :

❶ 聽說你的手機不見了，是不是被偷了？

Tīngshuō nǐ de shǒujī bújiàn le, shìbúshì bèi tōu le?

I heard your cell phone disappeared. Did it get stolen?

❷ 你知道我們學校電腦教室的窗戶被打破了嗎？

Nǐ zhīdào wǒmen xuéxiào diànnǎo jiàoshì de chuānghù bèi dǎpò le ma?

Did you know that the window in the computer room of our school got smashed?

❸ 我找不到我的本子，是不是被你帶回家了？

Wǒ zhǎobúdào wǒ de běnzi, shìbúshì bèi nǐ dàihuí jiā le?

I can't find my notebook. Was it taken home by you? (i.e., Did you take it home with you?)

Usage

(1) 被 passive can refer to instances either in the past as shown in ❶, ❷; in the future ❸, ❹; or to habitual instances as shown in ❺, ❻.

❶ 上個星期他的背包被偷了。

Shàng ge xīngqí tā de bēibāo bèi tōu le.

His backpack got stolen last week.

❷ 他花一萬塊買背包的事被爸爸發現了。

Tā huā yí wàn kuài mǎi bēibāo de shì bèi bàba fāxiàn le.

He spent NT$10,000 to buy a backpack and was found out by his dad.

❸ 按照臺灣的法律，你不能打工。要不然會被送回你的國家。

Ànzhào Táiwān de fǎlǜ, nǐ bù néng dǎgōng. Yàobùrán huì bèi sònghuí nǐ de guójiā.

According to Taiwan law, you can't work, or else you will be sent back to your country.

15

④ 明天這張桌子就會被搬到別的教室去了。
Míngtiān zhè zhāng zhuōzi jiù huì bèi bān dào biéde jiàoshì qù le.
Tomorrow this desk will be moved to a different classroom.

⑤ 他不想被人知道他結過婚了。
Tā bù xiǎng bèi rén zhīdào tā jiéguò hūn le.
He doesn't want anyone to know that he has been married before.

⑥ 媽媽每次買芒果蛋糕回來，馬上就被妹妹吃光了。
Māma měi cì mǎi mángguǒ dàngāo huílái, mǎshàng jiù bèi mèimei chīguāng le.
Every time Mom buys a mango cake, it gets eaten up instantly by my kid sister.

(2) The noun after 被, i.e., the subject, the actor, can be omitted.

① 我們打工的事被發現了。
Wǒmen dǎgōng de shì bèi fāxiàn le.
It's been found out that we are working part-time jobs.

② 出去旅行要小心，錢別被偷了。
Chūqù lǚxíng yào xiǎoxīn, qián bié bèi tōu le.
Be careful while traveling. Don't get your money stolen.

③ 小李常常被罵，因為他上班幾乎每天遲到。
Xiǎo Lǐ chángcháng bèi mà, yīnwèi tā shàngbān jīhū měi tiān chídào.
Xiao Li often gets reprimanded because he is late for work almost every day.

Or in some cases, it can be an indefinite noun, i.e., someone, somebody.

① 我的腳踏車被人偷了。
Wǒ de jiǎotàchē bèi rén tōu le.
My bike was stolen by somebody.

② 我們說的話被人聽見了。
Wǒmen shuō de huà bèi rén tīngjiàn le.
What we were talking about was overheard by somebody. (or Somebody overheard what we talking about.)

③ 小美發現自己被人騙了。
Xiǎoměi fāxiàn zìjǐ bèi rén piàn le.
Xiaomei found that she was tricked.

比, bǐ, (Prep), Comparison (1)

Function The 比 preposition indicates an explicit comparison between two items.

① 山上的風景比這裡漂亮。
Shān shàng de fēngjǐng bǐ zhèlǐ piàoliàng.
The view on the mountain is more beautiful than here.

❷ 我們學校比他們學校遠。

Wǒmen xuéxiào bǐ tāmen xuéxiào yuǎn.

Our school is farther away than their school.

❸ 坐捷運比坐火車快。

Zuò jiéyùn bǐ zuò huǒchē kuài.

Taking the MRT is faster than taking the train.

Structures　　A 比 B Vs

Negation :　　The 比 pattern can be negated by either 不bù or 不是búshì.

❶ 在家上網不比在學校快。

Zài jiā shàngwǎng bù bǐ zài xuéxiào kuài.

Using the internet at home is not faster than using it at school.

❷ 我的車不比他的車貴。

Wǒ de chē bù bǐ tā de chē guì.

My car is not more expensive than his.

❸ 坐公車不是比坐計程車快。

Zuò gōngchē búshì bǐ zuò jìchéngchē kuài.

Taking the bus is not faster than taking a taxi.

Questions :

❶ 他們學校比你們學校遠嗎？

Tāmen xuéxiào bǐ nǐmen xuéxiào yuǎn ma?

Is their school farther away than your school?

❷ 這種手機比那種貴嗎？

Zhè zhǒng shǒujī bǐ nà zhǒng guì ma?

Is this kind of cellphone more expensive than that kind?

Usage　　In the 比 pattern, intensifying adverbs like 很hěn 'very', 真zhēn 'really', and 非常fēicháng 'very' do not appear before the Vs. It is incorrect, therefore, to say:

❶ *我的手機比他的很貴。 （Should be: 我的手機比他的貴得多。）

*Wǒ de shǒujī bǐ tā de hěn guì. (Should be: Wǒ de shǒujī bǐ tā de guì de duō. 'my cellphone is much more expensive than his'.)

❷ *坐高鐵比坐火車非常快。 （Should be: 坐高鐵比坐火車快得多。）

*Zuò gāotiě bǐ zuò huǒchē fēicháng kuài. (Should be: Zuò gāotiě bǐ zuò huǒchē kuài de duō. 'Taking the High Speed Rail is much faster than the train.')

比, bǐ, (Prep), Intensifying a State with 一 M 比一 M, more and more X, more X than the last　(2)

Function　　This pattern intensifies a state by making a virtual comparison between nouns in question, 'more and more X'.

17

❶ 李老師喜歡教書，把這些學生教得一個比一個好。

Lǐ lǎoshī xǐhuān jiāoshū, bǎ zhèxiē xuéshēng jiāo de yí ge bǐ yí ge hǎo.

Teacher Li loves her job and each of the students she teaches gets better and better.

❷ 新年快到了，商店的生意一家比一家好。

Xīnnián kuài dào le, shāngdiàn de shēngyì yì jiā bǐ yì jiā hǎo.

Chinese New Year is approaching and the business at each shop you visit is more booming than the last.

❸ 城市發展太快，環境的問題一年比一年嚴重。

Chéngshì fāzhǎn tài kuài, huánjìng de wèntí yì nián bǐ yì nián yánzhòng.

The city has developed rapidly and environmental issues are growing worse with every year.

Structures

❶ 網路上的資料很多，現在學生問的問題一個比一個難。

Wǎnglù shàng de zīliào hěn duō, xiànzài xuéshēng wèn de wèntí yí ge bǐ yí ge nán.

There is so much information on the internet, the questions students ask these days are getting tougher and tougher.

❷ 她去法國的那些照片，風景一張比一張漂亮。

Tā qù Fǎguó de nàxiē zhàopiàn, fēngjǐng yì zhāng bǐ yì zhāng piàoliàng.

Each of the scenic pictures she took during her trip to France is more beautiful than the last.

❸ 現在手機的功能一支比一支多，當然也一支比一支貴。

Xiànzài shǒujī de gōngnéng yì zhī bǐ yì zhī duō, dāngrán yě yì zhī bǐ yì zhī guì.

Functionality is constantly rising with each new phone, and naturally so is the price.

❹ 為了保護自己國家的經濟，外國人打工的規定一年比一年多。

Wèile bǎohù zìjǐ guójiā de jīngjì, wàiguó rén dǎgōng de guīdìng yì nián bǐ yì nián duō.

The country has to protect its economy, so each year foreigners seeking employment face more and more rules.

❺ 這裡的大樓一棟比一棟高，房子一間比一間貴。有錢人才買得起。

Zhèlǐ de dàlóu yí dòng bǐ yí dòng gāo, fángzi yì jiān bǐ yì jiān guì. Yǒuqiánrén cái mǎideqǐ.

The condos here are being built taller and taller, and the housing prices are rising higher and higher. Only the well to do can afford to buy property.

***N**egation* : The negative form of 一 M 比 一 M is less common than the affirmative form, but many examples can still be found.

❶ 這幾個學生一個比一個不愛念書。
Zhè jǐ ge xuéshēng yí ge bǐ yí ge bú ài niànshū.
Each of these students is less studious than the last.

❷ 他的那幾個朋友習慣開車，一個比一個不喜歡走路。
Tā de nà jǐ gè péngyǒu xíguàn kāi chē, yí ge bǐ yí ge bù xǐhuān zǒulù.
His group friends are all used to driving. Each dislikes walking more than the last.

❸ 那一家人說起話來一個比一個不客氣。
Nà yì jiā rén shuōqǐ huà lái yí ge bǐ yí ge bú kèqì.
When that family gets to talking, each one becomes more impolite than the last.

❹ 父親年紀大了，身體沒有以前好，一天比一天不願意動。
Fùqīn niánjì dà le, shēntǐ méi yǒu yǐqián hǎo, yì tiān bǐ yì tiān bú yuànyì dòng.
My father is getting old. He is not as healthy as he once was, and every day he is less and less willing to move around.

❺ 小文一天比一天瘦，一天比一天不快樂。
Xiǎowén yì tiān bǐ yì tiān shòu, yì tiān bǐ yì tiān bú kuàilè.
Xiaowen is getting thinner by the day, and unhappier too.

***Q**uestions* :

❶ 經濟不好，想到外國念書的人一年比一年少嗎？
Jīngjì bù hǎo, xiǎng dào wàiguó niànshū de rén yì nián bǐ yì nián shǎo ma?
The economy is doing bad, does that mean fewer and fewer people want to study abroad every year?

❷ 為了到中國做生意，想學中文的人是不是一天比一天多？
Wèile dào Zhōngguó zuò shēngyì, xiǎng xué Zhōngwén de rén shìbúshì yì tiān bǐ yì tiān duō?
Has business opportunity in China caused the number of Chinese learners to grow day by day?

❸ 那家店的衣服是不是一件比一件好看，所以沒有幾天就賣完了？
Nà jiā diàn de yīfú shìbúshì yí jiàn bǐ yí jiàn hǎokàn, suǒyǐ méi yǒu jǐ tiān jiù màiwán le?
Does that clothing store sell off their stock every few days because the selections keep getting better and better?

④ 張教授對翻譯有很多年經驗。這幾年他翻譯的那幾本書是不是一本比一本賣得好？

Zhāng jiàoshòu duì fānyì yǒu hěn duō nián jīngyàn. Zhè jǐ nián tā fānyì de nà jǐ běn shū shìbúshì yì běn bǐ yì běn mài de hǎo?

Professor Zhang is an experienced translator. Of the books he has translated over the last few years, each one has sold better than the last, right?

Usage

In some contexts, this pattern can be replaced by 越來越 yuèláiyuè with roughly the same meaning, e.g.,

① a. 他的太極拳打得一天比一天好。
   Tā de Tàijí quán dǎ de yì tiān bǐ yì tiān hǎo.
   He gets better at Tai Chi every day.

   b. 他的太極拳打得越來越好。
   Tā de Tàijí quán dǎ de yuèláiyuè hǎo.
   He is getting better and better at Tai Chi.

② a. 學校附近的那家餐廳的生意一年比一年好。
   Xuéxiào fùjìn de nà jiā cāntīng de shēngyì yì nián bǐ yì nián hǎo.
   That restaurant close to school gets more and more business every year.

   b. 學校附近的那家餐廳的生意越來越好。
   Xuéxiào fùjìn de nà jiā cāntīng de shēngyì yuèláiyuè hǎo.
   Business is getting better and better for that restaurant close to school.

比較, bǐjiào, (Adv), Implicit Comparison (3)

Function

The adverb 比較 conveys implicit comparison. The comparison is understood based on the context.

① 今天比較熱。
   Jīntiān bǐjiào rè.
   Today is relatively hot.

② 越南餐廳很遠。坐捷運比較快。
   Yuènán cāntīng hěn yuǎn. Zuò jiéyùn bǐjiào kuài.
   The Vietnamese restaurant is very far. Taking the MRT would be faster.

③ 我們家，姐姐比較會做飯。
   Wǒmen jiā, jiějie bǐjiào huì zuòfàn.
   In our family, my sister cooks better.

Structures

Adverbs do not take negation directly. Negation goes with the main verb.

Negation :

① 昨天比較不熱。
   Zuótiān bǐjiào bú rè.
   Yesterday was less hot.

❷ 他比較不喜歡游泳。
Tā bǐjiào bù xǐhuān yóuyǒng.
He doesn't like swimming as much.
(compared to some other activity or to someone else)

❸ 我最近比較沒有空。
Wǒ zuìjìn bǐjiào méi yǒu kòng.
I have been relatively busy lately.

Questions :

❶ 咖啡和茶，你比較喜歡喝咖啡嗎？
Kāfēi hàn chá, nǐ bǐjiào xǐhuān hē kāfēi ma?
Coffee and tea, do you prefer drinking coffee?

❷ 你和哥哥，你比較會打棒球嗎？
Nǐ hàn gēge, nǐ bǐjiào huì dǎ bàngqiú ma?
Between you and your older brother, do you play baseball better?

❸ 他比較想去看美國電影還是日本電影？
Tā bǐjiào xiǎng qù kàn Měiguó diànyǐng háishì Rìběn diànyǐng?
Would he prefer to go watch an American movie or a Japanese movie?

Usage ▸ In mainland China, 比較 can be used as an adverb meaning 'quite, rather' without a sense of comparison. 他的法文說得比較好。Tā de Fǎwén shuō de bǐjiào hǎo. 'He speaks French rather well.' In Taiwan, 比較 bǐjiào always indicates a comparison. 哥哥和我，我比較高。Gēge hàn wǒ, wǒ bǐjiào gāo. 'Between me and my brother, I am taller.'

比起來, bǐqǐlái, Comparison (4)

Function ▸ Two nouns are compared with the phrase 比起來, and then a choice or a preference is made.

❶ 跟美國的書比起來，台灣的比較便宜。
Gēn Měiguó de shū bǐqǐlái, Táiwān de bǐjiào piányí.
Compared to American books, Taiwanese books are cheaper.

❷ 中文跟英文比起來，小李覺得中文容易一點。
Zhōngwén gēn Yīngwén bǐqǐlái, Xiǎo Lǐ juéde Zhōngwén róngyì yìdiǎn.
Comparing Chinese and English, Xiao Li feels Chinese is a bit easier.

❸ 跟大城市比起來，鄉下舒服多了。
Gēn dà chéngshì bǐqǐlái, xiāngxià shūfú duō le.
Compared to living in big cities, the countryside is much more comfortable.

Structures ▸ In this pattern, 比起來 is the main verb (phrase), and its preposition is 跟 that connects A and B. This pattern cannot be negated.

Questions :

❶ 巴黎跟紐約比起來，哪個城市的冬天比較冷？
   Bālí gēn Niǔyuē bǐqǐlái, nǎ ge chéngshì de dōngtiān bǐjiào lěng?
   When you compare Paris and New York, which city is colder in the winter?

❷ 打太極拳跟踢足球比起來，哪個比較累？
   Dǎ Tàijí quán gēn tī zúqiú bǐqǐlái, nǎ ge bǐjiào lèi?
   Comparing Tai Chi with soccer, which one would make you feel tired easily?

❸ 跟那家店的麵包比起來，這家店的怎麼樣？
   Gēn nà jiā diàn de miànbāo bǐqǐlái, zhè jiā diàn de zěnmeyàng?
   Compared to that shop's bread, how is this shop's?

Usage

(1) In the pattern 'A 跟 B 比起來, ...', A can be omitted if it is also the subject in the main clause.

❶ (你哥哥)跟我哥哥比起來，你哥哥高多了。
   (Nǐ gēge) Gēn wǒ gēge bǐqǐlái, nǐ gēge gāo duō le.
   (Your brother) compared to my brother, your brother is much taller.

❷ (泰國菜)跟法國菜比起來，泰國菜比較酸。
   (Tàiguó cài) Gēn Fǎguó cài bǐqǐlái, Tàiguó cài bǐjiào suān.
   (Thai cuisine) compared to French cuisine, Thai cuisine is more sour.

❸ (今年的夏天)跟去年的夏天比起來，今年的夏天更熱。
   (Jīnnián de xiàtiān) Gēn qùnián de xiàtiān bǐqǐlái, jīnnián de xiàtiān gèng rè.
   Compared to last summer, this summer is even warmer.

(2) The preposition 跟 gēn in this pattern can be replaced by 和 hàn. For example: 和烏龍茶比起來，咖啡真的比較貴。 Hàn Wūlóng chá bǐqǐlái, kāfēi zhēn de bǐjiào guì. 'Compared to Wulong tea, coffee is more expensive indeed'.

(3) In the main (the second) clause in the pattern, adverbs or (post-verbal) complements of degree must be used, such as 比較 bǐjiào 'relatively', 多了 duō le 'much more', or 一點兒 yìdiǎnr 'a little bit'.

❶ 跟你妹妹比起來，我妹妹比較矮。
   Gēn nǐ mèimei bǐqǐlái, wǒ mèimei bǐjiào ǎi.
   Compared to your younger sister, my kid sister is relatively short.

❷ 日本的冬天跟臺灣的比起來，日本冷多了。
   Rìběn de dōngtiān gēn Táiwān de bǐqǐlái, Rìběn lěng duō le.
   Compared to Taiwan's, Japan's winter is much colder.

❸ 跟陽明山比起來，玉山高得多了。
   Gēn Yángmíng Shān bǐqǐlái, Yù Shān gāo de duō le.
   Compared to Mt. Yangming, Mt. Jade is way taller.

畢竟, bìjìng, (Adv), after all, to Urge Concession

Function

With the adverb 畢竟, the speaker urges the addressee to accept what cannot be helped or avoided.

❶ 雖然現在很多年輕人批評他，但我認為我們都應該尊敬他。畢竟他對國家還是有不少貢獻。

Suīrán xiànzài hěn duō niánqīng rén pīpíng tā, dàn wǒ rènwéi wǒmen dōu yīnggāi zūnjìng tā. Bìjìng tā duì guójiā háishì yǒu bù shǎo gòngxiàn.

He has come under a lot of criticism among younger people, but I think we still ought to respect him. After all, he had done so much for our country.

❷ 我們餐飲業還算景氣，不過畢竟物價上漲了不少，所以我的生活還是苦哈哈的。

Wǒmen cānyǐnyè hái suàn jǐngqì, búguò bìjìng wùjià shàngzhǎng le bù shǎo, suǒyǐ wǒ de shēnghuó háishì kǔhāhā de.

Our food and beverage industry is doing well, but after all, commodity prices have risen quite a bit, so times are still hard for me.

❸ 聽古典音樂的人畢竟比較少。那場音樂會的票應該還買得到吧。

Tīng gǔdiǎn yīnyuè de rén bìjìng bǐjiào shǎo. Nà chǎng yīnyuèhuì de piào yīnggāi hái mǎidedào ba.

There aren't many people that listen to classical music after all, so there should still be tickets available for that performance.

❹ 整型畢竟還是有風險的。你再多考慮考慮吧。

Zhěngxíng bìjìng háishì yǒu fēngxiǎn de. Nǐ zài duō kǎolǜ kǎolǜ ba.

Cosmetic surgery does have its risks after all. Make sure you give it due thought.

Usage

As a member of the so-called 'movable adverbs', 畢竟 bìjìng can occur before a VP or at the beginning of a clause. Other such adverbs include 難道 nándào, 大概 dàgài, 居然 jūrán, 隨時 suíshí, 到底 dàodǐ.

別的, biéde, other

Function

其他的 qítā de, 別的 biéde, and 另外的 lìngwài de all occur before the noun as a modifier, referring to nouns other than what is being referred to. The three have distinct meanings: 其他的 'the others, the remaining', 別的 'other', and 另外的 'the other, another'.

❶ 他來台灣以後，只去過花蓮，沒去過別的地方。

Tā lái Táiwān yǐhòu, zhǐ qùguò Huālián, méi qùguò biéde dìfāng.

Since he came to Taiwan, he's only been to Hualien. He hasn't been to other places. (i.e., anywhere else)

❷ 我不喜歡吃牛肉，我們點別的菜吧。

Wǒ bù xǐhuān chī niúròu, wǒmen diǎn biéde cài ba.

I don't like to eat beef. Let's order something else.

❸ 李先生結婚的事，只有我知道。其他的人都不知道。

Lǐ xiānshēng jiéhūn de shì, zhǐyǒu wǒ zhīdào. Qítā de rén dōu bù zhīdào.

About Mr. Li getting married, only I know. No one else knows.

❹ 我只聽說她搬家了。其他的事我都沒聽說。

Wǒ zhǐ tīngshuō tā bānjiā le. Qítā de shì wǒ dōu méi tīngshuō.

I only heard that she moved. I didn't hear anything else.

❺ 除了這家民宿，另外的旅館都沒房間了。

Chúle zhè jiā mínsù, lìngwài de lǚguǎn dōu méi fángjiān le.

Aside from this B&B, none of the other hotels have vacancies.

❻ 現在的公司離家太遠。我打算找另外的工作。

Xiànzài de gōngsī lí jiā tài yuǎn. Wǒ dǎsuàn zhǎo lìngwài de gōngzuò.

My current place of work is too far away from where I live. I plan on looking for another job.

Structures   Give examples/sentences below.

	Omitting 的	Number	Measure	Noun
其他的 qítā de	✔	✔	✔	✔
別的 biéde	✕	✕	✕	✔
另外的 lìngwài de	✔	✔	✔	✔

(1) 別的 cannot combine with numbers, nor measures. See the chart on above.

❶ 另外三個人怎麼去？

Lìngwài sān ge rén zěnme qù?

How will the other three people go?

❷ 其他三個人怎麼去？

Qítā sān ge rén zěnme qù?

How will the other three people go?

❸ *別的三個人怎麼去？

*Biéde sān ge rén zěnme qù?

(2) 其他 combines with any number two (2) or greater, but not the number one (1).

❶ 這家百貨公司只賣台灣做的衣服，其他五家賣各國的衣服。

Zhè jiā bǎihuò gōngsī zhǐ mài Táiwān zuò de yīfú, qítā wǔ jiā mài gè guó de yīfú.

This particular department store only sells clothes made in Taiwan, but the other five sell international brands.

❷ 今天只有一個同學沒來，其他九個都來了。

Jīntiān zhǐyǒu yí ge tóngxué méi lái, qítā jiǔ ge dōu lái le.

Today, only one classmate didn't come. The other nine all came.

❸ *我借了三本書，兩本已經還了，其他一本還在我這裡。
*Wǒ jièle sān běn shū, liǎng běn yǐjīng huán le, qítā yì běn hái zài wǒ zhèlǐ.
I borrowed three books. I've returned two. The other one, I still have it.

別再…了, bié zài...le, stop doing it

Function The pattern '別再…了' is used to ask the addressee to stop doing something.

❶ 別再玩手機了！
Bié zài wán shǒujī le!
Stop playing on the cellphone.

❷ 別再抱怨工作了！
Bié zài bàoyuàn gōngzuò le!
Stop complaining about work.

❸ 別再考慮了！
Bié zài kǎolǜ le!
Don't think about it anymore.

❹ 別再麻煩他了！
Bié zài máfán tā le!
Don't bother him anymore.

❺ 姐姐跟妹妹說：「別再買新衣服了！」
Jiějie gēn mèimei shuō: 'Bié zài mǎi xīn yīfú le!'
The older sister said to her younger sister, 'Stop buying new clothes!'

❻ 你週末要多運動！別再忘了！
Nǐ zhōumò yào duō yùndòng! Bié zài wàng le!
You should take exercise over the weekend. Don't forget again.

Structures 別 is an imperative/command marker. 別再 could be used with most actions or a small number of states. The subject is often omitted.

❶ (你)別再生氣了！
(Nǐ) Bié zài shēngqì le!
(You) don't be angry anymore.

❷ 別再請我吃甜點了！我已經很胖了。
Bié zài qǐng wǒ chī tiándiǎn le! Wǒ yǐjīng hěn pàng le.
Stop treating me to sweets! I'm big enough already.

❸ 你已經掉過一次錢包了，別再不小心了！
Nǐ yǐjīng diàoguò yí cì qiánbāo le, bié zài bù xiǎoxīn le!
You've dropped your wallet once already, don't be so careless again.

並, bìng, (Adv), 並＋Negation, Contrary to Expectation

Function　The adverb 並 is typically followed by negation, forming 並不 or 並沒（有）. Its use suggests that a statement runs contrary to expectations or common assumptions. Used in dialogues, these expressions indicate the speaker's strong opposition to what was said previously.

❶ 你們為什麼都來問我？我並不知道怎麼包餃子啊。
Nǐmen wèishénme dōu lái wèn wǒ? Wǒ bìng bù zhīdào zěnme bāo jiǎozi a.
Why did you all come to ask me? I have no idea how to wrap dumplings.

❷ 這些菜的作法雖然簡單，但是味道並不差。
Zhèxiē cài de zuòfǎ suīrán jiǎndān, dànshì wèidào bìng bù chà.
Although these dishes are easy to make, they taste good.

❸ 這件事說起來容易，做起來並不容易。
Zhè jiàn shì shuōqǐlái róngyì, zuòqǐlái bìng bù róngyì.
This is easy to talk about, but it's not easy to do.
(This is easier said than done.)

❹ 網路雖然把世界變小了，但是人跟人的關係並沒有變得比較近。
Wǎnglù suīrán bǎ shìjiè biàn xiǎo le, dànshì rén gēn rén de guānxi bìng méi yǒu biàn de bǐjiào jìn.
The internet has made the world smaller, but it hasn't brought people closer together.

❺ 垃圾分類並沒有你想的那麼麻煩。
Lèsè fēnlèi bìng méi yǒu nǐ xiǎng de nàme máfán.
Sorting garbage isn't as much a hassle as you think it is.

Usage

(1) 並 is an adverb. It is placed after the subject and before the verb.

(2) When one wants to indicate 'it is not the case (that)…', the expression is 並＋不是. For example, 並不是所有的牌子都打七折。Bìng búshì suǒyǒu de páizi dōu dǎ qī zhé. 'It's not the case that all brands are 30% off.'

(3) The speaker uses 並 to indicate that what he is saying is contrary to what the addressee assumes or expects. By contrast, without 並, the speaker's statement is a straightforward one.

　　A：你們班上不是還有位子嗎？你怎麼沒叫我去旁聽？
　　　　Nǐmen bān shàng búshì hái yǒu wèizi ma? Nǐ zěnme méi jiào wǒ qù pángtīng?
　　　　Aren't there still empty seats in your class? Why didn't you tell me to go audit?

　　B：a. 我並不知道還有位子。(relatively tactful way of saying it)
　　　　　Wǒ bìng bù zhīdào hái yǒu wèizi.
　　　　　I had no idea there were any empty seats.

b. 我不知道還有位子。(more direct)
Wǒ bù zhīdào hái yǒu wèizi.
I had no idea there were any empty seats.

不, bù, vs. 沒, méi, Negation (1)

Function

Both 不 and 沒 are negative markers, but they are used differently. Negation is best understood in terms of how a negative marker interacts with various verb types.

Verb Types / Negator	不	沒 (有)
Action Verb	✓	✓
State Verb	✓	✗
Process Verb	✗	✓

A. Negation of action verbs

(1) In 不 negation, there are two interpretations:

❶ Habitual

a. 我們星期六不上課。
Wǒmen xīngqíliù bú shàngkè.
We don't go to school on Saturdays.

b. 學生常不吃早餐。
Xuéshēng cháng bù chī zǎocān.
Students often don't eat breakfast.

❷ Intention not to

a. 我不去圖書館。
Wǒ bú qù túshūguǎn.
I'm not going to go to the library.

b. 他不找工作。
Tā bù zhǎo gōngzuò.
He's not looking for a job.

(2) 沒 negation indicates a non-happening in the past.

❶ 昨天我沒打電話給他。
Zuótiān wǒ méi dǎ diànhuà gěi tā.
I didn't call him yesterday.

❷ 上個星期我沒跟同學去KTV。
Shàng ge xīngqí wǒ méi gēn tóngxué qù KTV.
I didn't go to KTV with classmates last week.

❸ 今天我沒坐捷運來上課。我坐公車。
Jīntiān wǒ méi zuò jiéyùn lái shàngkè. Wǒ zuò gōngchē.
I didn't come to class by MRT today. I took a bus.

B. Negation of state verbs

State verbs can only be negated by 不, i.e., the condition does not exist.

❶ 今天不熱，我想出去逛逛。
Jīntiān bú rè, wǒ xiǎng chūqù guàngguàng.
It is not hot today. I'd like to go out and look around.

❷ 他說中文不難學，可是中國字不好寫。
Tā shuō Zhōngwén bù nán xué, kěshì Zhōngguó zì bù hǎo xiě.
He said Chinese is not difficult to learn, but Chinese characters are hard to write.

❸ 我不舒服，今天不想出去。
Wǒ bù shūfú, jīntiān bù xiǎng chūqù.
I don't feel well. I don't want to go out today.

C. Negation of process verbs

Process verbs can only be negated by 沒, which indicates non-happening.

❶ 中文課還沒結束，所以我不能回國。
Zhōngwén kè hái méi jiéshù, suǒyǐ wǒ bù néng huíguó.
My Chinese classes have not ended yet, so I can't go back to my country.

❷ 我沒忘。你先去學校，我等一下去找你。
Wǒ méi wàng. Nǐ xiān qù xuéxiào, wǒ děng yíxià qù zhǎo nǐ.
I didn't forget. You go to school first and I will go see you later.

❸ 我還沒決定要不要去旅行。
Wǒ hái méi juédìng yào bú yào qù lǚxíng.
I still have not decided whether to take a trip or not.

Usage

In Taiwan, 沒 negation is less common than 沒有 negation. E.g., 我沒有買手機 Wǒ méi yǒu mǎi shǒujī 'I didn't buy a cell phone'. In mainland China, 我沒買手機 Wǒ méi mǎi shǒujī 'I didn't buy a cell phone' is more common.

不, bù, Negative Potential Complement (2)

Function

When 得 or 不 is inserted between the verb and the resultative or directional complement, the pattern expresses whether the result is potentially attainable.

❶ 我看得懂中國電影。
Wǒ kàndedǒng Zhōngguó diànyǐng.
I catch on to Chinese movies.

❷ 垃圾車的音樂雖然很小，但是我聽得見。
Lèsè chē de yīnyuè suīrán hěn xiǎo, dànshì wǒ tīngdejiàn.
The music played by the garbage truck isn't loud, but I can hear it.

❸ 早上八點，我當然起得來。
Zǎoshàng bādiǎn, wǒ dāngrán qǐdelái.
Of course, I can get up at 8am.

❹ 師父教的這個動作很容易，每個人都學得會。

Shīfù jiāo de zhè ge dòngzuò hěn róngyì, měi ge rén dōu xuédehuì.

The movement taught by the master was so easy that anyone could learn it.

Structures

Negation :　　Verb＋不＋complement

❶ 我認識他，但是他的名字我想不起來。

Wǒ rènshì tā, dànshì tā de míngzi wǒ xiǎngbùqǐlái.

I knew him, but I just can't recall his name.

❷ 夜市太吵了，他聽不見我叫他。

Yèshì tài chǎo le, tā tīngbújiàn wǒ jiào tā.

The night market is too noisy. He can't hear that I was calling him.

❸ 半夜三點太早了，誰也起不來。

Bànyè sāndiǎn tài zǎo le, shéi yě qǐbùlái.

3 a.m. is early for anybody to get up.

Questions :

❶ 老師上課，你聽得懂聽不懂？

Lǎoshī shàngkè, nǐ tīngdedǒng tīngbùdǒng?

Do you understand the teacher in class?

❷ 廣告上的字那麼小，你是不是看不見？

Guǎnggào shàng de zì nàme xiǎo, nǐ shìbúshì kànbújiàn?

The text on that advertisement is so small, can you even see it?

❸ 只有一個星期，他們學得會學不會一百個漢字？

Zhǐ yǒu yí ge xīngqí, tāmen xuédehuì xuébúhuì yìbǎi ge Hànzì?

Can they learn 100 Chinese characters in only one week?

Usage

There is a difference between '沒V_1V_2' and 'V_1不V_2'. The first pattern indicates that some result was not accomplished. The second pattern indicates that some result cannot be accomplished. Compare the following examples:

❶ 我沒看見那個人從七樓走上來。

Wǒ méi kànjiàn nà ge rén cóng qī lóu zǒu shànglái.

I didn't see that person walk up from the 7th floor.

❷ 我在十樓，所以看不見七樓的人。

Wǒ zài shí lóu, suǒyǐ kànbújiàn qī lóu de rén.

I'm on the 10th floor, so I can't see the people on the 7th floor.

❸ 他只上了一天的課，所以他還沒學會開車。

Tā zhǐ shàngle yì tiān de kè, suǒyǐ tā hái méi xuéhuì kāi chē.

He only took the lesson for one day, so he has not yet learned how to drive.

❹ 他已經上了半年的課了，還學不會開車。

Tā yǐjīng shàngle bàn nián de kè le, hái xuébúhuì kāi chē.

He has already taken the lesson for half a year, but he still couldn't drive.

-部 -bù, or -邊 -biān, Locative Markers

Function

-部 refers to 'sections' of a region, and -邊 to 'sides' of a point of reference. In terms of a country, -部 refers to domestic areas, and -邊 to areas beyond borders.

❶ 台灣的北部、南部有很多好玩的地方。

Táiwān de běibù, nánbù yǒu hěn duō hǎowán de dìfāng.

There are lots of fun places in northern and southern Taiwan.

❷ 台灣東部的風景很美。

Táiwān dōngbù de fēngjǐng hěn měi.

The scenery in eastern Taiwan is beautiful.

❸ 台灣東邊的大海非常乾淨。

Táiwān dōngbiān de dà hǎi fēicháng gānjìng.

The ocean to the east of Taiwan is very clean.

❹ 那個地方西邊有山，南邊有海。

Nà ge dìfāng xībiān yǒu shān, nánbian yǒu hǎi.

To the west of that place there are mountains and to the south there is ocean.

Structures

Cardinal And Intermediate Points	Locative Suffix
東 east	
西 west	
南 south	
北 north	邊/部
東南 southeast	biān / bù
東北 northeast	
西南 southwest	
西北 northwest	

Usage

There is 中部 zhōngbù for 'in the central region of', but there is no *中邊 *zhōngbiān.

不但 A，還 B, (búdàn (Conj) A, hái (Adv) B), not only A, but also B

Function

This pattern provides two pieces of information about the subject of a sentence.

❶ 他昨天買的那件外套不但輕，還很暖和。

Tā zuótiān mǎi de nà jiàn wàitào búdàn qīng, hái hěn nuǎnhuo.

The coat he bought yesterday is not only light, but also very warm.

❷ 陳小姐的中文不但聲調很準，說話還很流利。

Chén xiǎojiě de Zhōngwén búdàn shēngdiào hěn zhǔn, shuōhuà hái hěn liúlì.

Miss Chen's Chinese is not only spot on in terms of tones; she speaks very fluently.

❸ 我新辦的手機，不但月租便宜，還可以上網吃到飽。

Wǒ xīn bàn de shǒujī, búdàn yuèzū piányí, hái kěyǐ shàngwǎng chīdàobǎo.

The cell phone I just got not only has low monthly fees; I get unlimited internet usage.

❹ 外面不但下雨，還颳大風，你就別出去了。

Wàimiàn búdàn xià yǔ, hái guā dà fēng, nǐ jiù bié chūqù le.

It's not only raining outside; it's also very windy. Don't go out.

Usage

Remember that conjunctions are placed either pre- or post-subject, while adverbs occur before VP. If the conj 而且 érqiě appears after 不但 búdàn, 還 hái can be omitted, e.g.,

❶ 他買的外套，不但樣子好看，而且價錢（還）很便宜。

Tā mǎi de wàitào, búdàn yàngzi hǎokàn, érqiě jiàqián (hái) hěn piányí.

Not only is the style of his coat attractive, the price is really low.

❷ 他做的菜，不但顏色漂亮，而且味道（還）很香。

Tā zuò de cài, búdàn yánsè piàoliàng, érqič wèidào (hái) hěn xiāng.

Not only is the dish he made visually attractive, it tastes great too.

❸ 經常寫漢字不但能記住，而且（還）能寫得漂亮。

Jīngcháng xiě Hànzì búdàn néng jìzhù, érqiě (hái) néng xiě de piàoliang.

Frequently writing Chinese characters not only helps you remember, it helps you to be able to write beautifully.

不但 A，而且 B, (búdàn (Conj) A, érqiě (Conj) B), not only A but also B

Function

This pattern connects two clauses incrementally, not only A but also B, usually with the same subject.

❶ 這個房間，不但光線好，而且離捷運站不遠。

Zhè ge fángjiān, búdàn guāngxiàn hǎo, érqiě lí jiéyùn zhàn bù yuǎn.

This room is not only well lit, it is not far from an MRT station.

❷ 不少外國人喜歡逛夜市，他們覺得夜市不但熱鬧，而且有趣。

Bù shǎo wàiguó rén xǐhuān guàng yèshì, tāmen juéde yèshì búdàn rènào, érqiě yǒuqù.

Many foreigners like to visit night markets. They find night markets not only bustling, but also fun.

❸ 學中文不但能了解中國文化，而且對將來找工作有幫助。

Xué Zhōngwén búdàn néng liǎojiě Zhōngguó wénhuà, érqiě duì jiānglái zhǎo gōngzuò yǒu bāngzhù.

Learning Chinese not only can help you understand Chinese culture, but it will also be helpful in seeking employment in the future.

31

(1) If the subjects of the two clauses are identical, then the subject occurs once and appears before 不但. The subject in the second clause can be omitted. For example, 他不但會說中文，而且說得很流利。Tā búdàn huì shuō Zhōngwén, érqiě shuō de hěn liúlì. 'He can not only speak Chinese, but also speaks it fluently'.

(2) If the subjects of the two clauses are different, then each will appear after 不但 or 而且. For example, 我們家的人都喜歡看棒球比賽，不但爸爸喜歡看，而且媽媽也喜歡看。Wǒmen jiā de rén dōu xǐhuān kàn bàngqiú bǐsài, búdàn bàba xǐhuān kàn, érqiě māma yě xǐhuān kàn. 'Our families all like to watch baseball games. Not only my father likes to watch the games, but my mother does, too.'

(3) 不但 can be omitted when 而且 is used on its own. 不但 can also be used without 而且, but words such as 還hái or 也yě need to be inserted in the second clause.

❶ 他覺得找房子麻煩，而且覺得搬家更麻煩。
Tā juéde zhǎo fángzi máfán, érqiě juéde bānjiā gèng máfán.
He feels that looking for a place to live is a pain and moving is even more of a pain.

❷ 他不但沒買到衣服，錢還被偷了。
Tā búdàn méi mǎidào yīfú, qián hái bèi tōu le.
Not only did he not buy clothes, his money even got stolen.

❸ 多運動不但對身體好，也可能讓你長得更高。
Duō yùndòng búdàn duì shēntǐ hǎo, yě kěnéng ràng nǐ zhǎng de gèng gāo.
Exercising is not only good for your physical health, supposedly it helps you grow taller.

❹ 這支手機不但可以照相，也可以透過網路傳給別人。
Zhè zhī shǒujī búdàn kěyǐ zhàoxiàng, yě kěyǐ tòuguò wǎnglù chuán gěi biérén.
This cell phone can not only take pictures, but can also send them over the internet to others.

不到, búdào, less than

不到 is often followed by modifying a number, meaning 'less than...'.

❶ 博物院的人說不到 6 歲的小孩子，不可以進去參觀。
Bówùyuàn de rén shuō búdào 6 suì de xiǎo háizi, bù kěyǐ jìnqù cānguān.
The museum staff say that children less than 6-years old cannot go inside (and visit).

❷ 這支手機不到五千塊，真便宜。
Zhè zhī shǒujī búdào wǔqiān kuài, zhēn piányí.
This cell phone is less than NT$5,000. That's really cheap.

❸ 老師說成績不到 85 分，不可以申請獎學金。

Lǎoshī shuō chéngjī búdào 85 fēn, bù kěyǐ shēnqǐng jiǎngxuéjīn.

The teacher said that students with grades of less than 85 cannot apply for a scholarship.

❹ 他來台灣還不到半年，就認識了不少台灣朋友。

Tā lái Táiwān hái búdào bàn nián, jiù rènshì le bù shǎo Táiwān péngyǒu.

He has been in Taiwan less than half a year and he already has lots of Taiwanese friends.

❺ 昨天的作業那麼多，可是她不到一個小時就寫完了。

Zuótiān de zuòyè nàme duō, kěshì tā búdào yí ge xiǎoshí jiù xiěwán le.

There was all that homework yesterday, but she finished it in less than an hour.

不得不, bùdébù, have no choice but to...

Function The pattern 不得不 is used when one is engaged in doing something reluctantly, as a last resort. There are not other options.

❶ 我不喜歡吃魚，但是為了讓傷口恢復得比較快，不得不喝點魚湯。

Wǒ bù xǐhuān chī yú, dànshì wèile ràng shāngkǒu huīfù de bǐjiào kuài, bùdébù hē diǎn yú tāng.

I don't like fish, but if I want to heal my wound quicker I have no choice but to drink some fish soup.

❷ 因為小明去參加畢業旅行，媽媽不得不幫他照顧寵物。

Yīnwèi Xiǎomíng qù cānjiā bìyè lǚxíng, māma bùdébù bāng tā zhàogù chǒngwù.

Because Xiaoming went on a graduation trip, his mom has no choice but to take care of his pet for him.

❸ 現代人的飲食習慣改變了，很多傳統小吃店不得不改賣年輕人喜歡的食物。

Xiàndài rén de yǐnshí xíguàn gǎibiàn le, hěn duō chuántǒng xiǎochī diàn bùdébù gǎi mài niánqīng rén xǐhuān de shíwù.

The dietary habits of people today have changed. Many traditional eateries have had to change and sell foods that young people like.

❹ 他的腿受傷了，不得不放棄這場比賽。

Tā de tuǐ shòushāng le, bùdébù fàngqì zhè chǎng bǐsài.

He has an injured leg, so he has no choice but to sit out this match.

❺ 陳如美的父親生病住院，所以她不得不休學去工作，改善家裡的生活。

Chén Rúměi de fùqīn shēngbìng zhùyuàn, suǒyǐ tā bùdébù xiūxué qù gōngzuò, gǎishàn jiālǐ de shēnghuó.

Chen Rumei's father is sick and staying in the hospital, so she had no choice but to take a break from school and go to work to help improve her family's life.

不管 A 都 B, (bùguǎn (Conj) A dōu (Adv) B), regardless of whether or not

Function ▶ This pattern indicates that the consequence (following 都) remains the same no matter whether the condition (following 不管) is or is not met.

❶ 我爸爸不管工作忙不忙，天天都去健身房運動。
Wǒ bàba bùguǎn gōngzuò máng bù máng, tiāntiān dōu qù jiànshēnfáng yùndòng.
Regardless of whether or not he's busy at work, my dad goes to the gym every day to work out.

❷ 不管那裡的環境怎麼樣，他都要搬去那裡。
Bùguǎn nàlǐ de huánjìng zěnmeyàng, tā dōu yào bān qù nàlǐ.
Regardless of what the conditions will be like, he's going to move there.

❸ 不管是蒸魚還是炸魚，我都不吃。
Bùguǎn shì zhēng yú háishì zhá yú, wǒ dōu bù chī.
Whether it's steamed fish or fried fish, I won't eat it.

❹ 不管上幾點的課，他都會遲到。
Bùguǎn shàng jǐ diǎn de kè, tā dōu huì chídào.
No matter when his classes are, he's always late.

❺ 不管媽媽同不同意，我都要去美國念書。
Bùguǎn māma tóng bù tóngyì, wǒ dōu yào qù Měiguó niànshū.
I am going to go study in the US, no matter what my mom says.

Structures ▶ Note that whatever comes after 不管 is basically a question in concept, e.g., 忙不忙 (❶ above), 怎麼樣 (❷) and 蒸魚還是炸魚 (❸).

Usage ▶ The following expressions often appear after 不管：

(1) Interrogative pronouns like 什麼 shénme, 誰 shéi, 哪 nǎ.
要是你有問題，不管什麼時候都可以打電話給我。
Yàoshi nǐ yǒu wèntí, bùguǎn shénme shíhòu dōu kěyǐ dǎ diànhuà gěi wǒ.
If you have a question, no matter when, you can call me.

(2) A-not-A question
不管父母同不同意，他都要念會計系。
Bùguǎn fùmǔ tóng bù tóngyì, tā dōu yào niàn kuàijì xì.
Regardless of whether or not his parents agree, he is going to major in accounting.

(3) A or B, Choice question
老師說不管天氣好（還是）壞，學生都不可以遲到。
Lǎoshī shuō bùguǎn tiānqì hǎo (háishì) huài, xuéshēng dōu bù kěyǐ chídào.
The teacher says that whether the weather is good or bad, students are not allowed to be late.

不見得, bújiàndé, (Adv), not necessarily

Function

不見得 means 'It does not necessarily follow from the previous point'.

❶ 現在工作不好找。就算念理想的大學，也不見得找得到好工作。

Xiànzài gōngzuò bù hǎo zhǎo. Jiùsuàn niàn lǐxiǎng de dàxué, yě bújiàndé zhǎodedào hǎo gōngzuò.

Jobs are hard to find right now. Even graduates of top schools aren't necessarily guaranteed a good job.

❷ 學歷高的人不見得都可以當經理。

Xuélì gāo de rén bújiàndé dōu kěyǐ dāng jīnglǐ.

Being highly educated doesn't necessarily mean one will become a manager.

❸ 離開家鄉的人不見得都能在節日回家團聚。

Líkāi jiāxiāng de rén bújiàndé dōu néng zài jiérì huíjiā tuánjù.

Those who move away from home aren't necessarily able to come home for the holidays.

❹ 好吃的東西不見得對身體好。

Hǎochī de dōngxi bújiàndé duì shēntǐ hǎo.

Tasty food isn't necessarily healthy food.

❺ 有的人開茶店不見得是為了賺錢。

Yǒu de rén kāi chá diàn bújiàndé shì wèile zhuàn qián.

Some people don't necessarily open up tea shops just to make money.

Usage

(1) 不見得 has no affirmative form, i.e., *見得.

(2) Can combine with negative sentences, e.g., 今天不見得不會下雪。Jīntiān bújiàndé búhuì xiàxuě. 'It won't necessarily not snow today.'

(3) 不見得 can refute a previous claim or viewpoint. e.g.,

一天學五十個詞不見得能提高中文能力。

Yì tiān xué wǔshí ge cí bújiàndé néng tígāo Zhōngwén nénglì.

Studying 50 words a day won't necessarily improve your Chinese proficiency.

(4) 不見得 is used colloquially, and it can stand alone or in the middle of a sentence. Keep in mind that 不見得 is not always synonymous with 不一定. Both can be used to express disagreement, but when expressing uncertainty that is viewpoint neutral, 不見得 cannot be used. E.g.,

❶ A：他明天一定來。

Tā míngtiān yídìng lái.

He is sure to come tomorrow.

B：他明天不見得會來。/他明天不一定會來。
Tā míngtiān bújiàndé huì lái. / Tā míngtiān bùyídìng huì lái.
He won't necessarily come tomorrow.

❷ A：他明天來不來？
Tā míngtiān lái bù lái?
Is he coming tomorrow?

B：不一定來。Bùyídìng lái. /*不見得會來。Bújiàndé huì lái.
Not necessarily.

❸ A：我想小玲會在台灣上大學。
Wǒ xiǎng Xiǎolíng huì zài Táiwān shàng dàxué.
I think Xiaoling will go to university in Taiwan.

B：不見得。Bújiàndé. /不一定。Bùyídìng.
Not necessarily.

❹ A：小玲打算在台灣上大學嗎？
Xiǎolíng dǎsuàn zài Táiwān shàng dàxué ma?
Does Xiaoling plan to go to university in Taiwan?

B：不一定。Bùyídìng. /*不見得。Bújiàndé.
Not necessarily.

❺ A：颱風來的時候一定會放假。
Táifēng lái de shíhòu yídìng huì fàngjià.
When typhoons hit, we get the day off.

B：不見得。Bújiàndé. /不一定。Bùyídìng.
Not necessarily.

❻ A：颱風來的時候會不會放假？
Táifēng lái de shíhòu huì bú huì fàngjià?
When the typhoon gets here, will we get the day off?

B：不一定。Bùyídìng. /*不見得。Bújiàndé.
Not necessarily.

(5) 不見得 is an adverb and precedes other adverbs such as 都, 也 and 還 etc.

❶ 老師的說明，學生不見得都懂。
Lǎoshī de shuōmíng, xuéshēng bújiàndé dōu dǒng.

❷ 你欣賞的藝術表演，別人不見得也欣賞。
Nǐ xīnshǎng de yìshù biǎoyǎn, biérén bújiàndé yě xīnshǎng.

❸ 運動員過了四十歲以後，不見得還能參加比賽。
Yùndòngyuán guòle sìshí suì yǐhòu, bújiàndé hái néng cānjiā bǐsài.

不禁, bùjīn, (Adv), uncontrollably, cannot help but...

Function ▶ The adverb 不禁 refers to one's inability to control oneself from some action or desire as prompted by the circumstances.

❶ 看到小時候的朋友，他不禁想起童年的生活。
Kàndào xiǎoshíhòu de péngyǒu, tā bùjīn xiǎngqǐ tóngnián de shēnghuó.
Upon seeing his childhood friends, he couldn't help but think of his own childhood.

❷ 阿姨聽說表弟得到獎學金的消息，不禁高興得大叫。
Āyí tīngshuō biǎodì dédào jiǎngxuéjīn de xiāoxī, bùjīn gāoxìng de dà jiào.
When aunt heard that her son (my cousin) got a scholarship, she couldn't help but shout out for joy.

❸ 聽完王教授的演講，讓人不禁想出去留學，看看外面的世界。
Tīngwán Wáng jiàoshòu de yǎnjiǎng, ràng rén bùjīn xiǎng chūqù liúxué, kànkàn wàimiàn de shìjiè.
After listening to Prof. Wang's talk, everyone couldn't help but be inspired to go study abroad and see the world.

❹ 看到網路上模特兒穿的衣服那麼好看，李小姐不禁也想買來穿穿看。
Kàndào wǎnglù shàng mótèr chuān de yīfú nàme hǎokàn, Lǐ xiǎojiě bùjīn yě xiǎng mǎilái chuānchuān kàn.
Seeing how beautiful the outfit looked on the online model, Ms. Lee couldn't stop herself from wanting to buy it.

❺ 哥哥聽完小妹妹的話，不禁哈哈大笑。
Gēge tīngwán xiǎo mèimei de huà, bùjīn hāhā dà xiào.
He couldn't help burst out laughing at his little sister's words.

不如, bùrú, (Vst), not as good as

Function　The transitive state verb 不如 introduces a comparison between two items. The first noun is inferior to, or less desirable, than the second.

❶ 這件衣服的品質不如那件的好。
Zhè jiàn yīfú de pǐnzhí bùrú nà jiàn de hǎo.
The quality of this garment is not as good as that one.

❷ 這家火鍋店的海鮮不如那家的新鮮。
Zhè jiā huǒguō diàn de hǎixiān bùrú nà jiā de xīnxiān.
The seafood in this hot pot restaurant is not as fresh as that one.

❸ 搭捷運得轉兩趟車，不如坐公車方便。
Dā jiéyùn děi zhuǎn liǎng tàng chē, bùrú zuò gōngchē fāngbiàn.
Taking the MRT, you have to transfer twice. It's not as convenient as taking the bus.

❹ 考試以前才熬夜念書，不如平常就做好準備。
Kǎoshì yǐqián cái áoyè niànshū, bùrú píngcháng jiù zuòhǎo zhǔnbèi.
Staying up all night to study just before the test isn't as good as being prepared on a general basis.

⑤ 太陽這麼大，躺在沙灘上，不如回房間看電視舒服。

Tàiyáng zhème dà, tǎng zài shātān shàng, bùrú huí fángjiān kàn diànshì shūfú.

The sun is scorching. Lying on the beach isn't as comfortable as returning to the room and watching TV.

Usage

(1) The state verb at the end of a sentence with 不如 must indicate a desirable property. E.g., you cannot say *這支手機不如那支手機舊。Zhè zhī shǒujī bùrú nà zhī shǒujī jiù. 'This cellphone is not as old as that one.'

(2) If the context of a sentence using a state verb is clear, then the state verb can be omitted. For example:

A：我的手機壞了。你知道哪裡可以修理嗎？

Wǒ de shǒujī huài le. Nǐ zhīdào nǎlǐ kěyǐ xiūlǐ ma?

My cell phone is broken. Do you know where I can get it fixed?

B：你的手機已經那麼舊了。修理不如買一支新的（好）。

Nǐ de shǒujī yǐjīng nàme jiù le. Xiūlǐ bùrú mǎi yì zhī xīn de (hǎo).

Your cell phone is already so old. Rather than fix it, get a new one.

(3) 'A 不如 B' and 'A 沒有 méi yǒu B 那麼 nàme...' are similar, but there are differences:

❶ 不如 is frequently used in literary Chinese. A 沒有 B 那麼... is more colloquial.

❷ The state verb at the end of a sentence using 不如 can be omitted. The same is not true of A 沒有 B 那麼.... E.g., 坐巴士不如坐高鐵（快）。Zuò bāshì bùrú zuò gāotiě (kuài). 'Taking the HSR is faster than taking a bus.'; But you cannot say *坐巴士沒有坐高鐵那麼。(*Zuò bāshì méi yǒu zuò gāotiě nàme.)

不是, búshì, Negation

Function

不是 is not a regular negator. It negates what has been stated or assumed, i.e., 'it is not true that...,' for example,

❶ 小華覺得那支手機很貴。我覺得不是很貴。

Xiǎohuá juéde nà zhī shǒujī hěn guì. Wǒ juédé búshì hěn guì.

Xiaohua feels that cellphone is expensive. I think it's not all that expensive.

❷ 他不是點大碗的牛肉麵。他點的是小碗的。

Tā búshì diǎn dà wǎn de niúròu miàn. Tā diǎn de shì xiǎo wǎn de.

He didn't order a large bowl of beef noodles. He ordered a small one.

❸ 餐廳不是在學校裡面。餐廳在學校外面。

Cāntīng búshì zài xuéxiào lǐmiàn. Cāntīng zài xuéxiào wàimiàn.

The restaurant isn't on campus. The restaurant is off campus.

Structures ⟩ The 不是 negation can occur in either positive or negative sentences, e.g.,

❶ 他們不是在樓下喝咖啡。他們是在樓下買書。
Tāmen búshì zài lóuxià hē kāfēi. Tāmen shì zài lóuxià mǎi shū.
It's not the case they are drinking coffee downstairs. They are buying books downstairs.

❷ 我不是不來，我是週末來。
Wǒ búshì bù lái, wǒ shì zhōumò lái.
I am not not coming. I am coming on the weekend.

❸ 我不是不喜歡吃牛肉麵，可是這家的牛肉麵太辣了。
Wǒ búshì bù xǐhuan chī niúròu miàn, kěshì zhè jiā de niúròu miàn tài là le.
It's not that I don't like beef noodles; rather, it's that this shop's beef noodles are too spicy.

Usage ⟩ 不bù negation and 沒méi negation are presented separately. 不是búshì negation is quite different. It negates what has been said or claimed, 'It is not the case that...'.

他不要買包子。vs. 他不是要買包子，他是要買臭豆腐。
Tā bú yào mǎi bāozi. vs. Tā búshì yào mǎi bāozi, tā shì yào mǎi chòudòufǔ.
He isn't buying baozi. vs. It's not that he is buying baozi. He's buying stinky tofu.

不是 A 就是 B, (bú shì A jiù shì B), if it's not A, then it's B

Function ⟩ This construction, when used literally, indicates that either one of the two options offered must be true, and there are no other possibilities. It can also be used for hyperbole when describing a situation, often spoken out of frustration, e.g., ❹

❶ 我新買的手機不是收不到訊號，就是自動關機，我非拿去門市退換不可。
Wǒ xīn mǎi de shǒujī bú shì shōubúdào xùnhào, jiù shì zìdòng guānjī, wǒ fēi ná qù ménshì tuìhuàn bùkě.
If my new cell phone isn't having problems getting a signal, it's shutting itself off. I'm going to take it back to the store and exchange it if it's the last thing I do.

❷ 桌上這件外套我想不是小敏的，就是婷婷的。
Zhuō shàng zhè jiàn wàitào wǒ xiǎng bú shì Xiǎomǐn de, jiù shì Tíngtíng de.
I think that the coat on the table is either Xiaomin or Ting Ting's.

❸ 放假的時候，他不是上網玩遊戲，就是在家看漫畫，放鬆心情。

Fàngjià de shíhòu, tā bú shì shàngwǎng wán yóuxì, jiù shì zài jiā kàn mànhuà, fàngsōng xīnqíng.

When he's on break, he's either online playing games or reading comic books to relax.

❹ 他整天不是抱怨工作太多，就是抱怨薪水太少，讓人聽得好煩。

Tā zhěng tiān bú shì bàoyuàn gōngzuò tài duō, jiù shì bàoyuàn xīnshuǐ tài shǎo, ràng rén tīng de hǎo fán.

All day long, he's either complaining that he's overworked or underpaid. It's irritating to listen to.

❺ 暑假，他不是去打工，就是回家照顧爺爺，所以沒時間跟我們玩。

Shǔjià, tā bú shì qù dǎgōng, jiù shì huíjiā zhàogù yéye, suǒyǐ méi shíjiān gēn wǒmen wán.

He didn't have any time to go out with us during summer vacation. He was either working or at home taking care of his grandfather.

不是 A，而是 B, (bú shì A, ér shì B), not A; rather B

Function This structure negates a claim and presents the correct answer. 而 is an adverb.

❶ 他喜歡的人不是王小姐，而是白小姐。

Tā xǐhuān de rén bú shì Wáng xiǎojiě, ér shì Bái xiǎojiě.

The one that he likes isn't Miss Wang; rather, it's Miss Bai.

❷ 我不是不想去參加校外教學，而是因為最近忙死了。

Wǒ bú shì bù xiǎng qù cānjiā xiàowài jiāoxué, ér shì yīnwèi zuìjìn máng sǐle.

It's not that I don't want to take part in the field trip; rather, it's because I've been really busy lately.

❸ 這件衣服你不是用現金買的，而是刷卡買的，所以不能馬上退錢。

Zhè jiàn yīfú nǐ bú shì yòng xiànjīn mǎi de, ér shì shuākǎ mǎi de, suǒyǐ bù néng mǎshàng tuì qián.

You didn't purchase this garment with cash. You bought it with a credit card, so the money can't be refunded immediately.

❹ 他來台灣不是為了旅行，而是為了學中文。

Tā lái Táiwān bú shì wèile lǚxíng, ér shì wèile xué Zhōngwén.

He didn't come to Taiwan to travel around; rather, he came to study Chinese.

❺ 我換新工作，不是因為薪水比較高，而是新公司離我家比較近。

Wǒ huàn xīn gōngzuò, bú shì yīnwèi xīnshuǐ bǐjiào gāo, ér shì xīn gōngsī lí wǒ jiā bǐjiào jìn.

I changed jobs, not because the salary is higher; rather, it's because the new company is closer.

Usage 是 is a highly versatile element, sometimes a verb and sometimes a grammatical marker, like 'be' in English. As a marker, it is rather like 'do' in English, as in 'He did do it.' 是 is a marker in examples 2-5 above, in which 是 cannot be translated as 'be'. 而 is also a high frequency grammatical element, always an adverb, which is slightly literary in style.

不說, bùshuō, in S₁ 不說，S₂ 也 yě, not merely, but also (complaining)

Function This pattern is used to indicate a complaint about two issues, the second of which is more serious than the first.

❶ 那個地方吵不說，環境也很複雜。
Nà ge dìfāng chǎo bùshuō, huánjìng yě hěn fùzá.
Aside from the fact that the place is noisy, it's also a bit seedy.

❷ 他現在的工作是推銷產品。薪水低不說，也很辛苦。
Tā xiànzài de gōngzuò shì tuīxiāo chǎnpǐn. Xīnshuǐ dī bùshuō, yě hěn xīnkǔ.
His current job is selling products. The low salary aside, it's hard work.

❸ 那家店賣的商品種類少不說，價錢也很貴，難怪客人不多。
Nà jiā diàn mài de shāngpǐn zhǒnglèi shǎo bùshuō, jiàqián yě hěn guì, nánguài kèrén bù duō.
That shop has poor selection, not to mention high prices. It's no wonder they don't have many customers.

❹ 小林最近常遲到不說，功課也不寫。他怎麼了？
Xiǎo Lín zuìjìn cháng chídào bùshuō, gōngkè yě bù xiě. Tā zěnme le?
Xiao Lin has been late a lot recently; not to mention, he hasn't been doing his homework. What's up with him?

❺ 週年慶的時候，擠死了不說，也常常因為便宜買了一些沒有用的東西回家。
Zhōuniánqìng de shíhòu, jǐ sǐle bùshuō, yě chángcháng yīnwèi piányí mǎile yìxiē méi yǒu yòng de dōngxi huíjiā.
During anniversary sales the stores are overcrowded; not to mention, you often buy and bring home a lot of useless things just because they're cheap.

Usage Both 'S₁ 不說，S₂ 也' and '不但 A，還 B' patterns are incremental, i.e., they add one fact on top of another, but the latter can be used with either positive or negative instances, whereas the former can only be used in the negative. E.g., you can say: 他不但成績好，還很熱心 (Tā búdàn chéngjī hǎo, hái hěn rèxīn) 'His grades are not only good, he is also very enthusiastic.', but *他成績好不說，也很熱心 (*Tā chéngjī hǎo bùshuō, yě hěn rèxīn) isn't good Chinese.

41

不太, bútài, not very

Function

The pattern '不太＋state verb' expresses a polite, toned-down negation, when compared with a plain Neg＋Vs pattern, similar to English 'not terribly...'.

❶ A：騎機車去旅行太累了吧。
Qí jīchē qù lǚxíng tài lèi le ba.
Traveling by motorcycle is too tiring.

B：我覺得騎車去不太累，很好玩。
Wǒ juéde qí chē qù bútài lèi, hěn hǎowán.
I don't think going by motorcycle is too tiring. It's a lot of fun.

❷ A：高鐵票很貴，我們坐公車比較好。
Gāotiě piào hěn guì, wǒmen zuò gōngchē bǐjiào hǎo.
The HSR tickets are expensive. Why don't we take the bus?

B：高鐵票不太貴！
Gāotiě piào bútài guì!
The HSR tickets are not terribly expensive.

❸ A：多穿一點衣服。
Duō chuān yìdiǎn yīfú.
You should put on some more clothes.

B：今天不太冷！
Jīntiān bútài lěng!
It is not terribly cold today.

Structures

*Q*uestions：

❶ 放假的時候，高鐵票是不是不太好買？
Fàngjià de shíhòu, gāotiě piào shìbúshì bútài hǎo mǎi?
HSR tickets are not all that easy to buy during the holidays, right?

❷ 去西班牙的飛機是不是不太多？
Qù Xībānyá de fēijī shìbúshì bútài duō?
Are there not many flights to Spain?

❸ 台灣的秋天和日本的秋天是不是不太一樣？
Táiwān de qiūtiān hàn Rìběn de qiūtiān shìbúshì bútài yíyàng?
Are autumns in Taiwan and autumns in Japan not all that similar?

Usage

(1) 不太bútài＋Vs:

不太 has basically lost its literal meaning and simply means 'not very'. Depending on the context, 不太 can be used negatively or in a polite fashion.

❶ 這杯茶不太熱。
(1. Just the right temperature. 2. Not hot enough for me.)
Zhè bēi chá bútài rè.

This cup of tea is not very hot.

❷ 他的咖啡賣得不太好。(concerned)
Tā de kāfēi mài de bútài hǎo.
His coffee is not selling all that well.

❸ 今天不太冷，你不必穿那麼多。(comforting)
Jīntiān bútài lěng, nǐ búbì chuān nàme duō.
It's not so cold today. You don't need to wear that much.

(2) 不很bùhěn＋Vs:

不很 on the other hand is not as common as 不太. It is related in meaning to 不是很, which is also glossed as 'not very', causing confusion. Note that 不很 is more factual and straightforward, without any polite overtone.

不停, bù tíng, as in Verb＋個不停, keep on

Function　This pattern stresses the incessant happening of an instance, much to the displeasure of the speaker.

❶ 雨下個不停，真不知道什麼時候天氣才會變好。
Yǔ xià ge bù tíng, zhēn bù zhīdào shénme shíhòu tiānqì cái huì biàn hǎo.
It just keeps raining. I have no idea when the weather will change for the better.

❷ 什麼事讓你這麼生氣，罵個不停？
Shénme shì ràng nǐ zhème shēngqì, mà ge bù tíng?
You keep harping on and on. What's got you so pissed off?

❸ 她一走進百貨公司就買個不停，連跟我説話的時間都沒有。
Tā yì zǒujìn bǎihuò gōngsī jiù mǎi ge bù tíng, lián gēn wǒ shuōhuà de shíjiān dōu méi yǒu.
As soon as she stepped into the department store she just kept buying. She didn't even have time to talk to me.

❹ 我感冒了，鼻水流個不停。很不舒服。
Wǒ gǎnmào le, bíshuǐ liú ge bù tíng. Hěn bù shūfú.
I have a cold and my nose keeps running. I feel terrible.

❺ 你不是已經吃過晚飯了嗎？怎麼一看到蛋糕，還是吃個不停？
Nǐ búshì yǐjīng chīguò wǎnfàn le ma? Zěnme yí kàndào dàngāo, háishì chī ge bù tíng?
Haven't you already eaten dinner? How is it that as soon as you see cake, you just keep shoveling it in?

Usage

(1) This pattern only uses action verbs that can continue for a while. State verbs (Vs) and process verbs (Vp) do not participate in this pattern. The following two examples are not grammatical Chinese:
*他快樂個不停。*Tā kuàilè ge bù tíng. 'He's happy all the time.'

Or *這件事結束個不停。*Zhè jiàn shì jiéshù ge bù tíng. *This thing keeps stopping.

(2) In this pattern, 個 is not a measure word it usually is; rather, it's an 'instance marker'.

不再⋯了, (bú zài...le), not...any more

Function　The use of this structure indicates that the subject abandons an old routine/habit/belief.

❶ 他覺得自己長大了，可以獨立了，就不再接受父母的幫助了。
Tā juéde zìjǐ zhǎngdà le, kěyǐ dúlì le, jiù bú zài jiēshòu fùmǔ de bāngzhù le.
He feels that he has grown up and can be independent, so he doesn't accept his parents' help anymore.

❷ 我已經跟我男朋友分手了，我們不再見面了。
Wǒ yǐjīng gēn wǒ nánpéngyǒu fēnshǒu le, wǒmen bú zài jiànmiàn le.
I have broken up with my boyfriend. We no longer see each other.

❸ 那家店的東西品質不是很好，而且價錢很貴，我不再去了。
Nà jiā diàn de dōngxi pǐnzhí búshì hěn hǎo, érqiě jiàqián hěn guì, wǒ bú zài qù le.
The quality of the products in that store isn't all that good and the prices are expensive. I no longer go there.

❹ 漫畫不再吸引我了。現在我喜歡看談歷史的書。
Mànhuà bú zài xīyǐn wǒ le. Xiànzài wǒ xǐhuān kàn tán lìshǐ de shū.
Comics no longer have the draw on me than they used to. I now like to read books on history.

❺ 他現在越來越喜歡狗了，覺得養狗很快樂，不再是負擔了。
Tā xiànzài yuèláiyuè xǐhuan gǒu le, juéde yǎng gǒu hěn kuàilè, bú zài shì fùdān le.
He likes dogs more and more. He feels that raising dogs is a joy and no longer a burden.

不只, bùzhǐ, (Adv), not merely, exceeding

Function　The adverb 不只 means (1) 'not merely, exceeding', when modifying a noun. (2) 'not only', when modifying a sentence, associated with 也, an S₁ adverb.

❶ 這項政策已經施行了不只五年了。
Zhè xiàng zhèngcè yǐjīng shīxíng le bùzhǐ wǔ nián le.
This policy has been in implementation for over five years already.

❷ 最近教授一定很忙，因為不只我一個人找他寫推薦信。
Zuìjìn jiàoshòu yídìng hěn máng, yīnwèi bùzhǐ wǒ yí ge rén zhǎo tā xiě tuījiàn xìn.
My professor has been busy lately. I'm not the only one looking for a recommendation letter.

❸ 現在不只結婚的人比較少，結婚的年齡也比較晚。

Xiànzài bùzhǐ jiéhūn de rén bǐjiào shǎo, jiéhūn de niánlíng yě bǐjiào wǎn.

Not only are fewer people getting married these days, they are waiting longer to do so too.

❹ 最近不只大學招生困難，不少小學也關閉了。

Zuìjìn bùzhǐ dàxué zhāoshēng kùnnán, bù shǎo xiǎoxué yě guānbì le.

Enrollment isn't only low for universities. Lots of elementary schools have had to close.

❺ 這件事不只考驗他的智慧，也考驗他的信用。

Zhè jiàn shì bùzhǐ kǎoyàn tā de zhìhuì, yě kǎoyàn tā de xìnyòng.

This is not only a test of his intellect. It's also a test of his credibility.

不至於, búzhìyú, (Adv), but the situation would not be so bad as to...

Function The adverb 不至於 negates the worst possible scenario under the given circumstances, not to the extent of..., will not be as bad as....

❶ 路上車子雖然很多，但還不至於塞車。

Lù shàng chēzi suīrán hěn duō, dàn hái búzhìyú sāichē.

There are lots of cars on the road, but it's not congested yet.

❷ 他條件那麼好，不至於找不到工作吧？

Tā tiáojiàn nàme hǎo, búzhìyú zhǎobúdào gōngzuò ba?

He's certainly qualified. It's not so bad that he won't be able to find a job, right?

❸ 他個性是不太好，可是不至於害別人。

Tā gèxìng shì bútài hǎo, kěshì búzhìyú hài biérén.

He's a little volatile, but not so much so that he'd hurt anyone.

❹ 雖然我不太喜歡做飯，但還不至於每天都在外面吃。

Suīrán wǒ bútài xǐhuān zuòfàn, dàn hái búzhìyú měi tiān dū zài wàimiàn chī.

I don't particularly like cooking, but it's not to the point that I eat out every day.

❺ 我們兩個的意見是有一點不同，但我還不至於生他的氣。

Wǒmen liǎng ge de yìjiàn shì yǒu yīdiǎn bùtóng, dàn wǒ hái búzhìyú shēng tā de qì.

We may have conflicting viewpoints, but not to the point that I am upset at him over it.

❻ A：小華膽子很小，他是不是晚上不敢一個人在家？

Xiǎohuá dǎnzi hěn xiǎo, tā shìbúshì wǎnshàng bù gǎn yí ge rén zài jiā?

Xiaohua is a bit gutless. Do you think he's scared to be home alone at night?

45

B：不至於吧！

Búzhìyú ba!

It will never be that serious.

Usage

不至於 is an S₂-Adv, i.e., no utterance begins with it. It is used in the second, or later, sentence.

才, cái, (Adv), merely, only (1)

Function

The adverb 才 refers to merely/only... in quantity, which falls short of common expectation.

❶ 法國，我才去過一次。

Fǎguó, wǒ cái qùguò yí cì.

I've been to France only once. (When a lot of people go there often.)

❷ 一本書才五十塊。真便宜。

Yì běn shū cái wǔshí kuài. Zhēn piányí.

Only $50 each for a book. That's really cheap. (When they cost much more elsewhere.)

❸ 他才學了半年中文。

Tā cái xuéle bàn nián Zhōngwén.

He has studied Chinese for only half a year. (And his Chinese is super! When other people struggle for a long time.)

Structures

Questions :

❶ 你今天才吃了一個麵包嗎？

Nǐ jīntiān cái chīle yí ge miànbāo ma?

You've only had one piece of bread today?

❷ 他是不是才學了兩個星期的中文？

Tā shìbúshì cái xuéle liǎng ge xīngqí de Zhōngwén?

He has only studied Chinese for two weeks?

❸ 台北捷運，你才坐過一次嗎？

Táiběi jiéyùn, nǐ cái zuòguò yí cì ma?

You've only taken the Taipei MRT once?

Usage

(1) In the context of quantity, both 才 cái and 只 zhǐ mean 'only', so that 他才學了三個月的西班牙文 Tā cái xuéle sān gè yuè de Xībānyáwén is the same as 他只學了三個月的西班牙文 Tā zhǐ xuéle sān gè yuè de Xībānyáwén 'He studied Spanish for only three months'. However, while 只 is only factual, 才 further indicates that most people spend more time on foreign languages.

(2) Further, 才 can be followed by quantity expressions directly, whereas 只 cannot. So, 這本書才五十塊錢。Zhè běn shū cái wǔshí kuài qián. 'This book is only $50' is OK, but *這本書只五十塊錢 *Zhè běn shū zhǐ wǔshí kuài qián is not grammatical.

才, cái, (Adv), longer/later than expected (2)

Function

才 implies that the instance referred to in the sentence has taken longer than expected.

❶ 你現在才來，大家等你很久了。
　 Nǐ xiànzài cái lái, dàjiā děng nǐ hěn jiǔ le.
　 You're finally here. We've been waiting for you for a long time.

❷ 他是昨天才到台北的，所以睡得不好。
　 Tā shì zuótiān cái dào Táiběi de, suǒyǐ shuì de bù hǎo.
　 He just arrived in Taipei yesterday, so he did not sleep very well.

❸ 我等了十分鐘，捷運才來。
　 Wǒ děngle shí fēnzhōng, jiéyùn cái lái.
　 I waited 10 minutes before the MRT finally came.

Structures

Time expressions are nearly always used in 才 sentences. 才 itself cannot be negated. 不是 negation is used instead.

Negation :

❶ 我跟你一起住了十年了。我不是現在才了解你的。
　 Wǒ gēn nǐ yìqǐ zhùle shí nián le. Wǒ búshì xiànzài cái liǎojiě nǐ de.
　 I have lived with you for 10 years already. It's not like I just got to know you now.

❷ 他不是今天才告訴老闆他不能來上班的。
　 Tā búshì jīntiān cái gàosù lǎobǎn tā bù néng lái shàngbān de.
　 He didn't wait until today to tell his boss that he can't come in to work.

❸ 我們不是今天才認識的，是三年前就認識的。
　 Wǒmen búshì jīntiān cái rènshì de, shì sān nián qián jiù rènshì de.
　 We didn't just meet today. We met three years ago.

Questions :

❶ 王先生這個月才來上班的嗎？
　 Wáng xiānshēng zhè ge yuè cái lái shàngbān de ma?
　 Mr. Wang didn't come to work until this month?

❷ 你是不是昨天晚上10點才打電話給他的？
　 Nǐ shìbúshì zuótiān wǎnshàng 10 diǎn cái dǎ diànhuà gěi tā de?
　 You waited until 10 o'clock last night before calling him, didn't you?

❸ 你什麼時候才可以跟我去看電影？
　 Nǐ shénme shíhòu cái kěyǐ gēn wǒ qù kàn diànyǐng?
　 When will it be before you'll be able to see a movie with me?

Usage

While 才 indicates that the instance referred to has taken longer than expected, 就 jiù indicates that the instance referred to occurred sooner than expected. Compare the following.

❶ 我等了十分鐘捷運就來了。(pleased)
Wǒ děngle shí fēnzhōng jiéyùn jiù lái le.
I waited for the MRT and it came in just 10 minutes.

❷ 我等了十分鐘捷運才來。(displeased)
Wǒ děngle shí fēnzhōng jiéyùn cái lái.
I waited for the MRT, but it didn't come for 10 minutes.

才, cái, (Adv), then and only then (3)

Function ▸ When the adverb 才 is used in the second (consequence) clause, it indicates that the consequence takes place only when the condition or circumstance specified in the first clause is obtained successfully.

❶ 新人得選好日子，才能結婚。
Xīnrén děi xuǎnhǎo rìzi, cái néng jiéhūn.
The bride and groom-to-be have to select an auspicious day before they can get married.

❷ 做餃子得先準備好餃子皮和餡兒，才能包。
Zuò jiǎozi děi xiān zhǔnbèihǎo jiǎozipí hàn xiànr, cái néng bāo.
When making dumplings, the skins and filling have to be prepared first before the dumplings can be wrapped. (i.e., made)

❸ 大家為了幫你，才給你這些建議。
Dàjiā wèile bāng nǐ, cái gěi nǐ zhèxiē jiànyì.
We gave you these suggestions only because we wanted to help you.

Structures ▸ 才 is an adverb, and occurs before the auxiliary verb and other adverbials.

*Q*uestions :

❶ 我們一定要訂好旅館，才可以去旅行嗎？
Wǒmen yídìng yào dìnghǎo lǚguǎn, cái kěyǐ qù lǚxíng ma?
Do we have to book a hotel before we can go on the trip?

❷ 是不是要天天練習，太極拳才能打得好？
Shìbúshì yào tiāntiān liànxí, Tàijí quán cái néng dǎ de hǎo?
You need to practice every day before you can be good at Tai Chi, right?

❸ 這些新衣服你是不是都穿一下，才能知道哪件適合？
Zhèxiē xīn yīfú nǐ shìbúshì dōu chuān yíxià, cái néng zhīdào nǎ jiàn shìhé?
Only by trying on all these new clothes will you know which one suits you best, right?

Usage ▸ When 才 is used in the second clause, words such as 得 děi 'have to', 要 yào 'want to, need to', 為了 wèile 'for the sake of, because of', 因為 yīnwèi 'because' are often used in the first clause.

❶ 觀光客得先買票，才能參觀博物館。
Guānguāng kè děi xiān mǎi piào, cái néng cānguān bówùguǎn.
Tourists need to buy tickets before they can visit, i.e., look around, the museum.

❷ 因為合約快到期了，小李才找房子搬家。

Yīnwèi héyuē kuài dàoqí le, Xiǎo Lǐ cái zhǎo fángzi bānjiā.

Xiao Li looked for a new place to move to only because his lease was about to expire.

❸ 為了考試有個好成績，他才每天念那麼久的書。

Wèile kǎoshì yǒu ge hǎo chéngjī, tā cái měi tiān niàn nàme jiǔ de shū.

He only studies so long every day, because he wants to get a good score on the test.

才, cái, (Adv), to outrightly deny (4)

Function With the adverb 才, the speaker outrightly rejects the other party's viewpoint. It cannot be translated into English literally. See the various translations below.

❶ A：風水是種迷信。

Fēngshuǐ shì zhǒng míxìn.

Feng Shui is just a superstition.

　B：風水才不是迷信！

Fēngshuǐ cái bú shì míxìn!

No, it's not!

❷ A：那個餐廳在學校的右邊。

Nà gè cāntīng zài xuéxiào de yòubiān.

That restaurant is just to the right of the school.

　B：才不是在右邊，在左邊。

Cái bú shì zài yòubiān, zài zuǒbiān.

No it's not. It's to the left.

❸ A：你不是很喜歡吃臭豆腐嗎？我們去吃吧！

Nǐ bú shì hěn xǐhuān chī chòudòufǔ ma? Wǒmen qù chī ba!

You like stinky tofu right? Let's go get some.

　B：我才不喜歡（呢）！

Wǒ cái bù xǐhuān (ne)!

No way, I hate stinky tofu!

❹ A：101大樓是世界上最高的大樓。

101 dàlóu shì shìjiè shàng zuì gāo de dàlóu.

Taipei 101 is the tallest building in the world.

　B：101才不是最高的，已經有比101還高的了。

101 cái bú shì zuì gāo de, yǐjīng yǒu bǐ 101 hái gāo de le.

Actually it's not the tallest anymore. There are others that are taller.

❺ A：小籠包是台灣最好吃的食物。

Xiǎolóngbāo shì Táiwān zuì hǎochī de shíwù.

The best food in Taiwan has got to be those steamed meat buns.

B：小籠包算什麼，牛肉麵才是。

Xiǎolóngbāo suàn shénme, niúròu miàn cái shì.

Those buns are nothing, beef noodles is where it's at.

❻ A：那兩個人，高的是哥哥吧？

Nà liǎng ge rén, gāo de shì gēge ba?

Those two people over there, the taller one is older right?

B：不是，矮的才是。

Bú shì, ǎi de cái shì.

Nope, the shorter one is.

❼ A：既然你上網購物了，為什麼不用宅配的方法？宅配又快又方便。

Jìrán nǐ shàngwǎng gòuwù le, wèishénme bú yòng zháipèi de fāngfǎ? Zháipèi yòu kuài yòu fāngbiàn.

Since you are shopping online anyway, why don't you have your goods couriered? It's fast and easy.

B：宅配不方便，因為我常常不在家。我覺得超商取貨才方便。

Zháipèi bù fāngbiàn, yīnwèi wǒ chángcháng bú zài jiā. Wǒ juéde chāoshāng qǔhuò cái fāngbiàn.

I'm never home, so it's actually easier for me to pick up at the store than to have it couriered.

❽ A：我的壓力好大。要養家，薪水卻這麼低。

Wǒ de yālì hǎo dà. Yào yǎngjiā, xīnshuǐ què zhème dī.

It's a lot of stress having to raise a family on such low pay.

B：我的壓力才大（呢）！你只有一個孩子，我有三個孩子！

Wǒ de yālì cái dà (ne)! Nǐ zhǐ yǒu yí ge háizi, wǒ yǒu sān ge háizi!

You think you're under stress? You only have one kid, but I've got three!

才 A 就 B, (cái A jiù B), only just A, and B already　(5)

Function　This pattern is used to indicate the speaker's surprise at the occurrence of an instance so soon after another.

❶ 蛋糕才拿來，就被大家吃完了。

Dàngāo cái nálái, jiù bèi dàjiā chīwán le.

The cake was just brought here and it has already been eaten up by everybody.

❷ 他上星期才拿到薪水，就已經用了一半了。

Tā shàng xīngqí cái nádào xīnshuǐ, jiù yǐjīng yòngle yíbàn le.

He just got his salary last week and he's already used up half of it.

❸ 老師昨天才教過的字，學生今天就忘了。

Lǎoshī zuótiān cái jiāoguò de zì, xuéshēng jīntiān jiù wàng le.

The characters that the teacher just taught yesterday have already been forgotten by the students. (i.e., The students have already forgotten the characters that the teacher just taught yesterday.)

Structures　The subjects in the two clauses can be identical or different.

❶ 她上星期才開始找房子，昨天就搬家了。(same subject)
Tā shàng xīngqí cái kāishǐ zhǎo fángzi, zuótiān jiù bānjiā le.
She only started looking for a place last week, but she already moved yesterday.

❷ 透過朋友的介紹，大明、小美才認識三個月，下個月就要結婚了。(same subject)
Tòuguò péngyǒu de jièshào, Dàmíng, Xiǎoměi cái rènshì sān ge yuè, xià ge yuè jiù yào jiéhūn le.
Daming and Xiaomei were introduced to each other by a friend only three months ago and they're already planning to get married next month.

❸ 我們才說這幾天天氣不錯，颱風下個星期就要來了。(different subjects)
Wǒmen cái shuō zhè jǐ tiān tiānqì búcuò, táifēng xià ge xīngqí jiù yào lái le.
We were just saying that the weather has been nice these past few days and now a typhoon is going to be here next week.

❹ 老師才離開，學生就開始說話了。(different subjects)
Lǎoshī cái líkāi, xuéshēng jiù kāishǐ shuōhuà le.
The teacher just left and the students started chatting.

Questions :

❶ 那個字是不是你才教過，學生就忘了？
Nà ge zì shìbúshì nǐ cái jiāoguò, xuéshēng jiù wàng le?
Didn't you just teach that word and the students have already forgotten it?

❷ 他是不是才買了腳踏車，就被偷了？
Tā shìbúshì cái mǎile jiǎotàchē, jiù bèi tōu le?
Didn't he just buy that bike and it's already been stolen?

❸ 你是不是覺得才放暑假，就要上課了？
Nǐ shìbúshì juéde cái fàng shǔjià, jiù yào shàngkè le?
Don't you feel like you just started your summer break and it's already time to go back to school?

Usage　才 cái and 剛 gāng are similar adverbs. However, '才 A 就 B' indicates the speaker's surprise, regret, or negative attitude, while '剛 A, 就 B' is simply factual. In other words, 剛 refers to timing only, while 才 includes the speaker's attitude. Compare the following examples.

❶ 我才買車，車就被偷走了。
Wǒ cái mǎi chē, chē jiù bèi tōuzǒu le.
I just bought my car and it has already been stolen.

❷ 我剛買車，車就被偷走了。
Wǒ gāng mǎi chē, chē jiù bèi tōuzǒu le.
I just bought my car and it was stolen.

51

曾經, céngjīng, (Adv), experience in the past, V'ed before

Function　曾經 is an adverb that refers to experiences in the past, to have previously.

① 你曾經看過那位導演的電影嗎？
Nǐ céngjīng kànguò nà wèi dǎoyǎn de diànyǐng ma?
Have you ever seen any films done by that director?

② 媽媽以前曾經抱怨過爸爸每天都早出晚歸。
Māma yǐqián céngjīng bàoyuànguò bàba měi tiān dōu zǎochū wǎnguī.
Mom has complained about dad having to leave so early and come home so late.

③ 我曾經在一家室內設計公司工作。
Wǒ céngjīng zài yì jiā shìnèi shèjì gōngsī gōngzuò.
I have worked at an interior design company before.

④ 他的演技很好，曾經得過兩次獎。
Tā de yǎnjì hěn hǎo, céngjīng déguò liǎng cì jiǎng.
He's a brilliant actor, and he's won two awards before.

⑤ 你曾經在淡水老街看過街頭藝術的演出嗎？
Nǐ céngjīng zài Dànshuǐ lǎojiē kànguò jiētóu yìshù de yǎnchū ma?
Have you ever seen the street artists performing on Danshui Old Street?

Usage

(1) 過 is an experiential aspect, which can be used with 曾經. 過 always appears after the main verb, e.g., 他曾經當過英文老師。Tā céngjīng dāngguò Yīngwén lǎoshī.

(2) 曾經 can only be used in an affirmative sentence.
You can't say
*我沒有曾經工作。*他曾經沒去過西班牙。
*Wǒ méi yǒu céngjīng gōngzuò. *Tā céngjīng méi qùguò Xībānyá.

(3) 曾經 is used in formal speech, e.g.,
我記得你曾經跟我說過你的計畫。
Wǒ jìde nǐ céngjīng gēn wǒ shuōguò nǐ de jìhuà.

差不多, chàbùduō, (Vs, Adv), In Various Functions

Function　差不多, literally 'differ not much', functions variously as a state verb and adverb.

Structures　差不多 functions in many parts of speech and in various meanings, as illustrated below.

(1) 差不多Vs, as a predicate, about the same, roughly equivalent.

① 我們開始學中文的時間差不多。
Wǒmen kāishǐ xué Zhōngwén de shíjiān chàbùduō.
We started studying Chinese at about the same time.

❷ 那幾家超市賣的東西都差不多。
Nà jǐ jiā chāoshì mài de dōngxi dōu chàbùduō.
Those supermarkets all sell about the same things.

❸ 我們國家的夏天和這裡差不多。
Wǒmen guójiā de xiàtiān hàn zhèlǐ chàbùduō.
The summers in our country are about the same as here.

(2) 差不多 Vs, as a verb complement, almost completed.

❶ 我的功課寫得差不多了。
Wǒ de gōngkè xiě de chàbùduō le.
My homework is almost done.

❷ 我的旅行計畫得差不多了，你看一看吧！
Wǒ de lǚxíng jìhuà de chàbùduō le, nǐ kàn yí kàn ba!
My trip is pretty much all planned out, here, take a look!

❸ 找工作的事準備得差不多了。
Zhǎo gōngzuò de shì zhǔnbèi de chàbùduō le.
(I am) almost done preparing to look for work.

(3) 差不多 as an adverb, modifier of verbs, about, approximately.

❶ 從這裡到捷運站，差不多（走）十分鐘。
Cóng zhèlǐ dào jiéyùn zhàn, chàbùduō (zǒu) shí fēnzhōng.
From here to the MRT station, it's about a 10 minute walk.

❷ 哥哥和弟弟差不多高。
Gēge hàn dìdi chàbùduō gāo.
The older brother and the younger brother are almost the same height.

❸ 我差不多學了四個月的中文了。
Wǒ chàbùduō xuéle sì ge yuè de Zhōngwén le.
I have studied Chinese for about four months now.

Questions :

❶ 從學校到捷運站差不多得走多久？
Cóng xuéxiào dào jiéyùn zhàn chàbùduō děi zǒu duōjiǔ?
About how long does it take to walk from the school to the MRT station?

❷ 你的考試準備得差不多了嗎？
Nǐ de kǎoshì zhǔnbèi de chàbùduō le ma?
Are you almost done preparing for the exam?

❸ 這兩個房間的房租是不是差不多？
Zhè liǎng ge fángjiān de fángzū shìbúshì chàbùduō?
Is the rent for these two rooms about the same?

Usage

Sometimes it's common for Chinese people to respond with 差不多, making it difficult to figure out what the truth is.

❶ A：你新年要吃的東西都準備了嗎？

Nǐ Xīnnián yào chī de dōngxi dōu zhǔnbèi le ma?

Have you prepared the food for New Year's?

B：差不多了。

Chàbùduō le.

Just about.

❷ A：我們準備要去餐廳了嗎？

Wǒmen zhǔnbèi yào qù cāntīng le ma?

Are we ready to go to the restaurant?

B：差不多了。

Chàbùduō le.

Almost.

❸ A：你習慣花蓮的生活了嗎？

Nǐ xíguàn Huālián de shēnghuó le ma?

Are you used to life in Hualien?

B：差不多了。

Chàbùduō le.

More or less.

差一點（就）, chàyìdiǎn (jiù), (Adv), almost

Function　差一點（就）… means 'almost... (but did not)'. The ... part usually indicates a situation that, from the speaker's perspective, was not expected to take place. 就 in this pattern is optional, but its use marks urgency.

❶ 昨天的演講真沒意思，我差一點睡著了。

Zuótiān de yǎnjiǎng zhēn méiyìsi, wǒ chàyìdiǎn shuìzháo le.

The speech yesterday was really boring. I almost fell asleep.

❷ 上次我哥哥去爬山的時候，差一點迷路。

Shàng cì wǒ gēge qù páshān de shíhòu, chàyìdiǎn mílù.

The last time my brother went hiking in the mountains, he almost got lost.

❸ 為了健康，他差一點就搬到鄉下去住。

Wèile jiànkāng, tā chàyìdiǎn jiù bān dào xiāngxià qù zhù.

For the sake of his health, he nearly moved to the countryside.

❹ 上個星期他在圖書館念書，背包差一點被偷走。

Shàng ge xīngqí tā zài túshūguǎn niànshū, bēibāo chàyìdiǎn bèi tōuzǒu.

Last week, he was studying in the library and his backpack almost got stolen.

❺ 小美的生日，我差一點就忘了送她禮物。

Xiǎoměi de shēngrì, wǒ chàyìdiǎn jiù wàngle sòng tā lǐwù.

On Xiaomei's birthday, I almost forgot to give her a present.

Usage　差一點（就）… indicates that some situation almost took place but not. 差不多 chàbùduō, on the other hand, means 'about, close to', so that, for example, 差不多都 in ❷ below can be 90%.

❶ 外面的雨很大，我差一點來不了。
　Wàimiàn de yǔ hěn dà, wǒ chàyìdiǎn láibùliǎo.
　It's pouring outside. I almost couldn't get here.

❷ 他昨天告訴我的事情，我差不多都忘了。
　Tā zuótiān gàosù wǒ de shìqíng, wǒ chàbùduō dōu wàng le.
　I've forgotten just about everything he told me yesterday.

趁, chèn, (Prep), seize the moment

Function　The preposition 趁 refers to seizing an opportune moment for the implementation of an action.

❶ 林老師趁這個週末沒事到東部的海邊走走。
　Lín lǎoshī chèn zhè ge zhōumò méi shì dào dōngbù de hǎibiān
　zǒuzǒu.
　Ms. Lin is taking advantage of the fact that she has nothing to do
　this weekend to take a walk on a beach on the east coast.

❷ 他趁老師還沒來上課，出去買了一杯咖啡。
　Tā chèn lǎoshī hái méi lái shàngkè, chūqù mǎile yì bēi kāfēi.
　He took advantage of the fact that the teacher hadn't arrived for
　class yet to go out and buy a cup of coffee.

❸ 趁天氣好，小明和美美去河邊公園騎腳踏車。
　Chèn tiānqì hǎo, Xiǎomíng hàn Měiměi qù hébiān gōngyuán qí
　jiǎotàchē.
　Taking advantage of the nice weather, Xiaoming and Meimei went
　to Riverside Park to ride bikes.

Structures　趁 can introduce a noun phrase, a verb phrase, or a clause. The 趁
phrase can appear either sentence initially or before the main VP.

Questions :

❶ 趁這個週末，我們要不要搭捷運去看電腦展？
　Chèn zhè ge zhōumò, wǒmen yào bú yào dā jiéyùn qù kàn diànnǎo
　zhǎn?
　Should we take the opportunity this weekend to hop on the MRT
　and go see the computer exhibition?

❷ 趁年輕的時候你不打打工，怎麼會了解工作的情形呢？
　Chèn niánqīng de shíhòu nǐ bù dǎdǎ gōng, zěnme huì liǎojiě
　gōngzuò de qíngxíng ne?
　If you don't seize the opportunity to work part-time while you are
　young, how will you understand what work is really all about?

❸ 你是不是應該趁老師還沒來，趕快把作業寫完？
　Nǐ shìbúshì yīnggāi chèn lǎoshī hái méi lái, gǎnkuài bǎ zuòyè
　xiěwán?
　Shouldn't you take advantage of the fact that the teacher hasn't
　come back yet to hurry up and finish your homework?

Usage ▶ 趁 and 趁著 chènzhe mean practically the same thing. Either 趁 or 趁著 can be used in the following example, 我們趁（著）天氣好，去山上走一走 Wǒmen chèn (zhe) tiānqì hǎo, qù shān shàng zǒu yì zǒu. 'We took a walk in the mountain while the weather was nice'. 趁 alone is more colloquial and has a higher frequency of occurrence.

成, chéng, (Ptc), as Verb Complement, to become, to turn into (1)

Function ▶ The post-verbal 成 introduces a noun that denotes the new entity (or state) that derives from the action denoted by the verb, i.e. action＋result. English translations can be difficult in some cases.

❶ 你看！你把餃子包成什麼樣子了？
Nǐ kàn! Nǐ bǎ jiǎozi bāochéng shénme yàngzi le?
Look at you! What kind of dumplings are you making?

❷ 我看不懂西班牙文。你能不能幫我把這段話翻譯成中文？
Wǒ kànbùdǒng Xībānyáwén. Nǐ néng bù néng bāng wǒ bǎ zhè duàn huà fānyìchéng Zhōngwén?
I don't understand Spanish. Can you translate this section into Chinese for me?

❸ 你在我房間裡做了什麼事？怎麼把我的房間弄成這樣？
Nǐ zài wǒ fángjiān lǐ zuòle shénme shì? Zěnme bǎ wǒ de fángjiān nòngchéng zhèyàng?
What did you do in my room? How did it get so messed up?

❹ 她用蛋跟其他材料做成一個生日蛋糕，送給媽媽。
Tā yòng dàn gēn qítā cáiliào zuòchéng yí ge shēngrì dàngāo, sòng gěi māma.
She used eggs and some other ingredients and made them into a birthday cake for her mom.

❺ 這是用Word寫的。我幫你存成PDF，可以嗎？
Zhè shì yòng Word xiě de. Wǒ bāng nǐ cúnchéng PDF, kěyǐ ma?
This was written in Word. I saved it for you in a PDF file. Is that OK?

Usage ▶

(1) V＋成 is typically followed by a noun. If the new state is denoted by a state verb, then 成 is not inserted between the action verb and the state verb. So *他把我的杯子弄成破了(*Tā bǎ wǒ de bēizi nòngchéng pò le) is no good. Only 弄破 nòngpò is possible.

(2) Negation 沒 is placed before the action verb. For example, 她的手機沒換成月租型。Tā de shǒujī méi huànchéng yuèzūxíng. 'She didn't change her cell phone to a monthly plan.'

成, chéng, (Ptc), As a verb complement, successful(ly) (2)

Function

成 is a resultative complement referring to the successfulness of an undertaking, able to succeed at the verb.

① 要是你再不努力讀書的話，就念不成醫學系了。
Yàoshi nǐ zài bù nǔlì dúshū de huà, jiù niànbùchéng yīxué xì le.
If you don't start taking your studies seriously you'll never get into med school.

② 如果訂購不成的話，就只好換一個網站訂購了。
Rúguǒ dìnggòu bù chéng de huà, jiù zhǐhǎo huàn yí ge wǎngzhàn dìnggòu le.
If you can't complete the order, you'll have to try from a different website.

③ 他又參加了民意代表選舉，可惜這一次他沒連任成。
Tā yòu cānjiā le mínyì dàibiǎo xuǎnjǔ, kěxí zhè yí cì tā méi liánrènchéng.
He ran in the representative elections again, but unfortunately was not reappointed.

④ 上個月那場演唱會因為颱風而改時間了。等了一個月，今天我終於看成了。
Shàng ge yuè nà chǎng yǎnchànghuì yīnwèi táifēng ér gǎi shíjiān le. Děng le yí ge yuè, jīntiān wǒ zhōngyú kànchéng le.
The concert scheduled for last month was postponed due to a typhoon. I went to see it today, finally.

⑤ 高小美當得成當不成助教，得由系主任來決定。
Gao Xiǎoměi dāngdechéng dāngbùchéng zhùjiào, děi yóu xìzhǔrèn lái juédìng.
Whether or not Gao Xiǎoměi will become a teaching assistant is up to the chairman of the department.

Usage

(1) 成 can be used in both the actual mode (V 成, 沒 V 成) and the potential mode (V 得成, V 不成).

(2) Compare with 成 serving in other functions.

成語, chéngyǔ, 四字格, Four-Character Phrases

Function

The four-character expressions are ready-made phrases, e.g., 萬事如意 wànshì rúyì, 'May everything go your way.', 心想事成 xīnxiǎng shìchéng, 'May all your wishes come true.', 生日快樂 shēngrì kuàilè, 'Happy birthday.', 步步高升 bùbù gāoshēng, 'Keep advancing in your career.', 年年有餘 niánnián yǒuyú, 'Enjoy abundance every year.', and 恭喜發財 gōngxǐ fācái, 'Be happy and prosper.' Four-character expressions are frequently used due to their concise form but rich meaning. Different internal structures typically convey different meanings.

(1) In '大 A 大 B', A and B are two mono-syllabic units of similar meaning. The pattern usually serves as the predicate in a sentence, to indicate 'very A & B', 'greatly A & B', or 'having lots of A & B'.

❶ 吃橘子是希望新的一年大吉大利。(very)
Chī júzi shì xīwàng xīn de yì nián dàjí dàlì.
Eating tangerines represents the hope that the New Year will be a very lucky and prosperous one.

❷ 過年的時候，家家大魚大肉，慶祝新年。(abundance)
Guònián de shíhòu, jiājiā dàyú dàròu, qìngzhù xīnnián.
During the Spring Festival, every household prepares lots of fish and meat to ring in the New Year.

❸ 睡覺以前大吃大喝相當不健康。(in abundance)
Shuìjiào yǐqián dàchī dàhē xiāngdāng bú jiànkāng.
Eating and drinking a lot before bed is rather unhealthy.

❹ 張先生、張太太常因為小孩的事，大吵大鬧。(great noises)
Zhāng xiānshēng, Zhāng tàitai cháng yīnwèi xiǎohái de shì, dàchǎo dànào.
Mr. and Mrs. Zhang often have big fights because of issues surrounding their children.

(2) The pattern, '有 A 有 B', usually serves as the predicate in a sentence. A and B are two mono-syllabic units whose meanings can be opposite. They can be state verbs, nouns, or action verbs. The pattern may indicate 'some A, some B' as in **❶** and **❷**. The pattern may indicate 'have A and B', as in **❸** and **❹**. The pattern may indicate 'experience A and B', as in **❺** and **❻**.

❶ 那家店的水果有好有壞，得慢慢地選。
Nà jiā diàn de shuǐguǒ yǒuhǎo yǒuhuài, děi mànmàn de xuǎn.
Some of that store's fruit is good; some is bad. You have to select carefully.

❷ 這些小吃有甜有鹹，你想吃什麼就買什麼。
Zhèxiē xiǎochī yǒutián yǒuxián, nǐ xiǎng chī shénme jiù mǎi shénme.
There are both sweet and savory snacks here, so get whatever you are hungry for.

❸ 這附近有山有水，風景真美。
Zhè fùjìn yǒushān yǒushuǐ, fēngjǐng zhēn měi.
There are both mountains and water around here. The scenery is really beautiful.

❹ 他有名有姓，你不可以叫他「喂」，太不客氣了。
Tā yǒumíng yǒuxìng, nǐ bù kěyǐ jiào tā 'wèi', tài bú kèqì le.
He has a name, calling him 'hey you' is not good form.

❺ 我們昨天去參加學校的活動，有吃有喝，很開心。
Wǒmen zuótiān qù cānjiā xuéxiào de huódòng, yǒuchī yǒuhē, hěn kāixīn.
We took part in a school activity yesterday. There were things to eat and drink. We were happy. (i.e., We had great fun.)

❻ 大家一邊吃飯、一邊說話，有說有笑的。
Dàjiā yìbiān chīfàn, yìbiān shuōhuà, yǒushuō yǒuxiào de.
We ate and talked. There was good conversation and laughter.

Usage

(1) Different four-character formats have different productivity. For example, there are more expressions in the '有 A 有 B' format than in the '大 A 大 B' format. Further examples of '有 A 有 B' format include: 有高有低 yǒugāo yǒudī 'some high, some low', 有快有慢 yǒukuài yǒumàn 'some fast, some slow', 有新有舊 yǒuxīn yǒujiù 'some new, some old'.

(2) Some four-character expressions have specific meaning which resists analysis and requires memorization. Examples:

❶ 有頭有臉 yǒutóu yǒuliǎn (– of a situation or occasion, describes having been done properly, with dignity, or in a way that brings honor. – of a person, describes one who is respected and may be of status, prestige, or authority.)

❷ 有聲有色 yǒushēng yǒusè (– lit. having sound and color, describes an impressive display, something dazzling.)

(3) Not all units of similar meaning can fit into the '大 A 大 B' pattern. The following examples are not OK: *大平大安 dàpíng dàān, *大跑大跳 dàpǎo dàtiào, *大清大楚 dàqīng dàchǔ, *大快大樂 dàkuài dàlè. In fact, most four-character formats accept only a limited set of units.

(4) In addition to meanings, the most important things to learn about 成語 or 四字格 are their 'functions' in a sentence, i.e., they function as subject, object, modifier, adverbial, complement, commentary, or predicate.

出, chū, (Ptc), Verb Particle, to have emerged

Function

When the verb particle 出 is attached to an action verb, it carries the meaning of something coming into existence or consciousness.

❶ 我不好意思說出的話，他都幫我說了。
Wǒ bùhǎoyìsi shuōchū de huà, tā dōu bāng wǒ shuō le.
The things I was too embarrassed to say, he said for me.

❷ 一樣的衣服，他穿起來，總是能穿出跟別人完全不同的感覺。
Yíyàng de yīfú, tā chuānqǐlái, zǒngshì néng chuānchū gēn biérén wánquán bùtóng de gǎnjué.
When he wears the same garment as someone else, he always exudes a totally different feeling.

❸ 他用有機商店買回來的材料做出又酸又辣的泡菜。
Tā yòng yǒujī shāngdiàn mǎihuílái de cáiliào zuòchū yòu suān yòu là de pàocài.
He made sour and spicy kimchi out of ingredients purchased at an organic shop.

❹ 我寫不出這麼讓人感動的歌。
Wǒ xiěbùchū zhème ràng rén gǎndòng de gē.
I could never write such a powerful song.

❺ 那位教授花了十年的時間，才研究出這種新藥。
Nà wèi jiàoshòu huāle shí nián de shíjiān, cái yánjiūchū zhè zhǒng xīn yào.
That professor spent a decade on research before coming up with this type of new medicine.

Usage

(1) The particle 出 is different from 出 as a verb, which has the following properties.

❶ 出 indicates spatial movement from inside to outside, as V_1 in V_1V_2 (e.g., 出來 'come out', 出去 'go out').

❷ 出 as V_2 in $V_1V_2V_3$ (e.g., 拿出去 náchūqù 'take it out and away', 走出去 zǒuchūqù 'walk out of', 跑出來 pǎochūlái 'run out towards me', 把書拿出房間去 Bǎ shū náchū fángjiān qù 'get the books out of this room'.

(2) 來 is needed in forming $V_1V_2V_3$, when the particle 出 appears with 把 or when the object is moved to the front, e.g., 你應該把心裡的話說出來。Nǐ yīnggāi bǎ xīnlǐ de huà shuōchūlái. Or 心裡的話，你應該說出來。Xīnlǐ de huà, nǐ yīnggāi shuōchūlái. 'You should speak out what's on your mind.' In other situations, 來 is optional, e.g., 他研究了很久，才研究出（來）新的做法。Tā yánjiū le hěn jiǔ, cái yánjiūchū (lái) xīn de zuòfǎ. 'He researched it for a long time before he thought (out) a new way.'

(3) The complememt '出（來）' can also be used in the potential form. E.g.,

A：你想得出辦法嗎？
Nǐ xiǎngdechū bànfǎ ma?
Can you think out a way?

B：我想不出來。
Wǒ xiǎngbùchūlái.
I can't think one out.

(4) Watch out for the differences between the particles 出 and 起. The first refers to the emergence of something out of nowhere, while the second refers to something that used to be known but returns to his consciousness or awareness. Compare the examples below:

❶ 我想了很久才想出一個辦法來。
Wǒ xiǎngle hěn jiǔ cái xiǎngchū yí ge bànfǎ lái.
I thought for a long time before I thought of a way. (出 = from nothing to something, out of thin air)

❷ 他說過一個不錯的辦法，我差一點忘了。幸虧現在想起來了。
Tā shuōguò yí ge bùcuò de bànfǎ, wǒ chàyìdiǎn wàng le. Xìngkuī xiànzài xiǎngqǐlái le.
I almost forgot. He mentioned a good method. Luckily, I thought of it just now. (起 = already in existence, new awareness)

出來, chūlái, as Verb Complement, to figure out

Function

When 出來 serves as a complement to verbs of cognition and senses, it refers to a result of 'being figured out', ending a cognitive processing.

❶ 這張三十年以前的照片，你得看久一點，才能看出來是誰。
Zhè zhāng sānshí nián yǐqián de zhàopiàn, nǐ děi kàn jiǔ yìdiǎn, cái néng kànchūlái shì shéi.
You need to look awhile to figure out who the person in this 30-year-old picture is.

❷ 我聽出來那個人說的是臺灣話。
Wǒ tīngchūlái nà ge rén shuō de shì Táiwān huà.
I was able to tell that that person was speaking Taiwanese.

❸ 這個旅行路線的建議是他想出來的。
Zhè ge lǚxíng lùxiàn de jiànyì shì ta xiǎngchūlái de.
He is the one who came up with this suggested travel itinerary.

Structures

出來 can be used in all the four complement structures, i.e., V 出來, 沒 V 出來, V 得出來, and V 不出來.

❶ 美美喝得出來這杯是烏龍茶。
Měiměi hēdechūlái zhè bēi shì Wūlóng chá.
Mei Mei could tell (by tasting) that this cup is Oolong tea.

❷ 他寫得出來這個中國字。
Tā xiědechūlái zhè ge Zhōngguó zì.
He is able to write this Chinese character.

❸ 我吃不出來那種食物是什麼材料做的。
Wǒ chībùchūlái nà zhǒng shíwù shì shénme cáiliào zuò de.
I could not tell (by eating) what ingredients were used to make that type of food.

❹ 小李看不出來那個人是臺灣人還是韓國人。

Xiǎo Lǐ kànbùchūlái nà ge rén shì Táiwān rén háishì Hánguó rén.

Xiao Li cannot tell (by looking) whether that person is Taiwanese or Korean.

Negation :

❶ 他沒吃出來媽媽在水餃裡放了什麼菜。

Tā méi chīchūlái māma zài shuǐjiǎo lǐ fàngle shénme cài.

He could not tell (by tasting) what vegetable Mom put in the boiled dumpling.

❷ 美美沒喝出來飲料裡有什麼水果。

Měiměi méi hēchūlái yǐnliào lǐ yǒu shénme shuǐguǒ.

Mei Mei could not tell (by tasting) what the fruit was in that drink.

❸ 考試的時候，小明沒想出來那個複雜的漢字怎麼寫。

Kǎoshì de shíhòu, Xiǎomíng méi xiǎngchūlái nà ge fùzá de Hànzì zěnme xiě.

During the test Xiaoming could not recall how to write that difficult Chinese character.

Questions :

❶ 你聽不聽得出來說話的那個人是美國人？

Nǐ tīng bù tīngdechūlái shuōhuà de nà ge rén shì Měiguó rén?

（＝ 你聽得出來聽不出來說話的那個人是美國人？）

(= Nǐ tīngdechūlái tīngbùchūlái shuōhuà de nà ge rén shì Měiguó rén?)

Can you tell (by listening to him) that the person who is speaking is American?

❷ 你看得出來看不出來老師說的那個字？

Nǐ kàndechūlái kànbùchūlái lǎoshī shuō de nà ge zì?

Can you find the character that the teacher talked about?

❸ 我們上個月花了多少生活費，你算出來了沒有？

Wǒmen shàng ge yuè huāle duōshǎo shēnghuófèi, nǐ suànchūlái le méi yǒu?

Have you calculated last month's living costs?

Usage

(1) If the object is short, it can appear between 出 and 來.

❶ 是他想出那個建議來的。

Shì tā xiǎngchū nà ge jiànyì lái de.

It was he who came up with that suggestion.

❷ 你寫不寫得出這個字來？

Nǐ xiě bù xiědechū zhè ge zì lái?

Can you write this character?

(2) Also, when the pattern is used with non-cognitive verbs, 出來 simply refers to the ability of accomplishing something, 'able to', e.g.,

❶ 你們公司是不是有問題？這個月薪水還沒發出來！
Nǐmen gōngsī shìbúshì yǒu wèntí? Zhè ge yuè xīnshuǐ hái méi fāchūlái!
Is something wrong with your company? They haven't issued this month's salaries yet.

❷ 如果你沒說出來，沒有人會知道你幫過他。
Rúguǒ nǐ méi shuōchūlái, méi yǒu rén huì zhīdào nǐ bāngguò tā.
If you had not said so, no one would have known that you helped him.

❸ 小明拍得出來那麼好看的照片，可是我拍不出來。
Xiǎomíng pāidechūlái nàme hǎokàn de zhàopiàn, kěshì wǒ pāibùchūlái.
Xiaoming takes such amazing pictures, but I can't seem to.

除了 A，還 B, (chúle (Prep) A, hái (Adv) B), in addition to

Function

This pattern introduces additional elements to what is specified by the preposition 除了.

❶ 放假的時候，他除了常打籃球，還常踢足球。
Fàngjià de shíhòu, tā chúle cháng dǎ lánqiú, hái cháng tī zúqiú.
On days off, in addition to playing basketball, he also plays soccer often.

❷ 臺灣好吃的小吃，除了牛肉麵，還有小籠包。
Táiwān hǎochī de xiǎochī, chúle niúròu miàn, hái yǒu xiǎolóngbāo.
In addition to beef noodles, steamed dumplings are another tasty Taiwanese delicacy.

❸ 從學校到火車站，除了坐捷運，還可以坐公車。
Cóng xuéxiào dào huǒchē zhàn, chúle zuò jiéyùn, hái kěyǐ zuò gōngchē.
In addition to taking the MRT, you can also take the bus to get from the school to the train station.

Structures

除了 is a special preposition that can take a noun phrase or a verb phrase as its object.

Negation:

❶ 陳小姐除了不喜歡喝茶，她還不喜歡喝咖啡。
Chén xiǎojiě chúle bù xǐhuān hē chá, tā hái bù xǐhuān hē kāfēi.
In addition to not liking tea, Miss Chen does not like drinking coffee, either.

❷ 小明生病了，他除了沒寫作業，還沒準備考試。

Xiǎomíng shēngbìng le, tā chúle méi xiě zuòyè, hái méi zhǔnbèi kǎoshì.

Xiaoming is sick. In addition to not doing the homework, he did not prepare for the exam, either.

❸ 她除了不喜歡太辣的菜，還不喜歡太甜的甜點。

Tā chúle bù xǐhuān tài là de cài, hái bù xǐhuān tài tián de tiándiǎn.

In addition to dishes that are too spicy, she does not like desserts that are too sweet, either.

*Q*uestions :

❶ 你們除了去故宮，還去了哪些地方？

Nǐmen chúle qù Gùgōng, hái qùle nǎxiē dìfāng?

In addition to the Palace Museum, where else did you go?

❷ 我們除了點牛肉麵，還要點臭豆腐嗎？

Wǒmen chúle diǎn niúròu miàn, hái yào diǎn chòudòufǔ ma?

In addition to beef noodles, shall we also order stinky tofu as well?

❸ 除了芒果，他是不是還喜歡吃西瓜？

Chúle mángguǒ, tā shìbúshì hái xǐhuān chī xīguā?

In addition to mangoes, he also likes watermelon, right?

> Usage

In this pattern, the adverb 還, can often be replaced by 也 yě, expressing the same meaning.

❶ 感冒的人除了要吃藥，也要多喝水、多休息。

Gǎnmào de rén chúle yào chī yào, yě yào duō hē shuǐ, duō xiūxí.

In addition to taking medicine, people who are sick should also drink lots of water and rest.

❷ 陳小姐租的房子除了離捷運站很近，離超市也很近。

Chén xiǎojiě zū de fángzi chúle lí jiéyùn zhàn hěn jìn, lí chāoshì yě hěn jìn.

In addition to being close to the MRT station, the apartment Miss Chen rented is also close to the supermarket.

❸ 小明生日，媽媽除了買生日蛋糕，也訂了豬腳麵線。

Xiǎomíng shēngrì, māma chúle mǎi shēngrì dàngāo, yě dìngle zhūjiǎo miànxiàn.

In addition to buying a cake for Xiaoming's birthday, Mom also ordered pork knuckles with extra fine noodles.

Complement of Intensification in Comparison Structures (1)

> Function

Intensifiers can be presented either as a pre-verbal adverbial, or as post-verbal complement. The latter can include 一點 yìdiǎn, 得多 de duō, and 多了 duōle, which occur in high frequency.

❶ 他的房間比我的大一點。
Tā de fángjiān bǐ wǒ de dà yìdiǎn.
His room is just a little bigger than mine.

❷ 捷運站比公車站遠得多。
Jiéyùn zhàn bǐ gōngchē zhàn yuǎn de duō.
The MRT station is much farther away than the bus stop.

❸ 我覺得晚上比早上舒服多了。
Wǒ juéde wǎnshàng bǐ zǎoshàng shūfú duō le.
I think evenings are a lot more comfortable than mornings.

Structures

Questions :

❶ 哥哥是不是比弟弟高一點？
Gēge shìbúshì bǐ dìdi gāo yìdiǎn?
Is the older brother a bit taller than his younger brother?

❷ 房租可以便宜一點嗎？
Fángzū kěyǐ piányí yìdiǎn ma?
Can the rent be a little cheaper?

❸ 春天去旅行是不是比夏天舒服得多？
Chūntiān qù lǚxíng shìbúshì bǐ xiàtiān shūfú de duō?
It is much more enjoyable (lit. comfortable) to travel in the spring than in the summer, isn't it?

❹ 高鐵票比火車票貴多了嗎？
Gāotiě piào bǐ huǒchē piào guì duō le ma?
Are HSR tickets much more expensive than train tickets?

❺ 這家店賣的甜點是不是比別家賣的好吃多了？
Zhè jiā diàn mài de tiándiǎn shìbúshì bǐ bié jiā mài de hǎochī duō le?
This shop's desserts are tastier than at others' shops, aren't they?

Usage

Unless reduplicated, 一點 yìdiǎn does not occur pre-verbally. 多 duō occurs either pre- or post-verbally. 多了 duō le is always a complement.

Complements, 極了 **jíle,** 得不得了 **de bùdéliǎo,** 得很 **de hěn, terribly, extremely** (2)

Function

The intensification of states is usually marked with pre-verbal adverbs, such as 很 or 非常, but in a few instances, intensification is also possible by complements after the state verbs.

❶ 你做的日本菜好吃極了。
Nǐ zuò de Rìběn cài hǎochī jíle.
The Japanese dishes prepared by you are really delicious.

❷ 我沒吃中飯，現在餓極了。
Wǒ méi chī zhōngfàn, xiànzài è jíle.
I didn't have any lunch and I'm starving now.

❸ 張教授婚禮的氣氛熱鬧得不得了。
Zhāng jiàoshòu hūnlǐ de qìfēn rènào de bùdéliǎo.
The atmosphere at Professor Chang's wedding was incredibly lively.

Structures ▶ Intensification by complements comes in two patterns.

(1) Without 得 de: V＋(極了 jíle，多了 duō le，一點 yìdiǎn)

　　❶ 泰國菜比日本菜辣多了。
　　　Tàiguó cài bǐ Rìběn cài là duō le.
　　　Thai food is much more spicy than Japanese food.

　　❷ 大城市有捷運，交通會方便一點。
　　　Dà chéngshì yǒu jiéyùn, jiāotōng huì fāngbiàn yìdiǎn.
　　　With the metro, it's easy to get around in the city.

(2) With 得 de: V＋得＋(多 duō，不得了 bùdéliǎo，很 hěn)

　　❶ 打了太極拳以後，精神好得很。
　　　Dǎle Tàijí quán yǐhòu, jīngshén hǎo de hěn.
　　　Practicing Tai Chi makes me feel a lot more energetic.

　　❷ 房租便宜比光線好重要得多。
　　　Fángzū piányí bǐ guāngxiàn hǎo zhòngyào de duō.
　　　Cheap rent is more important than good lighting.

Questions : Usually only 是不是 quesitons are possible.

❶ 紐約的生活費是不是比這裡高得多？
Niǔyuē de shēnghuófèi shìbúshì bǐ zhèlǐ gāo de duō?
The cost of living in New York is much higher than here, right?

❷ 漢字對你是不是難得不得了？
Hànzì duì nǐ shìbúshì nán de bùdéliǎo?
Chinese characters are terribly difficult for you, right?

❸ 巴黎秋天的天氣是不是舒服得很呢？
Bālí qiūtiān de tiānqì shìbúshì shūfú de hěn ne?
I gather that fall weather in Paris is really nice.

Usage ▶

(1) Both 'Vs＋得很' (in examples ❷ and ❹ below) and '很＋Vs' (in examples ❶ and ❸ below) express intensification. 'Vs＋得很' is more spoken and provides a much stronger emphasis than pre-verbal adverbs. Also, it has been stated previously that when 很 acts as a necessary weak marker in front of state verbs there is no intensificatioin function.

　　❶ 檸檬魚的味道很酸。
　　　Níngméng yú de wèidào hěn suān.
　　　Lemon fish has very sour flavor.

❷ A：檸檬魚的味道酸嗎？

　　Níngméng yú de wèidào suān ma?

　　Is lemon fish sour?

　　B：是啊，檸檬魚的味道酸得很。

　　Shì a, níngméng yú de wèidào suān de hěn.

　　Yes, lemon fish is extremely sour.

❸ 打太極拳很累。

　　Dǎ Tàijí quán hěn lèi.

　　Tai Chi is very tiring.

❹ 我覺得打太極拳很輕鬆，可是他說累得很。

　　Wǒ juéde dǎ Tàijí quán hěn qīngsōng, kěshì tā shuō lèi de hěn.

　　I think Tai Chi is relaxing, but he said it is exhausting.

(2) The intensifiers 極了, 得不得了 and 得很 cannot be used together with 比 bǐ, as in examples ❶ and ❷ below.

❶ *巴黎的建築比高雄的漂亮極了。

　　*Bālí de jiànzhú bǐ Gāoxióng de piàoliang jíle.

　　Parisian architecture is extremely more beautiful than Kaohsiung's.

❷ *大城市的馬路比鄉下的寬得很。

　　*Dà chéngshì de mǎlù bǐ xiāngxià de kuān de hěn.

　　Big city roads are much bigger than rural ones.

❸ 這個小鎮的氣氛比以前熱鬧得多。

　　Zhè ge xiǎo zhèn de qìfēn bǐ yǐqián rènào de duō.

　　This little town is much more exciting than it used to be.

❹ 用提款機提錢比到銀行去便利多了。

　　Yòng tíkuǎnjī tí qián bǐ dào yínháng qù biànlì duō le.

　　Using an ATM to take out money is much easier than going to the bank.

從 A 到 B, (cóng (Prep) A dào (Prep) B), from A to B

Function

This pattern is used to indicate the 'from...to...' spatial or temporal distance between points A and B. A and B can refer to time or place, but never people.

❶ 我從早上十點二十分到下午一點十分有中文課。

　　Wǒ cóng zǎoshàng shídiǎn èrshífēn dào xiàwǔ yìdiǎn shífēn yǒu Zhōngwén kè.

　　I have Chinese class from 10:20am to1:10pm.

❷ 我今天從早上到晚上都有空，歡迎你們來我家。

　　Wǒ jīntiān cóng zǎoshàng dào wǎnshàng dōu yǒu kòng, huānyíng nǐmen lái wǒ jiā.

　　I am free from morning to night today. (You're) welcome to come to my house.

❸ 從我家到那個游泳池有一點遠。
Cóng wǒ jiā dào nà ge yóuyǒngchí yǒu yìdiǎn yuǎn.
From my house to that swimming pool is a little far.

❹ 我從我朋友家到這個地方來。
Wǒ cóng wǒ péngyǒu jiā dào zhè ge dìfāng lái.
I came to this place from my friend's house.

❺ 他從圖書館到那家餐廳去吃飯。
Tā cóng túshūguǎn dào nà jiā cāntīng qù chīfàn.
He went from the library to that restaurant to eat.

Structures

Negation :

❶ 我們的書法課不是從九點到十一點。
Wǒmen de shūfǎ kè búshì cóng jiǔdiǎn dào shíyīdiǎn.
Our calligraphy class is not from 9 to 11.

❷ 陳先生的媽媽昨天不是從早上到晚上都很忙。
Chén xiānshēng de māma zuótiān búshì cóng zǎoshàng dào wǎnshàng dōu hěn máng.
Mr. Chen's mom wasn't busy yesterday from morning to night.

❸ A：我什麼時候可以去你家？
Wǒ shénme shíhòu kěyǐ qù nǐ jiā?
When can I go to your house?

B：我今天從早上到晚上都沒有空。可是明天可以。
Wǒ jīntiān cóng zǎoshàng dào wǎnshàng dōu méi yǒu kòng, kěshì míngtiān kěyǐ.
I don't have time from morning to night today, but tomorrow is OK.

❹ 從這棟大樓到那家 KTV 不遠。
Cóng zhè dòng dàlóu dào nà jiā KTV bù yuǎn.
It is not far from this building to that KTV.

❺ 我不想從學校到那裡去，想從我家去。
Wǒ bù xiǎng cóng xuéxiào dào nàlǐ qù, xiǎng cóng wǒ jiā qù.
I don't want to go there from school. I want to go from my house.

Questions : Three different patterns can be employed in this construction.

❶ 你們老師後天從早上到下午都有空嗎？（嗎）
Nǐmen lǎoshī hòutiān cóng zǎoshàng dào xiàwǔ dōu yǒu kòng ma?
Is your teacher free from morning to afternoon the day after tomorrow?

❷ 請問從圖書館到你們宿舍遠不遠？（A-not-A）
Qǐngwèn cóng túshūguǎn dào nǐmen sùshè yuǎn bù yuǎn?
Excuse me. Is it far from the library to your dorm?

❸ 他們想從宿舍還是圖書館到教室去上課？（A or B）
Tāmen xiǎng cóng sùshè háishì túshūguǎn dào jiàoshì qù shàngkè?
Do they want to go from the dorm or from the library to the classroom for class?

從 A 往 B, (cóng (Prep) A wǎng (Prep) B), go B from A

Function

This pattern expresses directions of movements. 從 marks the beginning point and 往 marks the ending point of the movement.

❶ 你從這裡往前一直走，就到師大了。

Nǐ cóng zhèlǐ wǎng qián yìzhí zǒu, jiù dào Shīdà le.

Walk straight from here and you will arrive at NTNU.

❷ 從這個路口往右轉，你可以到學校宿舍。

Cóng zhè ge lùkǒu wǎng yòu zhuǎn, nǐ kěyǐ dào xuéxiào sùshè.

Turn right at this intersection and you will arrive at the school dorms.

❸ 從學校大門往裡面走十分鐘，可以到語言中心。

Cóng xuéxiào dàmén wǎng lǐmiàn zǒu shí fēnzhōng, kěyǐ dào yǔyán zhōngxīn.

Walk straight in from the school gate for 10 minutes and you will arrive at the language center.

Structures

If the beginning point of the movement is clear from the context, '從…' can often be omitted while '往…' is used alone. E.g.,

A：請問，圖書館怎麼走？

Qǐngwèn, túshūguǎn zěnme zǒu?

Excuse me. How do I get to the library?

B：你往前一直走，就到了。

Nǐ wǎng qián yìzhí zǒu, jiù dào le.

Just walk straight and you'll get there.

*N*egation：

❶ 你不能（從這裡）往前走，前面沒有路了。

Nǐ bù néng (cóng zhèlǐ) wǎng qián zǒu, qiánmiàn méi yǒu lù le.

You can't keep going straight, there's a dead end up ahead.

❷ 你不可以從這個路口往左轉，只可以往右轉。

Nǐ bù kěyǐ cóng zhè ge lùkǒu wǎng zuǒ zhuǎn, zhǐ kěyǐ wǎng yòu zhuǎn.

You can't turn left at this intersection. You can only turn right.

❸ 這公車不是往師大，是往火車站的。

Zhè gōngchē búshì wǎng Shīdà, shì wǎng huǒchē zhàn de.

This bus doesn't go to NTNU, it goes to the train station.

*Q*uestions：

❶ 我是不是從這裡往前面一直騎，就可以到花蓮？

Wǒ shìbúshì cóng zhèlǐ wǎng qiánmiàn yìzhí qí, jiù kěyǐ dào Huālián?

If I keep riding my bike straight ahead, will I end up in Hualien?

❷ 請問從師大，有沒有往故宮博物院的公車？

Qǐngwèn cóng Shīdà, yǒu méi yǒu wǎng Gùgōng Bówùyuàn de gōngchē?

Excuse me, are there any buses that go from NTNU to the Palace Museum?

❸ 請問，我要到銀行去，是從這裡往前一直走嗎？

Qǐngwèn, wǒ yào dào yínháng qù, shì cóng zhèlǐ wǎng qián yìzhí zǒu ma?

Excuse me. I want to go to the bank. Do I keep going straight from here?

從⋯起, (cóng (Prep)...qǐ (Ptc)), starting from...

Function　　This pattern specifies the beginning point of an instance.

❶ 學生總是說從明天起，我要好好地念書，不讓父母失望。

Xuéshēng zǒngshì shuō cóng míngtiān qǐ, wǒ yào hǎohǎo de niànshū, bú ràng fùmǔ shīwàng.

Students always say, 'I'll study hard starting tomorrow. I don't want my parents to be disappointed.'

❷ 那個語言中心規定從今年秋天起，申請獎學金的學生，成績要有85分。

Nà ge yǔyán zhōngxīn guīdìng cóng jīnnián qiūtiān qǐ, shēnqǐng jiǎngxuéjīn de xuéshēng, chéngjī yào yǒu 85 fēn.

The language center has stipulated that starting this fall, students applying for scholarships must have a grade average of at least 85.

❸ 因為放暑假的關係，學校的圖書館從後天起，上午九點才開門。

Yīnwèi fàng shǔjià de guānxi, xuéxiào de túshūguǎn cóng hòutiān qǐ, shàngwǔ jiǔdiǎn cái kāimén.

Due to summer vacation, starting tomorrow, the school library won't open until 9:00 in the morning.

❹ 你弄錯了。百貨公司打折活動是從十月十號起，不是十月一號。

Nǐ nòngcuò le. Bǎihuò gōngsī dǎzhé huódòng shì cóng shíyuè shíhào qǐ, búshì shíyuè yīhào.

You've got it wrong. The department store sales start from October 10th, not from October 1st.

❺ 那個展覽館從下星期一起到下個月三十一號，要舉行電腦展。

Nà ge zhǎnlǎn guǎn cóng xià xīngqíyī qǐ dào xià ge yuè sānshíyīhào, yào jǔxíng diànnǎoz hǎn.

That exhibition hall will be holding a computer exhibition starting next Monday, on until the 31st of next month.

Usage　　從⋯起 is relatively literary and formal. It's more colloquial to say 從⋯開始 cóng...kāishǐ. E.g., 從明天開始，我不再吃炸的東西了。Cóng míngtiān kāishǐ, wǒ bú zài chī zhá de dōngxi le. 'Starting tomorrow, I'm not eating fried foods.'

從來, cónglái, (Adv), 從來＋Negation, never

Function

The pattern 從來＋沒 refers to instances that never took place in the past (in which case, the main verb is followed by the aspect 過). And the pattern 從來不 refers to situations that do not generally happen.

❶ 他雖然是台灣人，可是從來沒吃過道地的台南美食。
Tā suīrán shì Táiwān rén, kěshì cónglái méi chīguò dàodì de Táinán měishí.
Although he's Taiwanese, he has never had authentic Tainan food.

❷ 我從來沒參加過跨年活動。難得今年有機會參加。
Wǒ cónglái méi cānjiāguò kuànián huódòng. Nándé jīnnián yǒu jīhuì cānjiā.
I've never taken part in a New Year's countdown. It's nice that I have the opportunity to go this year.

❸ 小美從來沒逛過24小時營業的書店，所以我今天要帶她去。
Xiǎoměi cónglái méi guàngguò 24 xiǎoshí yíngyè de shūdiàn, suǒyǐ wǒ jīntiān yào dài tā qù.
Xiaomei has never checked out a bookstore that's open 24/7, so I'm going to take her today.

❹ 我從來沒喝過雄黃酒，今天想喝喝看味道怎麼樣。
Wǒ cónglái méi hēguò xiónghuáng jiǔ, jīntiān xiǎng hēhēkàn wèidào zěnmeyàng.
I've never had realgar liquor before. Today, I would like to drink some and see what it tastes like.

❺ 我從來沒在餐廳打過工，不知道在餐廳打工累不累。
Wǒ cónglái méi zài cāntīng dǎguò gōng, bù zhīdào zài cāntīng dǎ gōng lèi bú lèi.
I've never worked in a restaurant. I don't know if it's tiring work.

❻ 妹妹年紀還小，媽媽從來不讓她一個人出門。
Mèimei niánjì hái xiǎo, māma cónglái bú ràng tā yí ge rén chūmén.
My little sister is still too little. Mom never lets her leave the house alone.

❼ 他說在山區騎摩托車不太安全，所以他從來不在山區騎。
Tā shuō zài shānqū qí mótuōchē bútài ānquán, suǒyǐ tā cónglái bú zài shānqū qí.
He says that riding a motorcycle in the mountains isn't all that safe, so he never does like that.

❽ 為了身體健康，他從來不吃炸的東西。
Wèile shēntǐ jiànkāng, tā cónglái bù chī zhá de dōngxi.
For the sake of his health, he never eats fried foods.

Usage

The use of 沒 and 不 in this pattern is summarised in the table below.

	Action Verb	State Verb	Process Verb
從來不	✓	✓	✗
從來沒 (…過)	✓	✗	✓

當…的時候, (dāng...de shíhòu), when, while, at the time of

Function

The preposition 當 refers to the time of an instance, represented by a sentence in this case.

❶ 當機會來的時候，你千萬別錯過。
Dāng jīhuì lái de shíhòu, nǐ qiānwàn bié cuòguò.
When the opportunity comes, you definitely mustn't let it slip away.

❷ 當別人對你説話時，你要仔細聽。
Dāng biérén duì nǐ shuōhuà shí, nǐ yào zǐxì tīng.
When someone is talking to you, you must listen carefully.

❸ 當他知道他得到獎學金時，高興地跳起來。
Dāng tā zhīdào tā dédào jiǎngxuéjīn shí, gāoxìng de tiàoqǐlái.
When he heard that he got the scholarship, he leapt for joy.

❹ 當你欣賞表演時，一定要關手機。
Dāng nǐ xīnshǎng biǎoyǎn shí, yídìng yào guān shǒujī.
When enjoying a performance, be sure to turn off your cell phone.

Usage

當 is often optional in conversations, e.g.,

❶ (當)孩子回家的時候，媽媽已經做了很多好吃的菜。
(Dāng) háizi huíjiā de shíhòu, māma yǐjīng zuòle hěn duō hǎochī de cài.
When the child gets home, his mother has already made many tasty dishes.

❷ (當)我住在香港的時候，認識了很多香港朋友。
(Dāng) wǒ zhùzài Xiānggǎng de shíhòu, rènshìle hěn duō Xiānggǎng péngyǒu.
When I lived in Hong Kong, I made many Hong Kong friends.

❸ (當)她寫功課時，發現了不少問題。
(Dāng) tā xiě gōngkè shí, fāxiànle bù shǎo wèntí.
When doing her homework, she discovered a number of problems.

到, dào, (Prep), Destination Marker (1)

Function

The preposition 到 indicates the destination of a movement.

❶ 他這個週末到臺灣來。
Tā zhè ge zhōumò dào Táiwān lái.
He is coming to Taiwan this weekend.

❷ 老師明天到臺北來。我們要和他一起吃晚飯。

Lǎoshī míngtiān dào Táiběi lái. Wǒmen yào hàn tā yìqǐ chī wǎnfàn.

The teacher is coming to Taipei tomorrow. We are having dinner with him.

❸ 想吃牛肉麵嗎？明天我們可以到那家店去。

Xiǎng chī niúròu miàn ma? Míngtiān wǒmen kěyǐ dào nà jiā diàn qù.

Would you like to have beef noodles? We can go to that shop tomorrow.

❹ 我可以教你中文，明天到我家來吧！

Wǒ kěyǐ jiāo nǐ Zhōngwén, míngtiān dào wǒ jiā lái ba!

I can teach you Chinese. Go ahead and come to my house tomorrow.

Structures

*N*egation : Negation is always done by placing a negator in front of a preposition, not the main verb.

❶ 王先生明天不到臺北來。

Wáng xiānshēng míngtiān bú dào Táiběi lái.

Mr. Wang is not coming to Taipei tomorrow.

❷ 那家的越南菜不好吃。他們不到那家餐廳去。

Nà jiā de Yuènán cài bù hǎochī. Tāmen bú dào nà jiā cāntīng qù.

That shop's Vietnamese food doesn't taste good. They don't go to that restaurant.

❸ 他晚上去看電影，不到我家來，你呢？

Tā wǎnshàng qù kàn diànyǐng, bú dào wǒ jiā lái, nǐ ne?

He is going to go to a movie tonight and will not be coming to my house. How about you?

*Q*uestions : 到 can be used to form A-not-A questions, as in the case of a certain number of Preps, e.g., 在 zài, 替 tì, 給 gěi, 跟 gēn.

❶ 你妹妹到不到臺灣來？

Nǐ mèimei dào bú dào Táiwān lái?

Is your younger sister coming to Taiwan?

❷ 他們到不到我家來？

Tāmen dào bú dào wǒ jiā lái?

Are they coming to my house?

❸ 你明天到不到學校來？

Nǐ míngtiān dào bú dào xuéxiào lái?

Are you coming to school tomorrow?

Usage

到 can also be a main verb in a sentence, similar to 來 lái 'come' or 去 qù 'go'. In Taiwan, 到 is mostly used as a verb, e.g.,

❶ 這麼多家餐廳，我們要到哪一家？

Zhème duō jiā cāntīng, wǒmen yào dào nǎ yì jiā?

There are so many restaurants. Which one should we go?

❷ 他們明天晚上要到王老師家。你想去嗎？

Tāmen míngtiān wǎnshàng yào dào Wáng lǎoshī jiā. Nǐ xiǎng qù ma?

They are going to teacher Wang's house tomorrow evening. Would you like to go?

❸ 歡迎你到我家。

Huānyíng nǐ dào wǒ jiā.

Welcome to my home.

到, dào, (Prep), Destination Marker for Movement Verbs (2)

Function The preposition 到 marks a destination, following a movement. As a result of the action performed, an item has been moved to a location marked by 到.

❶ 他在踢足球，踢著踢著就踢到學校外面了。

Tā zài tī zúqiú, tīzhe tīzhe jiù tī dào xuéxiào wàimiàn le.

He was playing soccer and ended up kicking the soccer ball outside the school grounds.

❷ 他上星期從台北騎機車騎到花蓮。

Tā shàng xīngqí cóng Táiběi qí jīchē qí dào Huālián.

Last week he rode his scooter from Taipei to Hualien.

❸ 這個蛋糕，我打算拿到學校請同學吃。

Zhè ge dàngāo, wǒ dǎsuàn ná dào xuéxiào qǐng tóngxué chī.

I plan to take this cake to the school to share it with my classmates.

Structures

Negation : The entire preposition phrase (PP) follows the main movement verb, which can be negated.

❶ 我在師大下車，沒搭到臺北火車站。

Wǒ zài Shīdà xiàchē, méi dā dào Táiběi huǒchē zhàn.

I got off the bus at NTNU. I did not ride as far as the Taipei Station.

❷ 張老師跟他太太決定不搬到西班牙了。

Zhāng lǎoshī gēn tā tàitai juédìng bù bān dào Xībānyá le.

Teacher Zhang and his wife decided against moving to Spain.

❸ 我太累了，沒走到故宮，就回家了。

Wǒ tài lèi le, méi zǒu dào Gùgōng, jiù huíjiā le.

I was too tired. I went home before I got to the Palace Museum.

Questions :

❶ 我的書，妳明天會拿到學校給我嗎？

Wǒ de shū, nǐ míngtiān huì ná dào xuéxiào gěi wǒ ma?

Will you give me my book back at school tomorrow?

❷ 那個電腦，你送到他家去了沒有？

Nà ge diànnǎo, nǐ sòng dào tā jiā qù le méi yǒu?

Did you take that computer to his home?

❸ 本子和筆，你是不是都放到背包裡了？

Běnzi hàn bǐ, nǐ shìbúshì dōu fàng dào bēibāo lǐ le?

Did you put the notebooks and pens into the backpack?

Usage

(1) Another PP, '從＋noun', can be added before the verb to indicate the starting point.

❶ 他從家裡走到學校，需要三十分鐘的時間。

Tā cóng jiā lǐ zǒu dào xuéxiào, xūyào sānshí fēnzhōng de shíjiān.

It takes 30 minutes for him to walk from his home to the school.

❷ 放假的時候，我從台北開車開到台南，真的太累了。

Fàngjià de shíhòu, wǒ cóng Táiběi kāi chē kāi dào Táinán, zhēn de tài lèi le.

During the holidays, I drove from Taipei to Tainan. It was really tiring.

(2) The '到 PP' can be placed either before or after the verb, with distinct meanings. Compare the following examples.

❶ 他到火車站搭高鐵。

Tā dào huǒchē zhàn dā gāotiě.

He went to the train station to take the high speed train.

❷ 他搭巴士搭到火車站附近。

Tā dā bāshì dā dào huǒchē zhàn fùjìn.

He took the bus to somewhere near the train station.

(3) Either 來 lái or 去 qù can be added after the location. 來 indicates a movement towards the speaker, whereas 去 indicates a movement away from the speaker.

❶ 球踢到公園裡去了。還好沒踢到人。

Qiú tī dào gōngyuán lǐ qù le. Háihǎo méi tī dào rén.

The ball was kicked (from here) into the park over there. Good thing it didn't hit anyone.

❷ 球踢到公園裡來了。

Qiú tī dào gōngyuán lǐ lái le.

The ball was kicked here into the park (from there).

到, dào, (Prep), Post-verbal Preposition, up to, till (3)

Function

When a verb is followed by the preposition 到, 到 marks the spatial or temporal end point, the terminal point.

❶ 中國人過年要一直過到一月十五號。
Zhōngguó rén guònián yào yìzhí guò dào yīyuè shíwǔhào.
The Chinese celebrate the Lunar New Year all the way to the 15th of the first lunar month.

❷ 我們吃年夜飯，吃到晚上快十二點。
Wǒmen chī niányèfàn, chī dào wǎnshàng kuài shí'èrdiǎn.
We eat New Year's Eve dinner until almost midnight.

❸ 這學期的課上到下星期五。
Zhè xuéqí de kè shàng dào xià xīngqíwǔ.
Classes for this semester will be held until next Friday.

❹ 他們想走到火車站。
Tāmen xiǎng zǒu dào huǒchē zhàn.
They want to walk to the train station.

❺ 他們爬到屋頂上。
Tāmen pá dào wūdǐng shàng.
They climbed to the roof.

Structures

*N*egation :

❶ 老師今天上課，沒上到五點就下課了。
Lǎoshī jīntiān shàngkè, méi shàng dào wǔdiǎn jiù xiàkè le.
Our teacher ended the class before 5 p.m. today.

❷ 小張沒做到月底，就決定不上班了。
Xiǎo Zhāng méi zuò dào yuèdǐ, jiù juédìng bú shàngbān le.
Xiao Zhang decided to quit his job without finishing out the month.

❸ 那家店的水果還沒賣到中午，就已經賣光了。
Nà jiā diàn de shuǐguǒ hái méi mài dào zhōngwǔ, jiù yǐjīng màiguāng le.
It wasn't even evening and the fruit in that store were already sold out.

*Q*uestions :

❶ 星期六你都睡到幾點才起床？
Xīngqíliù nǐ dōu shuì dào jǐ diǎn cái qǐchuáng?
What time do you sleep until on Saturdays? (i.e., What time do you finally get up at on Saturdays?)

❷ 這本書是不是可以借到下個月五號？
Zhè běn shū shìbúshì kěyǐ jiè dào xià ge yuè wǔhào?
This book can be checked out until the 5th of next month, right?

❸ 作業，你昨天寫到什麼時候才寫完？
Zuòyè, nǐ zuótiān xiě dào shénme shíhòu cái xiěwán?
Until what time did you work on your homework yesterday?

Usage　A 從cóng phrase can be added to this pattern to indicate the originating point.

❶ 中國人過年，要從除夕過到一月十五。
Zhōngguó rén guònián, yào cóng chúxì guò dào yīyuè shíwǔ.
Chinese people celebrate the lunar new year from New Year's Eve to the 15th of the first month of the lunar year.

❷ 他們包水餃，從下午包到晚上才包完。
Tāmen bāo shuǐjiǎo, cóng xiàwǔ bāo dào wǎnshàng cái bāowán.
They wrapped the dumplings starting from afternoon and did not finish until evening.

到, dào, (Ptc), as Verb Complement, to be successful in... (4)

Function

When the particle 到 serves as a verb complement, it has the meaning 'to be successful' in an action.

❶ 在台灣很容易買到外國東西。
Zài Táiwān hěn róngyì mǎidào wàiguó dōngxi.
In Taiwan, it is easy to buy foreign goods.

❷ 我找了很久，才找到了我的手機。
Wǒ zhǎole hěn jiǔ, cái zhǎodào le wǒ de shǒujī.
I looked for a long time before I found my cell phone.

❸ 我們答應老師以後要天天來上課，我們得做到。
Wǒmen dāyìng lǎoshī yǐhòu yào tiāntiān lái shàngkè, wǒmen děi zuòdào.
We promised the teacher that in the future we'll come to class every day, so we have to make good on that.

Structures

Negation:

The pattern V＋到 can only be negated by 沒.

❶ 他沒想到搬家麻煩極了。
Tā méi xiǎngdào bānjiā máfán jíle.
He did not expect moving to be such a big hassle.

❷ 今年我在台灣過生日，所以沒吃到媽媽做的蛋糕。
Jīnnián wǒ zài Táiwān guò shēngrì, suǒyǐ méi chīdào māma zuò de dàngāo.
This year, I had my birthday in Taiwan, so I didn't get to eat a cake made by my mom.

❸ 我在百貨公司看了半天，可是我沒找到我要的。
Wǒ zài bǎihuò gōngsī kànle bàn tiān, kěshì wǒ méi zhǎodào wǒ yào de.
I looked around the department store for a long time, but I didn't find what I wanted.

Questions:

❶ 十樓聽得到聽不到汽車的聲音？
Shí lóu tīngdedào tīngbúdào qìchē de shēngyīn?
Can you hear cars from the 10th floor?

❷ 你喜歡的水果，在台灣是不是買得到？
Nǐ xǐhuān de shuǐguǒ, zài Táiwān shìbúshì mǎidedào?
Can you buy the fruit you like in Taiwan?

❸ 小美的電話你找到了沒有？
Xiǎoměi de diànhuà nǐ zhǎodào le méi yǒu?
Did you find Xiaomei's phone number?

Usage

(1) Perception verbs like 看 kàn 'to see' and 聽 tīng 'to hear' can combine with either 到 dào or 見 jiàn with the same meaning. 到 is more common in Taiwan, whereas 見 is commoner on the mainland.

❶ 我看見他在打太極拳。
Wǒ kànjiàn tā zài dǎ Tàijí quán.
I saw him practicing Tai Chi.

❷ 我看到他在打太極拳。
Wǒ kàndào tā zài dǎ Tàijí quán.
I saw him practicing Tai Chi.

(2) The complement 到 can be used in all the complement structures, i.e., 看到 kàndào, 沒看到 méi kàndào, 看得到 kàndedào, 看不到 kànbúdào.

(3) 沒想到 méi xiǎngdào has become idiomatic. It often occurs at the beginning of a sentence to express the speaker's surprise. 想不到 xiǎngbúdào means and behaves the same as 沒想到.

❶ 沒想到你爸爸這麼會做菜。
Méi xiǎngdào nǐ bàba zhème huì zuò cài.
I had no idea your dad could cook so well.

❷ 想不到你爸爸這麼會做菜。
Xiǎngbúdào nǐ bàba zhème huì zuò cài.
I had no idea your father could cook so well.

到底, dàodǐ, (Adv), after all? how on earth...?

Function The adverb 到底 is used when the speaker is perplexed about something and is anxious to find out about the truth. The sentence carries a strong tone of inquisitiveness and impatience.

❶ 小陳幾天以前說想去麵包店當學徒，今天說想去鄉下種水果，他到底想做什麼？
Xiǎo Chén jǐ tiān yǐqián shuō xiǎng qù miànbāo diàn dāng xuétú, jīntiān shuō xiǎng qù xiāngxià zhòng shuǐguǒ, tā dàodǐ xiǎng zuò shénme?
The other day, Xiao Chen said he wanted to apprentice at a bakery. Today, he said he wants to go to the countryside and grow fruit. What does he really want to do?

❷ 你不要看到新型的電子產品就買，「貨比三家不吃虧」這句話的意思，你到底懂不懂？

Nǐ bú yào kàndào xīnxíng de diànzǐ chǎnpǐn jiù mǎi, 'huò bǐ sān jiā bù chīkuī' zhè jù huà de yìsi, nǐ dàodǐ dǒng bù dǒng?

Stop buying the latest electronic product whenever you see one. You understand the saying 'shop around and you won't get ripped off', don't you?

❸ 那家商店賣的鳳梨酥特別受歡迎，他們到底用的是什麼行銷方式？

Nà jiā shāngdiàn mài de fènglísū tèbié shòu huānyíng, tāmen dàodǐ yòng de shì shénme xíngxiāo fāngshì?

The pineapple cakes sold at that store are especially popular. What is their marketing scheme?

❹ 我昨天介紹給你的那位先生，到底你對他的印象怎麼樣？

Wǒ zuótiān jièshào gěi nǐ de nà wèi xiānshēng, dàodǐ nǐ duì tā de yìnxiàng zěnmeyàng?

What is your impression of the gentleman I introduced to you yesterday?

❺ 看到你有這麼多好朋友，真羨慕你。你到底是怎麼跟別人建立關係的？

Kàndào nǐ yǒu zhème duō hǎo péngyǒu, zhēn xiànmù nǐ. Nǐ dàodǐ shì zěnme gēn biérén jiànlì guānxi de?

You have so many friends. I really envy you. How in the world do you make friends like that?

Usage

到底 is a member of a sub-group of adverbs that can move to the sentence-initial position. It is only used in non-嗎ma questions. It can appear either before or after the subject, but when the subject is a question-word, 到底 can only occur sentence-initially.

❶ a. 你到底去不去？
   Nǐ dàodǐ qù bú qù?

b. 到底你去不去？
   Dàodǐ nǐ qù bú qù?
   Are you or are you not going?

❷ a. 他到底哪裡不舒服？
   Tā dàodǐ nǎlǐ bù shūfú?

b. 到底他哪裡不舒服？
   Dàodǐ tā nǎlǐ bù shūfú?
   Where, exactly, is he feeling pain?

❸ a. 你到底買菜了沒有？
   Nǐ dàodǐ mǎi cài le méi yǒu?

b. 到底你買菜了沒有？
   Dàodǐ nǐ mǎi cài le méi yǒu?
   Did you buy vegetables after all?

But you cannot say:

❶ *誰到底要去？

*Shéi dàodǐ yào qù?

Who on earth wants to go?

❷ *哪裡到底好玩？

*Nǎlǐ dàodǐ hǎowán?

Where after all fun place?

❸ *什麼人到底才能參加？

*Shénme rén dàodǐ cái néng cānjiā?

Who on earth can join?

Prior to saying a 到底 question like 臭豆腐到底臭不臭？Chòudòufǔ dàodǐ chòu bú chòu? 'Is stinky toufu really smelly?', one of the statements below must be true.

(1) Some say it is, while others say it is not.

(2) Someone keeps saying it is or it is not.

In the following situations, it cannot be used.

(1) Nobody is talking about 臭豆腐 chòudòufǔ 'stinky tofu'.

(2) Someone says it is or it is not, only once.

倒是, dàoshì, (Adv), on the other hand

Function ▶ 倒是 is an S_2 adverb, which presents a view that differs from, and contrary to, one previously stated.

❶ 不少人認為目前經濟不樂觀。我倒是覺得並沒那麼嚴重。

Bù shǎo rén rènwéi mùqián jīngjì bú lèguān. Wǒ dàoshì juéde bìng méi nàme yánzhòng.

Many people think that the economy is at a low point, but I happen to think it's not that bad.

❷ 我覺得連鎖咖啡店的咖啡不錯。我朋友倒是覺得小咖啡館的比較好喝。

Wǒ juéde liánsuǒ kāfēi diàn de kāfēi búcuò. Wǒ péngyǒu dàoshì juéde xiǎo kāfēi guǎn de bǐjiào hǎohē.

I think that the coffee in chain store cafes isn't that bad, but my friend prefers the coffee in independent shops.

❸ 你常說遠距教學不是個好方法。那些學生倒是覺得很不錯。

Nǐ cháng shuō yuǎnjù jiāoxué bú shì ge hǎo fāngfǎ. Nàxiē xuéshēng dàoshì juéde hěn búcuò.

You often say that distance learning isn't a good method of teaching, but those students seem to think it's great.

❹ 美國人認為減稅對經濟發展有幫助。對這件事北歐人倒是有不同的看法。

Měiguó rén rènwéi jiǎnshuì duì jīngjì fāzhǎn yǒu bāngzhù. Duì zhè jiàn shì Běi'ōu rén dàoshì yǒu bùtóng de kànfǎ.

Americans think that tax cuts help stimulate economic development, but Scandinavians hold a different viewpoint.

❺ 現代年輕人雖然不太迷信，但倒是相信風水。

Xiàndài niánqīng rén suīrán bútài míxìn, dàn dàoshì xiāngxìn fēngshuǐ.

The young generation is not really superstitious, but they do believe in Feng Shui.

Usage

(1) The '是' in 倒是 is often optional, e.g.,

有的家長認為念書時不要打工，免得影響成績。我倒認為打工有助於學習。

Yǒu de jiāzhǎng rènwéi niànshū shí bú yào dǎgōng, miǎnde yǐngxiǎng chéngjī. Wǒ dào rènwéi dǎgōng yǒu zhù yú xuéxí.

Some parents believe that you shouldn't work when you are a student, lest it affects your grades. I, on the other hand, think that having a part-time job facilitates learning.

(2) 倒是 often combines with conjuctions like 但是 or 不過, e.g.,

這學期我打工，每天忙得不得了，不過倒是交到了不少好朋友。

Zhè xuéqí wǒ dǎgōng, měi tiān máng de bùdéliǎo, búguò dàoshì jiāodàole bù shǎo hǎo péngyǒu.

I'm working part-time this semester, so I'm really busy every day. That said, I've actually made lots of good friends.

得, de, (Ptc), Complement Marker (1)

Function The complement marker 得 comes in between the verb and the complement, which describes the result or state of the action represented by the verb. In Chinese, results always come after actions.

❶ 他學中文學得不錯。

Tā xué Zhōngwén xué de búcuò.

He has learned Chinese quite well.

❷ 王伯母做越南菜做得很好吃。

Wáng bómǔ zuò Yuènán cài zuò de hěn hǎochī.

Auntie Wang cooks Vietnamese food very well.

❸ 這件事，你做得很好。

Zhè jiàn shì, nǐ zuò de hěn hǎo.

You did a great job, this time.

❹ 這種手機最近賣得很好。
Zhè zhǒng shǒujī zuìjìn mài de hěn hǎo.
This type of cell phone sells well recently.

Structures

When a complement is added to a transitive verb, several structural consequences follow.

(1) When its object directly follows the verb, the verb is repeated before 得 and the complement.

❶ 你做飯做得真好吃。
Nǐ zuòfàn zuò de zhēn hǎochī.
You cook really well.

❷ 我的老師教中文教得很好。
Wǒ de lǎoshī jiāo Zhōngwén jiāo de hěn hǎo.
My teacher teaches Chinese well.

❸ 他們吃晚飯吃得很早。
Tāmen chī wǎnfàn chī de hěn zǎo.
They eat dinner early.

(2) When the object is moved to the front of the sentence, the verb is not repeated.

❶ 飯，他做得真好吃。
Fàn, tā zuò de zhēn hǎochī.
He cooks really well.

❷ 中文，你說得很好。
Zhōngwén, nǐ shuō de hěn hǎo.
You speak Chinese well.

❸ 這種甜點，他做得很好吃。
Zhè zhǒng tiándiǎn, tā zuò de hěn hǎochī.
He makes this kind of dessert very tasty.

❹ 這支手機賣得很便宜。
Zhè zhī shǒujī mài de hěn piányí.
This cell phone is sold cheaply.

Negation : Negation occurs only within the complement.

❶ 他做甜點做得不好。
Tā zuò tiándiǎn zuò de bù hǎo.
He does not make desserts well.

❷ 王先生打網球打得不好。
Wáng xiānshēng dǎ wǎngqiú dǎ de bù hǎo.
Mr. Wang does not play the tennis well.

❸ 他的咖啡賣得不好。
Tā de kāfēi mài de bù hǎo.
His coffee does not sell well.

❹ 越南菜，這家店做得不好吃。
Yuènán cài, zhè jiā diàn zuò de bù hǎochī.
This shop does not cook Vietnamese food well.

Questions :

❶ 他做飯做得怎麼樣？
Tā zuòfàn zuò de zěnmeyàng?
How (well) does he cook?

❷ 他打籃球打得好嗎？
Tā dǎ lánqiú dǎ de hǎo ma?
Does he play basketball well?

❸ 中文，他說得好不好？
Zhōngwén, tā shuō de hǎo bù hǎo?
Does he speak Chinese well?

得, de, (Ptc), Complement Marker, used in comparing the results of actions (2)

Function

In this pattern, the complement marker 得 connects to a comparison of the results of actions.

❶ 哥哥吃牛肉麵吃得比弟弟多。
Gēge chī niúròu miàn chī de bǐ dìdi duō.
The older brother eats more beef noodles than the younger brother.

❷ 這種手機賣得比那種好。
Zhè zhǒng shǒujī mài de bǐ nà zhǒng hǎo.
This type of cell phone sells better than that type.

❸ 今年的雨下得比去年多。
Jīnnián de yǔ xià de bǐ qùnián duō.
It rains more this year than last year.

Structures

The pattern is called 'comparative adverbial'. The pattern comes in a variety of sub-patterns as illustrated below.

(1) Comparative＋Action＋得＋State

❶ 他比我做得快。
Tā bǐ wǒ zuò de kuài.
He does it faster than I do.

❷ 我比他走得快。
Wǒ bǐ tā zǒu de kuài.
I walk faster than he does.

❸ 弟弟比哥哥念得好。
Dìdi bǐ gēge niàn de hǎo.
The younger brother studies better than (is a better student than) his older brother.

(2) Action＋得＋Comparative＋State

❶ 他做飯做得比我快。
Tā zuòfàn zuò de bǐ wǒ kuài.
He cooks faster than I do.

❷ 我走路走得比他快。
Wǒ zǒulù zǒu de bǐ tā kuài.
I walk faster than he does.

❸ 弟弟念書念得比哥哥好。
Dìdi niànshū niàn de bǐ gēge hǎo.
The younger brother studies better than his older brother.

Negation :　The negation marker 不 precedes 比bǐ.

❶ 他做飯不比我做得快。
Tā zuòfàn bù bǐ wǒ zuò de kuài.
He doesn't cook faster than I do.

❷ 走路，我不比他走得快。
Zǒulù, wǒ bù bǐ tā zǒu de kuài.
I don't walk faster than he does.

❸ 弟弟念書念得不比哥哥好。
Dìdi niànshū niàn de bù bǐ gēge hǎo.
The younger brother doesn't study better than his older brother.

Questions :

❶ 你做飯做得比媽媽好嗎？
Nǐ zuòfàn zuò de bǐ māma hǎo ma?
Do you cook better than Mom?

❷ 他是不是走路走得比你快？
Tā shìbúshì zǒulù zǒu de bǐ nǐ kuài?
Does he walk faster than you do?

❸ 弟弟打網球打得比哥哥好嗎？
Dìdi dǎ wǎngqiú dǎ de bǐ gēge hǎo ma?
Does the younger brother play tennis better than the older brother?

得, de, (Ptc), Complement Marker, so...that... (3)

Function ▶　This pattern introduces an extent resulting from a state of affairs, 'so...that...', in which 'that' corresponds to 得, which brings in a complement.

❶ 我常常累得起不來，腿也痛得走不了路。
Wǒ chángcháng lèi de qǐbùlái, tuǐ yě tòng de zǒubùliǎo lù.
I am often so tired that I cannot get up and my legs are hurt so much that I cannot walk.

❷ 天氣冷得很多人不想去上班。
Tiānqì lěng de hěn duō rén bù xiǎng qù shàngbān.
The weather was so cold that many people did not want to go to work.

❸ 夜市裡到處都是人，熱鬧得像過年。
Yèshì lǐ dàochù dōu shì rén, rènào de xiàng guònián.
The night market is full of people. It is as bustling as Lunar New Year.

Structures

Negation :

❶ 林教授的演講，複雜得我聽不懂。
Lín jiàoshòu de yǎnjiǎng, fùzá de wǒ tīngbùdǒng.
Porfessor Lin's speech was so complicated that I was not able to understand.

❷ 他去夜市買了很多東西，多得拿不了。
Tā qù yèshì mǎile hěn duō dōngxi, duō de nábùliǎo.
He bought a lot of stuff at the night market, so much that he could not carry it all.

❸ 他腿痛得跑不完一百公尺。
Tā tuǐ tòng de pǎobùwán yìbǎi gōngchǐ.
His leg hurt so badly that he couldn't finish runnıng 100 meters.

Questions :

❶ 你是不是累得走不了了？
Nǐ shìbúshì lèi de zǒubùliǎo le?
Are you too tired to walk? (or Are you so tired that you can't walk?)

❷ 這個房子是不是小得住不了五個人？
Zhè ge fángzi shìbúshì xiǎo de zhùbùliǎo wǔ ge rén?
Is this house too small for five people to live in?

❸ 那家麵包店賣的蛋糕是不是甜得你吃不下？
Nà jiā miànbāo diàn mài de dàngāo shìbúshì tián de nǐ chībúxià?
The cakes from that bakery are so sweet that you can't even eat them?

Usage

This pattern is quite compatible with hyperbole or exaggerations, e.g.,

❶ 她精神差得好像三天沒睡覺。
Tā jīngshén chà de hǎoxiàng sān tiān méi shuìjiào.
She has so little energy that she looks as though she hasn't slept for three days.

❷ 我餓得吃得了一百個小籠包。
Wǒ è de chīdeliǎo yìbǎi ge xiǎolóngbāo.
I am so hungry that I could eat 100 steamed dumplings.

❸ 這個地方好玩得我不想離開。
Zhè ge dìfāng hǎowán de wǒ bù xiǎng líkāi.
This place is so much fun that I don't want to leave.

得, de, (Ptc), Positive Potential Complement Marker (4) (See 不(2))

的, de, (Ptc), Possessive Marker (1)

Function ▸ 的 is used to show possession and is placed between the possessor and the object possessed.

❶ 我的書
wǒ de shū
my book

❷ 你們的照片
nǐmen de zhàopiàn
your photo

❸ 李老師的姐姐
Lǐ lǎoshī de jiějie
teacher Li's sister

❹ 哥哥的老師
gēge de lǎoshī
brother's teacher

❺ 我媽媽
wǒ māma
my mom

❻ 我們老師
wǒmen lǎoshī
our teacher

Structures ▸ Notice that 的 is sometimes omitted, e.g., ❺ and ❻ above.

(1) If the relationship between the possessor and the possessed is close, 的 can be omitted, e.g., 我爸爸wǒ bàba 'my dad', 我哥哥wǒ gēge 'my brother', 我家wǒ jiā 'my home'. Furthermore, the possessor has to be a pronoun when 的 is omitted. So, one can say 李先生的爸爸Lǐ xiānshēng de bàba 'Mr. Li's dad', but not *李先生爸爸 *Lǐ xiānshēng bàba (omitting 的de).

(2) If the two nouns in a possessive relationship refer to an individual and his/her affiliated group, the noun referring to the individual usually appears in the plural rather than the singular form. For example, for 'his home', it is 他們家tāmen jiā (their home), 我們日本wǒmen Rìběn (our Japan).

的, de, (Ptc), Modifier Marker (2)

Function ▸ 的 is used between the modifier and the primary noun.

❶ 漂亮的小姐
piàoliàng de xiǎojiě
pretty young lady

❷ 好喝的咖啡
hǎohē de kāfēi
tasty coffee

❸ 很好看的房子
hěn hǎokàn de fángzi
beautiful house

Usage　　Notice that 的 can be omitted when the modifier and the head noun are used together frequently. For example, when talking about nationality, one says 哪國人 nǎ guó rén 'person from which country', rather than *哪國的人 *nǎ guó de rén. One says 臺灣人 Táiwān rén 'Taiwanese people' rather than *臺灣的人 *Táiwān de rén.

的, de, (Ptc), with the Head Noun Omitted　(3)

Function　　Nouns are always modified using this structure: modifier 的 ＋ head noun. When the head noun is clear from the context, it is usually omitted.

❶ A：你要買新手機還是舊手機？
Nǐ yào mǎi xīn shǒujī háishì jiù shǒujī?
Do you want to buy a new cell phone or an old one?

B：我要新的，不要舊的。
Wǒ yào xīn de, bú yào jiù de.
I want a new one. I don't want an old one.

❷ A：新手機貴不貴？
Xīn shǒujī guì bú guì?
Are new cell phones expensive?

B：新的比較貴。
Xīn de bǐjiào guì.
New ones cost more.

Structures

Negation：

❶ 你的手機不是新的。
Nǐ de shǒujī bú shì xīn de.
Your cell phone is not new.

❷ 咖啡，我不要熱的。
Kāfēi, wǒ bú yào rè de.
Coffee, I don't want a hot one.

❸ 房子貴，我不買大的。
Fángzi guì, wǒ bù mǎi dà de.
Houses are expensive. I won't buy a large one.

Questions：

❶ 房子，你喜歡新的嗎？
Fángzi, nǐ xǐhuān xīn de ma?
House, do you like a new one?

❷ 手機，他買不買舊的？
Shǒujī, tā mǎi bù mǎi jiù de?
Cell phone, will he buy an old one?

❸ 咖啡，你要熱的嗎？
Kāfēi, nǐ yào rè de ma?
Coffee, do you want a cup of hot one?

的, de, (Ptc), to Mark Assurance, co-occurring often with 會 huì (Vaux) (4)

Function

When 的 is used at the end of a sentence, it indicates the speaker's assurance about something to take place in the future. 會 co-occurs and expresses the likelihood of an action or a state.

❶ 你說話的聲音太大，會讓人討厭的。
Nǐ shuōhuà de shēngyīn tài dà, huì ràng rén tǎoyàn de.
You speak very loud; other people might find it annoying.

❷ 大家不常見面，關係會越來越遠的。
Dàjiā bù cháng jiànmiàn, guānxi huì yuèláiyuè yuǎn de.
(If) we don't see one another often, our relationships will become more and more distant.

❸ 你放心，我會把手機帶著的。
Nǐ fàngxīn, wǒ huì bǎ shǒujī dàizhe de.
Don't worry, I will take my phone with me.

Structures

Negation : Only 不 negation is used in this pattern. 沒 is not allowed.

❶ 你放心，你被老闆罵的事，我不會告訴別人的。
Nǐ fàngxīn, nǐ bèi lǎobǎn mà de shì, wǒ bú huì gàosù biérén de.
Don't worry. I won't tell anybody about what the boss laced into you for.

❷ 我的功課沒那麼好，老師不會讓我參加交換學生的計畫的。
Wǒ de gōngkè méi nàme hǎo, lǎoshī bú huì ràng wǒ cānjiā jiāohuàn xuéshēng de jìhuà de.
My grades are not that strong, the teacher won't allow me to take part in the exchange student program.

❸ 要是沒有教書的經驗，語言中心不會選你的。
Yàoshi méi yǒu jiāoshū de jīngyàn, yǔyán zhōngxīn bú huì xuǎn nǐ de.
If you don't have any teaching experience, the language center will not select you.

Usage

的 in this pattern indicates the speaker's assurance of the instance. Without a final 的, then the sentence is only a factual statement without personal commitment. Compare the following examples.

❶ 她會來參加我們的婚禮的。(I assure you...)
Tā huì lái cānjiā wǒmen de hūnlǐ de.
She will surely come attend our wedding.

② 她會來參加我們的婚禮。 (plain statement)
Tā huì lái cānjiā wǒmen de hūnlǐ.
She will come attend our wedding.

的話, de huà, if, supposing

Function

The pattern …的話, appears at the very end of the 'if' part, while the 'consequence' part appears in the second clause.

① 酸辣湯太辣的話，你就別喝了。
Suānlàtāng tài là de huà, nǐ jiù bié hē le.
If the hot and sour soup is too spicy, don't drink it.

② 你想轉系的話，最好先跟父母討論。
Nǐ xiǎng zhuǎnxì de huà, zuìhǎo xiān gēn fùmǔ tǎolùn.
If you want to change majors, it would be best if you discuss it with your parents first.

③ 學生要參加社團的話，得先上網填申請表。
Xuéshēng yào cānjiā shètuán de huà, děi xiān shàngwǎng tián shēnqǐng biǎo.
If students want to take part in school clubs, they have to first go online and fill out a form.

④ 我覺得外語能力不錯的話，念國際關係系比較適合。
Wǒ juéde wàiyǔ nénglì búcuò de huà, niàn guójì guānxi xì bǐjiào shìhé.
I believe that if one's foreign language skills are pretty good, it would be more suitable to study international relations.

⑤ 美美說拿到獎學金的話，就請我們看電影。
Měiměi shuō nádào jiǎngxuéjīn de huà, jiù qǐng wǒmen kàn diànyǐng.
Meimei said that if she gets a scholarhip, she will treat us to a movie.

Usage

Conjunctions 如果rúguǒ or 要是yàoshì can be used together with the pattern above. In such cases, 的話 can be omitted. 的話 is more colloquial, while 如果/要是rúguǒ/yàoshì…（的話）is more formal.

① 如果你覺得這裡太吵的話，我們可以換一個地方繼續聊。
Rúguǒ nǐ juéde zhèlǐ tài chǎo de huà, wǒmen kěyǐ huàn yí ge dìfāng jìxù liáo.
If you think it's too noisy here, we can continue our conversation somewhere else.

② 要是爸爸給我的生活費不夠的話，我就得去打工。
Yàoshì bàba gěi wǒ de shēnghuófèi búgòu de huà, wǒ jiù děi qù dǎ gōng.
If Dad doesn't give me enough allowance money I'll have to go work part time.

的時候, de shíhòu, when, at the time of

Function The 的時候 pattern indicates the time an instance takes, took, or will take place.

❶ 在山上看風景的時候，我覺得很舒服。
Zài shān shàng kàn fēngjǐng de shíhòu, wǒ juéde hěn shūfú.
I felt great when I was on the mountain looking at the scenery.

❷ 放假的時候，我喜歡去逛夜市。
Fàngjià de shíhòu, wǒ xǐhuān qù guàng yèshì.
I like visiting night markets on days off.

❸ 你有空的時候，請到我家來玩。
Nǐ yǒu kòng de shíhòu, qǐng dào wǒ jiā lái wán.
When you have time, please come to my place.

等, děng, (Ptc), enumeration particle, etc...

Function Used in enumeration, 等 may refer to a closed listing or an open-ended listing, depending on the contexts.

❶ 我去過美國、法國等兩個國家。(closed)
Wǒ qùguò Měiguó, Fǎguó děng liǎng ge guójiā.
I have been to the US and the France. (only two)

❷ 我和男朋友的興趣很不一樣，他對文學、繪畫、舞蹈等都沒有興趣。(open)
Wǒ hàn nánpéngyǒu de xìngqù hěn bù yíyàng, tā duì wénxué, huìhuà, wǔdào děng dōu méi yǒu xìngqù.
My boyfriend and I have dissimilar interests. He's not into things like literature, painting, and dance. ('Things like' implies that further examples could be given.)

❸ 我問過很多人，他們吃素大部分是因為宗教，也有不少是為了健康等原因。(open)
Wǒ wènguò hěn duō rén, tāmen chīsù dà bùfèn shì yīnwèi zōngjiào, yě yǒu bù shǎo shì wèile jiànkāng děng yuányīn.
I have asked many people why they are vegetarians, and for most it is because of religion. Others say they just want to eat healthier.

❹ 我們家要修理的地方很多，像客廳的窗戶、洗手間的門等。(open)
Wǒmen jiā yào xiūlǐ de dìfāng hěn duō, xiàng kètīng de chuānghù, xǐshǒujiān de mén děng.
There's a lot that needs fixing our house, the living room window and bathroom door, just to name two.

Usage

(1) The total number of listed items can be reiterated following the enumeration particle, e.g.,

這個大學熱門的科系有國際關係系、會計系、中文系、英文系等四個科系。

Zhè ge dàxué rèmén de kēxì yǒu guójì guānxi xì, kuàiji xì, Zhōngwén xì, Yīngwén xì děng sì ge kēxì.

There are four popular programs in this university, international relations, accounting, Chinese and English. (closed listing, only four)

(2) The enumeration particle may be reduplicated, e.g.,

生活中有很多事都離不開電腦，比方説：買東西、查資料等等。

Shēnghuó zhōng yǒu hěn duō shì dōu líbùkāi diànnǎo, bǐfāng shuō: mǎi dōngxi, chá zīliào děngděng.

There are many areas in life in which we cannot do without computers, such as on-line shopping and looking up information.

等 A 就 B, (děng A jiù B), when A comes, then B

Function

This pattern indicates that when A is done, B follows in sequence.

❶ 等客人都回去了，喜宴就結束了。
Děng kèrén dōu huíqù le, xǐyàn jiù jiéshù le.
When all the guests go home, the wedding reception is over.

❷ 等夏天到了，去海邊的人就多了。
Děng xiàtiān dào le, qù hǎibiān de rén jiù duō le.
When summer arrives, many people will go to the seaside.

❸ 等你準備找工作的時候，我就會給你一些建議。
Děng nǐ zhǔnbèi zhǎo gōngzuò de shíhòu, wǒ jiù huì gěi nǐ yìxiē jiànyì.
Once you are ready to look for a job I will give you some suggestions.

Structures

Negation :

Basically, this pattern connects two instances. In conjunction, either sentence can be in the negative. However, there's a special negative form of 不等 bù děng 'without waiting for', e.g.,

❶ 不等足球比賽結束，加油的學生就走了。
Bù děng zúqiú bǐsài jiéshù, jiāyóu de xuéshēng jiù zǒu le.
The students rooting for the team left without waiting for the soccer match to finish.

❷ 看到桌上有吃有喝的。不等爸爸回來，大家就先吃了。
Kàndào zhuō shàng yǒu chī yǒu hē de. Bù děng bàba huílái, dàjiā jiù xiān chī le.
Everyone started eating without waiting for Dad, since food and drinks were already on the table.

❸ 他常常練習沒學過的字,所以不等老師教他,他就都會了。

Tā chángcháng liànxí méi xuéguò de zì, suǒyǐ bù děng lǎoshī jiāo tā, tā jiù dōu huì le.

He often learns characters they've not studied so he knows them before his teacher teaches them in class.

Questions :

❶ 是不是等我結婚的時候,你就會來參加我的婚禮?

Shìbúshì děng wǒ jiéhūn de shíhòu, nǐ jiù huì lái cānjiā wǒ de hūnlǐ?

Will you come to my wedding ceremony when I get married?

❷ 等到了週末,交通是不是就會比較好?

Děng dàole zhōumò, jiāotōng shìbúshì jiù huì bǐjiào hǎo?

Will the traffic improve over the weekend?

❸ 是不是等美美從東部旅行回來,我們就請她介紹介紹那裡的風景?

Shìbúshì děng Měiměi cóng dōngbù lǚxíng huílái, wǒmen jiù qǐng tā jièshào jièshào nàlǐ de fēngjǐng?

When Meimei returns from the east coast (i.e., eastern Taiwan), shall we have her tell us all about the scenery there?

Usage

In the second clause expressing instance 2, there is often an adverb, either 再 zài, or 才 cái, or 就 jiù. The choice of the adverb depends on the context and meaning intended. Examples follow.

❶ 等他來了,我再離開。（再: next in sequence）

Děng tā lái le, wǒ zài líkāi.

Wait until he gets here, then I'll leave.

❷ 等他來了,我才離開。（才: condition）

Děng tā lái le, wǒ cái líkāi.

I won't leave until he gets here.

❸ 等他來了,我就離開。（就: immediately following）

Děng tā lái le, wǒ jiù líkāi.

I'll leave once he gets here.

的確, díquè, (Adv), indeed

Function

The adverb 的確 re-affirms a view previously presented.

❶ A：我聽說現在有不少大學生想延後畢業的時間,是真的嗎?

Wǒ tīngshuō xiànzài yǒu bù shǎo dàxuéshēng xiǎng yánhòu bìyè de shíjiān, shì zhēn de ma?

I've heard that a lot of college students are putting off graduation. Is that true?

B：現在的確有不少學生,因為要逃避就業而延後畢業的時間。

Xiànzài díquè yǒu bù shǎo xuéshēng, yīnwèi yào táobì jiùyè ér yánhòu bìyè de shíjiān.

Indeed, many students postpone graduation to avoid having to get a job.

❷ A：我覺得上網交友好容易喔！

　　　Wǒ juéde shàngwǎng jiāoyǒu hǎo róngyì o!

　　　Making friends online is real easy!

　　B：上網交友的確容易，不過要小心喔！

　　　Shàngwǎng jiāoyǒu díquè róngyì, búguò yào xiǎoxīn o!

　　　It is indeed, but be discerning!

❸ A：上次你說你以後要自己創業，為什麼呢？

　　　Shàng cì nǐ shuō nǐ yǐhòu yào zìjǐ chuàngyè, wèishénme ne?

　　　I remember you talked about starting your own business. Why is that?

　　B：我畢業以後，的確想自己創業，因為不想看別人的臉色。

　　　Wǒ bìyè yǐhòu, díquè xiǎng zìjǐ chuàngyè, yīnwéi bù xiǎng kàn biérén de liǎnsè.

　　　Indeed, I want to start my own business after graduation because I don't want to have to deal with bosses.

❹ A：現在的房價高漲，大多數人都買不起房子吧？

　　　Xiànzài de fángjià gāozhǎng, dà duōshù rén dōu mǎibùqǐ fángzi ba?

　　　Housing prices have risen sharply. Most people can't afford to buy, right?

　　B：的確，我跟很多人一樣買不起房子。我們都是「無殼蝸牛」。

　　　Díquè, wǒ gēn hěn duō rén yíyàng mǎibùqǐ fángzi. Wǒmen dōu shì 'wúké guāniú'.

　　　You're absolutely right. Like a lot of other people I too can't afford a house. We're all like a snail without a shell.

❺ A：最近我的眼睛非常疲倦，可能是因為工作時一直盯著螢幕看吧！

　　　Zuìjìn wǒ de yǎnjīng fēicháng píjuàn, kěnéng shì yīnwèi gōngzuò shí yìzhí dīngzhe yíngmù kàn ba!

　　　My eyes have been extremely sore lately, I think it's because I have to stare at a screen all day for work.

　　B：長時間一直盯著螢幕看，眼睛的確會很疲倦。

　　　Cháng shíjiān yìzhí dīngzhe yíngmù kàn, yǎnjīng díquè huì hěn píjuàn.

　　　Looking at a screen for extended periods of time will certainly do that to you.

Usage

(1) 的確 can be used at the beginning of a sentence, meaning 'I agree with you', e.g.,

的確，現在即使有碩士學位的人找工作也不容易。

Díquè, xiànzài jíshǐ yǒu shuòshì xuéwèi de rén zhǎo gōngzuò yě bù róngyì.

Indeed, even people with master's degrees are having a difficult time finding work.

(2) 的確 can be reduplicated: 的的確確, e.g.,

他的的確確是昨天才知道的。

Tā dídí quèquè shì zuótiān cái zhīdào de.

He really didn't know until yesterday.

(3) The reduplicated form of 的確 is quite colloquial and puts added stress on whatever follows it, making the tone stronger. It is worth noting that only very few disyllabic adverbs can be reduplicated, as below.

完全wánquán—完完全全 'completely'

幾乎jīhū—幾幾乎乎 'almost all'

隨便suíbiàn—隨隨便便 'casually, flippantly, in an offhand manner'

確實quèshí—確確實實 'actually, really'

掉, diào, (Ptc), Verb Particle, separated from

Function

The verb particle 掉 expresses the meaning that a noun is disposed of, separated from where it was before. Its precise meaning is determined by the main verb of the sentence.

❶ 廚房裡的垃圾，我拿出去丟掉了。(away and gone)

Chúfáng lǐ de lèsè, wǒ ná chūqù diūdiào le.

I removed the garbage from the kitchen.

❷ 誰把我的咖啡喝掉了？(up and gone)

Shéi bǎ wǒ de kāfēi hēdiào le?

Who drank my coffee?

❸ 他每次一走進房間就把鞋子踢掉。(off)

Tā měi cì yì zǒujìn fángjiān jiù bǎ xiézi tīdiào.

Every time, as soon as he walks into a room, he kicks off his shoes.

❹ 桌子上的茶，我還沒喝呢，他怎麼拿去倒掉了？(out and away)

Zhuōzi shàng de chá, wǒ hái méi hē ne, tā zěnme náqù dàodiào le?

The tea on the table, I hadn't drunk it yet. Why did he take it and pour it out?

❺ 他上個月把舊車賣掉，買了新車。(off)

Tā shàng ge yuè bǎ jiù chē màidiào, mǎile xīn chē.

Last month, he sold his old car and bought a new one.

Usage

(1) V＋掉 can also be used in the potential patterns, i.e., V＋得＋掉; V ＋不＋掉. For example, 衣服上的咖啡洗得掉嗎？Yīfú shàng de kāfēi xǐdediào ma? 'Can the coffee on the clothes be washed out?'

(2) Because 掉 indicates 'separation from', only action verbs that can cause something to 'be removed' in some way can be used with 掉. These verbs have an 'outward' (away from the subject) direction, e.g., 丟diū 'to throw', 脫tuō 'to take off, remove, undress', 忘wàng 'to forget', 賣mài 'to sell', etc. Most verbs that indicate the obtaining of something i.e., 'inward', cannot be used. For example, *他把車買掉 (*Tā bǎ chē mǎidiào 'He bought his car.') isn't grammatical.

(3) If the verb used in this pattern is an outward transitive action verb, like 喝hē 'to drink', 吃chī 'to eat', 忘wàng 'to forget', 賣mài 'to sell', 脫tuō 'to take off, remove, undress', 倒dào 'to pour, discard' (see 把bǎ entries), 掉 is often omitted. E.g., both 他上個月把機車賣掉了 (Tā shàng ge yuè bǎ jīchē màidiào le. 'He sold his car last month.') and 他上個月把機車賣了 (Tā shàng gè yuè bǎ jīchē mài le. 'He sold his car last month.') are equally good sentences.

(4) The semantic meaning of the verb particles 掉diào 'away, off' and 走zǒu 'away, off' overlaps a bit. Both suggest that an 'object' is removed in some way from the 'main body'. When using 掉, the agent does not accompany the object when it leaves the main body. Use of 走, on the other hand, indicates that the agent goes away with the object. E.g., 他離開的時候，不小心把我的悠遊卡帶走了。Tā líkāi de shíhòu, bù xiǎoxīn bǎ wǒ de Yōuyóu kǎ dàizǒu le. 'When he left, he inadvertently took my EasyCard with him.'

Directional Constructions V_1V_2 and $V_1V_2V_3$

Function

When a movement is referred to in Chinese, it is necessary to further indicate a direction towards or away from the speaker, the reference point, indicated by V_2 or V_3. All V_1, V_2 or V_3 are basically verbs themselves. They function differently in combinations.

Structures

There are two major directional constructions, V_1V_2 and $V_1V_2V_3$.

(1) Direction + Reference (V_1V_2)

Direction		Reference	
上 shàng	'up'	來 lái	'towards me'
下 xià	'down'	去 qù	'away from me'
進 jìn	'into'		
出 chū	'out of'		
回 huí	'back to'		
過 guò	'over'		

❶ 爸爸出去了。
Bàba chūqù le.
Dad went out.

❷ 他從火車站東邊的門進去。

Tā cóng huǒchē zhàn dōngbiān de mén jìnqù.

He went in through the entrance on the east side of train station.

❸ 我的房東還沒回來。

Wǒ de fángdōng hái méi huílái.

My landlord has not returned yet.

(2) Movement＋Direction＋Reference (V$_1$V$_2$ V$_3$)

Verb		Direction		Reference
走 zǒu	'walk'	上 shàng	'up'	來 lái 'to, toward the speaker'
跑 pǎo	'run'	下 xià	'down'	去 qù 'to, away from the speaker'
站 zhàn	'stand'	進 jìn	'into'	
坐 zuò	'sit'	出 chū	'out off'	
拿 ná	'take'	回 huí	'back'	
追 zhuī	'chase'	過 guò	'over, past'	
帶 dài	'carry, bring'	起 qǐ	'upward'	
開 kāi	'open, turn on'	etc.		
etc.				

❶ 弟弟從樓下跑上來。

Dìdi cóng lóuxià pǎo shànglái.

The younger brother ran up from downstairs.

❷ 我剛看見房東走出去，不知道他要去哪裡。

Wǒ gāng kànjiàn fángdōng zǒu chūqù, bù zhīdào tā yào qù nǎlǐ.

I just saw the landlord walk out. I don't know where he was going.

❸ 這麼多東西，我怎麼帶回去呢？

Zhème duō dōngxi, wǒ zěnme dài huíqù ne?

So many things! How am I going to bring them all back?

❹ 這個學校，公車可以開進去。

Zhè ge xuéxiào, gōngchē kěyǐ kāi jìnqù.

Buses can drive into this school.

(3) Placement of a Destination: The destination of a movement is inserted before the reference, i.e., V$_1$＋V$_2$＋destination＋V$_3$.

❶ 這些書，請你幫我拿上樓去。

Zhèxiē shū, qǐng nǐ bāng wǒ náshàng lóu qù.

Please take these books upstairs for me.

❷ 在展覽館拿的資料都得帶回美國去。

Zài zhǎnlǎn guǎn ná de zīliào dōu děi dàihuí Měiguó qù.

All the information collected at the exhibition needs to be taken back to America.

❸ 垃圾呢？拿回家去了嗎？

Lèsè ne? Náhuí jiā qù le ma?

And the garbage? Did you take it home?

④ 這個椅子要搬下樓去嗎？
Zhè ge yǐzi yào bānxià lóu qù ma?
Does this chair need to be moved downstairs?

⑤ 媽媽告訴他錢要記得放進皮包裡去。
Māma gàosù tā qián yào jìde fàngjìn píbāo lǐ qù.
Mom told him to remember to put his money into his wallet.

Negation :

V₁ can be negated by either 不/別 bù/bié or 沒 méi. 沒 refers to past, occurred, instances.

① 他訂的手機還沒拿回來。
Tā dìng de shǒujī hái méi ná huílái.
He hasn't gone to get the cell phone he ordered.

② 我太累了，不走上去了。
Wǒ tài lèi le, bù zǒu shàngqù le.
I'm too tired and am not going to walk all the way up there.

③ 要考試了，你別跑出去了！
Yào kǎoshì le, nǐ bié pǎo chūqù le!
You have a test coming up. Don't you go out!

Questions :

① 垃圾車就在前面，你為什麼不追過去？
Lèsè chē jiù zài qiánmiàn, nǐ wèishénme bù zhuī guòqù?
The garbage truck is right in front of us. Why don't you run over to it?

② 我不喜歡臭豆腐，請你拿出去，好嗎？
Wǒ bù xǐhuān chòudòufǔ, qǐng nǐ ná chūqù, hǎo ma?
I don't like stinky tofu. Please take it out of here, OK?

③ 你沒看見公車開過來嗎？
Nǐ méi kànjiàn gōngchē kāi guòlái ma?
Didn't you see the bus heading this way?

Usage

When the aspect 了 is used, it is placed after V₁, the primary movement verb.

① 他從家裡走了出來。
Tā cóng jiālǐ zǒule chūlái.
He walked out of his house.

② 公車開了過去。
Gōngchē kāile guòqù.
The bus drove by.

③ 小明在夜市看見小美，就趕快追了過去。
Xiǎomíng zài yèshì kànjiàn Xiǎoměi, jiù gǎnkuài zhuīle guòqù.
Xiaoming caught up to Xiaomei when he saw her at the night market.

Disposal Construction　(See 把 bǎ, 1-7)

懂, dǒng, (Vs, Vp), Complement Indicating Cognitive Ability as a Result

Function

When a verb is followed by 懂 as a result complement, the combination indicates that 'understanding' has taken place, i.e., 'understood' through listening (聽懂 tīngdǒng) or through reading (看懂 kàndǒng).

❶ 老師説的，我都聽懂了。

Lǎoshī shuō de, wǒ dū tīngdǒng le.

I understood everything that the teacher said.

❷ 老師給的功課我只聽了一次，就聽懂了。

Lǎoshī gěi de gōngkè wǒ zhǐ tīngle yí cì, jiù tīngdǒng le.

I understood the homework assigned by our teacher after listening to it only once.

❸ 老師寫的那些字，學生都看懂了。

Lǎoshī xiě de nàxiē zì, xuéshēng dōu kàndǒng le.

The students could make out all the characters written by the teacher.

Structures

Negation :

Negation is always 沒.

❶ 他説什麼？我沒聽懂。

Tā shuō shénme? Wǒ méi tīngdǒng.

What did he say? I didn't understand him.

❷ 那個電影我第一次沒看懂，第二次看懂了。

Nà ge diànyǐng wǒ dìyī cì méi kàndǒng, dìèr cì kàndǒng le.

I didn't understand that movie the first time I saw it, but I did after the second time.

❸ 老師説明了半天，我沒聽懂。

Lǎoshī shuōmíngle bàn tiān, wǒ méi tīngdǒng.

The teacher explained for a whole while, but I still didn't understand.

Questions :

❶ 他剛説的，你是不是聽懂了？

Tā gāng shuō de, nǐ shìbúshì tīngdǒng le?

Did you understand what he just said?

❷ 這些資料你都看懂了沒有？

Zhèxiē zīliào nǐ dōu kàndǒng le méi yǒu?

Did you understand all this information?

❸ 老師教的，你聽懂沒聽懂？

Lǎoshī jiāo de, nǐ tīngdǒng méi tīngdǒng?

Did you understand what the teacher was teaching us?

Usage

(1) 'Complement' is a cover term in Chinese grammar for a variety of functions.

(2) 懂 below is a process verb and can be used alone as a main verb. It often serves as a complement to such verbs as 看 and 聽 to express the result of 'understood'. Compare the following sentences. Comprehension is the same, but the process of it is different.

❶ 老師教的，你懂了嗎？
Lǎoshī jiāo de, nǐ dǒng le ma?
Do you now/did you understand what the teacher taught?

❷ 老師教的，你聽懂了嗎？
Lǎoshī jiāo de, nǐ tīngdǒng le ma?
Did you understand (in terms of listening) what the teacher taught?

❸ 老師教的，你看懂了嗎？
Lǎoshī jiāo de, nǐ kàndǒng le ma?
Did you understand (in terms of reading) what the teacher taught?

動, dòng, (Vp), used as a verb complement, capable of causing movement

Function　When the verb 動 'to move' is used as a verb complement, the construction refers to the (in)ability of moving something.

❶ 這個小冰箱，妳一個人搬得動嗎？
Zhè ge xiǎo bīngxiāng, nǐ yí ge rén bāndedòng ma?
Are you able to move this small fridge by yourself?

❷ 我們應該趁年輕的時候常去旅行。等老了就玩不動了。
Wǒmen yīnggāi chèn niánqīng de shíhòu cháng qù lǚxíng. Děng lǎole jiù wánbúdòng le.
We really should go traveling abroad while we are young, because we won't be capable once we're too old.

❸ 那輛汽車壞了，開不動了。
Nà liàng qìchē huài le, kāibúdòng le.
That car broke down and is not drivable.

❹ 王小姐只是小感冒，明天的現代舞蹈表演她還跳得動吧！
Wáng xiǎojiě zhǐshì xiǎo gǎnmào, míngtiān de xiàndài wǔdào biǎoyǎn tā hái tiàodedòng ba!
Ms. Wang only has a slight cold. I guess she will still be able to perform in the modern dance show tomorrow!

❺ 爸爸要帶小妹妹去參觀寺廟。我想路那麼遠，小妹妹恐怕會走不動。
Bàba yào dài xiǎo mèimei qù cānguān sìmiào. Wǒ xiǎng lù nàme yuǎn, xiǎo mèimei kǒngpà huì zǒubúdòng.
Dad wants to take sister to see a temple but I don't think she'll be able to walk that far down the road.

Usage

(1) 動 is used as a complement to verbs of movements.

(2) 動 complement can only be used in potential, not actual, forms, e.g.

❶ 我拿得動這些書。
Wǒ nádedòng zhèxiē shū.
I can pick up these books.

小孩拿不動那些東西。
Xiǎohái nábúdòng nàxiē dōngxi.
A child can not pick up those (heavy) things.

❷ *我拿動這些書。
*Wǒ nádòng zhèxiē shū.
*I take move those books.

*小孩沒拿動那些東西。
*Xiǎohái méi nádòng nàxiē dōngxi.
The child didn't move those things.

(3) 動 complement vs. 了 complement
There is semantic overlap between the two, both denoting the capability of achieving an action, and are thus often interchangeable, e.g.,

這個小冰箱，妳一個人搬得動嗎？(Are you strong enough to lift it?)
Zhè ge xiǎo bīngxiāng, nǐ yí ge rén bāndedòng ma?

這個小冰箱，妳一個人搬得了嗎？(Can you lift it?)
Zhè ge xiǎo bīngxiāng, nǐ yí ge rén bāndeliǎo ma?

(a) For actions that are not movement specific, only V得/了 can be used.

❶ 這些飲料，我喝不了了。
Zhèxiē yǐnliào, wǒ hēbùliǎo le.
I can't finish these beverages.

*這些飲料，我喝不動了。
*Zhèxiē yǐnliào, wǒ hēbúdòng le.
I can't finish these beverages.

❷ 這麼多書，你讀得了嗎？
Zhème duō shū, nǐ dúdeliǎo ma?
This is a lot of books. Can you read them all?

這麼多書，你讀得動嗎？
Zhème duō shū, nǐ dúdedòng ma?
Can you read this many books?

(b) When emphasizing capability over specific movement, only V得/不了 can be used.

❶ 他中午吃太飽了，現在已經吃不了了。（*吃不動
*chībúdòng）
Tā zhōngwǔ chī tài bǎo le, xiànzài yǐjīng chībùliǎo le.
He ate too much at lunch. He can't eat any more.

❷ 爺爺年紀大了，已經吃不動肉了。（*吃不了
*chībùliǎo）
（refering to chewing）
Yéye niánjì dà le, yǐjīng chībúdòng ròu le.
Grandpa is old. He can no longer eat meat. (i.e., can't sink his teeth into the meat)

(4) 走不動 'unable to make oneself move' vs. 走不了 (liǎo) 'unable to depart'

❶ 他已經走路走了一天了，現在他走不動了。(can't walk any more, too tired)
Tā yǐjīng zǒulù zǒule yì tiān le, xiànzài tā zǒubúdòng le.
He has been walking all day. He can't take another step.

❷ 大颱風來了，我看，你今天走不了了。(can't leave, strong winds)
Dà táifēng lái le, wǒ kàn, nǐ jīntiān zǒubùliǎo le.
The huge typhoon is here. I don't think you can leave today.

動不動就, dòngbúdòng jiù, whenever one pleases to do something impetuously

Function

The idiom 動不動 refers to doing something or getting into some state quite often and without good reason, ever so often. This pattern is used as a criticism.

❶ 現在年輕人動不動就換工作，怎麼能成功？
Xiànzài niánqīng rén dòngbúdòng jiù huàn gōngzuò, zěnme néng chénggōng?
Young people today change jobs at the drop of a hat. How are they going to succeed?

❷ 這是你自己的問題，不要動不動就怪別人。
Zhè shì nǐ zìjǐ de wèntí, bú yào dòngbúdòng jiù guài biérén.
This is your problem. Don't go blaming others at the drop of a hat.

❸ 你別動不動就打擾別人工作，等他們有空的時候再去請教他們。
Nǐ bié dòngbúdòng jiù dǎrǎo biérén gōngzuò, děng tāmen yǒu kòng de shíhòu zài qù qǐngjiào tāmen.
Don't interrupt others when they're working whenever you feel like it. Wait until they have time, and then ask them your questions.

❹ 你很健康，不要動不動就去醫院檢查身體。
Nǐ hěn jiànkāng, bú yào dòngbúdòng jiù qù yīyuàn jiǎnchá shēntǐ.
You're healthy, don't go to the hospital for checkups at the drop of a hat.

❺ 最近高鐵動不動就出問題，讓搭高鐵的人很不放心。

Zuìjìn gāotiě dòngbúdòng jiù chū wèntí, ràng dā gāotiě de rén hěn bú fàngxīn.

The HSR has been having all kinds of problems lately, causing anxiety among people who take it.

都, dōu, (Adv), totality, all (1)

Function　　都 is used to indicate that all items referred to by the subject or object noun have something in common.

❶ 我們都姓陳。

Wǒmen dōu xìng Chén.

We are all surnamed Chen.

❷ 他的兄弟姐妹都很好看。

Tā de xiōngdì jiěmèi dōu hěn hǎokàn.

His siblings are all good-looking.

❸ 這兩個房子都是他的。

Zhè liǎng ge fángzi dōu shì tā de.

Both of these two houses are his.

Structures　　都 is an adverb, which is placed after the noun it relates to and before the main verb phrase, i.e., in Noun＋都＋VP, the noun can be a subject or an object. When the noun is an object, it must be moved to the front of the sentence, see ❸.

❶ 我們都是美國人。

Wǒmen dōu shì Měiguó rén.

We are all American.

❷ 你爸爸、媽媽都要喝咖啡。

Nǐ bàba, māma dōu yào hē kāfēi.

Both your dad and mom want to drink coffee.

❸ 茶、咖啡，我都喜歡喝。

Chá, kāfēi, wǒ dōu xǐhuan hē.

I like to drink both tea and coffee.

Negation :　　The adverb 都 is negated by 不.

❶ 我們不都是美國人。

Wǒmen bù dōu shì Měiguó rén.

Not all of us are American.

❷ 我哥哥、我姐姐不都喜歡照相。

Wǒ gēge, wǒ jiějie bù dōu xǐhuan zhàoxiàng.

Not both of my brother and my sister like taking pictures.

The sequence 不都 is the same as 不是都.

Questions :

❶ 你們都是美國人嗎？
　 Nǐmen dōu shì Měiguó rén ma?
　 Are you all American?

❷ 你的家人是不是都要喝咖啡？
　 Nǐ de jiārén shìbúshì dōu yào hē kāfēi?
　 Do all the people in your family want to drink coffee?

Usage

(1) 都 is an adverb and appears before the verb and after the subject. It is not correct to say *都我們是臺灣人。*Dōu wǒmen shì Táiwān rén. '*All we are Taiwanese'.

(2) Members of a group indicated by 都 all have to appear before 都. For example, to say 'I like both teachers Li and Wang', one says 李老師、王老師，我都喜歡。Lǐ Lǎoshī, Wáng Lǎoshī, wǒ dōu xǐhuān. 'I like both Teacher Li and Teacher Wang.' It is incorrect to say *我都喜歡李老師、王老師。*Wǒ dōu xǐhuān Lǐ Lǎoshī, Wáng Lǎoshī. '*I both like Teacher Li and Teacher Wang.'

(3) In interrogatives, 都 works with the 嗎 ma question form but not with A-not-A question forms. For example, to say 'Are you all surnamed Wang?', one can say 你們都姓王嗎？Nǐmen dōu xìng Wáng ma? 'Are you all surnamed Wang?' but not *你們都姓不姓王？*Nǐmen dōu xìng bú xìng Wáng? '*Are you all surnamed or not surnamed Wang?'

(4) When 都 is modified by 不bù, the sentence means 'not all…', e.g., 他們不都是臺灣人。Tāmen bù dōu shì Táiwān rén. 'Not all of them are Taiwanese'.

都, dōu, (Adv), expressing displeasure, annoyance or surprise (2)

Function

The adverb 都 qualifies an unexpected or unusual state of affairs. With it, the speaker expresses displeasure, annoyance or surprise.

❶ 都幾點了？你還不起床！
　 Dōu jǐ diǎn le? Nǐ hái bù qǐchuáng!
　 Do you know what time it is now? Get out of bed!

❷ 我都等了你兩個鐘頭了，你還沒到。我要走了！
　 Wǒ dōu děngle nǐ liǎng ge zhōngtóu le, nǐ hái méi dào. Wǒ yào zǒu le!
　 I've been waiting for two hours already, and you're not here yet. I'm leaving!

❸ 我都給你五千塊錢了！還不夠嗎？
　 Wǒ dōu gěi nǐ wǔqiān kuài qián le, hái bú gòu ma?
　 I've given you 5,000 dollars, that's not enough!?

④ 風水學都用了一千多年了。應該有值得相信的部分吧？

Fēngshuǐ xué dōu yòngle yìqiān duō nián le. Yīnggāi yǒu zhíde xiāngxìn de bùfèn ba?

Feng Shui has been practiced for over 1,000 years. It must have at least some credibility, right?

⑤ 你都病得快起不來了。還想去上班！

Nǐ dōu bìng de kuài qǐbùlái le. Hái xiǎng qù shàngbān!

You're so sick you can barely get up. Forget going to work!

對, duì, (Prep), towards

Function

The preposition 對 means 'to, towards', introducing the target of the verb. It can combine with either action or state verbs.

(1) With action verbs.

❶ 陳主任對小明說明了辦公室的工作環境。

Chén zhǔrèn duì Xiǎomíng shuōmíngle bàngōngshì de gōngzuò huánjìng.

Director Chen explained the office environment here to Xiaoming.

❷ 李小姐對他說：「對不起，我不知道你是美國人。」

Lǐ xiǎojiě duì tā shuō: 'Duìbùqǐ, wǒ bù zhīdào nǐ shì Měiguó rén.'

Miss Li said to him, 'Sorry, I didn't know you were an American.'

❸ 他一看見我，就對我笑。

Tā yí kànjiàn wǒ, jiù duì wǒ xiào.

He always smiles at me whenever he sees me.

(2) With state verbs.

❶ 他對台北的交通情形很了解。

Tā duì Táiběi de jiāotōng qíngxíng hěn liǎojiě.

He understands the traffic situation (i.e., what the traffic is like) in Taipei well.

❷ 王主任對老師很客氣。

Wáng zhǔrèn duì lǎoshī hěn kèqì.

Director Wang is courteous to teachers.

❸ 張先生對這個事很關心。

Zhāng xiānshēng duì zhè ge shì hěn guānxīn.

Mr. Zhang is concerned about this matter.

Structures

Negation:

The negation appears before 對, a preposition.

❶ 你別對他說我找工作的事。

Nǐ bié duì tā shuō wǒ zhǎo gōngzuò de shì.

Don't say anything to him about my job search.

❷ 小明沒對他說「對不起」。

Xiǎomíng méi duì tā shuō 'duìbùqǐ'.

Xiaoming did not say 'sorry' to him.

❸ 黃主任沒對我說明鐘點費的事。

Huáng zhǔrèn méi duì wǒ shuōmíng zhōngdiǎnfèi de shì.

Director Huang didn't explain (give any details about) the hourly pay.

Questions :

❶ 醫生對你說了什麼？

Yīshēng duì nǐ shuōle shénme?

What did the doctor say to you?

❷ 你是不是對小明說了你要去看電腦展？

Nǐ shìbúshì duì Xiǎomíng shuōle nǐ yào qù kàn diànnǎo zhǎn?

Did you tell Xiaoming that you were going to the computer exhibition?

❸ 你的房東對你好不好？

Nǐ de fángdōng duì nǐ hǎo bù hǎo?

Does your landlord treat you well? (i.e., Is he nice to you?)

Usage

The prepositions 對 duì, 跟 gēn and 給 gěi all refer to the target of verbs, greatly overlapping in meanings. It is important to remember which verbs go with which prepositions.

	說 shuō 'speak'	說明 shuōmíng 'explain'	介紹 jièshào 'introduce'	笑 xiào 'smile'
跟 gēn	✓	✓	✓	✓
給 gěi		✓	✓	
對 duì	✓	✓		✓

(1) 給 gěi：

❶ 白小姐昨天給我介紹了一家綠島的旅館。

Bái xiǎojiě zuótiān gěi wǒ jièshàole yì jiā Lǜdǎo de lǚguǎn.

Yesterday, Miss Bai told me about a hotel on Green Island.

❷ 房東早上給美美打了電話，告訴她得付房租了。

Fángdōng zǎoshang gěi Měiměi dǎle diànhuà, gàosù tā děi fù fángzū le.

The landlord called Meimei this morning to tell her to pay rent.

(2) 跟 gēn：

❶ 我跟他說明了臺灣人吃飯的習慣。

Wǒ gēn tā shuōmíngle Táiwān rén chīfàn de xíguàn.

I explained Taiwanese dining customs to him.

❷ 小高跟老師說明天不能來上課。

Xiǎo Gāo gēn lǎoshī shuō míngtiān bù néng lái shàngkè.

Xiao Gao mentioned to his teacher that he can't come to class tomorrow.

(3) 對duì：

❶ 他對我說他沒打過工。
Tā duì wǒ shuō tā méi dǎguò gōng.
He told me that he has never worked part-time.

❷ 我對老闆說明為什麼昨天沒來上班。
Wǒ duì lǎobǎn shuōmíng wèishénme zuótiān méi lái shàngbān.
I explained to my boss why I didn't come to work yesterday.

對 A 有 B, (duì (Prep) A yǒu (Vst) B), to be B in A

Function

In this pattern, the preposition 對 occurs with the state verb 有, the object of 有 is always an abstract noun, such as 興趣xìngqù 'interests', 幫助 bāngzhù 'assistance', 好處hǎochù 'benefit', 影響yǐngxiǎng 'influence', 想法xiǎngfǎ 'thoughts', etc....

❶ 很多人對學中文有興趣。
Hěn duō rén duì xué Zhōngwén yǒu xìngqù.
Many people are interested in learning Chinese.

❷ 多看書，對充實我們的專業能力有幫助。
Duō kànshū, duì chōngshí wǒmen de zhuānyè nénglì yǒu bāngzhù.
If you read more, it will enhence your professional abilities.

❸ 多吃青菜、少吃肉對身體有好處。
Duō chī qīngcài, shǎo chī ròu duì shēntǐ yǒu hǎochù.
Eating more vegetables and less meat is good for the body, i.e., health.

Structures

(1) In this pattern, 對 is a preposition, the dummy state verb is 有, and such nouns as 興趣xìngqù 'interests', 幫助bāngzhù 'assistance', 好處hǎochù 'benefit', 影響yǐngxiǎng 'influence', 經驗jīngyàn 'experience', 想法xiǎngfǎ 'thoughts' serve as its objects. These abstract nouns can be modified, too. Example: 運動對身體健康有 很大的幫助。Yùndòng duì shēntǐ jiànkāng yǒu hěn dà de bāngzhù. 'Exercise has a great help to physical health'.

(2) Furthermore, the state verb 有 can be modified by 很hěn or 非常 fēicháng, e.g., 他對做菜很有興趣。Tā duì zuò cài hěn yǒu xìngqù. 'He is very interested in cooking.'

***N**egation* :

❶ 媽媽對又酸又辣的泡菜沒有興趣。
Māma duì yòu suān yòu là de pàocài méi yǒu xìngqù.
Mom is not interested in sour and spicy kimchi.

❷ 陳先生認為做廣告對企業沒有太大的幫助。
Chén xiānshēng rènwéi zuò guǎnggào duì qǐyè méi yǒu tài dà de bāngzhù.
Mr. Chen thinks it's not helpful for a company to make advertisement.

❸ 我只是喉嚨痛，對工作沒有影響。
Wǒ zhǐshì hóulóng tòng, duì gōngzuò méi yǒu yǐngxiǎng.
I just have a sore throat. It doesn't affect my work.

Questions :

❶ 馬老師是不是對教書很有經驗？
Mǎ lǎoshī shìbúshì duì jiāoshū hěn yǒu jīngyàn?
Teacher Ma has a lot of experience teaching, right?

❷ 一個人會說很多種語言，是不是對找工作有幫助？
Yí ge rén huì shuō hěn duō zhǒng yǔyán, shìbúshì duì zhǎo
gōngzuò yǒu bāngzhù?
If someone speaks many languages, it is helpful in finding work,
right?

❸ 你對跟外國人結婚有沒有什麼想法？
Nǐ duì gēn wàiguó rén jiéhūn yǒu méi yǒu shénme xiǎngfǎ?
Do you have any thoughts on marrying a foreigner?

Usage

When state verbs take a preposition, it must be 對, whereas action
verbs can take a whole variety of prepositions, e.g., 他對每件事都
很熱心。Tā duì měi jiàn shì dōu hěn rèxīn. 'He is enthusiastic about
everything.'

對…來說, (duì (Prep)…lái shuō), as far as…is concerned, for

Function

This pattern presents a fact that applies only to the object of 對. The
statement may not be true to others.

❶ 對台南人來說，早餐非常重要。
Duì Táinán rén lái shuō, zǎocān fēicháng zhòngyào.
For the people of Tainan, breakfast is very important.

❷ 對喜歡中國文化的人來說，故宮博物院是一個值得參觀的地
方。
Duì xǐhuān Zhōngguó wénhuà de rén lái shuō, Gùgōng Bówùyuàn
shì yí ge zhíde cānguān de dìfāng.
For people who like Chinese culture, the National Palace Museum
is a place worth visiting.

❸ 一件羊毛外套8000塊錢，對我來說，太貴了。
Yí jiàn yángmáo wàitào 8000 kuài qián, duì wǒ lái shuō, tài guì le.
For me, NT$8,000 for a wool coat is too expensive.

❹ 對日本人來說，寫漢字不難。
Duì Rìběn rén lái shuō, xiě Hànzì bù nán.
For Japanese, writing Chinese characters is not hard.

❺ 對中國人來說，春節、端午節、中秋節是一家人團聚的日子。
Duì Zhōngguó rén lái shuō, Chūnjié, Duānwǔ Jié, Zhōngqiū Jié shì
yì jiā rén tuánjù de rìzi.
For the Chinese, the Spring Festival, the Dragon Boat Festival, and
the Mid-Autumn Moon Festival are days that families get together.

對⋯講究, (duì (Prep)...jiǎngjiù (Vst)), to be discerning, discriminating, particular about

Function   The use of this pattern indicates that the subject is very particular about the object of 對 and wants nothing but the very best.

① 鈴木先生沒想到台南人對吃這麼講究。

Língmù xiānshēng méi xiǎngdào Táinán rén duì chī zhème jiǎngjiù.

Mr. Lingmu had no idea that the people of Tainan were so particular about foods.

② 高先生對住的環境非常講究，不但要離車站近，附近還要有公園。

Gāo xiānshēng duì zhù de huánjìng fēicháng jiǎngjiù, búdàn yào lí chēzhàn jìn, fùjìn hái yào yǒu gōngyuán.

Mr. Gao is very particular about where he lives. Not only does it have to be close to the public transportation, it also has to have a park nearby.

③ 小張對吃東西不怎麼講究，常常吃麵包或是超商的速食。

Xiǎo Zhāng duì chī dōngxi bù zěme jiǎngjiù, chángcháng chī miànbāo huò shì chāoshāng de sùshí.

Xiao Zhang isn't all that fussy about what he eats. He often has bread or fast food from convenience stores.

④ 李小姐對衣服的品質很講究，總是買名牌的。

Lǐ xiǎojiě duì yīfú de pǐnzhí hěn jiǎngjiù, zǒngshì mǎi míngpái de.

Miss Li is very particular about the quality of her clothes and always buys famous brand names.

⑤ 對吃很講究的人，不一定都胖。

Duì chī hěn jiǎngjiù de rén, bùyídìng dōu pàng.

People who care a great deal about eating aren't necessarily all over-weight.

對於, duìyú, (Prep, Ptc), towards, regarding (1)

Function   對於 is basically a prep, rather formal and advanced, meaning towards etc . But, it can also function as an object marker.

(1) 對於 as a prep: In this function, it marks the target, a direction at, of a state (esp attitudes) or an action, towards, regarding, as far as A is concerned.

① 對於城鄉學生，這都是福音。

Duìyú chéngxiāng xuéshēng, zhè dōu shì fúyīn.

For both urban and rural students, this is good news.

② 這對於教育過程也有指引作用。

Zhè duìyú jiàoyù guòchéng yě yǒu zhǐyǐn zuòyòng.

This also play a guiding role in the education process.

❸ 對於男友的疏遠感到不甘心而憤怒。

Duìyú nányǒu de shūyuǎn gǎndào bù gānxīn ér fènnù.

Her boyfriend is keeping her at a distance. She's angry and not taking it lying down.

❹ 對於國家來說，這是一種損失。

Duìyú guójiā lái shuō, zhè shì yì zhǒng sǔnshī.

This is a loss of sorts for the country.

(2) 對於 as an object-marker (particle): In this function, 對於 moves the object of a transitive verb to the front of a VP. This function is similar to the 'of' in 'the killing of wild animals'.

❶ 韓國人對於學歷的看重不次於中國人。(=看重學歷)

Hánguó rén duìyú xuélì de kànzhòng bú cìyú Zhōngguó rén. (= kànzhòng xuélì)

Koreans attach as much importance to degrees as the Chinese. (=importance attached to degrees)

❷ 那也可以緩和一下人們對於死亡的恐懼。(=恐懼死亡)

Nà yě kěyǐ huǎnhé yíxià rénmen duìyú sǐwáng de kǒngjù. (= kǒngjù sǐwáng)

That can also mitigate the fear of death people have. (=fear death)

❸ 對於那天的事，她仍然很在意。(=在意那天的事)

Duìyú nà tiān de shì, tā réngrán hěn zàiyì. (= zàiyì nà tiān de shì)

She still cares about what happened that day. (=care about the events of that day)

❹ 對於她的問句，我只用搖頭來回答。

Duìyú tā de wènjù, wǒ zhǐ yòng yáotóu lái huídá.

I merely shook my head in answer to her question.

Structures 對於 is not a typical preposition. It can be placed at the very beginning of a sentence, or following a subject, as can be seen above.

Negation : Negation never precedes 對於, except 不是. The primary verb receives negation, e.g.,

❶ 對於國家來說，這並不是一種損失。

Duìyú guójiā lái shuō, zhè bìng bú shì yì zhǒng sǔnshī.

This is no loss to the nation.

❷ 對於那天的事，她不是一點都不在意。

Duìyú nà tiān de shì, tā búshì yìdiǎn dōu bú zàiyì.

She isn't completely apathetic about the events of that day.

Questions : 對於 cannot itself occur in the A-not-A pattern. 是不是 must be used. 嗎 questions are always possible.

❶ 對於那天的事，她都不在意嗎？
Duìyú nà tiān de shì, tā dōu bú zàiyì ma?
Is she completely indifferent about what happened that day?

❷ 對於城鄉學生這都是福音嗎？
Duìyú chéngxiāng xuéshēng zhè dōu shì fúyīn ma?
Is this good news for both urban and rural students?

❸ 對於那天的事，她是不是都不在意？
Duìyú nà tiān de shì, tā shìbúshì dōu bú zàiyì?
Is she completely unconcerned about what happened that day?

❹ 是不是對於城鄉學生這都是福音？
Shì búshì duìyú chéngxiāng xuéshēng zhè dōu shì fúyīn?
Is this good news for both urban and rural students?

Usage

對於 is partly a formal counterpart of 對. They are interchangeable in many situations, but not all, e.g.,

❶ 請不要對不懂事的孩子生氣。
Qǐng bú yào duì bù dǒngshì de háizi shēngqì.
Please don't get angry with children who don't know any better.

*請不要對於不懂事的孩子生氣。
*Qǐng bú yào duìyú bù dǒngshì de háizi shēngqì.
Please don't get angry with children who don't know any better.

❷ 她總是對外國人不禮貌。
Tā zǒngshì duì wàiguó rén bù lǐmào.
She is always impolite to foreigners.

*她總是對於外國人不禮貌。
*Tā zǒngshì duìyú wàiguó rén bù lǐmào.
She is always impolite to foreigners.

對於⋯而言, (duìyú (Prep)...ér yán), as far as... is concerned (2)

Function

This pattern marks the focus of the entire sentence.

❶ 對於這些新移民而言，語言溝通的障礙最大。
Duìyú zhèxiē xīn yímín ér yán, yǔyán gōutōng de zhàng'ài zuì dà.
The most difficult thing for new immigrants is the language barrier.

❷ 一直要員工加班，對於公司而言，不見得有好處。
Yìzhí yào yuángōng jiābān, duìyú gōngsī ér yán, bújiàndé yǒu hǎochù.
Regularly requiring employees to work overtime is not necessarily advantageous to the company.

❸ 對於這些志工而言，能輔導這些學童是一件快樂的事。
Duìyú zhèxiē zhìgōng ér yán, néng fǔdǎo zhèxiē xuétóng shì yí jiàn kuàilè de shì.
As far as these volunteers are concerned, they are happy just to be able to mentor school children.

❹ 我想對於任何人而言，受到種族歧視都是無法接受的。

Wǒ xiǎng duìyú rènhé rén ér yán, shòudào zhǒngzú qíshì dōu shì wúfǎ jiēshòu de.

I think anyone would agree that being discriminated against because of race is unacceptable.

Usage

The pattern 對⋯來說 always applies to a person or group of people, e.g., 對台南人來說，早餐非常重要。Duì Táinán rén lái shuō, zǎocān fēicháng zhòngyào. 'Breakfast is very important to the people of Tainan.' This needn't be the case for the formal pattern 對於⋯而言, e.g., 對於高科技的發展而言，如何培養研究人員是最重要的議題。 Duìyú gāo kējì de fāzhǎn ér yán, rúhé péiyǎng yánjiù rényuán shì zuì zhòngyào de yìtí. 'When it comes to developing high tech, how to cultivate researchers is the most important issue.'

多, duō, (Vs), more than, over, and some (1)

Function

多 is used after numbers to indicate 'more than' or 'over'.

❶ 十多人

shí duō rén

10 some people

❷ 二十多個人

èrshí duō gè rén

20 some people

❸ 一百萬多支手機

yìbǎiwàn duō zhī shǒujī

1,000,000 plus cell phones

Structures

(1) When 多 is associated with a number greater than 10, 多 indicates the residual amount.

數詞 numeral	多 duō 'more'	量詞 measure	名詞 noun
二十 èrshí	多	個 ge	人 rén
五百 wǔbǎi	多	個 ge	包子 bāozi
一千 yìqiān	多	支 shī	手機 shǒujī
三萬四千 sānwàn sìqiān	多	塊 kuài	錢 qián

(2) When 多 is used with a number, it refers to what is greater than it and is not specified.

❶ 五塊多(錢)

wǔ kuài duō (qián)

more than five dollars (under 6)

❷ 一塊多(錢)

yí kuài duō (qián)

more than one dollar (under 2)

111

多, duō, (Adv), as in 多＋Verb, more... than planned (2)

Function

Pre-verbal 多 duō 'more' or 少 shǎo 'less' indicates 'more' or 'less/fewer' than pre-conception.

1. 我最近沒錢了，應該少買東西。
   Wǒ zuìjìn méi qián le, yīnggāi shǎo mǎi dōngxi.
   I haven't had any money recently, so I should spend less (than usual).

2. 我中文不好，應該多看書，少看電視。
   Wǒ Zhōngwén bù hǎo, yīnggāi duō kànshū, shǎo kàn diànshì.
   My Chinese is not good. I should study more and watch TV less.

3. 我們明天應該多穿衣服嗎？
   Wǒmen míngtiān yīnggāi duō chuān yīfú ma?
   Should we wear more clothes than usual tomorrow?

Usage

When a transitive verb occurs in this pattern, 一點 yìdiǎn 'a little bit' is often used with its object.

1. 他喜歡臺灣，想多學一點中文。
   Tā xǐhuān Táiwān, xiǎng duō xué yìdiǎn Zhōngwén.
   He likes Taiwan and wants to study Chinese a bit more.

2. 昨天我朋友來我家，我多做了一點菜。
   Zuótiān wǒ péngyǒu lái wǒ jiā, wǒ duō zuòle yìdiǎn cài.
   Friends of mine came to my house yesterday. I made a little extra food.

3. 她今天太累了，想少做一點功課。
   Tā jīntiān tài lèi le, xiǎng shǎo zuò yìdiǎn gōngkè.
   She is too tired today and wants to do less homework (than her teacher assigned.)

多, duó, (Adv), intensifying, how...! (3)

Function

多 expresses a high level of intensity, an exaggeration, or charged emotion. This type of sentence often ends with the particle 呀 or 啊.

1. 這裡的風景多美啊！真是百聞不如一見。
   Zhèlǐ de fēngjǐng duó měi a! Zhēnshi bǎiwén bùrú yíjiàn.
   The scenery here is so beautiful! It is something you have to see to believe.

2. 你看，老闆給我的薪水這麼少，多小氣呀！
   Nǐ kàn, lǎobǎn gěi wǒ de xīnshuǐ zhème shǎo, duó xiǎoqì ya!
   See! My boss is paying me a pittance, what a cheapskate!

3. 表弟每天搭計程車去學校上課。多浪費啊！
   Biǎodì měi tiān dā jìchéngchē qù xuéxiào shàngkè. Duó làngfèi a!
   Every day my cousin takes a taxi to school. How extravagant!

4. 你不知道導演他的脾氣多暴躁！動不動就罵人。
   Nǐ bù zhīdào dǎoyǎn tā de píqì duó bàozào! Dòngbúdòng jiù mà rén.
   You don't know how hot-tempered the director is! He'll lash out without warning.

⑤ 這棟建築多堅固啊！地震以後只有它沒倒。

Zhè dòng jiànzhú duó jiāngù a! Dìzhèn yǐhòu zhǐyǒu tā méi dǎo.

This building is so sturdy! It's the only one that didn't collapse during the earthquake.

多少, duōshǎo, (Adv), likely, at least

Function The adverb 多少 refers to the possibility of a vague and minimal amount, similar to English 'at least, somewhat, a little'.

❶ 你雖然不餓，可是媽媽準備了這麼多菜，你多少吃一點吧。

Nǐ suīrán bú è, kěshì māma zhǔnbèile zhème duō cài, nǐ duōshǎo chī yìdiǎn ba.

Even though you're not hungry, Mom prepared a lot of dishes for you, so you should eat something.

❷ 你在西班牙住了半年，多少能説幾句西班牙語吧。

Nǐ zài Xībānyá zhùle bàn nián, duōshǎo néng shuō jǐ jù Xībānyáyǔ ba.

You lived in Spain for half a year; you must be able to speak some Spanish.

❸ 你買的電腦這麼便宜，多少會有一點問題吧。

Nǐ mǎi de diànnǎo zhème piányí, duōshǎo huì yǒu yìdiǎn wèntí ba.

The computer you bought was so cheap, I reckon it's got to have something wrong with it.

❹ 那個店員是我朋友。我帶你去買東西，多少可以打一點折。

Nà ge diànyuán shì wǒ péngyǒu. Wǒ dài nǐ qù mǎi dōngxi, duōshǎo kěyǐ dǎ yìdiǎn zhé.

That employee is my friend. If I take you to buy something, he's going to give you some kind of discount.

❺ 我不常做飯，可是調味料多少準備了一點。

Wǒ bù cháng zuòfàn, kěshì tiáowèiliào duōshǎo zhǔnbèile yìdiǎn.

I don't cook often, but I do have some spices ready.

Usage In most cases, 多少 suggests possibility, thus making itself highly compatible with modal verbs like 能 néng, 會 huì, and 可以 kěyǐ, as illustrated in ❷, ❸, and ❹ above.

而且, érqiě, (Conj), furthermore

Function 而且 is a conjunction occurring in S_2. It can connect two short verb phrases, such as in ❶ and ❷, meaning 'and, as well as'. It can also connect two clauses, such as in ❸ and ❹, meaning 'furthermore'.

❶ 臺灣的夏天很熱而且很潮濕。

Táiwān de xiàtiān hěn rè érqiě hěn cháoshī.

Taiwan's summers are hot and humid.

❷ 如果多花一點時間找，一定能找到便宜而且合適的。

Rúguǒ duō huā yìdiǎn shíjiān zhǎo, yídìng néng zhǎodào piányí érqiě héshì de.

If one spends a little more time looking, one is sure to find an inexpensive and suitable one.

❸ 房東幫她裝了有線電視，而且還幫她裝了網路。

Fángdōng bāng tā zhuāngle yǒuxiàn diànshì, érqiě hái bāng tā zhuāngle wǎnglù.

The landlord installed cable TV for her, and also installed the internet for her.

❹ 做這個工作得會說中文，而且得有一些工作經驗。

Zuò zhè ge gōngzuò děi huì shuō Zhōngwén, érqiě děi yǒu yìxiē gōngzuò jīngyàn.

This job requires fluency in Chinese and some work experience.

Usage

In S₂ where 而且 érqiě is used, such adverbs as 還 hái or 也 yě typically co-occur.

Existential Sentence with Posture Verbs (1)

Function

Posture verbs refer to 'sit, stand, lie, kneel, squat etc…'. They can be used in action sentences or in existential sentences. The latter refers to the existence of a noun in that physical posture.

❶ 路口已經站了很多人。

Lùkǒu yǐjīng zhànle hěn duō rén.

There were already a lot of people standing at the street intersection.

❷ 餐廳裡坐著很多外國學生。

Cāntīng lǐ zuòzhe hěn duō wàiguó xuéshēng.

There are many foreign students sitting in the restaurant.

❸ 咖啡店裡坐著很多來做功課的中學生。

Kāfēi diàn lǐ zuòzhe hěn duō lái zuò gōngkè de zhōngxuéshēng.

A lot of secondary school students who came to do their homework are sitting in the café.

Structures

In existential sentences, posture verbs are typically used with aspect particles (esp. 了 and 著), and the post-verbal subjects are typically indefinite (one, three, many, etc…).

*Q*uestions :

❶ 那個展覽館前面是不是站著很多學生？

Nà ge zhǎnlǎn guǎn qiánmiàn shìbúshì zhànzhe hěn duō xuéshēng?

Are there many students standing in front of the exposition hall?

❷ 餐廳裡是不是已經坐著很多客人？

Cāntīng lǐ shìbúshì yǐjīng zuòzhe hěn duō kèrén?

Are there already a lot of customers sitting in the restaurant?

❸ 今天的新郎，是不是門口站著的那個人？

Jīntiān de xīnláng, shì bú shì ménkǒu zhànzhe de nà ge rén?

Is this guy who is standing in front of door today's groom ?

Usage　Non-posture verbs can also occur in this construction, including 放 fàng 'place', 走 zǒu 'walk', 來 lái 'come', 住 zhù 'live'. In addition, 掛 guà 'hang', 躺 tǎng 'lie (down)', 貼 tiē 'stick', can also appear in this construction with the co-occurrence of 著, e.g.,

❶ 牆上掛著不少畫。

Qiáng shàng guàzhe bù shǎo huà.

There are quite a few paintings on the wall.

❷ 床上躺著一個人，我不認識。

Chuáng shàng tǎngzhe yí ge rén, wǒ bú rènshì.

In the bed lies a man, whom I don't know.

Existential Sentence with 有 yǒu　(2)

Function　The existential verb 有 yǒu expresses the existence of somebody or something at some location.

❶ 那棟大樓(的)前面有很多人。

Nà dòng dàlóu (de) qiánmiàn yǒu hěn duō rén.

There are many people in front of that building.

❷ 我家附近有圖書館。

Wǒ jiā fùjìn yǒu túshūguǎn.

There is a library near my home.

❸ 山上有兩家很有名的咖啡店。

Shān shàng yǒu liǎng jiā hěn yǒumíng de kāfēi diàn.

There are two famous coffee shops on the mountain.

❹ 樓下有一家商店。

Lóuxià yǒu yì jiā shāngdiàn.

There is a shop downstairs.

Structures　The existential structure is: Location＋有 yǒu＋Noun. The internal structures of location here are the same as the location in the locative sentences.

***Negation* :**　The negation for existential sentences is 沒有 méi yǒu.

❶ 他家附近沒有游泳池。

Tā jiā fùjìn méi yǒu yóuyǒngchí.

There is no swimming pool near his home.

❷ 教室裡面沒有學生。

Jiàoshì lǐmiàn méi yǒu xuéshēng.

There is no student in the classroom.

❸ 那棟大樓的後面沒有餐廳。

Nà dòng dàlóu de hòumiàn méi yǒu cāntīng.

There is no restaurant behind that building.

Questions :

❶ 你家附近有海嗎？
Nǐ jiā fùjìn yǒu hǎi ma?
Is there ocean near your house?

❷ 學校(的)後面有沒有好吃的牛肉麵店？
Xuéxiào (de) hòumiàn yǒu méi yǒu hǎochī de niúròu miàn diàn?
Is there a good beef noodle shop behind the school?

Usage

(1) The object in existential sentences is usually indefinite, i.e., the identification of the object is not readily certain or familiar to the speaker.

(2) Note also that existential sentences and locative sentences are just the reverse in sequence, e.g.,
樓下有圖書館。Lóuxià yǒu túshūguǎn. vs.
圖書館在樓下。Túshūguǎn zài lóuxià.
'Downstairs there is a library.' vs. 'The library is downstairs.'

(3) In 我有一支手機。Wǒ yǒu yì zhī shǒujī. 'I have a cellphone.', the verb 有 is possessive and transitive and in 房子裡面有一支手機。Fángzi lǐmiàn yǒu yì zhī shǒujī. 'There is a cellphone in the house', the verb 有 is existential and intransitive. The possessive 有 is always transitive, while the existential 有 is always intransitive.

反而, fǎn'ér, (Adv), on the contrary

Function

The adverb 反而 introduces an action or situation that is contrary to the expectations of the speaker. 反而 brings in S$_2$.

❶ 你說了那麼多次。她不但沒聽懂，反而更糊塗了。
Nǐ shuōle nàme duō cì. Tā búdàn méi tīngdǒng, fǎn'ér gèng hútú le.
Even after you have repeated yourself so many times, she still doesn't get it. On the contrary, she's even more confused than before.

❷ 她本來很好看，化了妝以後反而不好看。
Tā běnlái hěn hǎokàn, huàle zhuāng yǐhòu fǎn'ér bù hǎokàn.
She is naturally pretty, and make-up actually makes her less attractive.

❸ 看了我寫的文章，老師不但沒罵我，反而說我寫得很好。
Kànle wǒ xiě de wénzhāng, lǎoshī búdàn méi mà wǒ, fǎn'ér shuō wǒ xiě de hěn hǎo.
The teacher didn't reproach me after reading my paper. On the contrary, she said I did a good job with my writing.

❹ 我運動以後不但不累，反而更有精神。
Wǒ yùndòng yǐhòu búdàn bú lèi, fǎn'ér gèng yǒu jīngshén.
I don't feel tired after a work out; on the contrary I have even more energy.

❺ 現在很多年輕人喜歡穿黑色的，反而是年紀大的人喜歡穿紅色的。

Xiànzài hěn duō niánqīng rén xǐhuān chuān hēisè de, fǎn'ér shì niánjì dà de rén xǐhuān chuān hóngsè de.

Black is in style among young people these days. On the contrary it is the older generation who wears red.

Usage

The 反而 clause is often preceded by a 不但 clause (S₁) in the negative.

❶ 他常常熬夜念書。成績不但沒進步，反而退步了。

Tā chángcháng áoyè niànshū. Chéngjī búdàn méi jìnbù, fǎn'ér tuìbù le.

He often stays up late studying. Not only have his grades not improved, they have actually gotten worse.

❷ 他去當兵不但沒變瘦，反而胖了。

Tā qù dāngbīng búdàn méi biàn shòu, fǎn'ér pàng le.

He went to serve in the military. Not only did he not lose weight, he actually gained.

❸ 我幫她打掃房間。她不但不覺得高興，反而生氣了。

Wǒ bāng tā dǎsǎo fángjiān. Tā búdàn bù juéde gāoxìng, fǎn'ér shēngqì le.

I cleaned her room for her. Not only did it not make her happy, she actually got displeased.

反正, fǎnzhèng, (Adv), at any rate, anyway

Function

反正 is an S₂ adverb, giving concession to or acceptance of a fact that cannot be altered.

❶ 不管你有沒有意願，反正我們已經決定要這麼做了。

Bùguǎn nǐ yǒu méi yǒu yìyuàn, fǎnzhèng wǒmen yǐjīng juédìng yào zhème zuò le.

It doesn't matter if you want to or not. Anyway we've all decided that this is how it's going to be done.

❷ 不管你跟他合得來合不來，反正你們得一起工作。

Bùguǎn nǐ gēn tā hédelái hébùlái, fǎnzhèng nǐmen děi yìqǐ gōngzuò.

It doesn't matter if you two get along or not. Anyway you have to work together.

❸ 你加入不加入沒關係，反正我們自己做也沒問題。

Nǐ jiārù bù jiārù méi guānxi, fǎnzhèng wǒmen zìjǐ zuò yě méi wèntí.

You can choose whether or not to help. At any rate we can take care of it ourselves.

❹ 不相信風水就算了，反正信不信由你。

Bù xiāngxìn fēngshuǐ jiù suànle, fǎnzhèng xìn bú xìn yóu nǐ.

That's fine if you don't believe in Feng Shui, and it's your decision to make anyway.

❺ 我還沒開始準備過年，反正還來得及啊。

Wǒ hái méi kāishǐ zhǔnbèi guònián, fǎnzhèng hái láidejí a.

I haven't started preparing for the new year yet. I still have time, anyway.

> **Usage**

反正 often combines with 不管 or 無論 in S₁, e.g.,

無論你怎麼說，反正我都不會答應。

Wúlùn nǐ zěnme shuō, fǎnzhèng wǒ dōu bú huì dāyìng.

No matter what you say, I won't agree to it/allow it any way.

方面, fāngmiàn, (N), as in 在…方面, with respect to; regarding

> **Function**

A sentence with the pattern （在）…方面 means that the sentence is true as far as '...' is concerned.

❶ 經過五十年的殖民統治，台灣人在飲食、生活習慣各方面都受到日本文化很深的影響。

Jīngguò wǔshí nián de zhímín tǒngzhì, Táiwān rén zài yǐnshí, shēnghuó xíguàn gè fāngmiàn dōu shòudào Rìběn wénhuà hěn shēn de yǐngxiǎng.

After 50 years of colonial rule, Taiwanese were deeply influenced by Japanese culture in the areas of dietary and living habits.

❷ 最近幾年，中國在經濟方面發展得很快，吸引了許多外國人到那裡工作。

Zuìjìn jǐ nián, Zhōngguó zài jīngjì fāngmiàn fāzhǎn de hěn kuài, xīyǐnle xǔduō wàiguó rén dào nàlǐ gōngzuò.

In recent years, China has developed very quickly with respect to its economy, attracting many foreigners there to work.

❸ 這棟大樓的環境，一般來説，還不錯。不過在衛生方面，還應該再改善。

Zhè dòng dàlóu de huánjìng, yìbān láishuō, hái búcuò. Búguò zài wèishēng fāngmiàn, hái yīnggāi zài gǎishàn.

This building's overall condition is, for the most part, pretty good. In terms of sanitation, however, it still needs some improvement.

❹ 明天李教授的演講談的是流行音樂。他在這方面相當有研究，應該很值得去聽。

Míngtiān Lǐ jiàoshòu de yǎnjiǎng tán de shì liúxíng yīnyuè. Tā zài zhè fāngmiàn xiāngdāng yǒu yánjiù, yīnggāi hěn zhíde qù tīng.

Professor Li's speech tomorrow will be on pop music. He has researched this area quite a lot. It should worth listening to.

❺ 他在門市服務快滿十年了，在處理消費糾紛方面很有經驗。你可以放心。

Tā zài ménshì fúwù kuài mǎn shí nián le, zài chǔlǐ xiāofèi jiūfēn fāngmiàn hěn yǒu jīngyàn. Nǐ kěyǐ fàngxīn.

He has been working in the sales office for almost 10 years and has a lot of experience in the area of handling consumer disputes. You don't need to worry.

Usage

(1) There are similarities between（在）…方面 and（在）…上, both referring to 'as regards', but there are significant differences. See below.

(2)（在）…上 can be used to indicate the foundation, standard, or principle upon which a statement is made, e.g.,

❶ 她跟男朋友只是同居。在法律上，還算是單身。

Tā gēn nánpéngyǒu zhǐshì tóngjū. Zài fǎlǜ shàng, hái suànshì dānshēn.

She is only living with her boyfriend. In terms of the law, she is still single.

❷ 對華人來説，中秋節是全家團聚的日子。習慣上，每個人都要回家。

Duì Huá rén lái shuō, Zhōngqiū Jié shì quánjiā tuánjù de rìzi. Xíguàn shàng, měi ge rén dōu yào huíjiā.

For the Chinese people, the Mid-autumn Moon Festival is a day when families get together. Customarily, everyone returns home.

❸ 雖然出車禍不是他的錯，可是他認為自己在道德上多少有一些責任。

Suīrán chū chēhuò bú shì tā de cuò, kěshì tā rènwéi zìjǐ zài dàodé shàng duōshǎo yǒu yìxiē zérèn.

Although the accident wasn't his fault, he feels that, morally speaking, he needs to take some responsibility.

(3) When used this way, only abstract nouns can be inserted into the pattern and it is not interchangeable with（在）…方面. E.g.,

❶ *他家在吃上很講究。

*Tā jiā zài chī shàng hěn jiǎngjiù.

❷ *她跟男朋友只是同居，在法律方面，還算是單身。

*Tā gēn nánpéngyǒu zhǐshì tóngjū, zài fǎlǜ fāngmiàn, hái suànshì dānshēn.

(4) When, however,（在）…方面 and（在）…上 are used to explain different aspects of the same topic, the two patterns are interchangeable. E.g.,

❶ a. 我們是好朋友，在興趣上完全一樣，可是在個性上，他比我活潑得多。

Wǒmen shì hǎo péngyǒu, zài xìngqù shàng wánquán yíyàng, kěshì zài gèxìng shàng, tā bǐ wǒ huópō de duō.

b. 我們是好朋友，在興趣方面完全一樣，可是在個性方面，他比我活潑得多。

Wǒmen shì hǎo péngyǒu, zài xìngqù fāngmiàn wánquán yíyàng, kěshì zài gèxìng fāngmiàn, tā bǐ wǒ huópō de duō.

We are good friends and share the same interests, but in terms of personality, we are completely different. He is much more lively than me.

❷ a. 有牌子的包包在價格上當然比沒有牌子的高一點，但是在品質上，比較能得到顧客的信任。

Yǒu páizi de bāobāo zài jiàgé shàng dāngrán bǐ méi yǒu páizi de gāo yìdiǎn, dànshì zài pǐnzhí shàng, bǐjiào néng dédào gùkè de xìnrèn.

b. 有牌子的包包在價格方面當然比沒有牌子的高一點，但是在品質方面，比較能得到顧客的信任。

Yǒu páizi de bāobāo zài jiàgé shàng dāngrán bǐ méi yǒu páizi de gāo yīdiǎn, dànshì zài pǐnzhí fāngmiàn, bǐjiào néng dédào gùkè de xìnrèn.

Of course a designer bag is higher priced than a non-designer brand, but in terms of quality, consumers are more likely to trust brands.

❸ a. 我來台灣快一年了。生活上差不多都習慣了，學習上也相當順利，中文進步了不少。

Wǒ lái Táiwān kuài yì nián le. Shēnghuó shàng chàbùduō dōu xíguàn le, xuéxí shàng yě xiāngdāng shùnlì, Zhōngwén jìnbùle bù shǎo.

b. 我來台灣快一年了。生活方面差不多都習慣了，學習方面也相當順利，中文進步了不少。

Wǒ lái Táiwān kuài yì nián le. Shēnghuó fāngmiàn chàbùduō dōu xíguàn le, xuéxí fāngmiàn yě xiāngdāng shùnlì, Zhōngwén jìnbùle bù shǎo.

I have been in Taiwan almost a year. In terms of day-to-day living, I'm just about used to it. In terms of study, things have been quite smooth; my Chinese has improved a lot.

非…不可, (fēi...bùkě), it is imperative that

Function　　With this pattern, the speaker indicates that something must be done. There are no alternatives.

① 哥哥已經兩年沒回國了。媽媽説今年除夕他非回來跟家人團聚不可。

Gēge yǐjīng liǎng nián méi huíguó le. Māma shuō jīnnián chúxì tā fēi huílái gēn jiārén tuánjù bùkě.

My big brother hasn't been back from abroad in two years. My mom says this year, he absolutely must come back and get together with the family on Chinese New Year's Eve.

② 想要找到好工作，非充實自己的專業能力不可。

Xiǎng yào zhǎodào hǎo gōngzuò, fēi chōngshí zìjǐ de zhuānyè nénglì bùkě.

If you want to get a good job, it is absolutely imperative that you hone your professional skills.

③ 台北這麼潮濕，我的鞋子都發霉了，非買除濕機不可。

Táiběi zhème cháoshī, wǒ de xiézi dōu fāméi le, fēi mǎi chúshījī bùkě.

Taipei is so humid; my shoes have grown mildew. I really have to buy a dehumidifier.

④ 最近發生很多不好的事情，我非去廟裡拜拜不可。

Zuìjìn fāshēng hěn duō bù hǎo de shìqíng, wǒ fēi qù miào lǐ bàibài bùkě.

A lot of bad things have happened lately. I have to go to the temple and worship.

⑤ 沒想到這份英文合約這麼複雜，公司非找人翻譯成中文不可。

Méi xiǎngdào zhè fèn Yīngwén héyuē zhème fùzá, gōngsī fēi zhǎo rén fānyì chéng Zhōngwén bùkě.

I had no idea that this English contract was so complicated. The company has to find somebody to translate it into Chinese.

Usage

Both 非 and 可 in this pattern are literary/formal in style. They are from classical Chinese originally.

否則, fǒuzé, (Conj), otherwise

Function

否則 is an S₂ conjunction, meaning 'otherwise'. The whole sentence has the meaning that S₁ must be true; otherwise, S₂, which is undesirable, would prevail.

① 我今年底必須把論文寫完，否則春節時沒辦法出國旅行。

Wǒ jīnniándǐ bìxū bǎ lùnwén xiěwán, fǒuzé Chūnjié shí méi bànfǎ chūguó lǚxíng.

I've got to finish my thesis by the end of the year; otherwise, I won't be able to go traveling abroad over Chinese New Year.

② 除非你願意改變你的觀念，否則我們無法錄取你。

Chúfēi nǐ yuànyì gǎibiàn nǐ de guānniàn, fǒuzé wǒmen wúfǎ lùqǔ nǐ.

Unless you change your mentality, we will not be able to accept your application.

❸ 政府必須有效改善台灣婦女生育的環境，否則無法提高生育率。

Zhèngfǔ bìxū yǒuxiào gǎishàn Táiwān fùnǚ shēngyù de huánjìng, fǒuzé wúfǎ tígāo shēngyùlǜ.

The Taiwan government must improve the circumstances surrounding raising children, otherwise birthrates will never rise.

❹ 你得改變你單身的想法，否則老了以後會覺得孤單寂寞。

Nǐ děi gǎibiàn nǐ dānshēn de xiǎngfǎ, fǒuzé lǎo le yǐhòu huì juéde gūdān jímò.

You have to change your philosophy about staying single, otherwise you will live a lonely old age.

❺ 面試以前，你一定要對這個職業有足夠的了解，否則不容易被錄取。

Miànshì yǐqián, nǐ yídìng yào duì zhè ge zhíyè yǒu zúgòu de liǎojiě, fǒuzé bù róngyì bèi lùqǔ.

Before an interview make sure you fully understand what the advertised position is about; otherwise it'll be hard to get the job.

Usage

In this pattern, S₁ can be preceded by 除非, e.g.,

❶ 除非你這個問題是針對成年者，否則未成年者大概沒有能力了解。

Chúfēi nǐ zhè ge wèntí shì zhēnduì chéngnián zhě, fǒuzé wèi chéngnián zhě dàgài méi yǒu nénglì liǎojiě.

Minors would probably not be able to understand this question of yours, unless it is targeted at adults and will not involve minors.

❷ 除非他不再抱怨，否則以後我不跟他一起去旅行了。

Chúfēi tā bú zài bàoyuàn, fǒuzé yǐhòu wǒ bù gēn tā yìqǐ qù lǚxíng le.

Unless he stops complaining; otherwise, in the future, I'm not going to travel with him anymore.

Four-Character Phrases (See 成語 chéngyǔ)

V 個夠, V ge gòu, to have a full dosage of an activity

Function

This pattern expresses one's great satisfaction in being able to indulge in some activity.

❶ 好久沒去 KTV 唱歌了。這次去，我要唱個夠。

Hǎojiǔ méi qù KTV chànggē le. Zhè cì qù, wǒ yào chàng ge gòu.

I haven't done KTV in ages, and this time I'm going to sing my heart out.

❷ 聽說下個禮拜百貨公司開始打折。我要去買個夠。

Tīngshuō xià ge lǐbài bǎihuò gōngsī kāishǐ dǎzhé. Wǒ yào qù mǎi ge gòu.

I heard that sales are on next week at the department stores, I'm going to spend, spend, spend!

❸ 我住在學校宿舍，好久才能吃一次媽媽做的菜。每次回家都想吃個夠。

Wǒ zhù zài xuéxiào sùshè, hǎojiǔ cái néng chī yí cì māma zuò de cài. Měi cì huíjiā dōu xiǎng chī ge gòu.

Living in dorm I don't get to eat mom's home cooking very often, so whenever I go home I really want to stuff my face.

❹ 沒關係！讓他罵個夠吧。罵夠了，他就不會那麼生氣了。

Méi guānxi! Ràng tā mà ge gòu ba. Màgòu le, tā jiù bú huì nàme shēngqì le.

It's OK. Just let him get it all out. That way he will be able to cool off.

❺ 這星期三晚上十點以後，啤酒打折。我跟朋友要去喝個夠。

Zhè xīngqísān wǎnshàng shídiǎn yǐhòu, píjiǔ dǎzhé. Wǒ gēn péngyǒu yào qù hē ge gòu.

This Wednesday beers are half off after 10 o'clock. My friends and I are going to drink to our heart's content.

Usage

(1) This pattern is more often used to refer to future activities than to past activities.

(2) This pattern is an instance of the general construction 'action 個 state', e.g., '吃個飽', '看個高興', '玩個痛快', in which 個 is not a measure.

(3) This pattern cannot be used in the negative, e.g.,*吃個不飽 *chī ge bù bǎo, *吃個不夠*chī ge bú gòu.

各 V 各的, (gè V gè de), each doing her/his own...

Function This pattern refers to each member of a given group engaged in her/his own pursuit.

❶ 他們結婚以後，因為在不同的城市上班，還是各住各的。

Tāmen jiéhūn yǐhòu, yīnwèi zài bùtóng de chéngshì shàngbān, háishì gè zhù gè de.

Since they've been married, because they work in different cities, each lives his or her own life.

❷ 他們各說各的，沒辦法一起討論。

Tāmen gè shuō gè de, méi bànfǎ yìqǐ tǎolùn.

Everyone was talking past each other. There was no way to get any discussion done.

❸ 我們雖然一起去故宮博物院，可是我們的興趣不同，各看各的。

Wǒmen suīrán yìqǐ qù Gùgōng Bówùyuàn, kěshì wǒmen de xìngqù bùtóng, gè kàn gè de.

Although we went to the Palace Museum together, each of us has his own interest, so each visited what he wanted to see.

❹ 他們同居好幾年了，可是晚飯常常是各吃各的。
Tāmen tóngjū hǎojǐ nián le, kěshì wǎnfàn chángcháng shì gè chī gè de.
They have lived together for many years, but they often eat their meals on their own.

❺ 他們一起去夜市，可是各逛各的。
Tāmen yìqǐ qù yèshì, kěshì gè guàng gè de.
They went to the night market together, but split so each could check out what they wanted to see.

給, gěi, (Prep), Various Meanings (1)

Function　　The preposition 給 has various meanings depending on contexts. Two are given below, and more will be presented later.

(1) 'to', the recipient of the action.

❶ 他給我們建議了臺東很多好玩的地方。
Tā gěi wǒmen jiànyìle Táidōng hěn duō hǎowán de dìfāng.
He suggested fun places in Taitung.

❷ 我昨天給房東打過電話。
Wǒ zuótiān gěi fángdōng dǎguò diànhuà.
I called the landlord yesterday.

❸ 小美給他介紹了很多臺灣朋友。
Xiǎoměi gěi tā jièshàole hěn duō Táiwān péngyǒu.
Xiaomei introduced many Taiwanese friends to him.

(2) 'for', the beneficiary of the action.

❶ 明天我想給你過生日。
Míngtiān wǒ xiǎng gěi nǐ guò shēngrì.
Tomorrow, I'd like to celebrate your birthday for you. (i.e., Tomorrow, I'd like to help you celebrate your birthday.)

❷ 小明給大家照相。
Xiǎomíng gěi dàjiā zhàoxiàng.
Xiaoming took photos of everybody.

❸ 他給同學們準備了西班牙咖啡。
Tā gěi tóngxuémen zhǔnbèile Xībānyá kāfēi.
He prepared some Spanish coffee for his classmates.

Structures　　給 is a preposition and all the structures to do with prepositions follow, except that when 給 means 'to', it can be placed after the main verb, especially in Taiwan. The same is true of 在 zài and 到 dào .

❶ 他建議了台南很多好玩的地方給我們。
Tā jiànyìle Táinán hěn duō hǎowán de dìfāng gěi wǒmen.
He suggested many fun places in Tainan to us.

❷ 我昨天打過電話給房東。
Wǒ zuótiān dǎguò diànhuà gěi fángdōng.
I called his landlord yesterday.

❸ 小美介紹了很多臺灣朋友給他。

Xiǎoměi jièshàole hěn duō Táiwān péngyǒu gěi tā.

Xiaomei introduced many Taiwanese friends to him.

Negation :　The negation is placed before 給.

❶ 我沒打電話給她。

Wǒ méi dǎ diànhuà gěi tā.

I didn't call her.

❷ 因為她的男朋友不高興，所以不給她打電話了。

Yīnwèi tā de nánpéngyǒu bù gāoxìng, suǒyǐ bù gěi tā dǎ diànhuà le.

Her boyfriend was unhappy, so he didn't call her.

❸ 媽媽感冒了，所以沒給我們準備早餐。

Māma gǎnmào le, suǒyǐ méi gěi wǒmen zhǔnbèi zǎocān.

Mom has a cold, so she didn't prepare breakfast for us.

Questions :

❶ 你是不是給他買了吃的東西？

Nǐ shìbúshì gěi tā mǎile chī de dōngxi?

Did you buy something for him to eat?

❷ 來臺灣以後，你給媽媽打過電話沒有？

Lái Táiwān yǐhòu, nǐ gěi māma dǎguò diànhuà méi yǒu?

Have you called your mother since you arrived in Taiwan?

❸ 妳可不可以給我介紹一個打工的機會？

Nǐ kě bù kěyǐ gěi wǒ jièshào yí ge dǎgōng de jīhuì?

Can you tell me of any part-time job opportunities?

Usage

(1) 給 can be a verb or a preposition (likewise 在 and 到), e.g., 給 is the verb in 他給我一本書。Tā gěi wǒ yì běn shū. 'He gave me a book'.

(2) When it means 'for', 給 can be replaced by 幫 or 替 with the same meaning, e.g., 我給/幫/替你準備了一本書。Wǒ gěi/bāng/tì nǐ zhǔnbèile yì běn shū. 'I have prepared a book for you'.

給, gěi, (Prep), Indirect Object Marker (2)

Function　There is a set of verbs called Double Object verbs, which take two objects, direct and indirect. Indirect objects are marked by the preposition 給, and direct objects are not marked.

❶ 他付給房東三個月的房租。

Tā fù gěi fángdōng sān ge yuè de fángzū.

He paid three months of rent to his landlord.

❷ 王先生賣給他一輛機車。

Wáng xiānshēng mài gěi tā yí liàng jīchē.

Mr. Wang sold him a motorcycle.

❸ 他從法國回來，送給李老師一些法國甜點。

Tā cóng Fǎguó huílái, sòng gěi Lǐ lǎoshī yìxiē Fǎguó tiándiǎn.

He's back from French and he gave Teacher Li some French pastries.

> **Structures**

給 marks the indirect object. The basic word order is: Verb＋給＋IndirectObj＋DirectObj. Variations in word order are illustrated below.

(1) Basic pattern

❶ 他想賣給我朋友這個電腦。

Tā xiǎng mài gěi wǒ péngyǒu zhè ge diànnǎo.

He wants to sell my friend this computer.

❷ 語言中心主任昨天才發給小陳上個月的薪水。

Yǔyán zhōngxīn zhǔrèn zuótiān cái fā gěi Xiǎo Chén shàng ge yuè de xīnshuǐ.

The language center director paid Xiao Chen last month's wage only yesterday.

❸ 我打算送給我同學這些桌子、椅子。

Wǒ dǎsuàn sòng gěi wǒ tóngxué zhèxiē zhuōzi, yǐzi.

I plan to give my classmates these desks and chairs.

(2) Indirect obj. moved to the back

❶ 他想賣這個電腦給我朋友。

Tā xiǎng mài zhè ge diànnǎo gěi wǒ péngyǒu.

He wants to sell this computer to my friend.

❷ 語言中心主任昨天才發上個月的薪水給小陳。

Yǔyán zhōngxīn zhǔrèn zuótiān cái fā shàng ge yuè de xīnshuǐ gěi Xiǎo Chén.

The language center director paid last month's wage to Xiao Chen only yesterday.

❸ 我打算送這些桌子、椅子給我同學。

Wǒ dǎsuàn sòng zhèxiē zhuōzi, yǐzi gěi wǒ tóngxué.

I plan to give these desks and chairs to my classmates.

(3) Direct obj. moved to the front

❶ 這個電腦，他想賣給我朋友。

Zhè ge diànnǎo, tā xiǎng mài gěi wǒ péngyǒu.

This computer, he wants to sell it to my friend.

❷ 上個月的薪水，語言中心主任昨天才發給小陳。

Shàng ge yuè de xīnshuǐ, yǔyán zhōngxīn zhǔrèn zuótiān cái fā gěi Xiǎo Chén.

Last month's wage, the language center director paid it to Xiao Chen only yesterday.

❸ 這些桌子、椅子，我打算送給我同學。

Zhèxiē zhuōzi, yǐzi, wǒ dǎsuàn sòng gěi wǒ tóngxué.

These desks and chairs, I plan to give them to my classmates.

*N*egation :

❶ 他只要租三個月，所以那個房間，房東不租給他了。

Tā zhǐyào zū sān ge yuè, suǒyǐ nà ge fángjiān, fángdōng bù zū gěi tā le.

He only wants it for three months, so the landlord isn't going rent him the room.

❷ 我還沒付給房東上個月的房租。

Wǒ hái méi fù gěi fángdōng shàng ge yuè de fángzū.

I haven't given my landlord last month's rent yet.

❸ 因為陳小姐快回國了，所以我不給她介紹工作了。

Yīnwèi Chén xiǎojiě kuài huíguó le, suǒyǐ wǒ bù gěi tā jièshào gōngzuò le.

Miss Chen is going back to her home country soon, so I needn't tell her of any jobs.

*Q*uestions :

❶ 你的腳踏車賣給他了沒有？

Nǐ de jiǎotàchē mài gěi tā le méi yǒu?

Have you sold him your bycicle?

❷ 那些芒果跟甜點，妳是不是送給小陳了？

Nàxiē mángguǒ gēn tiándiǎn, nǐ shìbúshì sòng gěi Xiǎo Chén le?

Did you give Xiao Chen those mangoes and sweets?

❸ 下個月中文課的學費，你付給學校了沒有？

Xià ge yuè Zhōngwén kè de xuéfèi, nǐ fù gěi xuéxiào le méi yǒu?

Have you paid the tuition for Chinese classes next month?

Usage

If the main verb in the structure involves 'outward, away from' actions from the actor, 給 can be deleted, such as in the following examples ❶ – ❸. Otherwise deletion is not possible. So, we cannot say *我做他一個蛋糕。*Wǒ zuò tā yí ge dàngāo. 或 *哥哥買我一本書。 *Gēge mǎi wǒ yì běn shū.

❶ 我要賣我朋友這個電腦。

Wǒ yào mài wǒ péngyǒu zhè ge diànnǎo.

I want to sell my friend this computer.

❷ 我打算送我同學這些桌子、椅子。

Wǒ dǎsuàn sòng wǒ tóngxué zhèxiē zhuōzi, yǐzi.

I plan to give my classmates these desks and chairs.

❸ 你知道公司付他多少薪水嗎？

Nǐ zhīdào gōngsī fù tā duōshǎo xīnshuǐ ma?

Do you know how much salary the company pays him?

A
B
C
D
E
F
G
H
I
J
K
L
M

給⋯帶來, (gěi (Prep)...dàilái), to bring...to (3)

Function   The preposition 給 points to the beneficiary of the instance mentioned.

❶ 好的生活習慣能給人們帶來健康。
Hǎo de shēnghuó xíguàn néng gěi rénmen dàilái jiànkāng.
Good habits in life can bring health to people.

❷ 朋友的關心給他帶來溫馨的感覺。
Péngyǒu de guānxīn gěi tā dàilái wēnxīn de gǎnjué.
His friends' concern brought him a feeling of warmth.

❸ 在天燈上寫下願望給人帶來新的希望。
Zài tiāndēng shàng xiěxià yuànwàng gěi rén dàilái xīn de xīwàng.
Writing wishes on sky lanterns brings people new hope.

❹ 大部分的中國人都認為拜神、祭祖能給家人帶來平安和幸福。
Dà bùfèn de Zhōngguó rén dōu rènwéi bài shén, jì zǔ néng gěi jiārén dàilái píng'ān hàn xìngfú.
Most Chinese believe that honoring gods and ancestors brings peace and happiness to their families.

❺ 科技發展給我們的生活帶來了很多的便利。
Kējì fāzhǎn gěi wǒmen de shēnghuó dàiláile hěn duō de biànlì.
Technological developments have brought a lot of convenience to our lives.

跟, gēn, (Prep), Companionship (1)

Function   The preposition 跟 brings in a companion is an undertaking.

❶ 我常跟哥哥去看棒球比賽。
Wǒ cháng gēn gēge qù kàn bàngqiú bǐsài.
I often go see baseball games with my brother.

❷ 我跟朋友在餐廳吃飯。
Wǒ gēn péngyǒu zài cāntīng chīfàn.
I am having a meal at a restaurant with friends.

❸ 我週末要跟同學去參觀故宮。
Wǒ zhōumò yào gēn tóngxué qù cānguān Gùgōng.
I'm going to go visit the Palace Museum this weekend with a classmate.

Structures   The '跟＋somebody' expression appears before the VP as do all prepositional phrases. The adverb 一起 yìqǐ is commonly associated with 跟 and is placed in front of the main verb.

Negation :   The negation marker 不 bù or 沒 méi appears before 跟.

❶ 我今天不跟同學去上書法課。
Wǒ jīntiān bù gēn tóngxué qù shàng shūfǎ kè.
I am not going to go to the calligraphy class with my classmate today.

❷ 他沒跟我一起去 KTV 唱歌。
Tā méi gēn wǒ yìqǐ qù KTV chànggē.
He didn't go to KTV with me.

❸ 妹妹沒跟我去吃越南菜。
Mèimei méi gēn wǒ qù chī Yuènán cài.
My sister didn't go with me to have Vietnamese food.

Questions :

❶ 你要跟他去日本嗎？
Nǐ yào gēn tā qù Rìběn ma?
Are you going to go to Japan with him?

❷ 你常跟誰去看電影？
Nǐ cháng gēn shéi qù kàn diànyǐng?
Who do you often go with to see movies?

❸ 你跟不跟我去圖書館看書？
Nǐ gēn bù gēn wǒ qù túshūguǎn kàn shū?
Are you going to go with me to the library to study?

跟, gēn, (Prep), Various Meanings of the Preposition (2)

Function 跟 can be variously translated in English, depending on contexts.

(1) 'to', recipient of the action.

❶ 老師跟學生說，明天要考試。
Lǎoshī gēn xuéshēng shuō, míngtiān yào kǎoshì.
The teacher told the students that there will be an exam tomorrow.

❷ 他剛跟我說明了他們國家的文化。
Tā gāng gēn wǒ shuōmíngle tāmen guójiā de wénhuà.
He just explained (part of) his country's culture to me.

❸ 語言中心主任跟小高介紹工作環境。
Yǔyán zhōngxīn zhǔrèn gēn Xiǎo Gāo jièshào gōngzuò huánjìng.
The language center director introduced Xiao Gao to the work environment.

(2) 'with', companion of the action.

❶ 小明昨天跟小美一起踢足球。
Xiǎomíng zuótiān gēn Xiǎoměi yìqǐ tī zúqiú.
Xiaoming played soccer with Xiaomei yesterday.

❷ 我是跟朋友一起來的。
Wǒ shì gēn péngyǒu yìqǐ lái de.
I came with my friends.

❸ 這個週末，我想跟朋友去台南玩。
Zhè ge zhōumò, wǒ xiǎng gēn péngyǒu qù Táinán wán.
I'd like to go to Tainan this weekend with my friends.

129

(3) 'from', source of the action of imparting.

❶ 小明想跟王老師學寫書法。
Xiǎomíng xiǎng gēn Wáng lǎoshī xué xiě shūfǎ.
Xiaoming would like to study calligraphy from (with) the teacher Miss Wang.

❷ 他打算跟麵包店老闆學做麵包。
Tā dǎsuàn gēn miànbāo diàn lǎobǎn xué zuò miànbāo.
He plans to learn how to make bread from the owner of the bakery.

❸ 我想跟朋友買他的那支舊手機。
Wǒ xiǎng gēn péngyǒu mǎi tā de nà zhī jiù shǒujī.
I would like to buy from my friend his old cell phone.

> **Structures**

Negation : The negation occurs before 跟 as in the case of all prepositions. Either 不 or 沒 can be used.

❶ 請你不要跟別人說起我的薪水。
Qǐng nǐ bú yào gēn biérén shuōqǐ wǒ de xīnshuǐ.
Please don't tell anyone how much money I make.

❷ 小明並沒跟臺灣朋友去看電腦展。
Xiǎomíng bìng méi gēn Táiwān péngyǒu qù kàn diànnǎo zhǎn.
Xiaoming didn't go to the computer exhibition with his Taiwanese friend.

❸ 我不是跟王老師學西班牙文，是跟別人學的。
Wǒ búshì gēn Wáng lǎoshī xué Xībānyáwén, shì gēn biérén xué de.
I did not learn Spanish from Teacher Wang. I studied with others.

Questions : The A-not-A pattern can be applied to prepositions including 跟, not to the verb. 是不是 is also commonly used.

❶ 你是不是跟李教授學書法？
Nǐ shìbúshì gēn Lǐ jiàoshòu xué shūfǎ?
Are you learning calligraphy from Professor Li?

❷ 你跟大家介紹辦公室環境沒有？
Nǐ gēn dàjiā jièshào bàngōngshì huánjìng méi yǒu?
Have you shown everybody around the office?

❸ 下個星期，你跟不跟我去爬山？
Xià ge xīngqí, nǐ gēn bù gēn wǒ qù páshān?
Are you coming with me when I go hiking next week?

跟⋯⋯一樣, (gēn (Prep)...yíyàng), Comparison

> **Function**

This pattern is used to compare two people or things and indicate whether they are the same (equal) or not the same. The similar/same quality of the persons or things being compared, if any, follow 一樣.

❶ 這支手機跟那支手機一樣。
Zhè zhī shǒujī gēn nà zhī shǒujī yíyàng.
This cellphone is exactly the same as that one.

❷ 我的生日跟她的生日一樣，都是八月十七日。
Wǒ de shēngrì gēn tā de shēngrì yíyàng, dōu shì bāyuè shíqīrì.
My birthday is the same as hers. They're both on August 17th.

❸ 他跟我一樣都常游泳。
Tā gēn wǒ yíyàng dōu cháng yóuyǒng.
He and I are the same. We both swim often. (We are alike)

Structures   A 跟 B 一樣（State VP），in which state VP is optional.

❶ 你點的菜跟我點的一樣。
Nǐ diǎn de cài gēn wǒ diǎn de yíyàng.
We both ordered the same dish.

❷ 我跟我妹妹一樣高。
Wǒ gēn wǒ mèimei yíyàng gāo.
I am as tall as my younger sister.

❸ 姐姐租的房子跟我租的一樣貴。
Jiějie zū de fángzi gēn wǒ zū de yíyàng guì.
The house that my older sister rents is as expensive as the one I rent.

❹ 我跟我朋友一樣喜歡看電視。
Wǒ gēn wǒ péngyǒu yíyàng xǐhuān kàn diànshì.
My friend and I are the same. We both enjoy watching TV.

***N**egation :*

(1) The negation 不 bù precedes 一樣 yíyàng to indicate that the two nouns are different in quality.

   ❶ 中國茶跟日本茶不一樣。
   Zhōngguó chá gēn Rìběn chá bù yíyàng.
   Chinese tea and Japanese tea are different.

   ❷ 我跟妹妹不一樣高。
   Wǒ gēn mèimei bù yíyàng gāo.
   My younger sister and I are not the same height.

(2) The negation marker 不 bù, can also precede 跟 gēn, but when it does, it negates the object to be compared with, i.e., the 跟 gēn… part, not the 'same' part. Typically, a 是 shì is inserted.

   ❶ 他不跟我一樣高，跟小王一樣高。
   Tā bù gēn wǒ yíyàng gāo, gēn Xiǎo Wáng yíyàng gāo.
   He and I are not the same height. He and Xiao Wang are the same height.

   ❷ 他不是跟我一樣高，是跟小王一樣高。
   Tā búshì gēn wǒ yíyàng gāo, shì gēn Xiǎo Wáng yíyàng gāo.
   He and I are not the same height. He and Xiao Wang are the same height.

131

Questions :　To ask a question, the A-not-A pattern can be used with 一樣yíyàng or 是不是shìbúshì can be placed in front of 一樣.

❶ 小籠包跟包子一樣不一樣？
Xiǎolóngbāo gēn bāozi yíyàng bù yíyàng?
Is a xiaolongbao the same as baozi?

❷ 小籠包跟包子是不是一樣？
Xiǎolóngbāo gēn bāozi shìbúshì yíyàng?
Are xiaolongbao the same as baozi?

❸ 今年的生意是不是跟去年的一樣好？
Jīnnián de shēngyì shìbúshì gēn qùnián de yíyàng hǎo?
Is business this year as good as it was last year?

❹ 說中文跟寫中文是不是一樣難？
Shuō Zhōngwén gēn xiě Zhōngwén shìbúshì yíyàng nán?
Is speaking Chinese as difficult as writing Chinese?

跟 B 有關的 A, (gēn (Prep) B yǒuguān de A), A that relates to B, A that concern B

Function　In this pattern, the preposition 跟 introduces an item (B) that relates to A. A in this pattern is the main topic.

❶ 上網買東西雖然方便，但是最近跟網購有關的糾紛很多。你還是小心一點。
Shàngwǎng mǎi dōngxi suīrán fāngbiàn, dànshì zuìjìn gēn wǎnggòu yǒuguān de jiūfēn hěn duō. Nǐ háishì xiǎoxīn yìdiǎn.
Going online to buy things is convenient, but there have been a lot of disputes related to online shopping lately. You still need to be careful.

❷ 我剛剛放在你桌上的是跟演講比賽有關的資料，請你收好。
Wǒ gānggāng fàng zài nǐ zhuō shàng de shì gēn yǎnjiǎng bǐsài yǒuguān de zīliào, qǐng nǐ shōuhǎo.
I just put some information about the speech contest on your desk. Please put it somewhere where you won't lose it.

❸ 他大學念的是歷史，而且輔系是經濟，所以跟臺灣經濟發展有關的歷史，你應該去請教他。
Tā dàxué niàn de shì lìshǐ, érqiě fǔxì shì jīngjì, suǒyǐ gēn Táiwān jīngjì fāzhǎn yǒuguān de lìshǐ, nǐ yīnggāi qù qǐngjiào tā.
He studied history in university and minored in economics, so any history questions related to Taiwan's economic development, you should direct to him.

❹ 想要了解跟原住民有關的風俗文化，你最好去一趟花蓮。
Xiǎng yào liǎojiě gēn yuánzhùmín yǒuguān de fēngsú wénhuà, nǐ zuìhǎo qù yí tàng Huālián.
If you want to better understand the customs and culture of aborigines, your best bet is to take a trip to Hualien.

❺ 我建議跟這一次校外教學有關的活動，都讓小王一個人安排。
Wǒ jiànyì gēn zhè yí cì xiàowài jiāoxué yǒuguān de huódòng, dōu
ràng Xiǎo Wáng yí ge rén ānpái.
I suggest that we let Xiao Wang make all arrangements for
activities related to the class excursion by himself.

根本, gēnběn, (Adv), not...at all, absolutely not

Function ▶ With the adverb 根本, the speaker emphatically presents a negative
view.

❶ 他每天在夜市裡擺地攤，收攤的時間都很晚。根本沒有時間去
約會。
Tā měi tiān zài yèshì lǐ bǎi dìtān, shōutān de shíjiān dōu hěn wǎn.
Gēnběn méi yǒu shíjiān qù yuēhuì.
He sets up a stand at the night market every day, and by the time
he packs up it is so late that there is no way he can make meet-up
afterwards.

❷ 你根本就看不懂現代舞。何必要買那麼貴的票？
Nǐ gēnběn jiù kànbùdǒng xiàndài wǔ. Hébì yào mǎi nàme guì de
piào?
You don't understand the first thing about modern dance, so why
go and buy such an expensive ticket?

❸ 台灣的房價那麼高。一般人根本買不起房子。
Táiwān de fángjià nàme gāo. Yìbān rén gēnběn mǎibùqǐ fángzi.
Housing prices in Taiwan are exorbitant. There is no way the
average joe can afford it.

❹ 現在是宅經濟時代。根本不必去百貨公司買衣服。線上購物就
好了。
Xiànzài shì zháijīngjì shídài. Gēnběn búbì qù bǎihuò gōngsī mǎi
yīfú. Xiànshàng gòuwù jiù hǎo le.
It's the on-line economy generation. There's no longer any need
to go to department stores for clothes. Everything can be ordered
online.

❺ 他們根本沒有什麼實力，只是運氣好而已。
Tāmen gēnběn méi yǒu shénme shílì, zhǐshì yùnqì hǎo éryǐ.
They have no actual prowess at all, just good luck.

更, gèng, (Adv), Intensification in Comparison, even more so

Function ▶ The adverb 更 presents a fact that is superior to a fact presented in a
previous statement. E.g., 星期天我更忙Xīngqítiān wǒ gèng máng
means that I am/will be even busier on Sunday than normally.

❶ 他很高，他哥哥比他更高。
Tā hěn gāo, tā gēge bǐ tā gèng gāo.
He is very tall. His brother is even taller than him.

❷ 今年比去年更冷。
Jīnnián bǐ qùnián gèng lěng.
This year is even colder than last year. (Last year was already very cold.)

❸ 我覺得芒果比西瓜更好吃。
Wǒ juéde mángguǒ bǐ xīguā gèng hǎochī.
I think mangos are even more delicious than watermelons. (Watermelons are (very) delicious as everyone knows.)

Structures　　更 is an adverb that modifies state verbs and is thus placed in front of state verbs.

Questions:　　The 是不是 pattern is typically used in this structure.

❶ 這次的颱風是不是比上次的更大？
Zhè cì de táifēng shìbúshì bǐ shàng cì de gèng dà?
Is this typhoon bigger than the one last time?

❷ 在學校上網是不是比在家裡更快？
Zài xuéxiào shàngwǎng shìbúshì bǐ zài jiā lǐ gèng kuài?
Is the internet at school even faster than at home?

更別説 B 了, (gèng bié shuō B le), let alone, never mind

Function　　This pattern presents a new topic, to which the previous statement applies even more effectively.

❶ 一到週末百貨公司裡人就很多，更別説百貨公司週年慶的時候了。
Yí dào zhōumò bǎihuò gōngsī lǐ rén jiù hěn duō, gèng bié shuō bǎihuò gōngsī zhōuniánqìng de shíhòu le.
The department stores are packed even on the weekends, not to mention during anniversary sales.

❷ 你這麼有學問的人都不懂，更別説我了。
Nǐ zhème yǒu xuéwèn de rén dōu bù dǒng, gèng bié shuō wǒ le.
If someone as highly educated as you doesn't understand it, what chance do I have.

❸ 他説的地方連我這個當地人都找不到，更別説你們了。
Tā shuō de dìfāng lián wǒ zhè ge dāngdì rén dōu zhǎobúdào, gèng bié shuō nǐmen le.
I grew up here and even I can't find it. How can you possibly find it?

❹ 我來台灣以後每天忙著念書，連101都還沒去過，更別説平溪老街了。
Wǒ lái Táiwān yǐhòu měi tiān mángzhe niànshū, lián 101 dōu hái méi qùguò, gèng bié shuō Píngxī lǎojiē le.
After I came to Taiwan I was so busy studying that I didn't have a chance to see Taipei 101, let alone the old street in Pingxi.

❺ 我連小獎都沒中過，更別説中大獎了。

Wǒ lián xiǎo jiǎng dōu méi zhòngguò, gèng bié shuō zhòng dà jiǎng le.

I've never even won a small prize, let alone a big one.

更別説 is followed by either an NP or a VP. See above. This pattern is often used together with 連 A 都 B or 就是 A 也 B patterns, e.g.,

❶ 連你都不清楚，更別説我這個新來的人了。

Lián nǐ dōu bù qīngchǔ, gèng bié shuō wǒ zhè ge xīn lái de rén le.

Even you don't understand it well, never mind a new person like me.

❷ 就是我也可能遲到，更別説他了。

Jiùshì wǒ yě kěnéng chídào, gèng bié shuō tā le.

Even I might be late, never mind him.

慣, guàn, (Ptc), indicating 'getting used to a routine'

The verb particle 慣 can be used in various ways and meanings. V 慣 and V 得慣 refer to routine activities that one is used to and feels comfortable with. They are used with plain, neutral statements, e.g.,

❶ 我從小吃慣了媽媽做的菜，所以吃不慣阿姨做的菜。

Wǒ cóng xiǎo chīguàn le māma zuò de cài, suǒyǐ chībúguàn āyí zuò de cài.

I've had mom's cooking since I was little, so I haven't been able to get used to that of my auntie.

❷ 他在台灣很多年了，已經用慣了筷子了。

Tā zài Táiwān hěn duō nián le, yǐjīng yòngguàn le kuàizi le.

He's been in Taiwan many years, so he's already used to chopsticks.

❸ 爺爺他不喝咖啡。他只喝得慣綠茶。

Yéye tā bù hē kāfēi. Tā zhǐ hēdeguàn lǜchá.

Grandpa doesn't take coffee. He is only accustomed to drinking green tea.

❹ 何先生每天騎腳踏車上班。他騎慣了，所以不覺得累。

Hé xiānshēng měi tiān qí jiǎotàchē shàngbān. Tā qíguàn le, suǒyǐ bù juéde lèi.

Mr. He rides his bike to work every day. He's gotten used to it, so it doesn't make him tired.

❺ 他聽慣了古典音樂，聽不慣流行音樂。

Tā tīngguàn le gǔdiǎn yīnyuè, tīngbúguàn liúxíng yīnyuè.

He's used to listening to classical music, and not pop music.

On the other hand, V 不慣, often carries negative overtones, e.g.,

❶ 林先生愛喝烏龍茶。他喝不慣冰紅茶。

Lín xiānshēng ài hē Wūlóng chá. Tā hēbúguàn bīng hóngchá.

Mr. Lin loves Oolong tea, but he hasn't acquired a liking for iced black tea.

❷ 奶奶喜歡住在鄉下老家。她住不慣大城市。

Nǎinai xǐhuān zhù zài xiāngxià lǎojiā. Tā zhùbúguàn dà chéngshì.

Grandma likes living at her home in the country. She is unaccustomed to living in the big city.

❸ 那種款式的衣服太短了。媽媽説她年紀大了穿不慣。

Nà zhǒng kuǎnshì de yīfú tài duǎn le. Māma shuō tā niánjì dà le chuānbúguàn.

That style of clothing is too short. Mom's not suited to it in her age.

❹ 有些民意代表只關心自己或是政黨的利益。人民真看不慣。

Yǒuxiē mínyì dàibiǎo zhǐ guānxīn zìjǐ huò shì zhèngdǎng de lìyì. Rénmín zhēn kànbúguàn.

Some public representatives are only concerned with personal or party benefit. The people can't stand it.

❺ 王教授一直在大學教書。他教不慣小學生。

Wáng jiàoshòu yìzhí zài dàxué jiāoshū. Tā jiāobúguàn xiǎoxuéshēng.

Professor Wang has always taught at university. He wouldn't know what to do with elementary school students.

光 A 就 B, (guāng (Adv) A jiù (Adv) B), just A alone...

Function ▸ This pattern consists of 2 adverbs, meaning 'even/just A alone exceeds common expectations'.

❶ 台灣的便利商店非常多。光我家外面那條街就有三家。

Táiwān de biànlì shāngdiàn fēicháng duō. Guāng wǒ jiā wàimiàn nà tiáo jiē jiù yǒu sān jiā.

There are tons of convenience stores in Taiwan. There are three on the street just outside my place alone.

❷ 他很愛吃甜點。光蛋糕一次就可以吃五個。

Tā hěn ài chī tiándiǎn. Guāng dàngāo yí cì jiù kěyǐ chī wǔ gè.

He loves sweets. Just speaking of cake, he can eat five slices in one sitting.

❸ 媽媽脾氣暴躁。光一件小小的事就能讓她生很大的氣。

Māma píqì bàozào. Guāng yí jiàn xiǎoxiǎo de shì jiù néng ràng tā shēng hěn dà de qì.

Mother's temper is volatile; even a minor thing can cause her to erupt.

❹ 老人動作比較慢。光上下公車就要比較長的時間。旁邊的人應該幫幫他們。

Lǎorén dòngzuò bǐjiào màn. Guāng shàng xià gōngchē jiù yào bǐjiào cháng de shíjiān. Pángbiān de rén yīnggāi bāngbāng tāmen.

The elderly have to move slowly; just getting on and off the bus alone takes quite a bit of time. Those close by ought to help.

❺ 那家新開的餐廳，聽說很有名。昨天我們光等位子就等了一個半鐘頭。

Nà jiā xīn kāi de cāntīng, tīngshuō hěn yǒumíng. Zuótiān wǒmen guāng děng wèizi jiù děngle yí ge bàn zhōngtóu.

I hear that new restaurant is quite popular. We went yesterday, and waiting for a table alone took an hour and a half.

關於, guānyú, (Vs, Ptc), about, regarding

Function 關於 is basically a state verb, meaning 'about, regarding, relating to', but it can also serve as a particle marking a topic.

(1) 關於 as a state verb: 關於 is used in contexts where it is the sole verb in that sentence or clause.

❶ 這本書也是關於語法的。
Zhè běn shū yě shì guānyú yǔfǎ de.
This book has to do with grammar.

❷ 我想買一本關於語法的書。
Wǒ xiǎng mǎi yì běn guānyú yǔfǎ de shū.
I would like to buy a book on grammar.

❸ 關於語法的書，滿街都是。
Guānyú yǔfǎ de shū, mǎn jiē dōu shì.
Grammar books are available everywhere.

(2) 關於 as a topic marker (Ptc), 'regarding, as far as A is concerned': To show that the object of 關於 is a true topic of the sentence, the following examples show the topics as not related meaningwise to the primary sentences.

❶ 關於大熊貓，這本書上的記載並不多。
Guānyú dà xióngmāo, zhè běn shū shàng de jìzài bìng bù duō.
As to giant pandas, this book doesn't cover much.

❷ 關於愛貓的死，我一點都不怪他。
Guānyú àimāo de sǐ, wǒ yìdiǎn dōu bú guài tā.
As to the death of my beloved cat, I don't place the blame on him at all.

❸ 關於我請客的事，我想麻煩你替我計劃一下。
Guānyú wǒ qǐngkè de shì, wǒ xiǎng máfán nǐ tì wǒ jìhuà yíxià.
I would like to trouble you to make the arrangements for the dinner that I will be hosting.

*N*egation : 不 and 沒 cannot be used with 關於. Only 不是 can.

❶ 不是關於語法的書，他不想買。

Búshì guānyú yǔfǎ de shū, tā bù xiǎng mǎi.

He is not interested in buying books that do not concern grammar.

❷ 這本書不是關於語法的。

Zhè běn shū búshì guānyú yǔfǎ de.

This book isn't on grammar.

*Q*uestions : 關於 itself cannot be made into a question pattern, *關不關於 *guān bù guānyú. 是不是 is the only possibility, in addition to the universal 嗎 questions.

❶ 這本書是關於王先生的嗎？

Zhè běn shū shì guānyú Wáng xiānshēng de ma?

Is this book about Mr. Wang?

❷ 關於愛貓的死，你一點都不怪他嗎？

Guānyú àimāo de sǐ, nǐ yìdiǎn dōu bú guài tā ma?

You don't blame him at all for the death of your beloved cat?

❸ 這本書是不是關於王先生？

Zhè běn shū shìbúshì guānyú Wáng xiānshēng?

Is this book about Mr. Wang?

❹ 是不是關於愛貓的死，你一點都不怪他？

Shìbúshì guānyú àimāo de sǐ, nǐ yìdiǎn dōu bú guài tā?

Is it the case that regarding your beloved cat's death, you don't hold him to blame at all?

Usage Unlike 對於, 關於 is commonly used in daily speech.

過, guò, (Ptc), Experience Aspect (1)

Function The particle 過 is suffixed to action verb and marks the subject's experience of the action depicted by the verb.

❶ 我在高中學過中文。

Wǒ zài gāozhōng xuéguò Zhōngwén.

I studied Chinese in senior high school.

❷ 我去過那個語言中心。

Wǒ qùguò nà ge yǔyán zhōngxīn.

I been to that language center.

❸ 我教過他兩年西班牙文。

Wǒ jiāoguò tā liǎng nián Xībānyáwén.

I taught him Spanish for two years.

Structures Experiential sentences usually include duration, frequency and non-specific past time.

❶ 我學過兩次西班牙文。
　Wǒ xuéguò liǎng cì Xībānyáwén.
　I've studied Spanish twice before.

❷ 他在越南住過三年。
　Tā zài Yuènán zhùguò sān nián.
　He lived in Vietnam for three years.

❸ 你已經去過這麼多國家，還想去哪裡？
　Nǐ yǐjīng qùguò zhème duō guójiā, hái xiǎng qù nǎlǐ?
　You've already been to so many countries. Where else would you like to go?

Negation :　Only 沒 negation is used in this pattern.

❶ 我以前沒學過中文。
　Wǒ yǐqián méi xuéguò Zhōngwén.
　I've never studied Chinese before.

❷ 我沒去過法國。
　Wǒ méi qùguò Fǎguó.
　I've never been to France.

❸ 我沒買過那家的麵包。
　Wǒ méi mǎiguò nà jiā de miànbāo.
　I've never bought bread at that store.

Questions :

❶ 你小時候去過日本沒有？
　Nǐ xiǎoshíhòu qùguò Rìběn méi yǒu?
　Did you ever go to Japan when you were young?

❷ 王老師的課，你上過嗎？
　Wáng lǎoshī de kè, nǐ shàngguò ma?
　Have you ever taken Miss Wang's class before?

❸ 他以前是不是看過那本書？
　Tā yǐqián shìbúshì kànguò nà běn shū?
　Has he read that book before?

Usage

(1) The experience marker, 過, usually combines with non-specific time references, such as 以前 yǐqián 'before', 小時候 xiǎoshíhòu 'when I was young', and not specific references, such as 昨天 zuótiān 'yesterday' or 上午十點半 shàngwǔ shídiǎnbàn '10:30am'.

(2) Verb＋過 vs. Verb＋了 :
The differences between 過 and 了 are often subtle, both referring to the occurrence of instances and activities in the past though 了 can be used with future actions. Remember that 過 refers to experience, which can repeat, whereas 了 refers to a single occurrence at a specific past. Please compare the following pairs of sentences.

❶ a. 他去過很多國家。(to date)
　　Tā qùguò hěn duō guójiā.

　b. 他去了很多國家。(during his last trip)
　　Tā qùle hěn duō guójiā.

❷ a. 他點過日本菜。(He is experienced. Let's ask him for his advice.)
　　Tā diǎnguò Rìběn cài.

　b. 他點了日本菜。(for our get-together last week)
　　Tā diǎnle Rìběn cài.

過, guò, (Ptc), Phase Aspect Marker, Completion of Action (2)

Function The 過 here follows an action verb, indicating that the said action is completed. It is different from the experiential 過.

❶ 你們吃過餃子再吃菜。
　Nǐmen chīguò jiǎozi zài chī cài.
　Eat the dished before you have done with the dumplings.

❷ 大家今天都跑過一千公尺了。
　Dàjiā jīntiān dōu pǎoguò yìqiān gōngchǐ le.
　Everyone ran 1000 meters today (as expected).

❸ 垃圾車剛剛來過了。
　Lèsè chē gānggāng láiguò le.
　The garbage truck has already been here (for the day).

Completion 過 is a member of 'phase' aspect. It refers to completion, not experience.

Structures V＋過

Negation :

❶ 他們還沒吃午飯。
　Tāmen hái méi chī wǔfàn.
　They haven't had lunch yet.

❷ 這個月他還沒付房租。
　Zhè ge yuè tā hái méi fù fángzū.
　He hasn't paid this month's rent.

❸ 今天我還沒練習太極拳。
　Jīntiān wǒ hái méi liànxí Tàijí quán.
　I haven't practiced Tai Chi today.

Questions :

❶ 你喝過咖啡了嗎？
　Nǐ hēguò kāfēi le ma?
　Have you had your coffee already?

❷ 新年大家見過面了沒有？
Xīnnián dàjiā jiànguò miàn le méi yǒu?
Has everyone already seen each other in the New Year?

❸ 那個電影你已經看過了嗎？
Nà ge diànyǐng nǐ yǐjīng kànguò le ma?
Have you already finished watching that movie?

Usage

The 過 indicating completion of an action is a phase maker, placed after an action verb in the form of V＋過. Despite indicating completion, 過 differs functionally from other phase markers 完wán and 好hǎo. Where as V 完 and V 好 simply indicate completion, implicit in V 過 is that something has been completed and repetition is unnecessary. Compare the following sentences:

❶ 我做完功課了。
Wǒ zuòwán gōngkè le.
I finished my homework. (and I can do something else now.)

❷ 我做好功課了。
Wǒ zuòhǎo gōngkè le.
I finished my homework. (and I am all set.)

❸ 我做過功課了。
Wǒ zuòguò gōngkè le.
I have already finished my homework (and I don't need to do it anymore).

The first two sentences (V 完 and V 好) simply state the fact that homework has been completed. The third sentence (V 過) has added implication, and is often used in response to suggestions like 'shouldn't you do your homework?' or 'go do your homework'. See below for further examples.

❶ A：要不要喝咖啡？
Yào bú yào hē kāfēi?
Would you like some coffee?

　B：我剛剛喝過（咖啡）了。
Wǒ gānggāng hēguò (kāfēi) le.
(No,) I just had some.

❷ A：快考試了，趕快去看書。
Kuài kǎoshì le, gǎnkuài qù kànshū.
There is a test coming up, you should be studying.

　B：我已經看過（書）了。
Wǒ yǐjīng kànguò (shū) le.
I have already studied (and I am ready for the test).

❸ A：等一下我們去跑步吧！
Děng yíxià wǒmen qù pǎobù ba!
Let's go for a run!

141

B：我們昨天不是已經跑過了嗎？

Wǒmen zuótiān búshì yǐjīng pǎoguò le ma?

Didn't we already go running yesterday?

還, hái, (Adv), still (unchanged, incomplete) (1)

Function
The adverb 還 indicates that a situation in question remains unchanged or in a certain state, 'still'.

❶ 現在時間還早，學生都還沒到。

Xiànzài shíjiān hái zǎo, xuéshēng dōu hái méi dào.

It's still too early. The students haven't arrived yet.

❷ 來的客人還太少，喜宴還不能開始。

Lái de kèrén hái tài shǎo, xǐyàn hái bù néng kāishǐ.

A lot of our guests are not here yet. The wedding reception can't start yet.

❸ 現在天氣還太冷，不可以去游泳。

Xiànzài tiānqì hái tài lěng, bù kěyǐ qù yóuyǒng.

It's still too cold yet for swimming.

Structures
When there is more than one adverb in a sentence, 還 occurs before other adverbs (except 也yě), including negation. This is referred to as 'hierarchy' of adverbs. 也 is on top, followed by 還.

Negation :

❶ 我的錢還不夠，不能付學費。

Wǒ de qián hái bú gòu, bù néng fù xuéfèi.

I still don't have enough money. I can't pay tuition.

❷ 現在天氣還不熱，我們去東部旅行吧！

Xiànzài tiānqì hái bú rè, wǒmen qù dōngbù lǚxíng ba!

It's not too hot (there) yet. Let's take a trip to the east. (i.e., eastern Taiwan)

❸ 他剛回國，找工作還不順利。

Tā gāng huíguó, zhǎo gōngzuò hái bú shùnlì.

He just returned from overseas. His job situation still isn't going smoothly.

Questions :
Whenever an adverb is used in a sentence, the 是不是shìbúshì question structure is used in front of it.

❶ 你的錢是不是還不夠租套房？

Nǐ de qián shìbúshì hái bú gòu zū tàofáng?

Do you not have enough money to rent a flat?

❷ 你喝得這麼慢，牛肉湯還很熱嗎？

Nǐ hē de zhème màn, niúròu tāng hái hěn rè ma?

You are eating that bowl of beef soup rather slowly. Is it still hot?

❸ 十二點的飛機，現在六點，去機場是不是還太早？

Shí'èrdiǎn de fēijī, xiànzài liùdiǎn, qù jīchǎng shìbúshì hái tài zǎo?

The flight is at 12:00. It's now six. Isn't it too early to go to the airport?

> **Usage**

The adverb 還 has a variety of meanings and English translations depend on context.

(1) 'still, yet'

❶ 我們還沒決定。你有什麼建議？

Wǒmen hái méi juédìng. Nǐ yǒu shénme jiànyì?

We haven't made the decision yet. Do you have any suggestions?

❷ 可是我說中文，還說得不夠流利。

Kěshì wǒ shuō Zhōngwén, hái shuō de bú gòu liúlì.

However, I still do not speak Chinese fluently enough.

❸ 菜還很多，你要多吃一點。

Cài hái hěn duō, nǐ yào duō chī yìdiǎn.

There's still plenty of food. Have some more.

❹ 這個工作的薪水還不夠付小孩的學費，他得再找另外一個工作。

Zhè ge gōngzuò de xīnshuǐ hái bú gòu fù xiǎohái de xuéfèi, tā děi zài zhǎo lìngwài yí ge gōngzuò.

The pay for this job is not enough to cover his child's school fees. He has to find another job.

(2) 'additionally, in addition to'

❶ 昨天晚上肚子很不舒服，還吐了好幾次。

Zuótiān wǎnshàng dùzi hěn bù shūfú, hái tùle hǎojǐ cì.

Last night, my stomach didn't feel well. I even threw up several times.

❷ 下了課要寫作業，還要準備第二天的課。

Xiàle kè yào xiě zuòyè, hái yào zhǔnbèi dìèr tiān de kè.

After class, homework has to be done and class for the following day prepared for. (Or After class, I/we/you have to do homework and prepare for class the next day.)

❸ 他還有兩個姐姐。

Tā hái yǒu liǎng ge jiějie.

He has two more sisters.

還, hái, (Adv), to my surprise (2)

> **Function**

This adverb expresses the speaker's surprise at something. Surprise comes not as expected.

❶ 我的鄰居太熱情了，我還真不習慣。

Wǒ de línjū tài rèqíng le, wǒ hái zhēn bù xíguàn.

My neighbors are a little too welcoming, and I'm really not used to it.

❷ 昨天的火鍋還真辣，害我肚子很不舒服。

Zuótiān de huǒguō hái zhēn là, hài wǒ dùzi hěn bù shūfú.

The hot pot we had yesterday was very spicy, so much so that it gave me a stomachache.

❸ 昨晚的地震搖得還真厲害，把我嚇了一大跳。

Zuówǎn de dìzhèn yáo de hái zhēn lìhài, bǎ wǒ xià le yídàtiào.

The earthquake last night shook something fierce and scared me half to death.

❹ 他每天都要運動一個小時，習慣還滿好的！

Tā měi tiān dōu yào yùndòng yí ge xiǎoshí, xíguàn hái mǎn hǎo de!

He excercises for an hour every day. What a great routine!

❺ 我以為他吉他彈得不好，其實他彈得還滿不錯的。

Wǒ yǐwéi tā jítā tán de bù hǎo, qíshí tā tán de hái mǎn búcuò de.

I thought he was lousy at guitar, but it turns out he is actually pretty good.

Usage　還 is often followed by an adverb of degree, such as 真 or 滿 (蠻). See examples above.

還是 A 吧, (háishì (Adv) A ba (Ptc)), it will be better if A, it would be best if A

Function　還是, an adverb, indicates that the A-sentence is the best option given the circumstances. The sentence always ends with the particle 吧.

❶ 我最近很忙，我們還是週末再出去吃飯吧！

Wǒ zuìjìn hěn máng, wǒmen háishì zhōumò zài chūqù chīfàn ba!

I've been very busy lately. It would be best if we went out to eat on the weekend.

❷ 已經晚上11點了。我還是明天早上再給老師打電話吧！

Yǐjīng wǎnshàng 11 diǎn le. Wǒ háishì míngtiān zǎoshàng zài gěi lǎoshī dǎ diànhuà ba!

It's already 11 o'clock, I should probabaly wait until tomorrow morning to call the teacher.

❸ 去學校，可以坐公車，也可以坐捷運，但是坐捷運應該比較快，我們還是坐捷運去吧。

Qù xuéxiào, kěyǐ zuò gōngchē, yě kěyǐ zuò jiéyùn, dànshì zuò jiéyùn yīnggāi bǐjiào kuài, wǒmen háishì zuò jiéyùn qù ba.

You can get to school by bus or MRT, but the MRT is faster, so that's what we should take.

Structures　還是, being an adverb (lexicalized), occurs between the subject and the verb, and 吧 is placed at the sentence-final position.

Negation :

❶ 坐公車很慢。我們還是不要坐公車吧！
Zuò gōngchē hěn màn. Wǒmen háishì bú yào zuò gōngchē ba!
Buses are slow. We probably shouldn't take the bus.

❷ 雨下得很大。今天你還是別回家吧！
Yǔ xià de hěn dà. Jīntiān nǐ háishì bié huí jiā ba!
It's raining hard. You probabaly shouldn't go home today.

❸ 他聽了一定不開心。你還是別告訴他吧！
Tā tīngle yídìng bù kāixīn. Nǐ háishì bié gàosù tā ba!
If he hears about it, he'll be upset. You probably shouldn't tell him.

> **Usage**

The use of 還是 adds much to politeness in communication. It's a mitigated suggestion, rather than a blunt command.

好, hǎo, as in 好＋Verb, nice to, easy to　(1)

> **Function**

(1) When 好 or 難 combines with sense verbs, they become single words, i.e., lexicalized.

好吃 hǎochī, nice to eat	難吃 nánchī, not nice to eat
好喝 hǎohē, nice to drink	難喝 nánhē, not nice to drink
好看 hǎokàn, nice-looking	難看 nánkàn, not nice-looking, ugly
好聽 hǎotīng, nice to listen to	難聽 nántīng, not nice to listen to

(2) When they combine with action verbs, 好 means 'easy to' and 難 'difficult/hard to', i.e., parts of special constructions.

好學 hǎo xué, easy to learn	難學 nán xué, hard to learn
好寫 hǎo xiě, easy to write	難寫 nán xiě, hard to write
好做 hǎo zuò, easy to do	難做 nán zuò, hard to do
好找 hǎo zhǎo, easy to find	難找 nán zhǎo, hard to find

❶ 日本菜好吃也好看。
Rìběn cài hǎochī yě hǎokàn.
Japanese food is both delicious and visually pleasing.

❷ 好工作很難找。
Hǎo gōngzuò hěn nán zhǎo.
Finding a good job is difficult.

❸ 這首歌好聽也好唱。

Zhè shǒu gē hǎotīng yě hǎo chàng.

This song is both nice to listen to and easy to sing.

Structures Intensification adverbs such as 很 'very' can modify both structures given above.

❶ 我媽媽做的菜很好吃。

Wǒ māma zuò de cài hěn hǎochī.

The food my mom makes is (very) delicious.

❷ 有人覺得中文很難學。

Yǒu rén juéde Zhōngwén hěn nán xué.

Some people think that Chinese is (very) hard to learn.

*N*egation :

(1) With sense verbs:

❶ 便宜的咖啡不好喝。

Piányí de kāfēi bù hǎohē.

Cheap coffee doesn't taste good.

❷ 學校餐廳的菜不難吃。

Xuéxiào cāntīng de cài bù nánchī.

School cafeteria food tastes okay.

❸ 這首歌，唱得太慢不好聽。

Zhè shǒu gē, chàng de tài màn bù hǎotīng.

This song does not sound nice if sung too slowly.

(2) With action verbs:

❶ 這家店賣的小籠包不好做。

Zhè jiā diàn mài de xiǎolóngbāo bù hǎo zuò.

The steamed dumplings sold at this shop are hard to make.

❷ 老師常常說中文不難學。

Lǎoshī chángcháng shuō Zhōngwén bù nán xué.

The teacher often says that Chinese is not difficult to learn.

❸ 學校附近便宜的套房不好找。

Xuéxiào fùjìn piányí de tàofáng bù hǎo zhǎo.

Suites near the school that are cheap to rent are hard to find.

*Q*uestions :

(1) With sense verbs:

❶ 旅館老闆買的水果好吃嗎？

Lǚguǎn lǎobǎn mǎi de shuǐguǒ hǎochī ma?

Does the fruit bought by the hotel owner taste good?

❷ 你覺得那個電影好不好看？

Nǐ juéde nà ge diànyǐng hǎo bù hǎokàn?

Do you think that movie was good or bad?

❸ 點烏龍茶的那個先生唱歌唱得好聽嗎？
Diǎn Wūlóng chá de nà ge xiānshēng chànggē chàng de hǎotīng ma?
Does the man who ordered Oolong tea sing well?

(2) With action verbs:

❶ 説中文的工作在你的國家好找嗎？
Shuō Zhōngwén de gōngzuò zài nǐ de guójiā hǎo zhǎo ma?
Are jobs in which you speak Chinese easy to find in your country?

❷ 又大又貴的房子好不好賣？
Yòu dà yòu guì de fángzi hǎo bù hǎo mài?
Are big and expensive houses easy to sell?

❸ 老師今天教的甜點難不難學？
Lǎoshī jīntiān jiāo de tiándiǎn nán bù nán xué?
Are the desserts that the teacher taught us (to make) today difficult to make?

好, hǎo, (Ptc), as Verb Complement, all set and ready (2)

Function

好 functions as a verb complement here, meaning the action has now been properly executed and properly concluded.

❶ 我昨天搬家。因為同學幫忙，很快就搬好了。
Wǒ zuótiān bānjiā. Yīnwèi tóngxué bāngmáng, hěn kuài jiù bānhǎo le.
I moved yesterday. Because my classmates helped, I moved very quickly.

❷ 明天的考試，我都準備好了。
Míngtiān de kǎoshì, wǒ dōu zhǔnbèihǎo le.
I am all prepared for tomorrow's exam.

❸ 我把去旅行的時候需要的資料都找好了。
Wǒ bǎ qù lǚxíng de shíhòu xūyào de zīliào dōu zhǎohǎo le.
I've collected all the information I'll need for my trip.

Structures

Negation :

Only 沒 negation can be used. This is the case whenever there are verb complements.

❶ 雖然我已經寫了三個小時的功課，可是還沒寫好。
Suīrán wǒ yǐjīng xiěle sān ge xiǎoshí de gōngkè, kěshì hái méi xiěhǎo.
Although I've been working on the homework for three hours, I still haven't finished it yet.

❷ 下星期我要參加太極拳比賽，但是我還沒準備好。

Xià xīngqí wǒ yào cānjiā Tàijí quán bǐsài, dànshì wǒ hái méi zhǔnbèihǎo.

Next week, I'm competing in a Tai Chi competition, but I'm not ready yet.

❸ 我還沒想好搭什麼車到台南去。

Wǒ hái méi xiǎnghǎo dā shénme chē dào Táinán qù.

I haven't decided what mode of transportation to take to go to Tainan.

*Q*uestions :

❶ 你是不是買好火車票了？

Nǐ shìbúshì mǎihǎo huǒchē piào le?

Have you already bought the train tickets?

❷ 她結婚需要的禮服，都準備好了沒有？

Tā jiéhūn xūyào de lǐfú, dōu zhǔnbèihǎo le méi yǒu?

Is the gown she'll need for the wedding all set and ready?

❸ 這個新的工作，你一個人做得好做不好？

Zhè ge xīn de gōngzuò, nǐ yí ge rén zuòdehǎo zuòbùhǎo?

Are you able to do this new work by yourself?

Usage

(1) The post-verbals 好hǎo and 完wán overlap somehow in meaning, both implying completion of tasks.

(2) Some verbs combine with 好 fully, while others do not. See the table below. Neat rules are not easily established.

	Actual		Potential	
	V 好	沒 V 好	V 得好	V 不好
搬bān 'to move'	✓	✓	✓	✓
寫xiě 'to write'	✓	✓	✓	✓
想xiǎng 'to think'	✓	✓	✗	✗
做zuò 'to do'	✓	✓	✓	✓
準備zhǔnbèi 'to prepare'	✓	✓	✓	✓
買mǎi 'to buy'	✓	✓	✗	✗
賣mài 'to sell'	✗	✗	✗	✗
吃chī 'to eat'	✗	✗	✗	✗

好不容易, hǎobù róngyì , (idiom), only after a tremendous amount of...

Function

The idiomatic phrase 好不容易 indicates the hard-won realization of a favorable situation. It means roughly 'only after much persuasion, much trying, much effort...'.

1 爸爸好不容易才答應讓我去美國念書。我一定要更用功。
Bàba hǎobù róngyì cái dāyìng ràng wǒ qù Měiguó niànshū. Wǒ yídìng yào gèng yònggōng.
After a great deal of effort (on somebody's part), Dad finally agreed to let me study in the US, so I'm going to make a point of working even harder.

2 你好不容易拿到獎學金,怎麼就要回國了?
Nǐ hǎobù róngyì nádào jiǎngxuéjīn, zěnme jiù yào huíguó le?
You finally managed to get a scholarship. How come you're going back home?

3 下了兩星期的雨,今天好不容易才停。
Xiàle liǎng xīngqí de yǔ, jīntiān hǎobù róngyì cái tíng.
After two weeks of rain, it finally managed to stop today.

4 好不容易看到一雙喜歡的鞋子,沒想到這麼貴。
Hǎobù róngyì kàndào yì shuāng xǐhuān de xiézi, méi xiǎngdào zhème guì.
I finally managed to find a pair of shoes that I like. I had no idea it'd be so expensive.

5 他做了一大碗豬腳麵線,我好不容易才吃完。
Tā zuòle yí dà wǎn zhūjiǎo miànxiàn, wǒ hǎobù róngyì cái chī wán.
He made a huge bowl of pork knuckle rice threads that I barely managed to finish.

何必, hébì, (Adv), why must

Function ▶ The adverb 何必 indicates that the speaker finds no justification for the subject's course of action.

1 東西丟了可以買新的。你何必那麼難過?
Dōngxi diūle kěyǐ mǎi xīn de. Nǐ hébì nàme nánguò?
You can buy a replacement for what you lost. Why must you be so upset?

2 外面天氣那麼好應該出去走走。何必在家看電視?
Wàimiàn tiānqì nàme hǎo yīnggāi chūqù zǒuzǒu. Hébì zài jiā kàn diànshì?
We should go out and enjoy the beautiful weather. Why sit at home and watch TV?

3 春天天氣已經不冷了。何必穿那麼多?
Chūntiān tiānqì yǐjīng bù lěng le. Hébì chuān nàme duō?
It's spring already, and it's warm outside. Must you wear so much?

4 他何必去打工?他的爸爸給他那麼多錢。
Tā hébì qù dǎgōng? Tā de bàba gěi tā nàme duō qián.
Does he really have to work part-time? His dad gives him plenty of money.

⑤ 何必買新的？舊的電腦還可以用啊！

Hébì mǎi xīn de? Jiù de diànnǎo hái kěyǐ yòng a!

Why buy a new one? The old computer still works!

Usage　Adding 呢 to the end of the above sentences softens the tone, making the statement more comforting and less abrupt, e.g., 只是小感冒，何必看醫生呢？Zhǐshì xiǎo gǎnmào, hébì kàn yīshēng ne? 'It's just a little cold. Why see a doctor?'

何況, hékuàng, (Adv), let alone, no need to mention

Function　The adverb 何況 states that if a previous statement is true, how about the next.

① 連膽子那麼大的人都怕，更何況我這個膽子小的人？

Lián dǎnzi nàme dà de rén dōu pà, gèng hékuàng wǒ zhè ge dǎnzi xiǎo de rén?

Even people who have guts get afraid, let alone someone as timid as me.

② 你那麼年輕都走不動了，更何況我這個銀髮族？

Nǐ nàme niánqīng dōu zǒubúdòng le, gèng hékuàng wǒ zhè ge yínfǎzú?

Even someone as young as you can't keep walking, never mind someone with grey hair like me.

③ 光布置一個小房間就花了那麼多時間，何況布置那麼大的客廳呢？

Guāng bùzhì yí ge xiǎo fángjiān jiù huāle nàme duō shíjiān, hékuàng bùzhì nàme dà de kètīng ne?

Decorating even a small room takes lots of time, never mind a big living room.

④ 在現實生活中，他們都會批評你，何況在網路的世界裡呢？

Zài xiànshí shēnghuó zhōng, tāmen dōu huì pīpíng nǐ, hékuàng zài wǎnglù de shìjiè lǐ ne?

Even in real life they'll criticize you, let alone on the internet.

⑤ 再大的困難我們都可以解決，更何況這一點小事？

Zài dà de kùnnán wǒmen dōu kěyǐ jiějué, gèng hékuàng zhè yìdiǎn xiǎo shì?

We could easily tackle a bigger problem yet, let alone this trivial one.

Usage

(1) 更 is often placed in front of 何況, see (**①**, **②** and **⑤**) above.

(2) 何況 often follows a 連 A 都 B pattern (even that is true) in the initial sentence, e.g.,

　　① 連那些藝術家都看不懂，更何況我呢？

　　　　Lián nàxiē yìshùjiā dōu kànbùdǒng, gèng hékuàng wǒ ne?

　　　　Even those artists don't understand, never mind me.

❷ 連你學了十年的小提琴都不敢表演了，更何況我才學了一年？

Lián nǐ xuéle shí nián de xiǎotíqín dōu bù gǎn biǎoyǎn le, gèng hékuàng wǒ cái xuéle yì nián?

Even somebody like you who has studied violin for ten years can't bring yourself to perform, how could somebody like me do it, who has only studied for one year?

❸ 連我都覺得穿這種衣服不足為奇，更何況你這種追求流行的人？

Lián wǒ dōu juéde chuān zhè zhǒng yīfú bùzú wéiqí, gèng hékuàng nǐ zhè zhǒng zhuīqiú liúxíng de rén?

Even I think nothing of wearing clothing like this, never mind somebody like you who is really into fashion.

很, hěn, (Adv), Intensification Marker

Function

The adverb 很 intensifies state verbs (Vs).

❶ 我很好。

Wǒ hěn hǎo.

I am fine.

❷ 他很喜歡臺灣。

Tā hěn xǐhuān Táiwān.

He likes Taiwan.

❸ 臺灣人很喜歡喝烏龍茶。

Táiwān rén hěn xǐhuān hē Wūlóng chá.

Taiwanese people like to drink Oolong tea.

Structures

The adverb 很hěn is placed before state verbs (Vs) as follows: Subject ＋很hěn＋State Verb.

❶ 烏龍茶很好喝。

Wūlóng chá hěn hǎohē.

Oolong tea tastes good.

❷ 他很喜歡日本人。

Tā hěn xǐhuān Rìběn rén.

He likes Japanese people.

❸ 我們很好。

Wǒmen hěn hǎo.

We are fine.

Usage

In general, adjectival state verbs as predicates must be preceded by either 不 or intensifiers. When no particular intensity is intended, they are preceded by a weak 很. When 很 is intended to actually mean 'very', it is typically stressed in speech and is frequently replaceable by 好hǎo 'very'. Lastly, note that the structure, 'The cat is pretty' is expressed as 'The cat 很 pretty'.

恨不得, hènbùdé, one really wishes one could...

Function　The phrase 恨不得 expresses a strong desire to do something against all odds.

❶ 住在美國時，我真恨不得每天早上都能吃到燒餅油條或中式飯糰。

Zhù zài Měiguó shí, wǒ zhēn hènbùdé měi tiān zǎoshàng dōu néng chīdào shāobǐng yóutiáo huò Zhōngshì fàntuán.

When I was living in the US, every morning I wanted so badly to have those deep fried breadsticks wrapped in a roll and Chinese style onigri.

❷ 他好不容易考上了熱門科系。念了一個學期卻發現興趣不合，念得很痛苦，恨不得能馬上轉系。

Tā hǎobù róngyì kǎoshàngle rèmén kēxì. Niànle yí gè xuéqí què fāxiàn xìngqù bù hé, niàn de hěn tòngkǔ, hènbùdé néng mǎshàng zhuǎn xì.

He worked so hard to get into a good department in university, but after struggling for one term he found out it wasn't for him, and wanted nothing more than to change majors.

❸ 水餃被我煮破了不少，不夠的話怎麼辦？真恨不得我們還有時間能再包一些。可是我們得出門了。

Shuǐjiǎo bèi wǒ zhǔpòle bù shǎo, bú gòu de huà zěnmebàn? Zhēn hènbùdé wǒmen hái yǒu shíjiān néng zài bāo yìxiē. Kěshì wǒmen děi chūmén le.

I over-boiled quite some of the dumplings, some split open. What if there isn't enough? I really wish we had the time to make some more, but we have to get going soon.

❹ 要不是我媽媽反對，我也恨不得能跟你們一起去參加反核遊行。

Yàobúshì wǒ māma fǎnduì, wǒ yě hènbùdé néng gēn nǐmen yìqǐ qù cānjiā fǎnhé yóuxíng.

Too bad my mom is against it. I really wish I could join up for the rally against nuclear energy.

❺ 走路走得腿痛死了，真恨不得能搭計程車過去，可惜錢包裡只有 50塊錢。

Zǒulù zǒu de tuǐ tòng sǐle, zhēn hènbùdé néng dā jìchéngchē guòqù, kěxí qiánbāo lǐ zhǐ yǒu 50 kuài qián.

My legs are so sore from walking, and I want nothing more than to take a taxi. Too bad I only have 50 dollars in my wallet.

Usage

(1) Most often used with auxiliary verbs like 想, 要, 可以, 能. This phrase cannot be used in the negative. E.g.,

＊我恨不得不可以馬上回家。

＊Wǒ hènbùdé bù kěyǐ mǎshàng huíjiā.

(2) All pronouns can serve as the subject, though 'I' is the commonest.

後來, hòulái, (Adv), next in sequence

Function

然後(Adv), 後來(Adv) and 以後(Noun) all refer to an instance next to another in occurrence. See the table below about their compatibility with the reference of time.

	Past	Future
然後	✓	✓
後來	✓	✗
以後	✗	✓

① 我們先去台中玩了一天，然後去了墾丁。
Wǒmen xiān qù Táizhōng wánle yì tiān, ránhòu qùle Kěndīng.
We first visited Taichung for a day, and then we went to Kenting.

② 請你把菜洗一洗，然後開始煮湯！
Qǐng nǐ bǎ cài xǐ yì xǐ, ránhòu kāishǐ zhǔ tāng!
Please wash the vegetables, and then start cooking the soup.

③ 我本來不想學太極拳，後來發現有趣得不得了，就去學了。
Wǒ běnlái bù xiǎng xué Tàijí quán, hòulái fāxiàn yǒuqù de bùdéliǎo, jiù qù xué le.
I originally had no interest in learning Tai Chi. Later, I discovered it was incredibly interesting, so I went and studied it.

④ 我以為弟弟今天回國，後來才知道他明天才回來。
Wǒ yǐwéi dìdi jīntiān huíguó, hòulái cái zhīdào tā míngtiān cái huílái.
I thought my younger brother was coming home today. I didn't know until later that he would not be back until tomorrow.

⑤ 雖然現在我還不會騎腳踏車，可是以後一定能學會。
Suīrán xiànzài wǒ hái bú huì qí jiǎotàchē, kěshì yǐhòu yídìng néng xuéhuì.
Although I can't ride a bike now, I will definitely be able to in the future.

⑥ 今年我們去日本，以後再去越南。
Jīnnián wǒmen qù Rìběn, yǐhòu zài qù Yuènán.
This year, we'll go to Japan. We'll go to Vietnam later.

Structures

Questions :

① 你本來想去日月潭，後來怎麼沒去呢？
Nǐ běnlái xiǎng qù Rìyuètán, hòulái zěnme méi qù ne?
You originally were thinking of going to Sun Moon Lake. How come you didn't later?

② 昨天你的錢包不見了，後來怎麼找到的？
Zuótiān nǐ de qiánbāo bújiàn le, hòulái zěnme zhǎodào de?
Yesterday, you lost your wallet. How did you find it later?

❸ 墾丁真的那麼浪漫嗎？值得你以後再去一趟啊？
Kěndīng zhēnde nàme làngmàn ma? Zhíde nǐ yǐhòu zài qù yí tàng a?
Is Kenting really that romantic? Would it be worth going again in the future?

❹ 學費越來越高了，我們的小孩以後會不會念不起大學？
Xuéfèi yuèláiyuè gāo le, wǒmen de xiǎohái yǐhòu huì bú huì niànbùqǐ dàxué?
With tuition steadily rising, I wonder if it will be affordable for our children to attend university in the future?

Usage

(1) Both 然後 and 後來 are adverbs and are used in similar situations. However, 然後 is used to connect two instances that take place consecutively, while 後來 indicates a lapse of time between two instances.

❶ 我們明天早上先去傳統市場買菜，然後再去超市買水果。
Wǒmen míngtiān zǎoshàng xiān qù chuántǒng shìchǎng mǎi cài, ránhòu zài qù chāoshì mǎi shuǐguǒ.
Tomorrow morning let's first go to the traditional market to buy vegetables, and then to the supermarket for fruit.

❷ 我們昨天早上去傳統市場買菜，後來又去超市買水果。
Wǒmen zuótiān zǎoshàng qù chuántǒng shìchǎng mǎi cài, hòulái yòu qù chāoshì mǎi shuǐguǒ.
Yesterday morning we first went to the traditional market to buy vegetables, and then to the supermarket for fruit.

(2) Also note that 以後 can also be used to connect two instances, either in the past or in the future.

❶ 白小姐到了臺灣以後，就沒回過國。
Bái xiǎojiě dàole Táiwān yǐhòu, jiù méi huíguò guó.
Miss Bai hasn't gone back to her home country ever since she came to Taiwan.

❷ 你們到了韓國以後，要打電話給我。
Nǐmen dàole Hánguó yǐhòu, yào dǎ diànhuà gěi wǒ.
Call me after you arrive in Korea.

會, huì, (Vaux), acquired skills, can, able to (1)

Function The modal verb 會 refers to skills that are acquired through learning, i.e., they are cognitive abilities, e.g., know how to.

❶ 陳小姐會做飯。
Chén xiǎojiě huì zuòfàn.
Miss Chen can cook.

❷ 他哥哥會踢足球。
Tā gēge huì tī zúqiú.
His older brother knows how to play soccer.

③ 他們兄弟姐妹都會游泳。
Tāmen xiōngdì jiěmèi dōu huì yóuyǒng.
All of those siblings know how to swim.

Structures　會 is an auxiliary verb and can be negated and can enter the A-not-A pattern.

*N*egation :

❶ 他的媽媽不會做飯。
Tā de māma bú huì zuòfàn.
His mom can't cook.

❷ 我媽媽不會做甜點。
Wǒ māma bú huì zuò tiándiǎn.
My mom does not know how to make desserts.

❸ 我的家人都不會打棒球。
Wǒ de jiārén dōu bú huì dǎ bàngqiú.
None of the members of my family knows how to play baseball.

*Q*uestions :

❶ 你會做甜點嗎？
Nǐ huì zuò tiándiǎn ma?
Do you know how to make desserts?

❷ 他弟弟會踢足球嗎？
Tā dìdi huì tī zúqiú ma?
Does his younger brother know how to play football?

❸ 你會不會說中文？
Nǐ huì bú huì shuō Zhōngwén?
Do you know how to speak Chinese?

❹ 你的姐姐會不會做飯？
Nǐ de jiějie huì bú huì zuòfàn?
Does your elder sister know how to cook?

Usage　會 can also be a main transitive verb, only in a small number of cases, e.g.,

❶ 我不會俄文。
Wǒ bú huì Éwén.
I can't speak Russian.

❷ 日語，我們都不會。
Rìyǔ, wǒmen dōu bú huì.
None of us can speak Japanese.

會, huì, (Vaux), likelihood (2)

Function　The modal 會 can also refer to the likelihood of an event, e.g.,

❶ 明天大概會下雨。
Míngtiān dàgài huì xiàyǔ.
It will probably rain tomorrow.

❷ 新出來的手機一定會漲價。
Xīn chūlái de shǒujī yídìng huì zhǎngjià.
Newly released cell phones will definitely cost more.

❸ 坐飛機會比開車快很多。
Zuò fēijī huì bǐ kāi chē kuài hěn duō.
Taking a plane will be much faster than driving.

Structures

The structure relating to this meaning of 會 are identical to those given under 會₁.

會, huì, (Vaux), as Verb Complement　(3)

Function

會 is most often an auxiliary verb, but it can also serve as a verb complement of such verbs as 學xué, 教jiāo, 練liàn to express the result of 'mastery', 'achievement' and 'proficiency'.

❶ 我在大學的時候學會怎麼開車。
Wǒ zài dàxué de shíhòu xuéhuì zěnme kāi chē.
I learned how to drive a car when I was in university.

❷ 只有一個鐘頭的課，老師要教會學生怎麼寫書法很難。
Zhǐ yǒu yí ge zhōngtóu de kè, lǎoshī yào jiāohuì xuéshēng zěnme xiě shūfǎ hěn nán.
It would be difficult to teach students how to write calligraphy (and do well) in just one 1-hour class.

❸ 學生學會了用中文介紹自己。
Xuéshēng xuéhuìle yòng Zhōngwén jièshào zìjǐ.
The students learned how to introduce themselves in Chinese.

Structures

*N*egation :

❶ 我學游泳只學了一個禮拜，還沒學會。
Wǒ xué yóuyǒng zhǐ xuéle yí ge lǐbài, hái méi xuéhuì.
I have been learning how to swim for only one week, I can't quite do it yet.

❷ 師父教了兩個星期了，還沒教會他太極拳最難的動作。
Shīfù jiāole liǎng ge xīngqí le, hái méi jiāohuì tā Tàijí quán zuì nán de dòngzuò.
After two weeks of classes the Master has yet to successfully teach him the most difficult Tai Chi move.

❸ 我們都沒學會怎麼騎腳踏車。
Wǒmen dōu méi xuéhuì zěnme qí jiǎotàchē.
None of us learned how to ride a bike.

Questions :

❶ 這些字你是不是都學會了？
Zhèxiē zì nǐ shìbúshì dōu xuéhuì le?
Have you learned all these characters?

❷ 太極拳學了這麼久，你還沒學會啊？
Tàijí quán xuéle zhème jiǔ, nǐ hái méi xuéhuì a?
You've been studying Tai Chi for such a long time and you haven't mastered it yet?

❸ 你教會了那些小孩踢足球了沒有？
Nǐ jiāohuìle nàxiē xiǎohái tī zúqiú le méi yǒu?
Have you succeeded in teaching those kids to play soccer?

既 A 又 B, (jì (Adv) A yòu (Adv) B), not only A, but also B

Function ▶

This structure indicates that the subject has two things associated at the same time.

❶ 打工的好處很多。既可以賺錢，又可以交朋友。
Dǎgōng de hǎochù hěn duō. Jì kěyǐ zhuànqián, yòu kěyǐ jiāo péngyǒu.
Working part time has a lot of advantages. Not only can you make money, but you can also make friends.

❷ 單親爸爸既要賺錢養家，又要照顧孩子，非常辛苦。
Dānqīn bàba jì yào zhuànqián yǎngjiā, yòu yào zhàogù háizi, fēicháng xīnkǔ.
Single dads not only have to make money to raise their families, they also have to take care of their kids. It's really tough.

❸ 廣告上這種最新型的手機，款式既新，功能又多，應該很快就會流行起來。
Guǎnggào shàng zhè zhǒng zuì xīn xíng de shǒujī, kuǎnshì jì xīn, gōngnéng yòu duō, yīnggāi hěn kuài jiù huì liúxíngqǐlái.
The latest cell phone being advertised not only comes in a new style, it also has a lot of functions. It's likely going to catch on fast.

❹ 她人既長得漂亮，外語能力又強，難怪是學校裡的風雲人物。
Tā rén jì zhǎng de piàoliàng, wàiyǔ nénglì yòu qiáng, nánguài shì xuéxiào lǐ de fēngyún rénwù.
She's not only pretty, but her foreign language skills are also very good. It's no wonder she is so well known throughout the school.

❺ 張先生對吃特別講究，他吃的東西既要味道好，顏色又要美。
Zhāng xiānshēng duì chī tèbié jiǎngjiù, tā chī de dōngxi jì yào wèidào hǎo, yánsè yòu yào měi.
Mr. Zhang is especially particular about eating. The food he eats has to be both delicious and colorful.

Usage

(1) 既 and 又 are both adverbs and sentences using this pattern refer to one and the same subject.

(2) The use of '既 A 又 B' and '不但 búdàn A 也 yě B' and '又 A 又 B' are very similar, but when a speaker uses 既 A 又 B, the addition is clearly incremental. Compare the following.

❶ 學習外語不但要練習聽和説，也要認字寫字。
Xuéxí wàiyǔ búdàn yào liànxí tīng hàn shuō, yě yào rèn zì xiě zì.
When studying a foreign language, you not only have to practice listening and speaking, you also need to learn to read and write. (Items are of similar importance.)

❷ 學習外語既要練習聽和説，又要認字寫字。
Xuéxí wàiyǔ jì yào liànxí tīng hàn shuō, yòu yào rèn zì xiě zì.
When studying a foreign language, you not only have to practice listening and speaking, you also need to learn to read and write. (Studying languages requires a lot of work.)

(3) Verbs being connected cannot have adverbs of degree. （*既很好看，又很漂亮 *jì hěn hǎokàn, yòu hěn piàoliàng）

(4) 既 A 又 B is more formal and literary than 又 A 又 B. Therefore, the number of syllables in the verbs following both 既 and 又 should be the same as symmetry is important in this pattern.

(5) The meaning of the words that follow 既 and 又 should be both positive or both negative in tone. You cannot say *農夫的社會地位既不高，收入又很穩定。(*Nóngfū de shèhuì dìwèi jì bù gāo, shōurù yòu hěn wěndìng. '*Famers' status is not only low but they have a steady income.')

既然 A 就 B, (jìrán (Conj) A jiù (Adv) B), Concession, since A then B

Function
This pattern presents the speaker's acceptance of the circumstances and her subsequent plans.

❶ 既然天氣這麼不穩定，我們就別去海邊了吧。
Jìrán tiānqì zhème bù wěndìng, wǒmen jiù bié qù hǎibiān le ba.
Since the weather is so unpredictable, let's not go to the seaside.

❷ 既然網路塞車，那就先去運動，晚一點再上網。
Jìrán wǎnglù sāichē, nà jiù xiān qù yùndòng, wǎn yìdiǎn zài shàngwǎng.
Since the internet is congested, let's go exercise first and go online later.

❸ 既然刷 Visa 卡，就可以再打九五折，當然要刷 Visa 卡。
Jìrán shuā Visa kǎ, jiù kěyǐ zài dǎ jiǔwǔ zhé, dāngrán yào shuā Visa kǎ.
Since I can get 5% off if I use a Visa Card, then, of course, I'll use my Visa Card.

❹ 既然吃素對保護地球環境有幫助，以後我們就常吃素食。

Jìrán chī sù duì bǎohù dìqiú huánjìng yǒu bāngzhù, yǐhòu wǒmen jiù cháng chī sùshí.

Since eating vegetarian food helps protect the earth's environment, we should eat vegetarian food more often.

❺ 既然你整天都會待在這裡，我就先去一趟銀行，再回來找你。

Jìrán nǐ zhěngtiān dōu huì dāi zài zhèlǐ, wǒ jiù xiān qù yí tàng yínháng, zài huílái zhǎo nǐ.

Since you'll be here all day, I'll go to the bank and come back later.

Usage

Like all conjunctions, 既然 can be placed before or after the subject. E.g., 既然你不去，我就不去了。～你既然不去，我就不去了。 Jìrán nǐ bú qù, wǒ jiù bú qù le. ~ Nǐ jìrán bú qù, wǒ jiù bú qù le. 'since you're not going, I'm not going either.'

見, jiàn, (Ptc), as Verb Complement, perceived

Function

When 見 follows a perceptual verb, it indicates that the object of an action (such as of seeing or hearing) is perceived.

❶ 昨天我在夜市看見小美了。

Zuótiān wǒ zài yèshì kànjiàn Xiǎoměi le.

Yesterday, I saw Xiaomei at the night market.

❷ 你跟別人說的話，我都聽見了。

Nǐ gēn biérén shuō de huà, wǒ dōu tīngjiàn le.

I heard everything that you said to others.

❸ 我們都看見你把書拿回去了。

Wǒmen dōu kànjiàn nǐ bǎ shū ná huíqù le.

We all saw that you took the book back with you.

Structures

Negation :

Only 沒-negation is possible.

❶ 東西在哪裡？我沒看見啊！

Dōngxi zài nǎlǐ? Wǒ méi kànjiàn a!

Where is it? I didn't see it.

❷ 我沒聽見他說什麼。

Wǒ méi tīngjiàn tā shuō shénme.

I didn't hear what he said.

❸ 請你再說一次，我沒聽見。

Qǐng nǐ zài shuō yí cì, wǒ méi tīngjiàn.

Please say that again. I didn't hear.

Questions :

❶ 我的背包，你看見了沒有？

Wǒ de bēibāo, nǐ kànjiàn le méi yǒu?

Did you see my backpack?

❷ 老師説的，你是不是聽見了？
Lǎoshī shuō de, nǐ shìbúshì tīngjiàn le?
Did you hear what the teacher said?

❸ 張先生呢？你看見他走出來了嗎？
Zhāng xiānshēng ne? Nǐ kànjiàn tā zǒu chūlái le ma?
What about Mr. Zhang? Did you see him come out?

Usage

There's a clear difference in meaning between using a perception verb alone or with the complement 見.

❶ a. 我沒聽他説話。
Wǒ méi tīng tā shuōhuà.
I was not listening to him.

b. 我沒聽見他説話。
Wǒ méi tīngjiàn tā shuōhuà.
I didn't hear him talk.

❷ a. 他想去動物園看熊貓。
Tā xiǎng qù dòngwùyuán kàn xióngmāo.
He wants to go to the zoo and see pandas.

b. 他在動物園看見兩隻熊貓。
Tā zài dòngwùyuán kànjiàn liǎng zhī xióngmāo.
He saw two pandas in the zoo.

漸漸, jiànjiàn, (Adv), gradually, slowly

Function

The adverb 漸漸 defines the gradual completion of a process.

❶ 這裡以前種族歧視的情況非常嚴重。現在這種現象可說已漸漸走入歷史了。
Zhèlǐ yǐqián zhǒngzú qíshì de qíngkuàng fēicháng yánzhòng. Xiànzài zhè zhǒng xiànxiàng kě shuō yǐ jiànjiàn zǒurù lìshǐ le.
Racism used to be a serious problem here, but that is slowly becoming history.

❷ 現在跨國企業的合作已漸漸成為一種趨勢了。
Xiànzài kuàguó qǐyè de hézuò yǐ jiànjiàn chéngwéi yì zhǒng qūshì le.
Cooperation between MNCs has become an emerging trend.

❸ 我回國後，因為工作忙碌，很少有機會跟那個組織聯絡，就漸漸失去了交流的機會。
Wǒ huíguó hòu, yīnwèi gōngzuò mánglù, hěn shǎo yǒu jīhuì gēn nà ge zǔzhī liánluò, jiù jiànjiàn shīqùle jiāoliú de jīhuì.
After coming back to my home country I became so busy with work that I stopped contacting that organization. Eventually exchange opportunities were forfeited.

❹ 台灣的生育率創下了歷史新低的紀錄，將來生產力會漸漸不足。

Táiwān de shēngyùlǜ chuàngxiàle lìshǐ xīn dī de jìlù, jiānglái shēngchǎnlì huì jiànjiàn bùzú.

The birth rate in Taiwan has set a record low, in the future productivity will dwindle.

❺ 透過大量地練習，他的口音已漸漸改善。

Tòuguo dàliàng de liànxí, tā de kǒuyīn yǐ jiànjiàn gǎishàn.

After extensive practice, his accent has slowly improved.

Usage

漸漸 is not a reduplicated form because *漸 does not exist. 漸漸 often combines with the adverb marker 地 and must do so if it precedes the subject. In this case 漸漸地 is also followed by a short pause. E.g.,

漸漸地，我越來越了解他了。

Jiànjiàn de, wǒ yuèláiyuè liǎojiě tā le.

I'm gradually getting to understand him.

簡直, jiǎnzhí, (Adv), to put it simply and plainly, it seems as if

Function

With this adverb, the speaker draws an untrue and hypothetical parallel, a hyperbole, a way of exaggeration.

❶ 昨天看的那個房子髒得要命，簡直不能住。我決定不租。

Zuótiān kàn de nà ge fángzi zāng de yàomìng, jiǎnzhí bù néng zhù. Wǒ juédìng bù zū.

The house we looked at yesterday was so terribly filthy and is simply unlivable. I have decided not to rent it.

❷ 他很愛狗，簡直把狗當自己的孩子。

Tā hěn ài gǒu, jiǎnzhí bǎ gǒu dāng zìjǐ de háizi.

He loves his dog. It's as if his dog is his child.

❸ 在這麼大的地方，沒有車簡直就像沒有腳。

Zài zhème dà de dìfāng, méi yǒu chē jiǎnzhí jiù xiàng méi yǒu jiǎo.

In a place this vast, not having a car is just like not having legs at all.

❹ 大明為了考試，最近每天熬夜看書，簡直快累死了。

Dàmíng wèile kǎoshì, zuìjìn měi tiān áoyè kànshū, jiǎnzhí kuài lèi sǐle.

Daming has been burning the midnight oil every day preparing for exams, and he's completely exhausted.

❺ 他又帥，個性又好，簡直就是我理想的男朋友！

Tā yòu shuài, gèxìng yòu hǎo, jiǎnzhí jiùshì wǒ lǐxiǎng de nánpéngyǒu!

He's handsome and a gentleman. He is the man of all my dreams!

叫, jiào, (V), Imperative Verb

Function　叫 here is a transitive verb to indicate that someone asks or makes someone else do something.

① 媽媽叫我先把包水餃的材料準備好。
Māma jiào wǒ xiān bǎ bāo shuǐjiǎo de cáiliào zhǔnbèihǎo.
Mom asked me to first get all the ingredients for wrapping dumplings ready.

② 房東叫我們把新家具都搬到樓上房間去。
Fángdōng jiào wǒmen bǎ xīn jiājù dōu bān dào lóushàng fángjiān qù.
The landlord asked us to move all the new furniture to the room upstairs.

③ 老師叫學生進教室參加考試。
Lǎoshī jiào xuéshēng jìn jiàoshì cānjiā kǎoshì.
The teacher told the students to go inside the classroom to take the exam.

④ 醫生叫我多休息。
Yīshēng jiào wǒ duō xiūxí.
The doctor told me to have more rest.

⑤ 媽媽叫我少吃油膩的食物。
Māma jiào wǒ shǎo chī yóunì de shíwù.
My mother asked me to eat less greasy food.

Structures

Negation:　沒 is used for instances in the past, 別 bié for instances to come and 不 bù for either.

① 別叫小孩一個人去超商買飲料。
Bié jiào xiǎohái yí ge rén qù chāoshāng mǎi yǐnliào.
Don't have the child go alone to the convenience store to buy a drink.

② 別叫新來的學生參加演講比賽。
Bié jiào xīn lái de xuéshēng cānjiā yǎnjiǎng bǐsài.
Don't tell new students to participate in the speech contest.

③ 你們不喜歡喝酒，我以後不叫你們來了。
Nǐmen bù xǐhuān hē jiǔ, wǒ yǐhòu bú jiào nǐmen lái le.
You guys don't like to drink, so I won't ask you to come in the future.

④ 爸爸不叫他看書，他是不會看的。
Bàba bú jiào tā kànshū, tā shì bú huì kàn de.
He doesn't study unless his father tells him to.

⑤ 老師沒叫你出去，你怎麼自己跑出去了？
Lǎoshī méi jiào nǐ chūqù, nǐ zěnme zìjǐ pǎo chūqù le?
The teacher didn't send you, so how come ran out on your own?

⑥ 主任沒叫小美介紹自己的工作經驗。
Zhǔrèn méi jiào Xiǎoměi jièshào zìjǐ de gōngzuò jīngyàn.
The director did not ask Xiaomei to introduce, i.e., talk about, her work experience.

Questions :

❶ 是不是主任叫你來參加這個活動的？
Shìbúshì zhǔrèn jiào nǐ lái cānjiā zhè ge huódòng de?
Did the director ask you to attend the instance?

❷ 醫生是不是叫你別天天喝酒？你還是少喝一點吧！
Yīshēng shìbúshì jiào nǐ bié tiāntiān hē jiǔ? Nǐ háishì shǎo hē yìdiǎn ba!
The doctor told you not to drink every day, right? You should ease up a bit then!

❸ 老師沒叫你把功課帶來嗎？
Lǎoshī méi jiào nǐ bǎ gōngkè dàilái ma?
Didn't the teacher ask you to bring your homework?

Usage

(1) As a verb, 叫 has several different meanings. Compare the meanings of the following examples.

❶ 他肚子痛得大叫。(to scream)
Tā dùzi tòng de dà jiào.
His stomach hurt so much he screamed.

❷ 你沒聽到我叫你嗎？(to call someone)
Nǐ méi tīngdào wǒ jiào nǐ ma?
Didn't you hear me call you?

❸ 她叫王美美。(to be named)
Tā jiào Wáng Měiměi.
She is called Wang Meimei. (i.e., Her name is Wang Meimei.)

❹ 腳踏車也叫自行車。(to be termed)
Jiǎotàchē yě jiào zìxíngchē.
Jiaotache is also known as zixingche.

(2) 請 qǐng is similar to 叫, but is more polite.

❶ 張老師叫你去找他。(plain command)
Zhāng lǎoshī jiào nǐ qù zhǎo tā.
Zhang Laoshi asked, or told, you to go see him.

❷ 張老師請你去找他。(polite request)
Zhāng lǎoshī qǐng nǐ qù zhǎo tā.
Zhang Laoshi requested that you go see him.

結果, jiéguǒ, (Adv), consequently, (Conj), in the end

Function

The 結果 connects a second clause to the first. In most cases, the second clause consists of an undesirable consequence.

(Adv. consequently)

❶ 他每天熬夜打電玩，結果成績不理想，被當了。

Tā měi tiān áoyè dǎ diànwán, jiéguǒ chéngjī bù lǐxiǎng, bèi dàng le.

He stayed up every night playing video games. Consequently, his grades weren't ideal, and he failed.

❷ 店員沒把合約的內容解釋清楚，結果害他多花了好幾千塊錢。

Diànyuán méi bǎ héyuē de nèiróng jiěshì qīngchǔ, jiéguǒ hài tā duō huāle hǎojǐ qiān kuài qián.

The store employee didn't explain the content of the contract clearly. As a result, he overpaid by a few thousand NT dollars.

❸ 他沒買除濕機，結果雨季的時候，衣服、鞋子都發霉了。

Tā méi mǎi chúshījī, jiéguǒ yǔjì de shíhòu, yīfú, xiézi dōu fāméi le.

He didn't buy a dehumidifier. As a result, during the rainy season, his clothes and shoes all mildewed.

(Conj. in the end)

❹ 他們在媒體上做了不少廣告，結果生意還是不好。

Tāmen zài méitǐ shàng zuòle bù shǎo guǎnggào, jiéguǒ shēngyì háishì bù hǎo.

They put a lot of ads in the media, in the end, however, their business was still poor.

❺ 他帶了發票，結果店員還是拒絕讓他退換。

Tā dàile fāpiào, jiéguǒ diànyuán háishì jùjué ràng tā tuìhuàn.

He brought the receipt. In the end, however, the store employee refused to let him exchange.

Usage

Sentences with 結果 always relate to instances in the past. Some 結果 sentences (consequences) can be paraphrased using 因為 A 所以 B.

❶ 他借錢常常不還，結果再也沒有人要借他了。

Tā jiè qián chángcháng bù huán, jiéguǒ zài yě méi yǒu rén yào jiè tā le.

He usually doesn't give back the money he borrows, As a result, no one wants to lend him money any more.

❷ 因為他借錢常常不還，所以再也沒有人要借他了。

Yīnwèi tā jiè qián chángcháng bù huán, suǒyǐ zài yě méi yǒu rén yào jiè tā le.

As he doesn't give back the money he borrows, no one wants to lend him money any more.

幾乎, jīhū, (Adv), almost

Function

The adverb 幾乎 indicates nearness. Its meaning is similar to 'almost, nearly' in English.

❶ 這幾天幾乎每天都下雨。

Zhè jǐ tiān jīhū měi tiān dōu xià yǔ.

It has rained almost every day lately.

❷ 他為了省錢幾乎每天都在學生餐廳吃飯。
Tā wèile shěng qián jīhū měi tiān dōu zài xuéshēng cāntīng chīfàn.
To save money, he has been eating in the student cafeteria almost every day.

❸ 這裡的人她幾乎都認識。
Zhèlǐ de rén tā jīhū dōu rènshì.
She knows almost everybody here.

❹ 他的婚禮幾乎花光了他所有的錢。
Tā de hūnlǐ jīhū huāguāngle tā suǒyǒu de qián.
He spent almost all of his money on his wedding.

❺ 他很節省。衣服幾乎都是朋友穿不下送他的。
Tā hěn jiéshěng. Yīfú jīhū dōu shì péngyǒu chuānbúxià sòng tā de.
He's very frugal. Almost all of his clothes were given to him by friends after they could no longer wear them.

Usage

(1) When 差不多 chàbùduō means 'almost', 幾乎 and 差不多 are interchangeable, indicating near-totality, e.g., 他差不多每天都運動～他幾乎每天都運動。Tā chàbùduō měi tiān dōu yùndòng ~ Tā jīhū měi tiān dōu yùndòng. 'He exercises almost every day.'

(2) 差不多 can mean 'approximately' when it is followed by a number. However, 幾乎 can not mean 'approximately'. So, 我吃了差不多二十個水餃。Wǒ chīle chàbùduō èrshí ge shuǐjiǎo. means 'I ate approximately/about 20 dumplings'. The person may have eaten more than or fewer than 20 dumplings. By contrast, 我吃了幾乎二十個水餃。Wǒ chīle jīhū èrshí ge shuǐjiǎo. means 'I ate almost 20 dumplings'. In this case, the person definitely ate fewer than 20 dumplings.

經過, jīngguò, (Prep), after

Function 經過 in this usage is a preposition meaning 'after' or 'subsequent to'.

❶ 經過父母多次的說明，她才明白要成功非努力不可。
Jīngguò fùmǔ duō cì de shuōmíng, tā cái míngbái yào chénggōng fēi nǔlì bùkě.
She didn't really understand that to succeed, you must work hard, until after her parents explained it to her numerous times.

❷ 他的喉嚨經過多天的休息，最近好一點了。
Tā de hóulóng jīngguò duō tiān de xiūxí, zuìjìn hǎo yìdiǎn le.
After several days of rest, his throat has gotten a bit better.

❸ 我是經過兩年的準備，才考上公務員的。
Wǒ shì jīngguò liǎng nián de zhǔnbèi, cái kǎoshàng gōngwùyuán de.
I passed the civil service test only after two years of preparation.

Usage　經過 can also be a verb meaning 'to pass a point', e.g., 從台北去高雄，要經過台南。Cóng Táiběi qù Gāoxióng, yào jīngguò Táinán. 'To get from Taipei to Kaohsiung, you need to pass through Tainan.'

竟然, jìngrán, (Adv), to the speaker's great surprise, unbelievably

Function　The S_2 adverb 竟然 expresses the speaker's amazement at some fact.

❶ 食品安全影響人民的健康，可是政府竟然不好好管理。

Shípǐn ānquán yǐngxiǎng rénmín de jiànkāng, kěshì zhèngfǔ jìngrán bù hǎohǎo guǎnlǐ.

Food safety affects people's health, yet somehow the government isn't doing a good job of controlling it.

❷ 政客為了自己的利益，竟然阻止公平的政策與制度。

Zhèngkè wéile zìjǐ de lìyì, jìngrán zǔzhǐ gōngpíng de zhèngcè yǔ zhìdù.

It's unbelievable. Politicians will impede fair policy and governance for the sake of personal benefit.

❸ 他擁有那麼大的企業，但是他的學歷竟然只是小學畢業。

Tā yǒngyǒu nàme dà de qìyè, dànshì tā de xuélì jìngrán zhǐshì xiǎoxué bìyè.

He is in charge of such a large enterprise, yet he is only an elementary school graduate.

Structures

(1) 居然 jūrán is more colloquial, while 竟然 is more formal. In most cases the two can be used interchangeably.

(2) 竟然 can be reduced to just 竟 jìng, but 居然 cannot be reduced, e.g., 沒想到現在每八個嬰兒中，竟有一個雙親之一不是本國國籍。(*居)

Méi xiǎngdào xiànzài měi bā ge yīng'ér zhōng, jìng yǒu yí ge shuāngqīn zhī yī bú shì běnguó guójí.

I didn't realize that for every eight babies born today, it turns out that one of the two parents is not a local.

(3) 竟然 is a regular adverb, always placed after the subject and before verb phrases, while 居然 is a non-typical, i.e., movable adverb, placed either before or after the subject. Other non-typical adverbs include 難道 nándào 'could it be that', 畢竟 bìjìng 'after all', 到底 dàodǐ 'after all', 難得 nándé 'rare, hard to come by', and 大概 dàgài 'probably', etc....

❶ 我說的都是真的，他居然不相信。/ 我說的都是真的，居然他不相信。

Wǒ shuō de dōu shì zhēn de, tā jūrán bù xiāngxìn./ Wǒ shuō de dōu shì zhēn de, jūrán tā bù xiāngxìn.

Everything I said was true. And you know what, he doesn't believe me.

❷ 我說的都是真的，他竟然不相信。/ *我說的都是真的，竟然他不相信。

Wǒ shuō de dōu shì zhēn de, tā jìngrán bù xiāngxìn. / *Wǒ shuō de dōu shì zhēn de, jìngrán tā bù xiāngxìn.

Everything I said was true. And you know what, he doesn't believe me.

就, jiù, (Adv), sooner than expected (1)

Function
When the adverb 就 refers to time or place, the instance being discussed takes place sooner than expected.

❶ 學校很近。走路十分鐘就到了。
Xuéxiào hěn jìn. Zǒulù shí fēnzhōng jiù dào le.
The school is close. Walking only ten minutes will get you there.

❷ 那個地方不遠。很快就到了。
Nà ge dìfāng bù yuǎn. Hěn kuài jiù dào le.
That place is not far. You'll get there very quickly.

❸ 他等一下就來。
Tā děng yíxià jiù lái.
He will be here in a bit.

Structures
就 often co-occurs with the sentence-final 了. See above. The sentences mean the same with or without 了.

Usage
就 is a high-frequency adverb, which has various functions and meanings. It can be used in a single sentence and it can be a linking adverb, connecting cause-effect sentences.

就, jiù, (Adv), in V 了 A 就 B, (V le A jiù B), do B right after doing A (2)

Function
The pattern 'V 了 A 就 B' indicates that instance 2 (B) occurs right after the completion of instance 1 (A). The pattern creates a feeling of immediacy, as soon as.

❶ 我放了假就去旅行了。
Wǒ fàngle jià jiù qù lǚxíng le.
I went on break (my break started) and I went traveling.

❷ 他吃了藥就睡覺了。
Tā chīle yào jiù shuìjiào le.
He took medicine and went to sleep.

❸ 我下了飛機就打電話給你。
Wǒ xiàle fēijī jiù dǎ diànhuà gěi nǐ.
I'll call you after I get off the plane.

Structures
The two instances can be independently in the affirmative or in the negative.

❶ 他到了臺北，就去臺北 101 看看。
Tā dàole Táiběi, jiù qù Táiběi 101 kànkàn.
He arrived in Taipei and checked out Taipei 101.

❷ 妹妹喝了一碗熱湯，就不覺得冷了。
Mèimei hēle yì wǎn rè tāng, jiù bù juéde lěng le.
My little sister stopped feeing cold right after she had a bowl of hot soup.

❸ 姐姐吃了臭豆腐，肚子就不舒服。
Jiějie chīle chòudòufǔ, dùzi jiù bù shūfú.
Sister ate stinky tofu then her stomach started acting up.

Questions : The A-not-A form is not possible. Either 嗎 ma or 是不是 shìbúshì can be used to form questions.

❶ 他們見了面，就去喝咖啡嗎？
Tāmen jiànle miàn, jiù qù hē kāfēi ma?
Did they go to drink coffee after they met?

❷ 你弟弟是不是下了課，就去 KTV 唱歌？
Nǐ dìdi shìbúshì xiàle kè, jiù qù KTV chànggē?
Your brother went to KTV to sing after class, right?

❸ 他是不是去紐約玩了兩個星期，就不想回來了？
Tā shìbúshì qù Niǔyuē wánle liǎng ge xīngqí, jiù bù xiǎng huílái le?
He visited New York for two weeks and didn't want to come back, right?

Usage The 'V 了 A 就 B' pattern is similar to and different from the '一 A 就 B', as explained below.

(1) The '一' is followed by a relatively short verbal phrase, e.g., 一出來 就… and 一看就…, to emphasize the immediate succession of the two actions. In contrast, the 'V 了' pattern is not as restricted in terms of what can follow it.

(2) 以後 yǐhòu can be used with 'V 了 A 就 B', but it cannot occur with the '一 A 就 B' pattern.

❶ 他吃了藥以後，就去睡覺。
Tā chīle yào yǐhòu, jiù qù shuìjiào.

❷ *他一吃了藥以後，就去睡覺。
*Tā yì chīle yào yǐhòu, jiù qù shuìjiào.

就, jiù, (Adv), on the contrary (3)

Function With the adverb 就, the speaker argues for an exception to a rule being talked about. This 就 is pronounced with a high stress.

❶ A：女生都不敢看恐怖片。
Nǚshēng dōu bù gǎn kàn kǒngbùpiàn.
Girls don't like horror flicks.

B：並不是所有的女生都不敢看恐怖片，我就很喜歡看。
Bìng búshì suǒyǒu de nǚshēng dōu bù gǎn kàn kǒngbùpiàn, wǒ jiù hěn xǐhuān kàn.
Not all girls. I for one love them!

❷ A：你的工作那麼忙。大概每天都要加班吧？
Nǐ de gōngzuò nàme máng. Dàgài měi tiān dōu yào jiābān ba?
With such a busy work schedule, you must have to put in a lot of overtime.

B：也不一定，今天就沒加班。
Yě bùyídìng, jīntiān jiù méi jiābān.
It depends. Today I didn't!

❸ A：小林家是不是每個人都瘦瘦的？
Xiǎo Lín jiā shìbúshì měi ge rén dōu shòushòu de?
Is everyone in Xiao Lin's family so slender?

B：不是，大兒子就胖胖的。
Búshì, dà érzi jiù pàngpàng de.
No, their oldest boy certainly isn't.

❹ A：看漫畫書對功課一點幫助都沒有。
Kàn mànhuà shū duì gōngkè yìdiǎn bāngzhù dōu méi yǒu.
Reading comics is of no help whatsoever to schoolwork.

B：誰說的！我看的漫畫書就可以讓我了解歷史。
Shéi shuō de! Wǒ kàn de mànhuà shū jiù kěyǐ ràng wǒ liǎojiě lìshǐ.
Are you kidding? The comics I read help me understand history!

❺ A：所有的限制級電影都是色情片。
Suǒyǒu de xiànzhìjí diànyǐng dōu shì sèqíngpiàn.
All restricted movies have pornographic content.

B：不一定吧。我們上星期看的那部就不是。
Bùyídìng ba. Wǒmen shàng xīngqí kàn de nà bù jiù bú shì.
Not necessarily. That movie we watched last week certainly wasn't.

就算S₁，也S₂, (jiùsuàn S₁, yě S₂), even if S₁, would S₂, no matter how

Function

The pattern indicates that even if a situation S_1 is true otherwise, S_2 would still be true.

❶ 我爸爸常說：就算我做不動了，也不要靠孩子。
Wǒ bàba cháng shuō: Jiùsuàn wǒ zuòbúdòng le, yě bú yào kào háizi.
My dad often says, 'Even if I can't move anymore, I don't want to depend on my kids.'

❷ 就算你的能力比老闆強，你也應該聽老闆的意見。
Jiùsuàn nǐ de nénglì bǐ lǎobǎn qiáng, nǐ yě yīnggāi tīng lǎobǎn de yìjiàn.
Even if you're more capable than the boss, you should still listen to his suggestions.

❸ 就算男人有養家的責任，家庭經濟也不能完全讓男人負擔啊。
Jiùsuàn nánrén yǒu yǎngjiā de zérèn, jiātíng jīngjì yě bù néng wánquán ràng nánrén fùdān a.
Even if men have the responsibility of taking care of their families, the household finances cannot be the sole responsibility of the man.

❹ 他的婚禮，我就算再忙，也要參加。
Tā de hūnlǐ, wǒ jiùsuàn zài máng, yě yào cānjiā.
No matter how busy I am, I will be at his wedding.

❺ 就算你覺得孤單，也不能隨便打擾別人。
Jiùsuàn nǐ juéde gūdān, yě bù néng suíbiàn dǎrǎo biérén.
Even if you feel lonely, you can't go around bothering others.

Usage

This is a highly colloquial pattern. The subject can appear before or after 就算. E.g., pre-subject in ❶ above and post-subject in ❹ above.

就要⋯了, (jiù yào... le), will soon

Function

This pattern is used to indicate an instance will soon take place.

❶ 我們已經四年級了，就要畢業了。
Wǒmen yǐjīng sì niánjí le, jiù yào bìyè le.
We're already seniors and will soon graduate.

❷ 林愛麗大學畢業以後，就要去念研究所了。
Lín Àilì dàxué bìyè yǐhòu, jiù yào qù niàn yánjiùsuǒ le.
After Lin Aili graduates from college, she will go to graduate school.

❸ 下個月就要放暑假了。
Xià ge yuè jiù yào fàng shǔjià le.
Next month, it will be summer vacation.

Structures

*Q*uestions :

❶ 你畢業以後，就要離開台灣了嗎？
Nǐ bìyè yǐhòu, jiù yào líkāi Táiwān le ma?
Will you be leaving Taiwan after you graduate?

❷ 爸爸今年是不是就要六十歲了？
Bàba jīnnián shìbúshì jiù yào liùshí suì le?
Dad is going to be sixty this year, right?

❸ 客人已經都到了，婚禮是不是就要開始了？
Kèrén yǐjīng dōu dào le, hūnlǐ shìbúshì jiù yào kāishǐ le?
The guests are already all here. The wedding is going to start now, right?

(1) In single sentences, 就要 jiù yào and 快要 kuàiyào are interchangeable with the same meaning, e.g.,

❶ a. 我們快要畢業了。　　　b. 我們就要畢業了。
Wǒmen kuàiyào bìyè le.　　Wǒmen jiù yào bìyè le.
We are about to graduate.

❷ a. 妹妹快要二十歲了。　　b. 妹妹就要二十歲了。
Mèimei kuàiyào èrshí suì le.　Mèimei jiù yào èrshí suì le.
Young sister is about to turn 20 years old.

(2) Only 就要 can be used to connect two clauses.

❶ a. 我們下了課，就要去吃晚飯。
Wǒmen xiàle kè, jiù yào qù chī wǎnfàn.
We are going to eat dinner after class.

b. *我們下了課，快要去吃晚飯。
*Wǒmen xiàle kè, kuàiyào qù chī wǎnfàn.

(3) When there is a time word, only 就要 can be used.

❶ a. 下個禮拜，我們就要考試了。
Xià ge lǐbài, wǒmen jiù yào kǎoshì le.
Next week, we will have a test.

b. *下個禮拜，我們快要考試了。
*Xià ge lǐbài, wǒmen kuàiyào kǎoshì le.

❷ a. 大家把餃子包好了以後，就要準備吃飯了。
Dàjiā bǎ jiǎozi bāohǎole yǐhòu, jiù yào zhǔnbèi chīfàn le.
When everyone finishes wrapping the dumplings, we'll get ready to eat.

b. *大家把餃子包好了以後，快要準備吃飯了。
*Dàjiā bǎ jiǎozi bāohǎole yǐhòu, kuàiyào zhǔnbèi chīfàn le.

究竟, jiùjìng, (Adv), I wonder

The adverb 究竟 expresses the speaker's desire to get to the bottom of something, of some inquiry.

❶ 萬一發生核能災害，我們究竟該如何應變？
Wànyī fāshēng hénéng zāihài, wǒmen jiùjìng gāi rúhé yìngbiàn?
In the event of a nuclear disaster, what on earth would we do?

❷ 那個問題究竟要怎麼解決？
Nà ge wèntí jiùjìng yào zěnme jiějué?
How in the world can this problem be solved?

❸ 雲端科技究竟會不會帶來負面的影響？
Yúnduān kējì jiùjìng huì bú huì dàilái fùmiàn de yǐngxiǎng?
Are there negative impacts of cloud techonology after all?

❹ 台灣究竟有多少家便利商店？
Táiwān jiùjìng yǒu duōshǎo jiā biànlì shāngdiàn?
How many convenience stores are there in Taiwan, I wonder?

❺ 李教授的理想究竟能不能實現？
Lǐ jiàoshòu de lǐxiǎng jiùjìng néng bù néng shíxiàn?
Is there really any way Prof. Li's ideals can come to fruition?

Usage

(1) 究竟 is more formal, while 到底 is more colloquial.

(2) 究竟, like 到底, is incompatible with 嗎.

　　*究竟什麼是微整型嗎？
　　*Jiùjìng shénme shì wéizhěngxíng ma?

(3) It can appear either before or after the subject, but when the subject is a question-word, 究竟 can only occur sentence-initially.

究竟誰了解這個問題？　　　　*誰究竟了解這個問題？
Jiùjìng shéi liǎojiě zhè ge wèntí?　*Shéi jiùjìng liǎojiě zhè ge wèntí?
Who on earth understands this type of situation?

究竟誰的條件比較好？　　　　*誰的條件究竟比較好？
Jiùjìng shéi de tiáojiàn bǐjiào hǎo?　*Shéi de tiáojiàn jiùjìng bǐjiào hǎo?
Whose qualifications are actually better?

居然, jūrán, (Adv), to one's surprise

Function　The adverb 居然 expresses the speaker's surprise that something happened the way it did. Compare the pair below.

A. 今天氣溫只有十度，可是小美沒穿外套。
Jīntiān qìwēn zhǐyǒu shí dù, kěshì Xiǎoměi méi chuān wàitào.
It's only 10 degrees today, but Xiaomei isn't wearing a jacket.
　（A plain and factual statement.）

B. 今天氣溫只有十度，可是小美居然沒穿外套。
Jīntiān qìwēn zhǐyǒu shí dù, kěshì Xiǎoměi jūrán méi chuān wàitào.
It's only 10 degrees today, but Xiaomei surprisingly isn't wearing a coat.
　（An unexpected exception to a rule.）

❶ 他是韓國人，居然不吃辣。
Tā shì Hánguó rén, jūrán bù chī là.
He's Korean but, surprisingly, doesn't like spicy food.

❷ 語言中心主任約他今天早上面談，他居然忘了。
Yǔyán zhōngxīn zhǔrèn yuē tā jīntiān zǎoshàng miàntán, tā jūrán wàng le.
The language center director made an appointment to interview him this morning. He surprisingly forgot.

❸ 我們看電影的時候，大家都感動得哭了，只有他居然睡著了。

Wǒmen kàn diànyǐng de shíhòu, dàjiā dōu gǎndòng de kū le, zhǐyǒu tā jūrán shuìzháo le.

When we were watching the movie everybody was moved to tears, except for him. Surprisingly, he fell asleep.

❹ 他收到帳單的時候，才發現「吃到飽」居然只是網路，不包括打電話。

Tā shōudào zhàngdān de shíhòu, cái fāxiàn 'chīdàobǎo' jūrán zhǐshì wǎnglù, bù bāokuò dǎ diànhuà.

When he got his bill, he realized that only internet access was unlimited, not phone calls.

❺ 他好不容易才找到一件他想要的外套，居然不買。

Tā hǎobù róngyì cái zhǎodào yí jiàn tā xiǎng yào de wàitào, jūrán bù mǎi.

He finally managed to find a jacket he liked and, to my surprise, he didn't buy it.

Usage

(1) 居然 is an adverb and is generally placed after the subject and in front of the verb.

(2) It frequently appears together with 沒想到. Reinforcement is a common strategy in Chinese, e.g., 今天天氣這麼冷。沒想到你居然沒穿外套。Jīntiān tiānqì zhème lěng. Méi xiǎngdào nǐ jūrán méi chuān wàitào. 'It's so cold today. I never imagined that you would (surprisingly) not wear a coat.'

看, kàn, (V), as in V V看, to try and see, to try out　(1)

Function　The verb 看 comes after reduplicated action verb. It suggests 'try (the verb) and see'. Because of the use of 看, the sentence carries a highly tentative tone.

❶ 這杯咖啡很香。你喝喝看。

Zhè bēi kāfēi hěn xiāng. Nǐ hēhēkàn.

This cup of coffee smells really good. Taste it.

❷ 聽說你唱歌唱得很好。我想聽聽看。

Tīngshuō nǐ chànggē chàng de hěn hǎo. Wǒ xiǎng tīngtīngkàn.

I've heard that you sing well. I'd like to hear.

❸ 那家餐廳的菜很好吃。我想去吃吃看。

Nà jiā cāntīng de cài hěn hǎochī. Wǒ xiǎng qù chīchīkàn.

The food in that restaurant is very good. I'd like to try it and see for myself.

❹ 臺灣的夜市很有名。這個週末我想去逛逛看。
Táiwān de yèshì hěn yǒumíng. Zhè ge zhōumò wǒ xiǎng qù guàngguàngkàn.
Taiwan's night markets are well known. I'd like to wander around this weekend and see for myself.

Usage

Basic monosyllabic action verbs can be used in this pattern, e.g., 吃 chī 'to eat', 喝 hē 'to drink', 打 dǎ 'to hit', 寫 xiě 'to write', 穿 chuān 'to wear', 學 xué 'to study, learn', 做 zuò 'to do', 聽 tīng 'to listen', 唱 chàng 'to sing', 逛 guàng 'to stroll', 住 zhù 'to live, stay'. Disyllabic verbs do not use this pattern.

看, kàn, (V), depend on (2)

Function

The verb 看 has many meanings. Here, it presents a factor that determines an issue.

❶ 考不考得上公職,除了努力以外,還得看運氣。
Kǎo bù kǎo de shàng gōngzhí, chúle nǔlì yǐwài, hái děi kàn yùnqì.
Whether or not you can pass the exam for the public service, in addition to studying hard, it also depends on luck.

❷ 傷口多久會好,得看是哪裡受傷。
Shāngkǒu duōjiǔ huì hǎo, děi kàn shì nǎlǐ shòushāng.
How long it takes for an injury to heal depends on where the injury is.

❸ 產品有沒有競爭力,要看價格。要是價格太高怎麼會有人想買?
Chǎnpǐn yǒu méi yǒu jìngzhēnglì, yào kàn jiàgé. Yàoshi jiàgé tài gāo zěnme huì yǒu rén xiǎng mǎi?
Whether or not a product is competitive depends on the price. If the price is too high, how is anyone going to want to buy it?

❹ 在網路上賣東西生意好不好,要看賣家的信用好不好。
Zài wǎnglù shàng mài dōngxi shēngyì hǎo bù hǎo, yào kàn màijiā de xìnyòng hǎo bù hǎo.
Whether or not an online sales business will do well depends on the trustworthiness of the seller.

❺ 台灣的學費貴不貴,很難說。得看是私立的還是公立的學校。
Táiwān de xuéfèi guì bú guì, hěn nán shuō. Děi kàn shì sīlì de háishì gōnglì de xuéxiào.
It's hard to say if tuition in Taiwan is high. It depends on whether the school is private or public.

Usage

All the sentences above have a 'whether... or not' segment, but this is not a requirement. Sentences below do not.

❶ 微整型沒有傷口,什麼時候都可以做,不必看什麼時候放假。
Wéizhěngxíng méi yǒu shāngkǒu, shénme shíhòu dōu kěyǐ zuò, búbì kàn shénme shíhòu fàngjià.
There are no abrasions with micro-cosmetic surgery, so it can be done anytime. You don't need to take into consideration when you have time off.

❷ 這是一件小事，不必看老闆的意見吧。

Zhè shì yí jiàn xiǎo shì, búbì kàn lǎobǎn de yìjiàn ba.

This is a small matter. No need to take the boss' views into consideration.

靠, kào, (V / Prep), to rely on, by means of

Function

As a main verb, 靠 means 'to rely on, to lean against', but when it is the first verb in a sentence with two verbs, its meaning is reduced to 'by means of' with 靠 acting more like a preposition.

(As a main verb)

❶ 有句話說，「在家靠父母，出外靠朋友」，說明了家人和朋友的重要。

Yǒu jù huà shuō, 'zài jiā kào fùmǔ, chū wài kào péngyǒu', shuōmíngle jiārén hàn péngyǒu de zhòngyào.

There's a saying, 'When at home, rely on your parents, when away from home, depend on friends.' It underscores the importance of family and friends.

(As a preposition)

❷ 他靠自己的努力賺錢買了這棟房子。

Tā kào zìjǐ de nǔlì zhuànqián mǎile zhè dòng fángzi.

He bought this house with his own hard-earned money.

❸ 現在工作非常難找。我是靠朋友幫忙才找到的。

Xiànzài gōngzuò fēicháng nán zhǎo. Wǒ shì kào péngyǒu bāngmáng cái zhǎodào de.

Jobs are hard to find now. I found mine through friends' help.

❹ 他靠打工賺的錢養家。生活過得並不輕鬆。

Tā kào dǎgōng zhuàn de qián yǎngjiā. Shēnghuó guò de bìng bù qīngsōng.

He supports his family with money earned with a part-time job. His life is by no means easy.

❺ 張太太的孩子在國外工作。她靠電子郵件跟網路電話了解孩子生活的情形。

Zhāng tàitai de háizi zài guówài gōngzuò. Tā kào diànzǐ yóujiàn gēn wǎnglù diànhuà liǎojiě háizi shēnghuó de qíngxíng.

Mrs. Zhang's children work abroad. She keeps up to date with their lives by means of email and internet phone.

可, kě, (Adv), but on the other hand, stating a mild warning

Function

可, an adverb, has two functions.

(1) It expresses the speaker's refutation of what people in general expect or assume.

❶ 你可是男生，怎麼膽子比我還小！

Nǐ kě shì nánshēng, zěnme dǎnzi bǐ wǒ hái xiǎo!

But you're a guy, where are your guts?

❷ 我可跟她們不一樣。我覺得恐怖片一點也不可怕。

Wǒ kě gēn tāmen bù yíyàng. Wǒ juéde kǒngbùpiàn yìdiǎn yě bù kěpà.

I'm not at all like those girls. I don't think horror movies are the least bit frightening.

❸ 那位畫家得獎以後，他的畫可貴了。我們怎麼買得起！

Nà wèi huàjiā dé jiǎng yǐhòu, tā de huà kě guì le. Wǒmen zěnme mǎideqǐ!

After that artist won an award, his paintings just got so expensive. How could we ever afford one!

❹ 台灣的大學生可很少人化了妝去上課的。

Táiwān de dàxuéshēng kě hěn shǎo rén huàle zhuāng qù shàngkè de.

In Taiwan, there are only very few university students who wear make-up to class.

(2) The speaker gives a suggestion, a mild warning or a reminder.

❶ 最近食品安全出了不少問題。買東西可要小心啊！

Zuìjìn shípǐn ānquán chūle bù shǎo wèntí. Mǎi dōngxi kě yào xiǎoxīn a!

There have been quite a few food safety issues of late. Beware what you buy!

❷ 開慢一點。你可別因為要趕時間而出車禍。

Kāi màn yidiǎn. Nǐ kě bié yīnwèi yào gǎn shíjiān ér chū chēhuò.

Drive slower. It's not worth spending the expense of an accident.

❸ 噓，小聲一點。這件事很重要，你可不能告訴別人。

Xū, xiǎo shēng yìdiǎn. Zhè jiàn shì hěn zhòngyào, nǐ kě bù néng gàosù biérén.

Hey, not so loud. This is very important, and you can't let anyone else know.

❹ 你可要表現得好一點。可別再出問題了。

Nǐ kě yào biǎoxiàn de hǎo yìdiǎn. Kě bié zài chū wèntí le.

You've got to do a better job. Don't let it happen again.

> **Usage**

可 is often used in imperative sentences and is followed by words like 要, 得, 不能, and 別, as illustrated above. On mainland China, 可 can also function as a conj, related to 可是. This is not observed in Taiwan.

可見, kějiàn, (Conj), it can thus be concluded that...

> **Function**

可見 is an S₂ conjunction, connected to an observation that follows naturally from S₁.

❶ 經過人民這麼多年的抗議，政府總算願意正視這個問題了，可見環境汙染的情況已很嚴重了。

Jīngguò rénmín zhème duō nián de kàngyì, zhèngfǔ zǒngsuàn yuànyì zhèngshì zhè ge wèntí le, kějiàn huánjìng wūrǎn de qíngkuàng yǐ hěn yánzhòng le.

After so many years of public protest the government is finally willing to address this issue. The problem of pollution has obviously become really bad.

❷ 連我那麼怕看恐怖片的人都不怕，可見這部電影一點也不可怕。

Lián wǒ nàme pà kàn kǒngbùpiàn de rén dōu bú pà, kějiàn zhè bù diànyǐng yìdiǎn yě bù kěpà.

Even a scaredy cat like me isn't scared by this horror movie. That tells you how mild it is.

❸ 李先生那麼年輕就在餐飲業擁有了一片天，可見他多麼努力。

Lǐ xiānshēng nàme niánqīng jiù zài cānyǐnyè yǒngyǒule yí piàn tiān, kějiàn tā duōme nǔlì.

Someone as young as Mr. Li is already a food and drink industry magnate. It goes to show how hard he works.

❹ 有錢的人越來越有錢，窮人越來越窮，可見貧富不均的情況越來越嚴重了。

Yǒuqián de rén yuèláiyuè yǒuqián, qióngrén yuèláiyuè qióng, kějiàn pínfù bùjūn de qíngkuàng yuèláiyuè yánzhòng le.

The rich are getting richer and the poor are getting poorer. Clearly the gap is widening.

❺ 現在有些碩士畢業生去夜市擺地攤，可見工作多難找啊！

Xiànzài yǒuxiē shuòshì bìyèshēng qù yèshì bǎi dìtān, kějiàn gōngzuò duō nán zhǎo a!

Some Master's graduates go on to sell at the night market. That's an indication of how hard it is to find a job!

可以, kěyǐ, (Vaux), Permission (1)

Function 可以 indicates permission to perform an action.

❶ 放假的時候，你們可以來我家打籃球。

Fàngjià de shíhòu, nǐmen kěyǐ lái wǒ jiā dǎ lánqiú.

During days off, you can come to my house to play basketball.

❷ 王老師說我們任何時候都可以找他討論期末報告。

Wáng lǎoshī shuō wǒmen rènhé shíhòu dōu kěyǐ zhǎo tā tǎolùn qímò bàogào.

Teacher Wang said that we can find him at any time to discuss the final report.

❸ 我叫王美美，你可以叫我小美。

Wǒ jiào Wáng Měiměi, nǐ kěyǐ jiào wǒ Xiǎoměi.

My name is Wang Meimei. You can call me Xiaoměi.

Structures

可以 is an auxiliary verb and it precedes the verb.

*N*egation :

❶ 這支手錶是我父親留給我的，不可以賣。

Zhè zhī shǒubiǎo shì wǒ fùqīn liú gěi wǒ de, bù kěyǐ mài.

This watch was left to me by my father. I can't sell it.

❷ 你不可以在圖書館裡面吃東西。

Nǐ bù kěyǐ zài túshūguǎn lǐmiàn chī dōngxi.

You cannot eat in the library.

❸ 先生，對不起，你不可以在這裡照相。

Xiānshēng, duìbùqǐ, nǐ bù kěyǐ zài zhèlǐ zhàoxiàng.

Sir, excuse me. You cannot take pictures here.

*Q*uestions :

❶ A：我可以不可以去看你們的籃球比賽？

　　Wǒ kěyǐ bù kěyǐ qù kàn nǐmen de lánqiú bǐsài?

　　Can I go watch your basketball game?

　B：沒問題！

　　Méi wèntí!

　　No problem.

❷ A：可以借一隻筆嗎？

　　Kěyǐ jiè yì zhī bǐ ma?

　　May I borrow a pen from you?

　B：可以啊。

　　Kěyǐ a.

　　Sure.

❸ A：這是你的書嗎？我可以看看嗎？

　　Zhè shì nǐ de shū ma? Wǒ kěyǐ kànkàn ma?

　　Is this your book? Can I check it out?

　B：對不起，那不是我的。

　　Duìbùqǐ, nà bú shì wǒ de.

　　Sorry, that's not my book.

Usage

When answering a question, 可以 alone suffices, like all cases of Vaux and V's.

　A：我可不可以後天開始上班？

　　Wǒ kě bù kěyǐ hòutiān kāishǐ shàngbān?

　　Can I start working the day after tomorrow?

　B：可以。

　　Kěyǐ.

　　Yes, of course.

可以, kěyǐ, (Vaux), Possibility (2)

Function

可以 as a Vaux can also refer to the possibility of an event.

❶ 這個字也可以這樣寫。
Zhè ge zì yě kěyǐ zhèyàng xiě.
This character can also be written like this.

❷ 二手車可以賣給朋友啊！
Èrshǒu chē kěyǐ mài gěi péngyǒu a!
Second-hand cars can be sold to friends.

❸ 我家不大，但可以住五、六個人。
Wǒ jiā bú dà, dàn kěyǐ zhù wǔ, liù ge rén.
My house isn't big, but it can accommodate five or six people.

Structures
Usage

As a Vaux, 可以₂ has exactly the same syntactic structures as 可以₁.

(1) Note that possibility-可以 can only be used in the positive. 不可以 can only be interpreted as the negation of 可以₁, e.g., 你不可以天天吃肉。 Nǐ bù kěyǐ tiāntiān chī ròu. 'You shall not eat meat every day.'

(2) 可以 can mean different things. Permission-可以 has been dealt with above. That is distinguished from possibility-可以, e.g., 你可以教我嗎？Nǐ kěyǐ jiāo wǒ ma? 'Can you teach me?'.

(3) 不可以 can only be used to indicate 'permission', not 'possibility'. The negative form can only be used to indicate permission. For example, '你不可以說老闆不好' Nǐ bù kěyǐ shuō lǎobǎn bù hǎo. 'You mustn't say anything bad about the boss.' When you use '可不可以' or '可以不可以', it can indicate either permission or possibility. For example,

❶ 你可不可以明天來？(possibility)
Nǐ kě bù kěyǐ míngtiān lái?
Can you come tomorrow?

❷ 我可以不可以買一支新手機？(permission)
Wǒ kěyǐ bù kěyǐ mǎi yì zhī xīn shǒujī?
Can I buy a new cellphone?

恐怕, kǒngpà, (Adv), probably, I'm afraid that

Function

The adverb 恐怕 introduces a situation that is likely to take place from the speaker's perspective. Usually the situation is a non-favorable one, similar to 'I am afraid that' in English.

❶ 壓力太大，恐怕會影響身體健康。
Yālì tài dà, kǒngpà huì yǐngxiǎng shēntǐ jiànkāng.
I'm afraid that too much stress will affect your physical health.

179

❷ 網路雖然把世界變小了，但是人跟人的關係恐怕更遠了。
Wǎnglù suīrán bǎ shìjiè biàn xiǎo le, dànshì rén gēn rén de guānxi kǒngpà gèng yuǎn le.
Although the internet has made the world smaller, I'm afraid that relationships between people are drifting further and further apart.

❸ 我租的房子，合約快到期了，恐怕得搬家。
Wǒ zū de fángzi, héyuē kuài dàoqí le, kǒngpà děi bānjiā.
The contract on the apartment I'm renting is almost up. I'm afraid I'll have to move.

❹ 走快一點吧。去晚了，恐怕小陳會生氣。
Zǒu kuài yìdiǎn ba. Qù wǎn le, kǒngpà Xiǎo Chén huì shēngqì.
Let's move faster. If we're late, Xiao Chen will probably get angry.

❺ 明天的報告，我還沒準備好，今天恐怕得熬夜。
Míngtiān de bàogào, wǒ hái méi zhǔnbèihǎo, jīntiān kǒngpà děi áoyè.
I haven't prepared the report for tomorrow, I'm afraid I'll have to burn the midnight oil tonight.

Structures

This adverb cannot be negated, nor can it be used in questions, as it is speaker-oriented.

Usage

(1) 大概 'approximately, about' and 可能 'probably' are also used to express an estimate. However, these expressions are neutral and don't usually suggest that the situation is non-favorable. For example: 我家離學校大概五百公尺。Wǒ jiā lí xuéxiào dàgài wǔbǎi gōngchǐ. 'my house is around 500 meters from school.' 我大概等了十分鐘就走了。Wǒ dàgài děngle shí fēnzhōng jiù zǒu le. 'I waited about 10 minutes, then I left.' 明天大概不會下雨。Míngtiān dàgài bú huì xiàyǔ. 'It probably won't rain tomorrow.' 今天晚上可能會下雨。Jīntiān wǎnshàng kěnéng huì xiàyǔ. 'It might rain tonight.'

(2) 恐怕 is used to indicate the speaker's conjecture. This contrasts with 怕, which can apply to anyone. 他怕熬夜會影響身體健康。Tā pà áoyè huì yǐngxiǎng shēntǐ jiànkāng. 'He's afraid that staying up late at night will affect (his) health.' 你怕下雨的話，就帶傘吧。Nǐ pà xiàyǔ de huà, jiù dài sǎn ba. 'If you're worried that it'll rain, go ahead and take an umbrella with you.'

快一點, kuài yìdiǎn, hurry up

Function

With this pattern, the speaker is urging the addressee to hurry up with something.

❶ 電影快開始了。我們快一點！
Diànyǐng kuài kāishǐ le. Wǒmen kuài yìdiǎn!
The movie is about to start. Let's hurry up.

❷ 哥哥跟弟弟說：「不要上網了，快一點去睡覺！」
Gēge gēn dìdi shuō: 'Búyào shàngwǎng le, kuài yìdiǎn qù shuìjiào!'
The older brother said to the younger brother: 'Get off the internet and hurry to bed!'

❸ 你最好快一點決定，這個房間可能很快就有人租了。
Nǐ zuìhǎo kuài yìdiǎn juédìng, zhè ge fángjiān kěnéng hěn kuài jiù yǒu rén zū le.
You'd better hurry up and decide. This room could be rented by someone very quickly. (i.e., Somebody might take this room any time.)

Structures

Negation: Only 不 can negate 快一點(V). The negated pattern indicates a mild alert, warning, 'If you do not hurry up and ....'

❶ 你不快一點吃完，我們就不能看電影了。
Nǐ bú kuài yìdiǎn chīwán, wǒmen jiù bù néng kàn diànyǐng le.
If you don't hurry up and finish eating, we won't be able to see the movie.

❷ 我們不快一點去吃飯，那家店可能就休息了。
Wǒmen bú kuài yìdiǎn qù chīfàn, nà jiā diàn kěnéng jiù xiūxí le.
If we don't hurry up and go eat, the restaurant might be closed (by the time we get there).

❸ 你不快一點來嚐嚐這個甜點，就被大家吃光了。
Nǐ bú kuài yìdiǎn lái chángcháng zhè ge tiándiǎn, jiù bèi dàjiā chīguāng le.
If you don't hurry up and try this dessert, it'll get eaten up by everybody else.

Usage

'快一點＋V' and 'V＋快一點' are two unrelated constructions. The first 快 refers to time (Hurry up!), while the second 快 refers to manner (fast vs. slowly).

❶ 快一點跑！
Kuài yìdiǎn pǎo!
Hurry up and run!

❷ 跑快一點！
Pǎo kuài yìdiǎn!
Run faster!

❸ 慢一點去！
Màn yìdiǎn qù!
Take your time and go later!

❹ 走慢一點！
Zǒu màn yìdiǎn!
Walk slower!

來, lái, (V), as in 來＋VP, to come to do something (1)

Function

'來＋VP' indicates the subject's intention of coming over to engage in something.

❶ 我來學中文。
Wǒ lái xué Zhōngwén.
I've come to study Chinese.

❷ 他來打籃球。
Tā lái dǎ lánqiú.
He came to play baseketball.

❸ 我和朋友來逛夜市。
Wǒ hàn péngyǒu lái guàng yèshì.
My friend and I came to wander around the night market.

Structures

Negation markers, auxiliary verbs, or adverbs are placed before the first verbal element 來.

Negation :

❶ 我明天有事不來上課。
Wǒ míngtiān yǒu shì bù lái shàngkè.
I have something to do tomorrow. I won't be coming to class.

❷ 那些學生都不來看電影。
Nàxiē xuéshēng dōu bù lái kàn diànyǐng.
None of those students will be coming to watch the movie.

❸ 他很忙，不來幫你裝有線電視了。
Tā hěn máng, bù lái bāng nǐ zhuāng yǒuxiàn diànshì le.
He is very busy. He can't come put cable television in for you.

Questions :

❶ 他不來吃晚飯嗎？
Tā bù lái chī wǎnfàn ma?
He's not coming to eat dinner?

❷ 你們常來游泳嗎？
Nǐmen cháng lái yóuyǒng ma?
Do you often come to swim?

❸ 你是不是來參觀故宮博物院？
Nǐ shìbúshì lái cānguān Gùgōng Bówùyuàn?
Are you coming to visit the Palace Museum?

Usage

The function of '來＋VP' is the same as that of '去＋VP'. The only difference is the direction of the subject's action, 來 towards and 去 away from the speaker's location.

❶ 我星期四來/去上書法課。
Wǒ xīngqísì lái/qù shàng shūfǎ kè.
I come/go take calligraphy classes on Thursdays.

❷ 我妹妹不想來/去吃牛肉麵。

Wǒ mèimei bù xiǎng lái/qù chī niúròu miàn.

My sister doesn't want to come/go eat beef noodles.

來, lái, as a verb complement, to get along well, to be able to relate to each other well (2)

Function ▶

When 來 is used as a non-directional complement, it conveys rapport, with V 得來 expressing good rapport and V 不來 the contrary.

❶ 他跟網友才見了一次面就覺得兩人很合得來，還約了下次一起去看電影。

Tā gēn wǎngyǒu cái jiànle yí cì miàn jiù juéde liǎng rén hěn hédelái, hái yuēle xià cì yìqǐ qù kàn diànyǐng.

He only met his online friend once but thought they got along famously. He even arranged for them to meet a second time at the movies.

❷ 我想我跟不愛乾淨的人一定合不來。

Wǒ xiǎng wǒ gēn bú ài gānjìng de rén yídìng hébùlái.

I don't think I would get along with someone who is messy.

❸ 他們很聊得來，尤其是一聊到吉他就聊個沒完。

Tāmen hěn liáodelái, yóuqí shì yì liáodào jítā jiù liáo ge méi wán.

They really hit it off, and once they got onto guitars they talked forever.

❹ 跟談不來的人說話，就連說一句話也嫌多。

Gēn tánbùlái de rén shuōhuà, jiù lián shuō yí jù huà yě xián duō.

It's hard talking to someone with whom you just don't click. Even a single sentence can feel like a lot of work.

❺ 別打擾他，他難得跟別人聊得來。你等一下再來找他吧。

Bié dǎrǎo tā, tā nándé gēn biérén liáodelái. Nǐ děng yíxià zài lái zhǎo tā ba.

Don't bother him. It's rare that he gets to talking like this with anyone. Come back in a bit.

Usage ▶

The complement 來 can only be used in the potential mode, and only with such social verbs as 談 tán, 合 hé, 聊 liáo, 處 chǔ.

了₁, le, (Ptc), Completed Action (1)

Function ▶

The verbal 了 is added after the verb to indicate that an action or instance was completed or had taken place. Compare the following.

我買了三張車票。　　　　vs.　　　我買三張車票。

Wǒ mǎile sān zhāng chēpiào.　vs.　Wǒ mǎi sān zhāng chēpiào.

I bought three tickets.　　　　　　　I buy three tickets.

183

❶ 我剛在便利商店喝了咖啡。
Wǒ gāng zài biànlì shāngdiàn hēle kāfēi.
I just had coffe at a convenience store.

❷ 我昨天吃了很多東西。
Wǒ zuótiān chīle hěn duō dōngxi.
I ate a lot of stuff yesterday.

❸ 今天早上我寫了一封信。
Jīntiān zǎoshàng wǒ xiěle yì fēng xìn.
I wrote a letter this morning.

❹ 他租了一個漂亮的房子。
Tā zūle yí ge piàoliàng de fángzi.
He rented a beautiful house.

Structures

Negation : The negation is marked by the negation marker 沒（有）méi (yǒu) before the verb. Note that the verbal 了 has been deleted in negative sentences.

❶ 我今天沒吃午餐。
Wǒ jīntiān méi chī wǔcān.
I didn't eat lunch today.

❷ 我最近很忙，一星期都沒看電視。
Wǒ zuìjìn hěn máng, yì xīngqí dōu méi kàn diànshì.
I have been very busy lately. I have not watched TV for a week.

❸ 昨天跟朋友去過生日，所以我沒寫功課。
Zuótiān gēn péngyǒu qù guò shēngrì, suǒyǐ wǒ méi xiě gōngkè.
Yesterday, I went to celebrate my friend's birthday so I did not do the homework.

Questions : To ask a question, 沒有 méi yǒu is added at the end of the sentence.

❶ 弟弟吃了午餐沒有？
Dìdi chīle wǔcān méi yǒu?
Did little brother eat his lunch?

❷ 下個月的學費，他付了沒有？
Xià ge yuè de xuéfèi, tā fùle méi yǒu?
Did he pay the tuition for next month?

❸ 今晚的籃球比賽開始了沒有？
Jīnwǎn de lánqiú bǐsài kāishǐle méi yǒu?
Has tonight's basketball game started yet?

Usage Note that the verbal 了 does not appear in negative sentences.

Wrong:	Correct:
*我沒吃了晚飯。	我沒吃晚飯。
*Wǒ méi chīle wǎnfàn.	Wǒ méi chī wǎnfàn.
	I didn't have dinner.

*我沒買了車票。
*Wǒ méi mǎi le chēpiào.

我沒買車票。
Wǒ méi mǎi chēpiào.
I didn't buy tickets.

了₁, le, (Ptc), Followed by Time-Duration (2)

Function

This pattern indicates the duration of a completed instance.

❶ 日本來的朋友在臺北玩了三天。
Rìběn lái de péngyǒu zài Táiběi wánle sān tiān.
My friend from Japan visited Taipei for three days.

❷ 老師在美國住了一年。
Lǎoshī zài Měiguó zhùle yì nián.
Our teacher stayed in the US for a year.

❸ 李小姐在語言中心工作了十個月。
Lǐ xiǎojiě zài yǔyán zhōngxīn gōngzuòle shí ge yuè.
Miss Li worked in the language center for ten month (and left).

Structures

The primary structure is verb＋Time Duration.

(1) If the verb is transitive and has an object after it, the verb must be repeated.

❶ 他租房子租了半年。
Tā zū fángzi zūle bàn nián.
He rented the house for half a year.

❷ 他住臺北住了三年。
Tā zhù Táiběi zhùle sān nián.
He lived in Taipei for three years.

(2) No verb repetition is needed if the object is moved to the very front of the sentence.

❶ 房子他只租了半年。
Fángzi tā zhǐ zūle bàn nián.
He rented the house for only half a year.

❷ 臺北他只住了三年。
Táiběi tā zhǐ zhùle sān nián.
He lived in Taipei for only three years.

Negation :

An intransitive verb receives the negation. If a transitive verb has its object following it, it must be repeated before it is negated.

❶ 他沒住幾天（就走了）。
Tā méi zhù jǐ tiān (jiù zǒu le).
He didn't stay very long and left.

❷ 他看書沒看多久，眼睛就痛了。
Tā kànshū méi kàn duōjiǔ, yǎnjīng jiù tòng le.
He didn't spend a long time reading, but his eyes started hurting.

Questions :

❶ 那間房子你租了一年半嗎？
Nà jiān fángzi nǐ zūle yì nián bàn ma?
Did you rent that house for one and half years?

❷ 你是不是在這裡等了一個鐘頭？
Nǐ shìbúshì zài zhèlǐ děngle yí ge zhōngtóu?
You waited here for an hour, right?

❸ 陳老闆去年是不是在紐約住了半年？
Chén lǎobǎn qùnián shìbúshì zài Niǔyuē zhùle bàn nián?
The Boss Chen stayed in New York for half a year last year, right?

了₂, le, (Ptc), Change in Situation (3)

| Function | The sentential 了 indicates a change in situations, i.e., some change has taken place, suggesting that things were not like this before.

❶ 咖啡貴了。
Kāfēi guì le.
Coffee is more expensive than before.

❷ 我會打網球了。
Wǒ huì dǎ wǎngqiú le.
I know how to play tennis now. (I didn't before.)

❸ 現在有手機的人多了。
Xiànzài yǒu shǒujī de rén duō le.
More people own cellphones now.

❹ 我現在喜歡吃越南麵了。
Wǒ xiànzài xǐhuān chī Yuènán miàn le.
I've come to like Vietnamese noodles. (I didn't before.)

| Structures | The sentential 了 appears at the very end of the sentence, which can be either affirmative or negative.

Negation :

❶ 我媽媽不喝咖啡了。
Wǒ māma bù hē kāfēi le.
My mom doesn't drink coffee any more.

❷ 他不想買那支手機了。
Tā bù xiǎng mǎi nà zhī shǒujī le.
He doesn't want to buy that cellphone any more.

❸ 我們不要去參觀故宮了。
Wǒmen bú yào qù cānguān Gùgōng le.
We don't want to visit the Palace Museum any more.

Questions :

❶ 現在學中文的學生多了嗎？

Xiànzài xué Zhōngwén de xuéshēng duō le ma?

Are more students studying Chinese now?

❷ 你們不去臺東了嗎？

Nǐmen bú qù Táidōng le ma?

You're not going to Taitung?

❸ 手機是不是又貴了？

Shǒujī shìbúshì yòu guì le?

Are cellphones more expensive now?

了₂, (Ptc), in 快…了, kuài...le, about to　(4)

Function　The sentential particle 了 often appears in sentences that contain adverbs, 快 kuài, 要 yào, or 快要 kuàiyào indicating 'something will soon happen'. This 了 suggests an imminent change of situations.

❶ 快下雨了。

Kuài xiàyǔ le.

It's going to rain soon.

❷ 電影要結束了。

Diànyǐng yào jiéshù le.

The movie is about to finish.

❸ 爸爸快要到家了。

Bàba kuàiyào dào jiā le.

Dad is almost home.

Structures　This pattern cannot be negated.

Questions :

❶ 你媽媽的生日快到了嗎？

Nǐ māma de shēngrì kuài dào le ma?

Is your mom's birthday coming soon?

❷ 比賽要開始了嗎？

Bǐsài yào kāishǐ le ma?

Is the game about to start?

❸ 哥哥的女朋友快要回法國了嗎？

Gēge de nǚpéngyǒu kuàiyào huí Fǎguó le ma?

Is brother's girlfriend going back to France soon?

Usage　This pattern indicates that an instance will soon take place. In Taiwan, the bi-syllabic 快要 kuàiyào is preferred. For example, 我的生日快要到了。Wǒ de shēngrì kuàiyào dào le. 'My birthday is coming soon.' If there is a time word, 快要 kuàiyào can not be used, e.g., *他明天快要回來了 *Tā míngtiān kuàiyào huílái le 'He will be coming home tomorrow'.

了₁…了₂, (le (Ptc)... le (Ptc)), Completion-to-date (5)

Function

The Double 了 ＋Time-Duration pattern indicates the completion of an action up to the time of speaking. The action may or may not continue, depending on the context.

❶ 她已經在臺灣玩了一年了。
Tā yǐjīng zài Táiwān wánle yì nián le.
She has already been in Taiwan for a year.

❷ 陳小姐在美國住了五年了。
Chén xiǎojiě zài Měiguó zhùle wǔ nián le.
Miss Chen has lived in the US for five years.

❸ 我工作了兩個月了。
Wǒ gōngzuòle liǎng ge yuè le.
I've been working for two months by now.

❹ 這間房子，他已經租了半年了。
Zhè jiān fángzi, tā yǐjīng zūle bàn nián le.
He has been renting this house for half a year.

❺ 他們學中文學了三個星期了。
Tāmen xué Zhōngwén xuéle sān ge xīngqí le.
They have studied Chinese for three weeks now.

離, lí, (Prep), distance from

Function

The preposition 離 marks the distance between two points.

❶ 我家離學校很遠。
Wǒ jiā lí xuéxiào hěn yuǎn.
My home is far away from the school.

❷ 離火車站很近的地方，有一家（牛肉）麵店的牛肉麵很好吃。
Lí huǒchē zhàn hěn jìn de dìfāng, yǒu yì jiā (niúròu) miàn diàn de niúròu miàn hěn hǎochī.
There is a very good beef noodle place close to the train station.

❸ 你從這裡往左邊走，離學校不遠的地方，可以看到海。
Nǐ cóng zhèlǐ wǎng zuǒbiān zǒu, lí xuéxiào bù yuǎn de dìfāng, kěyǐ kàndào hǎi.
Walk left from here. Not far from the school, you can see the ocean.

Structures

離 cannot be directly negated, unlike most other prepositions, unless 不是 is used.

*N*egation :

❶ 銀行離學校不遠。你應該走路去就可以了。
Yínháng lí xuéxiào bù yuǎn. Nǐ yīnggāi zǒulù qù jiù kěyǐ le.
The bank is not far from the school. You can walk there.

❷ 花蓮離台北不很遠，可是到那裡要花不少時間。
Huālián lí Táiběi bù hěn yuǎn, kěshì dào nàlǐ yào huā bù shǎo shíjiān.
Hualien is not very far from Taipei, but getting there takes a long time.

❸ 我要找的房子，不能離夜市太近。
Wǒ yào zhǎo de fángzi, bù néng lí yèshì tài jìn.
The house I want cannot be too close to the night market.

❹ 他家不是離公車站很遠。
Tā jiā búshì lí gōngchē zhàn hěn yuǎn.
His house is not far from a bus station.

*Q*uestions：

❶ 學校離郵局遠不遠？
Xuéxiào lí yóujú yuǎn bù yuǎn?
Is the school far from the post office?

❷ 你家離捷運站是不是很遠？
Nǐ jiā lí jiéyùn zhàn shìbúshì hěn yuǎn?
Is your home far from an MRT Station?

❸ 你們國家離臺灣遠嗎？
Nǐmen guójiā lí Táiwān yuǎn ma?
Is your country far from Taiwan?

離合詞, líhécí, Separable Verbs

Function

This is a special type of verb. The inherent property of all separable verbs is [V＋N]. The V and N can be separated and an element inserted in between them. This contradicts the inseparability of words in most languages, e.g., *under-a bit-stand. Examples of separable verbs are: 唱歌 chànggē 'to sing', 上班 shàngbān 'to work', 上網 shàngwǎng 'to go online', 上課 shàngkè 'to go to class', 生病 shēngbìng 'to be sick', 睡覺 shuìjiào 'to sleep', 看書 kànshū 'to read', 念書 niànshū 'to study', 滑雪 huáxuě 'to ski', 游泳 yóuyǒng 'to swim', 照相 zhàoxiàng 'to take photos', 吃飯 chīfàn 'to eat', 做飯 zuòfàn 'to cook', 見面 jiànmiàn 'to meet'.

Structures

Basically, there are three types of separable forms.

(1) 了 inserted. The 了 is the Verbal 了 here. (了₁)

❶ 他回了家以後，就開始工作。
Tā huíle jiā yǐhòu, jiù kāishǐ gōngzuò.
He started working after he got home.

❷ 我昨天下了課就跟朋友去看電影。
Wǒ zuótiān xiàle kè jiù gēn péngyǒu qù kàn diànyǐng.
I went to see a movie with friends after class yesterday.

189

❸ 他結了婚以後就放棄念書了。
Tā jiéle hūn yǐhòu jiù fàngqì niànshū le.
He gave up study after marriage.

(2) Recipients inserted. This noun refers to the recipient of an action.

❶ 我想見你一面。
Wǒ xiǎng jiàn nǐ yí miàn.
I want to meet with you once.

❷ 他總是生你的氣。
Tā zǒngshì shēng nǐ de qì.
He is always mad at you.

❸ 我們都應該幫別人的忙。
Wǒmen dōu yīnggāi bāng biérén de máng.
We should always help others.

(3) Time-Duration insterted.

❶ 我們每天上八個鐘頭的班。
Wǒmen měi tiān shàng bā ge zhōngtóu de bān.
We work eight hours a day.

❷ 你們新年的時候,放幾天的假?
Nǐmen xīnnián de shíhòu, fàng jǐ tiān de jià?
How many days do you get off for New Year's?

❸ 他唱了三小時的歌,有一點累。
Tā chàngle sān xiǎoshí de gē, yǒu yìdiǎn lèi.
He sang for three hours and is a little tired.

連 A 都 B, (lián (Prep) A dōu (Adv) B), even

Function　The preposition 連 introduces the focus of a sentence, highlighting a noun against all other related nouns in a given context. Positive sentences highlight a noun considered to be the best possible, whereas negative sentences highlight a noun considered to be the worst possible.

❶ 他喜歡到處吃小吃,連南部夜市都去過。
Tā xǐhuān dàochù chī xiǎochī, lián nánbù yèshì dōu qùguò.
He likes to go all around trying out the light repasts. He has even been to night markets in the south.

❷ 他把錢都花完了,現在連三十塊的咖啡都喝不起。
Tā bǎ qián dōu huāwán le, xiànzài lián sānshí kuài de kāfēi dōu hēbùqǐ.
He's spent all his money. Now he can't even afford a NT$30 coffee.

❸ 夏天去旅行真麻煩,連一家民宿都訂不到。
Xiàtiān qù lǚxíng zhēn máfán, lián yì jiā mínsù dōu dìngbúdào.
Traveling in the summer is a headache. You can't even book a B&B.

Structures　都 in this pattern can be replaced by 也. If the focus is the object, the '連＋focus' part can appear either before or after the subject.

❶ 他連你都忘了。
Tā lián nǐ dōu wàng le.
He even forgot you.

❷ 連你，他也忘了。
Lián nǐ, tā yě wàng le.
He even forgot you.

Negation : Unlike most prepositions in Chinese, 連 cannot be negated either by 不 or by 沒. Only 不是 negaiton is possible, e.g., 他不是連大學都沒上。Tā búshì lián dàxué dōu méi shàng. It's not true that he did not even attend college.

Questions :

❶ 你學過經濟，但是這本討論經濟的書，是不是連你也看不懂？
Nǐ xuéguò Jīngjì, dànshì zhè běn tǎolùn jīngjì de shū, shìbúshì lián nǐ yě kànbùdǒng?
You have studied Economics, but this book on economic issues is beyond even you, right?

❷ 你跟他認識，怎麼連他已經結婚了也不知道？
Nǐ gēn tā rènshì, zěnme lián tā yǐjīng jiéhūnle yě bù zhīdào?
The two of you know each other, so how can you not know that he is married?

❶ 這次考試太難了，連成績好的學生也考得不好？
Zhè cì kǎoshì tài nán le, lián chéngjī hǎo de xuéshēng yě kǎo de bù hǎo?
This exam was so difficult that even the top students did poorly?

Usage

(1) The noun introduced by 連 can be the subject or the object.

❶ 他學了兩年法文，連簡單的自我介紹都說不好。(object)
Tā xuéle liǎng nián Fǎwén, lián jiǎndān de zìwǒ jièshào dōu shuōbùhǎo.
He studied French for two years, but can't even introduce himself properly.

❷ 大家都去上課了，宿舍裡連一個人都沒有。(object)
Dàjiā dōu qù shàngkè le, sùshè lǐ lián yí ge rén dōu méi yǒu.
Everybody went to class. There is not even a single person in the dorms.

❸ 寫漢字不容易，連大學生都不一定寫得好。(subject)
Xiě Hànzì bù róngyì, lián dàxuéshēng dōu bùyídìng xiědehǎo.
Chinese characters are not easy to write. Even college students are not necessarily able to write them well.

❹ 餃子，連我都會包，媽媽當然包得更好。(subject)
Jiǎozi, lián wǒ dōu huì bāo, māma dāngrán bāo de gèng hǎo.
Even I can make dumplings, so of course mom makes them better.

191

(2) The noun introduced by 連 is the focus, highlighted against other nouns, with a hidden implication.

❶ 王老師什麼菜都會做，連義大利菜也會。(implication: Italian food is not easy to cook.)
Wáng lǎoshī shénme cài dōu huì zuò, lián Yìdàlì cài yě huì.
Teacher Wang can cook any type of dish. He can even cook Italian food.

❷ 誰都會做義大利菜，連王老師也會。(implication: Wang Laoshi is not a good cook.)
Shéi dōu huì zuò Yìdàlì cài, lián Wáng lǎoshī yě huì.
Anyone can cook Italian food; even Teacher Wang can.

(3) When a verb is to be highlighted, it is repeated in the negative. And the meaning of the sentence is negative, derogatory in tone.

❶ 我送了一本書給她，她連看都不看，我有點失望。
Wǒ sòngle yì běn shū gěi tā, tā lián kàn dōu bú kàn, wǒ yǒu diǎn shīwàng.
I gave her a book but she didn't so much as look at it, so I'm a little disappointed.

❷ 小李連問也沒問，就把我的筆拿走了。
Xiǎo Lǐ lián wèn yě méi wèn, jiù bǎ wǒ de bǐ názǒu le.
Without even asking, Xiao Li took my pen away.

了, liǎo, (Ptc), as Verb Complement, capability

Function 了 liǎo is a capability verb complement, used only in the potential pattern. 了 means that a result can be achieved.

❶ 這碗牛肉麵，我一個人吃得了。
Zhè wǎn niúròu miàn, wǒ yí ge rén chīdeliǎo.
I can finish this bowl of beef noodles.

❷ 這麼多書，我拿不了。
Zhème duō shū, wǒ nábùliǎo.
I cannot carry so many books.

❸ 颱風來了，今天晚上的喜宴我們去不了了。
Táifēng lái le, jīntiān wǎnshàng de xǐyàn wǒmen qùbùliǎo le.
There is a typhoon coming in so we won't be going to the wedding reception tonight.

❹ 到現在我還忘不了第一個筆友。
Dào xiànzài wǒ hái wàngbùliǎo dìyī ge bǐyǒu.
Even now, I still can't forget my first pen-pal.

Structures

*Q*uestions :

❶ 還要走半個小時，你走得了走不了？
Hái yào zǒu bàn ge xiǎoshí, nǐ zǒudeliǎo zǒubùliǎo?
We will still need to walk half an hour. Can you make it?

❷ 我們點了五道菜，吃得了吃不了？
Wǒmen diǎnle wǔ dào cài, chīdeliǎo chībùliǎo?
We ordered five dishes. Will we be able to finish them all?

❸ 雪這麼大，今天我們到得了山上嗎？
Xuě zhème dà, jīntiān wǒmen dàodeliǎo shān shàng ma?
With this much snow will we be able to reach the mountain today?

Usage

了 liǎo is an irregular complement. It can be used only in the potential mode, when regular complements can also be used in the actual mode, as indicated below.

	Actual		Potential	
	V-	沒 V-	V 得 -	V 不 -
了 liǎo	×	×	吃得了 chīdeliǎo 'can eat'	吃不了 chībùliǎo 'cannot eat'
完 wán	吃完 chīwán 'finish eating'	沒吃完 méi chīwán 'didn't finish eating'	吃得完 chīdewán 'able to finish eating'	吃不完 chībùwán 'unable to finish eating'

另外的, lìngwài de, another (See 別的 biéde)

亂, luàn, (Adv), as in 亂 + Verb, to do somethng in an irresponsible manner, risking undesirable consequences

Function

亂 is an adverb that refers to doing some action in a disorderly, irresponsible, destructive manner, risking undersirable consequences. The meaning originates from 亂 as a state verb.

Note the range of possible meanings through the translations below.

❶ 你不能亂倒垃圾，得等垃圾車來才能倒。
Nǐ bù néng luàn dào lèsè, děi děng lèsè chē lái cái néng dào.
You can't just dump your garbage anywhere. You need to wait for the garbage truck before you can dump it.

❷ 功課要好好地寫，不能亂寫。
Gōngkè yào hǎohǎo de xiě, bù néng luàn xiě.
You need to do a good job on your homework. You can't just do it haphazardly.

❸ 這些座位都有人坐，不能亂坐。
Zhèxiē zuòwèi dōu yǒu rén zuò, bù néng luàn zuò.
These seats are all occupied. You can't just sit anywhere you please.

❹ 你的感冒雖然不嚴重，可是不能自己亂買藥吃。
Nǐ de gǎnmào suīrán bù yánzhòng, kěshì bù néng zìjǐ luàn mǎi yào chī.
Your cold isn't serious, but you can't just go and buy any meds you want.

❺ 媽媽怕孩子亂花錢，不敢給孩子太多錢。
Māma pà háizi luàn huā qián, bù gǎn gěi háizi tài duō qián.
Moms are afraid their kids will spend money like there's no tomorrow, so they don't dare give them too much.

Usage

(1) 亂 is always negative in nature.
E.g., 亂寫 luàn xiě 'to write halfheartedly', 亂做 luàn zuò 'to do something carelessly', 亂選 luàn xuǎn 'to enroll in a course without thinking', 亂走 luàn zǒu 'to walk mindlessly', 亂交朋友 luàn jiāo péngyǒu 'to make friends indiscreetly', 亂打電話 luàn dǎ diànhuà 'to make phone calls mindlessly'… these phrases suggest a negative, halfhearted, or haphazard attitude or way of doing something. 亂, however, differs from 隨便 suíbiàn 'do as one pleases' in 隨便走走 suíbiàn zǒuzǒu 'to talk a walk casually without any intended destinations', 隨便拿一個 suíbiàn ná yí ge 'to take anyone that fancies you', 隨便坐 suíbiàn zuò 'to sit anywhere as you please'. 隨便 does not have the negative connotations.

(2) 亂＋V is also sometimes used in self-deprecation, often used to suggest humility.
E.g.,

❶ A：你真會穿，你的衣服都很講究。
Nǐ zhēn huì chuān, nǐ de yīfú dōu hěn jiǎngjiù.
You really know how to dress. You have very refined tastes when it omes to clothes.

B：哪裡，我是亂穿的。
Nǎlǐ, wǒ shì luàn chuān de.
Not at all. It's just something I threw on.

❷ A：你的報告寫得真好，拿到 A。
Nǐ de bàogào xiě de zhēn hǎo, nádào A.
Your report was written really well. You got an A.

B：哪裡，亂寫的，只是運氣好。
Nǎlǐ, luàn xiě de, zhǐshì yùnqì hǎo.
It was nothing. I just threw it together. It was just luck.

嗎, ma, (Ptc), Asking Questions (1)

Function

Questions can be formed using the question particle 嗎. It is usually used for short questions.

❶ 你好嗎？
Nǐ hǎo ma?
How are you?

❷ 你來接我們嗎？
Nǐ lái jiē wǒmen ma?
Are you here to pick us up?

❸ 他是日本人嗎？
Tā shì Rìběn rén ma?
Is he Japanese?

Structures sentence＋嗎？ The sentence in 嗎 questions can be either in the affirmative or negative.

*N*egation :

❶ 他不姓陳嗎？
Tā bú xìng Chén ma?
Isn't he surnamed Chen?

❷ 你不是臺灣人嗎？
Nǐ bú shì Táiwān rén ma?
Aren't you Taiwanese?

❸ 他不喝咖啡嗎？
Tā bù hē kāfēi ma?
Doesn't he drink coffee?

Usage The A-not-A question form involves no assumption, and is used for neutral inquiries or longer inquiries. It does not take a 嗎 question particle at the end of the sentence. One cannot say *這是不是茶嗎？ *Zhè shì bú shì chá ma? 'Is this tea?'. 嗎 questions, by contrast, are used for short inquiries.

❶ 你好嗎？
Nǐ hǎo ma?
How are you?

❷ 你要喝茶嗎？
Nǐ yào hē chá ma?
Do you want to drink tea?

❸ 你們要不要喝烏龍茶？
Nǐmen yào bú yào hē Wūlóng chá?
Do you want to drink Oolong tea?

嗎, ma, (Ptc), Confrontational (2)

Function In addition to making regular questions, 嗎 can also be used in mild confrontation. The speaker is not asking a question but is mildly challenging.

❶ 你覺得這個漢字很難寫嗎？
Nǐ juéde zhè ge Hànzì hěn nán xiě ma?
Do you think this Chinese character is difficult to write?

❷ 她不知道今天要考試嗎？
Tā bù zhīdào jīntiān yào kǎoshì ma?
Didn't she know there would be an exam today?

❸ 馬先生已經在這裡住了兩個月，還不知道丟垃圾的時間嗎？
Mǎ xiānshēng yǐjīng zài zhèlǐ zhùle liǎng ge yuè, hái bù zhīdào diū lèsè de shíjiān ma?
Mr. Ma has lived here two months and he still doesn't know when garbage is collected?

Structures　This pattern can be either positive or negative. Either 不 or 沒 negation can be used.

❶ 你不知道外國人不可以打工嗎？
Nǐ bù zhīdào wàiguó rén bù kěyǐ dǎgōng ma?
Don't you know that foreigners are not permitted to work?

❷ 他結婚的事，他沒告訴過你嗎？
Tā jiéhūn de shì, tā méi gàosùguò nǐ ma?
Didn't he ever tell you he's married?

❸ 你沒看見我正在忙嗎？
Nǐ méi kànjiàn wǒ zhèngzài máng ma?
Can't you see I'm busy?

Usage　Confrontational, or rhetorical, questions usually imply the speaker's surprise or annoyance. Such questions are uttered in a high-level intonation, as is also the case in English. Thus 嗎 questions are more complex than A-not-A questions.

嘛, ma, (Ptc), isn't it obvious that

Function　嘛 is a sentence-final particle that affirms what should be obvious, either to the speaker or from the context.

❶ 我願意幫你忙，因為我們是好朋友嘛！
Wǒ yuànyì bāng nǐ máng, yīnwèi wǒmen shì hǎo péngyǒu ma!
Of course I'm willing to help, because we are good friends!

❷ 王先生是為了做生意，才不得不喝酒嘛！
Wáng xiānshēng shì wèile zuò shēngyì, cái bùdébù hē jiǔ ma!
Mr. Wang only drinks because doing business requires it!

❸ 他的叔叔出來競選，是想為大家做事嘛！
Tā de shúshu chūlái jìngxuǎn, shì xiǎng wèi dàjiā zuòshì ma!
His uncle is running for an office, because it is obvious that he has the public's interest in mind!

❹ 看表演的時候穿著整齊，是為了尊重演出者嘛！

Kàn biǎoyǎn de shíhòu chuānzhuó zhěngqí, shì wèile zūnzhòng yǎnchū zhě ma!

You should look presentable when going to a performace. It shows respect to the performers!

❺ 哥哥常常打籃球，是因為他對籃球有興趣嘛！

Gēge chángcháng dǎ lánqiú, shì yīnwèi tā duì lánqiú yǒu xìngqù ma!

He often plays basketball. It's just what he loves to do!

滿, mǎn, (Vs), as Verb Complement, crowded with (1)

Function The state verb 滿 'full' serves as a result complement in this pattern. This pattern employs exaggeration to indicate a large number of items in a given location.

❶ 街道的兩邊蓋滿了新的大樓。

Jiēdào de liǎng biān gàimǎnle xīn de dàlóu.

Both sides of the road are bristling with new buildings.

❷ 101大樓前面擠滿了看跨年煙火的年輕人。

101 dàlóu qiánmiàn jǐmǎnle kàn kuànián yānhuǒ de niánqīng rén.

The area in front of Taipei 101 was packed with young people watching the New Year's Eve fireworks.

❸ 客廳牆上掛滿了他去花蓮拍的照片。

Kètīng qiáng shàng guàmǎnle tā qù Huālián pāi de zhàopiàn.

The living room wall was packed with photographs he took while in Hualien.

❹ 不到八點，教室裡就坐滿了學生。

Búdào bādiǎn, jiàoshì lǐ jiù zuòmǎnle xuéshēng.

It's not even eight o'clock yet and the classroom is filled with students.

❺ 這個袋子裡怎麼塞滿了垃圾？

Zhè ge dàizi lǐ zěnme sāimǎnle lèsè?

Why is this bag stuffed full of garbage?

Usage This type of existential sentence indicates the existence of a noun at a location.

滿, mǎn, (Vpt), to reach a ceiling (2)

Function Here, 滿 is a transitive process verb, suggesting 'to satisfy a required amount'. Some of the concepts in question may be puzzling or at least rather foreign to learners. This has to do with culture. When a baby is 滿月 mǎnyuè, it is exactly one month old. 30 full days are required for the concept of 滿月.

❶ 台灣的法律規定，滿 18 歲才可以接受醫美手術。
Táiwān de fǎlǜ guīdìng, mǎn 18 suì cái kěyǐ jiēshòu yīměi shǒushù.
Taiwan law stipulates that a person can only undergo cosmetic surgery after he or she is 18-years old. What about in your country?

❷ 按照我們公司的規定，服務滿一年可以休七天假。
Ànzhào wǒmen gōngsī de guīdìng, fúwù mǎn yì nián kěyǐ xiū qī tiān jià.
According to our company's rules, after serving in the company for one year, you can get seven days of vacation.

❸ 最近百貨公司週年慶，不但最高打五折，消費滿三千塊錢，還另外再送禮物。
Zuìjìn bǎihuò gōngsī zhōuniánqìng, búdàn zuì gāo dǎ wǔ zhé, xiāofèi mǎn sānqiān kuài qián, hái lìngwài zài sòng lǐwù.
The department store has been having its anniversary sale recently. Not only are they offering up to 50% off, if you spend NT$3,000, they will even give you a gift.

❹ 時間過得真快。再一個月，我來台灣就滿兩年了。
Shíjiān guò de zhēn kuài. Zài yí ge yuè, wǒ lái Táiwān jiù mǎn liǎng nián le.
Time passes really quickly. In another month, I'll have been in Taiwan for two years.

❺ 外國人在台灣住滿六個月就可以申請參加健康保險了。
Wàiguó rén zài Táiwān zhùmǎn liù ge yuè jiù kěyǐ shēnqǐng cānjiā jiànkāng bǎoxiǎn le.
After living in Taiwan for six months, foreigners can apply for health insurance.

Usage

(1) In most of the examples above, 滿 is a primary verb of the whole sentence. It can also be a complement to an action verb. For example:

❶ 服務生，麻煩你幫我把杯子加滿水。謝謝。
Fúwùshēng, máfán nǐ bāng wǒ bǎ bēizi jiāmǎn shuǐ. Xièxie.
Waiter, please fill my glass up with water. Thank you.

❷ 要是每天能睡滿八小時，身體一定會很健康。
Yàoshi měi tiān néng shuìmǎn bā xiǎoshí, shēntǐ yídìng huì hěn jiànkāng.
If one can sleep a full eight hours a day, one is sure to be healthy.

❸ 媽在屋子前面種滿了花。
Mā zài wūzi qiánmiàn zhòngmǎnle huā.
Mom planted tons of flowers in front of the house.

(2) 滿 as used in this pattern is different from another instance of 滿 where 滿 is consistently used as a verb complement in existential sentences. (see 滿(1))

Measures, (nominal), Units for Counting Nouns in Chinese (1)

Function

Nouns in Chinese are not directly countable. To count nouns, measures are used in between numbers and nouns.

❶ 一個朋友
yí ge péngyǒu
a friend

❷ 三本書
sān běn shū
three books

❸ 四張紙
sì zhāng zhǐ
four piece of papar

❹ 四枝毛筆
sì zhī máobǐ
four Chinese writing brush

Structures

(1) Number＋Measure＋Noun

❶ 三個人
sān ge rén
three people

❷ 幾張照片？
jǐ zhāng zhàopiàn?
How many photos?

(2) Determiner＋Number＋Measure＋Noun

❶ 那兩個人
nà liǎng ge rén
those two people

❷ 這三本書
zhè sān běn shū
these three books

When the number following 哪nǎ, 那nà, or 這zhè is 一yī 'one', the number is often omitted. For example, 哪一個人nǎ yí ge rén 'which person?' is the same as 哪個人nǎ ge rén. Likewise, 這個人zhè ge rén 'this person' and 那本書nà běn shū 'that book'.

Usage

(1) There are many measure words in Chinese. In linguistics, most of them are called classifiers. Different measure words are used with different nouns. 個ge is the most frequently used measure word and is used as the measure for many different kinds of nouns. When learning a new noun, we need to pay attention to the measure words that can be used with it.

(2) When the numeral is 'two', you do not say '二èr＋measure＋noun',
rather you say '兩liǎng＋measure＋noun',
i.e., 兩＋Measure＋Noun

兩	個	妹妹	liǎng ge mèimei (two sisters)
兩	個	日本人	liǎng ge Rìběn rén (two Japanese people)
兩	張	照片	liǎng zhāng zhàopiàn (two photos)

(3) Some common measures and their associated nouns.

1	個	朋友	老師	學生	人	妹妹
	ge	péngyǒu	lǎoshī	xuéshēng	rén	mèimei
		friend	teacher	student	person	sister
2	本	書	雜誌	小說	課本	日記
	běn	shū	zázhì	xiǎoshuō	kèběn	rìjì
		book	magazine	novel	textbook	diary
3	支	手機	傘	舞	牙刷	廣告
	zhī	shǒujī	sǎn	wǔ	yáshuā	guǎnggào
		cellphone	umbrella	dance	toothbrush	advertisement
4	塊	蛋糕	布	肉	玉	木頭
	kuài	dàngāo	bù	ròu	yù	mùtou
		cake	cloth	meat	jade	wood
5	條	魚	河	毛巾	裙子	馬路
	tiáo	yú	hé	máojīn	qúnzi	mǎlù
		fish	river	towel	skirt	road
6	種	水果	方法	情況	感覺	產品
	zhǒng	shuǐguǒ	fāngfǎ	qíngkuàng	gǎnjué	chǎnpǐn
		fruit	method	situation	feeling	product
7	隻	狗	小鳥	老虎	腳	眼睛
	zhī	gǒu	xiǎoniǎo	lǎohǔ	jiǎo	yǎnjīng
		dog	bird	tiger	foot	eye
8	家	公司	銀行	咖啡店	醫院	廠商
	jiā	gōngsī	yínháng	kāfēi diàn	yīyuàn	chǎngshāng
		company	bank	cafe	hospital	manufacturer
9	件	事	案子	外套	衣服	藝術品
	jiàn	shì	ànzi	wàitào	yīfú	yìshùpǐn
		thing	case	jacket	clothes	artwork
10	場	電影	比賽	音樂會	大雨	表演
	chǎng	diànyǐng	bǐsài	yīnyuè huì	dàyǔ	biǎoyǎn
		movie	competition	concert	heavy rain	performance

Measures, (verbal), 下xià, 趟tàng, 遍biàn, and 次cì (2)

Function Verb measures or classifiers, which usually appear after verbs, are used when the frequency or quantity of an action is expressed.

❶ 同學輕輕地打了他一下。
Tóngxué qīngqīng de dǎle tā yí xià.
His classmates hit him lightly. (i.e., tapped on/patted him)

❷ 泰國真好玩，我跟朋友去過兩趟。
Tàiguó zhēn hǎowán, wǒ gēn péngyǒu qùguò liǎng tàng.
Thailand is a lot of fun. My friend and I have been there twice.

❸ 那個電影我太喜歡了，所以看了好幾遍。
Nà ge diànyǐng wǒ tài xǐhuān le, suǒyǐ kànle hǎojǐ biàn.
I love that movie, so I watched it several times.

Structures

When both verb classifiers and objects appear in a sentence, the position of the object can vary. See below.

❶ a. 我存了兩次資料，怎麼不見了？ (after a verb classifier)
Wǒ cúnle liǎng cì zīliào, zěnme bújiàn le?
I saved the information twice. How can it be gone?

b. 那份資料，我存了兩次，怎麼不見了？ (moved to the front)
Nà fèn zīliào, wǒ cúnle liǎng cì, zěnme bújiàn le?
I saved the information twice. How can it be gone?

❷ 他打了我兩下。 (before a verb classifier)
Tā dǎle wǒ liǎng xià.
He hit me twice.

❸ 他把書看了一遍就去睡覺了。 (moved to become an object of 把)
Tā bǎ shū kànle yí biàn jiù qù shuìjiào le.
He read the book once before going to bed.

Questions :

❶ 你在台灣喝過幾次喜酒？
Nǐ zài Táiwān hēguò jǐ cì xǐjiǔ?
How many times have you been to a wedding receptions in Taiwan?

❷ 你昨天把第三課念過一遍了嗎？
Nǐ zuótiān bǎ dìsān kè niànguò yí biàn le ma?
Did you study chapter three (all the way through) once yesterday?

❸ 他很會打籃球，是不是參加過很多次籃球比賽？
Tā hěn huì dǎ lánqiú, shìbúshì cānjiāguò hěn duō cì lánqiú bǐsài?
He's very good at basketball. He's competed in many baseball games, right?

Usage

High-frequency verb classifiers include 下 xià (duration,frequency), 次 cì (frequency), 趟 tàng (frequency), and 遍 biàn (frequency).

(1) 次 is the most commonly used verb classifier to refer to the frequency of an action, i.e. number of times. It can be used with all action verbs, e.g., 看 kàn 'look, watch, read', 聽 tīng 'listen', 吃 chī 'eat', 去 qù 'go', 問 wèn 'ask', and 討論 tǎolùn 'discuss'.

(2) 趟 indicates one back-and-forth round for motion actions such as 來 lái 'come', 去 qù 'go', 走 zǒu 'walk', and 跑 pǎo 'run'.

(3) 遍 indicates the entirety of a process from beginning to end. Verbs that often go with 遍 include 看 kàn 'read', 聽 tīng 'listen', 念 niàn 'read', 寫 xiě 'write', 練習 liànxí 'practice', and 唱 chàng 'sing'. For example,

這本書，我看了一次。(I read this book once.)
Zhè běn shū, wǒ kànle yí cì.

這本書，我看了一遍。(I read this book once from beginning to end.)
Zhè běn shū, wǒ kànle yí biàn.

(4) 下 can refer either to the repeating of an action, or indicate brevity, depending on the verb involved. The second meaning goes with 去 qù 'go', 來 lái 'come', 問 wèn 'ask', 討論 tǎolùn 'discuss', 等 děng 'wait', where 一下 yí xià cannot be changed to, say, 三下 sān xià. The first meaning can go with 打 dǎ 'hit', 踢 tī 'kick', and 搖 yáo 'shake' where 一下 yí xià can be replaced by 兩下 liǎng xià or 三下 sān xià.

Measure 一M一M as Manner, one at a time

Function > This pattern modifies the verb to indicate the manner of 'one by one', 'one at a time'.

❶ 老師叫學生一個一個練習發音。
Lǎoshī jiào xuéshēng yí ge yí ge liànxí fāyīn.
The teacher had the students practice pronunciation one by one.

❷ 李太太把教室一間一間都打掃完了。
Li tàitai bǎ jiàoshì yì jiàn yì jiàn dōu dǎsǎowán le.
Mrs. Li cleaned up all of the classrooms one by one.

❸ 考試的時候，學生一遍一遍地檢查，怕不小心寫錯了字。
Kǎoshì de shíhou, xuéshēng yí biàn yí biàn de jiǎnchá, pà bù xiǎoxīn xiěcuòle zì.
After the exam, the students very thoroughly checked over their test papers, afraid they had written something wrong.

Structures > The adverbial marker 地, as in ❸ above, is optional in this pattern.

❶ 我把今天學的語法又一個一個地練習一遍。
Wǒ bǎ jīntiān xué de yǔfǎ yòu yí ge yí ge de liànxí yí biàn.
One by one I reviewed the grammar points I learned today.

❷ 他一個一個地給朋友打電話拜年。
Tā yí ge yí ge de gěi péngyǒu dǎ diànhuà bàinián.
He called his friends one by one to wish them a happy New Year.

❸ 麵包店的師父把蛋糕一層一層地做好了。
Miànbāo diàn de shīfù bǎ dàngāo yì céng yì céng de zuòhǎo le.
The baker at the bakery made the cake one layer at a time.

Negation : Either 不 or 沒 negation can be used.

❶ 學生的作業主任沒一本一本地檢查。

Xuéshēng de zuòyè zhǔrèn méi yì běn yì běn de jiǎnchá.

The director didn't check the students' work books one by one.

❷ 時間不夠了，這些店我們就不一家一家逛了。

Shíjiān bú gòu le, zhèxiē diàn wǒmen jiù bù yì jiā yì jiā guàng le.

There is not enough time, so we won't visit these stores one by one.

❸ 來面談的人太多了，他們的資料老闆不一個一個看了。

Lái miàntán de rén tài duō le, tāmen de zīliào lǎobǎn bù yí ge yí ge kàn le.

Too many people came for job interviews. The boss won't read their information one by one.

Questions :

❶ 買手機以前，你是不是都一支一支地試試看？

Mǎi shǒujī yǐqián, nǐ shìbúshì dōu yì zhī yì zhī de shìshìkàn?

Did you try out each cell phone one at a time before buying one?

❷ 那些照片，你是不是又一張一張上傳到網站了？

Nàxiē zhàopiàn, nǐ shìbúshì yòu yì zhāng yì zhāng shàngchuán dào wǎngzhàn le?

Did you upload the photos onto the webpage one by one again?

❸ 他是不是一家一家地逛這裡的百貨公司？

Tā shìbúshì yì jiā yì jiā de guàng zhèlǐ de bǎihuò gōngsī?

Did he go into each individual shop one by one at this department store?

沒有, méi yǒu, as used in Inferior Comparison

Function

The 'A 沒有 B (那麼 nàme/這麼 zhème)...' pattern is used to compare two things A & B and is used to indicate that A is not as (adjective) as B.

❶ 哥哥沒有爸爸高。

Gēge méi yǒu bàba gāo.

My older brother is not as tall as my dad.

❷ 火車沒有高鐵快。

Huǒchē méi yǒu gāotiě kuài.

The train is not as fast as the High Speed Rail.

❸ 我的中文沒有老師那麼好。

Wǒ de Zhōngwén méi yǒu lǎoshī nàme hǎo.

My Chinese is not as good as my teacher's.

❹ 這次的颱風沒有上次那麼可怕。

Zhè cì de táifēng méi yǒu shàng cì nàme kěpà.

This typhoon is not as scary as the last one.

Structures ▶ Note that this pattern is typically used in the negative, 沒(有) méi(yǒu). Sometimes, 那麼 nàme or 這麼 zhème can be omitted. Its positive counterpart is rarely used, except in 嗎 questions.

Questions: The A-not-A pattern is used for questions.

❶ 妹妹有沒有姊姊那麼漂亮？
Mèimei yǒu méi yǒu jiějie nàme piàoliàng?
Is the younger sister as pretty as the older sister?

❷ 花蓮的房租有沒有臺北的那麼貴？
Huālián de fángzū yǒu méi yǒu Táiběi de nàme guì?
Is rent in Hualien as expensive as in Taipei?

❸ 日本的工作有沒有美國的那麼難找？
Rìběn de gōngzuò yǒu méi yǒu Měiguó de nàme nán zhǎo?
Are jobs in Japan as hard to find as in the US?

❹ 夏天的天氣有沒有春天的舒服？
Xiàtiān de tiānqì yǒu méi yǒu chūntiān de shūfú?
Is the weather in the summer as pleasant as that in the spring?

Usage ▶ This pattern indicates that A is not as (adjective) as B, thus inferior so to speak. When A and B are the same, use the 'equal degree' pattern, i.e. 'A 跟 gēn B 一樣 yíyàng…'. The pattern for 'superior degree' is 'A 比 bǐ B…'. When you ask a question like 今天有沒有昨天熱？Jīntiān yǒu méi yǒu zuótiān rè? 'Is today as hot as yesterday?', it is assumed that yesterday was quite hot. Three different responses to this question are possible as shown below:

❶ 今天跟昨天一樣熱。　　　　(equal degree)
Jīntiān gēn zuótiān yíyàng rè.
Today is as hot as yesterday.

❷ 今天沒有昨天那麼熱。　　　(inferior degree)
Jīntiān méi yǒu zuótiān nàme rè.
Today is not as hot as yesterday.

❸ 今天比昨天熱。　　　　　　(superior degree)
Jīntiān bǐ zuótiān rè.
Today is hotter than yesterday.

每, měi, (Det), each and every　(1)

Function ▶ The determiner 每 měi indicates each and every.

❶ 他妹妹每天都上班。不休息。
Tā mèimei měi tiān dōu shàngbān. Bù xiūxí.
His sister works every days. She doesn't take days off.

❷ 他朋友每個週末都去游泳。
Tā péngyǒu měi ge zhōumò dōu qù yóuyǒng.
His friend goes to the swimming every weekend.

❸ 每一間教室都可以上網。
Měi yì jiān jiàoshì dōu kěyǐ shàngwǎng.
The internet can be accessed from every classroom.

❹ 他家人，每個人都會說法語。
Tā jiārén, měi ge rén dōu huì shuō Fǎyǔ.
Everyone in his family can speak French.

Structures 每 is a determiner. A determiner precedes numbers. Sentences with 每 almost always include the adverb 都 dōu 'all' to reinforce the sense of 'no exception'. 每＋M＋N＋都⋯. See the examples above.

*N*egation :

(1) Determiners themselves cannot be negated but the VPs that follow can.

❶ 他每天都不忙。
Tā měi tiān dōu bù máng.
He gets lots of free time every day.

❷ 我媽媽每個週末都沒空。
Wǒ māma měi ge zhōumò dōu méi kòng.
My mom is busy every weekend.

❸ 這家商店，每支手機都不便宜。
Zhè jiā shāngdiàn, měi zhī shǒujī dōu bù piányí.
Every cellphone (sold) in this store is not cheap.

(2) To indicate 'it is not the case that...', 不是 búshì is used before determiners.

❶ 他朋友不是每天都去看電影。
Tā péngyǒu búshì měi tiān dōu qù kàn diànyǐng.
His friend does not go to see a movie every day.

❷ 我們不是每天都有書法課。
Wǒmen búshì měi tiān dōu yǒu shūfǎ kè.
We don't have calligraphy class every day.

❸ 他的兄弟姐妹不是每個人都喜歡打球。
Tā de xiōngdì jiěmèi búshì měi ge rén dōu xǐhuān dǎ qiú.
Not all his siblings like to play ball.

*Q*uestions :

❶ 他每個週末都去哪裡運動？
Tā měi ge zhōumò dōu qù nǎlǐ yùndòng?
Where does he go every weekend to exercise?

❷ 你爸爸每天都在家吃晚飯嗎？
Nǐ bàba měi tiān dōu zài jiā chī wǎnfàn ma?
Does your dad eat dinner at home every day?

❸ 他的照片，每張都很好看嗎？
Tā de zhàopiàn, měi zhāng dōu hěn hǎokàn ma?
Does every one of his photos look nice?

Usage　每天měi tiān is the same as 每一天měi yì tiān 'every (single) day'. 一yī 'one' is often omitted. Similarly, 每個měi ge is the same as 每一個měi yí ge 'every (single) one', etc.

每, měi, (Det), as in 每＋Time Expression, Frequency　(2)

Function　This pattern indicates the happening of an instance at particular intervals of time, similar in meaning to the English sentence 'I clean the pool every 3 days'. Frequency consists of 每 followed by a time expression.

❶ 學校的游泳池每一個星期換一次水。
Xuéxiào de yóuyǒngchí měi yí ge xīngqí huàn yí cì shuǐ.
The school swimming pool changes water once a week. (i.e., The water in the school swimming pool is changed once a week.)

❷ 他每三天就去一次健身房。
Tā měi sān tiān jiù qù yí cì jiànshēnfáng.
He goes to the gym once every three days.

❸ 我姐姐每六個月就到外國旅行一次。
Wǒ jiějie měi liù ge yuè jiù dào wàiguó lǚxíng yí cì.
My elder sister takes a trip abroad once every six months.

Structures　每＋Time Expression＋VP

The subject can appear either before or after frequency phrase.

❶ 每一個星期我打一次電話回家。
Měi yí ge xīngqí wǒ dǎ yí cì diànhuà huí jiā.
Once a week, I call back home.

❷ 他每三天就去健身房運動一次。
Tā měi sān tiān jiù qù jiànshēnfáng yùndòng yí cì.
He goes to the gym to work out once every three days.

❸ 每一個月語言中心考兩次試。
Měi yí ge yuè yǔyán zhōngxīn kǎo liǎng cì shì.
The language center gives exams twice every month.

❹ 我每兩、三天就去吃一次牛肉麵。
Wǒ měi liǎng, sān tiān jiù qù chī yí cì niúròu miàn.
I eat beef noodles once every two or three days.

Negation :　不是 negation is the norm.

❶ 我們不是每半年交一次房租，是每兩個月交一次。
Wǒmen búshì měi bàn nián jiāo yí cì fángzū, shì měi liǎng ge yuè jiāo yí cì.
We pay rent once every two months, not once every half year.

❷ 他不是每兩年換一支手機。
Tā búshì měi liǎng nián huàn yì zhī shǒujī.
He doesn't update his cellphone once every two years.

❸ 我的電腦不是每三分鐘就存一次資料。
Wǒ de diànnǎo búshì měi sān fēnzhōng jiù cún yí cì zīliào.
My computer does not save data every three minutes.

Questions :

❶ 他每個月上幾次教堂？
Tā měi ge yuè shàng jǐ cì jiàotáng?
How many times does he go to church every month?

❷ 我們是不是每三個月有一次假期？
Wǒmen shìbúshì měi sān ge yuè yǒu yí cì jiàqí?
We have a vacation once every three months, right?

❸ 你去旅行的時候是不是每天都傳很多次簡訊給女朋友？
Nǐ qù lǚxíng de shíhòu shìbúshì měi tiān dōu chuán hěn duō cì jiǎnxùn gěi nǚpéngyǒu?
When you travel, do you send lots of texts to your girlfriend every day?

Usage

(1) In daily conversation, 每 is sometimes omitted, but then the time expression is spoken with a stress.

❶ 小明(每)半年跟大學朋友吃一次飯。
Xiǎomíng (měi) bàn nián gēn dàxué péngyǒu chī yí cì fàn.
Xiaoming dines with his friends from college every six months.

❷ 老師(每)三天就考一次聽寫。
Lǎoshī (měi) sān tiān jiù kǎo yí cì tīngxiě.
The teacher gives a dictation test every three days.

(2) Verb classifiers (like 次 and 趟), if any, are positioned either next to the verb or after the object. The former position is preferred.

❶ a. 張先生每半個月去一趟越南。
Zhāng xiānshēng měi bàn ge yuè qù yí tàng Yuènán.
Mr. Zhang goes to Vietnam every half month.

   b. 張先生每半個月去越南一趟。
Zhāng xiānshēng měi bàn ge yuè qù Yuènán yí tàng.
Mr. Zhang goes to Vietnam every half month.

❷ a. 你每個月上幾次教堂？
Nǐ měi ge yuè shàng jǐ cì jiàotáng?
How many times do you go to church every month?

b. 你每個月上教堂幾次？

Nǐ měi ge yuè shàng jiàotáng jǐ cì?

How many times do you go to church every month?

❸ 他每個月送兩次禮物給女朋友。

Tā měi ge yuè sòng liǎng cì lǐwù gěi nǚpéngyǒu.

He gives gifts to his girlfriend twice a month.

(*他每個月送禮物給女朋友兩次。)

(*Tā měi ge yuè sòng lǐwù gěi nǚpéngyǒu liǎng cì.)

(3) When 就 jiù is used in this pattern, it indicates that the frequency is higher than expected; if the frequency is lower than expected, 才 cái can be used. Please compare the following examples.

❶ 張主任每半年請我們吃一次飯。(factual statement)

Zhāng zhǔrèn měi bàn nián qǐng wǒmen chī yí cì fàn.

Director Zhang treats us to a meal every six months.

❷ 張主任每半年就請我們吃一次飯。(he's a generous person)

Zhāng zhǔrèn měi bàn nián jiù qǐng wǒmen chī yí cì fàn.

Director Zhang treats us to a meal (as frequently as) every six months.

❸ 張主任每半年才請我們吃一次飯。(he's a stingy person)

Zhāng zhǔrèn měi bàn nián cái qǐng wǒmen chī yí cì fàn.

Director Zhang treats us to a meal only every six months.

免得, miǎnde, (Adv), lest, so as to avoid

Function Advice is offered to avoid the occurrence of something undesirable. If what comes before 免得 is properly carried out, what comes after 免得 can be avoided.

❶ 你又咳嗽又發燒。快去看醫生吧，免得感冒越來越嚴重。

Nǐ yòu késòu yòu fāshāo, kuài qù kàn yīshēng ba, miǎnde gǎnmào yuèláiyuè yánzhòng.

You've got a cough and also a fever. You'd better go to a doctor right away, so that your cold will not get worse.

❷ 你有空的話去幫一下忙，免得他一個人忙不過來。

Nǐ yǒu kòng de huà qù bāng yíxià máng, miǎnde tā yí ge rén mángbúguòlái.

Give him a hand if you have a spare minute, otherwise he won't be able to handle it all by himself.

❸ 我們最好注意一下食材的產地，免得買到有問題的食品。

Wǒmen zuìhǎo zhùyì yíxià shícái de chǎndì, miǎnde mǎi dào yǒu wèntí de shípǐn.

We should keep an eye on where our food is produced so as to avoid buying anything suspect.

④ 我建議你多去參加一些社交活動，免得你一個人在家無聊。
Wǒ jiànyì nǐ duō qù cānjiā yìxiē shèjiāo huódòng, miǎnde nǐ yí ge rén zài jiā wúliáo.
You should go to more social functions, lest you grow bored at home.

⑤ 好好準備吧，免得口頭報告時太緊張而忘了要說什麼。
Hǎohǎo zhǔnbèi ba, miǎnde kǒutóu bàogào shí tài jǐnzhāng ér wàngle yào shuō shénme.
Be well prepared so that during your oral presentation you might avoid forgetting what to say because of nervousness.

明明, míngmíng, (Adv), it should be obvious to everyone that...

Function

The adverb 明明 indicates the speaker's annoyance at someone else's contradiction, whether explicit or implicit, of what seems to the speaker to be the plain truth.

① 小玉明明暗戀小王，可是不敢向他告白。
Xiǎoyù míngmíng ànliàn Xiǎo Wáng, kěshì bù gǎn xiàng tā gàobái.
It's so obvious that Xiaoyu has a thing for Xiao Wang, but she's just too shy to tell him that.

② 明明你們都知道他只在乎自己的利益，為什麼要選他？
Míngmíng nǐmen dōu zhīdào tā zhǐ zàihū zìjǐ de lìyì, wèishénme yào xuǎn tā?
You knew all along that he cares only for his own benefit, so why did you vote for him?

③ 小玉明明膽子很小，卻愛看恐怖片。
Xiǎoyù míngmíng dǎnzi hěn xiǎo, què ài kàn kǒngbùpiàn.
Xiaoyu is obviously a little scaredy cat, but she loves horror flicks.

④ 昨天的事，明明是你的錯。為什麼說是我的錯？
Zuótiān de shì, míngmíng shì nǐ de cuò. Wèishénme shuō shì wǒ de cuò?
About yesterday, it was obviously your fault, so why are you blaming me?

⑤ 這個房間裡都是垃圾。明明很髒，他還說很乾淨。
Zhè ge fángjiān lǐ dōu shì lèsè. Míngmíng hěn zāng, tā hái shuō hěn gānjìng.
His room is full of garbage. It's clearly a mess, but he insists it's clean.

Usage

By using the adverb 明明, the speaker confronts and challenges the addressee. This is rather impolite and should not be used lightly. 明明 is typically used in 2-clause utterances, with 明明 occurring with what the speaker believes to be the truth. More examples are given below.

❶ 你為什麼説這個蛋糕不好吃？明明很好吃啊！
　　Nǐ wèishénme shuō zhè ge dàngāo bù hǎochī? Míngmíng hěn hǎochī a!
　　Why did you say this cake doesn't taste good? It's obviously very
　　tasty!

❷ 誰説單身不好？她明明過得很好。
　　Shéi shuō dānshēn bù hǎo? Tā míngmíng guò de hěn hǎo.
　　Who says being single is not good? She's clearly getting along well.

❸ 她哪裡買不起房子？她明明是有錢人。
　　Tā nǎlǐ mǎibùqǐ fángzi? Tā míngmíng shì yǒuqiánrén.
　　Who says she can't afford a house? She's obviously rich.

❹ 你明明想買那種新手機，為什麼你説不想買？
　　Nǐ míngmíng xiǎng mǎi nà zhǒng xīn shǒujī, wèishénme nǐ shuō bù
　　xiǎng mǎi?
　　You obviously wanted to buy a new cell phone like that. Why did you
　　say you didn't want to buy one?

❺ 你明明去過日本，可是你為什麼説沒去過？
　　Nǐ míngmíng qùguò Rìběn, kěshì nǐ wèishénme shuō méi qùguò?
　　You've obviously been to Japan, but why did you say that you've
　　never been there?

❻ 小玉明明生病了，卻不去看醫生。
　　Xiǎoyù míngmíng shēngbìng le, què bú qù kàn yīshēng.
　　Xiaoyu is clearly sick, but she won't go see a doctor.

Multiple Verb Phrases

Function　　If there are more than one verb phrase in a sentence, the order of the verb
　　phrases reflects the temporal order in which the actions take place. This
　　construction is called Serial Verbs in linguistics.

❶ 我帶你們去你們的座位吧！
　　Wǒ dài nǐmen qù nǐmen de zuòwèi ba!
　　Let me take you to your seats.

❷ 他送美美回宿舍。
　　Tā sòng Měiměi huí sùshè.
　　He escorted Meimei to back to her dorm.

❸ 我跟弟弟去機場接朋友。
　　Wǒ gēn dìdi qù jīchǎng jiē péngyǒu.
　　My brother and I went to the airport to pick up a friend.

Structures　　The meaning of the sentence changes as the order of the verb phrases
　　changes. Compare the following sentences. However, only a handful of
　　verbs can do this.

❶ a. 我們送朋友去機場。
　　　Wǒmen sòng péngyǒu qù jīchǎng.
　　　We took our friends to the airport.

　　b. 我們去機場送朋友。
　　　Wǒmen qù jīchǎng sòng péngyǒu.
　　　We went to the airport to see our friends off.

❷ a. 他們坐巴士到台北。
　　　Tāmen zuò bāshì dào Táiběi.
　　　They took a bus to Taipei.

　　b. 他們到台北坐巴士。
　　　Tāmen dào Táiběi zuò bāshì.
　　　They went to Taipei to catch the bus.

❸ a. 小明送爸爸去高鐵站。
　　　Xiǎomíng sòng bàba qù gāotiě zhàn.
　　　Xiaoming took his father to the HSR Station.

　　b. 小明去高鐵站送爸爸。
　　　Xiǎomíng qù gāotiě zhàn sòng bàba.
　　　Xiaoming went to the HSR Station to see his father off.

Negation :　The negation occurs before the first verb.

❶ 我還有事。我不送她回家了。
　　Wǒ hái yǒu shì. Wǒ bú sòng tā huíjiā lc.
　　I still have something to do, so I won't be taking her back (to her) home.

❷ 他沒送我去郵局。我是自己去的。
　　Tā méi sòng wǒ qù yóujú. Wǒ shì zìjǐ qù de.
　　He didn't take me to the post office, I went there by myself.

❸ 我自己去機場比較方便。你別送我了。
　　Wǒ zìjǐ qù jīchǎng bǐjiào fāngbiàn. Nǐ bié sòng wǒ le.
　　It would be easier for me to go to the airport on my own. You don't need to take me there.

Questions :　The A-not-A pattern applies only to the first verb. 是不是 pattern can also be used.

❶ 你去不去圖書館看一下書？
　　Nǐ qù bú qù túshūguǎn kàn yíxià shū?
　　Are you going to the library to study for a bit?

❷ 你是不是搭捷運去山上喝茶？
　　Nǐ shìbúshì dā jiéyùn qù shān shàng hē chá?
　　Are you taking the MRT to the top of the moutain and have some tea?

❸ 王老師明天帶不帶我們去看電腦展？
　　Wáng lǎoshī míngtiān dài bú dài wǒmen qù kàn diànnǎo zhǎn?
　　Will Teacher Wang take us to see the computer exhibition tomorrow?

211

拿⋯來說, (ná (Prep)...lái shuō), take...as an example

Function With this pattern, the speaker presents a statement from a given perspective.

❶ 我們公司的產品最有競爭力。拿價錢來說,我們的產品是市場上最便宜的。

Wǒmen gōngsī de chǎnpǐn zuì yǒu jìngzhēnglì. Ná jiàqián lái shuō, wǒmen de chǎnpǐn shì shìchǎng shàng zuì piányí de.

Our company's products are highly competitive. Take prices as an example, our products are the cheapest on the market.

❷ 我最怕參加比賽了。拿上次演講比賽來說,我緊張得把要說的話全忘了。

Wǒ zuì pà cānjiā bǐsài le. Ná shàng cì yǎnjiǎng bǐsài lái shuō, wǒ jǐnzhāng de bǎ yào shuō de huà quán wàng le.

I hate taking part in competitions. Take the last speech contest for example; I was so nervous that I completely forgot everything I was going to say.

❸ 車禍的原因常常都是車速太快。拿王大明上次出車禍來說,他的車速幾乎超過規定的一倍。

Chēhuò de yuányīn chángcháng dōu shì chēsù tài kuài. Ná Wáng Dàmíng shàng cì chū chēhuò lái shuō, tā de chēsù jīhū chāoguò guīdìng de yí bèi.

Speeding is often the reason for car accidents. Take Wang Daming's accident earlier. He was going almost twice the stipulated speed.

❹ 這家公司的待遇真不錯。拿休假來說,只要工作兩年就能休十天的假。

Zhè jiā gōngsī de dàiyù zhēn búcuò. Ná xiūjià lái shuō, zhǐyào gōngzuò liǎng nián jiù néng xiū shí tiān de jià.

This company's terms of employment are really good. Take paid vacation for example. You only need to work here two years to get ten days of vacation.

❺ 麗麗對穿很講究。拿外套來說,黑色的就有十件不同的款式。

Lìlì duì chuān hěn jiǎngjiù. Ná wàitào lái shuō, hēisè de jiù yǒu shí jiàn bùtóng de kuǎnshì.

Lili is very fussy about clothes. Take coats for example; she has ten different styles of coat that are all black.

哪裡, nǎlǐ, (Adv), rhetorical question

Function 哪裡 can also express a rhetorical question in refuting or in doubt, i.e., 'how can it be possible?' or 'cannot possibly...'.

❶ 一般大學剛畢業的年輕人哪裡有錢買房子?

Yìbān dàxué gāng bìyè de niánqīng rén nǎlǐ yǒu qián mǎi fángzi?

How could young university graduates possibly afford to buy a house?

❷ 這件事哪裡稀奇了？這種現象越來越普遍了。
Zhè jiàn shì nǎlǐ xīqí le? Zhè zhǒng xiànxiàng yuèláiyuè pǔbiàn le.
What's so strange about it? It's become rather common actually.

❸ 我哪裡是盲目升學？我以後還要念博士呢。
Wǒ nǎlǐ shì mángmù shēngxué? Wǒ yǐhòu hái yào niàn bóshì ne.
What do you mean I keep studying just for the sake of studying? I have plans to do a PhD.

❹ 你穿起來哪裡不好看？你穿起來跟模特兒一樣漂亮。
Nǐ chuānqǐlái nǎlǐ bù hǎokàn? Nǐ chuānqǐlái gēn mótèr yíyàng piàoliang.
What do you mean it doesn't look good on you? You look like a model in that.

❺ 我媽媽連電腦都不會用，哪裡會上網購物？
Wǒ māmā lián diànnǎo dōu bú huì yòng, nǎlǐ huì shàngwǎng gòuwù?
My mom doesn't even know how to use a computer. How could she possibly shop online?

Usage

哪裡, though originally an interrogative spatial pronoun, refers to the meaning of 'cannot possibly' here. This 哪裡 should be distinguished from the common response to 'thank you'.

A： 「謝謝。」
'Xièxie.'

B： 「哪裡！哪裡！」
'Nǎlǐ! Nǎlǐ!'

難, nán, as in 難＋Verb, Special Meanings (See 好(1))

難道, nándào, (Adv), how could it possibly be true

Function

By using the adverb 難道, the speaker expresses his doubt that something he considers unlikely could ever take place. It is basically a rhetorical question.

❶ 動了微整型手術以後，難道就真能變得更有自信？
Dòngle wéizhěngxíng shǒushù yǐhòu, nándào jiù zhēn néng biàn de gèng yǒu zìxìn?
After undergoing micro-cosmetic surgery, are you telling me that a person really can gain self-confidence?

❷ 難道他是因為趕時間才出車禍的？
Nándào tā shì yīnwèi gǎn shíjiān cái chū chēhuò de?
Could it be that he only had the accident because he was in a hurry?

❸ 因為父母反對就放棄念理想的科系，難道你不覺得遺憾？

Yīnwèi fùmǔ fǎnduì jiù fàngqì niàn lǐxiǎng de kēxì, nándào nǐ bù juéde yíhàn?

Don't you think it a shame they had to give up studying in the department they wanted just because their parents opposed it?

❹ 這麼有名的鳳梨酥，難道你不想嚐嚐看？

Zhème yǒumíng de fènglísū, nándào nǐ bù xiǎng chángcháng kàn?

Pineapple cakes as famous as this, are you telling me that you don't even want to try one?

❺ 今天是星期一，你怎麼有空來看我？難道你真的辭掉工作了？

Jīntiān shì xīngqíyī, nǐ zěnme yǒu kòng lái kàn wǒ? Nándào nǐ zhēn de cídiào gōngzuò le?

Today's Monday. How do you have time to come see me? Are you telling me that you really quit your job?

Usage

(1) 難道 can co-occur with 嗎 in the same sentence. For example,

❶ 他寧可跟女朋友分手也不願意結婚。難道結婚真的那麼可怕嗎？

Tā níngkě gēn nǚpéngyǒu fēnshǒu yě bú yuànyì jiéhūn. Nándào jiéhūn zhēn de nàme kěpà ma?

He would rather break up with his girlfriend than get married. Could it be that marriage is really that scary?

❷ 阿姨讓小李每天喝魚湯。難道魚湯可以讓傷口好得快一點嗎？

Āyí ràng Xiǎo Lǐ měi tiān hē yú tāng. Nándào yú tāng kěyǐ ràng shāngkǒu hǎo de kuài yìdiǎn ma?

Xiao Li's aunt had Xiao Li drink fish soup every day. Are you telling me that fish soup can make your wound heal faster?

❸ 歐洲人很容易地佔領了台灣的土地。難道那時候台灣沒有政府嗎？

Ōuzhōu rén hěn róngyì de zhànlǐngle Táiwān de tǔdì. Nándào nà shíhòu Táiwān méi yǒu zhèngfǔ ma?

Europeans easily conquered in Taiwan. Are you telling me that Taiwan didn't have a government at that time?

(2) 難道 belongs to the same sub-category of adverbs such as 到底 dàodǐ and 居然 jūrán. This type of adverb can either precede or follow the subject, e.g., 你難道還下不了決心嗎？Nǐ nándào hái xiàbùliǎo juéxīn ma? ～難道你還下不了決心嗎？Nándào nǐ hái xiàbùliǎo juéxīn ma? 'Are you telling me you still can't make a decision?' In the former, the subject is prominently made the topic of the whole sentence. In the latter, 你 is a subject, but is not made a topic.

(3) In conversations, using 難道 etc, can be rather curt, confrontational, or even rude, where the speaker challenges the other party by enlisting an extreme case, a least probable situation, e.g.,

❶ 難道你要我把所有的錢都給你？
Nándào nǐ yào wǒ bǎ suǒyǒu de qián dōu gěi nǐ?
Are you telling me that you want me to give you all the money?

❷ 難道你窮得連一杯豆漿都喝不起？
Nándào nǐ qióng de lián yì bēi dòujiāng dōu hēbùqǐ?
Are you telling me that you are so poor that you can't even afford a cup of soy milk?

❸ 難道你預期他的得票率會超過百分之百？
Nándào nǐ yùqí tā de dépiàolǜ huì chāoguò bǎifēnzhībǎi?
Are you telling me that you anticipate he will receive a percentage of votes that exceeds 100%?

難得, nándé, (Adv), rarely

Function　難得 is an adverb, indicating the speaker's observation that such an instance is not commonly experienced.

❶ 他給自己很大的壓力。難得看到他輕鬆的樣子。
Tā gěi zìjǐ hěn dà de yālì. Nándé kàndào tā qīngsōng de yàngzi.
He is always putting so much pressure on himself, and it's rare to see him relaxed.

❷ 我難得來這附近的商業廣場。沒想到這裡這麼熱鬧。
Wǒ nándé lái zhè fùjìn de shāngyè guǎngchǎng. Méi xiǎngdào zhèlǐ zhème rènào.
I don't often come to this shopping district. I had no idea how bustling it is.

❸ 你們難得聽古典音樂吧？覺得怎麼樣？喜歡嗎？
Nǐmen nándé tīng gǔdiǎn yīnyuè ba? Juéde zěnmeyàng? Xǐhuān ma?
You don't often listen to classical music, do you? What do you think? Do you like it?

❹ 他的想法總是很正面，難得有負面的想法。
Tā de xiǎngfǎ zǒngshì hěn zhèngmiàn, nándé yǒu fùmiàn de xiǎngfǎ.
He's a very positive person, and it's rare that he is ever negative.

❺ 我難得看到他焦慮不安的樣子。發生了什麼事？
Wǒ nándé kàndào tā jiāolǜ bù'ān de yàngzi. Fāshēngle shénme shì?
I rarely see him anxious like this. What happened?

Usage 　難得 can also be a state verb modified by 很 or 真, e.g.,

真難得，那麼年輕就自食其力，不靠父母了。

Zhēn nándé, nàme niánqīng jiù zìshí qílì, bú kào fùmǔ le.

Now that's something you don't see every day. So young and standing on his own two feet and not relying on his parents.

難怪, nánguài, (Adv), no wonder

Function 　難怪, an adverb, introduces a 2nd clause in a 2-clause sentence. The second clause is concerned with the speaker's previous puzzlement, which has been clarified by a new observation presented in the first clause. The semantic structure is like this: 'new fact' clears away 'old puzzlement'.

❶ 他家過年過節都要拜祖先，難怪那麼早回家幫忙。

Tā jiā guònián guòjié dōu yào bài zǔxiān, nánguài nàme zǎo huíjiā bāngmáng.

His family venerates ancestors during Chinese New Year and other holidays. No wonder, he goes home so early to help out.

❷ 他下個星期有口頭報告，難怪這幾天都熬夜念書。

Tā xià ge xīngqí yǒu kǒutóu bàogào, nánguài zhè jǐ tiān dōu áoyè niànshū.

He has an oral report next week. No wonder, he's been burning the midnight oil lately.

❸ 美美要申請獎學金，難怪她請教授寫推薦信。

Měiměi yào shēnqǐng jiǎngxuéjīn, nánguài tā qǐng jiàoshòu xiě tuījiàn xìn.

Meimei wants to apply for a scholarship. No wonder, she asked the prof to write a letter of recommendation.

❹ 他剛才跟店員發生了一點糾紛，難怪說話的聲音那麼大。

Tā gāngcái gēn diànyuán fāshēngle yīdiǎn jiūfēn, nánguài shuōhuà de shēngyīn nàme dà.

He had a little dispute with the store employee just now. No wonder, his voice was so loud.

❺ 美美的爸爸最近沒工作了，難怪她哥哥放棄去法國留學。

Měiměi de bàba zuìjìn méi gōngzuò le, nánguài tā gēge fàngqì qù Fǎguó liúxué.

Meimei's dad has been out of work lately. No wonder, her brother gave up going to France to study.

難免, nánmiǎn, (Adv), inevitably, it is only natural that

Function 　難免 is an adverb, indicating that a situation is inevitable, that it cannot be helped or avoided.

❶ 很多學生好不容易考上了大學，難免想玩個夠，不想念書。
Hěn duō xuéshēng hǎobù róngyì kǎoshàngle dàxué, nánmiǎn xiǎng wán ge gòu, bù xiǎng niànshū.
Lots of students work extremely hard to get into university. Once they do, it's unavoidable that they'll want to let loose instead of studying.

❷ 有時候媒體的報導難免會有問題，所以大家要想一想，不能完全相信。
Yǒu shíhòu méitǐ de bàodǎo nánmiǎn huì yǒu wèntí, suǒyǐ dàjiā yào xiǎng yì xiǎng, bù néng wánquán xiāngxìn.
Errors in media reports are not always avoidable, so we ought to be discerning and not believe everything we hear.

❸ 張先生夫婦都失業了，難免會讓人擔心他們的未來。
Zhāng xiānshēng fūfù dōu shīyè le, nánmiǎn huì ràng rén dānxīn tāmen de wèilái.
Mr. Zhang and his wife both lost their jobs. That people are concerned for their future is inevitable.

❹ 年輕的一代已沒有重男輕女的觀念了，但老一輩的人難免還有這種想法。
Niánqīng de yí dài yǐ méi yǒu zhòngnán qīngnǚ de guānniàn le, dàn lǎoyíbèi de rén nánmiǎn hái yǒu zhè zhǒng xiǎngfǎ.
The younger generation may not be gender-biased, but among the elderly this way of thinking is to be expected.

❺ 由於「少子化」的關係，有些高中難免也受到了影響。
Yóuyú 'shǎozǐhuà' de guānxi, yǒuxiē gāozhōng nánmiǎn yě shòudào le yǐngxiǎng.
It is inevitable that the declining birth rate impacts some high schools.

Usage

難免 is rather versatile syntactically, unlike most adverbs, e.g.,

❶ 剛開始學中文時，難免會覺得很難。(pre-Vaux)
Gāng kāishǐ xué Zhōngwén shí, nánmiǎn huì juédé hěn nán.
When you first start studying Chinese, you're going to find it difficult. That's unavoidable.

❷ 剛開始學中文時，寫錯字是難免的。(as Predicate)
Gāng kāishǐ xué Zhōngwén shí, xiěcuò zì shì nánmiǎn de.
When you first start studying Chinese, it's inevitable that you write characters incorrectly.

❸ 雖然他的脾氣好，但對這件事也難免（會）生氣。(post-PP)
Suīrán tā de píqì hǎo, dàn duì zhè jiàn shì yě nánmiǎn (huì) shēngqì.
He has a good temper. That said, he's bound to get angry about this.

難以, nányǐ, (Vaux), to find it difficult to...

Function This Vaux indicates that it is difficult, almost impossible, to undertake something.

❶ 大學的學費漲了不少，使很多學生難以負擔。

Dàxué de xuéfèi zhǎng le bù shǎo, shǐ hěn duō xuéshēng nányǐ fùdān.

University tuitions have skyrocketed. A lot of students have a very hard time paying.

❷ 由於語言的障礙，他們兩個人一直難以溝通。

Yóuyú yǔyán de zhàng'ài, tāmen liǎng ge rén yìzhí nányǐ gōutōng.

The two of them have a difficult time communicating due to a language barrier.

❸ 政府的政策不夠有彈性，所以難以改善失業的情況。

Zhèngfǔ de zhèngcè bú gòu yǒu tánxìng, suǒyǐ nányǐ gǎishàn shīyè de qíngkuàng.

The government's policies are not flexible enough, so it is very difficult to improve unemployment.

❹ 要是該國再持續發展下去，我國將難以跟他們一較長短了。

Yàoshi gāi guó zài chíxù fāzhǎn xiàqù, wǒguó jiāng nányǐ gēn tāmen yíjiào chángduǎn le.

If that country in particular continues developing like this, our's will have a tough time keeping up.

❺ 這個週末他請我去吃他表哥的喜酒。我實在難以拒絕。

Zhè ge zhōumò tā qǐng wǒ qù chī tā biǎogē de xǐjiǔ. Wǒ shízài nányǐ jùjué.

He invited me to his cousin's wedding. How am I supposed to say no to that?

Usage

(1) 難以 is formal and is followed by a disyllabic verb, e.g.,

事情太複雜了，目前還難以處理。

Shìqíng tài fùzá le, mùqián hái nányǐ chǔlǐ.

The matter is really complicated and will be difficult to deal with at present.

(2) 難以 is always followed by VP, see examples above.

呢, ne, (Ptc), Contrastive tag Questions

Function The 呢 particle forms a tag question, i.e., 'how about'?

❶ 我要喝茶，你呢？

Wǒ yào hē chá, nǐ ne?

I want to drink tea, and you?

❷ 他不喝咖啡，陳小姐呢？

Tā bù hē kāfēi, Chén xiǎojiě ne?

He does not drink coffee. What about Miss Chen?

❸ 王先生是日本人，李先生呢？
Wáng xiānshēng shì Rìběn rén, Lǐ xiānshēng ne?
Mr. Wang is Japanese. What about Mr. Li?

> **Structures**

(1) Same predicate, different subjects
Subj.1 V Obj., Subj.2 呢？

❶ 他是美國人，你呢？
Tā shì Měiguó rén, nǐ ne?
He's American. And you?

❷ 他喜歡日本菜，你呢？
Tā xǐhuān Rìběn cài, nǐ ne?
He likes Japanese food. How about you?

(2) Same subject, different objects
Subj. V Obj.1, Obj.2 呢？

❶ 你喜歡喝茶，咖啡呢？
Nǐ xǐhuān hē chá, kāfēi ne?
You like to drink tea. How about coffee?

❷ 他不喝咖啡，茶呢？
Tā bù hē kāfēi, chá ne?
He doesn't drink coffee. How about tea?

能₁, néng, (Vaux), Capability (1)

> **Function**

The auxiliary verb 能 expresses some capability of the subject.

❶ 新手機能上網。
Xīn shǒujī néng shàngwǎng.
New cell phones can go online.

❷ 那支手機能照相。
Nà zhī shǒujī néng zhàoxiàng.
That cell phone can take photos.

❸ 他弟弟能吃四十個餃子。
Tā dìdì néng chī sìshí ge jiǎozi.
His younger brother can eat 40 dumplings.

❹ 我的車能坐八個人。
Wǒ de chē néng zuò bā ge rén.
My car can seat 8 people.

> **Structures**

Negation :

The negation marker 不 should be placed before, and not after the auxiliary verb.

❶ 我的手機不能上網。
Wǒ de shǒujī bù néng shàngwǎng.
My cell phone cannot access the internet.

❷ 我的小車不能坐那麼多人。
Wǒ de xiǎo chē bù néng zuò nàme duō rén.
My little car cannot hold that many people.

Questions :　　The auxiliary verb 能 is placed in the A position in the A-not-A pattern.

❶ 你的手機能不能照相？
Nǐ de shǒujī néng bù néng zhàoxiàng?
Can your cell phone take pictures?

❷ 那支手機能不能上網？
Nà zhī shǒujī néng bù néng shàngwǎng?
Can that cell phone go online?

❸ 你的手機能不能用十個小時？
Nǐ de shǒujī néng bù néng yòng shí ge xiǎoshí?
Can your cell phone last ten hours?

能₂, néng, (Vaux), Permission　(2)

Function　　能 can also refer to permission, e.g.,

❶ 明天，我能不能請假一天？
Míngtiān, wǒ néng bù néng qǐngjià yī tiān?
Can I take the day off tomorrow?

❷ 我能借一下筆嗎？
Wǒ néng jiè yíxià bǐ ma?
Can I borrow a pen?

❸ 他也能一起來嗎？
Tā yě néng yìqǐ lái ma?
Can he also come along?

Structures　　The same as for 能₁.

Usage　　能 permission overlaps with 可以 permission to such a great extent that 能 is often replaced by 可以, especially in negation, e.g., the negative answer to ❶ or ❸ above is often 不可以, especially in Taiwan. As a whole, 能 is used in greater frequency on mainland China than Taiwan where 可以 prevails.

能₃, néng, (Vaux), Possibility　(3)

Function　　能₃ refers to the possibility of implementing something when the circumstance is favorable.

❶ 我明天不能來開會。(otherwise engaged)
Wǒ míngtiān bù néng lái kāihuì.
I cannot make it to the meeting tomorrow.

❷ 咖啡也能外帶。(can be properly packed)
Kāfēi yě néng wàidài.
Coffee can also be taken to go.

❸ 小孩能不能在這裡玩手機？(any rules against it?)
　　Xiǎohái néng bù néng zài zhèlǐ wán shǒujī?
　　Can children use cell phones here?

❹ 他的腳受傷了，今天不能踢足球。
　　Tā de jiǎo shòushāng le, jīntiān bù néng tī zúqiú.
　　His foot got injured. He can't play soccer today.

Structures　　能₃ is also a Vaux and follows the regular syntax for Vaux. See under 能₁. Note that both 能₁ and 能₃ can be freely negated, whereas 能₂ negation is restricted. See under 能₂.

Usage　　As 能, 會, 可以 can all be translated into English 'can', it's imperative to make the correct choice in Chinese. The choice is strictly governed by meaning (i.e., semantics).

❶ You can come in now. → 可以

❷ Can you speak louder! → 能

❸ Can you cook? → 會

❹ Can you come for a minute? → 可以/能

❺ Can you hear it? → 得- complement

❻ Can her baby walk yet? → 會

❼ How many hamburgers can you eat? → 能

❽ Can he teach? → 能

❾ Sorry, I cannot come. → 能

❿ I can cook for you. → 可以

⓫ Can you wait for me? → 可以/能

寧可 A 也要 B, (níngkě (Adv) A, yě (Adv) yào (Vaux) B), would rather A , in order to B

Function　　In this pattern, 寧可 presents what the subject is willing to put up with, so that something more important could be accomplished.

❶ 父母寧可自己辛苦一點，也要讓孩子快樂。
　　Fùmǔ níngkě zìjǐ xīnkǔ yìdiǎn, yě yào ràng háizi kuàilè.
　　Parents would rather work a little harder, in order that their kids can be happy.

❷ 小農寧可收成少，也要種出安全、健康的食材。
　　Xiǎonóng níngkě shōuchéng shǎo, yě yào zhòngchū ānquán, jiànkāng de shícái.
　　Small farmers would rather the harvest be small, as long as they can raise safe and healthy food.

❸ 她寧可薪水少，也要做自己有興趣的工作。

Tā níngkě xīnshuǐ shǎo, yě yào zuò zìjǐ yǒu xìngqù de gōngzuò.

She would rather receive less money, if it means doing a job that she's interested in.

❹ 表哥寧可不睡覺，也要把報告寫完。

Biǎogē níngkě bú shuìjiào, yě yào bǎ bàogào xiěwán.

My cousin would rather not sleep, so that he can finish writing his report.

❺ 美美寧可餐餐吃麵包，也要省錢準備旅行。

Měiměi níngkě cāncān chī miànbāo, yě yào shěng qián zhǔnbèi lǚxíng.

Meimei would rather eat bread for every meal, so that she can save some money for her trip.

弄, nòng, (V), General Pro-Verb　(1)

Function　弄 is a general verb that can be used as a substitute for verbs of more specific meaning. Just like the English general pro-verb 'do' as in 'doing the dishes', 弄 is used when the precise meaning of the verb is not clear or not very important in a given context. 弄 can be followed by a noun indicating the object (e.g., 弄飯 'cooking a dinner').

❶ 你坐一下，我去弄飯。等一下就可以吃了。

Nǐ zuò yíxià, wǒ qù nòng fàn. Děng yíxià jiù kěyǐ chī le.

Have a seat. I'll go make supper. We'll be eating soon.

❷ 你別一直弄我的衣服。

Nǐ bié yìzhí nòng wǒ de yīfú.

Stop pulling on my clothes.

❸ 你休息一下。我去弄衣服。

Nǐ xiūxí yíxià. Wǒ qù nòng yīfú.

Take a break. I will do the laundry.

弄, nòng, (V), General Causative Verb　(2)

Function　弄 is a general causative verb like 'make' in English. The verb causes something to change its own properties.

❶ 是誰把我的玻璃瓶弄破的？

Shì shéi bǎ wǒ de bōlípíng nòng pò de?

Who was it that broke my glass bottle?

❷ 雨好大，把我的衣服弄濕了。

Yǔ hǎo dà, bǎ wǒ de yīfú nòng shī le.

The rain is really heavy and soaked my clothes.

❸ 這一課的語法好難，我看了半天還是弄不清楚。

Zhè yí kè de yǔfǎ hǎo nán, wǒ kànle bàn tiān háishì nòng bù qīngchǔ.

The grammar in this chapter is really hard. I've been studying it for a long time and I still can't figure it out.

Structures 弄 is always followed by state or process verbs, see examples above.

*N**egation*** : Only 沒 or negative potential are used, e.g., 沒弄清楚, méi nòng qīngchǔ 'did not get it right', 弄不清楚nòng bù qīngchǔ 'could not get it right'.

*Q**uestions*** :

❶ 你弄好了嗎？
Nǐ nòng hǎo le ma?
Are you done?

❷ 他弄乾淨了沒有？
Tā nòng gānjìng le méi yǒu?
Did he clean up?

❸ 這個東西，弄不弄得熟？
Zhè ge dōngxi, nòng bú nòngdeshóu?
This thing, can it be cooked well done?

Usage

(1) 弄 is typically used when the result of a process is informationally more important than the process itself, e.g., 弄乾淨nòng gānjìng 'make it clean', 弄好nòng hǎo 'make it right', or when the action taken is not known.

(2) When 弄 is followed by a state or a process verb, no further degree adverbs, such as 很, are used to modify the verb, so *弄很乾淨 *nòng hěn gānjìng is not grammatical, unless 得 is used after 弄. E.g., 弄得乾乾淨淨的nòng de gāngān jìngjìng de 'get it really clean', 弄得很濕nòng de hěn shī 'get it all wet', 弄得好極了nòng de hǎo jíle 'had it done nicely'.

Omission of Nouns at 2nd Mention

Function In Chinese, old information that has already been mentioned before or that is understood from the context is often omitted at 2nd and future mentions. The end result is called a 'zero pronoun' in linguistics.

Structures The most frequently omitted elements are the subject and the object.

(1) Subject predictable from contexts

❶ Ø請進！
Qǐng jìn!
(You) please come in.

❷ [store clerk asking customer]
Ø要買什麼？
Yào mǎi shénme?
What would (you) like to buy?

請問Ø外帶還是內用？

Qǐngwèn, wàidài háishì nèiyòng?

Excuse me, is this for here or to go?

❸ [A calling B]

今天晚上Ø要一起吃晚飯嗎？

Jīntiān wǎnshàng yào yìqǐ chī wǎnfàn ma?

Shall (we) eat dinner together tonight?

❹ Ø聽說臺灣有很多小吃。

Tīngshuō Táiwān yǒu hěn duō xiǎochī.

(I've) heard that Taiwan has lots of (different kinds of) light repasts.

(2) Subject previously mentioned

❶ 我姓王，Ø叫開文。

Wǒ xìng Wáng, jiào Kāiwén.

I am surnamed Wang. (I) am called Kaiwen.

❷ 我常打籃球，Ø也常踢足球。

Wǒ cháng dǎ lánqiú, Ø yě cháng tī zúqiú.

I often play basketball and (I) often play football.

(3) Object previously mentioned

昨天朋友給我一個芒果，我還沒吃Ø。

Zuótiān péngyǒu gěi wǒ yí ge mángguǒ, wǒ hái méi chī.

Yesterday, a friend gave me a mango. I have not tried it yet.

Usage

English allows reduction of nouns up to pronouns and no further. Chinese further reduces pronouns to zero. They are different process but the motivations are the same, i.e., avoiding redundancy.

偏偏, piānpiān, (Adv), contrary to expectation, deliberately, annoyingly

Function

偏偏 is an adverb that expresses the speaker's annoyance at the occurrence of a situation, against and contrary to his expectation.

❶ 我今天沒帶雨傘。希望別下雨，偏偏下午下起大雨來了。

Wǒ jīntiān méi dài yǔsǎn. Xīwàng bié xiàyǔ, piānpiān xiàwǔ xiàqǐ dàyǔ lái le.

I didn't bring an umbrella today. I was hoping it wouldn't rain but of course it poured in the afternoon.

❷ 真氣人，我準備的都是考古題。這次的考試偏偏一題考古題也沒有，害我沒考好。

Zhēn qìrén, wǒ zhǔnbèi de dōu shì kǎogǔtí. Zhè cì de kǎoshì piānpiān yì tí kǎogǔtí yě méi yǒu, hài wǒ méi kǎohǎo.

Unbelievable, I studied all the old recycled tests but there wasn't a single repeat question, and I got a bad mark because of it.

❸ 我請他別穿西裝來參加。他卻偏偏穿了黑色西裝來了。

Wǒ qǐng tā bié chuān xīzhuāng lái cānjiā. Tā què piānpiān chuānle hēisè xīzhuāng lái le.

I asked him not to come wearing a suit, but guess what, he showed up in a black suit.

❹ 我們告訴他應該配一條素色的領帶。他偏偏要配一條花的。

Wǒmen gàosù tā yīnggāi pèi yì tiáo sùsè de lǐngdài. Tā piānpiān yào pèi yì tiáo huā de.

We told him to wear a plain-colored tie, but he just had to wear a patterned one.

❺ 為了在這裡做生意，我告訴他最好先和本地人建立良好的關係。他偏偏不聽。

Wèile zài zhèlǐ zuò shēngyì, wǒ gàosù tā zuìhǎo xiān hàn běndì rén jiànlì liánghǎo de guānxi. Tā piānpiān bù tīng.

In order to get business done here, I told him it's best to first build good relationships with locals, but he didn't listen.

Usage

(1) This adverb has a stronger tone of annoyance than 倒 or 卻.

(2) When used for a deliberate action, 偏 can stand alone without duplication, but in this case it cannot be placed before the subject, e.g.,

❶ 我不想被家庭束縛，但她偏要生兒育女，所以我們就分手了。

Wǒ bù xiǎng bèi jiātíng shùfú, dàn tā piān yào shēngér yùnǚ, suǒyǐ wǒmen jiù fēnshǒu le.

I don't want to be tied down with a family, but she insisted on having children, so we broke up.

❷ 我希望他不要去參加晚會。他偏要去。

Wǒ xīwàng tā bú yào qù cānjiā wǎnhuì. Tā piān yào qù.

I'm hoping that he would not go to the party, but he insisted on going.

❸ 我跟她說會下雨，但她偏不帶傘。

Wǒ gēn tā shuō huì xiàyǔ, dàn tā piān bú dài sǎn.

I told her it was going to rain, but she insisted on not taking an umbrella.

Pronouns Interrogative to Refer to All-inclusion or All-exclusion (1)

Function

Interrogative pronouns can appear in declarative sentences in Chinese. When they do, they often co-occur with 都 dōu 'all' to indicate totality without exception, that is, total inclusion in affirmative sentences and total exclusion in negative sentences.

	Affirmative	Negative	Question
誰 shéi	everyone	nobody	who?
哪裡 nǎlǐ	everywhere	nowhere	where?
什麼 shénme	everything	nothing	what?
什麼時候 shénme shíhòu	anytime, always	never	when?
怎麼＋V zěnme＋V	whichever way	no way, never	how?

❶ 誰都喜歡去旅行。
Shéi dōu xǐhuān qù lǚxíng.
Everyone likes to travel.

❷ 哪裡都有好吃的東西。
Nǎlǐ dōu yǒu hǎochī de dōngxi.
There's delicious food everywhere you go.

❸ 他什麼都想買。
Tā shénme dōu xiǎng mǎi.
He wants to buy everything.

❹ 他們什麼時候都在上網。
Tāmen shénme shíhòu dōu zài shàngwǎng.
They are online all the time.

❺ 只要不叫我出錢，怎麼做都可以。
Zhǐyào bú jiào wǒ chū qián, zěnme zuò dōu kěyǐ.
As long as I don't have to fork out money, anything is O.K. with me.

> **Structures**

Negation : In negative sentences, question words are used with either 都 dōu or 也 yě to indicate total exclusion. The negation marker 不 bù or 沒 méi comes after 都 dōu/也 yě.

❶ 誰也不喜歡難看的東西。
Shéi yě bù xǐhuān nánkàn de dōngxi.
No one likes ugly things.

❷ 昨天我哪裡都沒去，在家看電視。
Zuótiān wǒ nǎlǐ dōu méi qù, zài jiā kàn diànshì.
I didn't go anywhere yesterday. I watched TV at home.

❸ 我今天什麼也不想吃。
Wǒ jīntiān shénme yě bù xiǎng chī.
I don't feel like eating anything today.

❹ 下個星期，我什麼時候都不在家。我要去旅行。
Xià ge xīngqí, wǒ shénme shíhòu dōu bú zài jiā. Wǒ yào qù lǚxíng.
Next week, I won't be home the whole time. I will be traveling.

❺ 中國菜很難做。我怎麼做都不太好吃。
Zhōngguó cài hěn nán zuò. Wǒ zěnme zuò dōu bú tài hǎochī.
Chinese food is hard to make. No matter what I do, it does not tastes good.

Questions : This pattern forms 嗎ma questions only, in addition to 是不是, 好不好, etc.

❶ 這家餐廳的東西什麼都好吃嗎？

Zhè jiā cāntīng de dōngxi shénme dōu hǎochī ma?

Is everything in this restaurant tasty?

❷ 你今天什麼時候都在公司嗎？

Nǐ jīntiān shénme shíhòu dōu zài gōngsī ma?

Will you be at the office all day today?

❸ 他們誰都去過法國，是不是？

Tāmen shéi dōu qùguò Fǎguó, shìbúshì?

They have all been to France, haven't they?

Pronouns Interrogative in Non-committal Stance (2)

Function When interrogative pronouns (e.g., 什麼shénme, 多少duōshǎo, 幾jǐ, 哪裡nǎlǐ, 什麼地方shénme dìfāng, 誰shéi, 什麼時候shénme shíhòu) occur in a declarative sentence, the sentence indicates a non-committal attitude on the part of the speaker who is avoiding giving a clear answer. Non-committal statements are always in the negative.

❶ 我沒有多少錢。

Wǒ méi yǒu duōshǎo qián.

I don't really have all that much money.

❷ 她沒有幾個朋友。

Tā méi yǒu jǐ ge péngyǒu.

She doesn't really have all that many friends.

❸ 你的感冒沒有什麼關係。

Nǐ de gǎnmào méi yǒu shénme guānxi.

Your cold really isn't all that serious.

❹ 我沒去哪裡。

Wǒ méi qù nǎlǐ.

I didn't really go anywhere.

❺ 我不想買什麼。

Wǒ bù xiǎng mǎi shénme.

I'm not buying things.

❻ 我昨天沒給誰打過電話。

Wǒ zuótiān méi gěi shéi dǎguò diànhuà.

I did not phone anyone yesterday.

起, qǐ, (Ptc), as Verb Complement, to be able to afford (1)

Function 起 is a verb complement, with the meaning 'to (have enough money to) afford doing something'.

❶ 公寓太貴，我當然買不起。
Gōngyù tài guì, wǒ dāngrán mǎibùqǐ.
Apartments are too expensive. Obviously, I cannot afford to buy one.

❷ 雖然套房不太便宜，但是我租得起。
Suīrán tàofáng bú tài piányí, dànshì wǒ zūdéqǐ.
Although the rent for a suite (i.e., a room with a bath) is not cheap, I can still afford one.

❸ 誰都吃得起臺灣小吃。
Shéi dōu chīdeqǐ Táiwān xiǎochī.
Anyone can afford eating Taiwanese delicacies.

> **Structures**

起 can only be used in the potential pattern,
i.e., V＋得＋起, V＋不＋起; *買起*mǎi qǐ, *沒買起*méi mǎi qǐ.

Negation :

❶ 我是學生，付不起一個月兩萬塊的房租。
Wǒ shì xuéshēng, fùbùqǐ yí ge yuè liǎngwàn kuài de fángzū.
I'm a student. I can't afford NT$20,000 a month for rent.

❷ 雖然我開始工作了，但是還買不起台北市區的房子。
Suīrán wǒ kāishǐ gōngzuòn le, dànshì hái mǎibùqǐ Táiběi shìqū de fángzi.
Even though I've started working, I still can't afford an apartment in central Taipei City.

❸ 有名的法國車，我開不起。
Yǒumíng de Fǎguó chē, wǒ kāibùqǐ.
I can't afford to drive a well-known French made car,.

Questions :

❶ 這件新娘禮服這麼貴，要結婚的人租得起嗎？
Zhè jiàn xīnniáng lǐfú zhème guì, yào jiéhūn de rén zūdeqǐ ma?
This bride's dress is so expensive. Can people getting married afford to rent one?

❷ 我們住得起住不起一個晚上一萬多塊的旅館？
Wǒmen zhùdeqǐ zhùbùqǐ yí ge wǎnshàng yíwàn duō kuài de lǚguǎn?
Can we afford to stay in a hotel room that costs more than NT$10,000 a night?

❸ 那種照相機，我們買得起買不起？
Nà zhǒng zhàoxiàngjī, wǒmen mǎideqǐ mǎibùqǐ?
Can we afford that kind of camera?

> **Usage**

(1) Only a limited number of verbs can combine with 起, including: 吃chī 'eat', 喝hē 'drink', 買mǎi 'buy', 住zhù 'live', 租zū 'rent', 穿chuān 'wear', 用yòng 'use', 付fù 'make payment'. The meaning of 起 is constant, i.e., to have financial capabilities for such pursuits.

(2) 起 can also combine with 看 kàn 'look', forming idiomatic 看得起 kàndeqǐ 'respect someone', and 看不起 kànbùqǐ 'look down upon someone', e.g.,

❶ 他做了那麼多壞事，朋友怎麼看得起他？
Tā zuòle nàme duō huàishì, péngyǒu zěnme kàndeqǐ tā?
He has done so many bad things, how can his friends think highly of him?

❷ 對父母不好的人，大家會看不起。
Duì fùmǔ bù hǎo de rén, dàjiā huì kànbùqǐ.
People don't think highly of people who treat their parents badly.

起, qǐ, (Ptc), as Verb Particle, to touch upon (2)

Function

When 起 combines with action verbs as their verb-particle, it refers to a meaning of 'to touch upon', e.g., 聊起 liáoqǐ 'to have talked about', 想起 xiǎngqǐ 'to have recalled, to have remembered', 談起 tánqǐ 'to have talked about', 說起 shuōqǐ 'to have spoken of'.

❶ 他常跟朋友說起在非洲的事。
Tā cháng gēn péngyǒu shuōqǐ zài Feizhōu de shì.
He often talks about Africa with his friends.

❷ 美美一個人在臺灣。她想起越南的家人時，有點難過。
Měiměi yí ge rén zài Táiwān. Tā xiǎngqǐ Yuènán de jiārén shí, yǒudiǎn nánguò.
Meimei lives in Taiwan alone. Whenever she thinks of her family in Vietnam, she feels a little sad.

❸ 小李跟朋友談起找房子的事，朋友告訴他可以上網找。
Xiǎo Lǐ gēn péngyǒu tánqǐ zhǎo fángzi de shì, péngyǒu gàosù tā kěyǐ shàngwǎng zhǎo.
Xiao Li brought up with his friend the topic of renting an apartment and his friend told him he could search online.

Structures

Negation:

❶ 老闆在辦公室的時候，別說起薪水的事。
Lǎobǎn zài bàngōngshì de shíhòu, bié shuōqǐ xīnshuǐ de shì.
Don't bring up the issue of salary while the boss is in the office.

❷ 他沒跟我談起結婚的事，所以我不能給他什麼建議。
Tā méi gēn wǒ tánqǐ jiéhūn de shì, suǒyǐ wǒ bù néng gěi tā shénme jiànyì.
He didn't bring up the issue of marriage, so I was unable to give him any advice.

❸ 我以為他會告訴我旅行的事，可是今天他來家裡都沒聊起。

Wǒ yǐwéi tā huì gàosù wǒ lǚxíng de shì, kěshì jīntiān tā lái jiā lǐ dōu méi liáoqǐ.

I thought he was going to tell me about his travels, but when he came to my house today, he didn't bring it up.

Questions :

❶ 中午的時候，她們是不是聊起昨天看的電影了？

Zhōngwǔ de shíhòu, tāmen shìbúshì liáoqǐ zuótiān kàn de diànyǐng le?

At noon did they chat about the movie they saw yesterday?

❷ 他又談起他從前的女朋友了？

Tā yòu tánqǐ tā cóngqián de nǚpéngyǒu le?

He talked about his ex-girlfriend, again?

❸ 我忘了我們是怎麼談起吃素的事了？

Wǒ wàngle wǒmen shì zěnme tánqǐ chīsù de shì le?

I forget how we got started talking about vegetarianism (or eating vegetarian food). (i.e., I forget how the topic of vegetarians/ vegetarian food came up.)

起來, qǐlái, as Verb Complement, assessment of situations (1)

Function   起來 as a verb complement conveys the speaker's judgment or evaluation about a situation.

❶ 白小姐笑起來很美。

Bái xiǎojiě xiàoqǐlái hěn měi.

Miss Bai looks pretty when she smiles.

❷ 那裡賣的小吃看起來很好吃。

Nàlǐ mài de xiǎochī kànqǐlái hěn hǎochī.

The snacks at that stand look delicious.

❸ 這個房子很小，我住起來不習慣。

Zhè ge fángzi hěn xiǎo, wǒ zhùqǐlái bù xíguàn.

This house is tiny. I am not used to tight spaces.

Structures

Negation :   The evaluative portion cannot be negated, but the state verbs that following, the judgment, can be negated.

❶ 王先生的臉色今天看起來不好。

Wáng xiānshēng de liǎnsè jīntiān kànqǐlái bù hǎo.

Mr. Wang does not look very well today.

❷ 越南菜看起來很辣，吃起來不太辣。

Yuènán cài kàn qǐlái hěn là, chīqǐlái bútài là.

Vietnamese food looks very spicy but does not taste very spicy.

❸ 你說的事聽起來不難。不過，做起來有點困難。

Nǐ shuō de shì tīngqǐlái bù nán. Búguò, zuòqǐlái yǒudiǎn kùnnán.

What you said sounds easy, but it will not be easy to do.

*Q*uestions :

❶ 臭豆腐吃起來怎麼樣？

Chòudòufǔ chīqǐlái zěnmeyàng?

How does stinky tofu taste?

❷ 你昨天買的衣服穿起來好不好看？

Nǐ zuótiān mǎi de yīfú chuānqǐlái hǎo bù hǎokàn?

Do the clothes you bought yesterday look good on you?

❸ 他的新車坐起來是不是很舒服？

Tā de xīn chē zuòqǐlái shìbúshì hěn shūfú?

His new car rides smoothly, right?

> Usage

Verbs appearing before 起來 in this function include, 看 kàn 'to look', 聽 tīng 'to listen', 吃 chī 'to eat', 喝 hē 'to drink', 坐 zuò 'to sit', 穿 chuān 'to wear', 寫 xiě 'to write', 笑 xiào 'to laugh, smile', 説 shuō 'to say, speak', 學 xué 'to study, learn', 念 niàn 'to study', 住 zhù 'to live, stay', 走 zǒu 'to walk, go'.

起來, qǐlái, as Verb Complement in 想起來 xiǎngqǐlái, to have remembered (2)

> Function

This pattern consists of the verb 想, followed by the verb particle 起 (來), referring to the fact that something has been recalled.

❶ 他的電話，我想起來了。

Tā de diànhuà, wǒ xiǎngqǐlái le.

I remembered his phone number.

❷ 那位小姐姓張，我想起來了。

Nà wèi xiǎojiě xìng Zhāng, wǒ xiǎngqǐlái le.

I recalled that young lady's last name is Zhang.

❸ 回到學校以後，以前的事我都想起來了。

Huí dào xuéxiào yǐhòu, yǐqián de shì wǒ dōu xiǎngqǐlái le.

When I went back to school, all the things that had happened there before came to mind.

> Structures

*N*egation :

❶ 他姓張，早上見面的時候我怎麼沒想起來。

Tā xìng Zhāng, zǎoshang jiànmiàn de shíhòu wǒ zěnme méi xiǎngqǐlái.

His last name is Zhang. How come I couldn't recall it this morning?

❷ 他是誰，我還沒想起來。

Tā shì shéi, wǒ hái méi xiǎngqǐlái.

Who is he? I still can't remember.

❸ 機車在哪裡，他一直沒想起來。

Jīchē zài nǎlǐ, tā yīzhí méi xiǎngqǐlái.

He couldn't recall where the motorcycle was the entire time.

Questions :

❶ 我們見過面。你想起來了嗎？

Wǒmen jiànguò miàn. Nǐ xiǎngqǐlái le ma?

We've met before. Do you recall?

❷ 他叫什麼名字？你是不是想起來了？

Tā jiào shénme míngzi? Nǐ shìbúshì xiǎngqǐlái le?

What is his name? Do you recall?

❸ 你的東西在哪裡，想起來了沒有？

Nǐ de dōngxi zài nǎlǐ, xiǎngqǐlái le méi yǒu?

Where is your stuff? Do you remember?

> Usage

起來 has many functions, and different interpretations depend largely on the verbs.

起來, qǐlái, as Verb Complement, with inchoative meaning (3)

> Function

When 起來 follows the verb as a complement, it indicates the beginning, the initial point, of an action or state, to begin to.

❶ 春節快到了，魚、肉都貴起來了。

Chūnjié kuài dào le, yú, ròu dōu guìqǐlái le.

The Lunar New Year is almost here. Prices for fish and meat have begun to go up.

❷ 一到夏天，旅行的人就多起來了。

Yí dào xiàtiān, lǚxíng de rén jiù duōqǐlái le.

As soon as summer arrives, the number of travelers begins to rise.

❸ 因為垃圾分類的關係，環境乾淨起來了。

Yīnwèi lèsè fēnlèi de guānxi, huánjìng gānjìngqǐlái le.

Because of garbage sorting, the environment has started to become cleaner.

> Structures

The verb before 起來 can be state verbs (as in the three examples above), or it can be action verbs (as in the three examples below). 了 can occur after the verb, or after 起來.

❶ 他們進了教室坐下來，就聊起來了。

Tāmen jìnle jiàoshì zuò xiàlái, jiù liáoqǐlái le.

They entered and classroom, sat down, and began to chat.

❷ 他想到昨天喜宴上的事，就笑了起來。

Tā xiǎngdào zuótiān xǐyàn shàng de shì, jiù xiàole qǐlái.

When he thought of the wedding banquet yesterday, he began to laugh.

❸ 他不等兄弟姐妹回來，自己吃了起來。

Tā bù děng xiōngdì jiěmèi huílái, zìjǐ chīle qǐlái.

He didn't wait for his siblings to come back before starting to eat by himself.

Negation : The negation of this pattern is done by 沒 and the potential form 'V 不起來'.

❶ 他身體不好，雖然吃得很多，可是還是胖不起來。

Tā shēntǐ bù hǎo, suīrán chī de hěn duō, kěshì háishì pàngbùqǐlái.

His is not in good health. Although he eats a lot, he never gains weight.

❷ 我吃藥吃了很久，可是身體一直好不起來。

Wǒ chī yào chīle hěn jiǔ, kěshì shēntǐ yìzhí hǎobùqǐlái.

I have been taking medicine for a long time, but my health has not improved.

❸ 他們兩個人的想法不一樣，所以聊不起來。

Tāmen liǎng ge rén de xiǎngfǎ bù yíyàng, suǒyǐ liáobùqǐlái.

The two of them have very different ways of thinking, so they don't get on well.

❹ 暖氣是剛剛才開的，所以房間還沒熱起來。

Nuǎnqì shì gānggāng cái kāi de, suǒyǐ fángjiān hái méi rèqǐlái.

I just turned on the heating, so the room is not warm yet.

Questions :

❶ 買了糖給弟弟，他是不是就高興起來了？

Mǎile táng gěi dìdi, tā shìbúshì jiù gāoxīngqǐlái le?

Did your younger brother cheer up when you bought candy for him?

❷ 他們是不是一見面就聊起來了？

Tāmen shìbúshì yí jiànmiàn jiù liáoqǐlái le?

They began to chat as soon as they met up, right?

❸ 你看，來旅行的人是不是多起來了？

Nǐ kàn, lái lǚxíng de rén shìbúshì duōqǐlái le?

Look, the number of travelers coming here has increased, right?

其他的, qítā de, the others (See 別的biéde)

去, qù, (Vi), as in 去＋VP, to go do something

Function The pattern 去＋VP indicates the intention to go elsewhere and do something.

❶ 我去打網球。

Wǒ qù dǎ wǎngqiú.

I am going to go play tennis.

❷ 他去踢足球。
Tā qù tī zúqiú.
He went to play soccer.

❸ 我們都要去看電影。
Wǒmen dōu yào qù kàn diànyǐng.
We are all going to go see a movie.

Structures Negation markers, auxiliary verbs, and adverbs are all placed in front of 去.

Negation:

❶ 他星期日不去打籃球了。
Tā xīngqírì bú qù dǎ lánqiú le.
He is not playing basketball Sunday.

❷ 明天早上我不去游泳。
Míngtiān zǎoshàng wǒ bú qù yóuyǒng.
I am not going to go swimming tomorrow morning.

Questions:

❶ 你要去看電影嗎?
Nǐ yào qù kàn diànyǐng ma?
Would you like to go see a movie?

❷ 你們是不是常去吃越南菜?
Nǐmen shìbúshì cháng qù chī Yuènán cài?
Do you often go eat Vietnamese food?

❸ 他去不去打棒球?
Tā qù bú qù dǎ bàngqiú?
Is he going to go play baseball?

卻, què, (Adv), however

Function In sentences indicating instances that are contrary to expectation, the adverb 卻 frequently occurs before the verb phrase in the second clause.

❶ 他的成績不錯,可是卻沒通過研究所的面試。
Tā de chéngjī búcuò, kěshì què méi tōngguò yánjiūsuǒ de miànshì.
His grades are good, but he didn't pass the interview for grad school. (Everyone expected him to pass.)

❷ 在那家麵包店當學徒,雖然辛苦,卻讓他大開眼界。
Zài nà jiā miànbāo diàn dāng xuétú, suīrán xīnkǔ, què ràng tā dàkāi yǎnjiè.
He served as an apprentice in that bakery. It was tough, but it really opened his eyes.

❸ 我昨天買的外套，裡面破了一個洞，但是店員卻不讓我退換。

Wǒ zuótiān mǎi de wàitào, lǐmiàn pòle yí ge dòng, dànshì diànyuán què bú ràng wǒ tuìhuàn.

The coat I bought yesterday has a hole on the inside, but the store employee wouldn't let me exchange it.

❹ 早上出門的時候還出太陽，沒想到現在卻下起雨來了。

Zǎoshàng chūmén de shíhòu hái chū tàiyáng, méi xiǎngdào xiànzài què xiàqǐ yǔ lái le.

It was sunny when I left the house this morning. I never expected it would rain now.

❺ 那家小吃店雖然沒有招牌，生意卻好得不得了。

Nà jiā xiǎochī diàn suīrán méi yǒu zhāopái, shēngyì què hǎo de bùdéliǎo.

That small eatery doesn't even have a sign, but its business is booming.

Usage 卻 is often used with 可是 kěshì, 但是 dànshì, or 沒想到 méi xiǎngdào in the sentences.

讓, ràng, (V), to let someone do something

Function The verb 讓 has several different but related meanings, depending on the sentence and on the context, e.g.,

❶ 租房子的事，請你讓我想一想。(let)

Zū fángzi de shì, qǐng nǐ ràng wǒ xiǎng yì xiǎng.

About the renting of the house, please let me think about it.

❷ 天氣這麼冷，冷得讓我感冒了。(make, cause)

Tiānqì zhème lěng, lěng de ràng wǒ gǎnmào le.

The weather is so cold that it caused me to have a cold. (i.e., It's so cold that I caught a cold.)

❸ 讓小孩一個人去旅行，不太安全吧！(permit)

Ràng xiǎohái yí gè rén qù lǚxíng, bútài ānquán ba!

Allowing children to travel alone is a bit unsafe, I should think. (i.e., Isn't it a bit unsafe to let children travel alone?)

❹ 老闆讓我做這份工作。(permit)

Lǎobǎn ràng wǒ zuò zhè fèn gōngzuò.

The boss is letting me do this work.

❺ 老師說我說中文說得很流利，讓我很高興。(make)

Lǎoshī shuō wǒ shuō Zhōngwén shuō de hěn liúlì, ràng wǒ hěn gāoxìng.

The teacher said that I speak Chinese fluently making me feel happy.

❻ 吃太辣會讓妹妹的喉嚨不舒服。(make)
Chī tài là huì ràng mèimei de hóulóng bù shūfú.
Your younger sister will get a sore throat if she eats too much spicy food.

❼ 這次旅行讓我更了解台東這個地方了。(make)
Zhè cì lǚxíng ràng wǒ gèng liǎojiě Táidōng zhè ge dìfāng le.
This trip allowed me to better understand Taitung.

Structures

*N*egation :

❶ 我跟小王借錢的事，我不讓他告訴別人。
Wǒ gēn Xiǎo Wáng jiè qián de shì, wǒ bú ràng tā gàosù biérén.
I didn't let him tell anyone that I borrowed money from Xiao Wang.

❷ 颱風來了，媽媽不讓我們出去踢足球。
Táifēng láile, māma bú ràng wǒmen chūqù tī zúqiú.
The typhoon was coming and mom didn't let us go out and play soccer.

❸ 他不讓我在泡菜裡放太多辣椒。
Tā bú ràng wǒ zài pàocài lǐ fàng tài duō làjiāo.
He didn't let me put too many peppers in the kimchi.

*Q*uestions : Either A not A or 是不是 can be used.

❶ 老闆讓不讓你把公司的車開回家去？
Lǎobǎn ràng bú ràng nǐ bǎ gōngsī de chē kāihuí jiā qù?
Does the boss allow you to drive the company car back home?

❷ 妳媽媽讓不讓妳跟我去潛水？
Nǐ māma ràng bú ràng nǐ gēn wǒ qù qiánshuǐ?
Will your mom let you go scuba diving with me?

❸ 你女朋友是不是讓你踢完足球再去找她？
Nǐ nǚpéngyǒu shìbúshì ràng nǐ tīwán zúqiú zài qù zhǎo tā?
Did your girlfriend have you go see her after you finished playing soccer?

然後, ránhòu, (Adv), next in sequence (See 後來 hòulái)

Reduplication of Verbs, to indicate softened action (1)

Function

Verb reduplication suggests 'reduced quantity, reduced force'. It also suggests that the action is easy to accomplish. When what is expressed is a request/command, verb reduplication softens the tone of the statement and the hearer finds the request/command more moderate.

❶ 他們學校很漂亮，我想去看（一）看。
Tāmen xuéxiào hěn piàoliàng, wǒ xiǎng qù kàn (yí) kàn.
Their school is pretty. I'd like to take a look.

❷ 我想學中文，請教教我。
Wǒ xiǎng xué Zhōngwén, qǐng jiāojiāo wǒ.
I'd like to study Chinese. Please teach me.

❸ A：我們今天晚上去哪裡吃飯？
Wǒmen jīntiān wǎnshàng qù nǎlǐ chīfàn?
Where are we going to go for dinner tonight?

B：我想（一）想。
Wǒ xiǎng (yì) xiǎng.
Let me think.

❹ A：你週末做什麼？
Nǐ zhōumò zuò shénme?
What do you do on weekends?

B：在家看看書、喝喝咖啡、上上網，也去學校打打籃球。
Zài jiā kànkàn shū, hēhē kāfēi, shàngshàng wǎng, yě qù xuéxiào dǎdǎ lánqiú.
I stay home and do some reading, have some coffee, and do some surfing on the internet. I also go to school and play some basketball.

Structures

Questions :

❶ 今天學校有人來演唱。我們去聽聽吧？
Jīntiān xuéxiào yǒu rén lái yǎnchàng, wǒmen qù tīngtīng ba?
There's a concert at school today. Let's go and see how it is.

❷ 聽說你換了手機。可不可以讓我看一看？
Tīngshuō nǐ huànle shǒujī. Kě bù kěyǐ ràng wǒ kàn yí kàn?
Heard that you got a new cellphone. Can I take a look?

Usage

(1) Not every verb can be reduplicated. Mainly action verbs can go undergo verb repetition. Of the verbs that can be reduplicated include 看 kàn 'to look', 想 xiǎng 'to think', 找 zhǎo 'to search for', 用 yòng 'to use', 熱 rè 'to heat', 量 liáng 'to measure', 坐 zuò 'to sit', 開 kāi 'to open, turn on', 聞 wén 'to smell'.

(2) Verb reduplication is mostly used in speech for requests and suggestions. Most reduplicated verbs are monosyllabic. When the verb takes an object, only the verb gets reduplicated, not the object. For example, 上網 shàngwǎng 'go online' is changed to 上上網 shàngshàng wǎng; 做飯 zuòfàn 'cook' is changed to 做做飯 zuòzuò fàn.

(3) VV is often interchangeable with V一下, e.g.,

看一看~看一下

坐一坐~坐一下

想一想~想一下

Both patterns shorten the engagement of activities.

Reduplication of State Verbs for Intensification (2)

Function

Reduplication intensifies the tone of a statement, much like the meaning of 很 intensification. It indicates the speaker's subjective feelings, as opposed to objective, factual observation. See the English translation below.

❶ 這碗牛肉湯香香的。

Zhè wǎn niúròu tāng xiāngxiāng de.

This bowl of beef soup smells really good.

❷ 熱熱的咖啡,真香。

Rèrè de kāfēi, zhēn xiāng.

Hot coffee smells really good.

❸ 那個地方有很多高高的大樓。

Nà ge dìfāng yǒu hěn duō gāogāo de dàlóu.

There are many really tall buildings there.

Structures

(1) No degree adverbs can be used with reduplication. For example, one cannot say *這杯茶很香香的Zhè bēi chá hěn xiāngxiāng de, since both 很 and reduplication intensify.

(2) Note that there is a 的 de after the reduplicated state verbs. So, it is not *這杯茶香香Zhè bēi chá xiāngxiāng, but rather 這杯茶香香的。 Zhè bēi chá xiāngxiāng de. 'This cup of tea smells good.' When there are two state verbs in a sequence, the first 的 de can be omitted. For example, we say 那種水果香香甜甜的Nà zhǒng shuǐguǒ xiāngxiāng, tiántián de 'That kind of fruit is aromatic and sweet'.

(3) Not all state verbs can be reduplicated. For example, those in the right column below cannot be reduplicated.

Yes	No
香xiāng 'fragrant', 甜tián 'sweet', 高gāo 'tall, high', 熱rè 'hot', 大dà 'big', 遠yuǎn 'far', 辣là 'spicy hot', 矮ǎi 'short'	多duō 'many', 貴guì 'expensive', 近jìn 'close', 忙máng 'busy', 新xīn 'new', 少shǎo 'few'

Usage

Subjective feelings are often expressed in praise or criticism, e.g., when we order coffee, we say 買一杯熱咖啡!Mǎi yì bēi rè kāfēi! and not *買一杯熱熱的咖啡!Mǎi yì bēi rèrè de kāfēi! as ordering is factual, not expressive.

Reduplication of Disyllabic State Verbs (3)

Function

Like monosyllabic adjectives, disyllabic adjectives in Chinese can be reduplicated to express intensified states. They occur as pre-VP adverbials marked by 地, as post-VP adverbial complements marked by 得, or as nominal modifiers marked by 的.

❶ 他們開開心心地一起吃飯。
Tāmen kāikāi xīnxīn de yìqǐ chīfàn.
They dined together happily.

❷ 王老闆客客氣氣地跟客人說話。
Wáng lǎobǎn kèkè qìqì de gēn kèrén shuōhuà.
Boss Wang talks to customers very politely.

❸ 美美每天都穿得漂漂亮亮的。
Měiměi měi tiān dōu chuān de piàopiào liàngliàng de.
Meimei dresses up beautifully every day.

Structures

(1) The reduplication of disyllabic adjectives is from AB into AABB.

❶ 開心→開開心心 happy → happily

❷ 輕鬆→輕輕鬆鬆 relaxed → in a relaxed manner

❸ 舒服→舒舒服服 comfortable → comfortably

(2) A reduplicated disyllabic adjective is followed by 地 when it modifies the verb.

❶ 大家開開心心地幫他過生日。
Dàjiā kāikāi xīnxīn de bāng tā guò shēngrì.
We all celebrated his birthday happily. (i.e., We had a good time celebrating his birthday.)

❷ 有了悠遊卡，就可以輕輕鬆鬆地到處逛逛。
Yǒule Yōuyóu kǎ, jiù kěyǐ qīngqīng sōngsōng de dàochù guàngguàng.
With the EasyCard, you can go anywhere and check things out easily.

❸ 大家舒舒服服地坐在餐廳裡。
Dàjiā shūshū fúfú de zuò zài cāntīng lǐ.
Everybody sat comfortably in the restaurant.

(3) A reduplicated disyllabic adjective is followed by 的 when it modifies a noun.

❶ 我要租一個乾乾淨淨的房間，比較舒服。
Wǒ yào zū yí ge gāngān jìngjìng de fángjiān, bǐjiào shūfú.
I want to rent a place that is spick and span, something comfortable.

❷ 小明是個客客氣氣的人，所以朋友很多。
Xiǎomíng shì ge kèkè qìqì de rén, suǒyǐ péngyǒu hěn duō.
Xiaoming is a very well-mannered person, and so has a lot of
friends.

❸ 大家都想找輕輕鬆鬆的工作。
Dàjiā dōu xiǎng zhǎo qīngqīng sōngsōng de gōngzuò.
Everyone wants a nice and easy job.

(4) When a reduplicated disyllabic adjective serves as the predicate, the
entire sentence ends with 的.

❶ 房間乾乾淨淨的，看起來真舒服。
Fángjiān gāngān jìngjìng de, kàn qǐlái zhēn shūfú.
The room is spick and span, it looks welcoming.

❷ 我看他早上開開心心的，沒因為昨天的事不高興。
Wǒ kàn tā zǎoshang kāikāi xīnxīn de, méi yīnwèi zuótiān de shì
bù gāoxìng.
He seemed to me in a good mood this morning. He wasn't upset
about what happened yesterday.

❸ 他對人客客氣氣的。
Tā duì rén kèkè qìqì de.
He is courteous.

(5) When a reduplicated disyllabic adjective serves as a post-verbal
complement, the entire sentence ends with 的, which can be optional.

❶ 他寫字寫得漂漂亮亮的。
Tā xiě zì xiě de piàopiào liàngliàng de.
He writes characters beautifully.

❷ 我聽得清清楚楚的，你別想騙我。
Wǒ tīng de qīngqīng chǔchǔ de, nǐ bié xiǎng piàn wǒ.
I've heard it very clearly. Don't try to fool me.

❸ 這個旅館房間很大，他住得舒舒服服（的）。
Zhè ge lǚguǎn fángjiān hěn dà, tā zhù de shūshū fúfú (de).
The hotel room is pretty big. He finds it very comfortable to stay
here.

Questions :

❶ 那裡的廚房是不是乾乾淨淨的？
Nàlǐ de chúfáng shìbúshì gāngān jìngjìng de?
Is the kitchen there clean?

❷ 學生是不是每天都快快樂樂的？
Xuéshēng shìbúshì měi tiān dōu kuàikuài lèlè de?
Do the students enjoy themselves every day?

❸ 房東對你們一直都客客氣氣的嗎？
Fángdōng duì nǐmen yìzhí dōu kèkè qìqì de ma?
Has the landlord always been so courteous to you?

Usage

(1) Not all disyllabic adjectives can be reduplicated. For example, those in the right column below cannot be reduplicated.

Yes	No
輕鬆 qīngsōng 'relaxed', 漂亮 piàoliàng 'pretty', 舒服 shūfú 'comfortable', 乾淨 gānjìng 'clean', 高興 gāoxìng 'happy', 快樂 kuàilè 'happy', 客氣 kèqì 'polite'	便宜 piányí 'inexpensive', 好看 hǎokàn 'good-looking', 傳統 chuántǒng 'traditional', 難看 nánkàn 'bad-looking, ugly', 好玩 hǎowán 'fun', 麻煩 máfán 'troublesome', 不錯 búcuò 'not bad', 可怕 kěpà 'scary', 年輕 niánqīng 'young', 好喝 hǎohē 'nice to drink', 有名 yǒumíng 'famous', 方便 fāngbiàn 'convenient', 特別 tèbié 'special', 討厭 tǎoyàn 'annoying'

(2) No intensification adverb can appear before a reduplicated adjective. Two structures with the same function, thus not co-occurring, incompatible. For example:

❶ *大家很開開心心地回家了。
*Dàjiā hěn kāikāi xīnxīn de huíjiā le.
Everybody returned home very happily .

❷ *她今天穿得非常漂漂亮亮。
*Tā jīntiān chuān de fēicháng piàopiào liàngliàng.
She is dressed very beautifully today.

Reduplication of Disyllabic Verbs for Tentative Action (4)

Function

When verbs, monosyllabic or disyllabic, are reduplicated, the commitment to the action is reduced. This pattern generally occurs in imperative sentences, with a polite overtone.

❶ 今天學的漢字,我還得練習練習。
Jīntiān xué de Hànzì, wǒ hái děi liànxí liànxí.
I still need to practice a bit more the Chinese characters I studied today.

❷ 你有空的時候,應該去旅行。多認識認識一些臺灣朋友。
Nǐ yǒu kòng de shíhòu, yīnggāi qù lǚxíng. Duō rènshì rènshì yìxiē Táiwān péngyǒu.
When you have time, you should travel and make some Taiwanese friends.

❸ 我想了解了解你是怎麼學中文的,為什麼說得這麼流利。
Wǒ xiǎng liǎojiě liǎojiě nǐ shì zěnme xué Zhōngwén de, wèishénme shuō de zhème liúlì.
I'd like to better understand how you learned Chinese, and why you can speak so fluently.

Structures

The reduplication of disyllabic action verbs is an expansion from AB to ABAB.

*N*egation :

❶ 下星期要考試，你怎麼不準備準備呢？
Xià xīngqí yào kǎoshì, nǐ zěnme bù zhǔnbèi zhǔnbèi ne?
There is a test next week. Why aren't you preparing for it?

❷ 你不練習練習寫字，聽寫怎麼考得好？
Nǐ bú liànxí liànxí xiě zì, tīngxiě zěnme kǎo de hǎo?
You don't practice writing. How are you going to do well on the dictation?

❸ 我們不參觀參觀，怎麼知道這個學校好不好？
Wǒmen bù cānguān cānguān, zěnme zhīdào zhè ge xuéxiào hǎo bù hǎo?
If we don't take a look around how are we going to know if this is a good school or not?

*Q*uestions :

❶ 我是妳男朋友，妳是不是應該多關心關心我？
Wǒ shì nǐ nánpéngyǒu, nǐ shìbúshì yīnggāi duō guānxīn guānxīn wǒ?
I'm your boyfriend. Shouldn't you show a little more concern?

❷ 這個週末，你要不要在家休息休息？
Zhè ge zhōumò, nǐ yào bú yào zài jiā xiūxí xiūxí?
Are you going to take a break at home this weekend?

❸ 我有什麼機會可以認識認識新朋友？
Wǒ yǒu shénme jīhuì kěyǐ rènshì rènshì xīn péngyǒu?
Are there any opportunities for me to really get to know some new friends?

> Usage

Since reduplication already indicates reduction (in commitment), reduplicated forms do not occur with 一下 yíxià 'a bit' or 一點 yìdiǎn 'a little', which also indicates reduction, i.e., incompatible or redundant.

❶ *我得練習練習一下。
*Wǒ děi liànxí liànxí yíxià.
I need to practice a bit.

❷ *你得關心關心她一點。
*Nǐ děi guānxīn guānxīn tā yìdiǎn.
You need to show her a little concern.

| Reduplication of Verbs in V了V　(5)

> Function

The 'V 了 V ' pattern indicates the completion of a repeated action in the past that was done briefly and tentatively.

❶ 媽媽穿了穿那件衣服，覺得很舒服。
Māma chuān le chuān nà jiàn yīfú, juéde hěn shūfú.
Mom tried on that dress and found it very comfortable.

❷ 朋友告訴我夏天芒果很甜，我就嚐了嚐。真的好吃。

Péngyǒu gàosù wǒ xiàtiān mángguǒ hěn tián, wǒ jiù cháng le cháng. Zhēn de hǎochī.

My friends told me that mangos are sweet in the summer, so I tried some. And they were good!

❸ 老闆看了看我寫的計畫，然後說沒問題。

Lǎobǎn kàn le kàn wǒ xiě de jihuà, ránhòu shuō méi wèntí.

My boss took a quick look at the proposal I wrote and said it was no problem.

Structures　The verb in this construction must be monosyllabic.

Questions :

❶ 王先生昨天來了以後，是不是坐了坐就走了？

Wáng xiānshēng zuótiān láile yǐhòu, shìbúshì zuò le zuò jiù zǒu le?

When Mr. Wang came by yesterday, he just sat for a bit and left, right?

❷ 他沒買那本書，是不是因為看了看就看不下去了？

Tā méi mǎi nà běn shū, shìbúshì yīnwèi kàn le kàn jiù kànbúxiàqù le?

After trying for a while he simply couldn't keep on reading the book, is that why he didn't buy it?

❸ 他是不是想了想，還是決定回到自己國家工作？

Tā shìbúshì xiǎng le xiǎng, háishì juédìng huí dào zìjǐ guójiā gōngzuò?

After thinking about it for a long time, he finally decided to return to his country to work, right?

Usage

(1) The reduplication pattern 'V 一 V' can relate to the past or to the future. On the other hand, 'V 了 V' is used only in relation to past actions.

❶ 他聽說墾丁海邊很漂亮，想去看一看。

Tā tīngshuō Kěndīng hǎibiān hěn piàoliàng, xiǎng qù kàn yí kàn.

He heard that the seaside at Kenting is beautiful, so he'd like to go check it out.

❷ 請你把老師今天給的功課做一做！

Qǐng nǐ bǎ lǎoshī jīntiān gěi de gōngkè zuò yí zuò!

Please do the homework that the teacher assigned today.

❸ 如果你要去旅行，應該先找一找網站上的資料。

Rúguǒ nǐ yào qù lǚxíng, yīnggāi xiān zhǎo yì zhǎo wǎngzhàn shàng de zīliào.

If you want to go on a trip, you should search for information on websites.

(2) While V 一 V can be used in a single sentence (see ❷ above), V 了 V can not. It must be used with another clause.

❶ *我到公園走了走。
*Wǒ dào gōngyuán zǒu le zǒu.

❷ 我昨天吃了飯以後，就到公園走了走。
Wǒ zuótiān chīle fàn yǐhòu, jiù dào gōngyuán zǒu le zǒu.
Yesterday after the meal, I went to the park and took a short walk.

❸ 我拿起一本語言學的書，看了看就覺得累了。
Wǒ náqǐ yì běn yǔyánxué de shū, kàn le kàn jiù juéde lèi le.
I picked up a book about linguistics and felt tired after reading for a while.

(3) If the verb is transitive, the construction often combines with the 把 construction.

❶ 媽媽把餃子餡兒嚐了嚐，覺得剛好。
Māma bǎ jiǎozi xiànr cháng le cháng, juéde gāng hǎo.
Mom tasted the filling for the dumplings and felt it was just right.

❷ 哥哥把那件衣服試了試，還是覺得不合適。
Gēge bǎ nà jiàn yīfú shì le shì, háishì juéde bù héshì.
My older brother tried on the shirt, but found it did not suit him.
(i.e., either in size, color, or style)

Relatve Clause A 的 B, Clause as Modifier of Noun

Function Clauses in Chinese can also be used to modify nouns.

❶ 你說的水果是西瓜。
Nǐ shuō de shuǐguǒ shì xīguā.
The fruit you're talking about is watermelon.

❷ 他喝的茶是烏龍茶。
Tā hē de chá shì Wūlóng chá.
The tea he drank was Oolong tea.

❸ 這些是我拍的照片。
Zhèxiē shì wǒ pāi de zhàopiàn.
These are photos that I took.

❹ 穿黃衣服的這個人是老闆。
Chuān huáng yīfú de zhè ge rén shì lǎobǎn.
The person in a yellow shirt is the (shop) owner.

❺ 現在去那裡玩的人比較少。
Xiànzài qù nàlǐ wán de rén bǐjiào shǎo.
Now, fewer people are visiting that place.

❻ 買這種手機的人很多。
Mǎi zhè zhǒng shǒujī de rén hěn duō.
A lot of people buy this kind of cellphone.

Structures Clauses (A), like all modifiers in Chinese, always precede the nouns (B) they modify. The modification marker 的 de comes directly in front of the noun modified. A relative clause itself can be either affirmative, or negative, see below.

Negation :

❶ 不能上網的手機很不方便。
Bù néng shàngwǎng de shǒujī hěn bù fāngbiàn.
Cellphones that cannot go online aren't that useful.

❷ 不去逛夜市的人可以去茶館喝茶。
Bú qù guàng yèshì de rén kěyǐ qù cháguǎn hē chá.
Those who do not want to go to the night market can go drink tea at the tea house.

❸ 不來上課的同學不能去看籃球比賽。
Bù lái shàngkè de tóngxué bù néng qù kàn lánqiú bǐsài.
Students who did not come to class can't go to watch basketall game.

Usage Modifiers of nouns in Chinese include clauses, nouns, adjectives, and verbs. These are all placed in front of the nouns they modify.

仍然, réngrán, (Adv), still the same, same as before

Function The adverb 仍然 indicates that a situation remains unchanged, still the same as before.

❶ 百貨公司週年慶雖然有折扣，可是價錢仍然很高。
Bǎihuò gōngsī zhōuniánqìng suīrán yǒu zhékòu, kěshì jiàqián réngrán hěn gāo.
There are discounts during department store anniversary sales, but overall the prices are still very high.

❷ 母親已經勸了他許多次，他卻仍然不聽。
Mǔqīn yǐjīng quànle tā xǔduō cì, tā què réngrán bù tīng.
He still did not heed his mother even after being urged by her many times.

❸ 王先生在生活上碰到很多困難，但是他仍然不放棄理想。
Wáng xiānshēng zài shēnghuó shàng pèngdào hěn duō kùnnán, dànshì tā réngrán bú fàngqì lǐxiǎng.
Despite having come across many an obstacle, Mr. Wang is still unwilling to give up on his ideals.

❹ 雖然現在科技發達，地震仍然是沒有辦法避免的天災。
Suīrán xiànzài kējì fādá, dìzhèn réngrán shì méi yǒu bànfǎ bìmiǎn de tiānzāi.
Techonology is very advanced, but earthquakes are still an unavoidable natural disaster.

❺ 政府已經提出多項鼓勵生育的措施，但是「少子化」的問題卻仍然很嚴重。

Zhèngfǔ yǐjīng tíchū duō xiàng gǔlì shēngyù de cuòshī, dànshì 'shǎozǐhuà' de wèntí què réngrán hěn yánzhòng.

The government has taken measures to promote population growth, but the declining birthrate is still a serious issue.

Usage

(1) 仍然 very often occurs in S₂, accompanied by 可是, 但是, or 卻.

(2) 仍然 is formal and is freely interchangeable with its colloquial counterpart 還是, e.g.,

❶ 雖然他來晚了，我們仍然/還是玩得很開心。

Suīrán tā lái wǎn le, wǒmen réngrán/háishì wán de hěn kāixīn.

Although he arrived late, we still had a good time.

❷ 爺爺雖然老了，仍然/還是很有精神。

Yéye suīrán lǎo le, réngrán/háishì hěn yǒu jīngshén.

Although grandpa is old, he still has lots of energy.

❸ 已經下課了，他仍然/還是捨不得離開教室。

Yǐjīng xiàkè le, tā réngrán/háishì shěbùdé líkāi jiàoshì.

Class is over, but he still can't pull himself away from the classroom.

Repetition of Verbs, as in V 來 V 去, (V lái V qù), repetitively, back and forth

Function

This pattern is used with action verbs and indicates repetitive execution, oftentimes in vain.

❶ 孩子總是喜歡打來打去，你別擔心。

Háizi zǒngshì xǐhuān dǎlái dǎqù, nǐ bié dānxīn.

Kids are always hitting each other. It's nothing to worry about.

❷ 他很講究吃，他說吃來吃去還是台南的牛肉湯最好喝。

Tā hěn jiǎngjiù chī, tā shuō chīlái chīqù háishì Táinán de niúròu tāng zuì hǎohē.

He's very particular about what he eats. He says he's eaten around and he still feels that the beef soup in Tainan is the best.

❸ 他們想來想去，最後決定帶狗去旅行。不送牠去狗旅館住。

Tāmen xiǎnglái xiǎngqù, zuìhòu juédìng dài gǒu qù lǚxíng. Bú sòng tā qù gǒu lǚguǎn zhù.

After thinking about it for a while, they decided to bring their dog along with them on their trip and not put him in a dog hotel.

❹ 他想換襯衫，可是換來換去都不適合。最後只好穿原來的。
Tā xiǎng huàn chènshān, kěshì huànlái huànqù dōu bú shìhé.
Zuìhòu zhǐhǎo chuān yuánlái de.

He wanted to change a shirt, but he changed several times and none
of them were a good fit. In the end, he had no choice but to return
to his original shirt.

❺ 老闆在辦公室裡走來走去，不知道在想什麼？
Lǎobǎn zài bàngōngshì li zǒulái zǒuqù, bù zhīdào zài xiǎng
shénme?

The manager was pacing back and forth in his office. Don't know
what was bothering him.

Usage

(1) If there is an object, it must be moved to the front of the sentence,
as a topic.

E.g.,

❶ 電腦，我不想帶來帶去，累死了。
Diànnǎo, wǒ bù xiǎng dàilái dàiqù, lèi sǐle.
I don't want to carry my computer around. It's exhausting.

❷ 他寫的文章，看來看去都跟文學有關。
Tā xiě de wénzhāng, kànlái kànqù dōu gēn wénxué yǒuguān.
After reading a lot of his articles it turns out they're all about
literature.

(2) The V 來 V 去 structure is followed by some kind of comments by
the speaker. In other words, this pattern does not end an utterance.
E.g.,

這幾個辦法，他想來想去，都覺得不好。
Zhè jǐ ge bànfǎ, tā xiǎnglái xiǎngqù, dōu juéde bù hǎo.
After tossing the methods about in his mind for a while, he feels
that none of them are any good.

Separable Verbs (See 離合詞 líhécí)

似乎, sìhū, (Adv), it seems that, it gives somebody the impression that

Function

This adverb expresses the speaker's judgment on or evaluation of a
situation.

❶ 看他跟妳說話的樣子，他似乎很喜歡妳。妳要不要給他一個機
會？
Kàn tā gēn nǐ shuōhuà de yàngzi, tā sìhū hěn xǐhuān nǐ. Nǐ yào bú
yào gěi tā yí ge jīhuì?
Seeing the way that he talks to you, it seems that he likes you. How
about giving him a chance?

❷ 聽你這麼說，你似乎不太相信他的話。

Tīng nǐ zhème shuō, nǐ sìhū bútài xiāngxìn tā de huà.

From the way you talk, it seems like you don't really believe what he said.

❸ 我以前根本沒來過這裡。為什麼我覺得似乎來過？

Wǒ yǐqián gēnběn méi láiguò zhèlǐ. Wèishénme wǒ juéde sìhū láiguò?

I've never been here in my life. Why does everything seem so familiar?

❹ 跟高中同學聊到以前在學校的事，讓大家似乎又回到十七、八歲。

Gēn gāozhōng tóngxué liáodào yǐqián zài xuéxiào de shì, ràng dàjiā sìhū yòu huídào shíqī, bā suì.

Chatting with my high school classmates about our school days then made it seem like we were all 17 or 18 years old again.

❺ 他每天吃喝玩樂，似乎都不需要擔心養家活口的問題。

Tā měi tiān chīhēwánlè, sìhū dōu bù xūyào dānxīn yǎngjiā huókǒu de wèntí.

Eat, drink, and be merry, that is what he does every day. It's as if he doesn't have to take care of his family.

所, suǒ, (Ptc), Verb Marker

Function ▶ The particle 所 marks the main verb of a relative clause, which modifies a noun.

❶ 這本書所介紹的方法，我早就學過了。

Zhè běn shū suǒ jièshào de fāngfǎ, wǒ zǎo jiù xuéguò le.

I have long since learned the methods outlined in this book.

❷ 他們所關心的價格問題，其實我們覺得並不重要。

Tāmen suǒ guānxīn de jiàgé wèntí, qíshí wǒmen juéde bìng bú zhòngyào.

The issue of price that they are concerned with is actually not so important to us.

❸ 我們已經把王先生所訂購的產品寄出了。

Wǒmen yǐjīng bǎ Wáng xiānshēng suǒ dìnggòu de chǎnpǐn jìchū le.

We have already mailed out the products Mr. Wang ordered.

Usage ▶ The usage of 所 is more formal, and its use is completely optional.

上, shàng, (V), Various Meanings of the Verb (1)

Function ▶ The verb 上 has various meanings, the most typical of which indicates an upward movement. Atypical cases will have to be learned as such. No general rules apply.

❶ 春天的時候，很多人上陽明山泡溫泉、欣賞櫻花。
Chūntiān de shíhòu, hěn duō rén shàng Yángmíng shān pào wēnquán, xīnshǎng yīnghuā.
In the spring, many people go up Yangming Mountain to soak in the hot springs and enjoy the cherry blossoms.

❷ 下課以後，我要上樓去找同學討論功課。
Xiàkè yǐhòu, wǒ yào shàng lóu qù zhǎo tóngxué tǎolùn gōngkè.
After class, I'm going upstairs to discuss homework with classmates.

❸ 車子來了。快上車吧！
Chēzi láile. Kuài shàng chē ba!
The bus is here. Hurry up and get on.

❹ 早點睡吧。明天 6 點要上飛機呢。
Zǎodiǎn shuì ba. Míngtiān liùdiǎn yào shàng fēijī ne.
Get to sleep a little earlier. You have to board the plane at 6:00 am tomorrow.

❺ 他習慣週末上超市買菜。
Tā xíguàn zhōumò shàng chāoshì mǎi cài.
He usually goes to the supermarket on the weekend to buy groceries.

❻ 為了身體健康，晚上最好 11 點以前上床。
Wèile shēntǐ jiànkāng, wǎnshàng zuìhǎo shíyīdiǎn yǐqián shàng chuáng.
For your health, it's best to get to bed before 11:00 pm.

❼ 上班時間，捷運上人很多，擠死了。
Shàngbān shíjiān, jiéyùn shàng rén hěn duō, jǐ sǐle.
When going to work, there are lots of people on the MRT. It's really crowded.

❽ 他每星期六都上教堂。
Tā měi xīngqíliù dōu shàng jiàotáng.
He goes to church every Saturday.

❾ 台北 101 跨年放煙火活動，昨天晚上上電視新聞了。
Táiběi 101 kuànián fàng yānhuǒ huódòng, zuótiān wǎnshàng shàng diànshì xīnwén le.
The Taipei 101 New Year's fireworks display was on the news last night.

上, shàng, (Ptc), as Verb Complement, coming into contact (2)

Function When 上 serves as a verb particle, it refers to the 'coming into contact' between two nouns.

❶ 王先生穿上西裝，準備去上班。
Wáng xiānshēng chuānshàng xīzhuāng, zhǔnbèi qù shàngbān.
Mr. Wang put on his suit and prepared to go to work.

249

❷ 新娘換上了另外一件漂亮的禮服。
Xīnniáng huànshàngle lìngwài yí jiàn piàoliàng de lǐfú.
The bride changed into another beautiful gown.

❸ 他跑了好久。最後，追上了垃圾車。
Tā pǎole hǎojiǔ. Zuìhòu, zhuīshàngle lèsè chē.
He ran a long time, and finally caught up with the garbage truck.

❹ 小林到臺灣以後就喜歡上了臺灣的芒果。
Xiǎo Lín dào Táiwān yǐhòu jiù xǐhuānshàngle Táiwān de mángguǒ.
After arriving in Taiwan, Xiao Lin fell in love with Taiwan's mangos.

❺ 我們一走進店裡去，姐姐就看上了那個紅色的背包。
Wǒmen yì zǒujìn diàn lǐ qù, jiějie jiù kànshàngle nà ge hóngsè de bēibāo.
As soon as we stepped into the shop, my big sister took a fancy for that red backpack.

❻ 哥哥愛上了她，想跟她結婚。
Gēge àishàngle tā, xiǎng gēn tā jiéhūn.
My older brother has fallen in love with her and wants to marry her.

Structures

*N*egation :

❶ 你不寫上你的名字，沒有人知道這本作業本是你的。
Nǐ bù xiěshàng nǐ de míngzi, méi yǒu rén zhīdào zhè běn zuòyèběn shì nǐ de.
If you don't write your name on this workbook, no one will know it's yours.

❷ 媽媽沒搭上最後那班捷運。
Māma méi dāshàng zuìhòu nà bān jiéyùn.
Mom didn't catch the last MRT train.

❸ 我沒追上垃圾車，只能明天再丟垃圾了。
Wǒ méi zhuīshàng lèsè chē, zhǐ néng míngtiān zài diū lèsè le.
I didn't catch up to the garbage truck, so I can only throw out the garbage tomorrow. (i.e., take the garbage out tomorrow)

*Q*uestions :

❶ 你是不是在履歷表上寫上了名字？
Nǐ shìbúshì zài lǚlì biǎo shàng xiěshàngle míngzi?
You wrote your name on the CV, didn't you?

❷ 爸爸看上的東西就一定很好嗎？
Bàba kànshàng de dōngxi jiù yídìng hěn hǎo ma?
Is everything that catches dad's fancy really nice?

❸ 老闆愛上王小姐了吧？要不然怎麼對她那麼好呢？
Lǎobǎn àishàng Wáng xiǎojiě le ba? Yàobùrán zěnme duì tā nàme hǎo ne?
I gather the boss has fallen in love with Miss Wang. Otherwise, why would he treat her so well?

Usage

(1) Only certain verbs can combine with 上. They must be verbs that can make two nouns come into contact with each other either physically or psychologically, e.g., 穿 chuān 'put on', 愛 ài 'love', and 追 zhuī 'chase, court' are typical cases.

(2) Not all 'V＋上' cominbations can have all the complement structures in the actual (positive, 沒 negative) or potential forms (can V₁ 得 V₂, cannot V₁ 不 V₂). See the chart below.

Verb ＋ 上	Actual (＿，沒)	Potential (得 / 不)
追 zhuī 'chase'	✓	✓
看 kàn 'see'	✓	✓
愛 ài 'love'	✓	✗
穿 chuān 'wear'	✓	✓
送 sòng 'give'	✓	✗
換 huàn 'exchange'	✓	✗
喜歡 xǐhuān 'like'	✓	✗

❶ 皮包雖然貴，可是不好看。媽媽還看不上呢。

Píbāo suīrán guì, kěshì bù hǎokàn. Māma hái kànbúshàng ne.

The bag is expensive, but it's not attractive. Mom won't take a fancy to it.

❷ 雖然很多人給他介紹女朋友，但是沒有一個他看得上的。

Suīrán hěn duō rén gěi tā jièshào nǚpéngyǒu, dànshì méi yǒu yí ge tā kàndeshàng de.

Although many people have introduced potential girlfriends to him, he hasn't taken a liking to any one of them.

上, shàng, (Ptc), as in 在 NP 上, regarding NP (3)

Function

This pattern '在 NP 上' applies the validity of the main predicate to the NP in question.

❶ 有機蔬果在價格上雖然比較貴一點。但是一般來說，它的品質，顧客也比較信任。

Yǒujī shūguǒ zài jiàgé shàng suīrán bǐjiào guì yìdiǎn. Dànshì yìbān láishuō, tā de pǐnzhí, gùkè yě bǐjiào xìnrèn.

As far as prices go, organic fruits and vegetables are a little more expensive, but generally speaking, customers trust the quality more.

❷ 有機蔬果在市場上的價錢雖然很高，但是實際上農夫的利潤並不高。

Yǒujī shūguǒ zài shìchǎng shàng de jiàqián suīrán hěn gāo, dànshì shíjì shàng nóngfū de lìrùn bìng bù gāo.

As far as prices on the market go, organic fruits and vegetables are expensive, but farmers don't actually make very high profits.

❸ 中國人習慣上都是先吃飯再喝湯。你們呢？

Zhōngguó rén xíguàn shàng dōu shì xiān chīfàn zài hē tāng. Nǐmen ne?

In terms of custom, Chinese have soup after eating the main meal. What about you?

❹ 我跟我最好的朋友在個性上很不一樣，她個性比我急。

Wǒ gēn wǒ zuì hǎo de péngyǒu zài gèxìng shàng hěn bù yíyàng, tā gèxìng bǐ wǒ jí.

My best friend and I are different in terms of personality. She is more impatient.

❺ 我來台灣快一年了，生活上都沒問題了，學習上也相當順利，中文進步了不少。

Wǒ lái Táiwān kuài yì nián le, shēnghuó shàng dōu méi wèntí le, xuéxí shàng yě xiāngdāng shùnlì, Zhōngwén jìnbùle bù shǎo.

I've been in Taiwan almost a year. In terms of my life, I have no problems. As far as my studies go, those are going smoothly, too. My Chinese has improved a lot.

Usage

(1) In most cases, a noun comes between 在 and 上.

(2) The 在 in this pattern can be omitted, but the 上 cannot, e.g., 在文化上 zài wénhuà shàng 'culturally' → 文化上 → *在文化.

少, shǎo, (Adv), as in 少＋Verb, less... than planned (See 多(2))

誰知道, shéi zhīdào, who would have thought that...?

Function   This pattern expresses the speaker's surprise at something has happened.

❶ 早上天氣那麼好。誰知道下午雨會下得那麼大，連鞋子都濕了。

Zǎoshang tiānqì nàme hǎo. shéi zhīdào xiàwǔ yǔ huì xià de nàme dà, lián xiézi dōu shī le.

The weather this morning was great. Who would have thought that it would rain so hard in the afternoon, soaking right through our shoes.

❷ 她親手做了巧克力，想送給小王。誰知道他桌上已經有一大堆巧克力了。

Tā qīnshǒu zuòle qiǎokèlì, xiǎng sòng gěi Xiǎo Wáng, shéi zhīdào tā zhuōshàng yǐjīng yǒu yí dà duī qiǎokèlì le.

She wanted to give to Xiao Wang some of her homemade chocolate. Who would have thought that he already had lots of chocolate on the table?

❸ 小王對女朋友那麼好。誰知道她居然想分開。

Xiǎo Wáng duì nǚpéngyǒu nàme hǎo, shéi zhīdào tā jūrán xiǎng fēnkāi.

Xiao Wang treated his girlfriend so well. Who would have thought that she wanted to split?

❹ 他以為永遠都回不去了。誰知道過了四十年後能再回到老家。

Tā yǐwéi yǒngyuǎn dōu huíbúqù le. Shéi zhīdào guòle sìshí nián hòu néng zài huídào lǎojiā.

He thought he'd never be able to return. Who would have thought that after forty years he was able to go back home?

Usage

That which follows 誰知道 can be either affirmative or negative, and either undesirable or desirable (less often).

❶ 他做的麵包看起來並不特別,誰知道得了世界麵包大賽冠軍。

Tā zuò de miànbāo kànqǐlái bìng bú tèbié, shéi zhīdào dé le shìjiè miànbāo dàsài guànjūn.

The bread he makes doesn't look special. You would never know that it actually won first place in a major world bread competition.

❷ 她說話的聲音不好聽,誰知道她唱歌唱得那麼好聽。

Tā shuōhuà de shēngyīn bù hǎotīng, shéi zhīdào tā chànggē chàng de nàme hǎotīng.

She has an unattractive speaking voice. Who would have guessed that she sounds so good when she sings?

❸ 他看起來很瘦,誰知道他吃那麼多。

Tā kànqǐlái hěn shòu, shéi zhīdào tā chī nàme duō.

He looks so thin. Who would have guessed that he has a huge appetite?

什麼都⋯,就是⋯, (shénme dōu..., jiùshì...), everything but...

Function

This pattern presents an exception to what has been said previously.

❶ 她什麼都買了,就是忘了買鹽。

Tā shénme dōu mǎi le, jiùshì wàngle mǎi yán.

She bought everything except for salt.

❷ 這家商店今天什麼都打八折,就是我要買的東西不打折。

Zhè jiā shāngdiàn jīntiān shénme dōu dǎ bā zhé, jiùshì wǒ yào mǎi de dongxi bù dǎzhé.

This shop has 20% off on everything except the things I want to buy today.

❸ 他對什麼都不講究,就是講究吃。

Tā duì shénme dōu bù jiǎngjiù, jiùshì jiǎngjiù chī.

He's not fussy about anything except food.

❹ 這條街上什麼店都有,就是沒有銀行。

Zhè tiáo jiē shàng shénme diàn dōu yǒu, jiùshì méi yǒu yínháng.

This street has any kind of store you could possibly need except a bank.

⑤ 他做什麼他父母都支持，就是不讓他休學去打工。
Tā zuò shénme tā fùmǔ dōu zhīchí, jiùshì bú ràng tā xiūxué qù dǎgōng.
His parents support everything he does, but they won't let him take time off school to work.

甚至, shènzhì, (Adv), even

Function   甚至 is an adverb which marks something in the sentence as extraordinary.

① 這種款式的包包非常受歡迎，甚至連續劇的女主角都拿過。我非買不可。
Zhè zhǒng kuǎnshì de bāobāo fēicháng shòu huānyíng, shènzhì liánxùjù de nǚzhǔjiǎo dōu náguò. Wǒ fēi mǎi bùkě.
This style of bag is quite popolar. Even the leading lady in a TV series had one. I have to buy one.

② 很多小農為了友善對待土地，最近甚至連農藥都不用了。
Hěn duō xiǎonóng wèile yǒushàn duìdài tǔdì, zuìjìn shènzhì lián nóngyào dōu bú yòng le.
For the sake of a healthy soil, recently, many small farmers are even going so far as to not use pesticides.

③ 鳳梨對臺灣經濟發展一直有很大的幫助，臺灣出口的鳳梨甚至曾經占世界第二位。
Fènglí duì Táiwān jīngjì fāzhǎn yìzhí yǒu hěn dà de bāngzhù, Táiwān chūkǒu de fènglí shènzhì céngjīng zhàn shìjiè dì'èr wèi.
Pineapples have always been a big help to Taiwan's economic development. Taiwan's pineapple exports were even once number two in the world.

④ 十六世紀時，歐洲人不但到中南美洲做生意，甚至到東方來從事貿易活動。
Shíliù shìjì shí, Ōuzhōu rén búdàn dào Zhōngnán Měizhōu zuò shēngyì, shènzhì dào Dōngfāng lái cóngshì màoyì huódòng.
During the 16th century, Europeans not only went to Central and South America to do business, they even came to the East to engage in trade activities.

⑤ 臺灣的微整型做得非常好，價錢又合理，甚至連外國人都利用假期來臺灣做微整型。
Táiwān de wéizhěngxíng zuò de fēicháng hǎo, jiàqián yòu hélǐ, shènzhì lián wàiguó rén dōu lìyòng jiàqí lái Táiwān zuò wéizhěngxíng.
Taiwan's micro-cosmetic surgery is very advanced and the prices are reasonable. Foreigners even use their holidays to come to Taiwan and undergo micro-cosmetic surgery.

Usage

(1) 甚至 is often followed by 連 lián, which marks exceptional circumstances. Please refer to 連 A 都 B.

(2) 甚至 is not related to 至於, which introduces a new topic to switch to, see 至於 zhìyú.

是, shì, (Ptc), it is indeed true that

Function 是 in this instance is not a full verb. Rather, it's an agreement marker. What follows 是 is old information. The speaker uses this pattern to indicate that his view is the same as that of the previous speaker.

❶ A：買鞋子是不是先試穿，才知道合適不合適？
Mǎi xiézi shìbúshì xiān shìchuān, cái zhīdào héshì bù héshì?
Shall I try the shoes on before I buy them to know if they fit or not?

B：是應該先試穿，而且還要穿著走一走。
Shì yīnggāi xiān shìchuān, érqiě hái yào chuānzhe zǒu yì zǒu.
You should indeed try them on first and even walk around in them.

❷ A：這位老師把語法解釋得很清楚，大家都很快地就了解了。
Zhè wèi lǎoshī bǎ yǔfǎ jiěshì de hěn qīngchǔ, dàjiā dōu hěn kuài de jiù liǎojiě le.
This teacher explains grammar very clearly. Everybody catches on quite quickly.

B：她解釋得是很清楚，而且她説話很有趣。
Tā jiěshì de shì hěn qīngchǔ, érqiě tā shuōhuà hěn yǒuqù.
She does explain very clearly and she's an interesting speaker too.

❸ A：你有居留證，可以打工了吧？
Nǐ yǒu jūliúzhèng, kěyǐ dǎgōng le ba?
You have an ARC, so you can work, right?

B：我是有居留證了，可是還不能打工，得再等八個月。
Wǒ shì yǒu jūliúzhèng le, kěshì hái bù néng dǎgōng, děi zài děng bā ge yuè.
I do have an ARC, but I can't work. I have to wait another eight months.

❹ A：你説話的聲音不對。你感冒了嗎？
Nǐ shuōhuà de shēngyīn bú duì. Nǐ gǎnmào le ma?
Your voice sounds a bit off. Do you have a cold?

B：我是感冒了，今天喉嚨好痛。
Wǒ shì gǎnmào le, jīntiān hóulóng hǎo tòng.
Yes, I do have a cold. My throat is really sore today.

❺ A：這個牌子的衣服品質很好。
Zhè ge páizi de yīfú pǐnzhí hěn hǎo.
The quality of this brand of clothing is good.

B：他們的品質是很好，可是打八折以後還很貴。

Tāmen de pǐnzhí shì hěn hǎo, kěshì dǎ bā zhé yǐhòu hái hěn guì.

The quality is indeed good, but even with 20% off, it's still expensive.

Usage

As an agreement marker, 是 is stressed slightly, e.g., 百貨公司的東西是比其他的商店貴，可是都是有名的牌子，品質跟樣子都比較好。Bǎihuò gōngsī de dōngxi shì bǐ qítā de shāngdiàn guì, kěshì dōu shì yǒumíng de páizi, pǐnzhí gēn yàngzi dōu bǐjiào hǎo. 'Things sold in department stores ARE more expensive than things in other stores, but it's all famous brand names, so the quality and styles are better.'

是…的, shì...de, to Focus, it was A that B

Function

This pattern highlights one of the elements in a sentence in a past instance and marks it as the focus, i.e., the main message of the sentence.

Structures

(1) In this pattern, the focus marker 是 is placed directly in front of the focused element and 的 is placed at the end of the sentence, i.e., Subject＋是＋Focus＋Activity＋的.

① 他是昨天晚上到臺灣的。

Tā shì zuótiān wǎnshàng dào Táiwān de.

It was last night that he arrived in Taiwan.

② 他是在學校附近吃晚飯的。

Tā shì zài xuéxiào fùjìn chī wǎnfàn de.

It was near the school that he had dinner.

③ 我是坐捷運來學校的。

Wǒ shì zuò jiéyùn lái xuéxiào de.

It was by MRT that I came to school.

(2) The object in this pattern is often moved to the very front of the sentence.

① 學費是公司替我付的。

Xuéfèi shì gōngsī tì wǒ fù de.

It is the company that pays my tuition.

② 這支手機是在夜市買的。

Zhè zhī shǒujī shì zài yèshì mǎi de.

It was in the night market that I purchased this cellphone.

(3) The focused element can be the subject, the expression for time, place, manner, and occasionally the verb, but never the object.

① 是我打電話給房東的。 (subject)

Shì wǒ dǎ diànhuà gěi fángdōng de.

It was I who called the landlord.

② 我是昨天晚上去看電影的。 (time)

Wǒ shì zuótiān wǎnshàng qù kàn diànyǐng de.

It was last night that I went to see a movie.

❸ 他是在那家便利商店買咖啡的。　　　　(place)
　　Tā shì zài nà jiā biànlì shāngdiàn mǎi kāfēi de.
　　It was in that convenience store that he bought coffee.

❹ 我是坐公車來上課的。　　　　　　　　(manner)
　　Wǒ shì zuò gōngchē lái shàngkè de.
　　It was by taking the bus that I came to class.

❺ *我是這間房間最近租的。　　　　　　　(object)
　　*Wǒ shì zhè jiān fángjiān zuìjìn zū de.

Negation :　The negation marker, 不 bú, always goes before 是 shì.

❶ 他不是今天早上去美國的。
　　Tā búshì jīntiān zǎoshàng qù Měiguó de.
　　It was not this morning that he went to the United States.

❷ 不是我打電話給房東的。
　　Búshì wǒ dǎ diànhuà gěi fángdōng de.
　　It was not I who called the landlord.

❸ 我不是在圖書館看書的。
　　Wǒ búshì zài túshūguǎn kànshū de.
　　It was not in the library that I studied.

Questions :

❶ 你是一個人來的嗎？
　　Nǐ shì yí ge rén lái de ma?
　　Did you come alone? (Was it by yourself that you came?)

❷ 他是不是坐高鐵去臺南的？
　　Tā shìbúshì zuò gāotiě qù Táinán de?
　　Was it by High Speed Rail that he went to Tainan?

❸ 你的房租是不是自己付的？
　　Nǐ de fángzū shìbúshì zìjǐ fù de?
　　Do you pay your own rent?

Usage

(1) Sometimes 是 can be omitted in the 是⋯的 pattern.

❶ 我（是）跟朋友一起來的。
　　Wǒ (shì) gēn péngyǒu yìqǐ lái de.
　　I came with friends. (It was with friends that I came.)

❷ 我（是）坐計程車來的。
　　Wǒ (shì) zuò jìchéngchē lái de.
　　I came by taxi. (It was by taxi that I came.)

(2) This pattern can be used to ask a wh-question (who, when, how, where) about an instance in the past. However, it does not work when 'what' is the object.

❶ 是誰打電話給你的？　　　　(who)
　　Shì shéi dǎ diànhuà gěi nǐ de?
　　Who called you?

257

❷ 他是什麼時候來學校的？　　(when)
Tā shì shénme shíhòu lái xuéxiào de?
When did he come to school?

❸ 你是怎麼去的？　　　　　(how)
Nǐ shì zěnme qù de?
How did you go?

❹ 你是在哪裡吃飯的？　　　(where)
Nǐ shì zài nǎlǐ chīfàn de?
Where did you eat?

❺ *你是什麼東西看的？　　　(object)
*Nǐ shì shénme dōngxi kàn de?

是不是, shìbúshì, is it the case that...?

Function　With this pattern, the speaker seeks confirmation for information already known or obvious from the context.

❶ 你是不是在家等我？
Nǐ shìbúshì zài jiā děng wǒ?
You are waiting for me at home, right?

❷ 那家餐廳是不是很有名？
Nà jiā cāntīng shìbúshì hěn yǒumíng?
That restaurant is well-known, right?

❸ 你是不是剛旅行回來？
Nǐ shìbúshì gāng lǚxíng huílái?
You just come back from a trip, right?

Usage

(1) 是不是 questions are quite different from 嗎 questions and A-not-A questions. It is not asking for new information but is asking for confirmation of old information. Please look at the differences below.

❶ 你銀行有錢嗎？
Nǐ yínháng yǒu qián ma?
(We're having problems. We need some money.) Do you have some money in the bank?

❷ 你銀行有沒有錢？
Nǐ yínháng yǒu méi yǒu qián?
same as above

❸ 你銀行是不是有錢？
Nǐ yínháng shìbúshì yǒu qián?
(We are having problems. We need some money.) You have some money in the bank, right?

(2) In the following sentences, A-not-A cannot be used. 是不是 shìbúshì or 嗎 ma is fine.

❶ 你比他高。　　*你比不比他高？　　*你比他高不高？
Nǐ bǐ tā gāo.　　*Nǐ bǐ bù bǐ tā gāo?　　*Nǐ bǐ tā gāo bù gāo?
You are taller than him.

你是不是比他高？
Nǐ shìbúshì bǐ tā gāo?
You are taller than him, right?

❷ 你最近太忙了。　　　　*你最近太忙不忙？
Nǐ zuìjìn tài máng le.　　*Nǐ zuìjìn tài máng bù máng?
You have been too busy lately.

你最近是不是太忙了？
Nǐ zuìjìn shìbúshì tài máng le?
You have been too busy lately, right?

使得, shǐde, (Vst), expressing causation, so as to make

Function

The state verb 使得 is a causative verb. What precedes it is the causer, which can be expressed by means of an NP or a clause. What comes after the causative is the result, which is always indicated by a sentence.

❶ 因為老闆決定裁員，使得他不得不另謀發展。
Yīnwèi lǎobǎn juédìng cáiyuán, shǐde tā bùdébù lìngmóu fāzhǎn.
The boss's decision to cut staff has forced him to explore other career avenues.

❷ 該國雖然已不施行一胎化政策，但並未使得少子化的問題得到解決。
Gāi guó suīrán yǐ bù shīxíng yìtāihuà zhèngcè, dàn bìngwèi shǐde shǎozǐhuà de wèntí dédào jiějué.
The country may have ended the one-child policy, but that hasn't solved the problem of a declining birth rate.

❸ 她的婆婆還有傳宗接代的觀念，使得她的壓力更大了。
Tā de pópo hái yǒu chuánzōng jiēdài de guānniàn, shǐde tā de yālì gèng dà le.
Her mother-in-law's traditional view of lineage is only added pressure.

❹ 今年因為奇怪的氣候，使得農民收成減少。
Jīnnián yīnwéi qíguài de qìhòu, shǐde nóngmín shōuchéng jiǎnshǎo.
Unusual weather this year has caused a decrease in harvest.

Usage

(1) 使得 and 使 are both causative verbs. They are often used interchangeably, e.g.,

❶ 聽說小王病得很嚴重,使/使得我們非常擔心。
Tīngshuō Xiǎo Wáng bìng de hěn yánzhòng, shǐ/shǐde wǒmen fēicháng dānxīn.
We understand that Xiao Wang is seriously ill. It has caused us to worry a great deal.

❷ 有話直說的人,有時真使/使得大家討厭。
Yǒu huà zhí shuō de rén, yǒushí zhēn shǐ/shǐde dàjiā tǎoyàn.
People who speak directly sometimes really annoy everybody.

❸ 因為沒念大學的關係,使/使得我一直害怕比不上別人。
Yīnwèi méi niàn dàxué de guānxi, shǐ/shǐde wǒ yīzhí hàipà bǐbúshàng biérén.
Because I didn't go to university, I'm afraid that I can never compare favorably with others.

(2) For 'virtual' instances (hypothetical situations), instances that have not already happened, 使 is often used.

❶ 人民希望政府能施行新政策,使物價穩定。
Rénmín xīwàng zhèngfǔ néng shīxíng xīn zhèngcè, shǐ wùjià wěndìng.
The people hope that the government will implement new policies to stabilize commodity prices.

❷ 如果想使頭髮看起來多一點的話,可以使用這種產品。
Rúguǒ xiǎng shǐ tóufà kànqǐlái duō yìdiǎn de huà, kěyǐ shǐyòng zhè zhǒng chǎnpǐn.
If you want your hair to look fuller, you can use a product like this.

❸ 如果去醫院動手術也不能使人恢復健康,那麼誰還願意去呢?
Rúguǒ qù yīyuàn dòng shǒushù yě bù néng shǐ rén huīfù jiànkāng, nàme shéi hái yuànyì qù ne?
If going to the hospital and undergoing surgery isn't going to make you regain your health, who would be willing to go?

(3) 使得 is often used with 'actual' instances, instances that have happened already.

❶ 這次颱風,由於民眾事前毫無準備,使得災情慘重。
Zhè cì táifēng, yóuyú mínzhòng shìqián háowú zhǔnbèi, shǐde zāiqíng cǎnzhòng.
This typhoon caused a disaster, because people were not at all prepared.

❷ 因為同學積極參與,使得這門課更加熱鬧、活潑。
Yīnwèi tóngxué jījí cānyù, shǐde zhè mén kè gèngjiā rènào, huópō.
The students actively participate, making this class more exciting and lively.

❸ 低所得、高物價的情況使得年輕人成了無殼蝸牛。

Dī suǒdé, gāo wùjià de qíngkuàng shǐde niánqīng rén chéngle wúké guāniú.

Low incomes and high prices have made it impossible for young people to afford homes.

(4) There are other causative verbs in modern Chinese, e.g., 讓 and 叫, which are highly colloquial. 使 is more formal, though not as formal as 使得.

❶ 漢堡吃多了對健康不好，而且容易讓你變胖。

Hànbǎo chī duō le duì jiànkāng bù hǎo, érqiě róngyì ràng nǐ biàn pàng.

Eating a lot of hamburgers is bad for the health and furthermore can make you fat.

❷ 這個消息叫我很難過。

Zhè ge xiāoxí jiào wǒ hěn nánguò.

This news has made me sad.

受, shòu, (Vst), a Passive Marker (see also 被 bèi entry)

Function   Sentences with the transitive verb 受 indicate a passive meaning, 'to be..., to get...'.

❶ 在台灣，教授是個受人尊敬的工作。

Zài Táiwān, jiàoshòu shì ge shòu rén zūnjìng de gōngzuò.

In Taiwan, teaching in university is a respected line of work.

❷ 五月天的歌很受大學生喜愛，他們演唱會的票很快就賣完了。

Wǔyuètiān de gē hěn shòu dàxuéshēng xǐ'ài, tāmen yǎnchànghuì de piào hěn kuài jiù màiwán le.

May Day's songs are loved by the college crowd. Their concert tickets sell out quickly.

❸ 他的能力很強，老闆很喜歡他，所以他在公司裡越來越受重視。

Tā de nénglì hěn qiáng, lǎobǎn hěn xǐhuān tā, suǒyǐ tā zài gōngsī lǐ yuèláiyuè shòu zhòngshì.

He is very capable and the boss likes him. He is valued more and more in the company.

❹ 有一位醫生常上電視，她不但經驗多，而且口才好，非常受歡迎。

Yǒu yí wèi yīshēng cháng shàng diànshì, tā búdàn jīngyàn duō, érqiě kǒucái hǎo, fēicháng shòu huānyíng.

There is a doctor that frequently appears on television. She is not only highly experienced, she is also eloquent. She is very well received.

❺ 他一向按照規定辦事情，今天不遵守規定，應該是受了很大的壓力。

Tā yíxiàng ànzhào guīdìng bàn shìqíng, jīntiān bù zūnshǒu guīdìng, yīnggāi shì shòule hěn dà de yālì.

He has always done things by the book. He didn't follow the rules today probably because he's under a lot of pressure.

Usage

A. Two structures are possible with 受. It either takes an object or it is followed by the subject of yet another verb.

(1) 受＋O

❶ 她受過很好的教育。

Tā shòuguò hěn hǎo de jiàoyù.

She received a good education.

❷ 他選擇放棄，應該是受了很大的壓力。

Tā xuǎnzé fàngqì, yīnggāi shì shòule hěn dà de yālì.

He decided to give up. He was probably under too much pressure.

(2) 受＋S＋V

❶ 他教書很活潑，很受學生（的）歡迎。

Tā jiāoshū hěn huópō, hěn shòu xuéshēng (de) huānyíng.

He teaches with a lot of energy and is very popular with students.

❷ 她寫的歌受大家（的）喜愛。

Tā xiě de gē shòu dàjiā (de) xǐ'ài.

The songs she writes are very well liked by everyone.

❸ 他提出的想法很受店長（的）重視。

Tā tíchū de xiǎngfǎ hěn shòu diànzhǎng (de) zhòngshì.

The ideas he proposes carry a great deal of weight with the store manager.

B. Comparing the passive with 受 and the passive with 被 bèi.

(1) 被 is a passive particle, and 受 is a verb. Words like 很, 非常, and 大 can be placed in front of 受 as adverbials. These cannot be placed in front of 被.

E.g.,

❶ 比賽的時候天氣不好，他的成績大受影響。

Bǐsài de shíhòu tiānqì bù hǎo, tā de chéngjī dà shòu yǐngxiǎng.

The weather was bad during the competition and his score was greatly impacted.

❷ 聽了李寶春的故事，他很受感動。

Tīngle Lǐ Bǎochūn de gùshì, tā hěn shòu gǎndòng.

Having heard Li Baochun's story, he was deeply moved.

❸ 他把學生當做孩子，非常受學生尊敬。

Tā bǎ xuéshēng dàngzuò háizi, fēicháng shòu xuéshēng zūnjìng.

He views students as his own children and is very much respected by them.

(2) 被-passives relate to instances that are often unfortunate for the subject or the speaker of the sentence, whereas 受-passives are free from this tendency.

E.g.,

❶ 她的手機被朋友弄壞了。

Tā de shǒujī bèi péngyǒu nòng huài le.

Her phone was broken by a friend.

❷ 這件事情被她發現就麻煩了。

Zhè jiàn shìqíng bèi tā fāxiàn jiù máfán le.

If she finds out about this, there'll be a lot of trouble.

❸ 他偷東西的時候被人看見了。

Tā tōu dōngxi de shíhòu bèi rén kànjiàn le.

Someone saw him stealing.

❹ 她很喜歡這個電影，看了以後很受感動。

Tā hěn xǐhuān zhè ge diànyǐng, kànle yǐhòu hěn shòu gǎndòng.

She likes this movie; she was really moved after watching it.

❺ 我喜歡接近自然，是受她影響。

Wǒ xǐhuān jiējìn zìrán, shì shòu tā yǐngxiǎng.

My affinity for nature is due to her influence.

❻ 她念書很專心，不受別人打擾。

Tā niànshū hěn zhuānxīn, bú shòu biérén dǎrǎo.

She is very focused when she studies. Other people can't disturb her.

(3) 受 is in most cases used with transitive state verbs. 被, on the other hand, is in most cases used with action verbs.

E.g.,

❶ 他把賣菜賺的錢都給了窮人，很受人尊敬。

Tā bǎ mài cài zhuàn de qián dōu gěile qióngrén, hěn shòu rén zūnjìng.

He is highly respected, because he gives all the money he makes from selling vegetables to the poor.

❷ 他說話很有意思，很受朋友歡迎。

Tā shuōhuà hěn yǒu yìsi, hěn shòu péngyǒu huānyíng.

He is a very interesting speaker. He is very popular with his friends.

❸ 這種遊戲很有意思，很受高中學生喜愛。
Zhè zhǒng yóuxì hěn yǒu yìsi, hěn shòu gāozhōng xuéshēng xǐ'ài.
This is a fun game and is very popular with high school students.

❹ 他沒把事情做好，被老闆罵了一頓。
Tā méi bǎ shìqíng zuòhǎo, bèi lǎobǎn màle yí dùn.
He didn't do a good job and was reamed out by the boss.

❺ 我的車上個週末停在路邊，結果被撞壞了。倒楣死了！
Wǒ de chē shàng gè zhōumò tíng zài lù biān, jiéguǒ bèi zhuànghuài le. Dǎoméi sǐle!
I parked my car on the side of the road last weekend, and it got smashed into. What rotten luck!

❻ 他安靜地走進辦公室，不想被發現。
Tā ānjìng de zǒujìn bàngōngshì, bù xiǎng bèi fàxiàn.
He walked quietly into the office. He didn't want to be noticed.

受到…影響, (shòudào...yǐngxiǎng), to be influenced by, affected by

> Function

In a sentence with this pattern, the subject is influenced by what comes after 受到.

❶ 王小明受到父母的影響，也很喜歡音樂。
Wáng Xiǎomíng shòudào fùmǔ de yǐngxiǎng, yě hěn xǐhuān yīnyuè.
Wang Xiaoming was influenced by his parents, and he too likes music.

❷ 台灣人受到西方文化的影響，喜歡喝咖啡的人越來越多了。
Táiwān rén shòudào xīfāng wénhuà de yǐngxiǎng, xǐhuān hē kāfēi de rén yuèláiyuè duō le.
Taiwanese have been influenced by western culture and more and more of them like to drink coffee.

❸ 他的公司受到經濟不好的影響，快要做不下去了。
Tā de gōngsī shòudào jīngjì bù hǎo de yǐngxiǎng, kuàiyào zuòbúxiàqù le.
His company has been impacted by the bad economy and soon won't be able to continue operating.

❹ 小孩子容易受到廣告的影響，總是要買一些對健康不好的東西。
Xiǎo háizi róngyì shòudào guǎnggào de yǐngxiǎng, zǒngshì yào mǎi yìxiē duì jiànkāng bù hǎo de dōngxi.
Kids are easily affected by advertisements and always want to buy things that are bad for their health.

❺ 颱風快要來了。天氣受到影響，變得很不穩定。
Táifēng kuàiyào lái le. Tiānqì shòudào yǐngxiǎng, biàn de hěn bù wěndìng.
A typhoon is approaching. The weather is being influenced by it and has become very unstable.

❻ 今年的氣溫特別高，雨又下得特別少。柚子的收成受到影響，比去年少了很多。

Jīnnián de qìwēn tèbié gāo, yǔ yòu xià de tèbié shǎo. Yòuzi de shōuchéng shòudào yǐngxiǎng, bǐ qùnián shǎole hěn duō.

The temperatures have been especially high this year and there has been little rain. The pomelo harvest has been affected. There are a lot fewer than last year.

❼ 地球的汙染越來越嚴重，有的人的健康已經受到影響了。

Dìqiú de wūrǎn yuèláiyuè yánzhòng, yǒu de rén de jiànkāng yǐjīng shòudào yǐngxiǎng le.

Pollution is worsening globally. Some people's health is already being impacted.

Usage

受到 is a bit formal, but is still used a great deal. It combines with many other nouns in addition to 影響, e.g., 教育 jiàoyù 'education', 鼓勵 gǔlì 'encouragement', 刺激 cìjī 'adversely impacted'.

説, shuō, (V), speak, vs. 談, tán, (V), talk

Function

In modern Mandarin Chinese, there are quite a few 'speak' verbs. Correct choice reflects mastery as well as politeness. In most cases, the type of object determines the verb, not the other way around. In rare instances, either choice is possible, with or without difference in meaning.

説話 shuōhuà (to speak, to utter)	vs.	談話 tánhuà (to chat, to have a conversation)
他説明天天氣會很好。 Tā shuō míngtiān tiānqì huì hěn hǎo. (said)	vs.	談天氣 tán tiānqì (talk about, discuss)
説外語 shuō wàiyǔ (speak)	vs.	談外語教育 tán wàiyǔ jiàoyù (talk about, discuss)
説故事 shuō gùshi (tell)	vs.	談理想 tán lǐxiǎng (talk about, discuss)
我們剛剛説了很多話。 Wǒmen gānggāng shuōle hěn duō huà. (said, talked about)	vs.	老師想找你談話。 Lǎoshī xiǎng zhǎo nǐ tánhuà. (speak with)
請你説一説這次旅行有趣的事。 Qǐng nǐ shuō yì shuō zhè cì lǚxíng yǒuqù de shì. (tell, talk about)	vs.	請你談一談你對這件事的想法。 Qǐng nǐ tán yì tán nǐ duì zhè jiàn shì de xiǎngfǎ. (tell us, explain)
他們正在説哪裡好玩。 Tāmen zhèngzài shuō nǎlǐ hǎowán. (saying)	vs.	他們正在談台北的經濟、建築。 Tāmen zhèngzài tán Táiběi de jīngjì, jiànzhú. (talking about, discussing)

> **Usage**

説 relates more to spontaneous instances, while 談 more to arranged and scheduled instances. 説 is almost always one-way and 談 two-way (back and forth between two or more people, so similar to talk with, discuss). In terms of frequency, 説 takes sentential objects more than 談.

説到, shuōdào, talking of

> **Function**

When a talk-verb combines with the particle 到, the pattern introduces a topic, 'speaking of ...', 'talking of...'.

❶ 説到台灣小吃，大家都會想起臭豆腐來。
Shuōdào Táiwān xiǎochī, dàjiā dōu huì xiǎngqǐ chòudòufu lái.
When Taiwanese light repasts are mentioned, people will think of stinky tofu, i.e., stinky tofu certainly comes to people's mind.

❷ 一談到旅行，我馬上想起墾丁的太陽。
Yì tándào lǚxíng, wǒ mǎshàng xiǎngqǐ Kěndīng de tàiyáng.
Whenever traveling is mentioned, I immediately think of the sun in Kenting.

❸ 説到台灣有名的飲料，外國學生都認為是珍珠奶茶。
Shuōdào Táiwān yǒumíng de yǐnliào, wàiguó xuéshēng dōu rènwéi shì zhēnzhū nǎichá.
Speaking of Taiwanese famous drinks, foreign students all think it is pearl milk tea.

❹ 談到怎麼教小孩，每個父母都有説不完的話。
Tándào zěnme jiāo xiǎohái, měi ge fùmǔ dōu yǒu shuōbùwán de huà.
(When the topic of) how to teach children comes up, every parent can talk endlessly.

> **Usage**

説到 or 談到 often appear at the very beginning of the sentence to introduce the topic.

❶ A：我喜歡去旅行，一放暑假就要去。
Wǒ xǐhuān qù lǚxíng, yí fàng shǔjià jiù yào qù.
I like to travel. As soon as summer vacation starts, I'll be going.

B：説到放假，我們還有多久才放假？
Shuōdào fàngjià, wǒmen hái yǒu duōjiǔ cái fàngjià?
Speaking of vacation, how long is it before the next break?

❷ 談到準備結婚的事，他有很多抱怨。
Tándào zhǔnbèi jiéhūn de shì, tā yǒu hěnduō bàoyuàn.
When talk turns to wedding preparations, he has a lot of complaints.

説 A 就 A, (shuō A jiù A), happening instantly without prior warning

> **Function**

This pattern means that something unexpected happens, without prior warning, or happens faster than expected (from the speaker's perspective). The pattern is roughly equivalent to 'just like that' and 'and before you know it' in English.

① 你不喜歡你的班嗎？怎麼說換班就換班？

　Nǐ bù xǐhuān nǐ de bān ma? Zěnme shuō huàn bān jiù huàn bān?

　You didn't like your class? Why did you change classes just like that?

② 台北的天氣真奇怪，說下雨就下雨。

　Táiběi de tiānqì zhēn qíguài, shuō xiàyǔ jiù xiàyǔ.

　The weather in Taipei is really strange. The rains can come at any moment.

③ 小明怎麼了？怎麼說走就走？

　Xiǎomíng zěnme le? Zěnme shuō zǒu jiù zǒu?

　What's up with Xiaoming? Why did he just up and leave?

④ 美美上個月剛來台灣，怎麼說回國就回國？

　Měiměi shàng ge yuè gāng lái Táiwān, zěnme shuō huíguó jiù huíguó?

　Meimei came to Taiwan just last month. How come she's going back home already?

⑤ 李老師很嚴，常常說考試就考試，學生都覺得壓力很大。

　Li lǎoshī hěn yán, chángcháng shuō kǎoshì jiù kǎoshì, xuéshēng dōu juéde yālì hěn dà.

　Our teacher, Mr. Li, is very strict. He often gives tests without prior warning. The students are under a lot of stress.

死了, sǐle, A Post-Verbal Intensifier, terribly

Function　The post-verbal intensifier 死了 indicates extreme degree and is usually used for complaining.

① 他念的是自己沒興趣的科系，痛苦死了。

　Tā niàn de shì zìjǐ méi xìngqù de kēxì, tòngkǔ sǐle.

　He's studying a major he has no interest in. He couldn't be more miserable.

② 申請居留證的手續麻煩死了，他不想辦居留證了。

　Shēnqǐng jūliúzhèng de shǒuxù máfan sǐle, tā bù xiǎng bàn jūliúzhèng le.

　Applying for an ARC is a royal pain. He doesn't want to apply anymore.

③ 這條路好長，走起來累死了。

　Zhè tiáo lù hǎo cháng, zǒuqǐlái lèi sǐle.

　This road is really long. It's exhausting to walk it.

④ 檸檬酸死了。我的烤魚上面不要加檸檬。

　Níngméng suān sǐle. Wǒ de kǎoyú shàngmiàn bú yào jiā níngméng.

　Lemon is way too tart. Don't put any on my grilled fish.

⑤ 你別再打電腦了，吵死了。

　Nǐ bié zài dǎ diànnǎo le, chǎo sǐle.

　Get off the computer. The noise is bugging the heck out of me.

Usage

(1) The post-verbal 死了 sǐle is similar to 極了 jíle, 得不得了 de bùdéliǎo, and 得很 de hěn. They all express intensity, but 死了 carries the highest intensity, though negatively.

(2) When 死了 is used, most of the time, it is about something negative with a handful of exceptions, e.g., 高興死了 gāoxìng sǐle 'terribly pleased', 羨慕死了 xiànmù sǐle 'terribly envious', 樂死了 lè sǐle 'extremely happy'.

(3) English has a similar pattern, e.g., He was frightened to death.

四字格, sìzìgé, Four-Character Phrases (See 成語 chéngyǔ)

算了, suànle, forget it, drop it

Function Use of the idiomatic pattern 算了 indicates the speaker's desire to disregard an unpleasant fact.

❶ A：你不是要跟女朋友去聽五月天的演唱會嗎？怎麼還在這裡？
　　Nǐ búshì yào gēn nǚpéngyǒu qù tīng Wǔyuètiān de yǎnchànghuì ma? Zěnme hái zài zhèlǐ?
　　Aren't you going with your girlfriend to the May Day concert? Why are you still here?

　 B：氣死我了。她說要準備明天的報告，不去了。
　　Qìsǐ wǒ le. Tā shuō yào zhǔnbèi míngtiān de bàogào, bú qù le.
　　I'm so mad. She said she has to prepare a report for tomorrow, so she's not going.

　 A：她不去算了，你不要生氣了。
　　Tā bú qù suànle, nǐ bú yào shēngqì le.
　　If she's not going then just forget about it. Don't be upset.

❷ A：你昨天會計的考試，成績怎麼樣？
　　Nǐ zuótiān kuàijì de kǎoshì, chéngjī zěnmeyàng?
　　How did you do on the accounting test yesterday?

　 B：真不好。算了，算了。今天不說這個。
　　Zhēn bù hǎo. Suànle, suànle. Jīntiān bù shuō zhè ge.
　　I did really poorly. Drop it, let's not talk about it today.

❸ A：小王說他對唱歌沒興趣，晚上不去KTV了。
　　Xiǎo Wáng shuō tā duì chànggē méi xìngqù, wǎnshàng bú qù KTV le.
　　Xiao Wang says that he's not a big fan of singing. He's not going to go to KTV tonight.

　 B：那就算了。我自己去。
　　Nà jiù suànle. Wǒ zìjǐ qù.
　　Then, forget it. I'll go myself.

❹ A：沒想到我最喜歡的羊毛外套破了一個大洞。

Méi xiǎngdào wǒ zuì xǐhuān de yángmáo wàitào pòle yí ge dà dòng.

I had no idea that my favorite wool coat would get a big hole in it.

B：既然破了一個大洞，就丟了算了。

Jìrán pòle yí ge dà dòng, jiù diūle suànle.

Since it's got a big hole in it, just toss it and forget about it.

❺ A：我告訴小明炸的東西對身體不好，不要常吃，他總是不聽。

Wǒ gàosù Xiǎomíng zhá de dōngxi duì shēntǐ bù hǎo, bú yào cháng chī, tā zǒngshì bù tīng.

I told Xiaoming that fried food is bad for his health, he shouldn't eat it so often, but he never listens.

B：他不聽算了，你別難過了。

Tā bù tīng suànle, nǐ bié nánguò le.

If he doesn't want to listen then just forget it. Don't be upset about it.

> **Usage**

Note that 算了 can occur at the very front, in the middle or even at the very end of a sentence. This type of grammatical flexibility is rather rare in modern Chinese.

算是, suànshì, (V), can be considered...

> **Function**

算是 is a verb that introduces an estimate after comparing the subject with other (comparable) things.

❶ 教書算是穩定的工作。

Jiāoshū suànshì wěndìng de gōngzuò.

Teaching is considered a stable job.

❷ 這裡的櫻花算是多的，所以來玩的人不少。

Zhèlǐ de yīnghuā suànshì duō de, suǒyǐ lái wán de rén bù shǎo.

You could say that there are a lot of cherry blossoms here, so many people have come to visit.

❸ 最近氣溫都很低，而且每天下雨。今天雨停了，天氣算是不錯的。

Zuìjìn qìwēn dōu hěn dī, érqiě měi tiān xiàyǔ. Jīntiān yǔ tíng le, tiānqì suànshì búcuò de.

It has been cold and rainy lately, but today the rain stopped so the weather is nice again.

❹ 台北的建築每一棟都差不多，101大樓算是有特色的。

Táiběi de jiànzhú měi yí dòng dōu chàbùduō, 101 dàlóu suànshì yǒu tèsè de.

The buildings in Taipei all look about the same. Taipei 101 is probably more distinctive.

❺ 國際關係系算是熱門的科系嗎？

Guójì guānxi xì suànshì rèmén de kēxì ma?

Would the department of international relations be considered a popular department?

Usage

The negative form of 算是 is 不算. So, it is fine to say 休學手續不算麻煩 Xiūxué shǒuxù bú suàn máfán 'The application process for taking leave of absence isn't really a hassle', but *休學手續算是不麻煩 *Xiūxué shǒuxù suànshì bù máfán is not acceptable.

❶ 跟鄉下比起來，這裡的蚊蟲不算多。

Gēn xiāngxià bǐqǐlái, zhèlǐ de wénchóng bú suàn duō.

Compared to the countryside there are not that many bugs here.

❷ 他只有一點發燒，感冒不算嚴重。

Tā zhǐyǒu yìdiǎn fāshāo, gǎnmào bú suàn yánzhòng.

He only has a low fever, I wouldn't say it is serious.

❸ 這家店的餃子不算好吃。我帶你去別家吃。

Zhè jiā diàn de jiǎozi bú suàn hǎochī. Wǒ dài nǐ qù biéjiā chī.

I wouldn't say that the dumplings in this shop are good. I'll take you to another shop to eat.

隨著 S_1，S_2 也, (suízhe (Prep) S_1, S_2 yě (Adv)), as a consequence of

Function

This pattern means that S_1 contributes significantly to the realisation of S_2.

❶ 隨著中國的經濟越來越好，中國在國際上的地位也越來越重要。

Suízhe Zhōngguó de jīngjì yuèláiyuè hǎo, Zhōngguó zài guójì shàng de dìwèi yě yuèláiyuè zhòngyào.

As a consequence of China's improving economy, the country's international position has been increasing in importance.

❷ 隨著她的中文越來越好，她參加的活動也越來越多。

Suízhe tā de Zhōngwén yuèláiyuè hǎo, tā cānjiā de huódòng yě yuèláiyuè duō.

As her Chinese improves, she is taking part in more and more activities.

❸ 隨著大家對農藥越來越了解，買有機產品的人也越來越多了。

Suízhe dàjiā duì nóngyào yuèláiyuè liǎojiě, mǎi yǒujī chǎnpǐn de rén yě yuèláiyuè duō le.

As people come to better understand pesticides, an increasing number of people are buying organic products.

❹ 隨著研究所考試的時間越來越近，他的壓力也越來越大。

Suízhe yánjiūsuǒ kǎoshì de shíjiān yuèláiyuè jìn, tā de yālì yě yuèláiyuè dà.

As the date for the grad school entrance test drew nearer, he grew increasingly stressed out.

❺ 隨著年紀越來越大，她越來越想在美國工作的孩子。

Suízhe niánjì yuèláiyuè dà, tā yuèláiyuè xiǎng zài Měiguó gōngzuò de háizi.

As she got older, she thought more and more about her child working in the US.

> **Usage** This pattern is not used in daily conversation. It is rather formal.

太⋯了, tài (Adv)...le, overly, excessively

> **Function** 太⋯了 indicates 'too', 'overly', or 'greatly', 'really', a negative or positive observation given by the speaker, depending on the Vs chosen.

Negative	Positive
太貴了。Tài guì le. Too expensive.	太好了。Tài hǎo le. Wonderful.
太大了。Tài dà le. Too big.	太漂亮了。Tài piàoliàng le. So beautiful.
太熱了。Tài rè le. Too hot.	太舒服了。Tài shūfú le. So comfortable.

> **Usage**

(1) '太＋Vs' presents a negative evaluation by the speaker. 那支手機太貴。Nà zhī shǒujī tài guì. 'That cell phone is too expensive'. Only the excessive meaning is possible in this structure.

(2) '太＋Vs＋了' is more subjective, indicating that the speaker feels that what is being talked about is either excessive (adj.) or praise-worthy. For example, 那支手機太貴了。Nà zhī shǒujī tài guì le. 'That cell phone is way too expensive'. 這支手機太便宜了。Zhè zhī shǒujī tài piányí le. 'This cell phone is so cheap.'

談, tán, (V), talk, vs. 說, shuō, (V), speak (See 說 shuō)

談到, tándào, talking of   (See 說到 shuōdào)

Time and Place of Events   (1)

> **Function** The time and place of instances are often specified in sentences using, the sequence Time＋Place＋Event. The subject of the sentence occurs either in front of or after Time.

❶ 他和他朋友下午在教室寫書法。

Tā hàn tā péngyǒu xiàwǔ zài jiàoshì xiě shūfǎ.

He and his friends practice calligraphy in the afternoons in the afternoon in the classroom.

❷ 昨天晚上我到我家附近的咖啡店喝咖啡。
Zuótiān wǎnshàng wǒ dào wǒ jiā fùjìn de kāfēi diàn hē kāfēi.
Last night, I went to a coffee shop near my house to have some coffee.

❸ 我們這個週末去圖書館看書。
Wǒmen zhè ge zhōumò qù túshūguǎn kànshū.
We will go to the library this weekend to study.

❹ 你們明天早上十一點到我家來吃牛肉麵。
Nǐmen míngtiān zǎoshàng shíyīdiǎn dào wǒ jiā lái chī niúròu miàn.
You guys come to my house to have beef noodles at 11:00 tomorrow morning.

Structures

_N_egation : The negative marker 不 appears before place elements.

❶ 我晚上不在家吃飯。
Wǒ wǎnshàng bú zài jiā chīfàn.
I don't eat dinner at home in the evenings.

❷ 他和他哥哥最近都不來學校上課。
Tā hàn tā gēge zuìjìn dōu bù lái xuéxiào shàngkè.
He and his brother haven't come to school for classes lately.

❸ 他們這個週末不去山上看風景。
Tāmen zhè ge zhōumò bú qù shān shàng kàn fēngjǐng.
They are not going up the mountain to view the scenery this weekend.

_Q_uestions :

❶ 你下午要不要來學校打籃球？
Nǐ xiàwǔ yào bú yào lái xuéxiào dǎ lánqiú?
Would you like to come to school to play basketball in the afternoon?

❷ 你們現在在我家附近的商店買手機嗎？
Nǐmen xiànzài zài wǒ jiā fùjìn de shāngdiàn mǎi shǒujī ma?
Are you buying a cell phone in the shop near my house right now?

❸ 你朋友晚上幾點去KTV唱歌？
Nǐ péngyǒu wǎnshàng jǐdiǎn qù KTV chànggē?
What time do your friends go to KTV to sing in the evening?

❹ 他們什麼時候到花蓮看籃球比賽？
Tāmen shénme shíhòu dào Huālián kàn lánqiú bǐsài?
When are they going to Hualien to watch the basketball game?

❺ 你和你妹妹明天早上要去哪裡看電影？
Nǐ hàn nǐ mèimei míngtiān zǎoshàng yào qù nǎlǐ kàn diànyǐng?
Where are you and your sister going to go see the movie tomorrow morning?

Usage

(1) Every instance involves a time and a place. While the time and place may not be explicitly stated in the sentence, they are typically evident from the context. If there is no context, the references are 'right now' and 'right here'.

(2) Note the word order. Time comes before place. For example, to express 'I don't eat dinner at home in the evening', we say 我晚上不在家吃飯。Wǒ wǎnshàng bú zài jiā chīfàn. or 晚上我不在家吃飯。Wǎnshàng wǒ bú zài jiā chīfàn., but not *我不在家吃飯晚上。*Wǒ bú zài jiā chīfàn wǎnshàng.

Time-When vs. Time-Duration (2)

Function Time-When expressions are words or phrases that indicate when an action takes place or a situation happens. They refer to a point in time, e.g., 6:30 this morning. Time-Duration expressions refer to a stretch of time, e.g., 2 hours. See examples below.

Time-When

	Past	Present	Future
Year	去年qùnián 'last year'	今年jīnnián 'this year'	明年míngnián 'next year'
Month	上個月shàng ge yuè 'last month'	這個月zhè ge yuè 'this month'	下個月xià ge yuè 'next month'
Week	上個星期/禮拜 shàng ge xīngqí / lǐbài 'last week'	這個星期/禮拜 zhè ge xīngqí / lǐbài 'this week'	下個星期/禮拜 xià ge xīngqí / lǐbài 'next week'
Day	昨天zuótiān 'yesterday'	今天jīntiān 'today'	明天míngtiān 'tomorrow'

Time-When vs. Time-Duration

	Time-When	Time-Duration
Year	2017年 '2017', 2018年 '2018', 2019年 '2019'…	一年yì nián 'a year', 兩年liǎng nián '2 years', 三年sān nián '3 years'…, 半年bàn nián 'half a year', 一年半yì nián bàn 'a year and a half'
Month	一月yīyuè 'January', 二月èryuè 'Feburary', 三月sānyuè 'march'…	一個月yí ge yuè 'a month', 兩個月liǎng ge yuè '2 months', 三個月sān ge yuè '3 months', …半個月bàn ge yuè 'half a month', 一個半月yí ge bàn yuè 'a month and a half'…
Week	星期一xīngqíyī 'monday', 星期二xīngqíèr 'Tuesday'…, 星期日/天 xīngqírì /tiān 'sunday'	一個星期yí ge xīngqí 'a week', 兩個星期liǎng ge xīngqí '2 weeks'…
Day	1日rì (號hào) 'first', 2日rì 'second', 3日rì 'third'…	一天yì tiān 'a day', 兩天liǎng tiān '2 days', 三天sān tiān '3 days'…, 半天bàn tiān 'half a day', 一天半yì tiān bàn 'a day and a half'
Hour	一點（鐘）yìdiǎn (zhōng) '1:00', 兩點（鐘）liǎngdiǎn (zhōng) '2:00', …, 六點半liùdiǎnbàn '6:30'	一個鐘頭yí ge zhōngtóu 'an hour', 兩個鐘頭liǎng ge zhōngtóu '2 hours'…, 半個鐘頭bàn ge zhōngtóu 'half an hour', 六個半鐘頭liù ge bàn zhōngtóu 'six and a half hours'…

Time-Duration 'for a period of time' (3)

Function   Time-Duration expressions indicate the length of time, i.e., 'how long', an action takes.

❶ 我要去花蓮玩一個星期。
Wǒ yào qù Huālián wán yí ge xīngqí.
I'll be in Hualien for a week.

❷ 這個電影很有意思，可是要看三個鐘頭。
Zhè ge diànyǐng hěn yǒu yìsi, kěshì yào kàn sān ge zhōngtóu.
This movie is interesting, but you have to watch it for three hours.

❸ 中文，我只能學一年半。
Zhōngwén, wǒ zhǐ néng xué yì nián bàn.
I can only study Chinese for one and a half years.

Structures

(1) Duration expressions follow the verb directly, i.e, subject＋verb＋duration.

❶ 我去日本旅行了一個多星期。
Wǒ qù Rìběn lǔxíngle yí ge duō xīngqí.
I went to Japan to travel for a little over a week.

❷ 這麼多甜點，我們要吃一個星期。
Zhème duō tiándiǎn, wǒmen yào chī yí ge xīngqí.
So many desserts! It'll take us a week to eat (it all).

❸ 我想坐高鐵去臺南玩兩天。
Wǒ xiǎng zuò gāotiě qù Táinán wán liǎng tiān.
I would like to take the HSR and kick around in Tainan for two days.

❹ 中文課，我們學校要上四年。
Zhōngwén kè, wǒmen xuéxiào yào shàng sì nián.
We need to take Chinese classes for four years at our school.

(2) If the verb has an object following it, you must repeat the verb, before saying a time-duration phrase.

❶ 他打算教中文教一年。
Tā dǎsuàn jiāo Zhōngwén jiāo yì nián.
He wants to teach Chinese for a year.

❷ 我每個星期學書法學兩天。
Wǒ měi ge xīngqí xué shūfǎ xué liǎng tiān.
I study calligraphy two days every week.

❸ 今年我想在臺灣學中文學九個月。
Jīnnián wǒ xiǎng zài Táiwān xué Zhōngwén xué jiǔ ge yuè.
This year, I would like to study Chinese in Taiwan for nine months.

(3) Time-Duration is placed in front of negation.

❶ 他太忙了，所以他兩天不能來上課。
Tā tài máng le, suǒyǐ tā liǎng tiān bù néng lái shàngkè.
He was too busy, so he did not come to class for two days.

❷ 這裡沒有網路，所以我兩個星期不能上網。
Zhèlǐ méi yǒu wǎnglù, suǒyǐ wǒ liǎng ge xīngqí bù néng shàngwǎng.
There is no internet here, so I can't go online for two weeks.

❸ 她要回美國，所以一個月不能上課。
Tā yào huí Měiguó, suǒyǐ yí ge yuè bù néng shàngkè.
She is returning to the US, so she will not be coming to class for a month.

(4) When a separable verb takes Time-Duration, the time expression is inserted into the separable verb, either with or without 的.

❶ 我每星期上五天的課。
Wǒ měi xīngqí shàng wǔ tiān de kè.
I have classes five days a week.

❷ 學校下個月放三天的假。
Xuéxiào xià ge yuè fàng sān tiān de jià.
Our school has three- days off next month.

❸ 我們打算明天去KTV唱三個鐘頭的歌。
Wǒmen dǎsuàn míngtiān qù KTV chàng sān ge zhōngtóu de gē.
We plan to go to KTV tomorrow to sing for three hours.

❹ 你決定在台灣學多久的中文？
Nǐ juédìng zài Táiwān xué duō jiǔ de Zhōngwén?
How long did you decide to study Chinese in Taiwan?

Topic in Sentence (1)

| Function |

When you want to describe, explain, or evaluate a person, instance, or thing, you place the person, instance, or thing at the beginning of the sentence as the 'topic'. The rest of the sentence serves as the 'comment'. The topic of a sentence is usually the person or thing that is placed at the beginning of the sentence.

❶ A：臺灣人喜歡喝烏龍茶嗎？
Táiwān rén xǐhuān hē Wūlóng chá ma?
Do Taiwanese people like to drink Oolong tea?

B：（烏龍茶，）臺灣人都喜歡喝。
(Wūlóng chá,) Táiwān rén dōu xǐhuān hē.
(Oolong tea,) Taiwanese people all like to drink (it).

❷ A：你有哥哥、姐姐嗎？
Nǐ yǒu gēge, jiějie ma?
Do you have any brothers and sisters?

B：（哥哥、姐姐，）我都沒有。
(Gēge, jiějie,) wǒ dōu méi yǒu.
(Brothers, sisters,) I have none.

❸ A：你想看美國電影還是臺灣電影？
Nǐ xiǎng kàn Měiguó diànyǐng háishì Táiwān diànyǐng?
Do you want to watch an American movie or a Taiwanese movie?

B：（美國電影、臺灣電影，）我都想看。
(Měiguó diànyǐng, Táiwān diànyǐng,) wǒ dōu xiǎng kàn.
(American movie, Taiwanese movie,) I would like to watch either.

Structures ▶ Topics are always placed at the very beginning of a sentence, and they are most often omitted in active conversations. Thus, topics on the whole do not contribute to the information being conveyed.

❶ 打棒球，我不喜歡。
Dǎ bàngqiú, wǒ bù xǐhuān.
Playing baseball, I don't like (it).

❷ 越南菜，我常吃。
Yuènán cài, wǒ cháng chī.
Vietnamese food, I often eat (it).

❸ 這張照片，我覺得很好看。
Zhè zhāng zhàopiàn, wǒ juéde hěn hǎokàn.
This photo, I think (it) is quite nice.

Usage ▶ The highest frequency of topics originates from the objects of transitive verbs.

❶ 中國菜，我都喜歡吃。
Zhōngguó cài, wǒ dōu xǐhuān chī.
Chinese food, I like to eat (them) all.

❷ 弟弟、妹妹，我都有。
Dìdi, mèimei, wǒ dōu yǒu.
Younger brothers and younger sisters, I've got both.

Topic as Contrastive (2)

Function ▶ A topic in Chinese can serve as the contrastive element in a sentence, i.e., 'this, but not that...'. Either a subject or an object can be so contrasted.

❶ A：台灣小吃，你都喜歡嗎？
Táiwān xiǎochī, nǐ dōu xǐhuān ma?
Do you like all Taiwanese snacks?

B：水餃、包子，我喜歡；臭豆腐，我討厭。
Shuǐjiǎo, bāozi, wǒ xǐhuān; chòudòufu, wǒ tǎoyàn.
Dumplings and steamed buns I like. Stinky tofu I dislike.

❷ A：你建議我們帶什麼東西去旅行？
Nǐ jiànyì wǒmen dài shénme dōngxi qù lǚxíng?
What do you suggest we bring on the trip?

B：錢、手機一定要帶；藥，不一定要帶。
Qián, shǒujī yídìng yào dài; yào, bùyídìng yào dài.
Wallet and cell phone, these are a must, but meds are optional.

❸ A：高小姐有教語言的經驗嗎？
Gāo xiǎojiě yǒu jiāo yǔyán de jīngyàn ma?
Does Miss Gao have any language teaching experience?

B：教法文的經驗，她有。教西班牙語的經驗，她沒有。
Jiāo Fǎwén de jīngyàn, tā yǒu. Jiāo Xībānyáyǔ de jīngyàn, tā méi yǒu.
Experience teaching French, yes. Experience teaching Spanish, no.

❹ A：小明是不是會騎車？
Xiǎomíng shìbúshì huì qí chē?
Can Xiaoming ride a bicycle/motorcycle?

B：機車，他不會騎，他只會騎腳踏車。
Jīchē, tā bú huì qí, tā zhǐ huì qí jiǎotàchē.
Motorcycles, he can't ride. He can only ride bicycles.

❺ A：他們都會包小籠包嗎？
Tāmen dōu huì bāo xiǎolóngbāo ma?
Can they all wrap steamed dumplings?

B：包小籠包，小陳不會，可是美美會。
Bāo xiǎolóngbāo, Xiǎo Chén bú huì, kěshì Měiměi huì.
Wrap steamed dumplings Xiao Chen can't, but Meimei can.

透過, tòuguò, (Prep), by means of

Function

The preposition 透過 indicates facilitation by an intermediate means; it describes the way, method, or mode by which something is accomplished.

❶ 我們能透過網路知道世界各地的消息。
Wǒmen néng tòuguò wǎnglù zhīdào shìjiè gè dì de xiāoxí.
We know what is happening worldwide through the use of internet.

❷ 他透過參加社團活動認識了很多朋友。
Tā tòuguò cānjiā shètuán huódòng rènshìle hěn duō péngyǒu.
He met many friends by going to student group activities.

❸ 我透過李教授才找到這個工作。
Wǒ tòuguò Lǐ jiàoshòu cái zhǎodào zhè ge gōngzuò.
I got this job thanks to Professor Li.

Structures

透過 belongs to a small sub-category of prepositions that can occur either sentence-initially or in front of VP.

❶ 透過這次參觀，外國學生知道怎麼做紙傘了。
Tòuguò zhè cì cānguān, wàiguó xuéshēng zhīdào zěnme zuò zhǐsǎn le.
Through this official visit, the international students learned how to make umbrellas (made of papers).

❷ 中國人相信透過食物能讓身體越來越健康。
Zhōngguó rén xiāngxìn tòuguò shíwù néng ràng shēntǐ yuèláiyuè jiànkāng.
Chinese people believe that diet is the key to good health.

❸ 很多人透過電視節目練習聽的能力。
Hěn duō rén tòuguò diànshì jiémù liànxí tīng de nénglì.
Many people practice their listening skills by watching television.

Negation :

❶ 不透過考試，有的老師不能了解學生學得好不好。
Bú tòuguò kǎoshì, yǒu de lǎoshī bù néng liǎojiě xuéshēng xué de hǎo bù hǎo.
Without tests, some teachers would not know how well their students are doing.

❷ 聽說不透過介紹是很難到那家公司工作的。
Tīngshuō bú tòuguò jièshào shì hěn nán dào nà jiā gōngsī gōngzuò de.
I've heard it's really hard to get into that company unless you are recommended.

❸ 你不透過長時間的練習是學不會的。
Nǐ bú tòuguò cháng shíjiān de liànxí shì xuébúhuì de.
You'll never learn without lots of practice.

Questions :

❶ 你們是透過美美介紹認識的嗎？
Nǐmen shì tòuguò Měiměi jièshào rènshì de ma?
Were you introduced to each other by Meimei?

❷ 他到國外旅行都是透過這個網站找到適合的旅館嗎？
Tā dào guówài lǚxíng dōu shì tòuguò zhè ge wǎngzhàn zhǎodào shìhé de lǚguǎn ma?
Did he use this website to find accommodations for his travels abroad?

❸ 是不是有很多公司都透過網路，替自己的產品做廣告？
Shìbúshì yǒu hěn duō gōngsī dōu tòuguò wǎnglù, tì zìjǐ de xīn chǎnpǐn zuò guǎnggào?
Do many companies promote their new products online?

Usage

The prep 透過 has a similar internal formation to other words such as 經過 jīngguò (Prep) 'via', 超過 chāoguò (Vp) 'to exceed', 越過 yuèguò (V) 'to cross over'.

完, wán, (Ptc), as Verb Complement, completion of action

Function

When the particle 完 follows an action verb, it indicates the completion of the action.

❶ 他們已經喝完咖啡了。
Tāmen yǐjīng hēwán kāfēi le.
They've already finished drinking their coffees.

❷ 你借給我的書，我都看完了。
Nǐ jiè gěi wǒ de shū, wǒ dōu kànwán le.
I've finished reading all the books you lent me.

❸ 這個月的薪水，我都用完了。
Zhè ge yuè de xīnshuǐ, wǒ dōu yòngwán le.
I have already spent this month's salary.

❹ 一千公尺我跑得完。
Yìqiān gōngchǐ wǒ pǎodewán.
I can run 1000 meters.

Structures

Negation :

❶ 別買水果了，家裡的還沒吃完呢！
Bié mǎi shuǐguǒ le, jiālǐ de hái méi chīwán ne!
Don't buy fruit. We haven't finished the fruit at home yet.

❷ 我還沒說完，可以再給我一點時間嗎？
Wǒ hái méi shuōwán, kěyǐ zài gěi wǒ yìdiǎn shíjiān ma?
I haven't finished what I want to say. Can you give me a little more time?

❸ 他工作沒做完，就去花蓮旅行了，所以老闆很不高興。
Tā gōngzuò méi zuòwán, jiù qù Huālián lǚxíng le, suǒyǐ lǎobǎn hěn bù gāoxìng.
He took a trip to Hualien before finishing his work, so his boss is very unhappy.

Questions :

❶ 你是不是考完試了？
Nǐ shìbúshì kǎowán shì le?
Are you finished taking your exams?

❷ 老師給的功課，你寫完了沒有？
Lǎoshī gěi de gōngkè, nǐ xiěwánle méi yǒu?
Have you finished the homework that the teacher gave you?

❸ 那些電影，你看完了沒有？
Nàxiē diànyǐng, nǐ kànwánle méi yǒu?
Did you finish watching those movies?

Usage

完 is a phase marker, to do with aspects, which is attached to an action verb. When combining with separable verbs, it is inserted into the verb.

279

❶ 我考完試，想去看電影。（*我考試完，想去看電影。）
Wǒ kǎowán shì, xiǎng qù kàn diànyǐng. (*Wǒ kǎoshì wán, xiǎng qù kàn diànyǐng.)
When I finish taking the exam, I'd like to go see a movie.

❷ 你們吃完飯，可以去夜市逛逛。
Nǐmen chīwán fàn, kěyǐ qù yèshì guàngguàng.
When you finish eating, you can go walk around the night market.

❸ 我們游完泳，就回家了。
Wǒmen yóuwán yǒng, jiù huíjiā le.
When we finished swimming, we went home.

萬一, wànyī, (Adv), supposing, in the event of something negative

Function This adverb literally means a 'one in 10 thousand' likelihood. It refers to something unlikely but possible nonetheless.

❶ 他請我幫他買一本詞典，萬一沒買到，那怎麼辦呢？
Tā qǐng wǒ bāng tā mǎi yì běn cídiǎn, wànyī méi mǎidào, nà zěnme bàn ne?
He's asked me to buy a dictionary for him. What should I do if I can't get my hands on one?

❷ 萬一別人知道是我們弄錯的，那就糟了。可能不會再信任我們了。
Wànyī biérén zhīdào shì wǒmen nòng cuò de, nà jiù zāo le. Kěnéng bú huì zài xìnrèn wǒmen le.
If other people found out it was our mistake, then we're finished. They'll never trust us again.

❸ 你別太早去。萬一她還沒準備好，就得在外面等了。
Nǐ bié tài zǎo qù. Wànyī tā hái méi zhǔnbèihǎo, jiù děi zài wàimiàn děng le.
Don't go too early. If she's not ready you'll have to wait outside.

❹ 多練習幾次吧。萬一我們表演得很糟，就太丟臉了。
Duō liànxí jǐ cì ba. Wànyī wǒmen biǎoyǎn de hěn zāo, jiù tài diūliǎn le.
Let's go over it a few more times. It would be really mortifying if our performance turned out atrocious.

❺ 帶本漫畫去吧。萬一得等很久，就可以看漫畫殺時間。
Dài běn mànhuà qù ba. Wànyī děi děng hěn jiǔ, jiù kěyǐ kàn mànhuà shā shíjiān.
Bring a comic book with you to kill some time in the event that we have to wait a while.

Usage 萬一 denotes the supposition of an undesirable instance, and can also be used with other adverbs or conjunctions. E.g.,

❶ 就算萬一發生什麼事，也不要緊張。
Jiùsuàn wànyī fāshēng shénme shì, yě bú yào jǐnzhāng.
Even if, on the off chance, something happens, don't be nervous.

❷ 要是萬一錢不夠的話，你可以跟朋友先借。
Yàoshi wànyī qián bú gòu de huà, nǐ kěyǐ gēn péngyǒu xiān jiè.
In the event that there isn't enough money, you can borrow some from a friend first.

往往, wǎngwǎng, (Adv), usually, tend to

Function

The adverb 往往 refers to the common and routine occurrence of something, relating to the subject.

❶ 我緊張的時候，往往會說不出話來。
Wǒ jǐnzhāng de shíhòu, wǎngwǎng huì shuōbùchū huà lái.
Whenever I get nervous, I tend to have trouble speaking.

❷ 跟能力比自己好的人一起工作往往會有壓力。
Gēn nénglì bǐ zìjǐ hǎo de rén yìqǐ gōngzuò wǎngwǎng huì yǒu yālì.
It's usually stressful working with people who are more capable than you.

❸ 對別人說出「對不起」往往是最難的。
Duì biérén shuōchū 'duìbùqǐ' wǎngwǎng shì zuì nán de.
Saying sorry tends to be the hardest part.

❹ 每年的新年，我父母往往會帶我們回老家跟平常不常見面的親戚拜年。
Měi nián de xīnnián, wǒ fùmǔ wǎngwǎng huì dài wǒmen huí lǎojiā gēn píngcháng bù cháng jiànmiàn de qīnqī bàinián.
Whenever the New Year comes around, my parents usually take us back to our hometown to celebrate with relatives.

❺ 有一句話說，快樂的時候如果不小心一點，往往就會有倒楣的事發生。
Yǒu yí jù huà shuō, kuàilè de shíhòu rúguǒ bù xiǎoxīn yìdiǎn, wǎngwǎng jiù huì yǒu dǎoméi de shì fāshēng.
As the saying goes, if you're not careful, extreme joy can beget sorrow.

Usage

往往 vs. 常常

(1) 往往 and 常常 are often used interchangeably, e.g.,

我跟朋友聊天，往往/常常聊到很晚。
Wǒ gēn péngyǒu liáotiān, wǎngwǎng/chángcháng liáo dào hěn wǎn.
When I chat with friends, more often than not/often, we chat until late.

(2) 常常 denotes high frequency, and can be used referring to past, present, or future instances, whereas 往往 cannot be used in reference to future instances, e.g.,

我到了美國以後會常常(*往往)給你打電話。

Wǒ dàole Měiguó yǐhòu huì chángcháng (*wǎngwǎng) gěi nǐ dǎ diànhuà.

After I arrive in the United States, I will frequently (more often than not) call you.

(3) 常常 refers to high frequency, while 往往 to a habitual routine.

(4) 往往 is contingent upon context, a condition must be established before it can be used, e.g.,

❶ 小玲常常去看恐怖片。

Xiǎolíng chángcháng qù kàn kǒngbùpiàn.

Xiaoling often goes to see horror movies.

❷ *小玲往往去看恐怖片。

*Xiǎolíng wǎngwǎng qù kàn kǒngbùpiàn.

❸ 小玲不開心的時候，往往去看恐怖片。

Xiǎolíng bù kāixīn de shíhòu, wǎngwǎng qù kàn kǒngbùpiàn.

When she's upset, more often than not, Xiaoling goes to see a horror movie.

(5) Negation can be placed either in front of or behind 常常, i.e., one can say either 不常常 (more commonly 不是常常…) or 常常不; however, 往往 cannot be negated, i.e., *不往往 *bù wǎngwǎng.

(6) Also c.f., 一向, 向來.

為, wèi, (Prep), Beneficiary Marker, beneficiary of an action

Function

The literary preposition 為 introduces a beneficiary noun into the sentence, a noun which benefits from the context of the following verb phrase. The term 'beneficiary' can have many meanings.

(1) Recipient of the action. In this usage, the object of 為 seems to be the real object of the verb, e.g., (1) 為人民服務 wèi rénmín fúwù 'serve on behalf of the people' (2) 為大家加油 wèi dàjiā jiāyóu 'root for everybody' (3) 為農夫帶來許多好處 wèi nóngfū dàilái xǔduō hǎochù 'bring many advantages to farmers'.

(2) On behalf of. In this usage, the verbs are mostly state verbs, e.g., (1) 為孩子擔心 wèi háizi dānxīn 'worry for/about the children' (2) 為家人難過 wèi jiārén nánguò 'feel bad for my family' (3) 為朋友高興 wèi péngyǒu gāoxìng 'happy for my friend'.

(3) For the sake of. In this usage, something has been done for the benefit of someone, e.g., (1) 為他們買健康保險 wèi tāmen mǎi jiànkāng bǎoxiǎn 'buy health insurance for their sake' (2) 為他翻譯 wèi tā fānyì 'translate for his sake' (3) 為誰辛苦 wèi shéi xīnkǔ 'work hard for whose sake'.

為了, wèile, (Prep), in order to

Function

The preposition 為了 refers to 'in order to, for the purpose of'.

① 為了保護環境，大家都應該做垃圾分類。
Wèile bǎohù huánjìng, dàjiā dōu yīnggāi zuò lèsè fēnlèi.
To protect the environment, everyone should separate their garbage.

② 為了去吃喜酒，美美買了一件新衣服。
Wèile qù chī xǐjiǔ, Měiměi mǎile yí jiàn xīn yīfú.
Gao Meimei bought a new dress for the wedding reception.

③ 為了早一點回到家，還是坐捷運吧！
Wèile zǎo yìdiǎn huí dào jiā, háishì zuò jiéyùn ba!
Let's take the MRT, so that we get home a little earlier.

Structures

The object of 為了 can be either a noun phrase or a verb phrase.

① 他為了父母，買了飛機票回去看他們。
Tā wèile fùmǔ, mǎile fēijī piào huíqù kàn tāmen.
He bought air tickets to go see his parents.

② 小明為了搬到便宜的套房去，花了很多時間找房子。
Xiǎomíng wèile bān dào piányí de tàofáng qù, huāle hěn duō shíjiān zhǎo fángzi.
Xiaoming spent a lot of time looking at apartments in order to move into a cheap studio.

Negation :

別 or 不是 negation can be used.

① 別只為了錢去打工。
Bié zhǐ wèile qián qù dǎgōng.
Don't work just for the money.

② 他不是為了錢回收汽水罐，是為了保護環境。
Tā búshì wèile qián huíshōu qìshuǐguàn, shì wèile bǎohù huánjìng.
He doesn't recycle soda cans for the money, but to protect the environment.

③ 你們別為了去旅行就不工作了。
Nǐmen bié wèile qù lǚxíng jiù bù gōngzuò le.
Don't put off work just so you can travel.

Questions :

① 你是不是為了跟同學討論功課，所以晚上沒回家吃飯？
Nǐ shìbúshì wèile gēn tóngxué tǎolùn gōngkè, suǒyǐ wǎnshàng méi huíjiā chīfàn?
Did you not come home for dinner because you were discussing homework with your classmates?

② 他為了什麼到台灣來？
Tā wèile shénme dào Táiwān lái?
For what purpose did he come to Taiwan?

❸ 你是不是為了幫女朋友照相，所以買了新的照相機？
Nǐ shìbúshì wèile bāng nǚpéngyǒu zhàoxiàng, suǒyǐ mǎile xīn de zhàoxiàngjī?
Did you buy a new camera so you could take pictures of your girlfriend?

Usage

為了 is one lexical item, not 為＋了. 為了 can be variously translated into English depending on contexts. Extra caution is recommended.

無論 A 都 B, (wúlùn (Conj) A dōu (Adv) B), regardless of what...

Function

This pattern refers to all-inclusive options, with no exceptions possible, such as no matter what, no matter who, no matter whether, no matter where...etc.

❶ 最近有食品安全的問題。無論吃什麼都要小心。
Zuìjìn yǒu shípǐn ānquán de wèntí. Wúlùn chī shénme dōu yào xiǎoxīn.
There have been food safety issues lately. No matter what you eat, make sure you take precautions.

❷ 工作了一天。無論是否疲倦都需要休息。
Gōngzuò le yì tiān. Wúlùn shìfǒu píjuàn dōu xūyào xiūxí.
After working for a whole day, you need to take a rest. It doesn't matter if you are tired or not.

❸ 無論學歷高還是學歷低，有實力、有資金的人都可以創業。
Wúlùn xuélì gāo háishì xuélì dī, yǒu shílì, yǒu zījīn de rén dōu kěyǐ chuàngyè.
No matter what your educational background, if you are capable and have the capital, you can start your own business.

❹ 風水師說：「無論是買房子還是租房子，都要注意風水。」
Fēngshuǐshī shuō: 'Wúlùn shì mǎi fángzi háishì zū fángzi, dōu yào zhùyì fēngshuǐ.'
The fengshui master said, 'It doesn't matter if you buy or rent. Make sure the house has good fengshui.'

❺ 在台灣無論什麼地方都可以買到鳳梨酥。
Zài Táiwān wúlùn shénme dìfāng dōu kěyǐ mǎidào fènglísū.
You can buy pineapple biscuits, no matter where you are in Taiwan.

Usage

(1) 無論 can be followed by a question word (QW), A-not-A, conjunction of antonymic words, or the addition of 多, as illustrated above. Regardless of structures, a sentence of this type has the meaning 'In spite of various circumstances, the following fact remains unaffected'.

❶ 無論 followed by a QW (who, what, when, where).

a. 無論什麼時候，他都很忙碌。
Wúlùn shénme shíhòu, tā dōu hěn mánglù.
No matter when it is, he's always busy.

b. 無論哪裡都有便利商店。

Wúlùn nǎlǐ dōu yǒu biànlì shāngdiàn.

No matter where you go, there are convenience stores everywhere.

❷ 無論 followed by A-not-A.

a. 無論能不能當選，李先生都要出來競選。

Wúlùn néng bù néng dāngxuǎn, Lǐ xiānshēng dōu yào chūlái jìngxuǎn.

Whether or not he can win, Mr. Li is going to run for office.

b. 無論學歷高不高，都應該自食其力。

Wúlùn xuélì gāo bù gāo, dōu yīnggāi zìshí qílì.

No matter how much education you have had, you should always rely on yourself.

❸ 無論 followed by an opposite pair.

a. 無論早晚，你總是得自食其力。

Wúlùn zǎo wǎn, nǐ zǒngshì děi zìshí qílì.

Sooner or later, you're going to have to stand on your own two feet.

b. 無論成績好壞，都可以升學。

Wúlùn chéngjī hǎo huài, dōu kěyǐ shēngxué.

Whether your grades are good or bad, you can still go further in your studies.

❹ 無論 followed by the adverb 多.

a. 無論他家多富裕，他都不浪費。

Wúlùn tā jiā duó fùyù, tā dōu bú làngfèi.

Regardless of how wealthy his family is, he doesn't waste.

b. 無論生活多困苦，吳先生還是很快樂。

Wúlùn shēnghuó duó kùnkǔ, Wú xiānshēng háishì hěn kuàilè.

No matter how hard life gets, Mr. Wu is always happy.

(2) 無論 and 不管 are synonymous. 不管 is more colloquial, while 無論 is more formal, and as a result 不管 is not often followed by formal or literary constructs such as 如何 or 是否.

❶ 無論別人如何批評他，他都無所謂。

Wúlùn biérén rúhé pīpíng tā, tā dōu wúsuǒwèi.

Regardless of how others criticize him, he doesn't care bit.

❷ 無論學生是否願意，都得參加考試。

Wúlùn xuéshēng shìfǒu yuànyì, dōu děi cānjiā kǎoshì.

Whether they want to or not, students all have to take the exam.

❸ 無論如何，你都不能放棄。

Wúlùn rúhé, nǐ dōu bù néng fàngqì.

No matter what, you should not give up.

無所謂, wúsuǒwèi, (Vs), does not matter

Function 無所謂, of classical Chinese, is now lexicalized into a state verb, meaning 'does not matter', 'of no consequence' or 'I do not much care', as far as the speaker or the subject is concerned.

❶ 候選人是什麼背景我無所謂，只要他有能力而且真的關心人民就好了。

Hòuxuǎn rén shì shénme bèijǐng wǒ wúsuǒwèi, zhǐyào tā yǒu nénglì érqiě zhēn de guānxīn rénmín jiù hǎo le.

I don't care what background each candidate has. As long as they are capable and genuinely care about people's well-being, that will be good enough.

❷ 總統的外表好不好看無所謂。能實現承諾最重要。

Zǒngtǒng de wàibiǎo hǎo bù hǎokàn wúsuǒwèi. Néng shíxiàn chéngnuò zuì zhòngyào.

It doesn't matter whether or not the president looks good. It matters that he can make good on his promises.

❸ 這件事他要怎麼做我無所謂，只要他盡到自己的責任就好了。

Zhè jiàn shì tā yào zěnme zuò wǒ wúsuǒwèi, zhǐyào tā jìndào zìjǐ de zérèn jiù hǎo le.

It doesn't matter how he gets it done, as long as he fulfills his responsibility to the best of his abilities.

❹ 她認為畢業以後能找到自己喜歡的工作就好了。薪資多少無所謂。

Tā rènwéi bìyè yǐhòu néng zhǎodào zìjǐ xǐhuān de gōngzuò jiù hǎo le. Xīnzī duōshǎo wúsuǒwèi.

She thinks that being able to find a fulfilling job after graduation is good enough, regardless of pay.

Usage As the sentence of this structure means it does not matter one way or another, the portion before or after (less often) contains a question, e.g., 什麼(❶), 好不好(❷), 怎麼(❸) and 多少(❹).

下, xià, (Ptc), as Verb Complement, enough space to accommodate

Function The construction, V＋得/不＋下, indicates whether there's enough room to accommodate something.

❶ 這個車子坐得下九個人。

Zhè ge chēzi zuòdexià jiǔ ge rén.

This car has enough room for nine people.

❷ 小李一個人喝得下大杯咖啡。

Xiǎo Lǐ yí ge rén hēdexià dà bēi kāfēi.

Xiao Li can drink a large cup of coffee all by himself.

❸ 三十個餃子，美美都吃得下。
Sānshí ge jiǎozi, Měiměi dōu chīdexià.
Meimei can eat 30 dumplings.

Negation :

❶ 背包太小了，裝不下這個電腦。
Bēibāo tài xiǎo le, zhuāngbúxià zhè ge diànnǎo.
The backpack is too small to fit this computer into.

❷ 這個資源回收桶放不下這麼多塑膠瓶子。
Zhè ge zīyuán huíshōu tǒng fàngbúxià zhème duō sùjiāo píngzi.
This recycling bin can't hold so many plastic bottles.

❸ 這個教室坐不下那麼多學生。
Zhè ge jiàoshì zuòbúxià nàme duō xuéshēng.
This classroom cannot seat that many students.

Questions : The potential form or to a lesser degree A-not-A form can be used.

❶ 這個房間放得下放不下一張大床？
（=這個房間放不放得下一張大床？）
Zhè ge fángjiān fàngdexià fàngbúxià yì zhāng dà chuáng?
(=Zhè ge fángjiān fàng bú fàngdexià yì zhāng dà chuáng?)
Is this room big enough to accommodate a big bed?

❷ 這間教室坐得下坐不下五十個學生？
Zhè jiān jiàoshì zuòdexià zuòbúxià wǔshí ge xuéshēng?
Can this classroom hold 50 students?

❸ 你的隨身碟存不存得下這些照片？
Nǐ de suíshēndié cún bù cúndexià zhèxiē zhàopiàn?
Can your flash drive hold these pictures?

The verb complements 下 and 了 liǎo can combine with the same verbs, and the differences in meaning are rather subtle.

❶ 我的車坐不下五個人。(room enough)
Wǒ de chē zuòbúxià wǔ ge rén.

❷ 我的車坐不了五個人。(can accommodate)
Wǒ de chē zuòbùliǎo wǔ ge rén.

The former refers to 'not enough space', while the latter 'inability to seat, incapable of seating'.

下來, xiàlái, a summary of the various meanings of the verb complement 下來

When 下來 serves as a complement to a verb, forming $V_1V_2V_3$, the meaning can be locational (downward, upward), temporal (to continue, to keep on), or a state (remain, still).

(1) Locational

❶ 王太太聽見王先生在樓下叫她，就從樓上走下來了。
Wáng tàitai tīngjiàn Wáng xiānshēng zài lóuxià jiào tā, jiù cóng lóushàng zǒu xiàlái le.
Mrs. Wang heard Mr. Wang call her from downstairs, so she walked down.

❷ 那本書在櫃子上，請你把那本書從櫃子上拿下來。
Nà běn shū zài guìzi shàng, qǐng nǐ bǎ nà běn shū cóng guìzi shàng ná xiàlái.
That book is up on the shelf. Please take it down.

(2) Temporal

❶ 他從十年前來這家公司，一直做下來，到現在已經當主任了。
Tā cóng shí nián qián lái zhè jiā gōngsī, yìzhí zuòxiàlái, dào xiànzài yǐjīng dāng zhǔrèn le.
He started at this company ten years ago and has stayed on ever since. He's a director now.

❷ 這些都是古代的人傳下來的習慣。
Zhèxiē dōu shì gǔdài de rén chuánxiàlái de xíguàn.
All these habits have been passed down from generation to generation.

(3) State

❶ 朋友想了很久，最後決定留下來。
Péngyǒu xiǎngle hěn jiǔ, zuìhòu juédìng liúxiàlái.
After much deliberation, my friend decided to stay.

❷ 畫家把鄉下美麗的風景畫下來。
Huàjiā bǎ xiāngxià měilì de fēngjǐng huàxiàlái.
The artist captured the idyllic countryside scenery in a painting.

> **Usage**

Typical $V_1V_2V_3$ can occur in both forms, as seen below.

(1) Actual form: V 下來，沒 V 下來

❶ 我把老闆說的話都寫下來了。
Wǒ bǎ lǎobǎn shuō de huà dōu xiěxiàlái le.
I wrote down everything the boss said.

❷ 你把髒衣服脫下來洗一洗。
Nǐ bǎ zāng yīfú tuōxiàlái xǐ yì xǐ.
Take your dirty clothes off and wash them.

❸ 雖然他看見山上有凶猛的動物，可是他還在山上，沒跑下來。
Suīrán tā kànjiàn shān shàng yǒu xiōngměng de dòngwù, kěshì tā hái zài shān shàng, méi pǎo xiàlái.
Although he saw ferocious animals on the mountain, he's still up on the mountain. He didn't come running down.

(2) Potential form: V 得下來，V 不下來

❶ 月亮怎麼摘得下來？
Yuèliàng zěnme zhāidexiàlái?
How can the moon be plucked?

❷ 車開得太快，停不下來。
Chē kāi de tài kuài, tíngbúxiàlái.
The car was going to fast. It couldn't be stopped.

❸ 那個衣櫥太大，我一個人搬不下來。
Nà ge yīchú tài dà, wǒ yí ge rén bānbúxiàlái.
The closet is too big. I can't move it down alone.

下去, xiàqù, as Verb Complement, to keep on doing something

Function 下去 is a locative V₁V₂. It is here used as a temporal complement to an action verb, with the meaning 'to continue to, to keep on'.

❶ 你說得很好。請你再說下去。
Nǐ shuō de hěn hǎo. Qǐng nǐ zài shuōxiàqù.
You have spoken well so far, please continue.

❷ 我們在夜市逛了很久了，你還要逛下去嗎？
Wǒmen zài yèshì guàngle hěn jiǔ le, nǐ hái yào guàngxiàqù ma?
We've walked the night market for a long time already. Do you want to continue?

❸ 雖然學費不便宜，但是我還想念下去。
Suīrán xuéfèi bù piányí, dànshì wǒ hái xiǎng niànxiàqù.
The tuition isn't cheap, but I still want to continue studying.

❹ 他還沒說完，請大家聽下去。
Tā hái méi shuōwán, qǐng dàjiā tīngxiàqù.
He hasn't finished yet, please let him speak.

❺ 這份工作不錯，雖然薪水少，可是我還要做下去。
Zhè fèn gōngzuò búcuò, suīrán xīnshuǐ shǎo, kěshì wǒ hái yào zuòxiàqù.
This job isn't bad. Although the pay is low, I want to continue doing it.

❻ 已經三個小時了，你還要等下去嗎？我想他不會來了。
Yǐjīng sān ge xiǎoshí le, nǐ hái yào děngxiàqù ma? Wǒ xiǎng tā bú huì lái le.
It's been three hours. Do you still want to keep on waiting? I don't think he'll come.

Structures When 下去 combines with transitive verbs, their objects are either moved to the front of the sentence or are omitted if the contexts are clear enough.

❶ 這個工作我想一直做下去。
Zhè ge gōngzuò wǒ xiǎng yìzhí zuòxiàqù.
I want to keep doing this job.

*我想一直做下去這個工作了。
*Wǒ xiǎng yìzhí zuòxiàqù zhè ge gōngzuò le.

❷ 念中文雖然很累，我還要念下去。
Niàn Zhōngwén suīrán hěn lèi, wǒ hái yào niànxiàqù.
Although I'm exhausted, I'm still going to keep on studying Chinese.

*雖然很累，我還要念下去中文。
*Suīrán hěn lèi, wǒ hái yào niànxiàqù Zhōngwén.

先 A 再 B, (xiān (Adv) A zài (Adv) B), first A, and then B

Function ▸ This pattern presents the temporal sequence of two consecutive instances.

❶ 弟弟打算先去旅行再找工作。
Dìdi dǎsuàn xiān qù lǚxíng zài zhǎo gōngzuò.
My brother plans to go traveling first and then look for a job.

❷ 我想先吃晚飯再給媽媽打電話。
Wǒ xiǎng xiān chī wǎnfàn zài gěi māma dǎ diànhuà.
I want to eat dinner first and then call my mom.

❸ 他計畫在臺灣先學語言再念大學。
Tā jìhuà zài Táiwān xiān xué yǔyán zài niàn dàxué.
He plans to study language in Taiwan first and then go to college.

Usage ▸ This pattern indicates the order of two instances either in the past or future.

❶ 我昨天晚上先寫功課，再看電視。
Wǒ zuótiān wǎnshàng xiān xiě gōngkè, zài kàn diànshì.
Last night, I did my homework first and then watched TV.

❷ 我明天先去圖書館看書，再去超市買東西。
Wǒ míngtiān xiān qù túshūguǎn kànshū, zài qù chāoshì mǎi dōngxi.
Tomorrow, I'll study in the library first and then go shopping at the supermarket.

向, xiàng, (Prep), to, toward

Function ▸ Directional preposition 向 indicates the target (either person or object) of an action. Often 向 can be replaced by 跟.

❶ 我想向那家公司爭取實習的機會。
Wǒ xiǎng xiàng nà jiā gōngsī zhēngqǔ shíxí de jīhuì.
I intend to vie for an internship placement with that company.

❷ 她居然敢向比她厲害的人挑戰。
Tā jūrán gǎn xiàng bǐ tā lìhài de rén tiǎozhàn.
She had the guts to challenge her superior.

❸ 警察向民眾說明塞車的原因。

Jǐngchá xiàng mínzhòng shuōmíng sāichē de yuányīn.

Police explained the reasons behind the congested traffic to the public.

❹ 新郎新娘向參加婚禮的人敬酒。

Xīnláng xīnniáng xiàng cānjiā hūnlǐ de rén jìngjiǔ.

The bride and groom toasted to the attendees.

Usage

(1) 向 can be followed by a directional word, such as 前 qián, 後 hòu, 左 zuǒ, 右 yòu, 東 dōng, 南 nán, 上 shàng, 下 xià, etc. to express the direction of an action, but cannot be substituted by 跟 in such a structure.

❶ 站在那棟房子前，向前看，會看到一條河；向後看會看到一座山。

Zhàn zài nà dòng fángzi qián, xiàng qián kàn, huì kàndào yì tiáo hé; xiàng hòu kàn huì kàndào yí zuò shān.

Standing in front of the house, looking forward, you will see a river. Looking behind you, you will see a mountain.

❷ 司機先生，請在下一個路口向右轉。

Sījī xiānshēng, qǐng zài xià yí ge lùkǒu xiàng yòu zhuǎn.

Mister (driver), please turn right at the next intersection.

(2) When 向 follows a verb, said verb is usually monosyllabic. This pattern is used mostly in formal language.

❶ 台灣大部分的河都流向大海。

Táiwān dà bùfèn de hé dōu liúxiàng dà hǎi.

Most rivers in Taiwan flow toward the ocean.

❷ 派對上來了一個美女，大家的目光都轉向她。

Pàiduì shàng láile yí ge měinǚ, dàjiā de mùguāng dōu zhuǎnxiàng tā.

A beautiful woman came to the party. All eyes turned toward her.

A 像 B 一樣, (A xiàng B yíyàng), A is just like B

Function

This pattern is used when we wish to point to the resemblances between two things or between two situations, i.e., A is just like B (in that...); A is true in the way that B is true. A/B may be NP, VP or S.

(1) A/B is an NP.

❶ 台灣的水果像越南的水果一樣好吃。

Táiwān de shuǐguǒ xiàng Yuènán de shuǐguǒ yíyàng hǎochī.

Taiwanese fruit tastes just as good as Vietnamese fruit.

❷ 花蓮的海邊像我的國家的海邊一樣漂亮。

Huālián de hǎibiān xiàng wǒ de guójiā de hǎibiān yíyàng piàoliàng.

The beach at Hualien is just as beautiful as the beach in my country.

❸ 現在的手機像電腦一樣方便，都可以上網。

Xiànzài de shǒujī xiàng diànnǎo yíyàng fāngbiàn, dōu kěyǐ shàngwǎng.

Now, cell phones are just as convenient as computers in that they can both go on-line.

(2) A/B is a VP.

❶ 他很有錢。買房子就像買車子一樣容易。

Tā hěn yǒu qián. Mǎi fángzi jiù xiàng mǎi chēzi yíyàng róngyì.

He's rich. He can buy a house as easily as he can buy a car.

❷ 學語言像學做菜一樣，多練習就會學得好。

Xué yǔyán xiàng xué zuò cài yíyàng, duō liànxí jiù huì xué de hǎo.

Learning a language is like learning how to cook: practice a lot and you'll learn it well.

❸ 他的體力很好。跑三千公尺就像走路一樣輕鬆。

Tā de tǐlì hěn hǎo. Pǎo sānqiān gōngchǐ jiù xiàng zǒulù yíyàng qīngsōng.

He's in good shape. Running 3,000 meters is as easy as walking for him.

(3) A/B is a clause.

❶ 泰國有很多廟，就像法國有很多教堂一樣。

Tàiguó yǒu hěn duō miào, jiù xiàng Fǎguó yǒu hěn duō jiàotáng yíyàng.

Thailand has many temples, just like France has many cathedrals.

❷ 哥哥喜歡喝咖啡，就像爸爸喜歡喝烏龍茶一樣。

Gēge xǐhuān hē kāfēi, jiù xiàng bàba xǐhuān hē Wūlóng chá yíyàng.

My big brother likes to drink coffee in much the same way that my dad likes to drink Oolong tea.

❸ 小李收到女朋友送的手機，就像他拿到獎學金一樣高興。

Xiǎo Lǐ shōudào nǚpéngyǒu sòng de shǒujī, jiù xiàng tā nádào jiǎngxuéjīn yíyàng gāoxìng.

Xiao Li was as happy when he received the cellphone from his girlfriend as he was when he received the scholarship.

> **Structures**

*N**egation* :

❶ 妹妹不像姐姐一樣，那麼常買新衣服。

Mèimei bú xiàng jiějie yíyàng, nàme cháng mǎi xīn yīfú.

The younger sister is not like her older sister, who often buys new clothes.

❷ 小明今年過生日的氣氛不像去年一樣熱鬧。

Xiǎomíng jīnnián guò shēngrì de qìfēn bú xiàng qùnián yíyàng rènào.

The atmosphere for Xiaoming's birthday party this year is not as fun and lively as last year's.

❸ 那個餐廳做的菜不像以前一樣那麼有特色。

Nà ge cāntīng zuò de cài bú xiàng yǐqián yíyàng nàme yǒu tèsè.

The food at that restaurant are not as unique as it once was.

Questions:

❶ 美美的中文是不是説得像台灣人一樣好？

Měiměi de Zhōngwén shìbúshì shuō de xiàng Táiwān rén yíyàng hǎo?

Does Meimei speak Chinese as well as Taiwanese people do?

❷ 你覺得教英文是不是像教西班牙文一樣容易？

Nǐ juéde jiāo Yīngwén shìbúshì xiàng jiāo Xībānyáwén yíyàng róngyì?

Do you think teaching English is as easy as teaching Spanish?

❸ 你們家準備結婚是不是像我們家準備結婚一樣麻煩？

Nǐmen jiā zhǔnbèi jiéhūn shìbúshì xiàng wǒmen jiā zhǔnbèi jiéhūn yíyàng máfán?

Are wedding preparations as much of a hassle in your family as they are in ours?

Usage

The A-not-A pattern can work with 'A 跟 B 一樣', but it does not work with 'A 像 B 一樣'. 跟 relates to comparison, while 像 relates to resemblance.

❶ 小籠包跟包子一樣不一樣？

Xiǎolóngbāo gēn bāozi yíyàng bù yíyàng?

Are steamed dumplings the same as steamed buns?

❷ *小籠包像包子一樣不一樣？

*Xiǎolóngbāo xiàng bāozi yíyàng bù yíyàng?

像…的＋Noun, (xiàng...de＋Noun), such (nouns) as

Function

This pattern adds special properties to either the subject or object of a sentence.

❶ 像小籠包、炸雞排、擔仔麵這樣的小吃，他都喜歡。

Xiàng xiǎolóngbāo, zhájīpái, dànzǎimiàn zhèyàng de xiǎochī, tā dōu xǐhuān.

He likes all kinds of light snacks, like steamed dumplings, fried chicken fillet, and danzai noodles.

❷ 像你這樣喜歡古蹟的人，一定要去台南看看。

Xiàng nǐ zhèyàng xǐhuān gǔjī de rén, yídìng yào qù Táinán kànkàn.

A person like you who likes historical sites really must go check out Tainan.

❸ 像她那樣有語言天分的人，一定能很快地學好中文。

Xiàng tā nàyàng yǒu yǔyán tiānfèn de rén, yídìng néng hěn kuài de xuéhǎo Zhōngwén.

A person talented in languages like her will most certainly learn Chinese quickly.

❹ 像他這樣友善對待土地的小農越來越多。

Xiàng tā zhèyàng yǒushàn duìdài tǔdì de xiǎonóng yuèláiyuè duō.

Small farmers like him who work the land in an environmentally conscious way are increasing in number.

❺ 像她這樣在農村長大的人都喜歡接近自然。

Xiàng tā zhèyàng zài nóngcūn zhǎngdà de rén dōu xǐhuān jiējìn zìrán.

People who, like her, grew up in a farming village all like to be close to nature.

Usage

This pattern is not related to 像⋯一樣, which compares two nouns, e.g., 他在鄉下買了一片田。每天吃的都是自己種的新鮮蔬菜。我羨慕他，希望能像他一樣。 Tā zài xiāngxià mǎile yí piàn tián. Měi tiān chī de dōu shì zìjǐ zhòng de xīnxiān shūcài. Wǒ xiànmù tā, xīwàng néng xiàng tā yíyàng. 'He bought a piece of farmland in the country and now his meals consist of the fresh vegetables he planted himself. I admire him. I wish I could do that.'

幸虧, xìngkuī, (Adv), fortunately

Function

The adverb 幸虧 introduces a situation that invalidates the possible negative effect of the previous clause. 要不然 yàobùrán or 才 cái often follows.

❶ 這幾天天天下雨。幸虧我買了除濕機，要不然衣服都發霉了。

Zhè jǐ tiān tiāntiān xiàyǔ. Xìngkuī wǒ mǎile chúshījī, yàobùrán yīfú dōu fāméi le.

It has been raining every day over the last few days. Luckily, I bought a dehumidifier; otherwise, my clothes would all mildew.

❷ 我弄丟了報告。幸虧朋友撿到了，才不用再寫一次。

Wǒ nòngdiūle bàogào. Xìngkuī péngyǒu jiǎndào le, cái búyòng zài xiě yí cì.

I lost my report. Fortunately, a friend picked it up (found it), so I don't have to rewrite it.

❸ 他爸爸常說幸虧這幾年生意還可以，才有錢付他的學費。

Tā bàba cháng shuō xìngkuī zhè jǐ nián shēngyì hái kěyǐ, cái yǒu qián fù tā de xuéfèi.

His dad often says it's a good thing business has been OK in recent years, that's why he has the money to pay his tuition.

④ 幸虧我一到車站，公車就來了，才沒有遲到。

Xìngkuī wǒ yí dào chēzhàn, gōngchē jiù lái le, cái méi yǒu chídào.

Luckily, the bus arrived just as I got to the bus stop, so I wasn't late.

⑤ 幸虧他有實際的經驗，才能這麼快地找到工作。

Xìngkuī tā yǒu shíjì de jīngyàn, cái néng zhème kuài de zhǎodào gōngzuò.

Fortunately, he has real-life experience; that is why he found a job so quickly.

要是 A 就 B, (yàoshì A jiù B), Condition and Consequence

Function

In this pattern, 要是 presents the condition, while 就 in the second clause presents the consequence.

❶ 要是我有錢，我就買大房子。

Yàoshì wǒ yǒu qián, wǒ jiù mǎi dà fángzi.

If I were rich, I would buy a big house.

❷ 我要是不回國，我就跟你們一起去玩。

Wǒ yàoshì bù huíguó, wǒ jiù gēn nǐmen yìqǐ qù wán.

If I do not go back to my country, I will go out with you.

❸ 要是我有空，我就跟朋友一起去KTV唱歌。

Yàoshì wǒ yǒu kòng, wǒ jiù gēn péngyǒu yìqǐ qù KTV chànggē.

If I am free, I will go sing with friends at a KTV.

Structures

要是 is a conjunction, which can be placed before or after the subject of the first clause. In the second clause, 就 is an adverb and is placed at the very beginning of the predicate.

❶ 你要是星期日有空，你就跟我去旅行吧！

Nǐ yàoshì xīngqírì yǒu kòng, nǐ jiù gēn wǒ qù lǚxíng ba!

If you are free on Sunday, go with me on a trip.

❷ 要是下個月不忙，她就回國。

Yàoshì xià ge yuè bù máng, tā jiù huíguó.

If she is not busy next month, she will return to her country.

❸ 你要是沒空，我們就不要去逛夜市。

Nǐ yàoshì méi kòng, wǒmen jiù bú yào qù guàng yèshì.

If you are not free, we will not go to the night market.

以, yǐ, (Prep), classical Chinese, indicating instrument

Function

The preposition 以 takes an instrument as its object, similar to modern 用.

❶ 1990年，她以很好的成績畢業，進入一家電腦公司工作。

1990 nián, tā yǐ hěn hǎo de chéngjī bìyè, jìnrù yì jiā diànnǎo gōngsī gōngzuò.

In 1990 she graduated with top marks and started working for a computer company.

❷ 聽到家裡出事了，媽媽以很快的速度跑回去。

Tīngdào jiā lǐ chūshì le, māma yǐ hěn kuài de sùdù pǎo huíqù.

Upon hearing that something had happened at home, mom came back as quickly as she could.

❸ 古代人用自己的東西跟別人換自己需要的東西，叫做「以物易物」（易 'trade' (formal)）。

Gǔdài rén yòng zìjǐ de dōngxi gēn biérén huàn zìjǐ xūyào de dōngxi, jiàozuò 'yǐ wù yì wù'.

During ancient times people acquired the things they needed by trading with each other in a 'commodity for commodity' system.

❹ 我在夜市以很低的價錢買到這件好看的衣服。

Wǒ zài yèshì yǐ hěn dī de jiàqián mǎidào zhè jiàn hǎokàn de yīfú.

I bought this nice piece of clothing for a really low price at the night market.

❺ 如果以簡單容易懂的句子來說明，孩子們比較容易了解。

Rúguǒ yǐ jiǎndān róngyì dǒng de jùzi lái shuōmíng, háizimen bǐjiào róngyì liǎojiě.

If you use simple, easy to understand sentences, kids will have a better time comprehending.

> **Usage**

In modern Chinese, the character 以 can form locational words, such as 以內 (within), 以外 (in addition, out of), 以下 (below), 以上 (above).

以後, yǐhòu, (N), in the future, after (Also see 後來 hòulái)

> **Function**

The word 以後 is basically a noun but covers 2 different functions. When it is used alone, it is just like a time word, meaning some time in the future. When it is used together with 2 instances, it connects them sequentially, i.e., after A, B....

> **Structures**

❶ 我們以後都得上班。

Wǒmen yǐhòu dōu děi shàngbān.

We will all have to work in the future.

❷ 他們以後還要再到台南去。

Tāmen yǐhòu hái yào zài dào Táinán qù.

They want to visit Tainan again in the future.

❸ 回國以後，我要找個有機會說中文的工作。

Huíguó yǐhòu, wǒ yào zhǎo ge yǒu jīhuì shuō Zhōngwén de gōngzuò.

After going back to my country, I want to look for a job that offers opportunities to speak Chinese.

❹ 來臺灣以後，我每星期上五天的中文課。

Lái Táiwān yǐhòu, wǒ měi xīngqí shàng wǔ tiān de Zhōngwén kè.

After coming to Taiwan, I have been going to Chinese class five days a week.

⑤ 我下課以後，常在圖書館上網。

Wǒ xiàkè yǐhòu, cháng zài túshūguǎn shàngwǎng.

After class, I often use the internet in the library.

⑥ 2010年以後，他就不教書了。

Èrlíng yīlíng nián yǐhòu, tā jiù bù jiāoshū le.

He stopped teaching as of 2010.

以及, yǐjí, (Conj), as well as

Function

以及 is a literary conjunction, which connects nouns or sentences.

❶ 我表哥念高中的時候最喜歡的課有英文、歷史以及藝術。

Wǒ biǎogē niàn gāozhōng de shíhòu zuì xǐhuān de kè yǒu
Yīngwén, lìshǐ yǐjí yìshù.

My cousin's favorite courses in high school were English, history, and art.

❷ 台北、台中以及高雄都是人口兩百萬以上的大城市。

Táiběi, Táizhōng yǐjí Gāoxióng dōu shì rénkǒu liǎngbǎi wàn
yǐshàng de dà chéngshì.

Taipei, Taichung and Kaohsiung are all cities with a population of more than 2 million people.

❸ 這個城市的交通很亂，怎麼改善交通問題以及減少車禍的發生，是這個城市的人民最關心的事情。

Zhè ge chéngshì de jiāotōng hěn luàn, zěnme gǎishàn jiāotōng
wèntí yǐjí jiǎnshǎo chēhuò de fāshēng, shì zhè ge chéngshì de
rénmín zuì guānxīn de shìqíng.

The traffic in this city is chaotic. The people of this city are most concerned with how to improve the traffic situation and reduce the number of accidents.

❹ 這次颱風，台灣東部以及南部都會受到影響。

Zhè cì táifēng, Táiwān dōngbù yǐjí nánbù dōu huì shòudào
yǐngxiǎng.

The eastern and southern part of Taiwan will both be affected by this typhoon.

❺ 明天要去旅行，請你把外套、鞋子以及日用品放在背包裡。

Míngtiān yào qù lǚxíng, qǐng nǐ bǎ wàitào, xiézi yǐjí rìyòngpǐn fàng
zài bēibāo lǐ.

We're going on a trip tomorrow. Please put your coat, shoes, and daily necessities in your backpack.

Usage

Conjunctions in Chinese can be of three types: those which connect nouns, those which connect sentences, and those which can connect either. 以及 belongs to the last category.

Type 1: connects noun, e.g., 和, 跟

❶ 那家商店賣青菜、水果和一些日用品。
Nà jiā shāngdiàn mài qīngcài, shuǐguǒ hàn yìxiē rìyòngpǐn.
That shop sells vegetables, fruit, and some daily necessities.

❷ 他剛去超市買了牛肉、魚跟麵包。
Tā gāng qù chāoshì mǎile niúròu, yú gēn miànbāo.
He just went to the supermarket where he bought beef, fish, and bread.

Type 2: connects sentences, i.e., 不過, 但是

❶ 這裡白天的溫度很高,不過剛剛下過雨,我覺得涼快多了。
Zhèlǐ báitiān de wēndù hěn gāo, búguò gānggāng xiàguò yǔ, wǒ juéde liángkuai duō le.
The temperature here during the day is high, but it just rained, (so) I feel a lot cooler.

❷ 她想去國外旅行,但是想到一個人旅行有點麻煩,就下不了決心。
Tā xiǎng qù guówài lǚxíng, dànshì xiǎngdào yí ge rén lǚxíng yǒudiǎn máfán, jiù xiàbùliǎo juéxīn.
She wants to travel abroad, but when she thought about how traveling alone is a bit of a pain, she couldn't make up her mind.

Type 3: connects nouns & sentences

❶ 去國外念書,當地的生活費以及學費,是學生最關心的事。
Qù guówài niànshū, dāngdì de shēnghuófèi yǐjí xuéfèi, shì xuéshēng zuì guānxīn de shì.
When studying abroad, students are most concerned with the local cost of living and tuition fees.

❷ 你要不要跟王先生見面,以及他來了以後,要跟他說什麼,你最好想清楚。
Nǐ yào bú yào gēn Wáng xiānshēng jiànmiàn, yǐjí tā láile yǐhòu, yào gēn tā shuō shénme, nǐ zuìhǎo xiǎng qīngchǔ.
It would be in your best interest to think clearly about meeting Mr. Wang or not and what you are going to talk to him.

以內, yǐnèi, within

Function This is a formal expression that indicates 'within a temporal, spatial or quantity range'.

❶ 他讓我在一個禮拜以內把這份報告寫完。這怎麼可能?
Tā ràng wǒ zài yí ge lǐbài yǐnèi bǎ zhè fèn bàogào xiěwán. Zhè zěnme kěnéng?
He's having me write this report within a week. How is that even possible?

❷ 在台灣宅配很快，一般來說，下訂單以後，24小時以內就能收到商品。

Zài Táiwān zháipèi hěn kuài, yìbān láishuō, xià dìngdān yǐhòu, èrshísì xiǎoshí yǐnèi jiù néng shōudào shāngpǐn.

Home delivery in Taiwan is very fast. Generally, products are received within 24 hours of putting in the order.

❸ 外套的價格，只要是在兩千塊以內，我都能接受。

Wàitào de jiàgé, zhǐyào shi zài liǎngqiān kuài yǐnèi, wǒ dōu néng jiēshòu.

I can accept a price for the coat as long as it's within NT$2,000.

❹ 他找的房子不但要在捷運站附近，而且離公司坐捷運一定要在十站以內。

Tā zhǎo de fángzi búdàn yào zài jiéyùn zhàn fùjìn, érqiě lí gōngsī zuò jiéyùn yídìng yào zài shí zhàn yǐnèi.

He's looking for a house that's not only near an MRT station, it has to be within 10 stops of his company.

❺ 我的體力還不錯，三千公尺以內，我想我都跑得完。

Wǒ de tǐlì hái búcuò, sānqiān gōngchǐ yǐnèi, wǒ xiǎng wǒ dōu pǎodewán.

I'm in pretty good shape. I think I could run any distance within 3,000 meters.

Usage

以內 literally means 'X and less' and X can refer to quantity (❸ above), spatial (❹, ❺), and temporal (❶, ❷).

一 A 就 B, (yì A jiù B), as soon as

Function

The pattern '一 A 就 B' indicates a sequence of instances with B taking place right after A.

❶ 我一下課，就回來。

Wǒ yí xiàkè, jiù huílái.

I will return as soon as class is over.

❷ 他一回國，就找工作。

Tā yì huíguó, jiù zhǎo gōngzuò.

He looked for a job as soon as he returned to his country.

❸ 我妹妹一回去，就給媽媽打電話。

Wǒ mèimei yì huíqù, jiù gěi māma dǎ diànhuà.

My sister called my Mom right after she got home.

Usage

The two instances can be the affirmative or in the negative. Both 一 and 就 are adverbs, which come after the subject. Note that a repeated subject can be omitted as below.

❶ 我一下課，就去吃晚飯。

Wǒ yí xiàkè, jiù qù chī wǎnfàn.

As soon as I get out of class, I'll go eat dinner.

❷ 他打算等那裡一沒人，就去拍照。
Tā dǎsuàn děng nàlǐ yì méi rén, jiù qù pāizhào.
He plans to go take pictures as soon as there is nobody there.

❸ 老闆今天早上一到公司，就不開心。
Lǎobǎn jīntiān zǎoshàng yí dào gōngsī, jiù bù kāixīn.
The boss was upset as soon as he arrived at the office this morning.

Questions : The A-not-A form is not possible. Both 嗎 ma or 是不是 can be used to form questions.

❶ 他一下課，就去學校找你嗎？
Tā yí xiàkè, jiù qù xuéxiào zhǎo nǐ ma?
Did he go to school to see you right after he got out of class?

❷ 我們今天是不是比賽一結束，就一起去KTV唱歌？
Wǒmen jīntiān shìbúshì bǐsài yì jiéshù, jiù yìqǐ qù KTV chànggē?
Are we going to KTV today together right after the game is over ?

一般來說, yìbān láishuō, generally speaking

Function ▶ This expression introduces a general setting for statements to be made. It is typically placed at the beginning of the sentence.

❶ 一般來說，個性活潑、外語能力好的學生很適合念國際關係系。
Yìbān láishuō, gèxìng huópō, wàiyǔ nénglì hǎo de xuéshēng hěn shìhé niàn guójì guānxi xì.
Generally speaking, students with vibrant personalities and good foreign language skills are suited to studying international relations.

❷ 在台灣，一般來說，退換商品的時候都得要帶發票。
Zài Táiwān, yìbān láishuō, tuìhuàn shāngpǐn de shíhou dōu děi yào dài fāpiào.
In Taiwan, generally speaking, when you exchange products, you need to bring the receipt with you.

❸ 一般來說，有牌子的商品比較貴，但是品質也比較好。
Yìbān láishuō, yǒu páizi de shāngpǐn bǐjiào guì, dànshì pǐnzhí yě bǐjiào hǎo.
Generally speaking, brand name products are more expensive, but they are also higher quality.

❹ 一般來說，菜的味道不要太鹹就比較健康。
Yìbān láishuō, cài de wèidào bú yào tài xián jiù bǐjiào jiànkāng.
Generally speaking, dishes that are less salty are healthier.

❺ 跟南部比起來，一般來說，台北市區大樓比較多，馬路也比較寬。
Gēn nánbù bǐqǐlái, yìbān láishuō, Táiběi shìqū dàlóu bǐjiào duō, mǎlù yě bǐjiào kuān.
Generally speaking, when you compare downtown Taipei with the south, there are more buildings and the roads are wider.

Usage　　一般來說 is interchangeable with 一般說來.

一邊 A 一邊 B, (yìbiān A yìbiān B), connecting two simultaneous events, doing A and B at the same time

Function　　This pattern is used to express two instances that take place at the same time.

❶ 我常常一邊走路，一邊聽歌。
Wǒ chángcháng yìbiān zǒulù, yìbiān tīng gē.
I often listen to songs while walking.

❷ 那個小姐喜歡一邊吃飯，一邊看電視。
Nà ge xiǎojiě xǐhuān yìbiān chīfàn, yìbiān kàn diànshì.
That young lady likes to eat while watching TV.

❸ 我們常常一邊逛夜市，一邊照相。
Wǒmen chángcháng yìbiān guàng yèshì, yìbiān zhàoxiàng.
We often takes pictures while wandering around night markets.

Structures　　The pattern 一邊 A 一邊 B connects two action verb clauses.

Negation :

❶ 你不可以一邊騎機車，一邊打電話。
Nǐ bù kěyǐ yìbiān qí jīchē, yìbiān dǎ diànhuà.
You can't ride a motorcycle while talking on the phone.

❷ 請你不要一邊上課，一邊吃早餐。
Qǐng nǐ bú yào yìbiān shàngkè, yìbiān chī zǎocān.
Please don't eat breakfast while in class.

❸ 他沒一邊工作，一邊玩手機。
Tā méi yìbiān gōngzuò, yìbiān wán shǒujī.
He wasn't using his cell phone while working.

Questions :

❶ 我們一邊看電視，一邊喝茶嗎？
Wǒmen yìbiān kàn diànshì, yìbiān hē chá ma?
Shall we drink tea while watching TV?

❷ 老闆，我可以一邊工作，一邊學西班牙文嗎？
Lǎobǎn, wǒ kěyǐ yìbiān gōngzuò, yìbiān xué Xībānyáwén ma?
Boss, can I work and study Spanish at the same time?

❸ 你是不是一邊上班，一邊念書？
Nǐ shìbúshì yìbiān shàngbān, yìbiān niànshū?
Are you working and studying at the same time?

一點 , yìdiǎn, (N), a bit, a little

Function　　The noun 一點 indicates a minimal quantity or degree.

❶ 他喝了一點咖啡。
Tā hēle yìdiǎn kāfēi.
He drank a little coffee.

❷ 這一點錢太少了。
Zhè yìdiǎn qián tài shǎo le.
This tiny amount of money is too little.

❸ 她要吃一點炒飯。
Tā yào chī yìdiǎn chǎofàn.
She wants to eat a little bit of fried rice.

Structures　　一點 can appear in a variety of structures as illustrated below.

(1) 一點＋NP: Before a noun as its modifier.

❶ 她在超市買了一點東西。
Tā zài chāoshì mǎile yìdiǎn dōngxi.
She bought some things at the supermarket.

❷ 我只喝了一點烏龍茶。
Wǒ zhǐ hēle yìdiǎn Wūlóng chá.
I only drank a little Oolong tea.

❸ 昨天下了一點雨。
Zuótiān xiàle yìdiǎn yǔ.
It rained a little yesterday.

(2) Vs＋一點: After a state verb as its complement, it indicates comparison, as in 'a little more/less...'.

❶ 他比我年輕一點。
Tā bǐ wǒ niánqīng yìdiǎn.
He is a little bit younger than I am.

❷ 請你早一點來！
Qǐng nǐ zǎo yìdiǎn lái!
Please arrive a little early.

❸ 明天我會晚一點回家。
Míngtiān wǒ huì wǎn yìdiǎn huíjiā.
I'll be home a little later tomorrow.

(3) 有（一）點＋Vs: Before a state verb but preceded by 有 as a modifier of the adjective, referring to degree.

❶ 牛肉麵有一點辣。
Niúròu miàn yǒu yìdiǎn là.
The beef noodles is a little spicy.

❷ 這裡，冬天有一點冷。
Zhèlǐ, dōngtiān yǒu yìdiǎn lěng.
Here, the winters are a bit cold.

❸ 這支手機有一點貴。
Zhè zhī shǒujī yǒu yìdiǎn guì.
This cell phone is a little expensive.

❹ 他有（一）點想睡。
Tā yǒu (yì) diǎn xiǎng shuì.
He is a little sleepy.

(4) V＋Vs＋一點：一點 can also occur behind a Vs combining into a verb complement, to an action verb, meaning do something more/ less ...ly!

❶ 你走慢一點！
Nǐ zǒu màn yìdiǎn!
Please walk more slowly!

❷ 你們吃快一點！
Nǐmen chī kuài yìdiǎn!
Please eat faster!

❸ 你的字要寫好看一點！
Nǐ de zì yào xiě hǎokàn yìdiǎn!
You need to write your characters more properly!

Usage

一點 can be reduplicated to form emphatic 一點點, indicating that something is 'just a tiny bit', e.g., 我只要一點點。Wǒ zhǐ yào yìdiǎndiǎn. 'I just want a tiny little bit.'

一點也不 V, (yìdiǎn yě bù V), emphatic negation

Function

This pattern suggests strong and exaggerated negation, something like 'not at all...', 'definitely not', or 'not a bit...' in English.

❶ A：你要坐公車去嗎？坐公車去故宮博物院比較慢。
Nǐ yào zuò gōngchē qù ma? Zuò gōngchē qù Gùgōng Bówùyuàn bǐjiào màn.
Are you going there by bus? Taking the bus to the Palace Museum is slower.

B：一點也不慢，比捷運方便。
Yìdiǎn yě bú màn, bǐ jiéyùn fāngbiàn.
It is not at all slow. It is easier than taking the MRT.

❷ A：他喝茶嗎？
Tā hē chá ma?
Does he drink tea?

B：他一點茶也不喝。
Tā yìdiǎn chá yě bù hē.
No. He doesn't drink tea at all.

❸ 夜市的東西一點也不貴。
Yèshì de dōngxi yìdiǎn yě bú guì.
The things sold at the night market are not expensive at all.
(Contrary to what people told me.)

❹ 已經晚上12點多了，他們一點也不想睡覺。

Yǐjīng wǎnshàng shí'èrdiǎn duō le, tāmen yìdiǎn yě bù xiǎng shuìjiào.

It's past 12 o'clock at night, but they are not at all sleepy.

Structures

This is a negative pattern, without a positive counterpart. The pattern can be used with action verbs or state verbs. The adverb 也 can be replaced by 都 dōu. If an object is not fronted to the beginning of the sentence to be the topic, it has to appear after the adverb 一點, before and not after the verb.

❶ 他昨天一點飯都沒吃。 （*他昨天一點都沒吃飯。）

Tā zuótiān yìdiǎn fàn dōu méi chī. (*Tā zuótiān yìdiǎn dōu méi chīfàn.)

He didn't eat anything at all yesterday.

❷ 我一點湯也沒喝。 （*我一點也沒喝湯。）

Wǒ yìdiǎn tāng yě méi hē. (*Wǒ yìdiǎn yě méi hē tāng.)

I didn't drink any soup at all.

*Q*uestions :

❶ 這種手機是不是一點也不好用？所以沒人買。

Zhè zhǒng shǒujī shìbúshì yìdiǎn yě bù hǎoyòng? Suǒyǐ méi rén mǎi.

This cell phone is not at all user-friendly? No wonder nobody buys it.

❷ 他生病這幾天一點東西都沒吃嗎？

Tā shēngbìng zhè jǐ tiān yìdiǎn dōngxi dōu méi chī ma?

Did he not eat anything during these last few days that he was sick?

❸ 他身體不好，是不是一點酒都不能喝？

Tā shēntǐ bù hǎo, shìbúshì yìdiǎn jiǔ dōu bù néng hē?

He's not well. He should not drink at all?

Usage

(1) 也 in this pattern is replaceable by 都.

　❶ 我一點都不累。

　　Wǒ yìdiǎn dōu bú lèi.

　　I'm not tired at all.

　❷ 捷運車票一點都不貴。

　　Jiéyùn chēpiào yìdiǎn dōu bú guì.

　　MRT ticket fares are not expensive at all.

　❸ 他一點都不想去。

　　Tā yìdiǎn dōu bù xiǎng qù.

　　He does not feel like going at all.

(2) In some case, 都 provides a stronger sense of total negation than 也.

　❶ 我剛剛一點西班牙文也/都沒說。

　　Wǒ gānggāng yìdiǎn Xībānyáwén yě/dōu méi shuō.

　　I didn't speak any Spanish at all just now.

❷ 王先生生病了，所以最近一點事也/都沒做。

Wáng xiānshēng shēngbìng le, suǒyǐ zuìjìn yìdiǎn shì yě/dōu méi zuò.

Mr. Wang fell ill, so he hasn't gotten anything done recently.

(3) The use of 也 has a higher frequency of occurrence than 都.

一方面 A，一方面 B, (yì fāngmiàn A, yì fāngmiàn B), doing A on the one hand, B on the other

Function ▶ This pattern presents two different perspectives on an instance, two different circumstances of one and the same instance.

❶ 她去聽五月天的演唱會，一方面想放鬆心情，一方面也想了解為什麼五月天這麼受歡迎。

Tā qù tīng Wǔyuètiān de yǎnchànghuì, yì fāngmiàn xiǎng fàngsōng xīnqíng, yì fāngmiàn yě xiǎng liǎojiě wèishénme Wǔyuètiān zhème shòu huānyíng.

She went to the May Day concert, on the one hand, to kick back and relax, on the other, to figure out why the band is so popular.

❷ 她暑假去打工，一方面想賺點錢，一方面也想學一些社會經驗。

Tā shǔjià qù dǎgōng, yì fāngmiàn xiǎng zhuàn diǎn qián, yì fāngmiàn yě xiǎng xué yìxiē shèhuì jīngyàn.

She's working part time during the summer, on the one hand, to make a little money, on the other, to get a little experience in society.

❸ 這個款式的包包賣得這麼好，一方面是因為連續劇裡的女主角拿過，一方面是價錢也不太貴。

Zhè ge kuǎnshì de bāobāo mài de zhème hǎo, yì fāngmiàn shì yīnwèi liánxùjù lǐ de nǚzhǔjiǎo náguò, yì fāngmiàn shì jiàqián yě bútài guì.

This style of bag sells really well, because, on the one hand, the female lead in a TV series had one, and on the other, it's not all that expensive.

❹ 去農夫市集買菜，一方面可以吃到最新鮮的蔬菜、水果，一方面也可以幫助小農。

Qù nóngfū shìjí mǎicài, yì fāngmiàn kěyǐ chīdào zuì xīnxiān de shūcài, shuǐguǒ, yì fāngmiàn yě kěyǐ bāngzhù xiǎonóng.

Going to the farmer's market, on the one hand, allows you to eat really fresh vegetables and fruit; on the other, it helps the small farmer.

⑤ 過節的時候回家鄉，一方面可以跟家人團聚，一方面還可以看看老同學。

Guòjié de shíhòu huí jiāxiāng, yì fāngmiàn kěyǐ gēn jiārén tuánjù, yì fāngmiàn hái kěyǐ kànkàn lǎo tóngxué.

Going back to your hometown during holidays allows you to, on the one hand, get together with your family, and on the other, see old schoolmates.

Usage　This is a somewhat literary construction, rarely used in colloquial speech.

一口氣, yìkǒuqì, in one breath, without interruption

Function　The phrase 一口氣 literally means 'in one breath', to accomplish an entire task without interruption.

❶ 今天我一口氣游了兩千公尺。
Jīntiān wǒ yìkǒuqì yóule liǎngqiān gōngchǐ.
Today I swam 2,000 meters in one go.

❷ 他可以一口氣喝完一大杯可樂。
Tā kěyǐ yìkǒuqì hēwán yí dà bēi kělè.
He can down an entire large Coke in one gulp.

❸ 她這學期一口氣修了28個學分。我看她是瘋了。
Tā zhè xuéqí yìkǒuqì xiūle 28 ge xuéfēn. Wǒ kàn tā shì fēng le.
She did 28 credits all in one term. She's nuts.

❹ 這位舞者一口氣跳了一個鐘頭，都沒休息。
Zhè wèi wǔzhě yìkǒuqì tiàole yí ge zhōngtóu, dōu méi xiūxí.
This dancer danced for an hour straight without taking a break.

❺ 我爺爺一口氣把他從年輕的時候到現在的事情都説給我聽。聽得我差一點睡著。
Wǒ yéye yìkǒuqì bǎ tā cóng niánqīng de shíhòu dào xiànzài de shìqíng dōu shuō gěi wǒ tīng. Tīng de wǒ chàyìdiǎn shuìzháo.
My grandpa gave me the entire story of his life from start to finish all in one go, and it nearly put me to sleep.

一來 A，二來 B, (yìlái A, èrlái B), on the one hand A, and on the other B; firstly A, secondly B

Function　This pattern offers two reasons or explanations for a statement already presented.

❶ 我不信任他，一來我們認識不久，二來聽説他會騙人。
Wǒ bú xìnrèn tā, yìlái wǒmen rènshì bù jiǔ, èrlái tīngshuō tā huì piàn rén.
I don't trust him. First, we have not known each other for very long. Second, I've heard that he cheats.

❷ 我不跟你們到綠島去玩，一來我怕坐船，二來我不會游泳，去了沒意思。

Wǒ bù gēn nǐmen dào Lǜdǎo qù wán, yìlái wǒ pà zuò chuán, èrlái wǒ bú huì yóuyǒng, qùle méiyìsi.

I'm not going to go with you to Green Island. On the one hand, I'm afraid of boat rides. On the other, I can't swim. It'll be boring if I go.

❸ 我最近吃素，一來天氣太熱，吃不下油膩的東西，二來吃青菜對健康比較好。

Wǒ zuìjìn chīsù, yìlái tiānqì tài rè, chībúxià yóunì de dōngxi, èrlái chī qīngcài duì jiànkāng bǐjiào hǎo.

I've been eating vegetarian food a lot lately. First of all, it's been too hot out, I can't handle oily food. Second, eating vegetables is better for you.

❹ 我們今年的收成不錯，一來天氣好，沒有颱風，二來我種的是新品種。

Wǒmen jīnnián de shōuchéng búcuò, yìlái tiānqì hǎo, méi yǒu táifēng, èrlái wǒ zhòng de shì xīn pǐnzhǒng.

Our harvest this year was pretty good. On the one hand, the weather was good--no typhoons. On the other, I planted a new strain of crops.

❺ 養寵物，一來讓我們不孤單，二來給我們很多快樂。所以現在養寵物的人越來越多。

Yǎng chǒngwù, yìlái ràng wǒmen bù gūdān, èrlái gěi wǒmen hěnduō kuàilè. Suǒyǐ xiànzài yǎng chǒngwù de rén yuèláiyuè duō.

Keeping pets, on the one hand, takes away loneliness, and on the other, brings us a lot of joy, so an increasing number of people are keeping pets.

Usage

The usage of this pattern is the same as 一方面 A，一方面 B, but 一來 A，二來 B can be used to offer more reasons. For example, 一來 A，二來 B，三來 C. In addition, 一來 A，二來 B is more colloquial than 一方面 A，一方面 B.

一連, yìlián, (Adv), without interruption, in rapid succession

Function

The adverb 一連 refers to the duration of an activity without interruption (❷, ❸), or to the occurrence of instances in rapid succession (❶, ❹, ❺).

❶ 學生一連問了五個問題，老師聽到第五個已經忘了第一個了。

Xuéshēng yìlián wènle wǔ ge wèntí, lǎoshī tīngdào dìwǔ ge yǐjīng wàngle dìyī ge le.

The students fired off five questions right in a row, and after hearing the fifth the teacher forgot what the first one was.

❷ 我已經一連三天沒睡覺了，都快生病了。
Wǒ yǐjīng yìlián sān tiān méi shuìjiào le, dōu kuài shēngbìng le.
It's been three full days since I've slept. I am going to be sick.

❸ 昨天她一連工作了十六個小時，回家的時候已經半夜一點了。
Zuótiān tā yìlián gōngzuòle shíliù ge xiǎoshí, huíjiā de shíhòu yǐjīng bànyè yìdiǎn le.
She worked for 16 hours straight yesterday, and by the time she got home it was already 1 o'clock in the morning.

❹ 最近一連來了兩個大颱風，上一個來的時候壞了的東西還來不及恢復，這一個就來了。
Zuìjìn yìlián láile liǎng ge dà táifēng, shàng yí ge lái de shíhòu huài le de dōngxi hái láibují huīfù, zhè yí gè jiù lái le.
The last two typhoons came in rapid succession. There wasn't enough time to fix the damages from the first before the second one landed.

❺ 為了找一本很舊的書，他一連問了好幾家書店，最後才在一家舊書店找到。
Wèile zhǎo yì běn hěn jiù de shū, tā yìlián wènle hǎojǐ jiā shūdiàn, zuìhòu cái zài yì jiā jiù shūdiàn zhǎodào.
He inquired at one bookstore after another after another, looking for a really old book, until finally he found it at a vintage bookstore.

Usage

(1) 一連 is always followed by a number phrase (五個…, 三天, 十六個小時, etc.). See examples above.

(2) When the verb is negated, the number phrase is moved to directly after 一連. See ❷ above.

(3) 一口氣 vs. 一連
一連 allows for interruption in between successive actions and instances. 一口氣 does not allow for interruption. 一連 is used in multiple instances, and 一口氣 in a single instance.

一下 A，一下 B, (yíxià A, yíxià B), referring to alternating events

Function 下 is a verbal measure, referring to very brief moments in time. This pattern describes the speaker's slight displeasure at fast-changing scenes, of usually two activities.

❶ 你別一下吃熱的，一下吃冰的，肚子會不舒服喔！
Nǐ bié yíxià chī rè de, yíxià chī bīng de, dùzi huì bú shūfú o!
Don't eat hot and cold foods in such close succession like that. You'll get a stomache ache.

❷ 這個地方天氣還真怪，一下冷，一下熱。
Zhè ge dìfāng tiānqì hái zhēn guài, yíxià lěng, yíxià rè.
The weather here is rather unpredictable; one moment it's cold, the next it's hot.

❸ 我女朋友一下要我陪她去看電影，一下要我陪她去逛夜市。她到底想去哪裡？

Wǒ nǚpéngyǒu yíxià yào wǒ péi tā qù kàn diànyǐng, yíxià yào wǒ péi tā qù guàng yèshì. Tā dàodǐ xiǎng qù nǎlǐ?

My girlfriend wants me to go with her to the movies one moment, then to the night market the next. I have no idea where she actually wants to go.

❹ 感冒的時候一下咳嗽，一下流鼻水，真不舒服。

Gǎnmào de shíhòu yíxià késòu, yíxià liú bíshuǐ, zhēn bù shūfú.

Having a cold is terrible, constantly coughing and having a runny nose.

❺ 你一下寫功課，一下跟朋友玩，功課當然寫不完。

Nǐ yíxià xiě gōngkè, yíxià gēn péngyǒu wán, gōngkè dāngrán xiěbùwán.

If while you are doing your homework you chat with your friends every few minutes, of course it'll never get done.

Usage

一下 as combined, serves like an adverb. As illustrated above, it does not connect instances in negation.

一向, yíxiàng, (Adv), all along, has always...

Function

The adverb 一向 means 'it has always been the case that', referring to habits or aptitudes.

❶ 他一向很熱心，總是喜歡幫助人。

Tā yíxiàng hěn rèxīn, zǒngshì xǐhuān bāngzhù rén.

He has always been passionate and has always liked helping others.

❷ 他對自己的能力一向有自信，他不會放棄的。

Tā duì zìjǐ de nénglì yíxiàng yǒu zìxìn, tā bú huì fàngqì de.

He has always been confident in his abilities. He won't give up.

❸ 這家公司一向重視品質。你可以放心買他們的產品。

Zhè jiā gōngsī yíxiàng zhòngshì pǐnzhí. Nǐ kěyǐ fàngxīn mǎi tāmen de chǎnpǐn.

This company has always attached a great deal of importance to quality. You can set your mind at ease when you buy their products.

❹ 他一向喜歡開玩笑，他說的話，都要打個折扣。

Tā yíxiàng xǐhuān kāiwánxiào, tā shuō de huà, dōu yào dǎ ge zhékòu.

He has always loved to joke around. You need to take what he says with a grain of salt.

❺ 他一向很照顧學生。不管學生碰到什麼問題，他都盡量幫忙。

Tā yíxiàng hěn zhàogù xuéshēng. Bùguǎn xuéshēng pèngdào shénme wèntí, tā dōu jìnliàng bāngmáng.

He has always looked after his students. No matter what problems they face, he does everything he can to help.

Usage

(1) Both 一向 and 一直 yìzhí indicate the continuation of an action or a state from the past to the present. 一向, however, stresses something being habitual, while 一直 emphasizes continuation, without interruption. They are thus not always interchangeable.

E.g.,

❶ 他一向一放假就出國旅遊。（*一直）
Tā yíxiàng yí fàngjià jiù chūguó lǚyóu. (*yìzhí)
He always takes a trip overseas as soon as a holiday begins.

❷ 他一向不相信我說的話。 （??一直）
Tā yíxiàng bù xiāngxìn wǒ shuō de huà. (?? yìzhí)
He has never believed what I say. (Habitual)

❸ 她一向不聽別人的建議，你別再說了。（*一直）
Tā yíxiàng bù tīng biérén de jiànyì, nǐ bié zài shuō le. (*yìzhí)
She never accepts other people's suggestions. Don't waste your breath.

❹ 他旅行以前，一向先計畫好。（*一直）
Tā lǚxíng yǐqián, yíxiàng xiān jihuàhǎo. (*yìzhí)
He always plans ahead before traveling.

(2) 一向 can only be used to describe something in the past, while 一直 can be used to express something in the future.

E.g.,

❶ 他會一直陪著你走到學校。（*一向）
Tā huì yìzhí péizhe nǐ zǒu dào xuéxiào. (*yíxiàng)
He will walk with you all the way to school.

❷ 他從昨天到現在一直在等你電話。（*一向）
Tā cóng zuótiān dào xiànzài yìzhí zài děng nǐ diànhuà. (*yíxiàng)
He has been expecting your call since yesterday.

❸ 小孩感冒了。媽媽今天會一直在家照顧他。（*一向）
Xiǎohái gǎnmào le. Māma jīntiān huì yìzhí zài jiā zhàogù tā. (*yíxiàng)
The child had a cold, and his mother will stay at home today, looking after him.

❹ 你要一直提醒他，他才記得。（*一向）
Nǐ yào yīzhí tíxǐng tā, tā cái jìde. (*yíxiàng)
He will just forget it, if you don't keep reminding him.

以為, yǐwéi, (Vst), to have wrongly thought that...

Function

The verb 以為, especially when used in colloquial conversations, confesses to a mistaken assumption on the part of the speaker or the subject.

❶ 我以為那會是一場美食的饗宴，結果，菜沒什麼特色不說，材料還不新鮮，真是讓人失望。

Wǒ yǐwéi nà huì shì yì chǎng měishí de xiǎngyàn, jiéguǒ, cài méi shénme tèsè bùshuō, cáiliào hái bù xīnxiān, zhēnshi ràng rén shīwàng.

Here I thought it was going to be a lavish feast, but not only was the food unremarkable, it wasn't even fresh. What a disappointment.

❷ 我原來以為你們不熟，沒想到他居然提到了你們小時候常一起玩的事。

Wǒ yuánlái yǐwéi nǐmen bù shóu, méi xiǎngdào tā jūrán tídàole nǐmen xiǎo shíhòu cháng yìqǐ wán de shì.

And here I thought you didn't know each other very well, but then he mentioned that you often played together as kids.

❸ 我們本來以為他會遲到；沒想到他今天很準時。

Wǒmen běnlái yǐwéi tā huì chídào; méi xiǎngdào tā jīntiān hěn zhǔnshí.

We thought he'd be late for sure; we never dreamed that today he'd be right on time.

❹ 我們都以為這家知名餐廳的服務生一定都很有禮貌，沒想到也有這麼糟的。

Wǒmen dōu yǐwéi zhè jiā zhīmíng cāntīng de fúwùshēng yídìng dōu hěn yǒu lǐmào, méi xiǎngdào yě yǒu zhème zāo de.

We all expected that the servers at this well-known restaurant would be very courteous, in reality ours was far from it.

❺ 我們以為這些番茄都是基因改造的，現在才知道這些都是有機番茄。

Wǒmen yǐwéi zhèxiē fānqié dōu shì jīyīn gǎizào de, xiànzài cái zhīdào zhèxiē dōu shì yǒujī fānqié.

We had been under the impression that these were GMO tomatoes, but just found out that they are organic tomatoes.

Usage

(1) In formal speech, 以為 and 認為 are freely interchangeable.

(2) 以為 is often used together with 其實, which presents the truth, e.g.,

❶ 我以為他還單身，其實他已經結婚了。
Wǒ yǐwéi tā hái dānshēn, qíshí tā yǐjīng jiéhūn le.
I thought he was still single. He was actually already married.

❷ 他以為我還住在淡水，其實我早就搬到台中了。
Tā yǐwéi wǒ hái zhù zài Dànshuǐ, qíshí wǒ zǎo jiù bān dào Táizhōng le.
He thought that I still lived in Danshui. I actually moved to Taichung a long time ago.

因為 A，所以 B, (yīnwèi (Conj) A, suǒyǐ (Conj) B), to express cause and effect

Function The '因為 A，所以 B' pattern links clauses to indicate cause (A) and effect (B), therefore.

❶ 因為現在去玩的人比較少，所以旅館不太貴。

Yīnwèi xiànzài qù wán de rén bǐjiào shǎo, suǒyǐ lǚguǎn bútài guì.

Because now fewer people go there, (therefore) the hotels are not that expensive.

❷ 因為火車太慢了，所以我想坐高鐵。

Yīnwèi huǒchē tài màn le, suǒyǐ wǒ xiǎng zuò gāotiě.

Because the train is too slow, so I'd like to take the HSR.

❸ 因為我不會做飯，所以常去餐廳吃飯。

Yīnwèi wǒ bú huì zuòfàn, suǒyǐ cháng qù cāntīng chīfàn.

Because I don't know how to cook, (therefore) (I) often go to eat at restaurants.

❹ 因為我不知道在哪裡買票，所以想請你幫我買。

Yīnwèi wǒ bù zhīdào zài nǎlǐ mǎi piào, suǒyǐ xiǎng qǐng nǐ bāng wǒ mǎi.

Because I don't know where to buy tickets, (so) (I)'d like to ask you to buy one for me.

Usage The two conjuctions, 因為yīnwèi and 所以suǒyǐ, almost always appear as pairs in sentences, while in English, for example, pairing does not happen. Pairing is a reinforcement strategy. In Chinese, cause almost always comes before effect.

因為 A 才 B, (yīnwèi (Conj) A cái (Adv) B), only because A, B...; B is true, only since A is like this

Function This pattern stresses that an instance happened only because of a particular reason. This is a typical cause-effect construction.

❶ 因為賣保險，收入不穩定，她才想換工作的。

Yīnwèi mài bǎoxiǎn, shōurù bù wěndìng, tā cái xiǎng huàn gōngzuò de.

She only wants to change jobs because she sells insurance and her income isn't stable.

❷ 因為教室裡沒人，我才把冷氣關掉。

Yīnwèi jiàoshì lǐ méi rén, wǒ cái bǎ lěngqì guāndiào.

I turned the air conditioner off, because there was no one in the classroom.

❸ 美美條件很好。因為工作一直很忙，才到現在還沒結婚。

Měiměi tiáojiàn hěn hǎo. Yīnwèi gōngzuò yìzhí hěn máng, cái dào xiànzài hái méi jiéhūn.

Meimei is a great catch. She's still unmarried only because she's always been busy at work.

❹ 因為工作壓力太大，健康出了問題，他才決定回鄉下種田的。
Yīnwèi gōngzuò yālì tài dà, jiànkāng chūle wèntí, tā cái juédìng huí xiāngxià zhòng tián de.
Stress from work caused him to have health issues, so he decided to go back to his village and work the fields.

❺ 因為他不但熱心，而且成績好，才拿到獎學金的。
Yīnwèi tā búdàn rèxīn, érqiě chéngjī hǎo, cái nádào jiǎngxuéjīn de.
He got a scholarship because he is both enthusiastic and has good grades.

Usage

才 can only be used in a sentence that describes a past instance. The 因為 A 所以 B pattern is used to indicate cause and effect. It is not necessarily used for instances that have already happened.

❶ A：你不是最喜歡看煙火的嗎？怎麼沒去？
Nǐ búshì zuì xǐhuān kàn yānhuǒ de ma? Zěnme méi qù?
Don't you love fireworks? Why didn't you go?

B：因為我不舒服，才沒去看煙火的。
Yīnwèi wǒ bù shūfú, cái méi qù kàn yānhuǒ de.
I didn't go, because I didn't feel well.

❷ A：你明天為什麼不去看煙火了？
Nǐ míngtiān wèishénme bú qù kàn yānhuǒ le?
Why aren't you going to see the fireworks tomorrow?

B：因為要去女朋友家，所以不能去看煙火了。
Yīnwèi yào qù nǚpéngyǒu jiā, suǒyǐ bù néng qù kàn yānhuǒ le.
I'm not going, because I'm going to my girlfriend's house.

因為 NP，S..., (yīnwèi (Prep) NP, S...), because of NP, S...

Function

This pattern presents an NP (a reason, an explanation or a motivation), for the subsequent clause. 因為 in this pattern is a preposition, not a conjuction, and is thus used with an NP.

❶ 因為氣溫的變化，今年的芒果熟得比較早。
Yīnwèi qìwēn de biànhuà, jīnnián de mángguǒ shóu de bǐjiào zǎo.
Due to changes in the temperature, mangoes are ripening relatively early this year.

❷ 因為工作的關係，我需要懂越南語的翻譯人員。
Yīnwèi gōngzuò de guānxi, wǒ xūyào dǒng Yuènányǔ de fānyì rényuán.
For the sake of my job, I need a translator in Vietnamese.

❸ 因為成家晚的關係，他的孩子年紀還很小。
Yīnwèi chéngjiā wǎn de guānxi, tā de háizi niánjì hái hěn xiǎo.
Because he didn't get married until later in life, his kids are still very young.

④ 因為週年慶的關係，百貨公司裡擠滿了人。
Yīnwèi zhōuniánqìng de guānxi, bǎihuò gōngsī lǐ jǐmǎnle rén.
The department stores are packed with people because the anniversary sale is on.

⑤ 因為連續劇的影響，街上賣韓國炸雞的店越來越多。
Yīnwèi liánxùjù de yǐngxiǎng, jiē shàng mài Hánguó zhájī de diàn yuèláiyuè duō.
Because of the influence of the TV series, an increasing numbers of street shops are selling Korean-style fried chicken

Usage

As indicated in the description above, 因為 in this pattern is a preposition but can be followed by a sentence with its own conjunction, e.g., 因為氣溫的變化，因此 (or 所以) 今年的芒果熟得比較早。Yīnwèi qìwēn de biànhuà, yīncǐ (or suǒyǐ) jīnnián de mángguǒ shóu de bǐjiào zǎo. 'Changes in weather conditions have caused mangoes to ripen earlier this year.'

因為 A 而 B, (yīnwèi (Conj) A ér (Adv) B), therefore, consequently

Function

The adverb 而 refers to a consequence resulting from a cause given elsewhere in the sentence.

① 我奶奶一個人住，因為怕孤單而養了兩隻狗。
Wǒ nǎinai yí ge rén zhù, yīnwèi pà gūdān ér yǎngle liǎng zhī gǒu.
My grandma lives by herself. She's afraid of being alone, so she has two dogs.

② 很多人因為想學道地的西班牙文而去西班牙。
Hěn duō rén yīnwèi xiǎng xué dàodì de Xībānyáwén ér qù Xībānyá.
Many people want to learn authentic Spanish, so they go to Spain.

③ 那個小鎮因為今年芒果收成很好而打算舉行慶祝活動。
Nà ge xiǎo zhèn yīnwèi jīnnián mángguǒ shōuchéng hěn hǎo ér dǎsuàn jǔxíng qìngzhù huódòng.
Because it had a good mango harvest this year, that town plans to put on some activities in celebration.

④ 她因為衣服、鞋子都發霉了而決定去買除濕機。
Tā yīnwèi yīfú, xiézi dōu fāméile ér juédìng qù mǎi chúshījī.
Because her clothes and shoes mildewed, she decided to go buy a dehumidifier.

⑤ 王小姐因為男朋友忘了送她生日禮物而氣得不想跟他說話。
Wáng xiǎojiě yīnwèi nánpéngyǒu wàngle sòng tā shēngrì lǐwù ér qì de bù xiǎng gēn tā shuōhuà.
Because her boyfriend forgot to give her a birthday present, Miss Wang is so angry that she doesn't want to talk to him.

Usage

The adverb 而 is frequently used in written documents or in formal venues.

314

由, yóu, (Prep), Introducing an Agent, an Actor

Function

由 is a literary preposition 'by', which marks an agent, or doer of an action.

❶ 今天晚上的演講，我們請到張主任，由他來介紹語言學最新的發展。

Jīntiān wǎnshàng de yǎnjiǎng, wǒmen qǐngdào Zhāng zhǔrèn, yóu tā lái jièshào yǔyánxué zuì xīn de fāzhǎn.

We've asked Director Zhang to speak tonight. He will be telling us about the latest developments in linguistics.

❷ 今天我們來包餃子。餃子餡兒，你準備，至於包呢，由我來吧。

Jīntiān wǒmen lái bāo jiǎozi. Jiǎozi xiànr, nǐ zhǔnbèi, zhìyú bāo ne, yóu wǒ lái ba.

Let's make dumplings tonight. You prepare the stuffing. As to the wrapping, I'll be responsible for that.

❸ 外交方面的問題，當然還是由專業的外交人員處理比較合適。

Wàijiāo fāngmiàn de wèntí, dāngrán háishì yóu zhuānyè de wàijiāo rényuán chǔlǐ bǐjiào héshì.

It is obviously more appropriate for professional diplomats to handle foreign affairs issucs.

❹ 張先生嗎？今天由我為您檢查身體。現在請您躺下。

Zhāng xiānshēng ma? Jīntiān yóu wǒ wèi nín jiǎnchá shentǐ. Xiànzài qǐng nín tǎngxià.

Mr. Zhang? I'll be giving you a health checkup today. Could you lie down please.

❺ 李先生退休以後，他的公司就由兩個女兒經營。

Lǐ xiānshēng tuìxiū yǐhòu, tā de gōngsī jiù yóu liǎng ge nǚ'ér jīngyíng.

After Mr. Li retired, his two daughters took over running his company.

Usage

(1) The order is generally thus: 由 ＋ agent ＋來. The 來 lái introduces the verb. E.g., 由他來照顧這片土地。Yóu tā lái zhàogù zhè piàn tǔdì. 'He is responsible for taking care of this piece of land.' But if the verb consists of two syllables, the 來 can be omitted. If it consists of just one syllable, then the 來 is required to form the four character combination 由 S 來 V, e.g., 由我來做 yóu wǒ lái zuò 'I'll do it.' More examples follow:

❶ 既然是選民的意見，還是由民意代表來反映吧。

Jìrán shì xuǎnmín de yìjiàn, háishì yóu mínyì dàibiǎo lái fǎnyìng ba.

Since it's the view of the voters, let it be voiced by our elected representative.

❷ 在傳統的華人社會，孩子念什麼科系多半不是由孩子自己決定，而是由父母決定。

Zài chuántǒng de Huá rén shèhuì, háizi niàn shénme kēxì duōbàn búshì yóu Háizi zìjǐ juédìng, ér shì yóu fùmǔ juédìng.

In traditional Chinese society, what department children studied generally wasn't decided by the children; rather, it was decided by the parents.

❸ 車禍受傷後的整型，一般來說，不是由外科醫生來做，而是請整型醫生處理。

Chēhuò shòushāng hòu de zhěngxíng, yìbān láishuō, búshì yóu wàikē yīshēng lái zuò, ér shì qǐng zhěngxíng yīshēng chǔlǐ.

Reconstructive surgery after car accidents isn't generally performed by general surgeons; rather, a plastic surgeon is called upon to handle it.

❹ 下一屆的電腦展應該由誰來舉辦？

Xià yí jiè de diànnǎo zhǎn yīnggāi yóu shéi lái jǔbàn?

Who should organize the next computer exhibition?

❺ 這些公共議題是不是由當地人來投票決定比較合適？

Zhèxiē gōnggòng yìtí shìbúshì yóu dāngdì rén lái tóupiào juédìng bǐjiào héshì?

Wouldn't it be more appropriate to have locals decide by vote on these public issues?

❻ 等一下是不是能由您代表說明大家的意見？

Děng yíxià shìbúshì néng yóu nín dàibiǎo shuōmíng dàjiā de yìjiàn?

Can you act as a representative and explain everybody's view in just a minute?

(2) 由 and 被 are related in that they both mark actor, but 被 has a wider range and can mark other nouns, e.g., 他被人發現了。Tā bèi rén fāxiàn le. 'His body was found.' vs. *他由人發現了。*Tā yóu rén fāxiàn le. 由 can only be used with action verbs, but 被 can be used with various verbs.

(3) Lastly, in terms of semantic meaning, 被 suggests something unfortunate or unpleasant happened. 由 doesn't. E.g., 手機被人買走了。Shǒujī bèi rén mǎizǒu le. 'someone bought the cellphone.' (a real loss for the speaker). For more information on 被, refer to the 被 entry.

尤其是, yóuqí shì, especially

Function The adverb 尤其 is used to show that what you are saying applies more to one thing or situation than to others. 尤其是 usually occurs in the latter part of a sentence.

❶ 這學期的功課給他很大的壓力，尤其是口頭報告。
Zhè xuéqí de gōngkè gěi tā hěn dà de yālì, yóuqí shì kǒutóu bàogào.
The homework this semester is really stressing him out, especially the oral reports.

❷ 過春節，小孩都很開心，尤其是拿紅包的時候。
Guò Chūnjié, xiǎohái dōu hěn kāixīn, yóuqí shì ná hóngbāo de shíhòu.
Kids really have a great time during the Spring Festival, especially when they get red envelopes.

❸ 中文很難學，尤其是聲調和發音，得花很多時間練習。
Zhōngwén hěn nán xué, yóuqí shì shēngdiào hàn fāyīn, děi huā hěn duō shíjiān liànxí.
Chinese is really hard to learn. In particular, you have to spend a lot of time practicing tones and pronunciation.

❹ 他對網路上好幾個徵求教師的廣告都很有興趣，尤其是去美國大學教中文的廣告。
Tā duì wǎnglù shàng hǎojǐ ge zhēngqiú jiàoshī de guǎnggào dōu hěn yǒu xìngqù, yóuqí shì qù Měiguó dàxué jiāo Zhōngwén de guǎnggào.
He is interested in a lot of ads for teachers on the internet, especially the ones for Chinese teachers in US universities.

❺ 最近他的中文進步了很多，尤其是發音。
Zuìjìn tā de Zhōngwén jìnbùle hěn duō, yóuqí shì fāyīn.
His Chinese has improved a great deal lately, especially his pronunciation.

有, yǒu, (Vst), to possess, to have, to own (1)

Function The verb 有 refers to possession or ownership.

❶ 我有很多照片。
Wǒ yǒu hěn duō zhàopiàn.
I have many photos.

❷ 他們有好喝的茶。
Tāmen yǒu hǎohē de chá.
They have good-tasting tea.

Structures

***Negation* :** 有 is always negated with 沒 méi.

❶ 他沒有房子。
Tā méi yǒu fángzi.
He does not have a house.

❷ 我沒有書。
Wǒ méi yǒu shū.
I don't have a book.

❸ 對不起,我們沒有烏龍茶.
Duìbùqǐ, wǒmen méi yǒu Wūlóng chá.
Sorry, we don't have any Oolong tea.

❹ 我沒有兄弟姐妹.
Wǒ méi yǒu xiōngdì jiěmèi.
I don't have any brothers or sisters.

Questions : The A-not-A form for the verb 有 is 有沒有 yǒu méi yǒu.

❶ 你們有沒有好喝的咖啡？
Nǐmen yǒu méi yǒu hǎohē de kāfēi?
Do you have good- tasting coffee?

❷ 你們有烏龍茶嗎？
Nǐmen yǒu Wūlóng chá ma?
Do you have Oolong tea?

❸ 你有幾張照片？
Nǐ yǒu jǐ zhāng zhàopiàn?
How many photos do you have?

有, yǒu, (Vs), in Existential Sentence, there's... (2) (See Existential Sentence with 有)

有, yǒu, (Vs), to mark the existence of a subject, there's someone, there's something... (3)

Function

The verb 有 introduces the existence of an indefinite subject. The subsequent VP in the sentence describes what the subject does.

❶ 有人住這裡。
Yǒu rén zhù zhèlǐ.
Somebody is living here.

❷ 有兩個學生來找你。
Yǒu liǎng ge xuéshēng lái zhǎo nǐ.
There are two students looking for you.

❸ 早上有一個小姐打電話給你。
Zǎoshàng yǒu yí ge xiǎojiě dǎ diànhuà gěi nǐ.
This morning some woman phoned you.

❹ 昨天有一個先生來裝有線電視。
Zuótiān yǒu yí ge xiānshēng lái zhuāng yǒuxiàn diànshì.
Some man came yesterday to install cable TV.

❺ 有一個人在外面唱歌。
Yǒu yí ge rén zài wàimiàn chànggē.
Someone is singing outside.

Structures

The subject in Chinese is usually a definite noun. If the subject is indefinite, it needs to be preceded by 有 to make it definite. Indefinite nouns cannot be subjects and stay behind intransitive existential verbs.

Negation :   有 is always negated with 沒.

❶ 這間沒有人住。
Zhè jiān méi yǒu rén zhù.
There is no one living in this room.

❷ 沒有人要跟我去逛夜市。
Méi yǒu rén yào gēn wǒ qù guàng yèshì.
Nobody wants to go walk around the night market with me.

❸ 沒有學生要去故宮。
Méi yǒu xuéshēng yào qù Gùgōng.
None of the students wants to visit the Palace Museum.

Questions :

❶ 有人在裡面看書嗎？
Yǒu rén zài lǐmiàn kànshū ma?
Is there someone inside studying?

❷ 有沒有人想去 KTV 唱歌？
Yǒu méi yǒu rén xiǎng qù KTV chànggē?
Is there anyone who wants to go to KTV to sing?

❸ 有沒有人要跟我一起去花蓮玩？
Yǒu méi yǒu rén yào gēn wǒ yìqǐ qù Huālián wán?
Is there anyone who wants to go to Hualien with me?

❹ 有沒有人不喜歡吃日本麵？
Yǒu méi yǒu rén bù xǐhuān chī Rìběn miàn?
Is there anyone who doesn't like to eat Japanese noodles?

Usage

'有＋NP＋在＋location' is equivalent in basic meaning to 'location ＋有＋NP'. However, the focuses of the two sentences are different. In sentence ❶ A below, which is called an existential sentence, the focus is on 'the cellphone', while in sentence ❷ A, the focus is 'the floor'. Compare the following dialogues.

❶ A：地上有一支手機。
Dì shàng yǒu yì zhī shǒujī.
There is a cellphone on the floor.

 B：是誰的？
Shì shéi de?
Whose is it?

❷ A：有一支手機在地上。
Yǒu yì zhī shǒujī zài dì shàng.
There is a cellphone on the floor.

 B：地上？為什麼放在地上？
Dì shàng? Wèishénme fàng zài dì shàng?
(On the floor? Why on the floor?)

有時候 A, 有時候 B, (yǒu shíhòu A, yǒu shíhòu B), sometimes A, and sometimes B

The 有時候 A, 有時候 B refers to two alternating possibilities of instances within a given situation.

❶ 我有時候吃中國菜，有時候吃越南菜。
Wǒ yǒu shíhòu chī Zhōngguó cài, yǒu shíhòu chī Yuènán cài.
Sometimes, I eat Chinese food and sometimes, I eat Vietnamese food.

❷ 在圖書館的時候，我有時候看書，有時候上網。
Zài túshūguǎn de shíhòu, wǒ yǒu shíhòu kànshū, yǒu shíhòu shàngwǎng.
When I am in the library, sometimes, I read, sometimes I use the internet.

❸ 放假的時候，我有時候在家寫功課，有時候出去玩。
Fàngjià de shíhòu, wǒ yǒu shíhòu zài jiā xiě gōngkè, yǒu shíhòu chūqù wán.
During days off, sometimes, I stay home and do homework, sometimes, I go out and enjoy myself.

有一點, yǒu yìdiǎn, slightly

有一點＋State Verb suggests a slightly negative evaluation and feeling, a mild criticism.

❶ 這碗牛肉麵有一點辣。
Zhè wǎn niúròu miàn yǒu yìdiǎn là.
This bowl of beef noodle is a little spicy.

❷ 那支手機有一點貴。
Nà zhī shǒujī yǒu yìdiǎn guì.
That cell phone is a little expensive.

❸ 他的房子有一點舊。
Tā de fángzi yǒu yìdiǎn jiù.
His house is a little old.

❹ 藥有一點苦。
Yào yǒu yìdiǎn kǔ.
The medicine has a bitter taste to it.

❺ 我有一點擔心了。
Wǒ yǒu yìdiǎn dānxīn le.
I am a bit worried.

❻ 他有一點驕傲。
Tā yǒu yìdiǎn jiāo'ào.
He is a bit proud of himself.

Since this expression suggests negative evaluation, there is no negative form for the pattern. If the Vs has a positive meaning, it can't be used in this pattern. For example, one can say, 這張照片有一點舊。Zhè zhāng zhàopiàn yǒu yìdiǎn jiù. 'This photo is a little old'. However, you cannot say *他妹妹有一點漂亮。Tā mèimei yǒu yìdiǎn piàoliàng. 'His younger sister is a little beautiful'.

有助於, yǒu zhù yú, be conducive to

Function The pattern 有助於 specifies that something or some instance is helpful in or conducive to the realization of something else.

① 有些人認為讓孩子去打工有助於訓練他們獨立。
Yǒuxiē rén rènwéi ràng háizi qù dǎgōng yǒu zhù yú xùnliàn tāmen dúlì.
Some people think that working part-time helps some children achieve independence.

② 有人說整型有助於改善人際關係。
Yǒu rén shuō zhěngxíng yǒu zhù yú gǎishàn rénjì guānxi.
Some people say that cosmetic surgery is conducive to better interpersonal relationships.

③ 多吃蔬菜、水果有助於身體健康。
Duō chī shūcài, shuǐguǒ yǒu zhù yú shēntǐ jiànkāng.
Eating fruits and vegetables is conducive to good health.

④ 媽媽說魚湯有助於傷口的恢復。
Māma shuō yútāng yǒu zhù yú shāngkǒu de huīfù.
Mom says that having fish soup helps speed up recovery time for wounds.

⑤ 有人說多打籃球有助於長高。你認為呢？
Yǒu rén shuō duō dǎ lánqiú yǒu zhù yú zhǎnggāo. Nǐ rènwéi ne?
Some people say that playing basketball is conducive to growing taller. What do you think?

Usage This pattern is rather formal. Its colloquial counterpart is 對⋯有幫助, e.g., 好的教育對提高國家競爭力有幫助。Hǎo de jiàoyù duì tígāo guójiā jìngzhēnglì yǒu bāngzhù. Good education helps enhance a country's competitiveness.

又 A 又 B, (yòu (Adv) A yòu (Adv) B), both A and B

Function The pattern 又 A 又 B, 'not only A but also B' is used to indicate two qualities, situations, or behaviors that are true of the person or thing being discussed.

① 這家餐廳的菜，又便宜又好吃，所以我們常來吃。
Zhè jiā cāntīng de cài, yòu piányí yòu hǎochī, suǒyǐ wǒmen cháng lái chī.
The food in this restaurant is both inexpensive and delicious, so we often eat here.

② 坐高鐵又快又舒服，可是有一點貴。

Zuò gāotiě yòu kuài yòu shūfú, kěshì yǒu yìdiǎn guì.

Taking the High Speed Rail is both fast and comfortable, but it's a little expensive.

③ 我又想喝茶又想喝咖啡，但是這裡沒有便利商店。

Wǒ yòu xiǎng hē chá yòu xiǎng hē kāfēi, dànshì zhèlǐ méi yǒu biànlì shāngdiàn.

I want to drink both tea and coffee, but there are no convenience stores here.

Structures　又＋Vs＋又＋Vs

***N**egation* :　The negation marker 不bù appears after both the first 又 and the second 又, forming 又不 A 又不 B, yòu bù A, yòu bù B.

① 老闆今天做的臭豆腐，又不臭又不辣。我覺得不好吃。

Lǎobǎn jīntiān zuò de chòudòufǔ yòu bú chòu yòu bú là. Wǒ juéde bù hǎochī.

The stinky tofu that the vendor made today tastes neither stinky nor spicy. I don't think it tastes any good.

② 我的舊手機又不能照相又不能上網。我想應該買新的了。

Wǒ de jiù shǒujī yòu bù néng zhàoxiàng yòu bù néng shàngwǎng. Wǒ xiǎng yīnggāi mǎi xīn de le.

My old cellphone cannot take photos, nor can it go online. I have to get a new one.

與其 A，不如 B, (yǔqí (Conj) A, bùrú (Conj) B), would rather B than A

Function　與其 presents (A) that is an action recommended against. The preference is given to B, presented by 不如. This is a formal pattern.

① 恐怖片那麼恐怖。與其看恐怖片，不如看愛情片。

Kǒngbùpiàn nàme kǒngbù. Yǔqí kàn kǒngbùpiàn, bùrú kàn àiqíngpiàn.

Horror movies are really scary. Why not watch a romance movie instead?

② 逛街那麼無聊。與其上街買東西，不如上網買。

Guàngjiē nàme wúliáo. Yǔqí shàng jiē mǎi dōngxi, bùrú shàngwǎng mǎi.

Window-shopping is rather boring. Shopping online is better than going out to buy stuff.

③ 百貨公司的東西那麼貴。與其去那裡買，不如去夜市買。

Bǎihuò gōngsī de dōngxi nàme guì. Yǔqí qù nàlǐ mǎi, bùrú qù yèshì mǎi.

It's expensive shopping in department stores. A good alternative is going to the night market.

④ 有人認為養孩子太貴太麻煩。與其養孩子，不如養隻寵物。

Yǒu rén rènwéi yǎng háizi tài guì tài máfan. Yǔqí yǎng háizi, bùrú yǎng zhī chǒngwù.

Some people say that raising kids is really expensive, a hassle too, and that opting for a pet is better.

⑤ 球賽現場人那麼多。與其去現場看，不如在家上網看。

Qiúsài xiànchǎng rén nàme duō. Yǔqí qù xiànchǎng kàn, bùrú zài jiā shàngwǎng kàn.

Going out to watch the game means dealing with crowds, and it's better to watch it online.

於是, yúshì, (Conj), thus, consequently, thereupon

Function 於是 is an S₂ conjunction, connecting a course of action (effect) motivated by the fact (cause) given in S₁.

① 媽媽看小明對音樂很有興趣，於是讓他去學鋼琴。

Māma kàn Xiǎomíng duì yīnyuè hěn yǒu xìngqù, yúshì ràng tā qù xué gāngqín.

Mom noticed Xiaoming taking an interest in music, so she enrolled him in piano lessons.

② 小林覺得這家公司的薪水太低，於是決定換工作。

Xiǎo Lín juéde zhè jiā gōngsī de xīnshuǐ tài dī, yúshì juédìng huàn gongzuò.

Xiao Lin thought the pay at this company was too low, so he changed jobs.

③ 因為小華成績太差了，於是媽媽決定幫他請個家教。

Yīnwèi Xiǎohuá chéngjī tài chā le, yúshì māma juédìng bāng tā qǐng ge jiājiào.

Xiaohua's marks are so bad that her mom decided to hire a tutor.

④ 上個星期才買的手機壞了，於是我拿到手機店要他們換新的給我。

Shàng ge xīngqí cái mǎi de shǒujī huài le, yúshì wǒ ná dào shǒujī diàn yào tāmen huàn xīn de gěi wǒ.

The cell phone I bought just last week stopped working, so I took it back to the store and had them replace it.

Usage 於是 vs. 所以

所以 is used in a pure cause/effect relationship. With 於是, S₂ is motivated rather than caused by S₁. 於是 suggests next in temporal sequence. E.g.,

因為颱風來了，所以/*於是 房子有好幾個地方壞了，於是/*所以 我們請人來修理房子。

Yīnwèi táifēng lái le, suǒyǐ/*yúshì fángzi yǒu hǎojǐ ge dìfāng huài le, yúshì/*suǒyǐ wǒmen qǐng rén lái xiūlǐ fángzi.

We were hit by a typhoon, so/whereupon the house is damaged in a lot of places. As a result, we have asked someone to come repair the house.

越 A 越 B, (yuè (Adv) A yuè (Adv) B), the more A, the more B

Function ▶ This pattern expresses that when A is true, B is also true.

❶ 學生租房子，離學校越近越方便。
Xuéshēng zū fángzi, lí xuéxiào yuè jìn yuè fāngbiàn.
For a student renting an apartment, the closer it is to school, the more convenient it is.

❷ 我聽說辣椒越紅越辣，是不是？
Wǒ tīngshuō làjiāo yuè hóng yuè là, shìbúshì?
I heard that the redder a pepper is, the hotter it is. Is that true?

❸ 很多台灣人說臭豆腐越臭越好吃。
Hěn duō Táiwān rén shuō chòudòufǔ yuè chòu yuè hǎochī.
Many Taiwanese say that, for stinky tofu, the stinkier it is the better.

Structures ▶ In this pattern, A can be an action or a state, but B can only be a state.

❶ 很多東西都是用得越久越容易壞。
Hěn duō dōngxi dōu shì yòng de yuè jiǔ yuè róngyì huài.
For a lot of things, the longer you use them, the easier, i.e., more likely, it is that they'll break.

❷ 他忘了把資料存在哪裡了，越急越找不到。
Tā wàngle bǎ zīliào cún zài nǎlǐ le, yuè jí yuè zhǎobúdào.
He forgot where he saved the information, and the more anxious he got, the more difficult it became to find.

❸ 他們越走越遠，已經不知道回民宿的路了。
Tāmen yuè zǒu yuè yuǎn, yǐjīng bù zhīdào huí mínsù de lù le.
They kept walking further and further away until they had no idea how to get back to the B&B.

❹ 弟弟現在包餃子，越包越好了。
Dìdi xiànzài bāo jiǎozi, yuè bāo yuè hǎo le.
The dumplings wrapped by my little brother are being wrapped better and better. (i.e., My little brother is getting better and better at wrapping dumplings.)

❺ 這個音樂，我越聽越喜歡。
Zhè ge yīnyuè, wǒ yuè tīng yuè xǐhuān.
The more I listen to this music, the more I like it.

Questions : 是不是 is the only structure possible for this pattern.

❶ 你的字是不是寫得越快越不好看？
Nǐ de zì shìbúshì xiě de yuè kuài yuè bù hǎokàn?
The faster you write, the uglier your characters become, right?

❷ 越健康的食物是不是越不好吃？

Yuè jiànkāng de shíwù shìbúshì yuè bù hǎochī?

The healthier the food, the worse it tastes, right?

❸ 禮物是不是越貴，大家越喜歡？

Lǐwù shìbúshì yuè guì, dàjiā yuè xǐhuān?

The more expensive a gift, the better it is received, right?

Usage

A and B can refer to either the same subject or to different subjects.

❶ 你越忙，越應該找時間運動運動。

Nǐ yuè máng, yuè yīnggāi zhǎo shíjiān yùndòng yùndòng.

The busier you get, the more you should find time to exercise.

❷ 泡菜放的時間越長，味道越酸。

Pàocài fàng de shíjiān yuè cháng, wèidào yuè suān.

The longer kimchi is stored, more sour it gets.

❸ 離捷運站越近的房子，房租越貴。

Lí jiéyùn zhàn yuè jìn de fángzi, fángzū yuè guì.

The closer an apartment is to an MRT station, the higher the rent.

❹ 垃圾分類做得越好，可以回收的資源越多。

Lèsè fēnlèi zuò de yuè hǎo, kěyǐ huíshōu de zīyuán yuè duō.

The better garbage sorting is done, the more resources (there are that) can be recycled.

在, zài, (Prep), Locative Marker, at, located at, situated at (1)

Function

在 introduces the location of someone or something.

❶ 我在臺灣。

Wǒ zài Táiwān.

I am in Taiwan.

❷ 他們學校在花蓮。

Tāmen xuéxiào zài Huālián.

Their school is in Hualian.

❸ 餐廳在宿舍的一樓。

Cāntīng zài sùshè de yì lóu.

The restaurant is on the first floor of the dormitory.

Structures

The primary structure is Noun ＋ 在 ＋ Location. There are three types of location as shown below:

(1) Type A:

Place Words
臺北Táiběi 'Taipei', 花蓮Huālián 'Hualien', 臺灣Táiwān 'Taiwan'… 學校xuéxiào 'school', 餐廳cāntīng 'restaurant', 宿舍sùshè 'dormitory'…

❶ 我們學校在臺北。
Wǒmen xuéxiào zài Táiběi.
Our school is in Taipei.

❷ 我爸爸早上在學校。
Wǒ bàba zǎoshàng zài xuéxiào.
My dad is at school in the mornings.

(2) Type B:

Localizers	Suffix
上 shàng 'top'	
下 xià 'down'	
前 qián 'front'	面 miàn or 邊 biān
後 hòu 'back'	
裡 lǐ 'inside'	
外 wài 'outside'	
旁邊 pángbiān 'next to'	
附近 fùjìn 'nearby'	

❶ 他在外面。
Tā zài wàimiàn.
He is outside.

❷ 圖書館在後面。
Túshūguǎn zài hòumiàn.
The library is in the back.

(3) Type C:

Noun	（的）	Location Type B	
		上 shàng	
		下 xià	
		前 qián	面 miàn or 邊 biān
		後 hòu	
		裡 lǐ	
		外 wài	
		旁邊 pángbiān	
		附近 fùjìn	

❶ 我在宿舍裡面。
Wǒ zài sùshè lǐmiàn.
I am in the dormintory.

❷ 那家店在你家附近嗎？
Nà jiā diàn zài nǐ jiā fùjìn ma?
Is that store near your house?

❸ 咖啡店在宿舍的旁邊，不在裡面。
Kāfēi diàn zài sùshè de pángbiān, bú zài lǐmiàn.
The coffee shop is next to the dorm, not inside.

❹ 游泳池在圖書館的後面，不在前面。
Yóuyǒngchí zài túshūguǎn de hòumiàn, bú zài qiánmiàn.
The swimming pool is behind the library, not in front.

❺ 他和朋友在圖書館後面的咖啡店。
Tā hé péngyǒu zài túshūguǎn hòumiàn de kāfēi diàn.
He and his friend are at the coffe shop behind the library.

Usage

(1) When the noun after 在zài is a common noun, a locative word has to be added after the common noun to turn it into a place noun. For example, in order to express 'He is in the house', you cannot say *他在房子Tā zài fángzi; rather, you need to say 他在房子裡面。Tā zài fángzi lǐmiàn. (房子裡面fángzi lǐmiàn is Type C with the 的 deleted.)

(2) When the noun after 在zài is a proper place name, a locative word is not allowed or necessary. For example, in order to express 'He is in Taiwan', one says 他在臺灣。Tā zài Táiwān, but not *他在臺灣裡面。Tā zài Táiwān lǐmiàn. On the other hand, in order to express 'He is in school', one can say either 他在學校。Tā zài xuéxiào, or 他在學校裡（面）。Tā zài xuéxiào lǐ (miàn). The addition of the locative word (裡面lǐmiàn, in this case) makes the location more explicit.

(3) The locative word 裡面lǐmiàn is a special case. Sometimes, it can be omitted. For example, 他在圖書館看書。Tā zài túshūguǎn kànshū means 'He's reading in the library'. There is no 裡面 lǐmiàn in the sentence, but the sentence still means inside the library. However, when the intended meaning is not 'inside', then a locative word is required. For example, in order to express 'He is reading outside the library', one has to say 他在圖書館外面看書。Tā zài túshūguǎn wàimiàn kànshū.

(4) Notice that the reference point is placed first and the locative word is placed after it. For example, 房子的前面fángzi de qiánmiàn 'in front of the house' is different from 前面的房子qiánmiàn de fángzi 'the house in front'. (The former is Type C, but the latter is modifier＋noun.)

(5) Abbreviations of locative phrases without 的 are common. For example, 'downstairs' is 樓下lóuxià, not *樓的下面lóu de xiàmiàn; 'on the floor' is 地上dìshàng, not *地的上面dì de shàngmiàn.

(6) When the 的 is omitted, the suffix 面miàn in 裡面lǐmiàn, 外面 wàimiàn, 上面shàngmiàn, etc, can be omitted. For example, 房子的裡面fángzi de lǐmiàn 'inside the house' is often just 房子裡 fángzi lǐ and 杯子上面bēizi shàngmiàn 'on the cup' is shortened to 杯子上bēizi shàng.

在, zài, (Prep), Marking the Location of an Activity (2)

Function 在zài 'at' marks the location where an activity takes place.

❶ 我爸爸在家做飯。
Wǒ bàba zài jiā zuòfàn.
My dad is cooking at home.

❷ 他和他朋友在七樓的教室上網。
Tàn hàn tā péngyǒu zài qī lóu de jiàoshì shàngwǎng.
He and his friends use the internet on the seventh floor.

❸ 我們老師常在學校附近的咖啡店喝咖啡。
Wǒmen lǎoshī cháng zài xuéxiào fùjìn de kāfēi diàn hē kāfēi.
Our teacher often has coffee at a café near the school.

❹ 我們很喜歡在這家餐廳吃牛肉麵。
Wǒmen hěn xǐhuān zài zhè jiā cāntīng chī niúròu miàn.
We love to eat beef noodles in this restaurant.

Structures Most sentences in Chinese follow this sequence: Time＋Place＋Action, where place is marked by 在.

Negation : The negation marker 不 is placed before preposition 在.

❶ 他們今天不在家吃晚飯。
Tāmen jīntiān bú zài jiā chī wǎnfàn.
They aren't eating dinner at home today.

❷ 他現在不在宿舍看書。
Tā xiànzài bú zài sùshè kànshū.
He is not studying in the dormitory now.

❸ 很多學生不在學校裡面的咖啡店買咖啡。
Hěn duō xuéshēng bú zài xuéxiào lǐmiàn de kāfēi diàn mǎi kāfēi.
Many students do not buy coffee at the coffee shop in the school.

Questions :

❶ 你們在不在家吃飯？
Nǐmen zài bú zài jiā chīfàn?
Will you be eating at home?

❷ 你們在哪裡打籃球？
Nǐmen zài nǎlǐ dǎ lánqiú?
Where do you play basketball?

❸ 他們是不是在英國上學？
Tāmen shìbúshì zài Yīngguó shàngxué?
Do they go to school in England?

Usage

(1) Note the word order. The location comes before the main verb. That is, the '在zài/到dào＋PLACE' phrase appears before the verb phrase as do all prepositional phrases. You do not say *他學中文在家 *Tā xué Zhōngwén zài jiā; rather you say 他在家學中文。Tā zài jiā xué Zhōngwén. 'He studies Chinese at home'.

(2) The negation is placed before the preposition rather than the main verb, e.g., 他不在家上網。Tā bú zài jiā shàngwǎng. 'He doesn't use the internet at home.'

在, zài, (Vs), Progressive, On-going Actions, at Ving, is in the middle of V＋ing (3)

Function

在 before a VP indicates an ongoing activity taking place at the present (default) or at a given time.

❶ 李老師在上課。
Lǐ lǎoshī zài shàngkè.
Teacher Li is in class right now.

❷ 陳先生在修理他的腳踏車。
Chén xiānshēng zài xiūlǐ tā de jiǎotàchē.
Mr. Chen is fixing his bike.

❸ 昨天下午五點我在聽演講。
Zuótiān xiàwǔ wǔdiǎn wǒ zài tīng yǎnjiǎng.
I was listening to a talk at 5:00 in the afternoon yesterday.

Structures

Negation :

Negation always proceeds 在, e.g.,

進來吧！他不在睡覺。
Jìnlái ba! Tā bú zài shuìjiào.
Come in! He is not sleeping.

Note that 不是 negation is more common than 不.

❶ 他不是在看書。他在看籃球比賽。
Tā búshì zài kànshū. Tā zài kàn lánqiú bǐsài.
He is not reading. He is watching a basketball game.

❷ 我不是在照相。我的手機不能照相。
Wǒ búshì zài zhàoxiàng. Wǒ de shǒujī bù néng zhàoxiàng.
I am not taking a picture. My cellphone can't take photos.

Questions :

❶ 他們老師不在上課嗎？
Tāmen lǎoshī bú zài shàngkè ma?
Is their teacher not in class now?

❷ 他們在打籃球嗎？
Tāmen zài dǎ lánqiú ma?
Are they playing the basketball ?

❸ 他們是不是又在滑手機？
Tāmen shìbúshì yòu zài huá shǒujī?
Are they playing with their phones again?

Usage

Only action verbs can be used with the 在 structure. State verbs cannot go with 在zài. It is not correct to say *手機在貴 *shǒujī zài guì. *Phones are being expensive.

在, zài, as Verb Complement, Resultant Location (4)

Function

The V＋在 pattern specifies the location of a noun resulting from an action.

❶ 那張椅子，請你放在樓下。
Nà zhāng yǐzi, qǐng nǐ fàng zài lóuxià.
Please put that chair downstairs.

❷ 這些複雜的漢字，我要寫在本子上。
Zhèxiē fùzá de Hànzì, wǒ yào xiě zài běnzi shàng.
I want to write these difficult Chinese characters in the notebook.

❸ 履歷表先留在我這裡。有適合的工作再告訴你。
Lǚlì biǎo xiān liú zài wǒ zhèlǐ. Yǒu shìhé de gōngzuò zài gàosù nǐ.
Leave your resume here with me, I will notify you of any suitable positions.

Structures

Negation :

Negation proceeds primary verbs, not 在, whether 不/別, 沒有 or 不是.

❶ 書別放在椅子上。請拿到房間去。
Shū bié fàng zài yǐzi shàng. Qǐng ná dào fángjiān qù.
Don't put the book on the chair, please take it into the room.

❷ 我沒留甜點在桌子上。我把甜點吃了。
Wǒ méi liú tiándiǎn zài zhuōzi shàng. Wǒ bǎ tiándiǎn chī le.
I didn't leave the dessert on the table. I ate it.

❸ 他的錢沒存在銀行裡。他太太很不高興。
Tā de qián méi cún zài yínháng lǐ. Tā tàitai hěn bù gāoxìng.
His wife was very upset that his money was not deposited in the bank.

❹ 錢不是放在銀行裡，匯到日本了。
Qián búshì fàng zài yínháng lǐ, huì dào Rìběn le.
He didn't put the money in the bank. He had it wired to Japan.

Questions :

❶ 電視，你打算放在哪裡？
Diànshì, nǐ dǎsuàn fàng zài nǎlǐ?
Where do you plan to put the TV?

❷ 這些家具，你是不是要留在這裡，不搬到新家？
Zhèxiē jiājù, nǐ shìbúshì yào liú zài zhèlǐ, bù bān dào xīnjiā?
Are you going to leave the furniture here instead of taking it to your new home?

❸ 我給你的資料，你存在電腦裡了沒有？
Wǒ gěi nǐ de zīliào, nǐ cún zài diànnǎo lǐ le méi yǒu?
Have you saved the information I gave you in the computer?

在⋯方面, (zài...fāngmiàn), with respect to; regarding (See 方面 fāngmiàn)

在⋯下, (zài...xià), under the..., due to the...

Function

The pattern 在⋯下 presents the circumstances, the pre-conditions of a given fact.

❶ 在學校的教育下，孩子學會了禮貌。
Zài xuéxiào de jiàoyù xià, háizi xuéhuìle lǐmào.
Under the school's education system, the pupils learned to be courteous.

❷ 在冰冷的氣候下，所有的動物都躲起來了。
Zài bīnglěng de qìhòu xià, suǒyǒu de dòngwù dōu duǒqǐlái le.
In a cold climate all sorts of animals hide during winter.

❸ 在高房價的情形下，年輕人都買不起房子。
Zài gāo fángjià de qíngxíng xià, niánqīng rén dōu mǎibùqǐ fángzi.
With such high property prices, young people cannot afford to buy.

❹ 在母親辛苦的照顧下，他的身體越來越健康了。
Zài mǔqīn xīnkǔ de zhàogù xià, tā de shēntǐ yuèláiyuè jiànkāng le.
Under mom's supervision, he is regaining his health.

Usage

Nouns that appear after 在 in this pattern are almost always abstract, e.g.,

❶ 在老師的鼓勵下，他的成績越來越進步了。
Zài lǎoshī de gǔlì xià, tā de chéngjī yuèláiyuè jìnbù le.
With the teacher's encouragement, his grades have continued to improve.

❷ 在少子化的情況下，補習班、幼稚園都減班了。
Zài shǎozǐhuà de qíngkuàng xià, bǔxíbān, yòuzhìyuán dōu jiǎn bān le.
(Faced with / Due to) With the low birth rate, cram schools and kindergartens have reduced the number of classes they offer.

❸ 在看不到遠景的情形下，年輕人都不想生孩子。
Zài kànbúdào yuǎnjǐng de qíngxíng xià, niánqīng rén dōu bù xiǎng shēng háizi.
Young people don't want to have children, because they don't know what the future holds.

再 A 也 B, (zài A yě B), no matter how A, still B

Function

This pattern indicates that a situation still holds true (after 也) regardless of circumstances (after 再).

❶ 學中文壓力再大，我也要繼續學。
Xué Zhōngwén yālì zài dà, wǒ yě yào jìxù xué.
No matter how much stress I get from studying Chinese, I'm going to keep studying.

❷ 你再生氣也不能罵人。
Nǐ zài shēngqì yě bù néng mà rén.
No matter how mad you get, you can't ream other people out.

❸ 豬腳麵線再好吃也不能天天吃。
Zhūjiǎo miànxiàn zài hǎochī yě bù néng tiāntiān chī.
It doesn't matter how delicious pork knuckle rice threads are. You can't eat the dish every day.

❹ 工作再穩定也可能發生變化。
Gōngzuò zài wěndìng yě kěnéng fāshēng biànhuà.
No matter how stable a job is, changes can still happen.

❺ 考試再簡單，也有人考不好。
Kǎoshì zài jiǎndān, yě yǒu rén kǎobùhǎo.
Regardless of how easy a test is, there's always someone who does poorly.

Usage

This pattern is similar to 不管bùguǎn A 都dōu B in usage. However, the 不管 pattern comes with 都 and suggests that the B situation always happens regardless of what circumstance A is. On the other hand, the 再 pattern comes with 也 and usually the A in this pattern refers to the most extreme circumstance. For example,

❶ 自己做的菜不管多麼難吃，都得吃光。
Zìjǐ zuò de cài bùguǎn duōme nánchī, dōu děi chīguāng.

❷ 自己做的菜，再難吃也得吃光。
Zìjǐ zuò de cài, zài nánchī yě děi chīguāng.
No matter how unpalatable the food you make is, you have to eat it all up.

Here, ❶ is more factual and non-emotional, while ❷ is an exaggeration.

再不 A 就 B 了, (zài bù A jiù B le),urgent conditional, if A doesn't happen now, B is sure to follow

Function

This pattern presents a condition first, and if the condition is not met, an undesirable consequence follows. 就 and 了 can be omitted in some contexts.

❶ 已經四個月沒下雨了。再不下雨，我們就沒水喝了。
Yǐjīng sì ge yuè méi xiàyǔ le. Zài bú xiàyǔ, wǒmen jiù méi shuǐ hē le.
It hasn't rained in four months. If it doesn't rain soon, we won't have any water to drink.

❷ 天氣這麼潮濕，再不買除濕機，衣服就要發霉了。
Tiānqì zhème cháoshī, zài bù mǎi chúshījī, yīfú jiù yào fāméi le.
It's so humid. If we don't buy a dehumidifier now, our clothes are going to mildew.

❸ 五月天演唱會很熱門。今天再不訂票，就訂不到了。
Wǔyuètiān yǎnchànghuì hěn rèmén. Jīntiān zài bú dìng piào, jiù dìngbúdào le.
May Day concerts are always a popular event. If you don't book tickets today, there won't be any left.

❹ 上次考試我只有60分。再不用功，恐怕會被當。
Shàng cì kǎoshì wǒ zhǐyǒu liùshí fēn. Zài bú yònggōng, kǒngpà huì bèi dàng.
On the last test, I only got 60 points. If I don't start studying hard, I'm afraid I'll be flunked.

❺ 發生什麼事了？你快説。你再不説清楚，我就要生氣了。
Fāshēng shénme shì le? Nǐ kuài shuō. Nǐ zài bù shuō qīngchǔ, wǒ jiù yào shēngqì le.
What happened? Tell me right now. If you don't explain yourself, I'm going to be mad.

Usage

It is common to have such adverbs as 就, 會, 要 to be used in the 2nd sentence, and it's also common to precede this pattern with conjunctions such as 如果rúguǒ or 要是yàoshì, e.g.,

❶ 他已經發燒好幾天了。要是再不去看醫生、吃藥，恐怕會越來越嚴重。
Tā yǐjīng fāshāo hǎojǐ tiān le. Yàoshi zài bú qù kàn yīshēng, chī yào, kǒngpà huì yuèláiyuè yánzhòng.
He's had a fever for quite a few days. If he doesn't see a doctor or take medicine soon, I'm afraid it's going to get increasingly serious.

❷ 知道這些傳統風俗的人已經越來越少了。要是我們再不重視，恐怕以後就沒有人能懂了。
Zhīdào zhèxiē chuántǒng fēngsú de rén yǐjīng yuèláiyuè shǎo le. Yàoshi wǒmen zài bú zhòngshì, kǒngpà yǐhòu jiù méi yǒu rén néng dǒng le.
Fewer and fewer people know these traditional customs. If we don't attach greater importance to them now, I'm afraid nobody will understand them.

再加上, zài jiāshàng, furthermore

Function

The phrase 再加上 adds a further item to a list just mentioned. The sentence can be an approval or a criticism, on the part of the speaker.

❶ 那件衣服的款式比較舊，顏色也太淺，再加上穿起來不舒服，所以雖然打五折，我也沒買。
Nà jiàn yīfú de kuǎnshì bǐjiào jiù, yánsè yě tài qiǎn, zài jiāshàng chuānqǐlái bù shūfú, suǒyǐ suīrán dǎ wǔ zhé, wǒ yě méi mǎi.
The style of that garment was relatively old and the color too light. In addition, it was uncomfortable, so even though it was half off, I didn't buy it.

❷ 陽明山上有很多很好的餐廳，再加上夜景很美，他決定帶女朋友上陽明山吃晚飯。

Yángmíng shān shàng yǒu hěn duō hěn hǎo de cāntīng, zài jiāshàng yèjǐng hěn měi, tā juédìng dài nǚpéngyǒu shàng Yángmíng shān chī wǎnfàn.

Yangming Mountain has a lot of good restaurants. What's more, the view at night is beautiful, so he decided to take his girlfriend there for dinner.

❸ 當老師生活穩定，再加上薪水比一般工作高，難怪他每天熬夜念書，準備考試。

Dāng lǎoshī shēnghuó wěndìng, zài jiāshàng xīnshuǐ bǐ yìbān gōngzuò gāo, nánguài tā měi tiān áoyè niànshū, zhǔnbèi kǎoshì.

A teacher's life is stable. In addition, the pay is higher than most jobs. No wonder he's staying up nights studying in preparation for the test.

❹ 在鄉下孩子可以接近土地，在田裡跑跑跳跳，再加上可以吃到最新鮮的蔬菜，所以父母週末都喜歡帶孩子到鄉下去玩。

Zài xiāngxià háizi kěyǐ jiējìn tǔdì, zài tián lǐ pǎopǎo tiàotiào, zài jiāshàng kěyǐ chīdào zuì xīnxiān de shūcài, suǒyǐ fùmǔ zhōumò dōu xǐhuān dài háizi dào xiāngxià qù wán.

In the country, kids can be close to the land and they can run and jump about in the fields. Furthermore, the vegetables there are the freshest you can get. That's why parents like to take their children to the countryside on weekends.

❺ 大家都很信任他，再加上他的麵包都是用最好的食材做的，所以很多人住得再遠也要去他的店買麵包。

Dàjiā dōu hěn xìnrèn tā, zài jiāshàng tā de miànbāo dōu shì yòng zuì hǎo de shícái zuò de, suǒyǐ hěn duō rén zhù de zài yuǎn yě yào qù tā de diàn mǎi miànbāo.

Everybody trusts him. What's more, he uses the best ingredients in his bread, so a lot of people, no matter how far away they live, go to his shop to buy bread.

再說, zàishuō, (Conj), besides, moreover

Function

The conjunction (S₂) 再說 introduces a new sentence that provides further clarification or elaboration about what was said in the preceding sentences.

❶ 還是刷卡吧。我沒帶那麼多現金。再說，刷卡還可以再打九五折。

Háishì shuākǎ ba. Wǒ méi dài nàme duō xiànjīn. Zàishuō, shuākǎ hái kěyǐ zài dǎ jiǔwǔ zhé.

I'm just going to use my credit card. I didn't bring that much cash. What's more, I can get another 5% off by swiping my credit card.

❷ 電信公司的中文合約那麼長。再說，他是外國人。怎麼可能看得懂？

Diànxìn gōngsī de Zhōngwén héyuē nàme cháng. Zàishuō, tā shì wàiguó rén. Zěnme kěnéng kàndedǒng?

The phone company's Chinese contract is so long. In addition, he is a foreigner. How is he possibly going to understand?

❸ 我女朋友一定會生我的氣的。這是我掉的第三支手機了。再說，手機是她送給我的生日禮物。

Wǒ nǚpéngyǒu yídìng huì shēng wǒ de qì de. Zhè shì wǒ diào de dìsān zhī shǒujīle. Zàishuō, shǒujī shì tā sòng gěi wǒ de shēngrì lǐwù.

My girlfriend is bound to be angry with me. This is the third cell phone I've lost. Besides, this was the cell phone she gave me for my birthday.

❹ 我準備的材料夠包一百多個餃子。再說，我還做了好幾道菜。大家一定都能吃飽。

Wǒ zhǔnbèi de cáiliào gòu bāo yìbǎi duō ge jiǎozi. Zàishuō, wǒ hái zuòle hǎojǐ dào cài. Dàjiā yídìng dōu néng chībǎo.

I prepared enough ingredients to make over 100 dumplings. In addition, I made several other dishes. Everybody is bound to eat their fill.

❺ 你應該趁學校放假到南部海邊看看。再說，你還沒玩過水上摩托車。值得去試一試。

Nǐ yīnggāi chèn xuéxiào fàngjià dào nánbù hǎibiān kànkàn. Zàishuō, nǐ hái méi wánguò shuǐshàng mótuōchē. Zhídé qù shì yí shì.

You should take advantage of the school break to go to the seaside down south and check it out. What's more, you've never ridden a jet ski. It's worth a try.

Usage

(1) Both 而且 érqiě and 再說 arc used to connect the current sentence with preceding sentences, both translatable as 'moreover'. 而且 suggests that what is said in the current sentence and the preceding sentence are on equal footing, while 再說 highlights that what is said in the current sentence is a further addition or elaboration on top of what was said in the preceding sentences. For example, the 而且 in 他的房間要有家具，而且光線要好。 Tā de fángjiān yào yǒu jiājù, érqiě guāngxiàn yào hǎo. 'He wants a room with furniture and good lighting.' cannot be replaced by 再說.

(2) 而且 can connect two words or two sentences. 再說 can connect only sentences. For example, the 而且 in 他一定能找到便宜而且合適的房子。 Tā yídìng néng zhǎodào piányí érqiě héshì de fángzi. 'He's bound to be able to find an inexpensive and suitable house.' in which 而且 cannot be replaced by 再說.

335

早就⋯了, (zǎo jiù...le), long since...

Function   This construction presents an exaggerated reference to the time in the past that an instance took place.

❶ 我只見過小陳幾次面，早就對他沒印象了。

Wǒ zhǐ jiànguò Xiǎo Chén jǐ cì miàn, zǎo jiù duì tā méi yìnxiàng le.

I only met Xiao Chen a few times. I have long since forgotten everything about him.

❷ 五月天演唱會的票，我早就買了，你不必擔心。

Wǔyuètiān yǎnchànghuì de piào, wǒ zǎo jiù mǎi le, nǐ búbì dānxīn.

I bought May Day concert tickets ages ago. No need to worry.

❸ 那條路上早就沒有日本人留下來的木造房子了，我們還要去嗎？

Nà tiáo lù shàng zǎo jiù méi yǒu Rìběn rén liúxiàlái de mùzào fángzi le, wǒmen hái yào qù ma?

It's been forever since there were any Japanese style wooden houses left on that street. Are we still going to go?

❹ 你的平板電腦我早就修理好了，你怎麼不記得呢？

Nǐ de píngbǎn diànnǎo wǒ zǎo jiù xiūlǐ hǎo le, nǐ zěnme bú jìde ne?

I fixed your tablet computer a long time ago. How is it you don't remember?

❺ 媽媽煮的水餃，早就被弟弟吃光了。你吃別的吧！

Māma zhǔ de shuǐjiǎo, zǎo jiù bèi dìdi chīguāng le. Nǐ chī biéde ba!

Little brother ate all the dumplings Mom made a long time ago. Go ahead and eat something else.

怎麼, zěnme, (Adv), asking how, asking about a manner of doing things, how, in what way

Function   怎麼, 'how?', is a question adverb, used to ask how something is done.

❶ 你們怎麼去？

Nǐmen zěnme qù?

How do you go there?

❷ 這個菜怎麼做？

Zhè ge cài zěnme zuò?

How do you make this dish?

❸ 這個歌怎麼唱？

Zhè ge gē zěnme chàng?

How do you sing this song?

❹ 這支新手機怎麼上網？

Zhè zhī xīn shǒujī zěnme shàngwǎng?

How do I access the internet using this new cellphone?

Usage　怎麼 'How?' is quite different from 怎麼樣 'How is it? What do you think?' 怎麼 is an adverb, whereas 怎麼樣 is a state verb. Compare 這個菜怎麼做？Zhè ge cài zěnme zuò? 'How is this dish made?' with 這個菜怎麼樣？Zhè ge cài zěnmeyàng? 'How is this dish? /What do you think of this dish?'

怎麼這麼, zěnme zhème, why so...?

Function　These two adverbs, 怎麼 and 這麼, are combined in this instance to convey the speaker's amazement. Only state verbs follow them.

❶ A：聽説小王每天都去夜市吃雞排。
　　 Tīngshuō Xiǎo Wáng měi tiān dōu qù yèshì chī jīpái.
　　 I hear that Xiao Wang goes to the night market for a chicken cutlet every single day.

　 B：他怎麼這麼愛吃雞排？！
　　 Tā zěnme zhème ài chī jīpái?!
　　 How can he love chicken that much!?

❷ A：這件羊毛外套一件賣三萬塊錢。
　　 Zhè jiàn yángmáo wàitào yí jiàn mài sānwàn kuài qián.
　　 This wool coat cost 30,000 dollars.

　 B：怎麼這麼貴？！
　　 Zěnme zhème guì?!
　　 Wow, why so expensive!?

❸ A：這位女明星得了今年的最佳女主角獎。
　　 Zhè wèi nǚmíngxīng déle jīnnián de zuìjiā nǚzhǔjiǎo jiǎng.
　　 This movie star won the award for best female actress.

　 B：她還這麼年輕。演技怎麼這麼好！
　　 Tā hái zhème niánqīng. Yǎnjì zěnme zhème hǎo!
　　 How can she be so talented at such a young age!?

❹ A：在荷蘭就算下雪，孩子們也會到戶外活動。
　　 Zài Hélán jiùsuàn xiàxuě, háizimen yě huì dào hùwài huódòng.
　　 In Holland the kids go out to play even if it's snowing.

　 B：怎麼這麼不怕冷？！
　　 Zěnme zhème bú pà lěng?!
　　 Wow, they really must not mind the cold!

❺ A：下訂單以後24小時就能收到訂購的東西。
　　 Xià dìngdān yǐhòu 24 xiǎoshí jiù néng shōudào dìnggòu de dōngxi.
　　 You will receive your order within 24 hours of placing it.

　 B：怎麼這麼快？！
　　 Zěnme zhème kuài?!
　　 How can it be so fast!?

占, zhàn, (Vst), to constitute

Function　The state verb 占 defines percentage or ranking.

❶ 這次考試的成績，口試、筆試各占一半。
Zhè cì kǎoshì de chéngjī, kǒushì, bǐshì gè zhàn yíbàn.
For this test, the oral and written tests will each account for one half of the grade.

❷ 電子產品的產值占台灣出口商品第一位。
Diànzǐ chǎnpǐn de chǎnzhí zhàn Táiwān chūkǒu shāngpǐn dìyī wèi.
Electronics hold top position when it comes to production value of Taiwan's exports.

❸ 我並不是整天都在公司裡上班；我在公司裡的時間只占工作時間的一小部分。
Wǒ bìng búshì zhěng tiān dōu zài gōngsī lǐ shàngbān; wǒ zài gōngsī lǐ de shíjiān zhǐ zhàn gōngzuò shíjiān de yì xiǎo bùfèn.
I don't work all day at the office. My time in the office only accounts for a small percentage of my work day.

❹ 我剛剛給你的資料還不完全；那些只占整份報告的一部分。
Wǒ gānggāng gěi nǐ de zīliào hái bù wánquán; nàxiē zhǐ zhàn zhěng fèn bàogào de yí bùfèn.
I didn't give you all of the information just now. That's just a small part of the entire report.

❺ 成本包括很多部分。實際上材料成本只占不到一半。
Chéngběn bāokuò hěn duō bùfèn. Shíjì shàng cáiliào chéngběn zhǐ zhàn búdào yíbàn.
Many things contribute to operating costs. (In reality) materials don't even account for half.

照, zhào, (Adv), deliberately, persist in

Function　The adverb 照 refers to the fact that the subject engages in some activity with total disregard for the given circumstances.

❶ 在這個展覽館裡不可以拍照，但這些觀光客還照拍！
Zài zhè ge zhǎnlǎn guǎn lǐ bù kěyǐ pāizhào, dàn zhèxiē guānguāngkè hái zhào pāi!
No pictures are allowed in this exhibition hall, but these tourists are taking pictures anyway. They are completely disregarding the rule.

❷ 老師說：先注意聽，不要寫，但是那些學生不聽，照寫。
Lǎoshī shuō: Xiān zhùyì tīng, bú yào xiě, dànshì nàxiē xuéshēng bù tīng, zhào xiě.
The teacher said: Listen closely before you start writing. The students, however, started writing immediately anyway.

❸ 奇怪，我不是已經關機了嗎？怎麼手機還是照響？

Qíguài, wǒ búshì yǐjīng guānjī le ma? Zěnme shǒujī háishì zhào xiǎng?

That's weird. I thought I turned my cell phone off, and how come it's still ringing?

❹ 我已經跟樓上鄰居抱怨了很多次，請他的孩子晚上10點以後別跳。但他的孩子不聽，照跳。

Wǒ yǐjīng gēn lóushàng línjū bàoyuànle hěn duō cì, qǐng tā de háizi wǎnshàng 10 diǎn yǐhòu bié tiào. Dàn tā de háizi bù tīng, zhào tiào.

I've already complained to the upstairs neighbours numerous times asking them to keep their kid quiet after 10 o'clock, but the kid just keeps jumping around.

❺ 最近食品安全出了好幾次問題，那些東西你怎麼還照吃？

Zuìjìn shípǐn ānquán chūle hǎojǐ cì wèntí, nàxiē dōngxi nǐ zěnme hái zhào chī?

With all the food safety issues recently, how can you still eat that?

Usage

(1) 照 sentences always refer to past instances.

(2) Verbs that follow 照 are most often monosyllabic, e.g., 照看zhào kàn 'to continue to look anyway (even though he was told not to)', 照寫zhào xiě 'to continue to write anyway', 照拍zhào pāi 'to continue to take photos anyway', 照拿zhào ná 'to continue to take something anyway', and 照摸zhào mō 'to continue to touch anyway', to name a few.

(3) 亂 V vs. 照 V

A monosyllabic verb or verb phrase can follow 亂, e.g., 亂寫luàn xiě 'write chicken scratch', 亂做luàn zuò 'do haphazardly', 亂花錢luàn huā qián 'blow money', 亂交朋友luàn jiāo péngyǒu 'make friends indiscriminately'. However, only a monosyllabic verb can follow 照, with the object left out, e.g.,

叫他別彈吉他了，但他還照彈。

Jiào tā bié tán jítā le, dàn tā hái zhào tán.

I told him not to play the guitar, but he continued to do so.

這麼説, zhème shuō, that being the case, in that case

Function The phrase 這麼説 presents a statement as a natural consequence of the previous statement.

❶ A：現在上網購物越來越普遍，這幾年大家的購物習慣真的改變了很多。

Xiànzài shàngwǎng gòuwù yuèláiyuè pǔbiàn, zhè jǐ nián dàjiā de gòuwù xíguàn zhēn de gǎibiànle hěn duō.

It is becoming increasingly common to shop online. In recent years, everyone's shopping habits have really changed a lot.

339

B：這麼說，將來我就不能開服裝店了，是不是？

Zhème shuō, jiānglái wǒ jiù bù néng kāi fúzhuāng diàn le, shìbúshì?

That being the case, I won't be able to open a clothing store in the future, right?

❷ A：醫生看了片子，說小王是骨折。

Yīshēng kànle piànzi, shuō Xiǎo Wáng shì gǔzhé.

After looking at the X-ray, the doctor told Xiao Wang that he had a broken bone.

B：這麼說，他得住院開刀嘍。

Zhème shuō, tā děi zhùyuàn kāidāo lou.

In that case, he'll have to be hospitalized and undergo surgery.

❸ A：我叔叔打算用穩定的價格跟當地小農購買芒果，做成芒果蛋糕來賣。

Wǒ shúshu dǎsuàn yòng wěndìng de jiàgé gēn dāngdì xiǎonóng gòumǎi mángguǒ, zuòchéng mángguǒ dàngāo lái mài.

My uncle plans to buy mangoes at stable prices from small farmers in the area, and use them to make mango cakes which he will then sell.

B：這麼說，那些小農就不需要擔心芒果賣不出去了。

Zhème shuō, nàxiē xiǎonóng jiù bù xūyào dānxīn mángguǒ mài bù chūqù le.

That being the case, those small farmers won't have to worry that they can't sell their mangoes.

❹ A：小陳從九月起，要到美國念 EMBA 研究所。

Xiǎo Chén cóng jiǔyuè qǐ, yào dào Měiguó niàn EMBA yánjiūsuǒ.

Xiao Chen is going to the US where he'll study in an EMBA graduate school program starting in September.

B：這麼說，他將來想成為企業家嘍。

Zhème shuō, tā jiānglái xiǎng chéngwéi qìyèjiā lou.

That being the case, I assume he wants to become an entrepreneur.

❺ A：我父母說大學念什麼系不重要，最重要的是要有興趣。

Wǒ fùmǔ shuō dàxué niàn shénme xì bú zhòngyào, zuì zhòngyào de shì yào yǒu xìngqù.

My parents say that it doesn't matter what major you study in. What matters most is that you find it interesting.

B：這麼說，你念服裝設計系，你父母應該不會反對。

Zhème shuō, nǐ niàn fúzhuāng shèjì xì, nǐ fùmǔ yīnggāi bú huì fǎnduì.

In that case, your parents wouldn't oppose you studying fashion design.

這下子, zhèxiàzi, that being the case, as a consequence

Function

The phrase 這下子 is used in S₂ and states that S₂ follows naturally from S₁.

① 那家便利商店倒閉了，這下子我得找新的地方買咖啡了。
Nà jiā biànlì shāngdiàn dǎobì le, zhèxiàzi wǒ děi zhǎo xīn de dìfāng mǎi kāfēi le.
That convenience store shut down. Now I have to find a new place to get coffee from.

② 聽說公司決定下個月開始裁員，這下子我們都可能失業。
Tīngshuō gōngsī juédìng xià ge yuè kāishǐ cáiyuán, zhèxiàzi wǒmen dōu kěnéng shīyè.
I hear that the company will be cutting staff next month, and we might all be out of a job!

③ 哇！沒想到受到問題牛肉的影響，來買雞排的人越來越多，這下子我們可發財了。
Wa! Méi xiǎngdào shòudào wèntí niúròu de yǐngxiǎng, lái mǎi jīpái de rén yuèláiyuè duō, zhèxiàzi wǒmen kě fācái le.
Wow, due to the influence of trouble beef, more and more people are lining up to buy chicken cutlets, and at this rate we're going to make a fortune in no time!

Usage

This is a highly colloquial phrase, pronounced in low intonation, used in conversations only.

這樣一來, zhèyàng yìlái, that being the case, that way

Function

The speaker uses this pattern to present a consequence that could result from the previous statement.

① A：聽說小陳這個學期有好幾門課被當。
Tīngshuō Xiǎo Chén zhè ge xuéqí yǒu hǎojǐ mén kè bèi dàng.
I heard that Xiao Chen flunked a number of his classes this semester.

　　B：這樣一來，他明年恐怕沒辦法畢業了。
Zhèyàng yìlái, tā míngnián kǒngpà méi bànfǎ bìyè le.
That being the case, there's probably no way he'll be able to graduate next year.

② A：我先生下星期要帶孩子去美國旅行一個月。
Wǒ xiānshēng xià xīngqí yào dài háizi qù Měiguó lǚxíng yí ge yuè.
Next week, my husband is taking the kids to the US for a one-month trip.

　　B：真的啊。這樣一來，妳就不必天天做飯了。
Zhēn de a. Zhèyàng yìlái, nǐ jiù búbì tiāntiān zuòfàn le.
Really? So I guess you don't have to cook every day.

❸ A：電視新聞說這個週末有颱風要來。

Diànshì xīnwén shuō zhè ge zhōumò yǒu táifēng yào lái.

The news on TV said that a typhoon is coming this weekend.

B：這樣一來，我們就不能去海邊玩了。

Zhèyàng yìlái, wǒmen jiù bù néng qù hǎibiān wán le.

In that case, we can't go to the seaside.

❹ A：媽媽建議讓弟弟下課以後去學游泳、書法跟網球。

Māma jiànyì ràng dìdi xiàkè yǐhòu qù xué yóuyǒng, shūfǎ gēn wǎngqiú.

Mom suggested having my kid brother go to swimming, calligraphy, and tennis classes after school.

B：太好了。這樣一來，他就不會整天在家看電視、打電玩了。

Tài hǎo le. Zhèyàng yìlái, tā jiù bú huì zhěng tiān zài jiā kàn diànshì, dǎ diànwán le.

Great. That way, he won't be in the house all day watching TV and playing video games.

❺ A：最近三個星期，我住的城市幾乎天天下雨。而且新聞還說，下個禮拜雨還不會停。

Zuìjìn sān ge xīngqí, wǒ zhù de chéngshì jīhū tiāntiān xiàyǔ. Érqiě xīnwén hái shuō, xià ge lǐbài yǔ hái bú huì tíng.

Over the past three weeks it has rained almost every day in the city I live in. And the news says that it's not going to stop next week either.

B：這樣一來，你的衣服、鞋子不是就都發霉了嗎？

Zhèyàng yìlái, nǐ de yīfú, xiézi búshì jiù dōu fāméi le ma?

If that's the case, aren't your clothes and shoes going to mildew?

著, zhe, (Ptc), ongoing, continuative action, in the state of V＋ing (1)

Function　　When the particle 著 is added to an action verb, it means the activity is ongoing, is being engaged, e.g.,

❶ 他在門口等著你，你快去吧。

Tā zài ménkǒu děngzhe nǐ, nǐ kuài qù ba.

He's waiting for you at the door. Please hurry!

❷ 小李拿著一杯冰咖啡。

Xiǎo Lǐ názhe yì bēi bīng kāfēi.

Xiao Li is holding a glass of iced coffee in his hand.

❸ 他看著我，什麼也沒說。

Tā kànzhe wǒ, shénme yě méi shuō.

He just stared at me, without uttering a word.

Structures　　The verb taking 著 is usually monosyllabic, and negation precedes the verb, e.g.,

Negation :

❶ 你不要一直坐著。我們去運動吧！
Nǐ bú yào yìzhí zuòzhe. Wǒmen qù yùndòng ba!
Don't just sit around all day. Let's get out and do some exercise!

❷ 你別帶著咖啡到圖書館去。裡面不能喝東西。
Nǐ bié dàizhe kāfēi dào túshūguǎn qù. Lǐmiàn bù néng hē dōngxi.
Don't bring your coffee into the library. You are not allowed to drink it there.

❸ 那裡的小巷子這麼多。要是我沒帶著地圖，一定會迷路。
Nàlǐ de xiǎo xiàngzi zhème duō. Yàoshi wǒ méi dàizhe dìtú, yídìng huì mílù.
There are so many small alleys. If I hadn't brought a map with me, I would have gotten lost.

Questions :

❶ 小陳是不是載著美美到圖書館去了？
Xiǎo Chén shìbúshì zàizhe Měiměi dào túshūguǎn qù le?
Did Xiao Chen take Meimei with him to the library?

❷ 他生病了。是不是有人陪著他？
Tā shēngbìng le. Shìbúshì yǒu rén péizhe tā?
He's sick. Is there somebody staying with him?

❸ 他是不是一直在學校門口等著他媽媽？
Tā shìbúshì yìzhí zài xuéxiào ménkǒu děngzhe tā māma?
Has he been waiting for his mother outside the school entrance this whole time?

| Usage |

著zhe vs. 在zài
Though both 著 and 在 can be interpreted in terms of V＋ing. 著 is static while 在 is dynamic. 'standing' is static. 'Eating' is dynamic. 'Putting on 在穿zài chuān' is dynamic, and 'wearing 穿著chuānzhe' is static. (See 在(3)).

著, zhe, (Ptc), used in Manner of an Action　(2)

| Function |

The pattern V-著 before the main verb, usually action, indicates the manner in which an action is carried out. It can be best understood as 'to do B while doing A'.

❶ 他笑著跟客人說話。
Tā xiàozhe gēn kèrén shuōhuà.
He is speaking to the guests with a smile on his face.

❷ 站著吃飯不好吧！
Zhànzhe chīfàn bù hǎo ba!
It's not good to stand while you eat.

❸ 那裡的路很複雜，你還是帶著地圖去吧！
Nàlǐ de lù hěn fùzá, nǐ háishì dàizhe dìtú qù ba!
The roads there are complex. You should probably bring a map.

Structures ▶ All the verbs before 著 are usually action verbs, whether transitive or intransitive.

Negation :

❶ 李老師站著上課。他沒坐著上課。
Lǐ lǎoshī zhànzhe shàngkè. Tā méi zuòzhe shàngkè.
Teacher Li stands when he teaches; he was not sitting.

❷ 爸爸説別看著電視吃飯。
Bàba shuō bié kànzhe diànshì chīfàn.
Dad says you shouldn't watch TV while you eat.

❸ 你站了多久了？怎麼不坐著等他？
Nǐ zhànle duōjiǔ le? Zěnme bú zuòzhe děng tā?
How long have you been standing? How come you don't sit while you wait for him.

Questions :

❶ 小明是不是聽著音樂騎機車？
Xiǎomíng shìbúshì tīngzhe yīnyuè qí jīchē?
Is Xiaoming listening to music while riding his motorcycle?

❷ 他是不是帶著兩個大背包去旅行？
Tā shìbúshì dàizhe liǎng ge dà bēibāo qù lǚxíng?
Is he taking two big backpacks with him to travel?

❸ 他是不是拿著雨傘下樓了？
Tā shìbúshì názhe yǔsǎn xià lóu le?
Was he holding an umbrella when he went downstairs?

Usage

(1) This construction is different from the '一邊yìbiān A，一邊yìbiān B' construction which gives two simultaneous actions. Compare the following examples. 一邊 A，一邊 B is used much more frequently, especially in Taiwan.

❶ a. 我常看著電視吃飯。
Wǒ cháng kànzhe diànshì chīfàn.
I often watch TV while eating.

b. 我常一邊看電視，一邊吃飯。
Wǒ cháng yìbiān kàn diànshì, yìbiān chīfàn.
I often watch TV and eat at the same time.

❷ a. 你不要聽著音樂做功課。
Nǐ bú yào tīngzhe yīnyuè zuò gōngkè.
Don't listen to music while doing your homework.

b. 你不要一邊聽音樂，一邊做功課。

Nǐ bú yào yìbiān tīng yīnyuè, yìbiān zuò gōngkè.

Don't listen to music and do your homework at the same time.

Not every verb can be used in both constructions. For example:

❸ **a.** 麵店沒有座位了，我們得站著吃麵。

Miàn diàn méi yǒu zuòwèi le, wǒmen děi zhànzhe chī miàn.

There are no seats available at the noodle stand. We have to stand while we eat.

b. *麵店沒有座位了，我們得一邊站，一邊吃麵。

*Miàn diàn méi yǒu zuòwèi le, wǒmen dé yìbiān zhàn, yìbiān chī miàn.

(2) Usually the V in the V-著 pattern is an action verb. However, some transitory state verbs can fall in this slot too, e.g., máng 'busy' (忙著mángzhe), and jí 'hurry' (急著jízhe), as shown below. Very few state verbs are transitory or temporary in nature.

❶ 他忙著找工作。

Tā mángzhe zhǎo gōngzuò.

He is busy looking for work.

❷ 陳小姐急著準備找工作的履歷表。

Chén xiǎojiě jízhe zhǔnbèi zhǎo gōngzuò de lǚlì biǎo.

Miss Chen is anxious to prepare her resume to look for work.

❸ 媽媽忙著給大家做飯。

Māma mángzhe gěi dàjiā zuòfàn.

Mom is busy cooking for everyone.

著, zhe, (Ptc), repeated, as in V 著 V 著，就…了, (V zhe V zhe, jiù...le), while doing A, B happens (3)

Function　This pattern refers to the meaning 'just as A is going on, B happens'.

❶ 大家吃著吃著，新郎、新娘和他們的父母就來敬酒了。

Dàjiā chīzhe chīzhe, xīnláng, xīnniáng hé tāmen de fùmǔ jiù lái jìngjiǔ le.

Just as everybody was eating, the bride, the bridegroom, and their parents came over and offered a toast.

❷ 我們等著等著，喜宴就開始了。

Wǒmen děngzhe děngzhe, xǐyàn jiù kāishǐ le.

As we were waiting, the reception started.

❸ 我小時候每天看媽媽做飯，看著看著，就會了。

Wǒ xiǎo shíhòu měi tiān kàn māma zuòfàn, kànzhe kànzhe, jiù huì le.

When I was young, I watched my mother cook every day and by watching, I was able to do it.

Structures　If the verb is transitive, its object must not be palced after the verb. It must be moved to the front to become a topic or is omitted if its identity is clear from the context.

❶ 這個歌，我聽著聽著，就會唱了。

Zhè ge gē, wǒ tīngzhe tīngzhe, jiù huì chàng le.

By listening to the song, I could sing it.

❷ 電視在介紹日本的風景，她看著看著就想家了。

Diànshì zài jièshào Rìběn de fēngjǐng, tā kànzhe kànzhe jiù xiǎng jiā le.

While watching a program about the beauty of Japan on TV, she started to miss home.

❸ 我在捷運上看書，看著看著，就忘了換車了。

Wǒ zài jiéyùn shàng kànshū, kànzhe kànzhe, jiù wàngle huàn chē le.

I was reading on the MRT and got so lost in his book that he forgot to change trains.

V 著玩, V zhe wán, do something just for fun

Function　This pattern presents a casual undertaking of something, not for any serious purposes.

❶ 有的事說著玩就好，不要太認真。

Yǒu de shì shuōzhe wán jiù hǎo, bú yào tài rènzhēn.

Some things are best spoken of in jest, not to be taken seriously.

❷ 我上線聊天只是聊著玩的，不會約網友出來玩的。

Wǒ shàngxiàn liáotiān zhǐshì liáozhe wán de, bú huì yuē wǎngyǒu chūlái wán de.

I chat online just for fun, but I never make arrangments to meet.

❸ 叔叔說他這次出來選舉是認真的，不是選著玩的。

Shúshu shuō tā zhè cì chūlái xuǎnjǔ shì rènzhēn de, búshì xuǎnzhe wán de.

My uncle is not kidding around. He said this time he is really running for office.

❹ A：你家裡有很多台灣歷史的書，你對台灣歷史有興趣嗎?

Nǐ jiālǐ yǒu hěn duō Táiwān lìshǐ de shū, nǐ duì Táiwān lìshǐ yǒu xìngqù ma?

There are many books on Taiwan history in your house. Does Taiwan's history interest you?

B：也不是特別有興趣，就看著玩。

Yě búshì tèbié yǒu xìngqù, jiù kànzhe wán.

Not particularly. I'm just reading for the fun of it.

❺ A：你書法寫得那麼好，簡直可以去比賽了。

Nǐ shūfǎ xiě dé nàme hǎo, jiǎnzhí kěyǐ qù bǐsài le.

Your calligraphy is amazing. You should enter a contest.

B：我只是寫著玩的，沒辦法參加比賽。

Wǒ zhǐshì xiězhe wán de, méi bànfǎ cānjiā bǐsài.

I just do it for fun. I'm not competition material.

只不過…(而已), (zhǐ búguò...(éryǐ)), merely...; nothing more than...

Function

This pattern consists of three elements: the adverb 只, the adverb 不過, and the sentence particle 而已. They are near synonyms, meaning 'only, merely.' Thus, this pattern is an instance of 3-way reinforcement and means 'merely, just'. 而已 can be omitted.

❶ 有些人認為，吳寶春只不過國中畢業而已，怎麼有能力念企管研究所呢？

Yǒuxiē rén rènwéi, Wú Bǎochūn zhǐ búguò guózhōng bìyè éryǐ, zěnme yǒu nénglì niàn qìguǎn yánjiūsuǒ ne?

Wu Baochun only graduated from junior high school. Some people think, 'How is he capable of studying in an MBA program?'

❷ 他只不過上烹飪課的時候做過一次蘿蔔糕而已，就到處告訴別人他做得多美味。

Tā zhǐ búguò shàng pēngrèn kè de shíhòu zuòguò yí cì luóbogāo éryǐ, jiù dàochù gàosù biérén tā zuò de duō měiwèi.

He merely made some daikon cakes once in a cooking class. Now, he goes around telling people how well he cooks.

❸ 他只不過說說而已，你難道認為他真的會辭掉工作？

Tā zhǐ búguò shuōshuō éryǐ, nǐ nándào rènwéi tā zhēn de huì cídiào gōngzuò?

He's was just talking (he didn't mean it). Did you actually think he really wants to quit his job?

❹ 只不過下了幾天的雨，衣服就全都發霉了。

Zhǐ búguò xiàle jǐ tiān de yǔ, yīfú jiù quán dōu fāméi le.

It merely rained a few days and the clothes are all mildewed.

❺ 這個學期你只不過選了三門課而已，怎麼就忙得連參加社團活動的時間都沒有了？

Zhè ge xuéqí nǐ zhǐ búguò xuǎnle sān mén kè éryǐ, zěnme jiù máng de lián cānjiā shètuán huódòng de shíjiān dōu méi yǒu le?

You're only taking three classes this semester. How come you're so busy that you don't even have the time to take part in any school club activities?

Usage

A. Omission in multiple reinforcement is always possible in Chinese. In this pattern, the omission goes like this: ending with 而已 alone, 不過…而已, and finally 只不過…而已. The first two options are illustrated below.

(1) …而已

    a. 他隨便說說而已，哪裡是真的想養狗？

    Tā suíbiàn shuōshuō éryǐ, nǎlǐ shì zhēn de xiǎng yǎng gǒu?

    He was just talking. He doesn't actually want to have a dog.

    b. 一個晚上沒睡好而已，就沒有精神上課了。

    Yí ge wǎnshàng méi shuìhǎo éryǐ, jiù méi yǒu jīngshén shàngkè le.

    You only had one bad night of sleep and you have no energy to go to class.

(2) 不過…而已

    a. 不過18度而已，你怎麼就穿起羊毛外套來了？

    Búguò shíbā dù éryǐ, nǐ zěnme jiù chuānqǐ yángmáo wàitào lái le?

    It's only 18 degrees. How come you're wearing a wool coat?

    b. 三號候選人不過是形象好而已，從政經驗其實並不多。

    Sān hào hòuxuǎn rén búguò shì xíngxiàng hǎo éryǐ, cóngzhèng jīngyàn qíshí bìng bù duō.

    Candidate number three merely has a good image. He doesn't actually have much political experience.

B. 只不過 vs. 才

  (1) If a sentence contains a number in the object position, either 只不過 or 才 can be used.

    E.g.,

    a. 雖然是百貨公司週年慶，可是商品只不過打八折而已。

    Suīrán shì bǎihuò gōngsī zhōuniánqìng, kěshì shāngpǐn zhǐ búguò dǎ bā zhé éryǐ.

    It's the department store's anniversary, but products are only 20% off.

    b. 雖然是百貨公司週年慶，可是商品才打八折而已。

    Suīrán shì bǎihuò gōngsī zhōuniánqìng, kěshì shāngpǐn cái dǎ bā zhé éryǐ.

    It's the department store's anniversary, but products are only 20% off.

    There is, however, a difference in attitude on the part of the speaker. Although 只不過 also stresses that the amount mentioned is small, it is more factual, while 才 further indicates that the quantity falls short of expectation. E.g., in example (1)a. above, although the speaker also thinks 20% off isn't quite enough and is a little dissatisfied, the speaker's attitude in (1)b. that the discount falls short of common expectation is very clear.

  (2) Therefore, when you want to stress something has fallen short of common expectation, you can only really use 才. See examples a, b, c, and d below.

a. *你擺了一個早上的攤子，怎麼只不過賺了幾百塊錢？

*Nǐ bǎile yí ge zǎoshang de tānzi, zěnme zhǐ búguò zhuànle jǐbǎi kuài qián?

b. 你擺了一個早上的攤子，怎麼才賺了幾百塊錢？

Nǐ bǎile yí ge zǎoshang de tānzi, zěnme cái zhuànle jǐbǎi kuài qián?

You've had your stall set up all morning; how come you've only made a few hundred dollars?

Most people feel that when you have had a stall up for hours, you should have made much more than a few hundred NT dollars, therefore, you can only use 才. You can't use 只不過.

c. *念醫學系只不過三年就畢業了？怎麼可能？

*Niàn yīxué xì zhǐ búguò sān nián jiù bìyè le? Zěnme kěnéng?

d. 念醫學系才三年就畢業了？怎麼可能？

Niàn yīxué xì cái sān nián jiù bìyè le? Zěnme kěnéng?

(He) graduated from medical school in just three years? How is that possible?

C. If, however, 只不過 is followed by something other than an amount, then 只不過 cannot be substituted with 才. E.g.,

a. 我只不過開開玩笑而已，你怎麼就生氣了？

Wǒ zhǐ búguò kāikāi wánxiào éryǐ, nǐ zěnme jiù shēngqì le?

I was just joking. How come you're angry.

b. *我才開開玩笑而已，你怎麼就生氣了？

*Wǒ cái kāikāi wánxiào éryǐ, nǐ zěnme jiù shēngqì le?

只好, zhǐhǎo, (Adv), concession, could only, have no choice but to

Function ▶ The adverb 只好 introduces the best possible option under the given circumstances.

❶ 電信公司的門市不能刷卡，顧客只好付現金。

Diànxìn gōngsī de ménshì bù néng shuākǎ, gùkè zhǐhǎo fù xiànjīn.

The telephone company's retail outlet doesn't let you pay with credit cards. Customers can only pay in cash.

❷ 他好不容易考上熱門科系，可惜念了一個學期發現興趣不合，只好轉系。

Tā hǎobù róngyì kǎoshàng rèmén kēxì, kěxí niànle yí ge xuéqí fāxiàn xìngqù bù hé, zhǐhǎo zhuǎn xì.

He managed to test into a really popular department. Unfortunately, after a semester, he discovered that it's not where his interests lie. He had no choice but to change majors.

❸ 水餃都煮破了，我只好留下來自己吃。
Shuǐjiǎo dōu zhǔpò le, wǒ zhǐhǎo liúxiàlái zìjǐ chī.
All of the dumplings split open during cooking. I had no choice but to keep them for myself to eat.

❹ 上課以前我才發現書被我弄丟了。我只好趕快去跟朋友借。
Shàngkè yǐqián wǒ cái fāxiàn shū bèi wǒ nòngdiū le. Wǒ zhǐhǎo gǎnkuài qù gēn péngyǒu jiè.
I didn't notice that I had lost my book until just before class. I had no choice but to quickly borrow one from a friend.

❺ 他快遲到了，只好搭計程車去上班。
Tā kuài chídào le, zhǐhǎo dā jìchéngchē qù shàngbān.
He was going to be late, so he had no choice but to take a taxi to work.

只要 A，就 B, (zhǐyào (Conj) A, jiù (Adv) B), B is true, as long as A is true.

Function ▶ 只要 is a conjunction presenting a condition in the first clause, which is followed by a second clause of consequence, introduced by an adverb 就. As long as the condition is met, the consequence follows.

❶ 只要坐捷運，就能到臺北很多地方去玩。
Zhǐyào zuò jiéyùn, jiù néng dào Táiběi hěn duō dìfāng qù wán.
As long as, i.e., if, you take the MRT, you can get to many places in Taipei.

❷ 你只要到郵局或是便利商店，就找得到提款機，可以提錢。
Nǐ zhǐyào dào yóujú huò shì biànlì shāngdiàn, jiù zhǎodedào tíkuǎnjī, kěyǐ tí qián.
As long as, i.e., if, you go to a post office or a convenience store, you can find an ATM to withdraw money.

❸ 只要你在説中文的環境裡，你的中文就會進步得快一點。
Zhǐyào nǐ zài shuō Zhōngwén de huánjìng lǐ, nǐ de Zhōngwén jiù huì jìnbù de kuài yìdiǎn.
As long as you are in a Chinese-speaking environment, your Chinese will improve a bit more quickly.

❹ 你只要去參觀故宮博物院，就可以看見很多中國古代的東西。
Nǐ zhǐyào qù cānguān Gùgōng Bówùyuàn, jiù kěyǐ kànjiàn hěn duō Zhōngguó gǔdài de dōngxi.
If you visit the Palace Museum, you will see many things from ancient China.

❺ 你只要多喝水、多休息，感冒很快就會好了。
Nǐ zhǐyào duō hē shuǐ, duō xiūxí, gǎnmào hěn kuài jiù huì hǎo le.
As long as, i.e., if, you drink a lot of water and rest a lot, your cold will be OK very quickly. (i.e., Drink plenty of fluids and get plenty of rest and you'll be over your cold very quickly.)

Structures 只要 is a (lexicalised) conjunction, which can appear before or after the subject. 就 is an adverb, and can only appear before a VP.

Questions : Only 是不是 can be used.

❶ 是不是只要他答應跟妳結婚，妳就願意留在臺灣？
Shìbúshì zhǐyào tā dāyìng gēn nǐ jiéhūn, nǎi jiù yuànyì liú zài Táiwān?
As long as he agrees to marry you, you would be willing to stay in Taiwan, right?

❷ 你是不是只要到一個新環境，就很容易感冒？
Nǐ shìbúshì zhǐyào dào yí ge xīn huánjìng, jiù hěn róngyì gǎnmào?
If you go to a new environment, you catch cold easily, right? (i.e., Whenever you change environments or go to a new place, you catch cold easily, right?)

❸ 是不是只要房東同意房租少一點，你就不搬家了？
Shìbúshì zhǐyào fángdōng tóngyì fángzū shǎo yìdiǎn, nǐ jiù bù bānjiā le?
As long as the landlord agrees to lower the rent a bit, you won't move out, right?

只有 A，才 B, (zhǐyǒu A, cái B), can not B, unless A

Function In this pattern, 只有 introduces a condition, which must be satisfied before the 才 cause can be carried out.

❶ 這家旅館，只有三個月前先訂，才訂得到房間。
Zhè jiā lǚguǎn, zhǐyǒu sān ge yuè qián xiān dìng, cái dìngdedào fángjiān.
You can only get a room at this hotel if you make reservations three months in advance.

❷ 我只有星期六，才有時間倒垃圾。
Wǒ zhǐyǒu xīngqíliù, cái yǒu shíjiān dào lèsè.
I only have time on Saturday to take the garbage out.

❸ 我家附近只有星期四，才回收汽水罐。
Wǒ jiā fùjìn zhǐyǒu xīngqísì, cái huíshōu qìshuǐ guàn.
In the area where I live, soft drink cans are recycled only on Thursdays.

Structures The two subjects in this pattern can be identical or different.

❶ 很多學生只有打工，才付得起學費。
Hěn duō xuéshēng zhǐyǒu dǎgōng, cái fùdeqǐ xuéfèi.
Many students can only afford to pay tuition by working part time.

❷ 你只有多休息，病才會好得快一點。
Nǐ zhǐyǒu duō xiūxí, bìng cái huì hǎo de kuài yìdiǎn.
You have to get a lot of rest. Only then will you get well more quickly. (i.e., You have to get a lot of rest if you want to get well more quickly.)

351

❸ 這個地方太吵，老師只有換到別的教室，才能上課。
Zhè ge dìfāng tài chǎo, lǎoshī zhǐyǒu huàn dào biéde jiàoshì, cái néng shàngkè.
This place is too noisy. The teacher can only conduct class if they change to another classroom.

Questions :

❶ 學生是不是只有考試以前才念書？
Xuéshēng shìbúshì zhǐyǒu kǎoshì yǐqián cái niànshū?
The students only study before tests, right?

❷ 你是不是只有在學校，才能上網？
Nǐ shìbúshì zhǐyǒu zài xuéxiào, cái néng shàngwǎng?
You can only get online at school, right?

❸ 你們只有週末，才有時間練習太極拳嗎？
Nǐmen zhǐyǒu zhōumò, cái yǒu shíjiān liànxí Tàijí quán ma?
You only have time to practice Tai Chi on the weekends, right?

Usage

'只有 A，才 B' and '只要 A，就 B' both indicate conditionals. However, in '只有 A，才 B' the said condition is (in the speaker's view) harder to meet. On the other hand, in '只要 A，就 B' the condition is not that difficult to attain. Compare the following examples.

❶ 只有懂法文，才能到那家公司工作。(few people understand French)
Zhǐyǒu dǒng Fǎwén, cái néng dào nà jiā gōngsī gōngzuò.
Only if you understand French can you work at that company.

❷ 只要懂法文，就能到那家公司工作。(many people unterstand French)
Zhǐyào dǒng Fǎwén, jiù néng dào nà jiā gōngsī gōngzuò.
If you understand French, you can work at that company.

至於, zhìyú, (Ptc), introducing a new topic, as to, as far as... is concerned

Function

至於 is a new-topic marker, introducing or shifting to a new topic that is related to a topic just mentioned in a previous sentence.

❶ 聽說小李受傷了。至於傷得怎麼樣，我就不清楚了。
Tīngshuō Xiǎo Lǐ shòushāng le. Zhìyú shāng de zěnmeyàng, wǒ jiù bù qīngchǔ le.
I hear that Xiao Li was injured. As to how serious the injury is, I don't know.

❷ 這件外套的大小、樣子都很合適。至於顏色，我覺得淺了一點。
Zhè jiàn wàitào de dàxiǎo, yàngzi dōu hěn héshì. Zhìyú yánsè, wǒ juéde qiǎnle yìdiǎn.
The size and style of this coat are both suitable. As for the color, I think it's a bit light.

❸ 我對醫學系完全沒興趣，我想當警察。至於我父母，他們當然
反對。我也沒辦法，我要做自己。

Wǒ duì yīxué xì wánquán méi xìngqù, wǒ xiǎng dāng jǐngchá.
Zhìyú wǒ fùmǔ, tāmen dāngrán fǎnduì. Wǒ yě méi bànfǎ, wǒ yào
zuò zìjǐ.

I have no interest in medical school, I want to be a policeman. As
for my parents, they obviously oppose the idea strongly. But I can't
help that, I want to be true to myself.

❹ 我吃東西只講究營養。至於味道好不好，沒關係。

Wǒ chī dōngxi zhǐ jiǎngjiù yíngyǎng. Zhìyú wèidào hǎo bù hǎo,
méi guānxi.

I am only fastidious about nutritious food. As to whether the taste
is good or not, that's irrelevant.

❺ 她喜歡個性好的人。至於外表，她覺得不重要。

Tā xǐhuān gèxìng hǎo de rén. Zhìyú wàibiǎo, tā juéde bú zhòngyào.

She likes people with good personalities. As to looks, she thinks
that's unimportant.

Usage

In learning Chinese, much confusion is observed relating to 對於
duìyú, 關於guānyú, and 至於. See relevant entries.

中, zhōng, a summary of the various meanings

Function

Spatial terms in Chinese, and indeed in many languages, can have
temporal meanings as well. 中 figures prominently in Chinese
people's life. 中國 means Middle Kingdom, the center of the world.

(1) Spatial meaning: amongst, short from 當中

❶ 這兩個人中，到底哪一個是你女朋友？

Zhè liǎng ge rén zhōng, dàodǐ nǎ yí ge shì nǐ nǚpéngyǒu?

Which of these two people exactly is your girlfriend?

❷ 你站在一群人中，當然不容易被找到。

Nǐ zhàn zài yì qún rén zhōng, dāngrán bù róngyì bèi zhǎodào.

Of course it's not easy to find you amid a crowd of people.

❸ 這次的面試在兩百個應徵者中，只選出三個，真的很不容
易考上。

Zhè cì de miànshì zài liǎngbǎi ge yìngzhēng zhě zhōng, zhǐ
xuǎnchū sān ge, zhēn de hěn bù róngyì kǎoshàng.

This time out of the 200 applicants who took the oral exam
only three were selected, qualifying was truly not an easy task.

(2) Temporal meaning 1: during

❶ 我去法國念書的那兩年中，不但學會了做飯，還學會了開
車。

Wǒ qù Fǎguó niànshū de nà liǎng nián zhōng, búdàn xuéhuìle
zuòfàn, hái xuéhuìle kāichē.

During the two years that I was studying in France, I not only
learned how to cook, but how to drive as well.

❷ 奶奶説她一生中最難忘的事，是17歲那年發生的戰爭。
Nǎinai shuō tā yì shēng zhōng zuì nánwàng de shì, shì 17 suì nà nián fāshēng de zhànzhēng.
Grandma said that the most unforgettable part of her whole life was the war broke out when she was 17.

❸ 大學四年是我的年輕歲月中最開心的一段時間。
Dàxué sì nián shì wǒ de niánqīng suìyuè zhōng zuì kāixīn de yí duàn shíjiān.
My four years of college life was the happiest period of my youth.

(3) Temporal meaning 2: in the process of

❶ 這個計畫已經在進行中了。現在喊停已經來不及了。
Zhè ge jìhuà yǐjīng zài jìnxíng zhōng le. Xiànzài hǎn tíng yǐjīng láibùjí le.
This proposal is already under way, and it's too late try stopping it now.

❷ 餐廳還沒開。門口掛著「準備中」的牌子。
Cāntīng hái méi kāi. Ménkǒu guàzhe 'zhǔnbèi zhōng' de páizi.
The restaurant hasn't open yet. There is a 'in prepartion' sign hanging in the door.

❸ 那個房間外面的燈寫著「手術中」，外面有好幾個家人焦慮地走來走去。
Nà ge fángjiān wàimiàn de dēng xiězhe 'shǒushù zhōng', wàimiàn yǒu hǎojǐ ge jiārén jiāolǜ de zǒulái zǒuqù.
Outside that door lit up by a sign, 'surgery in Progress', there are many family members pacing back and forth, in great anxiety.

自 , zì, (Prep), from (formal)

Function 自 is a classical Chinese preposition, corresponding to modern 從, meaning 'from' a location. It occurs after a main verb (as in classical Chinese).

❶ 世界各地都有來自中國的移民。
Shìjiè gè dì dōu yǒu láizì Zhōngguó de yímín.
Immigrants from China can be found all over the world.

❷ 現在中文裡像「超好吃」這樣「超……」的表達是來自日文。
Xiànzài Zhōngwén lǐ xiàng 'chāo hǎochī' zhèyàng 'chāo…' de biǎodá shì láizì Rìwén.
The characters '超', as used in modern Chinese phrases like '超好吃', is an expression that came from Japanese.

❸ 這本書裡的文章大多數選自美國作家的小説。
Zhè běn shū lǐ de wénzhāng dà duōshù xuǎnzì Měiguó zuòjiā de xiǎoshuō.
The selections in this book are mostly taken from American writers' novels.

❹ 這對夫婦的孩子領養自三個不同的國家。
Zhè duì fūfù de háizi lǐngyǎng zì sān ge bùtóng de guójiā.
This couple's children have been adopted from three different countries.

❺ 這本歷史故事書是翻譯自西班牙歷史故事。
Zhè běn lìshǐ gùshì shū shì fānyì zì Xībānyá lìshǐ gùshì.
This book on history is translated from Spanish.

Usage

The negative structure is '不是＋V 自', e.g.,

❶ 聽說那位畫家的很多畫都不是出自自己的手，而是學生畫的。
Tīngshuō nà wèi huàjiā de hěn duō huà dōu búshì chūzì zìjǐ de shǒu, ér shì xuéshēng huà de.
I've heard that many of that artist's paintings weren't even done by him. They were painted by his students.

❷ 這張圖片不是取自網路，而是我自己拍的。
Zhè zhāng túpiàn búshì qǔzì wǎnglù, ér shì wǒ zìjǐ pāi de.
This picture wasn't taken from the internet. I took it myself.

自從…以後, (zìcóng (Prep)...yǐhòu (N)), ever since...

Function

The preposition 自從 presents a time reference, from which point an instance began.

❶ 自從大學畢業以後，他就經營了一家網路公司。
Zìcóng dàxué bìyè yǐhòu, tā jiù jīngyíngle yì jiā wǎnglù gōngsī.
Ever since graduating from university, he has been running an online company.

❷ 自從有了網路商店以後，我們待在家裡也可以買東西。
Zìcóng yǒule wǎnglù shāngdiàn yǐhòu, wǒmen dāi zài jiā lǐ yě kěyǐ mǎi dōngxi.
Ever since the advent of online shops I have been able to shop from home.

❸ 自從她有了孩子以後，她的生活更忙碌了。
Zìcóng tā yǒule háizi yǐhòu, tā de shēnghuó gèng mánglù le.
Ever since having children, her live has been even busier.

❹ 自從她認識了新的網友以後，每天一回家就打開電腦，進入聊天室。
Zìcóng tā rènshìle xīn de wǎngyǒu yǐhòu, měi tiān yì huíjiā jiù dǎkāi diànnǎo, jìnrù liáotiānshì.
Ever since meeting her new online friend, first thing after coming home every day she opens her computer and goes into the chatrooms.

❺ 自從他到了南美洲念書以後，他就有機會天天跟同學說西班牙文
了。

Zìcóng tā dàole Nánměizhōu niànshū yǐhòu, tā jiù yǒu jīhuì tiāntiān
gēn tóngxué shuō Xībānyáwén le.

Ever since going to the South America for studies he has had the
opportunity to speak Spanish daily with his classmates.

Usage

以後 can sometimes be reduced to 後, but not very often, e.g.,

自從他搬家後，就再也沒見過他了。

Zìcóng tā bānjiā hòu, jiù zài yě méi jiànguò tā le.

I haven't seen him again since he moved.

總是, zǒngshì, (Adv), always, in all cases, without exception

Function This adverb modifies a very high frequency instance.

❶ 剛學中文的學生總是不清楚「的」和「得」有什麼不一樣。
Gāng xué Zhōngwén de xuéshēng zǒngshì bù qīngchǔ 'de' hàn 'de'
yǒu shénme bù yíyàng.
Beginning Chinese learners always have touble understanding the
difference between 的 and 得.

❷ 王太太總是趁百貨公司週年慶的時候買東西。
Wáng tàitai zǒngshì chèn bǎihuò gōngsī zhōuniánqìng de shíhòu mǎi
dōngxi.
Mrs. Wang always goes shopping at department stores when the
anniversary sales are on.

❸ 因為那家餐廳的海鮮很新鮮，所以門口總是有很多人排隊。
Yīnwèi nà jiā cāntīng de hǎixiān hěn xīnxiān, suǒyǐ ménkǒu zǒngshì
yǒu hěn duō rén páiduì.
That restaurant uses really fresh seafood, so there are always people
lined up at the door.

❹ 他的工作很忙。他總是九點多才下班。
Tā de gōngzuò hěn máng. Tā zǒngshì jiǔdiǎn duō cái xiàbān.
He has a very demanding job. Most days he only gets off at 9 o'clock
in the evening.

❺ 我和朋友去夜市總是吃臭豆腐、水煎包和炸雞。
Wǒ hàn péngyǒu qù yèshì zǒngshì chī chòudòufǔ, shuǐjiānbāo hàn
zhájī.
When my friends and I go to the night market, we always have stinky
tofu, pan-fried pork buns, and deep fried chicken.

總算, zǒngsuàn, (Adv), finally

Function The adverb 總算 refers to the meaning finally, eventually, said with a sigh
of relief after a period of anxiety, endurance, etc.,

❶ 下了兩個星期的雨。今天天氣總算變好了。

Xià le liǎng ge xīngqí de yǔ. Jīntiān tiānqì zǒngsuàn biàn hǎo le.

After two solid weeks of rain, the weather today has finally improved.

❷ 警察問了半天，都沒有人敢說話。最後總算有人說話了。

Jǐngchá wènle bàn tiān, dōu méi yǒu rén gǎn shuōhuà. Zuìhòu zǒngsuàn yǒu rén shuōhuà le.

The policeman pressed the issue but nobody dared speak out. Eventually somebody spoke up.

❸ 雖然這次考試也不是考得很好，但總算還可以。

Suīrán zhè cì kǎoshì yě búshì kǎo de hěn hǎo, dàn zǒngsuàn hái kěyǐ.

I may not have done amazingly well on the test, but I did good enough.

❹ 這次的報告我寫得不好，但總算寫完了。

Zhè cì de bàogào wǒ xiě de bù hǎo, dàn zǒngsuàn xiěwán le.

I didn't do a great job on this report, but at least it's done.

走, zǒu, (Ptc), as a Verb Particle, away

Function

走, when serving as a verb particle, usually indicates a movement of the object away from the speaker due to the subject's action.

❶ 我們都把客人送走了。

Wǒmen dōu bǎ kèrén sòngzǒu le.

We sent off all the guests.

❷ 請你把門口的那些東西推走。

Qǐng nǐ bǎ ménkǒu de nàxiē dōngxi tuīzǒu.

Please push away all those things from the door.

❸ 那件衣服已經被別人買走了。

Nà jiàn yīfú yǐjīng bèi biérén mǎizǒu le.

That dress (or blouse, garment, etc.) has already been purchased (and taken away) by someone.

Structures

Negation:

❶ 那幾本書我沒借走，還在圖書館裡。

Nà jǐ běn shū wǒ méi jièzǒu, hái zài túshūguǎn lǐ.

I did not take out those books; they are still in the library.

❷ 他沒騎走你的腳踏車，你的車還停在家裡呢。

Tā méi qízǒu nǐ de jiǎotàchē, nǐ de chē hái tíng zài jiā lǐ ne.

He didn't ride away on your bike. Your bike is still parked at home.

❸ 你不搬走門口這張桌子，我的家具搬不進去。

Nǐ bù bānzǒu ménkǒu zhè zhāng zhuōzi, wǒ de jiājù bān bú jìnqù.

If you don't move this desk away from the entrance, I can't move my furniture in.

*Q*uestions :

❶ 昨天的作業，老師收走了沒有？
Zuótiān de zuòyè, lǎoshī shōuzǒu le méi yǒu?
Has the teacher picked up yesterday's homework?

❷ 偷手機的那個人是不是跑走了？
Tōu shǒujī de nà ge rén shìbúshì pǎozǒu le?
Did the guy who stole the cell phone run off?

❸ 銀行的錢都被提走了嗎？
Yínháng de qián dōu bèi tízǒu le ma?
Has all the bank's money been withdrawn?

Usage

(1) 把 bǎ or 被 bèi constructions are often used with the verb particle 走.

❶ 他把我的腳踏車騎走了。
Tā bǎ wǒ de jiǎotàchē qízǒu le.
He rode away on my bike.

❷ 朋友把我的書帶走了。
Péngyǒu bǎ wǒ de shū dàizǒu le.
A friend took my book away.

❸ 我的手機被誰拿走了？
Wǒ de shǒujī bèi shéi názǒu le?
Who took my cell phone away?

(2) The following verbs combine with 走: 拿 ná 'take', 搬 bān 'move', 推 tuī 'push', 騎 qí 'ride', 借 jiè 'borrow', 買 mǎi 'buy', 帶 dài 'bring', 約 yuē 'have date/appointment with (someone)', 選 xuǎn 'select, choose', 送 sòng 'send', 偷 tōu 'steal', 提 tí 'to withdraw (as of money)' and 罵 mà 'scold'. The object can be a concrete thing, but can also be something abstract, e.g.,

❶ 警察把犯罪用的汽車帶走了。
Jǐngchá bǎ fànzuì yòng de qìchē dàizǒu le.
The police took the criminal's vehicle in custody.

❷ 他離開的時候把快樂的氣氛也帶走了。
Tā líkāi de shíhòu bǎ kuàilè de qìfēn yě dàizǒu le.
When he left, he took away with him the pleasant ambiance.

(3) 得/不 can be inserted for the potential form of the pattern.

❶ 這麼多書，你拿得走嗎？
Zhème duō shū, nǐ nádezǒu ma?
This many books! (i.e., There are so many books.) Are you able to take them all away?

❷ 他告訴大家他決定留在這裡，誰也罵不走他。

Tā gàosu dàjiā tā juédìng liú zài zhèlǐ, shéi yě màbùzǒu tā.

He told everyone he has decided to stay, so no matter who tells him off, it's no use.

❸ 家具太多了，你可能一次搬不走。

Jiājù tài duō le, nǐ kěnéng yí cì bānbùzǒu.

There is too much furniture. You probably won't be able to move it away all at once.

索 引
English to Chinese Index

English	Chinese	Page
successful complement	成chéng	57
successful complement	到dào	77
such as	像xiàng	293
suggestion particle	吧ba	4
supposing	萬一wànyī	280
supposing, if	要是yàoshì	295
surprised to have found out	還hái	143
surprised, displeased	都dōu	103
surprisingly, to one's great astonishment	居然jūrán	172
surprisingly, to one's great astonishment	竟然jìngrán	166

T

English	Chinese	Page
take ... as an example	拿...來說 ná...lái shuō	212
taking A as B	當做dàngzuò	12
talk about, mention	說到shuōdào	266
talk about, mention	談到tándào	271
terribly complement	死了sǐle	267
that being the case, because of it	這下子zhè xiàzi	341
that being the case, that way	這樣一來 zhèyàng yìlái	341
then and only then	才cái	48
thereupon, consequently	於是yúshì	323
thought wrongly	以為yǐwéi	310
thus, can be concluded that	可見kějiàn	176
time and place of events	時間詞shíjiān cí	271
time and place preposition	在zài	271
time at vs. time for	時點shídiǎn	273
to preposition	對duì	108
to preposition with you	對duì	106
to the extent of, even	甚至shènzhì	254
to, for, various gei	給gěi	124
to, up to	到dào	72

English	Chinese	Page
topic contrastive	對比主題duìbǐ zhǔtí	276
topic general	主題句zhǔtí jù	275
touch-upon complement	起qǐ	229
towards	對duì	104
towards, goal	向xiàng	290
towards, regarding	對於duìyú	108
try and see	看kàn	173

U

English	Chinese	Page
under, due to	在 …下zài...xià	331
understand complement	懂dǒng	98
until	等děng	91
up movement	起qǐ	95
up to, till as complement	到dào	75
up, various shang	上shàng	248
upward movement	上shàng	95
usually, always	往往wǎngwǎng	281

V

English	Chinese	Page
verb marker	所suǒ	248
very	很hěn	151
very in complement	得很de hěn	65

W

English	Chinese	Page
warning mild	可kě	175
what in statement	什麼shénme	227
when, at the time of	的時候de shíhòu	90
when, at the time of	當dāng	72
when, until	等děng	91
while	當dāng	72
whilst, take advantage of	趁chèn	55
who in statement	誰shéi	227
who would have thought that	誰知道shéi zhīdào	252
why must	何必hébì	149
why so	怎麼這麼zěnme zhème	337
wish desperately	恨不得hènbùdé	152
with	跟gēn	128
with (formal)	以yǐ	295
with preposition various meanings	跟gēn	129

English	Chinese	Page
with, to, various gen	跟 gēn	129
within a quota	以內 yǐnèi	298
without interruption, in one breath	一口氣 yìkǒuqì	306
wondering adverb	究竟 jiùjìng	171
would rather	寧可 níngkě	221
would rather	與其 yǔqí	322

Linking Chinese
當代中文語法點全集

策　　劃	國立臺灣師範大學國語教學中心	出版者	聯經出版事業股份有限公司
編　　著	鄧守信	發行人	林載爵
執行編輯	張莉萍、蔡如珮	社　長	羅國俊
編輯助理	許育凡、郭玫君	總經理	陳芝宇
翻　　譯	James Friesen、范大龍、傅思可、	總編輯	涂豐恩
	蔣宜臻	副總編輯	陳逸華
校　　對	陳昱蓉、張雯雯、蔡如珮	叢書主編	李芃

封面設計　林芷伊
內文排版　楊佩菱

2018 年 4 月初版・2019 年 5 月二版
2024 年 7 月二版六刷
版權所有 ・ 翻印必究
Printed in Taiwan.
ISBN　　978-957-08-5317-9　(平裝)
GPN　　1010700400
定　　價　600 元

地　　址　新北市汐止區大同路一段 369 號 1 樓
聯絡電話　(02)86925588 轉 5305
郵政劃撥　帳戶第 0100559-3 號
郵撥電話　(02)23620308
印刷者　文聯彩色製版印刷有限公司

著作財產權人　國立臺灣師範大學
地址：臺北市和平東路一段 162 號
電話：886-2-7734-5130
網址：http://mtc.ntnu.edu.tw/
E-mail：mtcbook613@gmail.com

感謝

丁國雲、王佩卿、王慧娟、王瓊淑、胡睦苓、孫懿芬、張黛琪、
陳淑美、陳慶華、黃桂英、劉崇仁、盧翠英、盧德昭

提供本書部分例句

（以上依姓氏筆畫順序排列）

國家圖書館出版品預行編目資料

> **當代中文語法點全集**/國立臺灣師範大學國語教學
> 中心策劃．鄧守信編著．二版．新北市．聯經．2019.05．
> 408面．17×23公分（Linking Chinese）
> ISBN　978-957-08-5317-9（平裝）
> [2024年7月二版六刷]
>
> 1.漢語語法
>
> 802.6　　　　　　　　　　　　　　　　108007453